NIGHT WIND

STEPHEN FRANCIS MONTAGNA

Printed in the United States of America
Published by: Stephen Francis Montagna

ISBN: 978-1-970301-04-5 PB
ISBN: 978-1-970301-05-2 HB

The inspiration for this novel came to me
On April 17th, 2001. My son's birthday so
I dedicate this book to my son, Stephen.
God bless you for all the love and enjoyment
you brought to my soul

PROLOGUE

THE COUNCIL OF KAMI

The unconquerable fighting spirit of the beautiful female Samurai Warrior known as Wind, was brought before the Council of Kami, the gathering of Japan's host of Gods; who Deities controlled the destiny of the Eight Islands of Japan and all her faithful people. Lord Takehiro Kawasomeru was standing by the right and honored side of his Wind, and she was brought before the Council because of the curse he had placed upon the sword he used to take her life back in the year of 1354. Although Lord Kawasomeru was not truly a Shogun but a powerful Daimyo (Important Person), a massive land owner who ruled over thousands of Samurai and vassals and Tami (the common people) and was regarded by many as a Shogun in his own right. Wind stood by her long ago Commander naked as the day she was born and fifteen of the gods sat in judgment of her actions when she was allowed to answer the call of the sword her spirit was attached to by Kawasomeru-Sama's (Sama-Lord) Command.

In the living world, whoever was in Command of Wind's Katana killing sword of the ancient past, was also in Command of her uncontrollable fighting spirit, and her body once called back to the land of the living. Was honored bound by the curse upon her sword to carry out any wishes of whoever held her sword in their hand. Wind was ordered before the Council to judge her and the gods would then decide if her spirit was going to be eliminated, or if she was going to be allowed to live on in the Ukiyo or the Floating World of spirits and the land of great myths. Many of the Kami were upset because Wind had attacked and she slaughtered the owner of her killing Katana sword and that went against the curse of her sword.

Izanagi and his sister Izanami were the ones who held her fate in their hands, and they were going to listen to Fujin, the always angry God of Wind who volunteered to represent Wind before the Council of Kami, and Hachiman, the fearful Kami of Warfare, was the God picked to try Wind for her crimes. Many other Gods were to sit in judgment of Wind, and Daisho jingi guri or band of all Gods would deal out the Tenchu or Heavenly punishment of her, if Wind was found guilty of any of the crimes she was accused of. The list of Gods to sit in judgment was long, and they all sat around the fabled Eight Fathom House with a Central Pillar. One of the first Gods to be created by Izanagi, Ninigi, his task was to direct the development of Japan and he became the first Divine Emperor to rule the Eight Islands of Japan.

The first Kami's born was the Heavenly Blowing Male later known as Fujin, or the God of Wind, other's there were the Sea Kami, Foam Waves, Foam Calm, and Ocean Wave and Heavenly Water Provider. The Sea Gods was Watatsumi or Sea Children. The Fire God Kagutsuchi, the Gods Kuramistsuha, the Dragon of Valleys and Kurayamatsumi, the Lord of Dark Munntains and Kuramistsuha, the Dark Water Snake was present. Mitsuhanome, or the Female Water Snake and a number of the fearsome Dragon Family, Mizuchi, or Water Fathers sometimes referred to as the Horned Deities, and Wani, one of the last Gods born, was a mighty Dragon who resembled a mix between a Crocodile and a shark. Also seated at the Council was Toyotamabime or Abundany Pearl Princess. One of the most powerful of Deities to be seated was Amaterasu, the Goddess of the Sun, and she was seated by Tsukiyomi, the God of the Moon. Susanowo, who was the younger brother of Fujin, the God of Wind and Wind's namesake.

Fujin took center stage and was roaring his defense of the only female Warrior to have ever been enlisted into the Samurai Caste by one of the powerful Daimyo's of the time. He started to explain the reason for Wind attacking the owner of the sword and of her soul, as long as the ancient killing sword was out of its wooden sheath. Every word he uttered was a roar and he was making the very best of his defense of the naked woman who was seated with her legs crossed under her rearend, and with her head slightly bowed forward. Wind understood she could not utter one single word in her own defense, unless one of the Deities asked her a direct question. Then and only then was she allowed to address any of the Council members.

Likewise, Lord Kawasomeru was also commanded to remain silent, and he was also not allowed to offer any sort of defense of his female Samurai Warrior, unless he was asked a direct question by one of the Gods seated in judgment of his ward.

CHAPTER ONE

Wind dared to looked over his shoulder and saw Hiromoai Hatanaka standing behind her, who was allowed to come from the pits of hell to testify against the savage attack on his person by the Samurai Warrior Wind. Instantly, her mind was flooded with hatred for the killer of her first and only true lover when she was a Warrior in Lord Kawasomeru's mighty Army of Samurai.

Fujin picked up the harsh glance and then he roared at the Council members. "Why has this inhuman animal to be allowed to attend this Council? He is the reason why this fine female Samurai Warrior is on trial here before us today. If it was not for his loathsome father's father who was the lowly assassin who killed Wind's mate like a lowly coward who attacked him in his sleep in the middle of the night, and did not offer that proud young Warrior the right to defend himself properly against his attack. We all would not be here deciding her future fate. I say we should send this evil dirt back to the pits of hell from whence he came, and leave the pure air of this Council in peace. I see no true reason for his foul presence before this Council meeting but to be a disruptive force to our intelligence..."

Hachiman stepped forward and he cut off Fujin's complaint by offering to the Council members in a rather heated tone of voice. "We are all well aware of Fujin's angry and wild outbursts, but it was I who has summoned this piece of filth to stand before this Council, so he can tell all of you how this unclean female Warrior had attacked and so savaged his body because of the sins of his father's, father's, father. No matter what the reason, he was in Command of Wind's killing sword and as such, he was in total Command of her spirit and according to the curse placed upon the great Katana blade by Lord Kawasomeru himself. No harm was to befall any such person who commanded this dishonored Samurai Warrior's being and Katana sword.

"I shall allow this most despicable and lowly person explain to each of you how this dishonored female Samurai Warrior took it upon herself to disobey the cursed placed upon her great killing sword by Lord Kawasomeru himself, and in doing so she has not only disrespected herself, but she has also disrespected her own Lord and Master of the time, and for this terrible a crime there is no possible defense against it. The loathsome spirit of this female Samurai Warrior known as Wind, must be put to death once and for all, and never again to be allowed to walk the lands of either the Ukiyo, or the earth ever again. Her death has to be total and all consuming, and her memory must forever be erased from the rolls of past great Samurai Warriors of our ancient times who had so faithfully honored their masters properly and completely. It is our sworn duty to honor all the past proud Samurai Warriors who have served their masters faithfully, not like the betrayal this one loathsome Samurai has committed against her Lord and Master's curse placed upon her spirit and killing sword.

If we allow this one Samurai to go unpunished then what president are we placing for the future Samurai of Japan? If we allow this Warrior to go without severe punishment then how could we possibly punish any future Samurai, if he disrespects his Lord and Master? We have to punish all or none of the foul fools. This worthless female has disrespected her Lord and for this she has forfeited her spirit to the pits of hell for all eternity. And she and this other piece of vile filth can serve their time in hell until Izanagi deems it fit the criminals served out their penance properly, and he allows them to return back to the lands of the faithful and pure. I believe it's time we hear from this lowly dog Hiromoai Hatanaka, and he can tell each of you how this worthless Warrior had betrayed the sacred oath of the killing sword. I say let him speak..."

Now it was Fujin's turn to interrupt Hachiman's hell fire speech as he offered to the Council in just as angry a tone of voice. "What good would it serve to hear from the foul mouth of such an evil person as Hiromoai Hatanaka? This evil man did nothing but use Wind's wonderful gifts for his own foul gains and evil wants and desires. The curse that was placed upon Wind's head by the honorable Lord Kawasomeru, was not made to give the owner of the killing sword to do evil with Wind's gifts and loyalty and of her body as well. It was placed upon Wind's head as a special reward for her loyal service to her Lord and Master of the past times, and if you remember correctly. Her death was ordered by the Shogun of the time to end the endless war that was being waging in central Japan for countless years and cost many honorable Samurai lives.

"The two powerful Daimyos, Lord Takehiro Kawasomeru who was in the right and Lord Motoshige Wakatsuki, who was the one in the wrong in that endless war, could not come to peaceful terms between themselves. It took the great Shogun of the time to send his most trusted General out to demand the war to end between the two. And you must also remember that it was the lowly dog Lord Wakatsuki who demanded the death of Wind to end the war. So to dishonor this fine female Samurai Warrior by allowing her good to be used by this evil man standing behind me, is a gross disservice and injustice aimed against this fine female Warrior. I for one have no wish to hear what this evil person has to offer to the Council members. I should demand he be removed from this Council immediately, and the foul thing be sent back to the Red Hell to serve out the rest of his penance properly as his crimes demand of his evil soul..."

"I see Lord Kawasomeru standing so proudly and strong before this Council in defense of his female Warrior. Why do I not see Lord Wakatsuki also standing here and prepared to defend his actions in this ongoing drama we are faced with here, Fujin-Sama?" Amaterasu, the Goddess of the Sun asked Fujin as she actually smiled first at him, and then at the Warrior Wind.

"I am most pleased to inform you why Lord Wakatsuki-Sama is not present before the Council members. It is this simply, he has refused to attend this meeting, and I actually ordered him to attend and he still refused my Command." Fujin nearly roared his reply at the Council.

"Well if that great fool has no interest in the finding of this Council! Then I say we have heard enough of this and I offer we end this trial here and now, and we allow Wind to go on her way with not even a slight punishment to carry. If he sees no crime in this Warrior's heart then who are we to find a crime and wrong doing where there is obviously none to be found..." Amaterasu remarked before she was rudely cut off by the extremely angry Hachiman, who actually dare to scream his remark back at the extremely dangerous female Sun Goddess.

"What is this foolishness I am hearing coming from the lips of the honored Goddess Amaterasu. Are you taking the side of this dishonored female Samurai Warrior just because she is of the same sex as you are, Amaterasu?"

"You better watch your step when you are addressing me, Hachiman-Sama. And how dare you accuse me of taking this honorable Samurai Warrior's side just because she is a woman. I offered what I did because I believe we are trying to be much too harsh with her, mainly because she is a female Warrior, and you male Warriors have still not gotten over the fact this woman Warrior was allowed to invade the Samurai Caste, and that's why you are still trying to have her destroy. And I warn you for a second time Hachiman-Sama, be very careful how you address me, it could very well cost all the ones who honor you an endless life with no sun shining on them until my anger for you has subsided. I do not take insults very lightly as you well know, so be very careful when dealing with me! I am no weak woman you can push around, Hachiman-Sama!"

Hachiman took a step backwards, and then he bowed slightly towards the suddenly extremely upset and powerful Goddess of the Sun.

"That is much better Hachiman-Sama. I am very pleased to discover you have seen the error in your way of addressing me and..."

"Enough of this madness, I have much better things I must attend to in my life, rather than sitting here and listening to this constant bickering being carried off between the Gods I myself have created to rule over these foolish Samurai. You!" Izanagi turned his attention towards Hiromoai Hatanaka and then he barked angrily at him. "You may leave this meeting, because the mere sight of your presence sickens me to my stomach."

With a sudden clap of his hands as loud as the thunder of a powerful thunderstorm itself, Hiromoai Hatanaka's form instantly disappeared from the Council meeting hall, and then Izanagi offered to the other Gods at the meeting hall. "And that ends that, and as for the fate of this female Samurai Warrior who is known to us Gods as Wind, I offer this. Wind-san, you may stand before me and hear you fate as I decree it to be. That is much better to see you standing tall before me. Wind-san, I see all and I hear all, and I have seen what that evil man has used your great gifts offered you from your honored Lord Kawasomeru standing proud by your side. He was wrong and the great fool has earned his just deserts, and I deem your actions as proper and correct. For this I find no crime committed by you against the evil one who commanded your sword and your spirit so foolishly even for the short time he was in Command of you.

"You will remain where your honored Lord and Master had placed you in the wonders of the Ukiyo, our Floating World of wonderment. Lord Takehiro Kawasomeru, I give you back your Samurai Warrior Wind-san, but not before I reward her myself for the terrible injustice she had suffered at the hands of that terrible and foolish master.

"Wind-san, you will step forward and receive this special amulet. It is my personal gift to honor you properly for what you were abused by the foul Master of your sword. It has the same powers as your cursed sword offers the next Lord and Master of your deadly killing sword. But it has one special power your sword does not possess. It will show you in your mind's eye what your new Lord and Master of your killing sword is doing. In that way, if your new Lord and Master of the cursed sword runs into any trouble while he is away from your protective side, and he is unable to properly summon you to his aide, you will see his dilemma and you will be able to locate him anywhere in the world, and then come to his aide. This amulet will enable you to be more of a service to the soon to be new Lord and Master of your killing sword.

"It is the only way I can possibly think of to properly honor you for the injustice you had suffered at the hands of the dishonored Hiromoai Hatanaka. I tell you this Wind-san, the dishonorable Hatanaka will suffer long periods of time trapped in the Red Hell, until I deem it fit he has suffered enough for the terrible injustice he has leveled upon the curse of your killing sword. The great fool had foolishly squandered such a powerful gift offered to you by your Lord and Master Kawasomeru-Sama, and enforced by my will and decree. What a sin he has committed against all the Gods who control the destiny of all the faithful Japanese people.

"Such a powerful gift if employed correctly would have brought great honor to the worthless fool who was too blind to see the magnificent gifts the Gods had bestowed upon your head for all your years of your faithful service to your Lord Kawasomeru. What a horrendous waste of this great gift the fool dishonored on his own want for personal glory. With the gift that was placed in his worthless hands, all the good he could have created for the faithful children of Japan, was wasted on his own want for revenge against an injustice he only believed was aimed at his foolish head. Here, take what I offer you and then go with your well respected Lord and Master who has served us Gods properly, and enjoy his great presence until the next call to you from your killing sword comes. You are dismissed from my presence and you may now go with your Lord Kawasomeru, and remain with him until the next call for your services is made of you."

With that said the still extremely powerful Lord Takehiro Kawasomeru along with his Samurai Warrior named Wind instantly disappeared from the presence of the Council members. They were both deposited in the area that was especially allotted by the Gods for Kawasomeru-Sama to enjoy his entire life spent in the Ukiyo, until the time of his rebirth was finally at hand, and he could once again walk the sacred lands of the Eight Islands of Japan in the living world. Lord Kawasomeru lead Wind towards a sitting area, suddenly she was surrounded with one of the finest light blue silk Kimono richly decorated with large painted locus flowers trimmed in gold. Just as they both were seated and Lord Kawasomeru was about to explain to her all of what had just transpired at the Council of Kami meeting. When her skin suddenly began to glow and then she slowly started to disappear from his presence.

Lord Kawasomeru smiled proudly as Wind's form fully disappeared from his sight, and then he mumbled to the slowly faded spirit of his Samurai Warrior. "Wind-san, I see someone else has just found your killing Katana sword, and he has now summoned you before his presence. After all these years that had passed, you are still cursed to the life of the deadly killing sword I forced your spirit to obey for all times to come. I hope the new owner of the deadly killing sword will treat you much better than the last owner of your Katana blade. Good luck my Wind-san, for you will always be locked in my heart and mind, and hopefully, you will once again be doing your new Lord and Master's faithful bidding. But he must also understand and be aware of, if he squanders the great gift that is now in his hands from the Gods who rule Japan like the foolish Hatanaka did. Then he will be subject to the same punishment as the great fool has just suffered."

FBI HEADQUARTERS, WASHINGTON D.C.
MONDAY JUNE 10th, 1996 3:30P.M.

FBI Special Field Agent Robert (Bob) Rossie reported to his Commander as ordered once he was called back to the United States to make his direct report on what had happened to the American Businessman Calvin Batterman. Who was killed by Wind in the empty construction plot along with Hiromoai Hatanaka in Japan. He left the Japanese Lieutenant Kenzaburo Motoshima and Sergeant Toshihiro Okamatsu investigating the death of the American in their country. Though he was extremely exhausted and suffering from jet lag, he reported to the headquarters straight from the Reagan International Airport, even before going home and resting and reporting in on the following day which was an option offered him from his Commander. He walked into Commander Ralph Murdock's office actually dragging is backside on the floor, he was so exhausted and tired from the long flight back to the United States.

"Jesus Christ Almighty Robert, you look like you were shot at and missed and shit at and hit mister. Why the hell didn't you go home and rest and report in tomorrow morning? I gave you that option if you remember right. Dammit, looking at you I don't think I'm going to be able to carry out a good conversation with you in your present condition, mister. You sure you don't want to go home and come in tomorrow morning to make your report about Batterman's death then. It's not that important we have this discussion today. We can have it tomorrow, you can report in tomorrow morning to make your opening report on Batterman's death. But what the hell since you're here we might as well get something accomplished today. I'll tell you this much though, once it was reported Batterman was killed in Japan, all sorts of hell has broken out here in the States, because he was that powerful a businessman in this country.

"Dammit to hell and all the back again, even the damn stock market had reacted to his death in Japan, and it had dropped over a hundred points over the news of his recent death. We're hoping the market will rebound sometime later on today and not keep dropping like it was doing. But the construction stocks have been taking a real hammering after the news of Batterman's death made the news waves. Before you left Japan, were there any sort of leads on who might have killed Batterman and why? Crap Bob, is the damn report of his fucking head missing from his body at all true man? I can't believe that crazy ass report I read, why the hell would anyone want to remove his damn head, and then cart it away with the murderer."

"I'm afraid you better believe that report, because as far as I was able to ascertain, Batterman's head was in fact removed from the damn place when he was killed, sir. The Japanese Detectives are still looking for his missing head, but as of yet they were unable to locate it for us sir." The extremely exhausted FBI Agent mumbled as he tried to gather some of his strength back.

"Damn, what the hell would anyone want with his fucking head anyway, dammit? You don't think the damn killer is part of some kind of Japanese cult faction operating over there, do you Bob? That's the only reason I can see for anyone wanting to remove Batterman's head from the damn crime scene. These damn Asian people are a real strange lot with all their foolish beliefs in so many different Gods and omens and crap like that." The surprised FBI Commander offered to his Field Agent with much concern lacing his voice this time.

"I don't really know at this time sir. All I do know is this entire case has some crazy ass things going down in it, Commander Ralph." Agent Rossie replied to his Commander.

"Like what, what the hell did you get involved in over there, Robert?"

"Beats the hell outta my ass sir, all I know for certain is, there was a crazy report stating some ancient female Samurai Warrior from Japan's past has somehow came back from the past, and she was killing a bunch of extremely important and very influential Japanese and now American businessmen, sir. Hell for a while there all fingers of blame were pointing directly at this one greatly honored Japanese businessman, a Hiromoai Hatanaka. But that ended real quick when it was discovered this Hatanaka fellow was slaughtered all to hell in the same pit where Batterman had met his end sir. So that removed the finger of blame aimed at him sir. So since we lost that one lead, the Japanese Detectives are desperately trying to find out what the hell was really going down over there sir. The last time I spoke to the Lieutenant, he informed me they were still bumping into a wall. Those Japanese people don't like to talk to any Police Officers, they'd rather die than help the police out over there sir." Rossie gave out an exhausted sigh.

"What the hell do you mean this Hatanaka fellow was slaughtered in the same pit Batterman was killed in, Rossie?" the Commander looked at his agent like he just lost his mind on him.

"I mean this poor Hatanaka fellow was slaughtered, and I mean really slaughtered sir. There wasn't one piece of him left larger than my damn hand. Someone really went after him with a fucking sword, Ralph. I don't think there was a piece of him left larger enough to make another slice of. He was actually chopped into small pieces, and I mean small pieces at that sir. And to top it all off, the remains of this poor Hatanaka was obviously pissed on by his murderer, who took this time to punish him even in death. That move was the worst possible insult the murderer could have possibly offered his remains, and a powerful insult any Japanese person could suffer. Whoever killed the bastard really enjoyed themselves at his expense I can tell you Ralph. It was a terrible mess we had to watch where the hell we were stepping on the crime scene, because his remains were all over the pit from wall to wall, sir." Agent Rossie announced as he shifted his weight in the chair as he tried to get more comfortable and remain awake at the same time.

"Are you trying to pull my damn leg here or what mister? This is the Twentieth Century for crap sake, and no one is hacked to death with a god damn sword any longer like they were when these damn Japanese buggers were roaming all over their damn country carrying two swords, and looking for anyone to chop their heads off their shoulders for no reason at all, mister. Man you really look like a can of crushed assholes here son, are you sure you don't want to go home and finish with this report tomorrow morning, Agent Rossie? Or at least I can order you up a strong cup of coffee so you can keep your damn eyes open as we talk this mess over, Bob."

"I can really use a cup of strong coffee to get my heart thumping again sir, because I want to get this damn report off my back while everything is still rather fresh in my mind, and I can still remember all the shit that took place over there in Japan, Ralph. There's so much to go over and with Batterman's death, it's got the Japanese Lieutenant I was working with running around in circles, and he's really concerned how we're going to react over here to Batterman's death. The Lieutenant was actually quite a bit concerned if this killing could end up as a major international incident, and we here in the States start blaming the Japanese government for Batterman's death. He was desperately trying to wrap up the entire murder case even before I left Japan to report back to you over the Batterman's situation, Ralph. Man did I drink that coffee already?'

"Yeah, yeah I got the message you pain in the ass you." Ralph moaned and then he hit the intercom and grumbled into it. "Say Grace, sorry for bugging you this late in the afternoon, but is it possible for you to fine two cups of coffee hanging around out there for us in here. Agent Rossie is having a bit of trouble keeping his damn eyes open, and he needs a strong shot of caffeine in the arm to get his blood flowing again in his body, honey?"

"Thanks, you're a real doll and yes a few pieces of cake would help out real fine for us. I own you a big one, young lady." When he was off the intercom Ralph offered to his agent. "Grace will be here in a few moments with some cakes and coffee for us, so now where were we when I was interrupted with what we were speaking about mister?"

"I was telling you how hard the Japanese Detectives were working on trying to solve the damn murder of Batterman before I left Japan to make my report to Headquarters, sir. I'm afraid the Detectives are taking it to heart that Batterman was killed in Japan, and so quickly after he brought a Japanese Construction Company to boot, sir."

"What was that you just said Agent Rossie, Batterman brought himself a fricking Japanese Construction Company? When the hell did that take place, I thought the lousy bastard was going over to Japan to have himself a little fling with one of those white faced painted up Japanese chicks for a change of pace from the American chicks he was always porking over here, dammit. We all know how he liked the girls and drink and some reports I read about him stated he sometimes used drugs, and I thought this was one of those sex visits it's always reported the old bastard was well known in doing every once in a while. How soon was he killed after buying the damn Japanese Construction

Company, Agent Rossie? Hey wait a minute mister, I thought an outsider couldn't buy a fricking Japanese business. It's supposed to be against their damn laws if I'm not correct. Am I correct here with that last assumption Rossie?"

"You're absolutely right spot on Ralph, and I don't know how the hell he was able to pull the transaction off in Japan. But the sonofabitch was successful and he brought himself a well known and highly honored Japanese Mining and Construction Company with a number of contracts still in effect for work projects in the country that company had signed up. I even read the report of the transaction before it was allowed to go though, and I couldn't find a damn thing wrong with it, and it was giving the finally okay by their Minister of Foreign Affairs Representative, sir. I don't know how he pulled it off and cleared all the hurdles the damn Japanese government has about a cursed Gai Jin taking over one of their damn construction companies and..."

"What the hell is a damn Gai Jin crap you just mentioned, Agent Rossie? I never heard that word used before, mister." His Commander asked him with a snap in his voice.

"Sorry Ralph, a Gai Jin is a foreigner to the Japanese, and their laws are rather strict about a Gai Jin owning one of their businesses. So I don't know how Batterman was able to pull it off, but he was successful. I guess if you throw enough money at anything, you can get what you want." The young FBI Agent offered with a bit of concern lacing his voice.

"Hummm... then allow me to ask you another question if you don't mind after all this information you have just offered me, Agent Rossie. Do you think it might be possible this Hiromoai guy, or someone else in the construction field in Japan, might have gotten insulted by this Gai Jin you like to call Batterman, and he took it upon himself to kill him to stop Batterman from owning one of their damn construction companies in Japan, sir?" His Commander asked.

"I threw that question out to Lieutenant Kenzaburo Motoshima myself, and he quickly brushed that suggestion aside. He didn't believe any other construction owner would ever stoop that low as to kill off one of their competition off, all that is but this Hiromoai Hatanaka fellow, sir. According to the Japanese Lieutenant, he didn't think anything was past this guy's intentions. That's why he concentrated all his attention and efforts on finding this guy guilty of Asahiko and his son Tsutomu-san and his wife's murder, or should I call it a slaughter, sir."

"You mean to tell me there were other deaths you were investigating while you were stationed in Japan, Agent Rossie? It seems like three others were killed excuse me, slaughtered to use your words like this Hiromoai fellow was with Batterman, Mr. Rossie. Was there any solution in those other deaths you were also working on in Japan?"

"I'm terribly sorry but you obviously have misunderstood what I was saying sir. I wasn't involved in investigating the other three deaths in the least sir. The Lieutenant and his Sergeant were doing all the investigations of those three deaths, sir. I only became involved in the last investigation, because that one involved the American Batterman, sir. The Lieutenant called me in on that one once he realized one of the bodies in the pit was that of Batterman, sir. Once I was involved in that investigation, the Lieutenant informed me of the other three deaths. Even though I was already aware of the deaths through a number of reports I read, and what I was able to pick up on the local news station." Rossie reported to his Commander with concern in his voice.

"I got it, by the way I was meaning to ask you another question Robert. If this Hiromoai fellow was so badly chopped to pieces where you couldn't even find enough of him to cut a second time, how the hell did you people ever identify all the gore as this Hiromoai fellow?" Ralph offered as he went silent for a moment while trying to collect his thoughts.

"Lieutenant Motoshima was able to identify the mess because we found his hand and part of his arm, it was the largest pieces we found of his slaughtered body, and on the part of the arm was this Rolex watch that the Lieutenant was able to identify as Hiromoai. Because he looked at the watch the other day to find out what time it was when he was interviewing Hiromoai Hatanaka over the other deaths he was investigating, sir." Agent Rossie reported to his control.

"It seems like you have all the damn answers to any question I might ask of you, Bob. I guess now you're back here in the States, we can start investigating what Batterman was up to for the past few weeks, before he went over to Japan and brought the Japanese Construction Company. I'm looking at maybe someone from the States took an exception to Batterman taking his business across the damn Ocean, and that one person might have trailed him to Japan and killed him there, so as to throw us off the track back here, sir. And cause all sorts of hell for the damn Japanese government at the same time by having so an important American businessman as Batterman was, killed in their stinking country. I don't know but obviously someone killed the lousy prick, so it's up to us to find out who that someone was, and why the hell he decided to kill an American businessman, and where he killed him for crap sake."

The Commander let out his breath in a rush as he went deep in thought for a few moments, and then he added to his orders to Agent Rossie. "Look Bob, I'm going to tag you with investigating Batterman's death, by starting you off here in the States. I want you to go over all his business records and transactions, find out if he was having any stinking problems with any other construction company here in the States. Also check and see if he was being sued by anyone, see if you can find anyone who might have had a grudge against him, or even maybe threatened his life in an argument. You know what I want and needed checked out. Hummm, I think I'm going to attach Special Agent Shinnosuke Fugiwara to this investigation with you as well. He understands and speaking this Japanese gibberish perfectly and I see in the future, you two will most likely end up back in Japan while continuing this damn investigation of Batterman's death.

"We are sure as hell going to end up back in Japan in order to investigate if any possible American businessman, Japanese or otherwise might have trailed Batterman over to Japan to kill him in that miserable country. You're going to get stuck checking out all the damn airlines, commercial and private and I'm certain you two will have to go to Japan to find out all the information you're going to need to solve this fricking murder case, Bob. I see this one turning out to be one helluva mess for us, and I also see even the President getting on my ass to solve this murder case faster than quick enough, and you can only guess who I'm going to get on if the heat's placed on my damn ass, mister." The Commander put on the biggest smile as he cocked his head to the side and then stared at Rossie until he got the message he was trying to send him.

"I hear you loud and clear with that last warning sir. I know Investigator Fugiwara and I have even worked on a couple other cases in the past when we were investigation the Japanese gangs operating out of L.A. a couple of years back sir. He's very easy to work with and he's damn good at what he does sir. Are you going to contact him and have him get in touch with me, or do you want me to contact him myself and find out when he can join me in this investigation sir? I take it I'm going to be the Lead Agent on this murder case sir?"

Agent Rossie was searching to see if he was going to be the Lead Agent in the case, or if he was going to end up working for Fugiwara because he spoke and understood the Japanese lingo perfectly. Even though he was able to pick up much of the Japanese language while he was stationed in Japan for the past three years to get by in the country. He did not know how to write it, or understand if the talker was speaking too quickly for him to follow his words, so he was well pleased he was going to be working with the Japanese Agent.

"What the hell are you talking about here Bob? Of course you're going to be the Lead Agent on this murder case. Why the hell do you think I'm speaking to you for, for my damn health for crap sake? Agent Fugiwara is going to be the second Agent on the job with you, Bob. Besides, if you two end up back in Japan, at least you know the Japanese Lieutenant who is already off and investigating Batterman's death in Japan. That's one of the main reasons I want you as the lead in this damn case, mister. I guess I'll make contact with Agent Fugiwara and order him to get in contact with you as soon as possible. I'll leave it up to you to bring him up to speed on this murder case, Bob. You can at least take that much off my damn back for me, mister. I know he was working a case up in New York for the past six months, but if I remember right. He finished up that case, and he's been reported taking a week off after that case concluded, sir.

"I'll find out where the hell he's at and what he's doing, and I'll order him to make contact with you at his earliest possibility time. I know he was coming up for an additional assignment and I'll cut him off that investigation and assign another Agent to the case I was going to assign him to. I need and want him working on this case with you, Bob. I know somewhere down the line you're going to end up back in Japan, and I want someone who knows and speaks and even writes the damn lingo of that country with you, Bob. I know you're up to some time off, but since this case showed up, I need you on this damn thing. Believe me Agent Rossie I'll make it up to you later on once this case is finished and I don't end up with the President riding my damn ass into the ground on me, mister. I need this damn murder case closed as soon as possible, Bob.

"I just wish this damn pain in the ass Batterman couldn't have stay in the States where he belonged and get knocked off here so we don't get stuck trying to head off a possible international murder incident for crap sake. I can see it now with the President getting on my case to solve this damn case as soon as possible, and that's why I'm going to rely heavily on you and Fugiwara on this case. I want my best Operatives working on this one so I know it won't take years to get this damn thing solved." Suddenly, his Commander looked over Rossie's shoulder at his belongings he brought into his office with him, and he grumbled at him.

"What the hell is that damn thing sticking out of your luggage over there, mister? Did you smuggle something you shouldn't have outta Japan with you mister? What the hell is that damn thing anyway, Bob?" His control asked because he was that interested in the package

Agent Rossie turned around and looked at his luggage and saw the wrapped up sword sticking out of the suitcase, and he offered his control. "No way Ralph, when I started investigating Batterman's death in that pit, while I was looking for any possible evidence. I happened to discover this ancient Samurai Sword stuck under a load of wood. I pulled it out and Motoshima checked it out and said it was worthless to the Antiquities Minister, and he told me he'd clear the way for me to get it out of Japan legally and take it home with me, you want to see it Ralph?'

"Why the hell would I want to see some old rusted fricking sword for? I'm not the least bit interested in them Japanese pig stickers, Bob. Now if you were to come home with a stack of naked pictures of them painted Japanese broads then you'll have my undivided attention I tell you, mister. What the hell are you going to do with the damn thing anyway, Agent Rossie?"

"Well I know the first thing I'm going to do when I get it home, I'm going to get the blade out of the ancient sheath then I'm going to clean the damn thing up the best I could and then I'm going to place it in the top of the mantle of the fake fireplace in my apartment. Then I'm going to brag to any women I bring home with me for the night on how I took it away from a Japanese Samurai Warrior after I have to fight him to the death. How could any women refrain from making love to me after hearing that whopper I'm gonna spin for them?" the young FBI Agent smirked back at his control and then he gave him a quick wink of the eye.

"Boy what a crock of shit you got yourself going there mister. I think you'd have much better luck getting a chick in bed with you, if you ply her with a chilled bottle of good wine and some soft music in the background, and a helluva lot of foreplay and skip all the damn drama about the sword if I was you, mister." His control offered Rossie with a smirk.

"Yeah, I think you have a pretty good point there Ralph, and I'm going to do what you have just suggested my friend. Anyway, I'm going to have some fun with the damn sword when I get it back to my apartment, cleaning it up and all and I think it's going to look real great sitting on my mantle. Besides it'll give me something to do when I end up with some extra time on my hands, and when I'm bored to death at the same time, sir. You're going to get in contact with Agent Shinnosuke Fugiwara and have him make contact with me as soon as he can call me sir, right? I don't have his contact number any longer ever since the last time I worked with him, and if you don't get him, at least give me his contact number and then I'll call him for myself to take some of this crap offa your back, Ralph."

"Jesus Christ Almighty, I already told you I'll make contact with him and order him to call you first thing for crap sake. What the hell do you think I'd forget to make that damn call for you, mister? You just worry about your old fricking sword and any young chicks you might be able to talk into visiting your apartment, and leave that pain in the ass Agent Fugiwara to me. I want to you head home and forget about any chicks for tonight, and I want you to get a good night's rest, because as soon as I get hold of Agent Fugiwara, I'm going to get the both of you busy on this damn murder case.

I'm not going to wait until I have the damn President breathing down the back of my neck on this one mister. I want it done with even before I receive the first call from the big Boss Man. Do you hear me mister, do you understand what I want you to do tonight?

"I don't want you to get too involved in any stinking hankie pinkie tonight with any stinking broads you might pick up along your way home mister. Just rest up because once you start on this damn murder case, there'll be no letting up until you two solve the damn thing for me, mister. So why the hell don't you get the hell out of my office, and go and get some rest for yourself tonight. I'll be expecting you back in my office tomorrow morning at exactly 10 A.M. sharp. No if and or buts about it my friend. I'll hope to make contact with Agent Fugiwara and with any luck, I can have him report to my office around the same time you're scheduled to arrive here to start in this damn case tomorrow morning, mister."

"Okay I'm leaving, but boy are things getting tight around here lately Ralph. I didn't even get my damn cup of coffee and piece of stinking cake before you're dismissing me, mister. Don't forget you owe me that..." Before he could even finish his complaint with his control, Ralph's secretary walked in the office with the coffee and cakes, and she was already apologizing because of how long it took for her to get the requested coffees and cakes.

"I'm terribly sorry Mr. Murdock Sir, but the coffee was left in the pot was old and smelt a little burnt, and I knew you wouldn't enjoy a cup of that mess. So I brewed a new pot and I had to go all the way down to the canteen to get you some cakes for you to enjoy. I hope I didn't take too long and now you two no longer want the coffee and cakes I got for the both of you to enjoy."

"No, you did real fine, I was just about ready to throw this bum out of my office anyhow, but I'd like to share a cup of coffee with him before he leaves. That way I'll know he'll stay awake long enough to get home safely for crap sake. Sit back down Bob and enjoy the coffee, there are a few other things I'd like to go over with you before you take off and I lose you for the rest of the damn day. Thank you Grace and you can go now please." Ralph waited until his secretary was out of the office before he spoke to Agent Rossie again.

"Okay now that she's out of the damn office Bob, can you think of anything you might need or want, to help you with this damn murder case you're about to start for me, mister? Anything at all you can think of, all you have to do is ask for it and I'll get it for you. You still have the service car at your disposal for a vehicle is no problem. Can you think of anything you might need, Bob?" His control asked as he took the first sip of the steaming brew.

"Yes, I can think of one thing I'm going to need okay, Ralph. What's my cash limit on this Batterman case. I know I'm going to need some money for traveling, gas, food and anything else I might need along the way, sir. I won't need a vehicle, I can always use the one that was left for my use at the airport I used to get over here at the office sir." Agent Rossie offered his control as he looked at the man to see if this request was going to upset him.

"That's no worry there, you still have the department credit card on your person, and you have an open credit line with it for anything you require throughout this entire case, mister. Just keep a good running tag for bookkeeping this time around will you please. I received so many damn complaints over your last expenditures list from the other case you worked on, mister. I though the damn GAO

(Government Accounting Office) was going to come over here and take all your charges out of my fucking paycheck, because you were so damn sloppy with keeping a good record of the expenses you incurred on that case, mister. Is that all you can think of that you might need for this case, Agent Rossie? Don't forget there are going to be two of you working on this damn case until it's solve, so you're going to be responsible for all the charges the both of you guys ring up on this one. It goes with being the Lead Agent in a murder case, mister." Rossie's control warned the young agent in no uncertain terms this time.

"No, I can't come up with anything else I might need with this case. I guess I'll handle anything that crops when it shows itself sir. And I have no problem keeping control of all expenses for the both of us during this case. I got it covered okay sir." Agent Rossie bragged as he quickly drained his coffee then he wolfed down the small cake. Once he was done he stood up and reached out and shook Murdock's hand then he turned in his heels and rushed out of the control's office.

All the while he was speaking with his control in his office and receiving his further orders, in the back of his mind he was dying to see what the ancient sword really looked like. When he first found the old sword out in the field at the murder site, Lieutenant Motoshima immediately grabbed the obviously useless sword away from him so quickly, and checked it out to make certain it was worthless. Then he handed it back to him, but when they were heading back for their cars, Lieutenant Motoshima requested the sword back, and he never saw it again until he was about to board the plane back to the United States. So he never really got a chance to really check out the old sword properly.

Lieutenant Motoshima met him at the airport and handed him the sword back wrapped in an evidence bag, and handed it to him as he boarded the plane. So he never got a chance to look at the sword, and now he had to wait until he was home. Then he could finally uncover the ancient sword and really see what it truly looked like, and see just how old it truly was at the same time.

He rushed to the parking lot and jumped in his Agency's car and started it up and drove out of the north parking lot. The traffic was rather heavy at this time of the day, and he was forced to take his time heading home. In his mind's eye he was seeing the sword all cleaned and polished up and proudly displayed on his mantle. His apartment was a good half an hour away from the office, and with this traffic he knew it was going to take him almost an hour to get home.

It took him the better part of an hour to finally reach his apartment. He was so tired by the time he opened the door to his apartment, he merely threw his luggage on the floor and rushed to the fridge and took out a cold Pepsi and placed the ice cold can up against his forehead to try and wake himself up a little. The cold can revived him enough for him to go off and look for the sword. He pulled it out of his luggage and ripped into the wrapping that covered the sword. He was so excited to finally see the sword he threw the wrapping on the floor. Finally looking at the ancient sword, he could actually smell the oldness of the blade, even the wood sheath was actually crumbling in his hands, even though he was trying to be extremely careful with the ancient weapon. He then walked over to the small kitchen and placed the sword down on the table then he started to try and release the sword from its wooden prison

CHAPTER TWO

FBI SPECIAL AGENT ROBERT ROSSIE'S APARTMENT

Agent Robert Rossie carefully laid the ancient sword down on his small kitchen table, and began to closely examine the terribly crumbling wood prison of the old sword. All the once exquisite carving and god and silver inlay of the sheath had been long ago lost to the endless ravages of time. Now the wood scabbard was barely able to remain together. He rolled the sword slowly over and examined the other side of the sheath and exposed handle of the once deadly killing sword. The brocade of silk cord that once wrapped the handle had long ago unraveled and the few gold decorations that held the cord in place, had likewise lost their luster to time and the elements. He smiled as he again studied the ancient weapon then wiping his hands of the side of his pants, he brought them up and took the handle of the sword in one hand, and with the other hand he grasped the sheath of the old weapon, and then he started to apply some pressure, to try and free the sword from the sheath of the weapon.

Neither side of the ancient weapon would release the gripe they had on each other, and quickly the FBI Agent found himself applying more and more increased pressure of both the handle of the sword and the sheath still protecting the age old weapon. Beads of sweat appeared on his forehead as he continued to struggle in his attempt to separate the sword from its wooden prison. Quickly, what was left of the badly crumbling wood sheath began to crumble more in his hand as he tugged, twisted and pulled on the two ends of the weapon. Slowly, he felt the wooden sheath weakening to the point he believed it was going to free the sword from its grasp. With a grunt of added pressure, the two ends suddenly separated and he ended up with the wooden sheath in his left hand, and the badly rusted sword end in his right hand. But even before he could place the two ends back down on the table, they both started to slightly vibrate in his hands.

Not understanding what the tingling in his hands meant, the concerned agent placed the two ends of the weapon down on the table, and then he began to examine with metal of the sword. In many places on the shaft, a number of small pieces of wood were stuck to the metal of the blade. He had no idea where the wood was stuck to the sides of the sword, it was Wind's blood that glued the wood to the once deadly shaft. Slowly he began to pick at the wood with the fingernails of his right hand, while holding the sword in place with his left hand. Picking most of the wood off from this side of the sword, he rolled the ancient weapon over in his hands, and began picking off the remaining small chunks of wood from the shaft of the sword from this side.

He was so involved in picking at the wood pieces, he failed to notice the slight bit of light that was developing in the center of the kitchen behind his back. The more he continue to pick at the pieces of wood, the more the glow increased, and now a slight draft was developing behind his back. Getting more and more involved with picking off every small piece of wood stuck to the shaft of the sword, his excitement for the weapon grew. Letting his breath out in a rush he stood up and stretched his back. All the once exhaustion assaulting his body left instantly when he started working on the ancient sword. It was at this point the slight breeze ruffled the small hairs on the back of his neck, and it drew his attention and he finally looked behind himself.

He was stunned when he noticed the glowing ball of light that seemed to be floating in the middle of the air about mid chest level. He cocked his head to the side and stared mystifyingly at the glowing and floating ball of light. Suddenly he smelt dust, and he could swear he heard in his mind, beating hooves of charging horses and he shook his head to try and get what he believed he was feeling out of his mind. Now he thought he heard the cried of charging soldiers as they rode their horses to battle against their enemy. Louder and louder this thought to be noises grew until he had to finally admit something strange was happening right in the center of his kitchen.

He reached for his pistol that hung from his hip when he was dressed, and then he remembered he put his weapon in his luggage when he boarded the aircraft from Japan. Finding himself without a weapon to protect himself from what was taking place in the center of his apartment, he reached behind himself and picked up the old and ancient sword, and then held it out before him in order to protect his life with the weapon. Instantly, his eyes opened wide and he found himself starting at what was moments before, a crumbling and terribly rusted, nicked and even slightly bent old weapon no one would have given a second glance at. Now he was holding an ancient Katana killing blade that seemed like it was just made. The once rusted shaft of the sword was as gleaming and razor sharp as the day it was born in the fire of the ancient sword maker.

The agent removed his eyes from the glowing ball then he stared at the sword, flipping it over in his hands and checking out the other side of the sword. He could not understand how and why the once severely damaged and worthless weapon was now worth a King's ransom, and looked as good as new. Even the once missing brocade wrap of the handle of the sword, and the ten small gold shapes that head the cord in place on both sides of the handle of the weapon, was back in all its beauty. He actually took a swing with the weapon, and it immediately warned the user of its deadly song, as the edge of the sword cut through the air as easily as the once ancient weapon would cut through any enemy it was ordered to attack by the master of the sword.

Stunned at what he was seeing, he mumbled at the sword locked in both his hands now. "What the hell's going on in here for the love of God? What the hell's going on with this damn thing? Shit, should I throw the damn thing out the window or keep it for my own protection?"

Instantly the once soft glowing light grew in its intensity, and a sweet sounding female voice nearly sang her reply to his words in old Japanese. "Is my Lord and Master asking this worthless Samurai Warrior a question? I am bound by my oath once sworn before you on the edge of my sword, and my bloody fingertip was placed on the scroll that bound my oath to your service for as long as I was allowed to breathe the air that gave me life, my Liege Lord." With each word the spirit of Wind asked, the glowing light pulsated brighter and brighter, and then the glow lessened when she stopped speaking and waited for who she thought was her Lord and Master Kawasomeru who just asked her a question. According to the curse of the sword, anyone who held the ancient sword in their hands was in her eyes and mind, her beloved Lord Kawasomeru.

Agent Rossie was having a hard time following what whoever was speaking to him was saying, because whoever it was, the obvious female speaking was speaking in Japanese to him as he cried at the speaker. "What the hell is going on here for God's sake? Who the hell are you and what the hell do you want from me, dammit? Show yourself to me at once!"

"I fear once again my honorable Liege Lord is employing words that I am most unfamiliar in knowing what is being asked of me. Please my honored Liege Lord, use the ancient words of Japan, so that I might know what is being asked of me by my Lord and Master."

TOKYO JAPAN, DETECTIVE AND HOMICIDE DEVISION OF THE TOKYO POLICE DEPARTMENT

Tokyo Police Detective Lieutenant Kenzaburo Motoshima was busy in his office going over the latest reports just filed with his office over the death of both Hiromoai Hatanaka, and the American businessman Calvin Batterman. At the end of his investigation and Hiromoai's elderly father was cleaning out Hiromoai's apartment, he was standing by and the elderly gentleman offered the Lieutenant a number of the well rusted and ancient junk pieces of age old armor his son found at one of their dig sites. The old man had no use for the terribly rusted, bent and crumbling weapons, so the Lieutenant took several of the ancient pieces and had them decorating his officer at the police department ever since receiving them from the old man.

At the same instant Agent Rossie was dealing with what was happening to the ancient and rusted sword the Lieutenant allowed him to remove from Japan. The same thing was happening to the number of pieces of ancient armor and weapons he had scattered about his office.

As he was working on the report, he suddenly picked up the strong smell of dust, and he felt a slight breeze also on the back of his neck in his office that caught his attention. He looked up from the report and was instantly stunned when he looked at the ancient and slightly bent Kama, the sickle like weapon once used in battle by the ancient Samurai of Japan's proud past, and it suddenly looked like it was just created. He immediately went around his office and looked at everything the old man gave him from Hiromoai's private collection of badly rusted and old weapons. The Toboko short hand spear also looked like it was just made, so he moved over to the next piece and discovered the same thing. The long handle Hachiwara paring weapon with the vicious hook like projection constructed at the base of the deadly weapon, also looked like it was just made and all the shine to the metal and sharp edge was back in all its glory.

He stepped away from the weapon and then grumbled at himself. "What the hell's gone on around here? How the hell did this just happen and what the devil does it mean to me, and possibly to this murder case I'm working on?" The Lieutenant bent down and pressed the button on his intercom and growled at the on duty Desk Sergeant. "Yes Sergeant Yamaguchi, is Sergeant Okamatsu hanging around anywhere out there? Is he by chance in his office? If you see him out there, inform him I need to see him in my office ten minutes ago, Sergeant."

"Err... Lieutenant, I just saw him around here a moment ago, let me see if he's in his office. Yes Lieutenant, I see him sitting in his office, I'll get him for you right off sir."

"Never mind that, I'll get him on his phone for myself I guess Sergeant, thanks anyway." With that said the Lieutenant broke off the connection and then he picked up the phone and hit the Sergeant's office number as he grumbled at himself that he should have called him right off, instead of bothering the Desk Sergeant.

When the bored Japanese Sergeant picked up the phone, the Lieutenant immediately growled at him. "Sergeant Okamatsu-san, I need to see you in my office as soon as possible mister. You won't believe what the devil is happening in here, mister. Get in here right away in case this is just a dream I'm seeing happening in here, and I need you to witness it as well mister."

The concerned Sergeant got up and rushed for the Lieutenant's office, fearing something was going down with the murder case they were investigation over Batterman's death. When he rushed into the office and looked at the Lieutenant. He did not say a word to the Sergeant. He merely pointed at the Kama weapon resting on the stand over one of his filing cabinets, and he allowed the instantly worried Detective Sergeant to draw his own opinion of what he was seeing happening to the once rusted and bent ancient weapon."

Also stunned over what he was seeing in the Lieutenant's office, the Sergeant absentminded mumbled more to himself. "What the hell..." As he slowly walked over to the weapon and he lightly rested his hand on the handle of the implement of death to see if what he was seeing was real or not. It was perfect, like new, with all the gold inlay and carving so neatly carved deep into the handle of the weapon again. Then he turned to the Lieutenant and asked him with concern lacing his tone of voice. "What the hell does this mean? Is this possibly connected to the case of Calvin Batterman, Lieutenant? If it is then nothing would surprise me about this unending case any longer, Lieutenant. With all the weird stuff that has happened with ancient Samurai Warrior from the past coming back and slaughtering our businessmen. A female Samurai Warrior at that, so if this is part of the case then it doesn't surprise me in the least, Lieutenant."

"I don't know, I was kind of hoping you could answer some of the same questions I was asking myself when I first noticed this crap happening to these old weapons and stuff I got from Hiromoai's private collection, from his honored father a while ago. I can't possibly answer any of the questions you just asked of me, when I'm asking the same questions of myself, Sergeant. I have no idea what this might mean and if it could be possibly connected to the

Batterman's murder case or not. But I have to say this to you, since I'm seeing this shit taking place with the stuff from Hiromoai's collection. I'm once again believing he was truly the one who was behind this supposed female Samurai Warrior from our past, and he was controlling her killing spirit to do his dirty work for him by killing his strongest competition in the construction field."

Taking a quick breath in, the Lieutenant again looked at some of the weapon that now looked like they were just created, and groused at his Sergeant. "How the hell do I write this one up in my report? If I put down what we both are seeing here and by the end of the day we'll surely either both be discharged from the Police Department, or we'll both find ourselves sitting on the top floor of the hospital in the nut ward, being filled with all sorts of head drugs. Looking at this unbelievable happening, I don't think for the time being I'm going to include it in any of my reports to the Commander's office. I'm not going to put my future with the Department on the chopping block because I'm seeing the impossible taking place right before my eyes, Sergeant."

"I'm seeing the same thing you are obviously seeing, and I can't believe it for myself sir, and I don't blame you in the least if you omit this happening from any report you have to file for upstairs, Lieutenant. I'll tell you this much Lieutenant, as soon as I'm off work tonight, I'm buying myself a bottle of Sake then I'm going to get blinded, stinking drunk tonight, and maybe I'll be able to forget what I think I'm seeing sitting right before my foolish eyes, Lieutenant." The still stunned Detective Sergeant offered to his Commanding Officer.

"And I think I'm going to join you in getting blinded drunk tonight as well Sergeant Okamatsu-san. Damn, I still can't believe what I'm seeing taking place here, mister. This is why

I called you into my office for in the first place, Sergeant, I wanted you to see this crap for yourself. That way if I was losing my mind, I was going to take you along with me mister." The Lieutenant mumbled as he slowly shook his head no over what he was looking at.

"Thanks a lot Lieutenant, you had to take me along with you, and now I won't be able to sleep for a week before I can forget what I'm looking at here, sir." Sergeant Okamatsu complained.

"I just can't believe what the devil I'm looking at here Sergeant. This has to be part of what Hiromoai has introduced into this nightmare, and it also has to be part of the Batterman murder case. You know what Sergeant, since I believe this has to have something to do with the Batterman case. I think I'm going to place a call to FBI Agent Robert Rossie, and see what he thinks of what we're seeing here today, Sergeant. I'm certain he still working on the Batterman case even though he was ordered to return to the United States by his Commanding Officer. So if he's still working on this case back in the States then I want to hear what he thinks this might be all about. Hummm... it has to be damn early in the States, so I think I'll put my call to Agent Rossie off for another few hours so I don't wake him early in the morning over there, Sergeant."

"That sounds about right to me Lieutenant." Sergeant Okamatsu offered with a smile.

BACK AT FBI AGENT ROBERT ROSSIE'S APARTMENT

Agent Rossie was still holding on to the ancient sword out before his face in a self protective stance, as he now found himself staring at the small floating orb of light, and trying to figure out who was speaking to him from within the glowing light as he called out to it. "Who and what are you and why the hell are you here? I'm warning you, I'm armed and I know how to protect myself from any attack so be aware of that warning."

"Once again my wise Lord and Master is using words that I am not familiar with. Please my Liege Lord, use the ancient words of Japan so that I can understand what you are saying to me." The spirit of Wind was actually begging the FBI Agent to speak to her in Japanese.

Hearing whatever was trying to commutate with him from within the glowing light, he understood if he wished to speak with it, he was going to have to use his limited knowledge of the Japanese language, as he offered in almost perfect Japanese. "Whoever you are, who are you and what the hell do you want from me? Why can't I see who is trying to talk to me from within this strange light that is filling my room? How can I see who or what you are?"

Wind smiled over the poor Japanese her Lord and Master was speaking at her, and what was missing from his words she kind of filled in for herself as she replied to his questions. "My honorable Liege Lord, have the many passing years not been very kind to your wonderful memory that you no longer can remember your loyal Samurai Warrior Wind?"

The concerned Agent Rossie had to cock his head to the side again and aim his ear at the orb in order to hear and try and figure out what whoever was trying to speak to him, was saying. Figuring more of her words out, he replied to what he was now feeling was the spirit he heard about, when he started investigating the Batterman murder back in Japan. Thinking about his words more carefully before offering them to this spirit he began. "I remember when I was working in Japan, a story about a female Samurai Warrior who was brought to the future from the past by some Master, are you that spirit I heard mentioned about, Samurai Warrior?"

Trying to fill in the words that were said wrong or missing from her Lord and Master's words, she finally replied to him. "Yes my wise Lord and Master, I am that person you are speaking about." Again the spirit of Wind almost sang her words to her believed to be Lord and Master.

"Damn, how was this possible, I mean you coming from the past to be allowed to come to the future? Are you a spirit of this Samurai Warrior you say you are?" Rossie asked as he slowly lowered the sword to a less threatening stance, as he continued to start at the glowing orb.

"Thank you for lowering your killing sword my Liege Lord, because you have nothing to fear from me. I am still your most loyal subject who would die a hundred deaths before I ever thought of any treachery aimed against my Lord and Master. What is it my Lord and Master requests from his loyal Warrior? All you have to do is request of me and I shall move Heaven and earth to accomplish what you desire of me my Master?" Wind offered to the still stunned man standing before her as if he was actually scared to death of her spirit, something she could not understand.

"Spirit of this long ago Samurai Warrior, why is it I cannot see your true form? Why are you choosing to hide yourself inside that glowing circle that hides you from my view? Is there certain reasons why I cannot or am not allowed see what and who you truly are, voice of the light? Are you a possible threat against me? Am I supposed to be in fear of you?" Agent Rossie asked the spirit, still remaining in fear of whatever was hiding itself inside the glowing circle. Even though the voice was that of a female speaking to him from within the light, his mind was still not linking it up to the fact this spirit he was speaking with, might be that of a woman.

"I could no more be a possible threat against my honored Liege Lord than I can change the fact I am Samurai! Now if I am understanding your words, although you are replying to me with broken Japanese, and you are also omitting many certain words that would make your sentences much more complete for my limited understanding my Liege Lord. I am trying to complete those sentences for you in my mind, before responding to your many questions of me my Lord. I hope I am not insulting you by my poor efforts of trying to understand everything you are offering to me, my Liege Lord. I only wish to communicate with my Master more clearly, so we both can understand each other, Kawasomeru-Sama." Wind offered in her own defense, because it was sometimes taking her a little time to organize his words into a proper sentence, so she could understand what he was trying to tell her, and respond properly to his questions of her.

"Spirit, I don't care how long it takes you to respond to any of my questions of you, as long as you finally reply to me. Once again I find myself be forced to ask you for a second time, why it is I cannot see your true form? Are you that ugly you don't wish I see you in true form? Are you not of solid form? Is it not possible for you to take a more solid form before me, so that I might see who I am speaking with?" Agent Rossie asked as he got more and more comfortable with speaking to this spirit he was still unable to see in true form. And more and more he was beginning to trust this spirit, and he was less concerned with this spirit was there to harm him.

"My honorable Liege Lord, there is only one way the Gods of my ancestors will allow me to assume a true and solid form before your honorable eyes as you must remember, because of the many times you Commanded my spirit to appear before you, Lord Kawasomeru. And that one way is if my spirit was able to become in constant contact with my Katana blade that you now hold within your hands, my Master of time and earth." Wind replied to her Master's question.

"You mean I have to hand you this sword, and that's the only way you can assume a solid form before me, spirit?" Rossie asked, no so confident any longer. Now he was worried if he allowed this spirit to take possession of the sword, was she going to attack him with it. Was he to be so foolish as to disarm himself, only to trust a spirit he can't even see with the only weapon in the room. Could he really trust this spirit, especially if this is the same spirit who might have killed Batterman and Hiromoai, and the other three murders that happened when he was in Japan?

Wind was easily able to see the turmoil her Lord and Master was suffering with and she offered him in a very trusting sounding tone of voice. "My most honorable and respected Lord and Master, why is it I read such mistrust of this most loyal Samurai Warrior, written so deeply within your all seeing eyes? I assure you my Liege Lord you have absolutely nothing to be in fear of me for. If anything, I would do anything within my power to protect your life from all danger and harm, even at the cost of my worthless life. I am only allowed life by the Gods as long as my life is committed to the protection and welfare of my Lord Kawasomeru. That is my life and my only want, to serve and protect your life from all harm my Lord." Wind stopped speaking at this point, and she settled down and hoped her Master would trust her with his sword.

FBI Agent Rossie found himself staring so intensely at the small floating orb of almost blinding light, while his mind raced over what he was to do. On one hand he wanted to see what this spirit looked like more than he wanted to bed his next girlfriend. But on the other hand, how could he possibly trust this extremely dangerous spirit. Especially if she truly had anything to do with the deaths of Batterman, or the other four Japanese people who lost their lives to this believed to be Samurai Warrior for the ancient past of Japan's proud history.

Again, Wind's spirit offered to the worried Agent in a calm voice. "My Liege Lord, though I wish to be standing before you in my true form, I shall also be willing to end my spirit's worthless life if you continue to mistrust the only person who had ever walked the face of the earth, who you could truly trust with your honorable life. I could not possible request to remain alive in spirit only if my wonderful Lord and Master did not truly trust his most loyal of subjects to ever be retained by my Master's most honorable hand and word. This would be too much of an insult for me to continue to wish to visit the living world from the Ukiyo, or the forever Floating World and myth and wonderment. If I do not own your sacred trust then I own nothing, not even life in the living world or the world of spirits."

Agent Rossie swallowed hard, and then he lit out his breath in a rush as he finally offered to the spirit of the light. "Okay, I'm going to trust you with the sword you need to be in contact with, so I might view your true form. Do you swear to me you'll not attack me with the sword once you're in Command of the weapon?" He asked as he began to speak more and more like the spirit was speaking to him. He did not even realize he was understanding much more of her Japanese words than he ever understood before, or was able to speak before in his life.

"Does my Liege Lord think of me as a lowly and forever wandering worthless Ronin, a Masterless Warrior who had no allegiance to any one Master of life and death over his being? No my Lord and Master, my spirit remains as loyal as my earthly form was loyal to you in life."

"In that case I'm going to allow you to take Command of your sword. What do you want me to do with it, spirit of the ancient past times?" Agent Rossie asked of the spirit of the light.

"All my faithful Lord and Master has to do is just simply lay my great Katana killing sword on the floor at your honorable feet, and then watch as I take my earthly form right before your worried eyes. Then you shall see nothing but sheer loyalty written deeply within my honorable eyes, and your soul we be set at easy with the knowledge I mean nothing but complete trust and loyalty from your always loyal Samurai Warrior of Japan's great past times. My loyalty's heavier than the world and my life is lighter than a feather. Please my Master of life and death, I wait patiently for the ability for me to assume my earthly form once again before you, so that I can again breathe the pure sweet smelling air of the living world. I long to feel the warmth of the sun and the chill of the stiff breeze that comes from clouds that surround Mount Fuji again, and hear the birds sing, and the dogs bark and the children play. All these pleasures are reserved for the living. Oh to be part of the living world again, my wise Master over time and earth."

"I shall offer you your sword then, here, take it." Agent Rossie replied as he bent down and laid the ancient sword carefully out on the floor right at the tips of his feet then he straightened up and watched the reaction of the glowing orb and the spirit floating within the light.

Almost instantly, the light rapidly expanded until it took over the entire interior of the small kitchen area of his apartment. Then four long fingers of the light wrapped its glow around the hilt of the sword resting on the floor. The breeze in the room picked up in its intensity, and so did the sounds of wildly charging Samurai Warriors, as they and their horses engaged in war against their enemy of the past times. The dust that suddenly filled the room was almost chocking, and it even threatened to take Rossie's breath away from him. A dish suddenly went flying across the room as a glass fell to the floor and shattered. Paper was lifted and drifted softly in the air, and the sword of Wind started to float in the air within the strong circle of light.

Slowly, a human form began to struggle in the light to take a solid form. The more the shape struggled, the stronger the light grew to the point Rossie had to put his hand over his eyes it was so strong a light now. The sword was moving around in the light then suddenly, an arm holding the Sagahara crafted sword appeared clearly in the center of the light, as the heat of the light lessened, and more of a human shape was taking a good form before him.

When the face, neck and upper chest of the spirit took on a more solid form, Rossie was finally able to make out the spirit was that of a beautiful and naked young Japanese woman. More and more of her body took on a solid form as the light grew dim, and her full body was finally exposed to his view. The Samurai called Wind stood naked and unashamed before him as she lowered her head in silent homage of him as she brought the deadly killing sword across her outstanding shape and she actually saluted him with the blade. The moment she was whole, she immediately dropped down to her knees and rested her rearend on her crossed ankles and rested her full weight on them. She then laid the sword out before her knees, allowing the very tip of the blade to tough one of her knees. Then she rested her hands on her legs, palms up.

This was to display to her concerned Lord and Master that her hands were free of any possible weapons, and her whole body was exposed to his view, to prove she was no possible threat against his person. Her beautiful hair was shaped in the old style of the Kama no Sagariba, cut short to the length of her shoulders on the sides of her face, and the back of her hair went all the way down to the swells of her perfect shaped rearend. Her hair circled her face like a black mist, and her back was held straight, and it made her breasts stick out more and larger than they really were. Her stomach was flat and her abs showed through her skin. Her rearend was small, and her long and slender legs were perfect, and her feet were small. But Agent Rossie could easily see the sheer strength in her legs and arms over the way she held herself for his inspection.

He tried to see her face, but the way her head was bent and her eyes cast down towards the floor, was making it impossible for him to see what her face looked like, so he called out to the female Samurai Warrior. "Spirit of the past times of Japan, I want you to look at me so I can see what your face looks like. I cannot see your eyes the way you're looking."

"Please forgive my foolish stupidity my Lord and Master, your wish is my only desire." Wind replied as she lifted her eyes then she looked right at Rossie's face.

Agent Rossie had to take a step backwards because he was not ready to see such a beautiful woman as this Warrior was. Her chin was sharp, her nose small and her forehead was split in the center by her hair, but the most striking feature of her face was her eyes. They were captivating, perfectly circled by the black makeup he was surprised she wore, and the ends of her eyes were accented by the black liner drawn out longer than her eyes. Her eyes were narrow as was all Japanese women, but they were so striking so all seeing, so prepared to react to a lover or enemy. He smiled and she returned the smile, remembering not to bare her teeth before who she thought was her Lord and Master. Rossie nodded slightly to her and he finally allowed his entire body to relax before her, because he no longer fears this extremely dangerous female Samurai Warrior

Suddenly, his mind was flooded with thousands of questions for this Warrior from the past, as he continued to drink in her raw beauty and taught and dangerous body perfected for making love, or fighting her Master's enemy. Trying to collect his thought, he mumbled at Wind. "Samurai, you may get more comfortable because I have many questions to ask of you."

"I beg my Master's pardon, but I am perfectly comfortable with the way I am presently resting. I am also ready to answer any questions my honorable Lord and Master demands to know from my worthless mind, my Lord Kawasomeru. Please ask of me anything you wish to know of my life of the past or of now. I shall answer all your questions of me as truthfully as I can possible answer them for you, my Lord and Master over life and death."

"Okay Samurai, what is the name you like to be addressed by. I don't feel very comfortable with calling you Samurai all the time when speaking with you." Rossie asked, amazed he was able to understand so much of what she was saying to him. Somehow she had the ability of being understood even by someone who understood so little of her Japanese language.

"My Lord and Master, I fear you are playing with me, because of the foolish question you have just asked of me. Was it not by your own breath you have bestowed my name on me my Master? Do you toy with me to ask such a question of me? Nevertheless, who am I to question anything you ask of me? I am honor bound to answer any questions you ask of me. On the day of my Gembuku, the ceremony of my entering manhood even thought I was of the female life, you allowed me to enter the close knitted Samurai Caste of the male world. You had bestowed the name of Wind upon my head, and you further ordered me to name my deadly Katana killing sword Wind's Breath because you once said my sword was merely an extension of my arm. I was so very deeply honored you were so kind as to bestow such a powerful and worthy name as that upon my honorable sword, my Lord and Master." Wind announced proudly to her Master.

"I feel that was a perfect name to brand you and your sword with, and I'm pleased you have shared that bit of information with me, Wind. How was it you became so well trained in a man's world, and how was it you were allowed to invade that man's world, you being a woman I mean, Wind?" Rossie asked as he moved over and then pulled a chair away from the table and sat down then he continued staring at this female weapon as he prepared himself to hear her story of life.

"It all started with my most honorable father, he was your Master Trainer responsible for training your most elite of young Samurai Warriors. He was one of your most trusted Vassals who you relied upon heavily to train many countless of your future Samurai Warriors for all the future battles your world would soon be trapped within, mostly defending your great lands against the always troublesome and very foolish Lord Motoshige Wakatsuki. The once great Warlord was always trying to engage your Samurai Army in battle, because he demanded certain areas of your land that would give him access to the waters of the seas, or paths through much of your lands to make his trade much more profitable to him and his foul lands. Yet he constantly refused to pay the taxes for you to happily open your lands to his trade, my Lord and Master.

"Nevertheless, my father was told by the old seer of our village when he discovered my mother was pregnant with her eighth child, me. The old seer assured both my father and mother I was to be a male child. Well the Gods decided to play the trick on them, and I turned out to be a female child. When my father discovered I was a female, he was going to kill me and my mother, but my mother stopped him by showing him my wrist, see." Wind offered as she raised her arm and showed him the birthmark that looked so much as a shooting start then she went on with her story to who she still believed was her Lord and Master.

"My father saw the mark of the Samurai on my wrist, and he had no choice but to train me as a Samurai. He trained me harder and longer than any young male Warriors sent to our village to be trained by the Master Trainer of your realm. I spent long days learning Bushido, the code of conduct, chivalry, literally the Way of the Warrior. My nights were spent many hours engaging my father in the game of Go, where I learned how and where to deploy my Warriors where they would do the best to defeat our enemy when we were forced to engage in war with our enemy.

"Every waking minute was used by my father to train me in surviving on the battlefield. My father built up my body strength, my ability to understand my enemy and how to control my Armies who and how to properly defeat my enemy. Day and night was used by my father, until he felt there was no General who could best me on the battlefield. All the while my father was training me, he kept the secret I was a female, and then on the day of Gembuku where my father presented me to Lord Kawasomeru to become one of his trusted Samurai. But behind my back, some other Samurai spoke to the General and complained they thought me unclean, a leaper.

"The General dared to complain to my Lord and Master as you well know. But you in your great wisdom, refused to have me stripped and checked out. But you also decreed I should be tattooed in your honor of the Claw. I was forced to drop my top and upon doing so, my breasts were exposed. One of the Samurai rushed up and tried to stuff his mighty dragon into my mouth before all the other gathered Samurai. I reacted by cutting off his offending member, that caused a second Samurai to attack me. He would have done great damage to me, but another Samurai who was loyal to me, killed the other Samurai before he could attack me. Then you ordered the ceremony to end and you ordered me to remain until you sent for me.

"It took many hours for you to send for me and when you finally did, you brought me before all your Generals and informed them you were going to make me a General over your horse Warriors. Two of your General's refused to work with me, and you immediately ordered them to commit Suppuku and once they were dead, you ordered me to take over the horse Warriors. But you decided to end your relationship with my most honorable father. First you ordered my father to put his terrible suffering wife and my mother to death by giving her a poison elixir, and once she was dead and her body turned to ashes. You ordered my honorable father to cut off the finger he swore his sacred oath to you many years ago, and he did as you ordered him.

"Once you received his slivered finger, you ordered him to climb Mount Fuji and find an active volcano vent and once he discovered the vent, there before that vent he was to commit Suppuku with General Kobayashi-san to act as his second, and at the turn of the blade in my father's stomach, The General carried out his duty and cut my father's head from his shoulders. At the time of his death I heard his cry in my mind, and this upset me. While I cried in my private living quarters and upon hearing my cry, my one and only true lover in life, Captain Katsunoke Seisakajo-san begged entrance to see why I was so stressed. He was ill prepared for what I did to him, what I needed from him. I actually attacked him and nearly ripped his clothes from his back.

"For the first time in my life I was with a man and he fulfilled my desperate need of the moment, but he was really gentle with our first pillowing, because he realized I was never with a man before in my life. From that time on he was always riding at my side, and we pillowed every chance we got when we were alone from the rest of the Samurai

Warriors under my command. Then on that horrible night when we were set upon by a number of Lord Wakatsuki's loathsome manure eating coward Samurai attacked my encampment, and they killed my Captain and lover in the middle of the night without giving him a fair chance to try and defend himself against their attack. By the time my Warriors fought off these attackers, my Captain was left to die in his own pool of blood. Over the passing days I was able to discover who was in command of the lowly attackers and murderers of my Captain, and it was then I swore to myself a death threat on this one Samurai Warrior who was named Tetsuo Hatanaka, and all his future god cursed offspring.

"It took me many sticks of time (One stick of time was a day) for me to get over the terrible loss of my Captain and only lover I have ever known in that time of my life. For many weeks I moped around like I had lost my true fighting spirit. My understanding Lord and Master realized this and he called me before him and ordered me to find my brains again and get back to my old myself. To help me crawl out of my dilemma, he gave me a special order for me to take a number of my trusted Warriors and you sent me out to kill Lord Wakatsuki-san's leading General. You informed me with the death of this one well feared General, was going to force the worthless Lord Wakatsuki-san down to his knees and sue for peace between the two warring houses of Central Japan. So I departed and hunted and then destroyed this powerful and feared enemy General, and you were so correct with these thoughts. But it wasn't Lord Wakatsuki-san who ordered or requested peace between your two houses.

"Instead of Lord Wakatsuki-san requesting peace talks between you and he, he instead turned his anger towards our Emperor enjoying life in his capital city. The powerful warlord dared to threaten to march his Armies of dogs into the capital city and destroy the capital in its entirety. The Emperor ordered his most powerful General to come to your vast encampment and he also ordered Lord Wakatsuki-san to appear at your encampment with a hundred of his Samurai to protect him on his travels. The most insulting warlord entered your encampment wearing the Green Kimono of victory over his enemy. He stomped his way into your command tent and between the three of you, there was a peace solution arrived at. But over that agreement, Lord Wakatsuki-san demanded as one of the terms of peace between your two houses. He demanded the head of what he called me the Assassin Samurai who killed his most important General.

"This demand of Lord Wakatsuki-san's created much strain in your mind and at first you fought against the General from granting Lord Wakatsuki-san's demand. But in the end the General agreed with Lord Wakatsuki-san's demand, and thus I was ordered by you to meet with you the next sunrise to enjoy the awaking of the sun on that glorious day. And just as we both enjoyed the birth of that day, you suddenly ordered me to commit Suppuku. I was momentarily stunned by that order because I had no memory of committing any infraction against your person, and as I prepared to commit Suppuku in the true Samurai way by slicing open my innards. I turned and asked you why I was ordered to die and to this day I remember your reply. You told me my death was ordered by fate, so peace can once again return to the entire realm of Japan.

"With that said I began the sacred act of Suppuku, and to my surprise you offered to be my faithful second, and your duty in this act was to end my life swiftly so I did not suffer for a long period of time. The first part of Suppuku was not as painful as I once feared, and only when I turned the blade in my stomach and started to draw the blade the other way in my belly, did the first real signs of pain appear with the act. It was at this exact time you struck me with the blade and separated my head from my shoulders and you ended my life as ordered. But this is part of the act of Suppuku that truly surprised my soul. As life quickly drained from my body, my ears were still open and I heard the words you spoke to my severed head. As you still held in your hands the great blade that had just ended my life as I had enjoyed it, you said to my spirit.

"'Body of Wind, I know not what the Gods of Japan had in mind when they first allowed life to enter your spirit. But I understand some special hand is at work and is resting and guiding you in this world, and now in the spirit world. So I'm going to honor you in your noble death in much the same way you have honored me in your short and obedient life to my will and Commands. I'll have you buried in the ways of the old, in the great Samurai Warrior tradition of long ago. I'll bury you in your finest armor, your trusted steed will accompany you on your endless journey to the faithful lands of our ancestors dwelling beyond imagination and thought and wonder.

"Your steed's reins will be held by your hand for eternity. I'll place your head after viewing by the detestable Wakatsuki, dressed in your battle helmet on your chest. I'll order it to be tucked in the great gash of obedience you opened with your own hand across your belly, to help guard your honorable body against all evil and harm for life everlasting. I bid you well and nothing but peace that you have never enjoyed in the living world and in the land of wonderment and hope, my beloved Samurai Warrior General Masahiko, Yuriko, Tanizaki-Sama, my forever faithful Wind.

"You have brought great honor and respect in your short lifetime even from your hated enemy to yourself and to your family's well honored and respected name. I must curse your fighting spirit forever to this earth, in case your heart and Warrior spirit and the Gods will has not yet finished shaping Japan's faithful future and fate by your hand. Soul and spirit of Wind, I order you to be linked to my sword that has just caused your honorable death in body only, for the life of the great blade. Wind! I curse you to this Katana sword of justice forever!

"When the sword is drawn from its sacred sheath, your fine spirit will be again called back to the earth in order to carry out the bidding of the new owner of my Katana blade. Your heart, your soul, your spirit is too strong to be conquered by mere Gods of wonder, or these lonely moments of death you are experiencing at this time. This curse I have just placed upon your honorable head, will forever doom your unconquerable spirit to the land of the living in forever servitude of this, my mighty Katana sword. To be used only in respect and honor, and to the call of the next proud owner of the sword that just took your life. Wind, whoever owns my Katana sword in the future, will be continuing my orders and desires, and you are bound by your sacred oath to me, to respect anyone who holds my sword in their hands, and calls you back to the land of the living from the Ukiyo or Floating World, to serve them as well as you have always served me."

"It was at this time my ears finally closed to the words you were still speaking to my spirit. But my spirit remained hovering over my body, and I was allowed to listen to all the preparations you had ordered to honor my body of the living world. I watched my honoring warlord Kawasomeru-Sama, as you had used the great Sugahara crafted Katana sword that you used to dispatch my life, and you held it high over the frozen in death, sitting perfectly body of myself as you spoke your final words of the curse you had just placed upon my spirit, and to the Gods of Japan. I stared at the honored Katana blade still locked within your honorable hands, while enjoying the sheer power being emitted from the blade, before you replaced the still blood soaked steel shaft back within its wooden scabbard prison, without cleaning the great blade of my blood from it first.

"Thus you have further locked my amazing fighting spirit to the sword's steel, and it's now wooden prison. As you finished speaking to what you believed was the spirit of my body. And as you continued speaking your words of honor to my spirit, another earth rattling crack of thunder suddenly shook the earth beneath your feet, and it was quickly followed by a blinding stalk of lightening, as it struck the face of the earth a mere fifteen feet away from my resting body, and so near the body of my Lord and Master as you continued to hold onto the sword of my death.

"I remember how the sudden and loud crash of thunder and the following blinding lightening made my powerful warlord flinch ever so slightly. Then I remember you thinking it was the powerful Kami of Thunder who came to collect my spirit and then help guide me safely to the Floating World, and you thought this so strongly that you actually bowed towards the earth where the lightening had just struck it. With this final action of respect for the sake of your dead Samurai, you forever linked my fine spirit to the living earth, by allowing my blood to drip from the very tip of your mighty Katana blade onto the ground under your feet, before returning the wonderful blood soaked killing blade to its sheath. Then in your further respect of my spirit, you kicked a fine layer of soil over the few drops of my blood, believing in your mind you were further locking my soul and spirit to the land of the living forever.

CHAPTER THREE

"All the while you were so proudly honoring my spirit and memory, General Shimbo Kobayashi-san was sent out by your order to locate the proper Kofun, the sacred burial mound or ancient tomb where you were going to order my body to be safely laid in place and protected for all eternity to come. The very wise and concerned General selected a few chosen loyal and well trusted Samurai Warriors to assist him in his task. Other trusted Warriors carefully picked up my headless body, and the General after you my powerful warlord left with my head locked within your hands for private viewing by Lord Wakatsuki-san, as was his right to demand of you. The respecting Warriors carefully placed my body in the hastily prepared crypt after properly dressing me in my full body armor for the last time to adorn my body.

"My great Lord and Master then ordered my severed head cleaned and richly perfumed, and then mounted properly upon the honored Gunyoki spiked plate and displayed before the hated Lord Wakatsuki-san, and the powerful General who was sent out by the Shogun to force peace between the two warring houses of Central Japan. Immediately upon you setting your honorable eyes upon my head resting on the Gunyoki spiked plate for the last time in your life, my well respecting Lord and Master snapped angrily at the face of your young female Samurai Warrior. "With your proud and honored death, peace has once again been returned to the great realm of Central Japan and your Shogun and myself, my beloved Warrior Wind.""

All the while Wind was speaking to the Agent Robert Rossie, in her mind she believed she was speaking to Lord Kawasomeru, because anyone in possession of her ancient Katana killing sword was her true Lord and Master, as she continued with her explanation to the new owner of her sword. "As you were paying homage to my spirit my Lord and Master of time, General Kobayashi-san ordered my steed moved into my Kofun, and as soon as the horse was inside my crypt, he slit the animal's throat. He allowed the horse to bleed to death while it was being held down by other Samurai who accompanied him preparing the tomb for your Warrior. The General discreetly positioned the horse on the ground after he had that horse dressed in her battle armor and neck protector, to lay alongside my body also clad in my armor. Then Kobayashi-san looped the leather reins around my right wrist and he weaved it through the fingers of my hand. The General then placed the honored Katana blade rest perfectly on the center of my right shoulder.

"My matching shorter Wakizashi blade was placed in my left hand by the General, and he allowed the sheathed blade to barely touch my shoulder on the left side. My still strung Yumi (bow) was carefully laid across my body, and my Katakama Yari sear was placed across and over my bow and chest alike. All this respect and honor was carried out by the specially chosen Samurai Warriors to honor your dead Warrior for all times to come inside my burial tomb.

"My countless numbers of throwing stars, skewers, Tanto blades and other of my honored weapons I had accumulated over my short life span were carefully laid about on the ground or in other areas of respect to my body, surrounding my body properly in their everlasting honor and respect of my spirit. My weapons of all sorts would forever pay great homage to my fallen body. My account of long bamboo shafted arrows were so perfectly laid out in a fan shaped pattern with the hardened brass points barely touching my shoulders where my head should have rested.

"My body armor was ordered by your lips to be left unattached across my chest, the terrible gash across my entire belly was exposed and outlining the horrifying gash allowed to remain opened, so it could receive my head still shrouded by my mighty battle helmet, once my head was returned to my body for proper burial. Thus your order would forever seal the great wound from any and all evil trying to enter my fallen body through the mighty gash of total respect.

"When my greatly respecting Lord Kawasomeru cautiously entered my crypt for the first and last time in your great life, as if the interior of my tomb was going to rob you of your very soul, while carefully carrying my decorated head dressed in my battle helmet and still resting upon the Gunyoki spiked plate. The number of chosen and trusted Samurai Warriors working inside my hastily prepared crypt, knelt and bowed their heads respectfully towards my head and their Lord and Master at the same time. You my Lord Kawasomeru, ceremoniously removed my head from the hidden spike with your bare hands, and then you very respectfully placed it carefully into the open wound of my belly. Then you my great warlord looked at General Kobayashi-san who was likewise dressed in his full and well honored battle armor, and you nodded politely at him.

"Every Samurai who worked in my secret crypt quickly filed outside without words as General Kobayashi-san reverentially approached my lifeless body. He looked deeply into my closed eyes, to discover my face was caked with the pure white rice powder, and my lips were covered with the deep blood red paint of the respected Geisha women of the time, and my eyes were circled in the delicate black painted sharp lines, adding to the length of my once beautiful eyes. My head was also delicately perfumed with the finest of fine scented oils of the times.

The well pleased General Kobayashi-san turned and he actually smiled at his Lord and Master, not daring to bare his teeth before my powerful warlord, for allowing my body to be buried as the true woman I was in life. He fully understood it was the overly polite and attentive wife of my Lord and Master, the Lady Yuko who took her time to dress my head properly for burial, a great honor further offered to my worthless body, and the memory of this most unworthy young female Samurai Warrior. General Kobayashi-san nodded his approval of Lady Yuko's outstanding handiwork with my head. Then the General performed his last duty in life by moving over to where my head should have rested on my body, and then he went a little further distance from my body to my left side, the side of respect and honor to all Samurai Warrior's of ancient Japan.

"General Kobayashi-san next knelt down on a short and raised natural stone ledge perfectly overlooking my prone body, and then he slowly and very respectfully opened his body armor to completely expose his stomach to the call and bite of the deadly Wakizashi short stabbing blade. General Kobayashi-san then took the time to carefully tie his legs crossed under his body in place with two long rawhide straps, forever locking his body in the honored seated position still overlooking the prone body of myself and my trusted horse for all eternal life.

"General Kobayashi-san then mumbled the mandatory prayers to the Lord Buddha, and he made his final peace with the White Heaven and earth and his true Lord and Master of the time. Then the highly respectful General Kobayashi-san sliced his belly wide with the smaller stabbing blade. Then my wise Lord Kawasomeru moved a little nearer to his most loyal General, and you carefully rested your right hand lightly on the greatly honored General's shoulder, and you held him as the honored General slowly bled to death right before your honored eyes. My powerful warlord actually stayed with your General as he suffered greatly through his slow and agonizing and very painful death. When my Lord and Master was certain General Kobayashi-san was dead, you took the time to fix the slightly out of place armor and made certain his battle helmet rested properly on his head, and then you released his body to the long rest of eternity.

"My forever concerned for his faithful Warriors, Lord Kawasomeru took your time and you positioned Kobayashi-san's armor correctly and his body resting properly, forever protectively, perfectly watching over my body for all time. In one of your private and rare shows of emotion, my sadden warlord lightly touched my face one last time with the trembling fingers of your right hand, as you bent over my body and whispered a prayer to my memory. Then you stood erect and proud and you bowed for the last time in your life, towards the two dead and highly respected and loyal Samurai Warriors who so proudly served you throughout their respected lives.

"Then you merely turned and you quickly left my crypt forever my Lord. I fully understood you needed fresh air to breathe, the smell of death hung heavy inside my crypt, and you wanted to put a quick end to this never-ending nightmare that was my life. But you were unaware that my spirit had followed you out of my crypt, and I hovered over the opening to my Kofun and my eyes watched as you ordered your other Warriors to gather at the very mouth of my tomb.

"You had a great number of Samurai stationed in the mountain over the opening of my tomb. But first you had the Samurai who worked and knew where the opening to my Kofun laid, and you ordered them to assembly in an area away from the opening and you had them slaughtered, and then had their bodies set ablaze to forever silence their lips, so the secret of my tomb was protected for time everlasting. Once this order was carried out, you raised your hand in the air and the horde of Samurai spread throughout the mountain, started a landslide, sending tons of earth down, completely hiding the mouth of my crypt from view. Once you were certain the secret of my crypt was protected, you ordered these Samurai out of the mountains.

"Then you ordered this small Army of Samurai to mount and you road off a good distance from my tomb, and when you felt you were far enough away from my crypt, your small Army joined up with a much larger group of trusted Samurai Warriors. At this meeting place, you had all the Samurai who caused the landside put to the sword, and their bodies burned and their ashes carried back to your encampment to be interned in the pit of Samurai who died in the service of your command. I am sorry to add this, but it was at this point when my protector Kami, Fujin-Sama, the always angry God of Wind came and collected my spirit and he escorted my spirit to the Ukiyo. There he released me in the wonderment of the Floating World, and I was no longer able to see what my Lord and Master was doing with his vast Armies, and his great lands.

"For countless sticks of time, I cursed myself because I worried I was letting my Lord down, by my not being able to continue protecting my warlord. I cannot think of the vast sticks of time that past and then on that glorious day, you appeared before me in the Floating World. What a joyous meeting that stick of time was for the both of us, but the time was short because my Lord was removed from this area of the Floating world, and your spirit was deposited in that certain area of the Floating World that was reserved for only the very elite of Japans proud history."

It was at this point the spirit of Wind slightly bowed her head towards the new owner of her sword and then she went silent, like she was deep in thought for the moment.

Agent Rossie found himself staring at this spirit with is mouth hanging open. He could not believe what he just heard come from this spirits mouth. The story was almost too hard to believe and he would not believe a single word of it, if it was not for the fact this spirit was kneeling before him in a solid form. He was struggling to get his breathing under control as his mind flashed a hundred questions he wanted to ask this female Warrior, but he did not know where he wanted to start asking her of her past life. Suddenly he took a deep breath in and then he spoke.

"Spirit, you obviously had an interesting past life if I'm to believe what you just told me..."

"My Lord and Master, please address my by the name you have placed upon my person. My name is Wind and if you want to honor me so, you can call me Wind-san. I must correct my Lord and Master though, because I am and have always been a most loyal and trusted Samurai Warrior General in the proud service of you. I would no sooner utter a falsehood before your presence, as I would commit any treachery aimed against my Liege Lord. My past life is my past life, and even a falsehood could not change one iota of how I have lived my past life. What would I possibly gain by adding any falsehoods to the story of my past life?" Wind offered to who she thought was her Lord Kawasomeru as she raised her eyes and looked and then spoke to him.

"Wind-san, I thank you for informing me of your right name to address you with. I guess you have a good point there, what would you gain by telling me a lie about your past life. Err... judging the way you have lived your life, I seriously doubt you could tell a lie. I must tell you, I'm deeply impressed over all you have told me about your life. I'm sorry your life seemed to be filled with nothing death and killing and people ordering you around and telling you how to live your life and what to do with it. I'm truly sorry you have only enjoyed one lover throughout your entire life, what a shame that must have been for you to endure Wind-san..."

"That is not exactly true my wonderful Liege Lord, I have had other lovers who I have shared the pillow with in my endless life. I have even shared the pillow with your spirit on numerous occasions, whenever you wanted to relieve yourself. I have also shared the pillow with the other owner of my sword, before I took his worthless life in my fit of anger I aimed at him, once I had discovered he was the offspring of the hated coward of a Samurai Warrior Tetsuo Hatanaka..."

"What was that you offered me, Wind-san? You just said you have shared the pillow with the other owner of your sword, you said it was the offspring of a Tetsuo Hatanaka. Are you telling me you were the one who might have slaughtered Hiromoai Hatanaka?" Rossie asked the ancient Samurai Warrior as he interrupted her words, and then he stared deeply into her lovely eyes.

"I am afraid I must reply in the affirmative to your last question that I was the Kaishaku, his executioner my Liege Lord, as I have mentioned when I was telling you of my past life. My one and only ancient lover was Captain Katsunoke Seisakajo-san, and he was killed in the middle of the night by the evil and coward of a Samurai Warrior as Tetsuo Hatanaka was in life."

"I was wondering how you ended up here in the future, if you lived way back in the history of Japan. Now you have told me how you lived in the past, you now have to tell me how you ended up in the Twentieth Century and how and why you lived now. You also have to tell me how and why you killed who you killed in my time. Wind-san, you have to be absolutely truthful with me when you start telling me how you were brought to my time of life. You must tell me everything, and why you might have done what you did and under who's Command while you're at it." Agent Rossie offered to the female Japanese Samurai Warrior from the ancient past.

"As I have already informed my honorable Liege Lord, I could no more tell you a falsehood than I can carry out any possible treachery against my Lord and Master. But I must admit to my Lord Kawasomeru, this part of my life is extremely confusing to myself, and I can only imagine how you are going to react when I begin this part of the history of my life, my Liege Lord. I clearly remember being placed within my Kofun, and I cannot tell you how long I had rested in my tomb. I remember the thunder of countless thunder storms, and I remember light. Then one day I was awoken from my long sleep to find myself standing before my Lord and Master in a long and filthy metal tunnel (the construction trailer).

"It was at that time you asked me countless questions of my past life. As I began to tell you of those times, but suddenly you stopped me from speaking any further and then you put me back to sleep, only to bring me to another place that was so much more comfortable and clean to be at. There I met another man you called a four man, and Lady Yoke who took great care of me, she bathed me and honored me greatly in many different ways..."

"I'm sorry for interrupting you again Wind-san, but I don't need to know about this. I'm more interested in who found you and was commanding you to do the terrible things you were doing in my times." Agent Rossie could not believe what he might have found in this ancient Samurai. In his mind he was starting to believe he found the person or spirit who killed Hiromoai Hatanaka, and maybe even the killer of Asahiko and his son Tsutomu Yurkowa and his lovely wife.

"As I have already mentioned this part of my new life is extremely confusing to my worthless memory. I was found by the new master of my sword, and his name was Hiromoai, and he refrained from ever telling me his last name until that faithful day when I turned from a loyal Samurai Warrior into the Kaishaku, his executioner once he told me of his last name..."

"You already told me this part of your life's story, and I take it Hiromoai was your new Lord and Master of your sword and your spirit, and he was the one who commanded you to dispatch a number of other Japanese people, and if I'm correct in this assumption. Then I want to know why he was ordering you to kill these other people. Did he give you any reason for demanding you to kill these other people, Wind-san?" Agent Rossie could not believe his luck, here he was in the United States, and he has obviously just solved the deaths in Japan of Hiromoai Hatanaka, The old Asahiko Yurkowa, and his son Tsutomu and his wife, and of course, the American businessman Calvin Batterman in one breath, as he added to his words for the ancient Warrior.

"Please Wind-san, you must go over everything about how Hiromoai found you, and how he ordered you to kill all these people and why he wanted you to kill them. You must not omit anything from your story. It's extremely important for me to know everything about how, when and why Hiromoai was commanding you to do the things he was ordering you to do for him. I can't tell you how important it is for me to know of everything Hiromoai ordered you to do for him. So you must tell me everything about him and his orders to you, Wind-san."

"I shall be most honored to tell you of everything that Hiromoai had ordered me to do for him to the best of my memory, my honorable Lord and Master. As I have already told you, Hiromoai was the one who woke me from my eternal sleep. When he brought my sword to his new castle and he again woke me from my long sleep by removing my well honored Katana sword from its sheath. I was pleased to see his castle and all the fine pleasures it offered to my Lord and Master and all the visitors to his castle. Much like you he requested me to tell him of my past life in ancient Japan. My time in the past was in the years of the thirteen hundreds.

"Once Hiromoai had me in his castle and I told him of my life, he had me display my skills with the Katana. He was impressed and asked me of the power he held over my spirit, and when I informed him I was at his service to carry out any wish and desire he might want to have carried out. He asked me if I would eliminate his competition and I replied I would eliminate any of his enemy no matter where they tried to hide from their final fate at the end of my sword..."

"Wind-san, obviously Hiromoai was the one who sent you out to kill his first target of Tsutomu Yurkowa and his wife, and the three bodyguards you killed and the four one you badly injured when you went after Tsutomu. Did Hiromoai tell you why he wanted him dead and if he did, you must tell me why he wanted these two people dead, Wind-san?"

Agent Rossie asked the female Samurai Warrior with concern lacing his voice as he interrupted her words.

"Yes my Lord and Master, Hiromoai did in fact tell me why he wanted this young Warrior and his wife dead. He told me he wanted him dead, because he was standing in his way of acquiring a certain construction company, and this young Warrior had cost him vast sums of money by taking certain work away from my Lord and Master of the time. He ordered me in no uncertain terms how and why he wanted this Tsutomu-san and his wife dead. I was ordered to kill his wife in a disgusting way, and I was ordered to slay Tsutomu-san in a most savage way as possible. Hiromoai ordered me to slice Tsutomu-san into small pieces. He further ordered me to enter his living compound and stop anyone who tried to stop me from completing my orders.

"Hiromoai showed me a map and location of Tsutomu-san's compound, and then he told me how I was to get into the compound and where this young Warrior slept with his wife. Then I was sent on my way to follow out my orders. I left Hiromoai's castle and worked my way to the compound, I climbed over the wall and was attacked and I killed a vicious dog then I climbed a wall to the second floor and bumped into two guards. I easily dispatched one and the other I allowed to live by just wounding him with my sword. I carefully entered Tsutomu-san's room and went right to his sleeping wife. I silently bent her head back and sliced her throat and waited for her to quickly bleed to death. Then I went around the massive sleeping bedroll and woke the sleeping Tsutomu-san by tapping his chin with the tip of my sword. He woke and began to curse me and he reached behind himself and found his hand covered with his wife's blood.

"With Tsutomu-san saw his wife's blood on his hand, this infuriated him and he cursed me more. He cursed me for killing an unarmed woman, and I was going to kill him without allowing him to try and defend himself. I thought his words were most honorable and I looked around the room and saw a pair of worthless Katana blades, and I pointed towards them with the tip of my sword. He smiled when I offered to allow him to arm himself, and he threatened to kill me by telling me he was well skilled with the worthless pair of weapons. So I engaged him in a duel to the death, and I quickly found out he was indeed very skilled with the Katana blade.

"I played with him for a few small breaths of time, cutting him here and there to follow my Master's orders to make him suffer before I dispatched his life. When I played with him long enough, I grew tired and killed him quickly. As we fought, one of his bodyguards tried to enter his room and was banging on the door. He finally forced his way into the large room and I had to dispatch him quickly, so I could escape and return to my Lord and Master, Hiromoai. As I escaped the compound of Tsutomu-san, I was confronted by another bodyguard and I did not waste my time to enter a duel with him, I merely dispatched him as quickly as possible. I made it back over the wall and returned to Hiromoai's castle, and then I reported to him I successfully followed his orders and killed the two he wanted to go to the Floating World."

Rossie picked up the fact every time Wind mentioned someone name in her story she always added the 'San' to the end of their names, except for Hiromoai. She never honored him when she mentioned his name. Now he was certain Hiromoai was responsible for the deaths that occurred in

Japan. He cannot believe he solved the murders by finding this one Samurai. He decided to take a break before he pressed Wind on why and how he killed the old Asahiko and then Batterman. He wanted a cold drink and he was certain Wind also needed something to drink as well. He got up and went to the fridge and took out a cold Pepsi, and he asked Wind.

"Wind-san, do you need something to drink, or maybe something to eat? You do need food and drink when you're visiting the living world you call this time, Warrior of the past."

"Yes my Lord and Master, I do thirst at that my Lord."

"Would you like to enjoy a soda, they're ice cold and enjoyable to drink?"

"A soda what is a soda my Liege Lord? I do not know of what you offer me my Lord"

"I'll get you one and you'll find out. Here you go, I put it in a glass for you. Enjoy Wind-san."

"It is cold. By the Gods, the liquid tickles my nose and hurts my throat, but I must admit it is a very enjoyable drink to enjoy. What did my Lord and Master call this so cold liquid I am drinking?" Wind asked as she moved the glass out before her eyes and then stared at the liquid.

"It's called a soda, a Pepsi in fact. It's a fun drink to enjoy, Wind-san."

"I must agree with my most wise Lord and Master, it is truly a drink to enjoy my Lord." Wind replied as she quickly finished off her drink, and then she watched every move her new Liege Lord was doing within his apartment.

"Would you like something to eat, maybe some cheese, or some cold cuts, bread, anything you want? Do you need any food at all, Wind-san?" Agent Rossie asked the ancient Warrior.

"Cheese, it that as enjoyable as this Pepsi water you offered me I just drank. If it is as enjoyable too one's spirit then yes my Lord and Master. I would truly like to enjoy some cheese." Wind replied as she got a little excited over the offered cheese to eat.

Agent Rossie cut up a number of bit size pieces of some cheddar cheese, and he put them on a plate and stuck toothpicks in the pieces for easier handling, and then he walked the plate over to the still kneeling Warrior and held the plate out before him.

Wind cautiously picked up one of the pieces and she slowly twirled the toothpick between her fingers as she carefully studied the yellow looking piece of cheese. Rossie placed the plate down on the side table and he sat on the sofa and smiled as he watched Wind carefully study the piece of cheese and then he announced. "Wind-san, that's cheese, it's made from the milk of a cow. Try it, you'll like it, it's good to nibble on before you have your main meal of the night."

Wind kind of shrugged and then she placed the small piece of cheese in her mouth and smiled over the interesting taste of what her Lord and Master was calling a piece of cheese. When she swallowed she looked at the plate still mostly covered with the small pieces of cheese.

Agent Rossie picked up her slight glance and he offered the ancient Samurai. "Please Wind-san, help yourself. You can enjoy as much of the cheese as you wish to eat. I have plenty more of it in the fridge. By the way, what do you like to eat for supper, Wind-san?"

"Supper my Liege Lord? What is supper you offer me my Lord and Master?"

"Oh brother this is going to take a long time I see. Wind-san, supper is what we call the last meal of the day. It's usually the largest meal of the day as well. What do you like to eat? Do you eat meat, chicken, pork? Or do you only eat vegetables and fruit and nuts and stuff like that?"

"My Liege Lord, I'm afraid I'm not very familiar with what you are offering me to eat. What is meat? I know of Chicken, and don't know what pork is though. Yes, I enjoy vegetables, fruit and nuts and enjoy eating them my Lord and Master, and I also know of the last meal of the night my Lord." Wind offered to Rossie who was staring so intensely back at her.

"By meat I mean Cow, you know Wind-san. Moooo."

Wind immediately started to laugh over the way Rossie just described meat to her, but she automatically brought her hand up mouth so she did not bare her teeth to her Lord and Master which is a terrible insult in her world as she finally replied. "Yes my Lord and Master, I truly enjoy eating what you call meat. But what you call meat is usually offered to only the most elite of the ruling class of Japan. But I have tasted and enjoyed eating meat. Mooooo."

Her response and copying his 'Moooo' call, made Rossie laugh as he added. "Now I know you like beef and chicken, how about pork, you know pig. Oink, oink, you understand, Wind-san?"

"Wakarimasu, I understand, pork, oink, oink. Yes, I also enjoy what you call pork to eat my Lord. That was more abundant and cheaper to purchase back in the old world." She smiled at Rossie because she was trying to please him, and when she made the cow sound he laughed hardily and she copied the sound of the pig to try and please him a second time.

Wind received the same response from Rossie as he laughed over her making the pig sound, and he responded to her words. "Well at least you're going to be easy to feed I guess, Wind-san. Would you want to enjoy eating something a little more substantial than just cheese at this time? I can fix you anything you desire to eat. I have cow, chicken and pork in my fridge and it would be nothing for me to prepare a good meal for you to enjoy at this time, Wind-san."

Wind thought for a few moments, although she was a little hungry, the cheese took the edge off her hunger, and she was a little uncomfortable over the fact of allowing her Liege Lord to prepare a meal for her to enjoy. It was she who should be preparing a meal for her Lord and Master to enjoy, when none of his usual servants were not around to properly look after him. Finally she replied to her master's last question of her. "No my Liege Lord, I am in no further need for any solid food at this time. What you called this enjoyable cheese was more than enough to satisfy my needs for any nourishment for the time being my Liege Lord."

"Suite yourself Wind-san. But I'm hungry and I'm going to make myself a small steak to enjoy. Errr... excuse me Wind-san, before you ask me, a steak is part of the cow, errr... Moooo. Do you Wakarimasu-ka. (Do you understand)

"Yes my Liege Lord, I Wakarimasu (Understand) Moooo." She added as she laughed because her Master looked happy as he prepared to make his meal, and she was pleased because when she made the sound of the cow again, it caused her Lord and Master to roar with laughter. And she was never so happy with herself as when she was able to make her Lord Kawasomeru laugh.

When his steak was finished he placed it on a plate and carried it over to the same side table he placed the dish of cheese on, and then he began to enjoy his steak. Wind did not realize just how hungry she truly was, and when he started to eat the steak in front of her, her mouth started to water for some of the meat. He glanced up at Wind and noticed she was staring at him while he ate, so he cut a fork full of steak off and offered it to the female Samurai.

Wind leaned forward and enjoyed the smell of the meat, and when he offered her the fork, she took it greedily. She placed the small morsel of steak in her mouth, and covered her mouth with the back of her hand and enjoyed the meal.

He really enjoyed watching her eat and he cut up a small section of the steak into little pieces and left them on the side of his dish, and then he got up and took another fork and returned to his seat and began eating the larger piece of steak. When Wind gave him back the fork he gave her, and he stabbed another one of the pieces of steak and gave her back the fork and steak. She again took the offer greedily because she was that hungry.

The FBI Agent smiled as she ate the steak and when she went to return the fork to him he offered. "No Wind-san, you use the fork and eat these small pieces of steak from my dish. And when you finish those pieces, I'll cut you up some more until you ate enough to satisfy your need for some real food. Please, help yourself and enjoy my meal with me."

Wind smiled because she felt so blessed to be eating from her Lord's dish of the meal he prepared for himself. She could not help but feel this new Master of the sword was treating her specially, and she was beginning to form a real kinship with her new Master. Every once and a while she would look up and smile at her Master and when she was finished eating enough of the meat, she leaned back and went back to resting her full weight on her crossed legs, and then she lowered her head, giving her Lord and Master the privacy to finish his meal in peace.

He noticed Wind move away from the small table and he asked her with some concern in his tone of voice. "What is the meaning of this Wind-san, did you get enough to eat already?"

"Yes my most caring Lord, I have eaten enough of the cow to satisfy myself for this day. This worthless Samurai thanks her kind Liege Lord for his concern of this foolish female Vassal of yours, Lord Kawasomeru." She offered and immediately lowered her head and stared at the floor.

"I guess I also have eaten enough food today myself." With that said he got up and picked up the plate and went to walk to the kitchen. But Wind sprang up to her feet so quickly it caused him to hesitate, and she reached out and took the edge of the dish and said. "No my honorable Lord and Master please allow this worthless person to care for the plate for you. Do you want me to keep this left over cow for you to enjoy later when you hunger again, my Liege Lord?"

"Yes Wind-san, just leave the plate and food on the counter and I'll look after it when we have finished speaking together on this tonight." He was really impressing himself after he realized how much Japanese he picked up over the few years he was working in Japan, and he was using that knowledge speaking with this ancient Samurai Warrior. While he was speaking with her, he was even picking up more and more of the language, and it was making it much easier for him to understand what Wind was telling him.

Now he was full, he wanted to get back to Wind's saga of her past life, and find out why Hiromoai wanted so many people dead around him.

He waited until Wind returned to the small living room area of his apartment, and again was kneeling on the floor with her rearend resting on her crossed legs. Once she looked comfortable for a second time, Agent Rossie spoke to her. "Wind-san, are you able to continue telling me why Hiromoai wanted so many people killed around him, and why he used your spirit to kill these people. Maybe you can tell me what he wanted to get out of ordering these people to their death. Are you okay to continue with this story for me, Wind-san?"

"All my Lord and Master has to do is ask this worthless Samurai a question and it is my Yoshi gi (duty) to carry out your wish. I am willing to continue with my story for as long as you wish to hear my worthless words of no account. Please my Liege Lord, make yourself comfortable and I will tell you all you want to know from this worthless person." She stopped speaking at this point and she immediately look down at the floor again then she waited until her master was comfortable and ready to hear more of what the detestable Hiromoai ordered her to do for him.

When he was ready, the FBI Agent smiled at the female Warrior then he offered to her in a pleasant tone of voice. "Please Wind-san, I'd like you to continue with the story and why Hiromoai wanted you to kill all these people for him. I want to know it all, the reasons, the wants and what was behind his driving madness. Errr... you do understand it's an evil thing and it's also against the law to take another person's life in my time, Wind-san? I don't understand how it was back in your time of life, but now you just can't go off and kill someone you don't like, because we have police and laws, and those laws will punish what we call now a murderer, and a murderer is someone who takes another person's life. Here in my time, the only people who can take a person's life is the law, and the police who enforce our laws for us."

"I don't understand this what you call the law and not being able to kill one's enemy when one might come across that one enemy in my footfalls. If my life is so unimportant then the life of my enemy is absolutely worthless to me. Throughout my entire life I was always taught I was supposed to destroy my Lord and Master's enemy no matter where I might find them hiding from your mighty wrath. Yes, in my time we also had laws that governed our actions, but the most important law I was taught was, it was my sacred duty to destroy your enemy, and if one was your enemy then that one was my sworn enemy for my entire life, and that one enemy was a stain on my soul. The only way I could ever erase that stain from my soul, was to kill that one enemy, until there were no more one enemy left to ever threaten my Lord and Master's life again.

"All the laws that governed my life was all made for we faithful Samurai Warriors to protect our Lord and Master's life, because our Liege Lord was the law of the land and when he desired, demanded and wanted from his Samurai Warriors was their loyalty to his laws and his being. Now in your time is against the law to kill one's enemy, why is this true my Lord? Throughout my short lifetime in the land of the living, I have created countless enemy, and if I did not kill those enemy when I found them hiding and wanting to kill me. My life time though short as it was, would have been much shorter if I was not allowed to vanquish my enemy at will.

"What a foolish law your time has created in this time, to allow one's enemy to live is just begging fate to intervene and allow that enemy to kill me. I don't understand if one is not allowed to kill one's enemy where he finds that enemy then what do you do with your enemy. Surely you cannot possibly allow your enemy to breed, because then there will be no end to the number of enemy that would be stalking you throughout your foolish life if this is allowed in your time. Please tell me what you do with your enemy my wise Lord and Master?" She asked of her concern looking Liege Lord as she waited for his rely to her question.

"I shall tell you what we do with the criminals in my time. Wind-san, in my time we don't call these law breakers our enemy, we call them criminals..."

"As it was a fact in my time as well I offer to you my honorable Liege Lord." She interrupted and then she smiled at her Lord and Master.

"I understand that but in my time the only ones we put to death after a trial, and if he was found guilty of that crime, is anyone who killed another person. There are a few other reasons a criminal would be put to death, but his crime would have to be one committed again my country. Wind-san, for me to try and explain the laws of my time to you, would take all the breath that is within my body. Let's just take it as a fact that it's against the law for anyone to take another one's life in my time and let it go at that. If we're together for long enough time, I'll surely be happy to explain all the laws that govern us in this time. But right now I'm more interested in what Hiromoai wanted from you, and why he wanted you to do what you did for him. I can't tell you how important it is for me to know of these reasons. It's an absolute necessity for me to understand what was driving Hiromoai's madness. But first I'd like to know how Hiromoai found and then how he enlisted you to be his Kaishaku? (Executioner)"

CHAPTER FOUR

Wind let her breath out in a rush and went on with her story for who she believed was her Lord. "I shall start at how Hiromoai had found me. As I was told and what I remember of his discovery, Hiromoai was in Command of what you call a construction company, and in his quest to fine the metal to make what is a horseless wagon. He was digging the mountains region of Central Japan where many battles once raged between the warlords of Japan's ancient past. The time honored but all forgotten fields of battles and respect of the past time was laid out over the ancient vast Kugyo plain, and covered over by the passing time. In the area where Hiromoai's workers toiled was the exact position were massive Armies of Samurai Warriors loyal to their Shogun and Lord Kawasomeru and Lord Wakatsuki shared their lives with their chosen warlords.

"I must remind my Lord and Master, your massive encampment was Ocean wide, along with the endless battlefield as you prepared your Warriors for the final battle to be waged between the two houses of Central Japan. The two Samurai Armies readied themselves for the battle of their lives. But now in your time of life the respected encampment and Samurai who fought so bravely in the past of Japan's history, and died on the reverent land your workers were making their lives, was replaced by the crawling sea of yellow painted steel and wire earthmoving monsters. Along with an endless Army of your modern day workers dressed in their protective battle helmets, overalls and thick work hand covers, and now armed with tooth shaped picks and shovels. These workers waged a new war, this time carried out against the very earth itself, to discover the vast hidden treasures and wealth of their greedy land owners and new Daimyos.

"I was told a rich deposit of iron ore was discovered in the Kai mountain ranges, and thus the age old plunder of the earth and battlefield began in earnest. Your workers offered no respect or consideration displayed for Japan's proud history to the past. The long time silenced and deadly war cries of the wildly charging Samurai and their trusted steeds were replaced by the destructive explosive sticks the workers used to break apart the earth. Along with the deafening roar emitted from the earthmoving metal monsters that polluted the clean air of Japan with their black, eye burning and chocking foul breath. As your workers assaulted the earth under the constant cursing of the angry what you call four men (foremen), as these new Commanders screamed at their toiling Heimin (Commoners) to produce more of the vast wealth for their owners and company.

"Some of the more luckier Heimin uncovered numerous ancient brass arrowheads, rusted and snapped and worthless Katana killing blades, and countless parts of discarded body armor that was once used to protect the lives of your loyal and honored Samurai Warriors from the biting edge of the sword's call, along with the scattered bones of long ago dead Warriors and their horses that carried their Masters to the honor of dying for their Lords and Masters of the time.

"A few pieces of discarded Warrior body armor was bent or otherwise destroyed, were uncovered by some of your low class workers, and they were saved by these people as keepsakes. But the owners of the metal monsters and companies were far more interested in searching for the prized iron ore, than in what they believed were worthless trinkets of the past glory of Japan's great history. The account of Japan's memory, and the Samurai who carved out a harsh living in Japan's savage past, had all been forgotten. Just as all honored histories of other great nations of the world were also lost in the constant quest for personal riches and greed of the earth.

"But as I was told, on this Tuesday morning, the crews of your workers were ordered to destroy a certain section of low lying ridges at the very base of the Kai Pass. This work was ordered to allow easier access to the much needed waters of the Kai River. The water would be used to wash away the lose earth and other debris broken away from the earth to expose the rich deposits of iron ore buried in the rocks and hard packed earth of the area. Despite how rich modern Japan was, she was forever forced to rely on imports of steel and iron ore from other nations of the world, to manufacture their horseless wagons and various other commodities and personal fortunes. This reliance on other nations went against the very fiber of the honorable Japanese peoples. We Japanese do not enjoy relying on anyone but themselves."

"C'mon Wind-san, you're drifting away from what I wanted to know from you. Tell me more of how Hiromoai found you, and what he did with you once he owned your fine spirit." Rossie groused as he shifted his weight on the sofa, and then settled in to hear more of Wind's saga.

"Please excuse this foolish Samurai for causing confusion in your mind. If I insulted my Lord then I am prepared to commit Suppuku to make amends for my errors committed against your honor, Lord Kawasomeru." Wind lowered her head in homage to her new Lord and Master.

"C'mon Wind-san, you didn't insult me in the least, all you were doing was getting off the subject I was interested in hearing about. I order you finish what you were telling me, so I know what and how Hiromoai was able to enlist you in his madness and murder plans." FBI Agent Rossie fired back at her then he stared at her until she started speaking again.

"Yes, I shall continue my story my Master. On the day I was first discovered, it was a cloud shrouded sun as it rose to the Heavens over the distant mountain range on this damp and overcast day, and a light mist of a rain was soaking the ground, as your workers tried to make the best of the day's work. Your workers understood later in the day, heavier rain was expected and that would place an end to their work. So your workers set of to plant their explosive sticks, and they tried to make the most of the morning hours, and the time they had to work and earn their living.

"One of your massive earthmoving metal monsters was working at trying to move the lose rock and dirt recently blasted away from the base of the ridge the day before their work ended. Many behemoth, yellow painted horseless wagons moved in like a swarm of angry bees, as the earthmoving monsters scooped up bucket loads of the lose rocks and earth, and dumped it in the rear of the waiting large wagons for removal from the worksite as fill for other projects your company had going on. All this I was able to see as my spirit came to defend my Kofun from any possible invasion from the foul workers toiling so near the covered mouth of my tomb.

"I witnessed a number of your troubleshooting spotters who kept a constant vigil before the slow crawling earthmoving monsters, as they dug deep into the crumbling ridge, making certain the monster did not fall victim to any uncovered crevasses the monster might tumble into and get damaged of stuck. This region of Japan was well noted to be honeycombed with steep hidden caves and deep rivets that could easily trap and or otherwise damage the mammoth and obviously expensive commercial monster of steel and wire. Many horseless wagons were lined up and waiting for its next supply of rock and earth the monster was digging up..."

"Wind-san, I don't wish to interrupt your story on you, but I must correct you at this point. The things you're calling steel monsters are in reality known as bulldozer machines. And what you call horseless wagons, those are what we call trucks, and they're powered by what we call motors that run on diesel fuel, and that is what causes the huge, black clouds of thick eye burning smoke." Agent Rossie offered so she understood what she was speaking about.

Wind bowed her head as she replied politely. "I thank my honorable Lord and Master for educating this worthless Samurai Warrior, from now on I shall refer to the metal monster as a machine and the horseless wagons as trucks. Shall I continue with my story my Liege Lord?"

Agent Rossie nodded his head yes, he was having a hard time concentrating on her story, mainly because he was constantly being distracted because as Wind drew in a breath, it would make her naked breasts sway slightly, and also be pushed out and making her breasts look larger than they actually were. It was a pleasant distraction, one he was truly enjoying.

"Thank you my Liege Lord, and I shall continue, and by the end of the first full hour of work for your crews, the once fine mist slowly turned into a much steady and heavier drizzle, with who you call your lead four man considering calling an early end to the day's work. Your wise four man obviously did not want any of his work crews getting hurt or injured foolishly, by slipping on the wet and loose stones, or on the mud the rain was quickly creating on the worksite.

"My spirit hovered and watched as he glanced to the sky and sadly shook his head, and just as he was about to blow his whistle to end the day's work, one of his spotters began to call out and create all sorts of excited disruption right where one of your massive bulldozer machines was digging in the side of the mountain before the mouth of my hidden tomb. I saw the suddenly worried four man leave his perch on top of the side of what you called a truck, and he immediately rushed over to where his spotter was working. I could easily tell by his actions that he was worried if what you call the bulldozer machine, might have lost the heavy chain that propelled the heavy machine forward, or the machine somehow got damaged or stuck on the site.

"It seemed your four man was doing everything in his power to protect the massive bulldozer machines, to the cost of his workers. Nevertheless, your four man rushed for the spotter and by the time he reached the excited worker and looked to where he was pointing. The older four man noticed what looked to be a mouth to a cave that seemed to have been carved out by human hands in the side of the mountain, and covered over by an ancient avalanche years before."

Wind was confusing her story and she was sometimes referring to Agent Rossie as the owner of the construction company in her long story, instead of Hiromoai Hatanaka as the true owner of the company and her spirit of the time. Every now and then as she continued the long story for her new Lord and Master. "Your most cunning four man immediately ordered the heavy bulldozer machine to move away from the opening in the side of the mountain. Then he ordered the spotter to run off and retrieve him what he called a flashlight from the field office trailer parked on the worksite, if my memory serves me correctly my Lord and Master.

"Your most wise and highly concerned four man quickly realized there was something very eerie about the deep cave that both interested and scared him at the same time, and he cautiously and carefully climbed into the narrow opening and he peered deeper into the dark, dank smelling void of pitch blackness. In his wandering and very confused mind, he was fearful something immortal and extremely dangerous was lurking within the mouth of the cave and darkness, just waiting to drag him deeper inside the dark cave and then devour his foul soul completely, to give the evil within a new life at his expense.

"When the spotter returned with the flashlight in his hand, his eyes displayed the excitement taking over his heart and mind. Your four man grabbed the flashlight from the spotter's hand and he shinned the light into the opening. He immediately noticed the light reflect off something hidden deep within the dank cave, his still not realizing it was an ancient Kofun burial chamber. Now greed and the want for great personal worth and riches for him to enjoy, took over his once fears of the most foreboding cave opening, and what horror might be lurking within. The four man started to cautiously probe a little further into the hidden underground chamber.

"I watched with amusement as the foolish old man carefully placed one foot before the other, as he cautiously entered the feeling dreaded void of darkness and fear. His breathing was labored in the dust filled cave, because of the stale air so long ago trapped inside the sealed chamber of my death, and because of the heavy dust raised by all what you call blasting in the area. The extremely fearful four man suddenly pulled back as if he was frightened by what he had just noticed hiding within the cave opening. But his foolish dreams of personal wealth filled his mind, and gave him the courage to continue on deeper into the cave that was my tomb.

"You're scared to death and actually shaking four man looked over his shoulder back at the equally as scared and worried spotter, and he ordered him to move the bulldozer machines further away from this certain section of the ridge.

Then he ordered most of the work crews home for the rest of the day, offering he did not want them working in the heavier rain. Your four man who was named Utsumi-san, was going to keep a few of his chosen crew workers he understood he could trust with his life, to remain in case they were needed if there was anything to be found hidden inside the cave of any worth to them or the owner of the great company. His mind was spinning as he tried to look even deeper into the cave now.

"Once the overly cautious Utsumi-san was certain the workers he did not trust to keep a secret to their foolish death were gone from the worksite. Your old four man Utsumi-san removed the little box from his pocket he was always talking into, and he placed a call out to you who was staying at your mighty castle in Tokyo. He wanted to inform you of what he believed he had found on the worksite, and wanted to see what you wanted to do about his discovery if anything, and he also wanted new orders from you over the find he believed he had discovered.

"Hiromoai Hatanaka was resting in his plush office on the twenty seventh floor of the luxurious and elite Hatanaka Towers. The magnificent structure was built by his honorable father when he first became successful in the construction field in Japan. When the call came in from your excited four man, you gave out with a disgusted sigh as you glanced at the phone as if it had just insulted you. As I remember it, you were enjoying a cup of Cha (tea). You were the oldest son of three of Hatanaka and Son's Mining and Construction Corporation, one of the oldest mining and construction companies in all of Japan, and you possessed more money than you could spend in three lifetimes. I have witnessed in my mind's eye as you removed your feet from the top of the cabinet you had your feet resting upon, and you picked up what is called a phone and you grumbled into it as if you were already angry at the voice trapped in the small box.

"Yes, yes Utsumi was his name, and you even failed to honor the old man by adding the 'san' to the end of his name, and you snapped at him as you asked him what he wanted from you. You tried to tell the old man you were busy and you did not have the time to talk to him, unless he was suffering an emergency over at the worksite. You barely allowed him to talk, it seemed like you just wanted not to hear from this old man. I can remember everything he told you to finally get your attention, and when he started speaking you listened to what he had to tell you. He told you would not believe what he thought he had uncovered at the worksite. He told you Machine Five, Three, Three had uncovered something hidden in the side of the mountains of Kai, and he thought you should come out to the worksite to see what it was for yourself."

"I also remember what you told the old man, you told Utsumi, you did not have time or patience to waste on this kind of word I do not remember. Then you added you did not wish to drive all over Japan looking at worthless items uncovered by one of your machines. You even yelled at the old man and told him to have the machine dig up whatever it was he found, and if it had any worth to it, you ordered him to bring it to you over the weekend. But he was so excited he dared to interrupt you, and he cried that you would not believe what they had uncovered at the worksite and he told you the value was beyond thought and belief. The excited words of the old man finally got your interest and you placed the paper you were reading down.

"You rose and barked in the handset because you known this old worker most of your life and he was not the type of man who would get excited over anything he found. His excitement forced you to growl at the old man. You said Utsumi-san, what do you think you might have discovered at the site. Then you asked him what he thought the value of his find that he was bringing it up to your attention, and why was he demanding you should visit the worksite. You also told him you never heard him so excited about anything in his life before. I was able to hear all you said by listening to the small box Utsumi-san held in his hand, and I heard his reply to your words.

He cried as he told you he himself could not believe what they might have discovered at the worksite. He told you he thought they might have uncovered an ancient burial site of a highly honored Samurai buried back when. Utsumi-san offered to you he believed the crypt was completely intact, and it seems to be laden down with many ancient pieces of armor and Katana blades from what you were able to see from the mouth of the cave. Utsumi-san further told you he was able to see bones, bones and helmets and swords laid out respectfully in the cave. He further offered it looked to him there were a few Samurai buried in the crypt. And according to our ancient laws and beliefs that usually meant there must be a well respected Warrior of great worth buried deep inside the tomb. He cried a find like this could mean riches beyond your wildest dreams, more than any amounts of iron ore could bright to you and your company.

"I heard your reply to Utsumi-san, you growled at him as you asked what about the other workers from the worksite. You asked what they were doing and he replied he sent most of the unworthy workers home for the rest of the day, because it was raining heavily at the site. The old Utsumi-san also said tomorrow he was going to start the work crews in a different section of the site, well away from the cave opening, so you could examine the tomb in private...”

“Again I find myself of being forced to interrupt you because your story is beginning to drag on long. Is there any way for you to get to the point on what Hiromoai found in your tomb, and how he brought you to his apartment, and how he sent you to kill his competition? I fear I might die of old age by the time you finish telling me of what happened when Hiromoai first discovered you, Wind-san.” He smiled at the female Warrior to show her he wasn’t really upset with her, he just want her to rush her story a little quicker than she was telling him about her past.

“I am so sorry for daring to bore you with my past, but I was trying to be as thorough as possible, so you can understand everything that had transpired between Hiromoai and myself, my Lord and Master. I shall continue my story at a much faster pace for your pleasure my Liege Lord. The old Utsumi-san was finally able to talk you into visiting the site and upon your arrival there, you rushed to my tomb. You entered after the workers had removed the thick layer of dust that covered my body and the body of my horse, and you discovered all the weapons and other items buried with me inside the tomb. You carefully examined my vast horde weapons and you found all except for my deadly Katana killing sword. You search my tomb and could not locate it and you finally confronted Utsumi-san about it, and he told you he had removed my killing sword from my tomb to have it cleaned then he was going to give it to you as a special gift.

“But my wise Lord and Master was too sharp to believe the tall tale he was trying to make you believe. You knew he was trying to take my sword for his to keep. He gave you the sword and all the while you were ordering your workers around, you held my sword and was constantly tapping your shoulder with my sheathed sword. You ordered Utsumi-san to make contact with another worker and he was ordered to bring his horseless... excuse me, his truck over to the site, and the few workers still at the site was to pack up all my weapons and armor and bring all my things to your castle for safe keeping. The workers quickly removed all my military equipment, everything that was but for my Katana killing sword. You held onto my sword and when you felt your workers had everything under their control, you walked down to what I believe was the field construction trailer, you wanted to see what my sword looked like in private.

"You entered this structure and you began to remove my sword from its ancient wooden prison. You struggled mightily because you were unaware my blood that was coating the sword when it was used to free my head from my shoulders, was welding the wood of my Katana Zutsu that is the tubular highly lacquered wood case for my sword to the metal of my blade. My blood was stopping the sword from being freed from the Zutsu. I'm afraid to offer, but the Zutsu was in dire shape from age as was the Tsuka, the hilt of my killing sword, even the Tsuba, the gold sword guard was badly tarnished from the ravages of time. You tried for a long period of time to free my great sword from the Zutsu, almost to the point of completely destroying the wooden sword cover. But all your efforts was finally rewarded when my sword was released, and I was suddenly called back to the living world from the forever Floating World of the lonely Ukiyo.

"Then the unsuspected happened. Just as the light of my spirit was called back to the living world, all my weapons and armor returned to their original newness. Even my Katana blade was like it was just crafted by the greatest sword maker in all Japan, the great Sugahara...

"Now I know what happened to your sword while I was holding it in my hands when you first started to appear before me, Wind-san." Agent Rossie offered as he glanced down at the ancient sword and was amazed it looked like it was truly just crafted by the maker of the deadly sword.

"Yes, I must believe this is just another of the great gifts the Gods of the Floating World has bestowed upon my worthless spirit. Getting back to my life story my Liege Lord, I feel we have covered everything that was discovered in my tomb, my weapons and such. I also believe I have explained how Hiromoai was able to call me back from the Floating World, just as you yourself have just called me back to the living world from the Floating World, my Lord and Master. So now what do you want me to speak further of my Liege Lord?" She asked, actually growing a little tired of sitting the way she was seated, and she started to shift her weight to try and get a little more comfortable still kneeling on the hard wood floor of his apartment.

Agent Rossie picked up her discomfort and offered a second time. "Wind-san, if you'd like, you can sit in that chair, it's well padded and comfortable and you'll be more comfortable seated there. Will you remember what we are speaking about, I need to get something from my room."

Wind merely nodded and she rose and walked over to the chair and sat and she smiled because her new Lord and Master was correct. It was a very comfortable chair to be seated in.

Agent Rossie walked back into the small living room of his apartment, and he was carrying one of his old robes. He smiled as he offered it to the female Samurai Warrior.

She realized what it was and although she never suffered from modesty, she liked the feel of the fabric and she was a little cool so she took the offered robe then she rose and slipped into the garment. Once she was covered as much as she wanted to cover of her body, she sat down in the chair and waited for Rossie to get comfortable again on the couch he was seated on.

He sat and looked at Wind and was pleased because she left the front of the robe open, and he was able to still see much of her breasts. He smiled and asked the female Samurai. "I believe you're correct, we covered enough of your past life, your tomb, the weapons found in your crypt and how Hiromoai called you back to what you call the living world from the land of the Floating World. So why don't we start covering how Hiromoai forced you into his world of murder. We have already covered the death of the bodyguards and Tsutomu Yurkowa-san and his wife well enough for the time being. But there were other deaths you were involved in under Hiromoai's direction. I want to know why Hiromoai ordered you to kill that poor old man, Asahiko Yurkowa-san, and most importantly, why he ordered you to kill Mr. Calvin Batterman."

He decided to add the 'san' to honor Asahiko and his son, because when Wind mentioned any Japanese name, she added the 'san' at the end of the name. He also omitted the 'san' at the end of Hiromoai's name, because Wind never added it to his name, and he felt she was disrespecting his memory because of what he forced her to do. If she was disrespecting his memory he sure was not going to respect him by adding the 'san' to his name to follow Wind's lead over these matters that seemed so important to her. He was finding Wind's story very captivating, and he was amazed he was sitting in his apartment and he was actually speaking to someone who was put to death by her Lord Kawasomeru, way back in the Thirteenth Century. He was never one who believed in the hereafter, he always felt once you were death you were dead.

But now, sitting here speaking to someone who has been death for centuries sure as hell shot his once belief all to hell and back again. He could not stop staring at this female spirit who had a solid form, and was so beautiful and looked so young, yet she was as old as dirt he felt. He wanted to tell everyone he knew about Wind and her story, but he understood if he tried to tell someone about her, there was a good chance he would end up in a padded cell waiting to see a doctor. Right now he was going to be content to hear her story, and then try and figure out a way to tell Lieutenant Kenzaburo Motoshima he was able to solve both Batterman and Asahiko-san's murders, and if the Japanese Lieutenant was going to believe what he was going to tell him about Wind, without him calling his Commander and have him check his sanity.

He actually smiled because he felt he could see the look on the Japanese Lieutenant's face when he started telling him about how Hiromoai used this ancient spirit to kill everyone he wanted dead. He knew if someone came to him with the story he was hearing from this Warrior, how he would react and he slowly shook his head and smiled again, because he knew he would not believe such a tale he was hearing right from the lips of the person who lived this tall tale.

"Yes my Liege Lord, we must talk about the men I sent to the Floating World under the orders of Hiromoai. After I had dispatched poor Tsutomu Yurkowa-san and his wife who was only guilty of being his wife, yet she died because of that fact. I returned to Hiromoai's castle and rested for many days in a row. Then one day Hiromoai announced he was going to see Asahiko-san and see if he could buy his construction company from the old man, now that his son was no longer able to run the company for the old and well honored man. He left for the meeting and in many short sticks of time he returned to his vast castle, but he was unable to be controlled. Something had gone terribly wrong with their meeting that I was unable to understand, and suddenly all he wanted to talk about was he wanted Asahiko-san dead, and he wanted me to slaughter him in much the same fashion that I had destroyed his honored son.

"I am sorry to offer my honorable Liege Lord, but I did not see the need to destroy such a well honored and respected old gentleman as Asahiko-san seemed to be. I wanted to tell Hiromoai to allow the old man to live out the rest of his years in peace. But Hiromoai was in such a foul state of anger I dared not breach my true feeling to him at that time. I merely sat with my eyes cast to the floor and listened as Hiromoai cursed and ranted and raved against the honored old man with words I had never hear said before in my entire life. His anger against this old man was beyond description and belief and bounds. For a number of days he roared angrily against Asahiko-san unabashed until he finally ordered me to come before him and he laid out a map of an ancient castle on the floor, and he told me here was where this hated old man lived.

"When Hiromoai showed me what he called a picture of the castle, I was stunned to my soul, because the castle he showed me where his enemy dwelled, was the well honored Engakuji Castle that was my Lord Kawasomeru's Castle, and I could not understand how this supposed hated man was able to live in your dwelling. Hiromoai wanted me to know my way to the old castle so when I was sent out to destroy the old man, I would know where I was going. Hiromoai asked me if I was going to be able to get inside the castle to kill Asahiko-san, and I informed my wise Lord Kawasomeru had a secret passageway so he could leave the castle at times of siege.

"Hiromoai was greatly pleased to know of this secret passageway, and he ordered me to wait till he returned and he left to see if the old passageway still existed. I instructed Hiromoai to go around the castle keep and search for the white rock that had the deeply carved shape of the dreaded Shibi Sea Monster upon the face of the stone. I informed Hiromoai that protective stone covered the passageway, and if the great stone was still there then the old passageway still existed and would make my entire into the castle easy to accomplish. It took Hiromoai a number of small sticks of time (Hours) to return with the news the stone and passageway were still there. When Hiromoai return to his castle, he ordered me to dispatch Asahiko-san on that night.

"I was forced to wait until the first call of the cock that signified the start of the new day, it was at that time Hiromoai demanded Asahiko-san die, so his ears heard the call of the new day, but his eyes would never see the start of that day. It was a further punishment he ordered me to deliver against the old man. As ordered I left on my quest to dispatch him. I found the old castle and the Shibi stone. I struggled against the stone's weight but was successful moving the stone out of my way and I entered the castle. I worked my way to the third floor and there I discovered Asahiko-san as he was reciting the first prayers to start the well honored respect of Suppuku. I was honor bound to respect what the old man was about to do to honor the Gods of Japan.

"Seeing the old man did not have a second to free his head from his shoulders, I offered to second his great death. It was the sin of sins for a Warrior to commit Suppuku without being second by his closest friend. If a Samurai committed Suppuku without being seconded and have his head released from his body then when the soul of that Samurai was freed from his earthly form, his spirit could be high jacked by the dredged wood goblins and they would eat his soul, thus ending the Samurai's hope of being reborn Samurai when the Gods felt he had wandered the Floating World long enough, and they decided to return that Warrior back to the world of the living so he could once again serve his Master faithfully. In my heart I just could not allow the old man to take his own life so honorably, only to have his spirit lost to the hated wood goblins.

"So I decided to go against my faithful Lord and Master's orders, and I honored the old man, but I was ill prepared for his terrible reaction he harbored against my being. When I waited until he finished reciting the beginning prayers to open the path his spirit had to follow in order to find the Ukiyo World safely, I let him acknowledge my presence in the room with him and much to my surprise over what I offered him. He verbally attacked me and said such harsh words of anger aimed against my honorable spirit. But I was honored bound to accept his unfettered anger aimed at myself for as long as he wanted to express it against my spirit, because he was the one who was going to soon honor the Gods greatly, by feeding the earth his sacred blood and innards. This placed his earthly being well above all others walking the sacred lands of Japan.

"Yes my Liege Lord, his act elevated him about your being until the final act of Suppuku was completed by his hand. So I allowed him to vent his anger against my spirit as long as he cared to attack me. Twice during his attack he was able to anger me, but I held my temper because of what he was prepared to do to honor the Gods. When his anger reached its limit we began to speak to each other properly. I stunned him by offering to second his death and he became more reasonable to speak with. I moved to his right side and used the pure water he set aside to wash the blade he was going to open his stomach with. I dipped the scoop in the water and showed the old man I faithfully washed both sides of my sword so he knew it was pure and clean.

"Then he recited the rest of the prayers. When he finished praying he picked up the small razor sharp Tanto blade, washed the blade clean in the pure water and he wrapped it in clean rice paper after he had pulled down his Kimono and bared his belly to the call of the blade. I watched as the old man carefully guided the blade through his skin and he displayed little if any pain in the act. Then he turned the blade in his skin and started to pull the blade across his stomach for a second time. It was at this point he suddenly let out is breath in a rush of air and blood spray and displayed terrible pain. I swiftly reacted and with on swipe of my mighty blade I released his body of the pain he was suffering from the sacred act of committing Suppuku for the Gods.

"I am sorry to offer for your ears to hear my wise Lord and Master, but when I acted and freed his head from his shoulders, his head fell into his innards and blood. So I bent down and picked up his head and looked into the still seeing eyes. and I bowed to his strength and honor. Then I began cleaning his head of the blood and gore and he looked at me until life as he understood finally left his brain, and his spirit left to find the direction it was going to use to fine the opening to the Floating World. When I cleaned his head well enough of his blood I then placed it on the floor and allowed his face to stare at his body that was still locked perfectly in his kneeling position. Showing his eyes the old man was still honoring the Gods correctly. Then I bowed to his earthly remains for the last time and left his body still honoring the Gods of Japan.

"I quickly worked my way out of the ancient castle, returned the Shibi so the Sea Monsters can once again protect the secret passageway into the castle, and worked my way back to Hiromoai's castle. It took me many short sticks of time to return to Hiromoai's home, and when I reported the old man was dead, he questioned me on the savagery I released on his worthless body and I hesitated for a brief moment. Hiromoai instantly picked up my hesitation and he roared at me if I savaged his body. Again I hesitated. he then demanded of me to explain how Asahiko-san had met his fate, and when I told him I found Asahiko-san in the start of committing Suppuku, and I seconded the old man's honored death. Hiromoai grew extremely upset with me until I told him the old man was dead, and dead was dead no matter the way he had died.

"After thinking about my words for a few clicks of time, Hiromoai agreed with them, then he saw the light of my actions and told me maybe it was a good thing the old man committed Suppuku. That way the police authorities could not say Asahiko-san was murdered. Then Hiromoai finally relaxed and he allowed me to go and wash the blood and sweat from my body. For the next sticks of time there was little for me to do, Hiromoai did what he did for his duty for his business. Then one day he came home and announced he was going to do something against Asahiko-san's business, he called it an offer to buy and if he could not buy the company, he said he was going to perform a hostile takeover of that company. His woman helper offered that Hiromoai should visit Asahiko-san's lawyer and offer to buy the leaderless company from the lawyer. Hiromoai thought that was a good idea and he left his castle in a great mood.

"I am unaware what had transpired at the meeting held between Asahiko-san's lawyer and Hiromoai, all I know was he returned to his castle in the most foul of mood I had ever witnessed him in before. He was in such a terrible mood he broke many items in the room, he cursed and threw things about the room. I left and so did his woman helper and we hid together from Hiromoai's wrath. He was worried the police were going to come and visit him and he sent me back to the Ukiyo while he waited to be interviewed by the police. While I was away, Hiromoai attacked his woman helper physically and sexually, and he beat her black and blue.

"It took a number of sticks of time for Hiromoai to call me back from the Floating World, and when I returned he told me some American I believe he called him Gai Jin, somehow brought Asahiko-san's business out from under him, and he wanted this Gai Jin dead above all his other desires. Together we worked out a way for me to be there and could dispatch this lowly Gai Jin so Hiromoai could then acquire

Asahiko-san's company. On the day I was supposed to destroy this Gai Jin, I was sent back to the Ukiyo so Hiromoai could hide my sword where this Gai Jin could find it, and Hiromoai was to allow this Gai Jin to call me from the Floating World.

"Everything worked out as we suggested, and when the Gai Jin called my from the Floating World, my sword was given me and I went to attack the Gai Jin. To my surprise the Gai Jin held the iron hand (gun) and he fired a number of Dragon's teeth into my body before I attacked him, the Dragon's teeth did not hurt me in the least and I moved on to attack and kill the Gai Jin..."

"Wind-san, I believe what you're calling the iron hand was a pistol, and the Dragon's teeth were the bullets from the weapon. Do you mean to tell me bullets have no effect on your body? The bullets will not harm you? How is this possible? What will easily kill me, has no effect on your person, Wind-san?" Agent Rossie said as he found himself staring at the ancient female Samurai Warrior as he waited for her to reply to his last questions of her.

"This is true my Lord and I have no explanation. All I know is when the Dragon's teeth strike what they were aimed at, many small explosions take place and wherever they hit is destroyed..."

"Everything but you is destroyed you mean, Wind-san." He interrupted her again as he suddenly stared at her like he was in disbelief of what she was telling him.

"Yes, you are most correct to make that remark my honorable Lord and Master, everything is destroyed but me and as I have already offered to you. I have no true explanation for this wonder to take place my Lord. Do you

wish for me to continue with my story now my Liege Lord?"
She asked her new owner of the sword

103

CHAPTER FIVE

"Yes, please Wind-san. I'm beginning to understand everything Hiromoai had put you through, and why he did that to your fine spirit and self." He replied as he smiled at the Warrior again then he waited for her to go on with what she was telling him before he interrupted her.

Wind bowed politely to her new Lord and Master then she began to finish her story for him. "When the Gai Jin fired his Dragon's teeth at myself and they did not stop me, I immediately struck out with my sword, and I chopped off the offending arm that held the iron hand he aimed at me.

Then I raised my sword and prepared myself to hack the lowly Gai Jin to death as was my orders from Hiromoai, but for some strange reason he stopped me from slaughtering this Gai Jin as he called out to me, and then he ordered me not to be so brutal against this guiltless Gai Jin.

"Hiromoai told me he was an innocent victim in this drama, and I could not understand why he still wanted this innocent Gai Jin dead. I listened to his words and he ordered me to dispatch this Gai Jin quickly with little pain as possible offered to the Gai Jin's body. So with one swift swing of my sword, I easily separated the Gai Jin's head from his shoulders so he did not suffer.

"It was at this point Hiromoai bragged and he called out that he, Hiromoai Hatanaka was now the most powerful construction owned of all Japan. I have to admit this was the first time in my being I heard his last name being mentioned, and upon hearing his last name, my breath was robbed from my body instantly. It was now I realized I was allowing a cursed and hated offspring of the loathsome coward of a Samurai Warrior of the lowly dog who attacked and killed my Captain Katsunoke Seisakajo. The only lover I had even known when I was a living being in the living world. When I discovered who killed my Captain and I found and slaughtered the lowly Warrior with my sword. I swore a curse on all his future offspring and I was going to hunt them all down and slaughtered them all for what their father, grandfather and grandfathers might give birth to. I was actually frozen to the ground and could not move and could only stare at him.

"Then when my wits came back to my body, all I could think was to strike out with my sword and I keep striking until there was not a piece of Hiromoai's body left enough for me to strike another time. I raged at his disgust while I was striking him. I wanted to block out his face locked so deeply in my eyes. I was having trouble breathing as I ended up standing in the middle of the gore once Hiromoai. I was so exhausted I had to go down to a knee and I had to stick my Wind's Breath in the ground to help me steady myself as I struggled to get my rampaging emotions back under my control. As I was breathing deep breaths in to help me calm down, there was a sudden small glow developing in the bottom of the pit near the tip of my sword Wind's Breath.

"I was instantly concerned what this small glow was about. At first I thought it might by my namesake Fuji the always angry God of Wind coming to take all the Gods revenge out against me for destroying the owner of my sword. Because of the curse Lord Kawasomeru had placed on my sword that whoever held my sword in their hands was my Lord and Master and I was not allowed to harm that Master under any circumstances. But in my mind my own curse overrode the curse my Lord and Master slaved my spirit to my sword. So I felt I was in the right to take my revenge out against Hiromoai's foul body so I took his worthless life. But I found myself staring into the bubbling, churning mass of an angry cloud and boiling flames trying to take shape before my stunned eyes. Tears of fear and sorrow were streaming down my cheeks and washed some of the blood from my face while I waited for the horrifying wrath of Fujin to befall my head and soul.

"I remained kneeling in the gore because I was at peace with myself, and if the Gods wanted to end my spirit's life so be it. I lived my oath to myself. As I waited for the God's wrath to befall my shoulders, I stared at the light as it grew larger until it engulfed the interior of the pit. A strong breeze developed and instead of the unimagined punishment and pain from within the boiling mass of turbulence. A voice I had long ago remembered, called out tenderly, charmingly, protectively to me. The voice caused instant harmony and peace to come from within my troubled and confused spirit, as I continued to stare in awe then waited for the spirit causing all the turbulence starting to surround my being. It was the voice of my Lord Kawasomeru.

"When I heard his voice, all fear left my body and I found myself waiting to see his face again. Finally, his form took on solid shape and again I was able to lay my eyes upon my Lord's face. What peace his face brought to my body as he began to speak to me. I will never forget what he said to me. He uttered 'My Wind-san it is I, Lord Kawasomeru of countless years past, my most loyal Samurai Warrior of all times. I now dwell within the honored Floating World as does your uncontrollable spirit. I dwell separate from you and the other Samurai who have served me well throughout my life on the great battlefield, and on the living earth. I now dwell within the land placed aside in the never, an honored and sacred place, and served by the honored Kami who protect all Shoguns who have served Japan's great past so honorable and true. I command your fighting spirit do not be angry at yourself my faithful Samurai Warrior of countless years past. I have returned from the place without thought to bring you back home, Wind, my Wind.

"My honorable and beyond loyal female Samurai Warrior of time long ago forgotten and honored by all children of Japan, Wind-san your unhampered and forever wandering spirit is still unable to be confined by the mere traps of mortal man, or the Gods who command them so. Wind-san, my Wind-san, I want to tell you Fujin-Sama is not angry with your spirit in the least, because you were only guilty of following your own sworn oath, and it was by my curse that had caused you this indecision you have suffered from over your deed of honor. You were bound to the land of the living and earth by your sacred oath to kill the one who had destroyed your noble Samurai Warrior and only lover, Captain Katsunoke Seisakajo-san, and all who were sired by this detestable murderer of the middle of the night who dispatched your lover, Tetsuo Hatanaka.

"It was a just and most honorable oath you had once sworn long ago to the countless Gods of wonderment as it should have been uttered, a noble and honorable curse indeed that even overrode my strong curse I had rested upon your head and sword of justice and vengeance. An oath of vengeance is far more important, far more powerful than any other curse from I could ever attain, Wind-san. Come with me your true Lord and Master of fate and time, my always faithful female Samurai Warrior of forever, give me your honorable hand. I shall be extremely proud to safely take you home, to rest among the clouds until the next time you are needed by the next new Lord and Master of the sword dwelling within the lands of the living. Yes Wind-san, your curse has not been lifted from your faithful shoulders, or has been fulfilled by time and honor, for the sword remains whole as one still my Wind-san.

"When Lord Kawasomeru finished speaking, I reached to retrieve his Katana blade, but I was stopped in my efforts by my Master of the sword's words. 'No my Wind-san, you must not, do not dare try and pick up the sword in your hand again, because the sword of justice will no longer recognize your faithful touch and respect. You must leave the great blade lying behind, because I am the only one in the entire universe who can possible touch it now. Wind-san, you shall continue to exist deep within the hearts and minds of all honorable Japanese peoples, until the last star gives up its endless existence in the Heavens, and it falls from the nighttime sky to be silenced of its light for eternity, and the earth itself begins its everlasting sleep of death and none-existence. Come with me my loyal and most honorable and trusted Samurai Warrior Wind-san.

"My powerful Lord Kawasomeru then tenderly reached his hand out to me from within the fine mist of the cloud that was now engulfing my spirit and the slight depression I stood in, and when I greedily extended my hand to greet his and lightly touched his comforting hand with mine. The instant when our hands touched together, my ungovernable spirit instantly disappeared in the still boiling cloud of mist. My spirit was bathed in a cool, refreshing relaxing light, and I was then placed in a special waiting area for Lord Kawasomeru to finish with his short visit to the living world. Though I was set in this sequestered place, I was still able to see everything my honorable Lord and Master was doing in the land of the living. All the blood and gore that once covered my naked body instantly vanished, the instant my spirit entered the cloud of mist. I was now cool, refreshed and very comfortable, and I was dressed in the most exquisite Kimono I have ever saw in my long and exhausting existence in the both worlds of greatness.

"When my spirit was gone from the blood soaked death scene, my once mighty and well feared warlord known as Lord Kawasomeru, took on a more solid earthly form, and I watched as he picked up my still blood soaked Katana blade. The very blade my Lord and Master used to dispatch my life so many centuries back in his living life. It was good for him to once again feel the fine heft of his fearsome killing sword locked in his powerful hands. The Katana blade that had served my Master so well on many past battlefields, the one my Liege Lord buried with my body. My Lord Kawasomeru took a few moments to look around and view the terrible carnage created by me, until he finally noticed the scabbard of his Katana resting on the bloody ground.

"But even before my Lord an Master retrieved the scabbard for the blade, he was forced to move a piece of Hiromoai's head out of his way with the tip of his ancient sword, as I heard him growl at the piece of ugly flesh lying on the ground before his feet. He snarled 'Fool of the evil fool, how dare you to believe that you, a mere and worthless mortal of the earth, a foul man as desperate as you could possibly control and tame what was not meant to be tamed and controlled by any mere mortal dwelling within either worlds of existence. You have received your just reward for daring to use the wonderful gift that the Gods had bestowed upon Wind-san's fine spirit in this life for all your evil and personal gains, your evil wants of this earth. Then you said you shall find the most proper way to so dishonor your cursed memory correctly in much the same way you have dishonored my faithful female Samurai Warrior of the past of Japan."

"My powerful warlord then slowly walked all over the gore without care or concern for the remains of both slaughtered men, and you stopped and respectfully picked up the scabbard and you placed the sword back in its ancient protective home. For the briefest of moments, I watched my indescribable warlord allow yourself a few seconds to enjoy the sweet smells of the living world, before you were called back to the Floating World forever. I witnessed how good for the great stalwart warlord of myth and wonderment, to again tread upon the dismembered bodies of the fallen enemy to your realm and laws and beliefs. These two killed honorably by one of your Warriors forever loyal to your commands over these many past centuries.

"When the killing sword of my Lord Kawasomeru was set in its rightful place in its ancient wood scabbard, you took the time to hide the weapon in the same place where Hiromoai had placed the great blade earlier in his ambush of the unsuspecting Gai Jin invader from another land. Then my warlord of the past left it for the next master of the sword to discover, and to control the spirit of your Wind honorably. You were aware Hiromoai was a most dishonorable and detestable man, and he used my great power and spirit for his evil gains on the land of the living world. My angry warlord wanted to carry out your own revenge played out against the man who had hurt your Wind so badly, and it overrode your will to leave the land of the living, as the laws that commanded you to do at the allotted time of your demanded departure time.

"I witnessed your final act of disgust and disrespect and loathing you could possibly display against the disrespected memory and remains of Hiromoai. The great spirit of my powerful warlord slowly hitched your Fundoshi, your loincloth to the side, and you desecrated Hiromoai's remains scattered about the slight depression by pissing on them. It was the only thing my well respected warlord could think of doing to the most evil man, to insult the enemy of his Wind for all eternity, and to honor your Warrior for my faithful service to your commands and desires.

"It was plain to see my Lord Kawasomeru fondly remembered when I did much the same thing when I caught up with and killed the cast down dishonored assassin who murdered my beloved younger sister so terribly in my father, the Master Trainer Tanizaki-san's home so many centuries ago. My sister was murdered because the assassin took her for me, and Lord Wakatsuki ordered this assassin out to dispatch me to take my sword from my Lord. It was a proper and deserving insult, one well worthy of repeating for the sake of your honorable Wind's spirit to witness from my waiting area, locked in the fabled Floating World of amazement and wonderment.

"Once my wise Lord Kawasomeru was finished disgracing the foul remains of Hiromoai, my Lord and Master then turned and you found the head of the slaughtered and guiltless American Gai Jin. And I listened to your honorable words as you muttered them to the spirit as you picked up the severed head of the dead Gai Jin by the crop of his almost white hair. You looked deeply into the non-seeing eyes of the stranger to your lands, and my ancient warlord said in your always commanding voice. "You! Gai Jin who came to Japan from another world, from another land, from another wonder, from another time, you are about to be honored as no other Gai Jin of the past has ever been honored by any Japanese Shogun. For your worthy but innocent spirit will forever be allowed to dwell within the great lands of wonderment of the Ukiyo World in peace and harmony, and with the greatest of respect offered you by all the spirit and Gods that give worth to the Floating World, and all who honor the powerful Kami of the Ukiyo.

"Gai Jin, it is a very special place in which to dwell for all eternity, and it was solely once reserved for only the honored and respected Japanese Samurai Warriors of the great past, and of the future years yet to be displayed for

Japan's history, Gai Jin. Since you were killed by my Wind-san's hand, an honorable Samurai Warrior of the past times for reasons beyond your blame or control, or of your own fault or cause. The Kami who rule over such decisions, have deemed it proper and correct for you to be allowed to dwell in peace forever with me in the great void of life. You shall be standing proudly by my side, so we can both watch the future of my world yet to be played out before our foolish eyes together. I will teach you my language so you will understand all that is about to be displayed before your non-believing eyes.

"I heard my great Liege Lord tell the Gai Jin's head you shall take good care of his honorable soul for all eternity yet to be unfolded in your memory, Gai Jin. You further said you shall teach him of all the many fine ways and great respect of the honorable Japanese Samurai Warrior Class. You also told the Gai Jin to come with you, because it was time you came home to fulfill the final destiny to your honorable memory and spirit. You said together the two of you shall go and collect your beloved Wind's unconquerable spirit, and then you two will bring me to stand proud before the Council of Kami, so they might again honor my spirit justly.

"Because I was still your most loyal and trusted Vassal, your retainer for time ever after, and it was a time for an unwise Gai Jin to witness and learn of the proper respect a true Lord and Master expects, and deserves from all his loyal Samurai retainers. Who serve you faithfully in life and in death as well, and how that Lord and Master repays the loyal Warriors who has honored you for the so many years of his useless existence upon this great rock of earth.

"When my powerful and ancient Lord Kawasomeru finished speaking to the hovering spirit of the American Gai

Jin Calvin Batterman through the head you were still holding in your hand through the unseeing eyes of his severed head. My warlord's spirit likewise rapidly dissolved to nothingness, while carefully guiding the newly forming spirit of Calvin Batterman to his resting place within the clouds of wonder, along with your loving Wind. Batterman's head was still held tightly in my Lord Kawasomeru's right hand as the ancient laws demanded it be carried to the Council of Kami, left the earth with them both. Once my Lord's spirit left the earth to be reunited with the countless spirits of the past of Japan that once owned the unseen world of wonder and legions, my Lord Kawasomeru led the two honored spirits forth until we both stood before the great Council of Kami, and the many Lords of the past began to honor us properly..."

"Well you have just answered one of the questions I was going to ask of you Wind-san. I wanted to know what happened to Batterman's head, but you have answered that question clearly for me. I hate to say this to you Wind-san, but I'm afraid I'm exhausted. It's been one helluva day and I'm having a little trouble keeping my eyes opened. I don't even know what time it is." Agent Rossie checked his watch and he was stunned to find out it was already 3:30 in the morning. That meant he was speaking with the female Samurai Warrior for over nine hours.

Drawing in a deep breath and he held it for a few moments then he let his air out and he told ancient female Warrior. "Wind-san, I want to turn in for the rest of the night. I have orders to report to my work later on this morning so I do need some sleep. I'm lucky though, because even though I was ordered to report to work at a certain time, it's flexible and when I show up, I show up. Yes, it's true my boss might get a little testy if I'm late but in the end it'll be okay. Tell you what, I'll fix you a place to sleep here on the couch. That's my room over there. How are you Wind-san, are you sleepy yet, do you need anything else to eat or drink?"

"I thank my kind and concerned Lord and Master for his worry for this worthless Samurai Warrior. I do not need any food, I am well there, but much like you, I am extremely tired and can use some sleep myself, my Liege Lord." Wind offered to the young and good looking FBI Agent.

"Good, let me get you some bed covers then." With that said, he got up and went to a closet and removed two blankets and walked back to the couch, straightened the pillows and covered the couch with one of the blankets. Then he flipped the other blanket over the back of the sofa. He took a step back and examined his handiwork then smiled as he turned to Wind and said, "There you go Wind-san, and if you get cold tonight, just pull the other blanket down and cover yourself with it. Well, I guess that about that, I'm turning in, I'm beat out and need some sleep. Good night Wind-san, sleep well and I'll see you in the morning."

Rossie smiled at the female Warrior, and he turned and walked in his bedroom and used the facilities then he crawled into bed, pulled the covered over him and by the time he rested his head on the pillow, he was snoring away. He slept like he was dead for the rest of the night, and when his alarm clock went off at 8 A.M. to give him enough time to shower and eat something before he left for the office so he could arrive at the agreed upon time of 10 A.M. He cursed because he was still exhausted because he was suffering from jetlag, and talking to Wind for most of the night. He reached out and hit the clock so hard he nearly knocked it off the night table. With a grown like a wounded bear, he flung the covers off him then sat up and swung his legs off the bed and nearly stepped on Wind sleeping on the floor right by the side of his bed.

"What the hell is this about?" He groused at Wind's sleeping body as he gently pushed her rearend with his foot, so she would move her body enough so he could put his feet on the floor and get out of bed. He smiled as Wind's eyes sprang opened and she immediately went to a sitting position, rubbed her eyes with the palms of her hands and looked up at him.

Again he repeated, but this time to Wind because she was now awake and she could reply to his question. "Hey Wind-san, why are you sleeping on the damn floor, wasn't the sofa comfortable enough for you to sleep a little better in the living room?"

"My Lord and Master, the bedroll you had prepared for my sleep was more comfortable than this foolish Warrior deserved." Wind replied as she returned Rossie's smile with one of her own.

"Then why the devil are you sleeping on the damn floor for, Wind-san?" the confused FBI Agent grumbled at the ancient Samurai Warrior with a snap in his voice this time.

"My Liege Lord, the reason I have decided to sleep on the floor was because when I was sleeping in the other room, I was unable to see you while you were sleeping. Since I was unable to see you then I was unable to protect your life against any treachery that was displayed against your person. So I removed this cover and brought it into your sleeping room and slept on the floor, so I could better protect your honorable life as you slept peacefully. What was that terrible bell I heard that woke me from my sleep it scared me to wake my Liege Lord?"

"You're really getting to be something Wind-san. The bell as you called it was my alarm clock, I use it to wake me in time for me to look after what I have to accomplish for my body, before I leave to report for my day's work. I have to get up because I want to take a quick shower before I leave then get myself something to eat first. Excuse me Wind-san." He offered to the ancient Warrior as he got out of bed, stood up completely naked before he, and then he stretched his arms over his head and again, growled like a wounded bear.

She intensely watched everything her new master of the sword and her spirit did as he got out of bed, and her spirit enjoyed looking at his naked body. Especially because he was semi-hard and she could tell he was rather well endowed. But his mighty dragon looked much different than that of the Japanese dragons of old. There was no skin hiding the might head of his dragon, and she found it most pleasing to see the difference. His member was more pleasing to look at than the Japanese members were to see. Now she found herself wondering how it would be to allow her new master's member to part her waiting Jade Gate, wondering if she would be able to tell the difference between the dragons. She smiled because she vowed to herself she was going to make it her business to find out if it did feel differently to her. She stared at him as he walked naked to the bathroom like he did not have a care in the world.

In seconds she could hear the water of the shower running, and heard him singing as he washed his body. When the water stopped, she got up and walked to the door of the bathroom and watched as her new master put white on his face then he dragged a blue handle thing across his face. But she found herself looking at his lightly swaying and a little harder member more than she watched him shave. Now she found herself yelling at her because she wanted to reach out and touch his member, to see if it felt differently because it looked so much better than her Japanese Warriors' members did. She so wanted to see what his member did when it is standing ready to penetrate the Jade Gate of any woman who wanted to pillow with her new Liege Lord.

He came out of the bathroom and quickly dressed then he looked at Wind and slowly shook his head because he did not know what to do with her. He went deep in thought for a few moments then he offered to the ancient Warrior. "What am I going to do with you while I'm at work Wind-san? I just can't leave you roaming around my apartment, I'd be concerned if you left the apartment and got yourself in some trouble outside. Damn, well anyway, I guess I have to find you something to wear. You can't remain without any clothes on all day."

He walked over to his closet and fished around and he found an old pair of pants he outgrew and wanted to throw them away but forgot about them. Then he took one of his shirts from the hanger and handed them to her, figuring she would want to get dressed. But instead she merely tossed the clothes on his bed, put her hands on her hips and almost glared at him,

"What's this all about now? Please don't tell me you don't like to be in clothes. I can't

have you walking around my apartment in the buff, someone might come by for a visit..."

"Excuse me for interrupting my Liege Lord, but I fear I do not understand what buff means?"

"Sorry Wind-san, buff means naked with no clothes on, do you understand now?"

"Of course I understand what naked means, does my wise Lord think me slow of mind?"

"No Winds-san, by no means could I ever suggest you might be slow of mind, if anything you're too swift. Wind-san, I do have a problem on my hands, I have to report to work, but I can't possibly leave you roaming around my apartment alone. No telling what kind of trouble you might get yourself into while I'm gone. I don't know what to do with you until I return later on tonight, and then we can speak further about all that has happened in your life. What to do?"

"I am so sorry I am suddenly such a heavy burden to my Liege Lord. I know what you might do if you do not mind my suggestion my Lord and Master." She offered with concern.

"Please, I'm open to any suggest you can possibly offer me, Wind-san."

"My Liege Lord, you can always send me back to the Floating World until you return from your work period, and you wish to see and speak to me any further about my past life."

"That is the answer to this problem, but how do I send you to this Floating World, Wind-san?"

"I am sorry this worthless Warrior failed to explain further the rewards of the sword, even though I would believe my Liege Lord should understand what your curse had bestowed upon my Katana blade. To send me back to the Floating World, all you have to do is place my killing sword back in its scabbard, and I will be instantly sent to the Floating World to wait forever for the next call of my Lord to serve him. So I would be freed to carry out the desires or demands my Liege Lord." She relaxed then she waited to see what her new master was going to do with her.

"That's all I have to do you tell me Wind-san, is just place your sword back in its scabbard? By the way Wind-san, how come when you came to stand before me, I was holding a rusted and worthless sword. But the moment you came before me, your sword and its scabbard instantly turned into looking like it was just crafted by the ancient sword maker."

"Again you test me foolishly you know when you call me from the Floating World everything I owned will return to its original luster like it was just crafted by the makers. It's more of the curse and gifts my Lord bestowed on my Katana blade, my Lord and Master over life and death."

"Okay I got it and that solves one part of the problem Wind-san, errr... does it hurt you when you're either called back from the Floating World, or when you're returned back to the Floating World, because if it does. I don't think I want to cause you any pain and we'll have to figure out another way to keep you out of any trouble when I'm working, Wind-san. Err... this will only be until I learn more about you, and find out if I can trust you to stay out of any trouble while I'm working. If I find out I can trust you while I'm working, I won't have to think about sending you back to the Floating World to keep you safe until I returned from work, Wind-san."

"My Lord, how can you mistrust one who has done nothing in my life other than protecting you and your property and worth throughout my life? I could no more cause you displeasure than I could overlook destroying one of your enemy. I am as trusted to your being as sure as the sun will awake from its night sleep and again soar within the Heavens of tomorrow's morning sky my Master." Wind pleaded in her own defense to who she believe was her Lord Kawasomeru.

"I understand that but I still have to be positive about you, before I can trust you to remain from the Floating World while I'm busying carrying out the duties of my job, Wind-san."

"I can understand how my Lord and Master feels, and will obey any decision you make on my fate my Lord and Master." Wind replied, but she could not keep the hurt she was feeling because her Lord wanted to send her back to the Floating World because he felt he could not trust her yet.

"Okay then Wind-san, I have to send you back to the Floating World now, or I'm going to be late for work and I'll get in some trouble with my boss if I end up coming in late. Before I send you back to the Floating World, is there anything you might need or want to eat, drink or enjoy before you go back to the Floating World. I really hate like hell to send you back to that obviously very lonely place, but I promise you Wind-san it'll only be for a short time."

"I understand and there are no wants or needs of my spirit, I am prepared to return to the Floating World of the forever waiting, my kind Lord and Master." She offered as she lowered her head and then looked at the floor, because she felt her heart breaking over the fact of her being returned to the place of long waiting to return to the living world and again enjoy the countless enjoyments and wonders the living share with their Lords and Masters and loved ones.

"I feel so bad to send you back to the Floating World Wind-san, but for the time being I have no other choice in the matter. Please forgive me, are you ready to return to where you were staying before I called you before me, Wind-san?" He offered, feeling her pain.

"There is one thing I wish to do before you send me away, my Lord and Master."

"Yes, anything Wind-san? What do you wish, now is the time to speak up, Wind-san?"

"Dozo (Please) I wish to give my Lord and Master a gift before I leave your presence. It is a very special gift handed to me personally by the mighty and all powerful Creator of the Eight highly honored Islands of Japan, Izanagi. It was specially given to me when I was ordered to stand before the entire Council of Kami, so they could judge if I was right to break the curse that governed my spirit to the life of my Katana blade. As I stood before the Council of Kami, they could have ordered the death of my spirit if I was found guilty of the crime of my dispatching the Master of my sword. Obviously, I was found guiltless of the crime because my sworn oath to my dead Samurai Captain Katsunoke Seisakajo-san superseded the curse you had placed upon the sword and my worthless head, my Lord and Master..."

"Quite obviously you were found guiltless, or I'm certain you would surely not be standing before me at this time, Wind-san?" He kind of snorted at her because he wanted to send this extremely dangerous female Samurai Warrior back to where she came from. So he could be off for his work for the day and time was fast running out on him, and if this dragged on any longer. Then he was going to be late to report to his Commander Ralph Murdock, and that would surely put him on the Commander's shit list for the rest of the day.

"Obviously my Lord and Master, nevertheless, I would like for you to have this amulet, it will help keep my Lord and Master safe, even when I am not standing within my Liege Lord's presence. Please my Master, take what I offer you in the light of why I am offering you such a powerful gift from the Creator of the Heavens and the earth that Japan exists upon. Not every spirit is so honored by the Creator's hand. Any Kami of the Floating World would honorably give up their spirit to have such a gift from the Creator. It was the honor of honors to have this amulet bestowed upon my worthless head, and now I wish for you to possess it." She said as she suddenly held her hand out and offered the great gift to her new Lord and Master.

"What is it, wow it's carved of the finest Jade I have ever seen in my life? I thank you very much for the wonderful gift Wind-san. I shall honor it as you have. Why do you say it will help protect me even when you're not with me, Wind-san?" He remarked as he carefully studied the fine work of art with an equally beautiful gold chain, so he could wear in around his neck.

"Because my wise Lord and Master, this sacred amulet has very special powers, it will enable me to see where and what you are doing when you are away from my side, and if you are suddenly attacked by any possible assassins, it shall bring me to your feet within the amount of time for you to mumble my name and call me to your side, my Liege Lord. This gift was given me by the Creator so I might better protect the ward of my sword and my spirit." She offered, hoping this information would stop her new master from sending her back to the Floating World.

"Huh, this means I'll have no privacy if I have this amulet with me, Wind-san." He groused as he rolled the piece of Jade and realized on the face of the small amulet that measured around three by two inches. Had a richly and deeply carved dragon, with its tail protectively wrapped around a lone Samurai Warrior who held a killing blade lifted well over his head.

"That is not exactly true I offer to my most honorable Liege Lord, the sacred amulet will only activate and communicate with my mind's eye at times when your life might be in any danger of attack from your Teki (Enemy). Then it is commanded to alert and then bring my spirit to you so that I might carry out my Yoshi gi, my duty of protecting your life no matter where you are. In this way you will still be able to maintain your private life without my eyes tampering into your privacy, my powerful Liege Lord." She offered her new and young master of the sword.

"Thank you for the gift and I'll wear it proudly. By the way Wind, when I'm finished work today, I'll stop at a store and buy you clothes so you can have women clothes to wear. I'm afraid my clothes don't flatter your exquisite body properly and they don't do you justice, Wind-san."

"My most pleasing Lord and Master I beg that will not be necessary, because when you return me to the Floating World when you leave for your workday. I will be granted to pick up many of my clothes and weapons and armor. It will be granted to me by my Lord Kawasomeru..."

"That's another thing I was meaning to talk to you about Wind-san, but now is not the time for that conversation to be had, I have to leave for work or I'll be late as I told you. But when I return and call you back from the Floating World, I want to talk to you about all the confusion you're giving me by referring to me as your Lord and Master. Then you call me Lord Kawasomeru and everyone else you refer to as your Lord and Master, your Liege Lord and Lord Kawasomeru and anything else. I'm sorry but I have to go, please forgive me for sending you back to the Floating World, Wind-san." With that said, he walked across the room and picked up the scabbard, and he was amazed it looked as good as the day it was first created. All the rich, gold inlay was back in all its lusted, and the lacquer was as shinny as the day it was born.

He took it back to the sofa and stopped right in front of Wind who was standing with her head slightly lowered, and she was staring at the floor. She was desperately begging the Kami to stop her new Master from sending her back to the lonely Ukiyo. The young FBI Agent bowed politely towards her as he picked up her sword and then he swiftly slipped it back in its sheath. Within less than a heartbeat Wind immediately started to fade into the rapidly developing and again nearly blinding light, and then she and the glow were gone in an instant.

He cocked and then shook his head as he wondered what he might have got himself into when he first found the ancient sword and this extremely dangerous female Samurai Warrior. Then he looked down at the sword and was stunned to see it had already returned to its ancient and rusted and crumbling state. Dust from the handle of the blade actually coated his hand, and he could easily smell the oldness being emitted from the sword and scabbard again. He walked over to his hall closet and quickly hid the ancient sword well in the back of the tiny closet. Then he closed the door and rushed out of the building. He went behind the building and climbed into his FBI vehicle and took off for the FBI Headquarters about a half an hour ride away from his apartment as quickly as the morning rush hour traffic would allow him to drive.

CHAPTER SIX

Agent Robert Rossie was five minutes early to report to his Commander's office. He walked in the office because the door was open and Ralph was seated behind his desk. When Murdock looked up from the report he was reading, he smiled and offered at the same time. "As I live and breathe, the great FBI Agent Bob Rossie is alive and moving under his own power this morning."

Two other agents working in the outer office laughed over the way the Commander just addressed his agent when he walked into the office.

"Enough of that shit out there, you two birds better be working on your caseload if you know what's good for you two." Murdock called out to the other agents with a snap in his voice.

Rossie took a seat and smiled at the Commander as he grumbled at him. "I see you're in your usual lovable good mood this morning Ralph. How are you doing today sir?"

"I think the real question is how are you doing today, mister? Did you catch up on your sleep last night? You better not have used last night to play patty cake with some chick instead of getting some sleep. Hummmm..." The Commander mumbled and then he went on with his words. "You do look a little rested at that mister, you still suffering from any jet lag, Bob?"

"Not really sir, but I sure as hell coulda used another five hours of sleep, sir."

"Couldn't we all mister, FYI (For Your Information) I have your new partner reporting here this morning, and Sergeant Toshihiro Fugiwara said he could be here before Twelve, Bob. I'll give you two the rest of the day to get caught up on this damn Batterman case, and then I want the two of you to put your noses to the grind stone, and get this damn case toot sweet before anyone placed the damn heat on my ass, mister. I already got my first inquiry from the DOJ, (Department of Justice) and they wanted to know who I assigned to the Batterman murder. I'm going to allow you two to use Agent Patterson office on this floor to work out of because Richard is in Montana working on a case that's going to take him a couple of months to finish that one off, a fraud case. I don't think he'd mind you two guys using his office.

"How's it going with you mister, you think you have any damn leads on this fricking case yet, Bob? I need this damn thing ended yesterday if you catch my frift my friend. Oh, by the way mister, I was contacted earlier this morning by a Japanese Lieutenant let me see, ahhh... yes here we go," The Commander offered as he searched the mess of papers cluttering his desk, and he found the slip of paper he wrote the Lieutenant's name on. "Kenzaburo Motoshima and he asked me to have you make contact with him at your earliest free time. Now can you think of any reason for some Jap cop from the Detective and Homicide Division of the Tokyo Police Department would want from your ass, mister?"

"He's the Officer who's working on the Batterman's murder case back in Japan, maybe he found something he wanted to tell me about. That's the only reason I could possibly think of for him trying to make contact with me this early in the case, sir. I just left the Investigator yesterday to be exact, and I'm certain he wasn't able to solve the case that quickly for us, sir."

"Nevertheless, I want you to get in contact with this damn Japanese Detective as soon as you're comfortable in Patterson's office. Look Bob, you're gonna have to hit the ground running on this case as fast as possible sir. If I already have the damn DOJ breathing down my stinking back, how long do you think before I'm gonna get a call from the big Boss, and the President starts demanding we solve this damn case yesterday? I know it's only a matter of time before he starts putting the pressure on me, especially when the Board of his damn Construction Company starts to cry for permission to carry on their work and things start getting locked up in probate on them. That's when these powerful people are gonna start crying to the President for him to get involved in this mess, so they can take over Batterman's junk and start working again, dammit."

"I hear you and I'm on it Ralph, but I can only move as fast as I discover any possible evidence on this damn case, sir. But I assure you I'm on it sir. Err..." He started and then he went deep in thought for few moments. He was debating with himself on if he should breach the fact of Wind and what she had to do with this murder case, and he had just about solved the entire case already. Then he thought about it for a second longer, and all he could see in his mind was his Commander laughing his ass off at him over the story about Wind. Then he would be ordering him to take a drug screen, and he might even end up in the padded room for a couple of weeks being checked out by a horde of doctors. He's thoughts were interrupted by his Commander as he cleared his throat, and then his Commander called out to him.

"Errr...Earth to Bob, come back to earth Bob. You crapping out on me mister or what?"

"I'm okay Ralph, I was just trying to go over some of the evidence I had, to see if I could show you the direction I was heading off in sir." He offered to his Commander.

"Okay, look Bob I know I'm dumping a helluva lot of pressure on your ass so quickly sir, especially since you just returned to the States yesterday. I'm going to back off some on you until you get your sea legs under you, and you know what's you're doing with this damn case. Hell Bob, Batterman was slaughtered just two damn days ago and here I am, demanding you solve this case yesterday. You want a cup of coffee and maybe a piece of cake. We can head down to the luncheonette and grab something to eat and drink until Fugiwara get's his ass down here."

"Yes sir, I can sure use a cup of coffee to get my blood moving sir."

"Fine, let's go I can use a cup of Joe myself, Bob. I was here first thing this morning at 7 A.M. I wanted to get here early to see if I heard anything from Agent Fugiwara. I was pleased to see he checked in already with the office." Ralph announced as he stood and then he lead Rossie out of his office, and they both headed for the elevator.

As they walked into the luncheonette the Commander was upset when he noticed Agent Shinnosuke Fugiwara was at a table reading the newspaper and enjoying a cup of coffee and plate of bacon and eggs. He rushed for the table, pulled the chair out and plopped down so noisily that Fugiwara looked over the edge of the paper to see who sat down at his table. When he saw the Commander glaring at him, he carefully folded the newspaper, put it down on the table and then he began eating his breakfast like his boss was not sitting at the table and giving him the evil eye.

"Why you lousy pain in the damn ass you, what the hell are you doing sitting down here when you knew damn well I was waiting for your stinking ass to get in my damn office this morning mister. So I can brief you on this new murder case I want you to work with Bob here on, buddy? I should give you a helluva swift boot in the damn ass for keeping me waiting for you backside to arrive at my office, mister." The Commander snarled hotly at the other FBI Agent

"What does it look like I'm doing here Ralph, I'm enjoying my breakfast. Look Ralph, you just pulled me in from my week off and I still had three days left to my week off. So the least you can do is to wait until I had my breakfast, before you get on my case, sir." Fugiwara was an Agent of high enough rank to be a little quick with his boss, as he returned to eating his breakfast.

"You got some damn Bravoes there buster, and I warn you mister, don't allow your balls go to your head. You could end up chocking on the damn things. Well Bob...," the Commander turned the Rossie and offered to him. "We might as well have some breakfast ourselves. Okay you two, breakfast is one me and we might as well start discussing this murder case as we eat."

"Why was murdered is that, Ralph?" Fugiwara asked as he allowed his fork covered with eggs to hover before his mouth, as he waited for the Commander to tell him who was killed,

"Calvin Batterman had his damn head chopped off his shoulders over there in Japan, and Bob here was brought into the case by some damn Japanese Investigator..."

"You're shitting me Ralph, if someone killed that man it's going to create all sorts of hell in the construction field. That man was in charge of one of the largest construction companies in the United States. I investigated the man on two incidents. He was a sonofabitch to work with or for, and he didn't care who he stuck his dick in, man, woman or beast. That guy woulda put it to his mother if she owed him any money, any idea who did him in and why did they take his head?"

"Funny you would say someone took his head, because that's exactly what happed to the poor man, Agent Fugiwara. The damn killer that chopped his head off actually did carry the damn thing off with him when he or she left the crime scene. What the hell he's going to do with Batterman's head beats the crap outta my ass? You're a Jap, why the hell would any damn assassin carry off his targets noggin for, Agent Shinnosuke?"

"If the assassin took off with his head then the murderer has to obviously be a Ninja, and he took off with Batterman's head to show the person who sent the Ninja out to kill Batterman that he has faithfully carried out his orders, and then he would get paid once he proved he killed his target. Man, Batterman must have really pissed off someone who was very powerful in Japan, for the man to send out Ninja, and ordered that Ninja to take his head from the crime scene. That's a very real rare occurrence to have someone's head removed from their shoulders. In fact sir I can't remember the last time anyone employed a Ninja, and ordered the target's head to be taken. Even the Yakuza (Gangsters) or the Bossozokus (Biker gangs) or even the Kaminari (Thunder Tribes) who usually wage war with other Kaminari's, never employ a Ninja to kill someone.

"Man Ralph, if a damn Ninja was employed to kill Batterman then this case is going to be a real messy one to solve. We're going to find ourselves going back and forth from the United States to Japan and back again, because of whoever used a Ninja to kill Batterman, isn't afraid to send one of them murderers over to the United States to carry out that Master's targets. Have you notified The DOJ that Batterman's head was removed from his shoulders? Those people would be as concerned over that fact as much as I am, Ralph. This is very serious Ralph!"

"The DOJ made contact with me and they wanted a report of Batterman's murder. I never informed the caller that Batterman's head was removed from his shoulder though, Fugiwara..."

"Then I suggest you get back on the horn to the DOJ and inform them about Batterman having his head chopped off, someone over there will sure as hell understand the severe ramifications of that move. I think they're going to have a stake in this case when they hear Batterman lost his head in Japan sir. Wow, say Bob, what do you know about this case, this is serious people?"

Agent Rossie was just about to start speaking when the waitress came over and asked if they wanted anything to eat. So both Rossie and Ralph ordered breakfast and as soon as the young waitress was out of ear shot, Rossie informed Fugiwara all he knew about the case. Everything that was accept for fact that Wind was involved in the case, and she was the one who murdered Batterman, and her Lord Kawasomeru fellow walked off with Batterman's head.

The three men quickly finished off their breakfast with just some minor small talk being carried off between the three of them. Now that Agent Fugiwara had informed them this was a sudden extremely serious murder case, they decided to finish speaking in either Murdock's office, or the office the two agents were going to be working out of at the headquarters, once they truly started working on the murder case. Murdock paid for the meals and the three of them rushed off for Murdock's office to finish discussing the case.

After three hours of both Murdock and Fugiwara picking Rossie's mind apart over what he knew of the Batterman's murder case so far, they called it an early end to the day's work and Rossie and Fugiwara vowed to earnestly start working on the case the following morning.

Agent Shinnosuke Fugiwara headed for his apartment he held in Washington though he lived in New Jersey, and Agent Robert Rossie headed for home. He stopped to pick up three pounds of shrimp he was certain Wind would enjoy for supper with him, and then he rushed for his apartment. He entered and placed the shrimp in the fridge then he hurried to take a quick shower to wash off the sweat from the day's work. He changed into his lounging clothes and rushed around the apartment and straightened it up some. He put away the blanket that was left on the sofa when Wind came into his room to protect him while he slept last night.

He found it thrilling to have a beautiful naked woman sleeping on the floor by the foot of his bed protecting him. In all his days he never dreamed of such a thing happening to him, neither did he dream about finding a beautiful woman who was older than dirt, under his command and she would do anything he demanded of her. Now his thoughts went to if that command even went so far as to her sharing his bed with him at night. Now he was more than thrilled with himself, and all he was thinking about now was making love to the beautiful Japanese woman.

When he had the apartment back to the way he always liked it, he slowly walked over to the small hall closet and went fishing around for Wind's Katana killing sword. He actually asked himself why he did not look for her sword when he first came home. For a brief moment while he could not find her sword, he feared someone might have sneaked into his apartment and took the sword on him. He breathed out a deep sigh of relief as he found the sword that had fallen to the floor and he pulled it out. Again he could smell the oldness of the ancient weapon as he rushed for the sofa and plopped down and began to carefully study the age old sword again.

Fighting his overwhelming want to recall Wind from what she called the Floating World as quickly as possible, he continued to stare at the ancient sword in total awe. Again he started to pick but this time at the badly damaged scabbard, digging some of the deeply embedded dirt from one of the countless cracks marring the wood case of the sword. Finally giving in to his want to see Wind's face and naked body again, he stood and gave a good pull on the sword's handle, and it finally released its grasp on the scabbard when he applied enough pressure on each side of the sword. Almost instantly the light started to grow in its intensity and size until it completely filled the interior of the apartment where he was standing.

Wind's voice almost instantly called out to him in her usual singing voice as she offered. "I am so pleased my Lord and Master had called me back for the so lonesome Floating World to smell the sweet smells of the living world. Does my Liege Lord have any demands of me, some Teki you wish vanquish or any other need or desire from your always loyal and most obedient Samurai Warrior? I am at your command both day and night Lord Kawasomeru as always..."

"Yes Wind-san, I want you to take a solid form as quickly as you can return to me from the Floating World. It seems to take you so long to come back to the living world." He suddenly ordered her, he did not even realize he was starting to employ the same demanding voice he always saw and heard in the movies any time the Shogun spoke to his Samurai.

"I shall try and hurry the wonders of the Floating World, but I fear I really do not have any control or command over these things my Lord and Master, I long to again be dwelling within the living world, as soon as I am allowed to return to your honorable presence, my Liege Lord." All the while she was speaking to him from within the blinding and growling light.

He was trying this best to see Wind's form in the light, and was only able to make it out when the light had reached it brightest point and then it began to soften. The more the light faded, the easier it was for him to see her rapidly taking on her solid form until finally she was whole, and she instantly dropped down to her knees and bowed politely towards her new Lord and Master.

"Thank you for appearing before me Wind-san, I have some surprises for you tonight..."

"My Lord and Master, I fear I have many surprised in store for you on this night as well. Look and behold and see what your eyes shall enjoy viewing my Liege Lord." She looked up and waved her arm out before her and the bright light returned, but not another spirit came out of the light and mist. This time a number of pieces of her ancient body armor and a number of her weapons also came out of the light along with a few beautiful Kimonos' and the outfit her and Hiromoai's female had helped her fashion out of her heavy Yoroi Hitatare battle robe. All these items were scattered around the room as they came out of the light one after the other.

He was forced to move twice to get out of the way of the items suddenly appearing before him from out of the bright light as she announced to her Liege Lord. "My honorable Lord and Master, if you remember correctly, I told you the Kami was going to allow me to bring some of my many possessions back to the living world, so I can be comfortable in both worlds I share."

"I understand that, but I hope I have enough room in my apartment for all this stuff you brought from the Floating World. Is this it or is there more?' He asked from the other side of a pile of ancient weapons and stuff in cloth bags lying on the floor and he smile at the female Warrior.

"I would have brought more with me, but I remembered how small your new castle is, so I left most of the other items behind my Liege Lord." She replied as she returned his smile.

"I didn't know you were able to store things in the Floating World like these items you brought with you, Wind-san." He remarked as he looked around his now overcrowded apartment.

"Oh no my wonderful and honorable Liege Lord, when you sent me back to the Ukiyo while you were busy working at your job, I was actually allowed to return to Japan to collect a number of my other belongings from Hiromoai's huge modern day castle. I looked at what was left of my belongings and I picked and chose what I might need when I was now serving my new Lord and Master in your castle. Although I had so much my Liege Lord showered upon my foolish shoulders by Lord Kawasomeru for my many deeds on the battlefield, and serving him in other ways, I could not more take all my belongings than I can change the direction of the flowing waters of a swift running river. But many of my once prized possessions had also been removed from Hiromoai's castle. I was even allowed to check the Police Detective's office, because he was allowed to remove some of my belongings for his personal enjoyment from Hiromoai's apartment when they were emptying his dwelling..."

"Oh crap, I forgot all about calling the Lieutenant back. For some reason he placed a call for me, but I didn't report to work in time to answer his call and my Commander fielded the call for me. Ralph ordered me to call the Japanese Detective to see if he found out anything more about Batterman and Hiromoai's death." He made certain he did not refer to the deaths as a murder before her, because he did not want to call her a murderer under any circumstance.

A few words her new master was using she did not understand what they meant, but the Kami made it so much easier for the two for them to communicate better, when they bestowed the understanding and speaking of the Japanese language into her new Lord's mind.

"Wind-san, I want you to look after all this mess while I go to my bedroom for privacy and I return the call to Lieutenant Motoshima over there in Japan. You can stick much of it in the closet, the rest of your stuff you can put it anywhere you can find a spot for it. I plan to make supper for us once I finished speaking with the Detective, if you'll excuse me Wind-san."

"Hai, (Yes) I shall have everything cleaned up for you by the time you have finished your call to the Japanese Police Officer my Lord and Master." She offered pleasantly to him.

Rossie nodded and then walked between Wind's belongings lying all over the floor, and headed into his bedroom. He closed the door behind him and sat down on the edge of the bed, picked up his small phone book and found Motoshima's number then took the phone and quickly dialed it. He did not pay any attention to the time and lucky for him it was 11:25 A.M. in the morning in Japan. It was answered on the forth ring by the Lieutenant."

"Detective Motoshima here, who's this I'm kind of busy right now."

""Kenzaburo-san, this is Bob Rossie back here in the States, I'm returning you call sir. What's up, did you find out anything new on the murders you're investigating, sir?"

"Ahhhh… Rossie-san, how are you doing? It is so good to hear your voice again."

"I'm doing rather well thank you for asking me sir. Why did you place a call to me, did something happen with the Batterman case over there, Kenzaburo-san?"

"Rossie-san, I placed that call to you in the States because the craziest thing happened here, sir. As you know after the death of Hiromoai-san, his father ordered his apartment cleaned out. Of course he kept the most exquisite pieces of ancient weapons and armor and they're still in the apartment. He donated most of the stuff to the Historical Sociality and allowed me to take some of the stuff in such poor shape he was just going to throw away. Well Rossie-san, I took fifteen pieces and even I considered throwing it away once I got it back to my office, but I just couldn't throw away any of Japan's ancient and proud history no matter how bad a shape it was in.

"Anyway Agent Rossie-san, yesterday I was working a little late and while I was in my office, it was suddenly bathed in a strong, bright light that came out of nowhere for a few moments, and then when the light evaporated back to where it came from. I'd be damn but the fifteen pieces of worthless and crumbling armor and two small Tanto blades suddenly looked like they were just fashioned by the ancient Master Crafter's of Japan. Yeah, yeah I know it sounds crazy and I'm not going nuts I assure you my friend, but that's what happened. I can't explain it, and I don't have any idea why or how it happened, it just happened and I just about watched it as it happened. I have two of my forensic people carefully checking the few items out, and they're at a complete loss over how to try and explain why and how this happened.

"As crazy as it sounds to you, it happened. I'm preparing to head over to Hiromoai's apartment and see it the stuff still in that place had this drastic rebirth. In all days and going over of Japan's history, I never once read or heard of this type of thing happening, sir. This has to be the craziest thing to every happened in Japan's history. But as sure as I'm going to solve Hiromoai and Batterman's murder, I'm going to find out how this crazy transformation has happened as well, Rossie-san." The Japanese Lieutenant informed his counterpart working in the United States.

"I guess stranger things might have happened in the world, Lieutenant Motoshima-san."

"I'm certain it has but not to me I tell you Rossie-san." The Lieutenant laughed into the phone.

"How is the Batterman murder investigation going on over there for you, Lieutenant?"

"I'm afraid I keep running into a stone wall with each and every twist and turn I make in this cursed case, Rossie-san. I haven't been about to turn up one minor thing on this supposed ancient female Samurai Warrior who's running all over downtown Tokyo killing all of Japan's and even the United States most powerful and elite people. I can't wait until I finally get my hands on this damn female murderer, what a day of reckoning that day will be I assure you Rossie-san."

"Well Kenzaburo-san, I'm just starting an investigation of Mr. Batterman here in the States. My Commander wants me to go over all his business dealings for the past fifteen years, and see if anyone might have threatened his life because of some slipshod workmanship, or his failure to finish a project and was sued. My Commander is of the believe that maybe someone from the United States might have followed Batterman to Japan and killed him there, to get the heat off himself here in the States. I know my boss is looking under the wrong rocks because we know of this female Samurai killing everyone, and my boss thinks that story is all hogwash. He doesn't believe in ghosts and people coming back from the grave and killing people under someone else's command. He told me he wants this case solve by tomorrow night, Kenzaburo-san.

"He gave me Agent Shinnosuke Fugiwara-san to work with, because he believes we're going to end up back in Japan to solve this case and I happen to agree with his assumption. Fugiwara-san has already done a number of investigations of Batterman and his dealings in the construction field; so he's kind of familiar with the man and how he conducted business. That's going to help me with this case big time I can tell you, Kenzaburo-san. Anyway, you'll get a chance to meet Fugiwara-san when we come back to Japan, and then the three of us can work together and maybe solve this case and then we can all tie one on and celebrate the end of this case together, sir." He informed the Japanese Detective of his future plans in the Batterman murder case.

"Well Rossie-san, I can think of no one better I'd rather to be with on a night out on the town that you, sir. I'm only sorry we have to put that date off until we finish this damn murder case sir. Hey, while you're back there in the States, have you been able to come up with anything on this damn female killer. The tracks here in Japan are as cold as ice over here, Rossie-san."

"Even though I have only been back here in the States for less than two days, I haven't been able to even begin any work on this case as yet. Hell, I was just linked up with Fugiwara-san early this morning and all we did was discussed this case between the two of us and the Commander. Give me a few days to get my feel back on the ground and I'm certain I'll come up with something on this supposed female Samurai." He said as he was biting the tip of his tongue, he was dying with the want to tell Kenzaburo all he found out about Wind, and why she did what she did and what happened with Batterman's head. But after hearing what the detective believed about the ancient weapons and armor returning to their new state, he knew the Japanese Detective would not believe a single thing he would have to tell him about Wind.

"I guess I'm just guilty of kind of pulling at straws over this endless case, Rossie-san. We still haven't found hide nor hair of Batterman's head. Usually by now someone would report they found a head either floating in the water or rolling around on the streets. I need some kind of damn break in this murder case, or I'm never going to be able to solve it, Rossie-san.

"Have some fate my friend, I sure you're going to get that break you're looking for soon enough Kenzaburo-san." He offered pleasantly, trying to cheer the detective up some.

"Rossie-san, I believe you're not to upset or concerned or even surprised about these ancient pieces of worthless junk turning into pieces of outstanding works of art now worth a small fortune. What gives with you anyhow Rossie-san, you seem like you were even expecting them to be returned to the condition they had when they were first created. Are you holding something back on me, Rossie-san? If you know something about this murder case, you can't hold it back you have to tell me what you might have discovered over there in the United States, Rossie-san. Although I can figure out what you might have discovered over there in the United States. The theory is there is some ancient female Samurai Warrior running around all over Japan killing people at will. And I know for a damn fact there's no way in hell if this is a fact.

"The United States never gave birth to any Samurai Warriors, especially a female one at that Rossie-san. Come on Rossie-san, if you know something about this case please let me know what you have discovered. I need a break in this case and if you have the break I need, give it up to me now, Rossie-san." Lieutenant Motoshima said as he actually looked at the receiver locked in his hand like he was trying to see the FBI Agent's face through the phone.

"Okay Lieutenant Motoshima-san, I think I might have found something out about Batterman, but I have to work out all the finer details first, before I can go off and start telling you what I might have discovered over here sir. I don't want to say something now and take you off the path you're working on, only to find out later it was a dead end I was working on all along."

"I'll give you that my friend, but the first second you think you might have discovered a possible lead for me to pick up on. You have to share it with me right off sir. Like I told you already in this conversation, I'm at a complete dead end with this murder case as it stands. All I know is, ever since Hiromoai and Batterman were murdered by this supposed female spirit of the damn sword, no one else in all Japan even suffered a damn starch from the bit of an ancient sword, Rossie-san." Motoshima groused into the phone as he let his breath out in a rush.

"I promise you Kenzaburo-san, if I get something working on this case you'll be the second to know. Any leads I uncover so far have to be discussed with my control first, before I can share them with anyone if he okay's it and you understand that. Because you would expect nothing less from your Sergeant Toshihiro Okamatsu-san, if he uncovered something important to this murder case and if he wasn't ready to lay out what he had discovered, he'd sure as hell hold it back, sir."

"Yes, I guess you're right at that Rossie-san. I think I had no right to believe you might be holding something back on me that was important to this murder case at that. Why the hell would you, you have just as much to gain as I do to solve this murder case Rossie-san." Lieutenant Motoshima replied, kind of sorry he pressed the agent so hard a few moments ago.

"Thank you for understanding that and it takes a lot of pressure off my shoulders Kenzaburo-san. Say Lieutenant it's getting kind of late over here and I still haven't eaten my supper as yet, sir. Besides, I'm expecting a fine looking young lady over for supper, and I want to be showered and a little rested before she arrives if you know what I mean sir." Rossie gave out with a slight chuckle and then he waited for the Lieutenant to reply to him.

"Say no more about it Rossie-san I know what you mean. I keep forgetting the time difference between Japan and the United States. I'll give you some time to get your teeth back into this murder case, and then we shall speak again I'm certain, Rossie-san. Please Rossie-san, enjoy you supper and your young lady even more on this night, until we speak again Rossie-san.”

“Yes Kenzaburo-san I’ll call you in a few days once I get into this murder case from over here sir. Thank you again for the call and the most interesting developments you witnessed over there, Kenzaburo-san. Talk to you later.” With that said he hung up on the Japanese Detective.

As soon as he was off the phone with the detective, he rose and went back out into his small living room, and he was instantly amazed at how well Wind had done with cleaning and putting all her stuff away. He smiled at the female Warrior and she immediately dropped down to her knees and bowed politely to her new Lord and Master as she replied.

“Yes my most honorable Liege Lord, you were speaking for so long into the small black box that it gave me more than enough time for me to put most of my belongings away properly. I wanted to have everything put away before you came out of your sleeping area my Lord.”

“Well Wind-san, you have done an outstanding job of cleaning up the room and I thank you for that. Are you hungry Wind-san?” He offered as he smiled and enjoyed the fact the beautiful young woman was walking around his apartment naked as the day she was born, and it did not seem to bother her in the least he was watching her every move.

“Although I am in need of nourishment, I am in need of a bath more. Visiting the Floating World there are but a few luxuries for one to enjoy. It is a very arid place to dwell and one needs no feed to substance them when they are in the spirit world. Most of the time you are alone in the world of wonderment, and one is supposed to meditate all the while visiting the Floating World. In constant thought on how to better honor your Lord and Master once you are reborn Samurai, and allowed to again dwell within the land of the living. There is so much want when you are in the Ukiyo, yet there is absolutely nothing one needs in the Floating World. One cannot truly describe it, one cannot picture it, one cannot admire it and one cannot feel it. It is your real self which has no hiding place from your eyes. When the world is destroyed, it will not be.

"If my Lord and Master would allow this worthless Samurai Warrior to indulge her foolish self to enjoy one of the countless pleasures the living world has to offer their faithful children, I would truly like to wash the coating of stardust from my body while I was dwelling within the Ukiyo. It is not a very pleasant odor for one to have adorning their bodies my Lord. After I have bathed and washed the smell of death from my body then I would be most pleased to share the last meal of the day with my so overly kind to this worthless person, Lord and Master."

"Yes, by all means you're free to enjoy a bath, and I'll get you something to wear once you finished bathing. That'll give me a chance to prepare our meal so we can eat when you're done bathing. I'm going to surprise you with what I'm preparing for us on this night, Wind-san..."

"This is what really upsetting my soul my honorable Lord and Master..." She was interrupted by Rossie this time as he asked her with concern lacing his voice.

"What is upsetting you Wind-san? I hope it is nothing I have done that's upsetting you so on this night that has all the earmarks of being a very enjoyable night for us to enjoy together."

"My generous as always Liege Lord had done nothing to upset me, nothing you can do to or against me could ever upset me my Lord. I am beyond getting upset by any of your actions. I am only dwelling upon this earth to serve you, and that is not what this foolish Warrior is doing. It is I who should be preparing and worrying about your last meal of the day, not you caring for this worthless person my Liege Lord. I should have my hair shaved from my foul head and then I should be forced to care for the Monks who would use my body for their evil pleasures, for my failure to my Lord and Master." She again sadly lowered her head and she stared at the floor.

Rossie laughed as he smiled at the beautiful Wind then announced. "I understand what you're saying Wind-san and when all things are right that is what you should be doing. But for the time being, allow me to repay you for your future service, by doing some things to please you for a change. Besides, I enjoy cooking, and if I am your Lord and Master then I am supposed to do only the things I truly enjoy doing to bring pleasures to myself. So it seems you're kind of stuck with allowing me to enjoy myself by cooking you a meal to enjoy for this time, Wind-san."

Wind could not come up with a proper answer to rebuff her Liege Lord's wise words that had so completely disarmed her complaint. So all she could thinking of doing was she just bowed slightly towards the young man smiling so proudly at her for the moment.

"Ahhh... I see you agree with what I just said to you Wind-san, and I thank you for allowing me to prepare our evening meal for us. So go and enjoy your bath and I'll get the supper going for the both of us to enjoy. But first I'll lay out some towels and face cloths and soap so you can wash your body, and I'll put something in the bathroom for you to wear after your bath. Because the water is going to cool your body and you might catch a chill if you're still damp from your bath, and you have nothing to wear to warm yourself with, Wind-san." He replied with a grin on his lips, feeling like he was winning another small victory over this extremely dangerous ancient female Samurai Warrior standing before him and staring back at him.

"The perfect Samurai Warrior employs one's mind as a mirror. It grasps nothing and yet it refuses nothing at the same time. It receives but it does not retain. Sitting quietly, doing nothing, spring comes and the grass grows by itself. My wise Liege Lord, the cloth you speak of I shall need to enjoy my bath, but for something to wear on my body. I brought three of my very best silk Kimonos once given to me by Lord Kawasomeru's hand for some of the accomplishments I had won upon the field of battle for his pleasure, to adorn my body when back from the Floating World. Because I was aware you wished me to cover my body from your view the last time you called me back to the land of the living from the Floating World, my Lord and Master. I am so sorry my foul body offends your worthy eyes so." She offered as she rested her hands on her hips, adding greatly to her outstanding beauty by standing the way she was doing.

"Wow Wind-san, I'm afraid you have me all wrong there. Your exquisite body doesn't offend my eyes in the least. In fact Wind-san, I can't get enough of looking at you this way. It was I just want you to have something to wear in case someone else comes around to visit me. I don't want to share your loveliness with anyone else. If I had my way about it and we were romantically involved, I'd surely want to keep you all to myself, Wind-san." He said to her with his smile.

She could not hide the smile that instantly crossed over her lips as she looked deeply into her new Master's eyes. Now she felt he was interested in her for more than her serving to protect him from all harm. But her short lived trance was interrupted when he offered to her.

"Okay, enough, why don't you take your bath and I'll get supper cooking for us, Wind-san."

"Yes my Liege Lord, I need to bathe because I am getting hungrier now, and I believe we have talked between us for long enough and we could always finish our conversation while we are enjoying our last meal on this fast approaching night, my honorable Liege Lord."

With that said Rossie took off to get the towels and soap, and Wind went to the closet where she placed most of the items she brought out of the Floating World, and she went hunting for the three Kimonos, finding the one she liked best and felt accented her body the best. She picked it up and went to the room her Liege Lord called the bathroom. To her surprise Rossie was already in the room and he was running the water for her bath.

When he saw her come into the bathroom he offered her. "Wind-san how do you like your water, warm, hot or very hot?"

"Hot will do very nicely for my pleasure of the bath my Liege Lord."

"You got it, errr... the bowl is over there and I hope you know what you do in it? Good here's soap to wash with. I'm sorry it's not feminine soap but tomorrow I'll pick you up some soap women like for your pleasure Wind-san. I see you have something to put on once you finished your bath. I guess I'll leave you so you can get on with your bath and I'll get supper going." He smiled again at the female Warrior and then he rushed out of the bathroom, almost sad because he understood once she finished her bath, she was going to cover her body on him.

When she was alone in the bathroom she did her business and then slowly climbed into the steaming hot water and she let her breath out as she enjoyed the sweet smells and water of the living world. She was very happy with herself, now that she was aware her new Lord and Master was interested in her in a romantic way. She could not wait for supper to be over, because she was going to pay close attention to his mood, and if he showed any interest in making love with her on this night, she was going to take full advantage of it and him tonight.

She put her head back and closed her eyes and enjoyed the warmth of the bath then she hurried washing herself that's how much she wanted to be with her young Liege Lord on this night.

CHAPTER SEVEN

When she was finished washing herself, she climbed out of the tube and stared at the water. She was waiting for it to disappear, but when it would not go, she shrugged and quickly dried herself off with the towel then she wrapped her best Kimono around her exquisite body and looked at herself in the mirror. She fussed a little with her hair using her hands because she did not see a hair pick to work her hair properly with. When she was finally satisfied with her appearance she strolled out of the bathroom, but she left the

Obi tying slash lying over the bathroom sink, because she had no interest in keeping her Kimono closed on this night.

She already decided she was going to do all she could possibly do to drive her new Lord absolutely wild with passion on this night. She could not help it and she actually started feeling a little sorry for the trap she was planning to lay out before her new Master, but she was going to have her way with him tonight, one way or the other. She came out of the bathroom with a smile on her lips, and it grew even brighter once she noticed her Master had the supper table set and there was two candles burning for them to enjoy and set the mood properly.

She walked up to the table and sat and he placed shrimp on her dish. She loved the feeling of having her new Master serving her, it was thrilling for her to be honored so by her Lord.

Wind sat modishly after she gave him a quick flash of her breast, and she could see him already tripping over his tongue and she smiled to herself. She knew she had fully captured his attention already and she was planning to make the best of it.

He sat down after serving them both and then prepared to eat. He smiled at her but he sure was not looking at her eyes. He popped a shrimp in his mouth without covering his mouth and this shocked Wind, she was not use to seeing anyone teeth as they ate. He swallowed and then asked her. "Wind-san, you have to tell me how you like the way I fixed the shrimp for you."

She looked at the shrimp and carefully picked at the strange coating and asked her Lord and Master. "I have eaten shrimp before in my unending life, but what is this you have wrapped around it, and why is the shrimp so red and what is this white power sprinkled on them?"

"I'm sorry Wind-san, I wrapped the shrimp in bacon, you know, oink, oink, and then I sprinkled some Paprika, that's the red stuff and the white is Parmesan Cheese. I hope you enjoy the way I made them for you." He watched her until she tasted one of the shrimp.

She did not know if she should peel off what he called bacon from the shrimp. Throwing all caution to the wind she picked up one of the small critters and popped it in her mouth with the implement she watched him pick up one of the shrimp up with. She was amazed, she did not know which she enjoyed more, the shrimp or the bacon, and the shrimp left a sharp, almost hot taste in her mouth, and she enjoyed the taste of the cheese as well. She quickly finished everything on her plate, not realizing just how hungry she really was, and how much she enjoyed the shrimp the way her Lord had prepared it for her.

Once their meal was done, Rossie left the dishes sitting on the table and he led her to the living room and asked her if she wanted to watch some television, or listen to some music. She had no idea what a television was so she said she would like to hear some music so he put the radio on, all the while watching every move she did and each time she moved he saw more of her outstanding body. They both sat on the sofa and kind of stared forward faking they were both listening to the soft music then he had an idea and asked her." Would you care for a glass of red wine, Wind-san? Now he wanted to get her drunk to see if he could maybe get her in bed.

Not knowing what wine was she just shook her head yes and he was on his feet in a flash. He opened a new bottle of wine, poured them both a large glass and then he handed one proudly to her. She sipped it and loved the taste. It reminded her of Sake, but it was much more enjoyable and soon she held up her glass and he immediately filled it a second time for her. In no time flat the bottle was empty and he opened a second bottle and poured her fourth glass of wine. Now the way she was sitting her Kimono was wide open and he was enjoying her body being draped in a cloud or rich, deep purple, and flowers hand painted on the bottom, one side and on one sleeve of the exquisite and extremely old Kimono, and she was beginning to slur her words.

They were sitting so close together and he moved and accidently brushed her right breast with his elbow, they both instantly stopped moving around and stared at each other. No words passed between them as they both instantly gave into their passion being fueled by the wine. They started kissing on the couch and pawing at each other's bodies, grabbing anything they could grab with their hands. But when she suddenly grabbed his dick through the thin silky lounging pants he had on, they fell to the floor and he was all over her body with his hands and mouth. He started by passionately kissing her lips, and when he forced his tongue into her mouth, she responding by opening her mouth and meeting his tongue with hers.

He kissed her eyes, her forehead, and then the nape of her neck, her shoulders and the top of her breasts while working ever so close towards her waiting nipple. When his lips sucked her nipple into his mouth, the first moan escaped her lips. He ran his tongue over her harden nipple, drew it into his mouth by sucking hard on it and then he let go and then kissed her nipple again and drew it back into his mouth and circled the nipple with his tongue, starting to drive her wild.

He left her breasts and at this point ran his tongue over her body, dragging it between her breasts, down the center of her chest until he found her belly button. He played here, dipping his tongue in the tiny opening, and circling it with his tongue. Then he slid his tongue out to the side of her body and tickled and made her jump and laugh. He licked her hip then ran his tongue on the outside of her body to her hip then down the outside of her leg. He stopped by her knee and lightly lifted her leg so he could kiss the inner of her knee. She jumped again from the pleasure, he then worked down to her feet and kissed her ankle then he suddenly sat up and put his fingers between her toes and massaged her toes, driving her wild with anticipation.

He released her leg and kissed her inner ankle, working his way up her leg. She was forced to spread her legs to make room for his head as he kissed the inside of her knee, and when he started to kiss her inner thigh, a second but louder moan escaped her lips as she moved her legs so he had more access and opening her Jade Gate to his interest. As he worked his way to the top of her inner leg and passed his mouth over her opening he blew his breath on her pearl of pleasure, making her arched her back in anticipation of his tongue replacing his breath on her.

Instead of bring her to new heights of pleasure by running his tongue over her pearl, he went over to her other leg and started kissing the upper part of her inner thigh. Then when she least expected it, he suddenly left her inner leg and ended up where she was trying to guide his probing tongue. When he first licked the tiny pearl, she cried out in pleasure, but when he drew it in his mouth she really went wild, rolling her hips to the rhythm of his mouth and tongue.

He stayed here for a few moments then he pulled away and started crawling up her body until he kissed her and entered her at the same time. She against arched her back, making it easier for him to enter her, and he took his time slowly rolling his hits and driving her crazy with passion. He felt her need and increased his tempo, driving himself fully into her, a little quicker with each thrust until he was equally caught up in his own passion until he came. Exhausted, he dropped his full weight down of top of her and she loved feeing him lying on top of her still panting and breathing heavily. She was also breathing heavily as her passion slowly subsided from their lovemaking with her new Lord and Master. She smiled, thinking how easy it was for her to trap her new Liege Lord into making love with her and he not even realizing she was doing it to him.

He finally rolled off the top of her, and he lied on his side and lightly ran his hand over her breast as he moaned. "That was absolutely beautiful, Wind-san. I tried to take my time with you, but I lost it over how beautiful you are and forgot myself and couldn't control myself and let go. I hope you were able to catch up with me before I came, Wind-san."

She smiled dreamy eyed at him and offered. "It has been too long since the last time I had the honor of pillowing with my Lord. But this worthless Samurai is sorry to offer to my Master. You said something I did not understand. Why did you ask me if I caught up with you? I was not running and neither were you, so why did I have to catch up with you for my Liege Lord?"

"Oh brother Wind-san, what was it I just said to you, ahhh yes... it was just a figure of speech. I asked you if you were able to share as much pleasure as I did when I came as we ended our lovemaking tonight." He said as he looked her in the eyes.

"You came, where did you come from? I thought we were pillowing together, I had no idea you were coming from someplace. Where did you come from I ask you again my Liege Lord." Now she returned his stare with questioning eyes as she waited for him to explain.

"Ahhh... let me see how I can explain this to you so you understand what I'm talking about, Wind-san. When I asked you if you came, I meant if you shared your essences with me like I shared my seeds of birth with you. Here we call that coming. It's the fluid that makes women with child. It's a great feeling when one shares his essence with another. Do you understand what I'm trying to tell you Wind-san? Is it clear now and did you come with me Wind-san?"

"Wakarimasu, I understand now what you are saying my Liege Lord. As it is said, what brings you pleasure do often, for it gives lightness to your head and wonders for your soul. I hope my Lord and Master will be looking as forward as I will to our next pillowing, my Liege Lord."

He did not reply he just smiled. His back bothered him so he got up to his feet and looked at the clock and was stunned to see it was so late, and he had to start work on the Batterman case, even though he knew everything that had to do with the case, tomorrow with his partner Shinnosuke Fugiwara. He stretched and raised his hands over his head and Wind enjoyed the view as he announced. "Wind-san, I have to go to sleep, my day starts at eight tomorrow and it's near midnight. Do you want me to set up the sofa for you, or do you want to sleep with me?"

"I would be most honored to share your bedroll for the night, my Liege Lord." She replied as she gave him one of the best smiles she could muster. She too was feeling her need to get some sleep. She followed him by standing and followed him into the room leaving her Kimono lying on the floor was it was discarded by them. They shared the bed together and she wrapped her body around her Lord and basically hugged him to her all night long.

The both of them were woke by the shrill call of the alarm clock at 6 A. M. and she jumped out of bed and headed for the kitchen, she ordered herself to get out of bed first and make eggs for her Lord and Master to enjoy, before he went off to work. This time he followed her, but he headed for the bathroom did his business and took a shower to help him wake up some.

He came out of the bathroom just as she was placing his eggs on a dish, seeing him she smiled and placed the dish before the chair her Liege Lord always seemed to sit in, whenever he was eating. He smiled and then remarked to her. "Gees, I didn't know you could cook?"

"My foolish Liege Lord, just because I am a Samurai Warrior, does not mean I cannot cook. I hope you enjoy the meal I have prepared especially for you to go to work, my Lord and Master." Again, she smiled at Rossie as she waited for him to sit and eat his morning meal.

Fine." He ate quickly, stood and looked at her and then went deep in thought for a few moments before he offered to her. "Wind-san, I really hate to have to send you back to the lonely Floating World, especially after last night and us sleeping together. What am I to do with you? Do you have to go back to the Floating World at all if I don't send you back there?"

"My Liege Lord, I have to report back to the Floating World once every seven sticks of time (a week) and if I don't return in the allotted amount of time. Then I will quickly get weaker and weaker until I grow so weak my spirit will die and my life in both worlds will cease to exist, and then I'll truly be dead in body and spirit and my history will end on that day." She replied and then she sadly lowered her head slightly.

"Then we'll have to make certain we don't let you miss the time you have to report back to the Floating World. All this is good for me to understand, but it still doesn't answer what I should do with you while I'm at work today. Look Wind-san, if I was to let you remain here while I'm at work, would you give me your word you'll not step foot out of this apartment, and not allow anyone to see you in the apartment. If you promise me this then I won't send you back to the Floating World until you have to go back and I guess recharge your batteries there. Wind-san, you have to understand you can't possible let anyone know you're in my apartment."

She looked deeply into his eyes, and then she offered. "My Liege Lord, I shall obey your orders as I have always done throughout my entire service to you my Lord and Master."

"Very well then Wind-san, I'm going to trust you this time and leave you here in the living world. You're welcome to enjoy the apartment, but you're forbidden to leave the apartment or open the door to anyone but myself under any circumstances. If someone is outside and knocking on the door, you'll not open the door unless it's me outside. Wind-san, it's getting late so I have to run. I shall return around six tonight." With that said he picked up his backpack with his weapon hidden inside and he was out the door after locking Wind inside his apartment.

FBI HEADQUARTERS, WASHINGTON D.C.
ZERO, SEVEN THIRTY HUNDRED HOURS

Agent Robert Rossie walked into FBI Headquarters fifteen minutes early for work, and he stopped just long enough to grab himself a cup of coffee, and then he headed for Agent Patterson's office on the third floor where both he and Agent Shinnosuke Fugiwara were going to conduct the Batterman murder case. He plopped down at the larger desk, put his coffee down and then flipped on the computer. As he waited for the computer to boot up, Agent Fugiwara walked into the office and he sat as the second desk and watched what Rossie was doing. When he looked at the other agent in the office, he immediately offered.

"Good morning Rossie-san, did anything crop up with this Batterman case since the last time we spoke together? Man it's getting hot early, it's only June and I'm sweating my ass off."

"Not very much since yesterday…" Their conversation was suddenly cut off when the phone rang and he answered it. It was his Commander calling and the moment he heard Rossie's voice on the other end of the phone he started right off on him.

"Agent Rossie, I was just checking on you to make certain you and Agent Fugiwara were in and starting work on this damn Batterman murder case. I just heard from the Senator from Batterman's State, and he was demanding to know what we're doing about this damn murder case. I warned you the lousy politicians were going to get on my case over this damn thing, and they sure as shit are for crap sake. I guess the President's going to be the next guy who'll get on my stinking backside, demanding to know what the hell we're doing to solve this damn case." Commander Murdock groused at Agent Rossie over the phone as he looked at his computer.

"We're both in the office and ready to start working on the Batterman murder case sir. These people have to give us a chance to sink our teeth into this damn case before they start busting our fricking horns over it like they're already doing. Christ sake, Batterman was killed just five days ago and there's no way in hell we could possibly solve this murder case that quickly, sir. Don't these people realize Batterman was killed in Japan, and that's going to make solving this murder case a whole lot more complicated for us to solve between the two nations, sir?"

"These people don't give a damn where Batterman was killed. They just know he was murdered and they want to know why. We also have to find his head for crap sake!"

"I feel ya there Commander and we'll do our best to solve this damn case as soon as possible Ralph." He replied with a sort of snap in his tone of voice because he was upset over the pressure Murdock was placing on him and his partner. His mind screaming at him, telling him what his boss would think if he tried to tell him about Wind, and how she had returned to the future from the ancient past, and how she was used by Hiromoai to kill his competition in Japan. Again, he talked himself out of telling his Commander about her and what she did in this Batterman murder case, he was that concerned what his Commander would think of his story about Wind

"I hear in your tone you're pissed off because of the pressure I'm putting on you on this case, and I don't give a shit. I warned you when you started on this case I was going to be on your ass over it. Just find me something I can tell the next prick who bugs my ass over this case to get some heat off my ass for a change." Murdock hissed at his agent as he hung up the phone on him.

Agent Fugiwara leaned back in his chair and smiled at Rossie as he offered to the other agent. "I can see in your face that dear old Murdock just reamed your ass out but good, Rossie-san. Pay no attention to him, he barks loud but he rarely if ever bites anyone working for him. I take it he's putting the heat on us to get on with this damn murder case, Rossie-san?"

"Putting the heat on us to solve this case is putting it mildly. Errr... when we really get in this case, I have things I'm going to dump on you that's going to make your head spin, Shinnosuke."

"What the hell are you telling me Rossie-san? If you know something about this case that might help us to solve it, you have to tell me what it is. For Christ sake I'm your damn partner, so there's no sense to hold anything back on my ass, Rossie-san." He grumbled at his partner.

"Naw, it's way too early for me to bring you in on that part of this damn murder case, Shinnosuke-san. We have to get over to Batterman's office before the members of his company board clean out the office of any possible evidence we might need to give us any potential leads in this case. Look Fugiwara-san, I want you to head over to Judge Harrison's office and get us a search warrant for Batterman's office. You know what to include, any locked file cabinets and safes, locked desk draws, the works. While you're doing that I'll get in contact with two other Agents because I think we're going to need little extra help to toss Batterman's office."

"Yes Rossie-san, Judge Harrison is best man to contact, he always backs us a hundred percent. Its 9:10 and it should take me fifteen minutes to get over to the judge's chamber and by the time he gives me this warrant it should be between 11 and noon. Do you think you can have the two other Agents ready to come with us to Batterman's office? Don't forget we have to get to Denver to get at his main office if that's the one you want to search, Rossie-san?" Fugiwara remarked.

"I have no problem with the Agents I want with us they both work out of the Denver office. I'm going to order Agents Richard Spaulding and Peter Hasler to link up with us when we arrive in Denver. I'll order our plane ready for an afternoon flight. I have to run home and look after a few things and pack and I'll meet you at the airport at 7 P.M. Once you're done with the judge, head home and pack for three to five days at Denver until we pick Batterman's office clean."

"Spaulding's a damn good Agent, but Hasler's last name fits him to a tee, he a real pain in the ass to work with man. He always acts like he knows it all and won't listen to anyone once he makes up his damn mind about something, Rossie-san. I'll do what you suggested, when I'm done with the judge I'll look after what I have to look after then I'll meet you at the airport at seven, Rossie-san. I'm going to take off now I want to get over to the judge before he gets involved in something that'll cause him to put off seeing me until later this afternoon, Rossie-san." Fugiwara rose and picked up his car keys then nodded and quickly left the office.

Agent Rossie watched him leave and once he was out of the office, he picked up the phone and placed a call to the FBI quarters stationed at the Reagan International Airport and requested the smaller private jet reserved for a 7 P.M. flight to their Denver office. Once he received the commitment for the aircraft, he hung up then rushed out of the office. He headed for his apartment, opened the door and found Wind busy checking and cleaning her armor and weapons.

He walked into the apartment and sat by her side on the floor and watched her for a few minutes, and then he offered to her. "Wind-san, I'm terribly sorry but I'm going to be forced to send you back to the Floating World for from three to seven sticks of time..."

"Has this foolish Warrior displeased my honorable Lord and Master for you to want to send me back to the lonely world of forever waiting and wanting? I have stayed to my word and have not left your castle, and I have not opened the door to anyone, even though no one wanted to come into your castle my Lord." She replied in an extremely sad tone of voice.

"Noooo... you haven't displeased me in any way Wind-san. It's just my work has me leaving my home for a few sticks of time, and I can't possibly leave you alone for that long because something is bound to take place that'll expose you to someone who could cause you some harm. I promise you Wind-san, when I return you won't ever have to go back to the Floating World until you have to return to recharge your spirit, and I'll send for you as soon as you're allowed to return to the living world again. Maybe we can figure out a way where you'll no longer have to report back to the Floating World ever Wind-san." He looked deeply into her eyes while trying to reassure her he was not the least bit upset with her in any manner.

Her shoulders sagged a bit and her eyes lost their shine as she let out her breath in a soft sigh. She was that upset over being sent back to the Floating World for this amount of time. She was so looking forward with sharing her Master's bed again on this night.

"I'm sorry, but I'll allow you to remain here in the living world while I pack for my trip, but when I have to leave, I'll have to send you back to the Floating World. You can help me pack if you would like." She followed him to his bedroom without a word and he pulled a few shirts and pants from their hangers and handed them to her and she placed them on the bed. He picked out some underwear and socks and threw them on the bed as well. Then he looked under the bed and pulled his suitcase out and dropped it down on the bed. He flipped it open and started to put his clothes inside the case he then picked out the toiletries he'd need for the trip.

Once he felt he had everything he needed for his trip, he closed the case and carried it out to the living room then he turned and looked at Wind and smiled at her as he offered. "Well Wind-san, I have everything I need so it looks like I have to leave you now. Sorry, but you have to return to the land of forever waiting. I promise you the moment I return, I'll send for you and we can share good times together." He hugged her to him for a few moments and then let her go and started looking for her sword. He found it lying on the sofa and went to it, picked up the sword and the case right next to the sword. He gave her one last long look and his heart sank when he saw the sad look etched deeply in her eyes then he slid the sword home.

Almost instantly the light grew and her shape started to fade. In five deep breaths she was gone and he walked out of his apartment almost as sadly as she looked when he sent her back to the lonely world. It was late enough for him to head for the airport. The traffic was heavy as it always was anywhere around the Reagan International Airport. He pulled into the FBI area and entered the building and had an early supper there. Just as he finished eating, Agent Fugiwara strolled into the building, he spotted Rossie and headed right for him and sat down at his table

"How did you make out with the search warrant and Judge Harrison, Agent Fugiwara-san?"

"Real good Rossie-san, the judge had no problem with giving me the search warrant when he found out I was investigating Batterman's murder. I got it right here." The agent patted his breast pocket and then went on. "I told you getting a warrant from Harrison was no problem. Mind if I get me something to eat, Rossie-san? I'm starving and we still have some time to kill before having to leave for Denver. By the way Rossie-san, I got a few numbers of women in Denver who are always up for a good time. We might as well make the best of being away from home."

"What's your wife going to say about you wanting to have a little patty cake out there with other women, mister?" He asked as he gave Agent Fugiwara the look like he was a criminal.

"What can I tell you Rossie-san, what she don't know won't hurt her any."

"If she finds out you're out there screwing around on her, she's not going to be very happy my friend. She'll divorce your ass and then where are you going to be, just because you had to screw around on her." He smirked as he held the Japanese Agent in his hash stare for a moment.

"Naw, my wife will never divorce me, she'd just kill me and then take the kids and head back for Japan and forget all about my ass, Rossie-san. She has no real sense of humor."

A pretty woman came to their table and asked him." Sir, are you Agent Robert Rossie, sir."

"Yes Ma'am, can I help you please?" he replied pleasantly to her.

"I thought you were sir, I was sent over here to find you sir. The Captain of the aircraft wanted to talk to you sir. He sent me out to find you, he said there was a good opening and he wondered if he could see you to see if you wanted to take off a little early sir."

"We're both here waiting to kill some time off, if we can take off now is just fine with us, Ma'am." He replied as he smiled at the young woman.

"That's great Agent Rossie sir, if you'd be so kind as to follow me then sir. I take it this other gentleman with you is obviously FBI Agent Shinnosuke Fugiwara, sir? Am I correct with that assumption, I have never met Agent Fugiwara before, sir." She asked and offered at the same time as she looked at the young and good looking Japanese man also sitting at his table.

"Yes he is Ma'am." He replied to the young female agent.

"That's great, now I don't have to go off looking for Agent Fugiwara in the crowd sir." With that said she straightened up, turned on her heels and looked behind herself for a second to make sure the two other agents stood, and they were now following her over to the hanger and the waiting Captain and aircraft the agents would use to get out to Denver.

Once inside the hanger, the private small FBI aircraft was just being towed out and onto the tarmac and once the aircraft was ready for boarding. The small ladder was lowered and a second female climbed down the ladder and stood on the side and announced to the two young agents waiting to board the plane it was ready for boarding. As they were connecting their seatbelts, the aircraft moved out to the main runway and when the Captain received permission to take off, the small plane shot down the runway until she reached full takeoff speed.

DENVER COLORADO. ZERO, TWO, FORTY, TWO HUNDRED HOURS,
FBI HEADQUARTERS IN THE CAPITAL OF DENVER

The flight was so quick it did not give Rossie and Fugiwara a chance to suffer jet lag. They were picked up at the Denver Airport by another Agent dispatched to pick up the two agents from Washington. Once they reached the Denver HQ they met with the Commander waiting for these two Washington Agents to arrive, and informed him what they needed and the Commander immediately called his two agents in he ordered to be at the headquarters when the other two agents were scheduled to arrive, Agent Richard Spaulding and Agent Peter Hasler sat in with the briefing. Both those agents were familiar with Batterman and his company and Agent Spaulding offered to lead the way to deliver the search warrant for Batterman's office. After they left the Commander's office, all four agents had something to eat to kill off some time, until when they could serve the search warrant on the board members of Batterman's construction company.

The agents were aware the board members never showed up for their work before 9 A.M. so they had plenty of time to kill off. One of the Denver Agents went so far as to offer maybe they should go home while the two Washington Agents checked in a hotel and they could all meet at Batterman's building at Ten A.M. to make certain the board members were at the building.

They agreed to do what was suggested by Agent Spaulding. Rossie and Fugiwara were driven to the Best Western Hotel and took a room together with separate beds. They put their luggage in the room and settled in because it was 5:20 A.M. They made themselves comfortable and as soon as he lied down, Fugiwara was sound asleep. He called the clerk and told he needed an 8 A.M. wake up call. When he was finished speaking to the clerk, he turned in for a few hours sleep.

8 A.M. AT THE DENVER BEST WESTERN HOTEL

The phone by his bed rang three times before an extremely groggy Agent Robert Rossie answered the call it was the desk clerk informing him it was eight in the morning. He thanked him and hung up and he looked at Fugiwara who was sound asleep and he called out to him. "Fugiwara-san 8 A.M. and time to get up." When he did not get a response to his call out, he took one of the pillows from his bed, sat up and pitched the pillow at Fugiwara.

"Huh, what the hell's with you this morning Rossie-san, dammit? I feel like I just fell asleep for crying out loud and here you are bothering me." Fugiwara moaned as he kicked Rossie's pillow off his bed, and then he sat up and swung his legs off the bed and leaned forward and rubbed the sleep out of his eyes with the palms of his hands. He drew in his breath and then looked up and stared at Rossie like he was going to take his head off his shoulder.

"That was the desk clerk he just gave us our wakeup call, its 8 A.M., Fugiwara-san.:

"Arrr... crap, I really hate this shit I need some more sleep. Damn, I'm still supposed to be enjoying my short week off and here I am, sharing a room with one ugly sonofabitch Gai Jin (non-Japanese person) male. Damn, I'm away from my wife and I should be sharing a room with some hot ass good looking bitch, and we should be screwing like two dogs in heat. I'm going to take a shower, maybe that'll wake me up some this morning. How are we going to link up with Agent's Spaulding and Hasler? We don't have any wheels to get around this damn city with, Rossie-san?" Fugiwara got up and started walking towards the bathroom in his jockies.

"Agent Spaulding is supposed to pick up Hasler and then he's going to come over here and pick us up and take us over to Batterman's office. When we finish up at his office, Spaulding's going to take us back over to Headquarters, and we're supposed to pick up a civilian car for our use all the while we're investigating Batterman's murder here in Denver."

"That's good to know." Fugiwara replied as he closed the bathroom door and almost immediately Rossie heard the shower water running. He was going to put off his shower until he returned to the room after work. He placed a call to Spaulding to make certain their plans did not change on him since Spaulding dropped the both of them off at the hotel early this morning.

"Agent Spaulding, what's up Bob?"

"Just checking in with you to make sure everything was still a go for 10 A.M. this morning. We're both up and we're going to grab something to eat from the hotel and we'll meet. Damn, I don't know how long it'll take us to get to Batterman's office from here, Richard?"

"It'll only take us about twenty minutes from you hotel to Batterman's office."

"Then Agent Fugiwara and I will be out front the hotel by nine thirty and wait for you to pick us up." He replied to the other FBI Agent over the phone.

"What's the big rush for Bob, we don't have a set time to raid Batterman's office? I take it as when we get there, that's when we start the damn raid. After all we're the ones running this operation, so we can set the time and the terms to act, Robert."

"Yeah, I guess you're right at that, when do you want us out front the hotel then Richard?" He asked Spaulding, he still refused to use the short name of Dick for Richard, because he just could not call someone 'Dick' unless they were acting like a dick.

"I'll pick you up in front of the hotel at 9:30 sharp Bob." Spaulding replied as he started laughing in the phone and then he hung up on him.

"Why you lousy dick you!" Rossie said in the phone as he hung up while laughing himself.

Agent Fugiwara just came walking out of the bathroom with a towel wrapped around his waist and he asked. "Who was that on the phone Rossie-san?"

"I just made contact with Agent Spaulding to see when he was picking us up? We have to be outside the hotel by 9:30 because that's when they're going to pick us up."

"Good, that gives us time to eat, I'm starved. Are you going to take a shower, Rossie-san?"

"I was going to put it off until after work, but we have time so I might as well take one now."

"Good, I'll get dressed and then have room service sent something up for us to eat."

"I don't think they have room service here, when I first came in I noticed a sign stating self serve breakfast served from six to ten in the morning, Fugiwara-san."

"Shit then I guess I'll have to run downstairs and pick up two trays of food, so we can eat something before starting work today, Rossie-san." Agent Fugiwara said to the closed door of the bathroom. He then quickly dressed and headed down to get them some food.

Rossi came walking out of the bathroom as naked as the day he was born, just as Fugiwara came in with two bags of food. He put the meals on the side table and then moaned at Rossie. "This is not quite the idea I had in mind of my having some fun while we're in Denver, Rossie-san. I'd much rather see a naked chick that your ass walking around with nothing on. Do me a favor and put some clothes on so I can enjoy my morning meal please."

"Ha ha Mr. Wiseguy, if you didn't get back here so quickly I would've been dressed and we could have both avoided this embarrassment buster. Why the bags, Fugiwara-san?"

"They wouldn't let me walk out of the room with any trays. They told me it was against the hotel policy. Some shit about walking around the hotel with exposed food or something like that who cares. I got ya a coffee and an egg, bacon and cheese bagel, the same for me Rossie-san."

"We better eat quick we're running outta time, Fugiwara-san." Rossie offered as he quickly dressed, and then looked into the bag and took out the coffee and sandwich and started eating.

When they were done they both started for outside the hotel, Rossie was still drinking his coffee. As they exited the hotel, Agent Spaulding's car was sitting outside. He and Fugiwara climbed in with Rossie remarking. "How long you guys out here? You're early."

"A few seconds at the longest, we just pulled up Agent Rossie." Spaulding replied.

"Great, let's get going then, I don't want any of the workers removing any more papers from Batterman's office then they might have already done, Richard."

CALVIN BATTERMAN'S MAIN OFFICE, 432 BLEACHER DRIVE
DOWNTOWN DENVER

"It took a little longer that first expected to reach Batterman's office, because the traffic was still a little heavy after rush hour traffic. The four agents pulled up to the building and they immediately headed for the third floor. Then exited the elevator and a pretty secretary was seated by a desk and she asked the four. "Good morning gentlemen, how my I assist you today, sirs?"

Agent Rossie stepped up and he flashed his gold shield as he announced and flash a paper in the secretary's face at the same time. "Good morning young lady, I'm FBI Agent Robert Rossie, and the man to my left is Agent Shinnosuke Fugiwara-san, the man to his left is FBI Agent Robert Spaulding and the fourth man is Agent Peter Hasler. I'm here to serve a search warrant for us to search Mr.

Batterman's office. Who do I see to gain access to his office, please?"

"Oh, I see, will you please wait a moment. The man you need to speak with is Mr. Fred Coughlin. I'll page him for you right away, I know he's in his office, I saw him as he came in for work today, Officer." The secretary picked up the phone and dialed a number and then started speaking. Then she returned her attention to the agent speaking to her and she announced. "Please wait a moment Mr. Coughlin will be right with you people momentarily please."

No sooner did she stop speaking and a man came out of an office in a rush, and he smiled as he offered. "Good morning gentlemen, how may I help you people please? It's not every day that we are visited by the FBI, sir"

Agent Rossie immediately offered him his hand as he replied to the overly polite company man he had no idea was a lawyer. "Good morning Mr. Coughlin Sir, please allow me to introduce myself to you sir. I'm Agent Robert Rossie, sir. I'm here to serve you with a search warrant for Mr. Batterman's private office. The warrant covers any and all file cabinets, safes and desks and locked draws, cabinets or other paper or document cabinet, desk, file cabinets or boxes that might contain any further paperwork, contracts or contacts that involved Mr. Batterman's dealings, sir."

"I'm pleased to meet you Agent Rossie Sir, and please allow me to introduce myself to you as well sir. I'm Mr. Fredrick Coughlin Esquire sir."

"You're a lawyer, that's good for me to know Mr. Coughlin Sir, this way we won't be forced to wait for a legal representative to come out and read the warrant, before being allowed in Batterman's office, sir." He immediately handed the lawyer a copy of the cover sheet of the warrant, and the lawyer quickly read it over and then he replied to the young agent.

"Everything seems to be all in proper legal order sir, may I ask you what you might be searching for, Agent Rossie Sir?"

"Mr. Coughlin, we're here investigating the murder of Mr. Batterman, sir. We want to search the office and see if we can discover anyone who might have recently threatened Mr. Batterman's life over a work project, a possible upset husband, an angry woman or anyone else who might be harboring a grudge against Mr. Batterman. Anyone who was dealing with him legally, or business wise or emotionally like a woman who might have taken things into their own hands and followed him to Japan and killed your boss, sir." Agent Rossie offered the lawyer.

"I see what you might be looking for in Mr. Batterman's private office sir, and I can't tell you how upset we board members were over hearing someone had killed Mr. Batterman in Japan on us sir. Many of us still can't believe he's gone. We're all seriously concerned about a possible hostile takeover attack of his company, and we're busy preparing to fend off any possible takeover bid for Mr. Batterman's company, Agent Rossie Sir."

"That's it and I need to know if any other company might gain big time over Mr. Batterman's death, and someone trying to take over his company with a hostile bid, sir. There has to be a reason for his death and we need to find out what that reason was as soon as possible, Mr. Coughlin Sir." Agent Rossie offered while he was having a little trouble with some of his lies, because he knew everything there was to know about this murder case already. All he was doing was making a show of it for his Commander, and also trying to keep the secret of Wind to himself for as long as possible.

CHAPTER EIGHT

"Yes Agent Rossie, I understand completely what you might be looking for in his office and I'm more than willing to assist you in any way possible your investigation of Mr. Batterman's office if you wouldn't mind, sir." Coughlin offered with concern to the agent.

"I think you would be much more of a help if you would just kind of stay out of our way and allow us do what we know best, sir. But what you could do for us if you wouldn't mind that is sir, is if you could compose a list of possible suspects, and add why you think these suspects might have been a serious threat against Mr. Batterman's life in the past three years, sir." Agent Rossie offered with a sort of smile on his lips. He wanted to get rid of the lawyer, yet give him something to do to keep him out of the way of their search.

"Í can do that easy enough Agent Rossie. I know of a couple of people who had a reason to want Mr. Batterman dead." The excited lawyer offered the agent, wanting to assist them.

"You do that for me Mr. Coughlin and if I have any further need of you for any reason whatsoever while we're searching Mr. Batterman's office, I'll call on ya at once sir. Now if you would be so kind as to lead us over to Mr. Batterman's office, sir." He asked.

"Yes, yes, by all means if you'd so kind as to follow me Agents, I'll be pleased to take you to Mr. Batterman's office. It's on the fifth floor of the building and it takes over half of that floor, sir. I hope you have enough people to help you with this search Agent Rossie Sir. The office is rather large and there are over twenty file cabinets in the office if I remember correctly as well sir." The lawyer grumbled as he turned and started to lead the small group of FBI Agents towards the three elevators that serviced the building.

CALVIN BATTERMAN'S OFFICE

Rossie stopped the lawyer from entering the office as the other agents walked in like they own the place as he said to the lawyer. "I guess we'll take it from here on in Mr. Coughlin Sir."

"Oh, I was going to show you were the safe is hidden and the keys to the filing system are in the right hand top draw of Mr. Batterman's desk. And the key for the center draw is hanging in the bathroom vanity, sir." Coughlin offered the Lead FBI Agent.

"I thank you for that last bit of information and you just made my job easier to accomplish, Mr. Coughlin. But we don't want you in the office when we start our search sir. One; you'll be in the way and two; you might get upset with us when we're getting into everything Mr. Batterman was doing with his company, sir. We don't need anyone getting upset with any of our actions and making our job any harder than it's going to be for us to accomplish sir."

"I understand and I'll start on that list of possible people who might have had a problem with Mr. Batterman and might have been a serious threat against him sir."

"You do that for me Mr. Coughlin Sir, I'd really appreciate that very much, now if you'll excuse me sir. I'd like to get on with the start of this search as soon as possible. As of this moment, no one is allowed in Mr. Batterman's private office, or allowed to remove anything from the office until we have finished our search, sir." Agent Rossie replied to the lawyer as he gave him the look that informed him he was finished speaking with him.

Coughlin turned on his heels and walked away as Rossie entered the office that was larger than his entire apartment it even had its own bathroom and small kitchen area and sitting room. There was a glass door leading into a large off room that must have been used as a conference room for private meetings with people doing business with the owner of the company.

He walked over to Agent Fugiwara who was already digging into one of the filing cabinets, and asked him. "What do you have there, Shinnosuke-san, anything important?"

"Boy this Batterman was some shit, look at some of these pictures he has here." He remarked as he held up a fist full of naked pictures of Batterman with a number of different and beautiful women and then added. "This guy sure had his pick of the best looking women in the States. Look at this one, this chick has his whole dick swallowed down her throat all the way up to his nuts. What a luck bastard this old man was to be able to play around with all these different great looking women. There must be a coupla hundred snapshots in the draw..."

"If you think you got some pictures of a bunch of hot looking chicks in your hands over there, you should see the mess in his desk over here, Agent Fugiwara." Agent Hasler called out to the other agents just starting their search of the office.

"C'mon you guys, we're not here to look at a mess of sex pictures. We need to find out if anyone wanted to harm Batterman. It figures you'd find them if any were to be found in here, Fugiwara-san..." Rossie started to complain at hi partner until the other agent called out to him.

"That's not quite right Agent Rossie, it seems anywhere you look there's another stack of pictures of Batterman hammering some young chick in cars, boats, on furniture and even in pools and hot tubs. It seems this guy fucked a chick on everything and anything he could drop a chick on, Rossie. Batterman even has some of these pictures on or in just about everything in the office. So Fugiwara doesn't have to go looking for any of these pics, they're all over the office."

"Whatever, just keep looking in any files to see if he made any personal notes on someone who might have threatened his life in any way. I want to look if he was being sued by anyone, and maybe he made a side note on that someone threatening him. In his line of work I'm certain he has many law suits filed against his company or him personally." Agent Rossie felt so foolish ordering his helpers to search for a possible person who might have killed Batterman, when he knew all along who and why she killed Batterman, Hiromoai, Asahiko and his son. But he still could not think of any possible way to breach the subject of Wind with his Commander, without Murdock looking at him as if he lost his mind. So he had to continue with looking like he was searching for someone who might have killed Batterman.

The search took the rest of the day and the four FBI Agents did not find anything or one to point their fingers at, so at 5 P.M. they called it a day with Rossie being the last one to walk out of Batterman's office. But before he left the floor, he ran his FBI 'Do not enter' tape across the door to stop anyone from entering the room after he locked the door with the key he found inside the office. The agents planned to return to the office the following morning at around 9 A.M. to start their next day searching for a possible name of anyone who they could aim their attention at in the Batterman murder case. But even before he could leave the building, he was stopped by Batterman's lawyer who was obviously waiting for him to come out of the office.

"Ahhh... Agent Rossie Sir, I wanted to speak with you before you left the building for the day sir. I was wondering how long your search might be sir..."

"However long it takes us to go through the tons of stacks of papers in there Mr. Coughlin Sir." Agent Rossie replied with a snap in his voice to show the lawyer he was not only exhausted, but he was kind of upset the lawyer was stopping him from leaving the building. The agent wanted to get back to his apartment and get himself some real sleep for a change. Ever since he first discovered the ancient female Samurai warrior, he was missing a lot of sleep.

"I'm sorry for detaining you Agent Rossie, but there's a lot for us board members to do to continue with Mr. Batterman's business opportunities, and the longer it's going to take us to be able to get in Mr. Batterman's office and get the proper papers we need to carry on with the company, the longer the company will be open for a hostile takeover attempt. Right now we can't accept any future work until we can restructure the company and elect a new CEO to run the company for the board members. So maybe you can understand why I was interested in when this search warrant will be satisfied, and we can get on with Mr. Batterman's company, sir."

"I see what you're driving at here Mr. Coughlin Sir, and I also understand how important it is that we wrap up our search of Batterman's office as quickly as possible for both our sakes, sir. Damn, I'm hoping to be completed with the search within the next two days, sir. Now if you can get me that list of names of a possible threat against Mr. Batterman's life then the faster we might be able to conclude our search of his private office, Mr. Coughlin sir. If you can't get me a list, then we'll have to go through every lick of paper in the office and see if we can come up with some names of a possible threat to Mr. Batterman's life, sir."

"Yes, yes Agent Rossie Sir, I'll have a list completed by tomorrow afternoon for you sir. I have already been working on the list and I was successfully able to come up with at least seven different names so far for you, Agent Rossie. Does the length of time hinge on the list you want from me sir?" Batterman's lawyer asked the smug looking young FBI agent.

"No, not really sir, but if you're able to complete that list for me by tomorrow afternoon, it'll help shorten my search of his office quite a bit, sir." He replied to the lawyer.

"Then I promise you that I'll have the list completed for you by tomorrow afternoon, Agent Rossie." The lawyer replied as he moved out of his way, and then followed him over to the elevators to try and keep their conversation going for a while longer.

"Look Mr. Coughlin Sir, I'm dead tired and would like to get the devil outta here and see if I can catch up on some of my sleep, sir. I promise you sir I'll do my very best to get this search of Mr. Batterman's office done with as soon as possible, sir." Agent Rossie walked into the elevator, turned and smiled at the lawyer as he nodded, and then pushed the first floor button.

FBI HEADQUARTERS, DENVER CALARADO

Agent Rossie went in the building, leaving Agent Fugiwara outside smoking. He walked in the Commander's office and reported everything they did at Batterman's office and what they did not find. When he finished his report, the Commander gave him keys for a vehicle so the agents from Washington had wheels to get them around the city. He collected the car, pulled around the building and picked up Fugiwara and they drove to the Best western and their room. Once inside the room, Fugiwara let his breath out in an exhausted sight and complained at the other agent.

"Man Rossie-san, I can't help but feel today was a complete waste of our damn time. We found absolutely nothing but a ton of naked pictures of Batterman having sex with just about every female in the damn world for Pete's sake. I only wish I was half as lucky as that old bastard was with the fine looking ladies. I'd die a very happy man I tell you Rossie-san."

Agent Rossie laughed as he took off his jacket, tie and then kicked off his shoes and asked his partner. "Are you hungry, if so what do you want to do about it? You want to go out and eat, or do you want to have something delivered to the room. It's up to you, but I'm so damn tired I don't know if I even want something to eat at this point, Fugiwara-san" He was making certain he offered the same respect Agent Fugiwara was giving him by adding the 'San' to his name whenever the Japanese Agent spoke to him.

"What do you want to order out from?" Fugiwara asked his partner.

"I don't know, a pizza maybe, on our way over here I noticed a Jason's and then have helluva sandwiches and one damn good salad bar and I know they deliver, or we can order Chinese food, err... skip the Chinese stuff..." He immediately corrected because his partner was Japanese.

"Thank you Rossie-san, Chinese food give me gas all the time I eat it. I think I'd like to order from this Jason's, I never ate there before."

"Jason's it is, I'll call for our meal." Agent Rossie called down to the front desk and asked if they had Jason's number, he got it and called and then asked Agent Fugiwara what he wanted after repeating the menu to his partner as the waiter read it off to him over the phone. After they ordered their supper, the two agents settled down to wait for their food to arrive. Rossie put the TV on and then laid down in his bed as Fugiwara sat across from him and he sort of just kind of stared at the young American Agent.

Getting the feeling someone was staring at him, he took his eyes off the TV and looked at his partner and found him staring at him with a funny look on his face. Looking at Agent Fugiwara for a few seconds he finally barked at him. "What?"

"What what?"

"What's up with the look you're giving me, Fugiwara-san? My fly open or what my friend?"

"I don't know but there's something about you lately that's starting to bug the living crap outta my ass, Rossie-san. What's going on with you my friend, you look preoccupied?"

"Like what, Fugiwara-san?"

"Like we just got back from searching Batterman's office and I tried to engage you in conversation over what we didn't find at his office. You didn't bite at what I said and you even acted like you knew we were not going to find anything of worth at the damn office. Why is that my friend? I swear Agent Rossie-san, I just can't get it outta my stinking mind that you know a little something more about this damn murder case than you're letting on, and for some reason you're keeping it from me, my friend. Why am I getting this weird feeling from you Rossie-san? Can you tell me, partner?" Shinnosuke sharpened his stare of the other special agent.

"I have no idea what you're talking about Fugiwara-san. I'm just as disappointed as you are over finding anything that might help us with this murder case. As for keeping anything away from my partner in this case, I'm afraid you're a little off base here my friend." He replied.

"C'mon man, look at you damn puss, you got a half ass smug look like the damn cat that swallowed the bird thing. What the hell do you know about this damn murder case, and why the devil won't you tell me everything you know about it, Rossie-san. Now more than ever I believe you know a lot more about this damn case and you won't clue me in on it. C'mon Rossie-san, I'm your damn partner, and you can tell me anything and it'll remain between us. You didn't kill Batterman while both you and he were in Japan, did ya my friend?"

He actually laughed over Agent Fugiwara asking him if he killed Batterman in Japan. He hesitated for a brief moment and almost started to tell him about Wind, and how he found her and how she was the one who actually killed Batterman, along with a number of other people in Japan. But then he caught himself and clammed up, because first of all: he did not want to tell anyone about Wind at this point, and second all: he was worried if Fugiwara would believe him or not, or if he might think he lost his mind. The story of Wind was almost too hard for him to believe it, and it was happening to him. He shook his head and drew in a large gulp of air and was just about ready to tell him something to feel him out and maybe breach the subject about Wind, when there was a knock on the door to the apartment. They both looked at the door.

"Saved by the damn bell Rossie-san, it must be our supper."

"Thank God, I'm starving to death." He replied as he let his breath out in a rush. Happy with the interruption, so he did not have to tell Fugiwara about Wind, not at this point yet. He paid for the food, laid it out and the two agents enjoyed their meal. The baseball game was on and they ended up watching the Mets play the Dodgers and Agent Fugiwara forgot all about the conversation they were having before the food arrived.

The next morning came and they got up and headed for the local MacDonald's for breakfast, and then headed for Batterman's office again. They linked up with Spaulding and Hasler who were both waiting for the other two agents to arrive, before entering the building again. Rossie checked the tape and was satisfied no one tampered with the tape or door, and then he pulled it down, opened the door and they quickly entered the room and started working again.

Outside the office, the people who worked for Batterman and Batterman Construction Company went about their daily work, and about completely ignored what the FBI Agents were doing in their dead boss' office. This day was about as productive as the day before, the agents found the names of two people who filed law suits against Batterman, one was personal, the other over business. Agent Rossie took the woman's name suing Batterman over a breach of promise, and Fugiwara took the name of the man who was suing Batterman over a failed construction project. But more of the day was spent with the agents looking at the stacks and stacks of naked sex act pictures of Batterman with a bevy of different women, young, middle aged and older women. That's how boring the search of the office got for the agents.

It was rounding 4 P.M. and Rossie wanted to call an early end of the search for the day. He called out and announced. "Well people, what say we end this boring ass day? I'm dead tired and I can't look at another page of work projects, or naked pictures of this old man putting it to some young chicks." He snapped as he looked directly at Agent Fugiwara and gave him the look.

"What Rossie-san, I don't think we're going to find anything that might help us out with this damn murder case in here. It seems all this old bastard liked to do with his time, was take some pictures of hot looking women he was porking, for Pete's sake. At least it gave us something better to look at than all these endless work contracts, proposals and people who were either pissed off, or damn happy with the work this old man's company was doing out there, dammit. I didn't find one stinking person who seemed angry enough to go after this old man and want to kill him, dammit. I think we're just wasting our lousy time looking in this office if you ask me Rossie-san. I think we'll be much better off speaking with some of the Japanese gangs roaming all over the country. I know of three different gangs that call Denver home to the groups. I think we'd be far better served by speaking to some of the gang members.

"We can speak to some of the gang members and see if anyone might have approached them and was looking to pay them to kill Batterman..."

"That's a damn good idea you just got there Shinnosuke-san. Do you think you might be able to approach any of these gang members and ask them that last question you just belted out to the rest of us here my friend? You said it and if it's possible then I'm going to assign you to the gangs and see if you can come up with anything that might help us from them." Rossie asked the Japanese Agent as he stared and then waited for him to reply to his last question of him.

"Yes Rossie-san, I think I can approach some of these gangs. I worked with a few Japanese gangs in Chicago and a few cities in California. It seemed like I got along with them. I guess because I'm a fellow Jap they looked at me as one of their own. I don't care either way why they seem to trust me, all I know was I never had serious problems approaching them. It's funny, even though I'm Japanese, these damn gang members can pick out any law authorities from a mile away from them. It's uncanny how easily they pick us out from the rest of the crowd."

"Then it's settled, tomorrow you'll drop me off here at the office, and you take the car and located some of the gang members and interview them. See if you can get any leads from them people, Fugiwara-san." Agent Rossie more or less ordered his partner for tomorrow's workday.

"You got it, I'll make contact with some of my people and I'm certain at least one of them can get me to a gang leader here in Denver, Rossie-san." Agent Fugiwara offered as he smiled back at Rossie then he got out of the chair and made it known he wanted to leave for the day.

The other three FBI Agents got up and prepared to leave Batterman's office, again they filed out of the room with Rossie stopping just long enough to run the yellow do not enter, FBI crime scene tape out cross Batterman's door, and then he locked up the office. And just like last night, as soon as he locked the door, the company lawyer approached him with a file folder locked in his hand, and he kind of cleared his throat to get Rossie's attention.

"Oh, Mr. Coughlin Sir, nice to see you again today sir, and how did you make out with that list I wanted from you, sir?" He asked kindly of the company lawyer.

"Rather well I offer you Agent Rossie. I was able to locate fifteen names of people who at least once in their lives threatened to kill Batterman one way or the other, sir. I have three people who I felt were extremely serious threats against Mr. Batterman, sir." The lawyer smiled at him.

"Well if you had this damn list finished earlier in the day, why the devil didn't you give it to me earlier in the day then sir? I might have sent two of my Agents out to start checking on these people if they live in the damn area, Mr. Coughlin Sir." Agent Rossie used his disgusted tone of voice as he was addressing the company lawyer, he was that upset because for the second day in a row, the lawyer was going to delay him from leaving the building for the day's work.

"I'm terribly sorry to say this Agent Rossie, but I refrained from disturbing your search of Mr. Batterman's office, and I was waiting until you finished for the day before I interrupted you sir. You know how hard pressed I am to get back in the office, so I can get his company back on track and his workers working again on the projected Mr. Batterman started before he was murdered in Japan, sir." The lawyer announced like he did something to help the agent.

"That's all fine, well and good Mr. Coughlin Sir, but you should have knocked on the door as soon as you compiled the list for me sir. If I had it a little earlier I could have split up my forces and sort of killed two birds with one stone, sir. Can I see the list and I want to know the names of the people you have classified as the most serious threats against Mr. Batterman's life, sir." The young FBI Agent Rossie offered as he put his hand out and almost instantly, the company lawyer handed the file folder over to him. He opened the folder and glanced at the list of names, and then he asked him which were the names you were most concerned with, sir?"

"I know I told you there were three names I was most concerned with on the list, but I did expand it to the first five names on the top of the list who are the ones I was most concerned with, Agent Rossie Sir. The most serious of threats is the first name and the next two were the three most serious, and then as they go down the list the threat lessens, but these five first names are the most serious ones I'd offer for you to check them out first, sir."

"I thank you very kindly for compiling the list of names for me so quickly Mr. Coughlin Sir, and the first five names on the last will get most of my Agent's attentions I assure you sir. Now as you can see for yourself sir, I'm about done for the day and I'd like to head for my apartment and get some rest and go over this list of names and then sent my Agents out to start checking these names out for me sir. Thank you again Mr. Coughlin Sir and have a good night sir." With that said, he headed for the elevator in a rush to get away from the pain of a lawyer.

BACK AT THEIR APARTMENT AT THE BEST WESTERN HOTEL

Agent Rossie sat on the edge of his bed and went over the list of names with Agent Fugiwara the company lawyer gave him. The first five names interested him the most, and there was a brief history of each name and why they made the lawyer's list. The first name was Tom Montgomery and the problem he was having with Batterman extended from a completed job and Batterman paid him half the agreed price, and Montgomery was suing Batterman for the rest of the contract, and the lawyer states twice Montgomery got into a fist fight with Batterman. It was a messy suit with Montgomery threatening a number of times to kill Batterman, and once he was stopped by Batterman's home, and Montgomery was found carrying a pistol and detained by the police after someone reported a strange man hanging around the area. The only reason the police did not pursue criminal actions against him was because Batterman refused to press criminal charges.

Fugiwara asked Rossie. "I wonder who won the fights, I met Batterman on a few occasions and I know I wouldn't want to tangle with him unless I had a pipe in my hands, he was that big."

"Ha ha, can't you be serious for once in your life, Fugiwara-san!" He snapped at him.

"Fugiwara completely ignored the nasty remark Rossie just aimed at him as he went on with his words. "What do you think about this one, sure seems like he had a real hardon against Batterman if you ask me, Rossie-san? I think we should aim our attention on this man."

"It's rather interesting this one's anger actually forced him to carry a weapon and obviously stalked Batterman a few times. I wonder if he really would have killed Batterman if he came across the man on the night this event took place. Look Agent Fugiwara-san, I think we're going to skip searching Batterman's office for tomorrow. I think I'll allow Agents Spaulding and Hasler to continue ripping his office apart tomorrow and we'll start checking out the names on this list. This second guy on the list is no better than the first one, and I think I'll take the first two people and you can have the next two. This second guy an Alan Larson outright threatened to kill Batterman if he ever came across him walking around the streets of Denver. The lawyer wrote about this guy he states Larson and Batterman were partners on a joint construction project, and Larson accused Batterman of draining all the profits from the job, and it caused Larson to lose over five million on the joint project.

"The Lawyer stated Larson's law suit was thrown out of court over some missing paperwork, and Larson came right back with a second lawsuit against Batterman, and that one also failed. But Larson wouldn't give up and he filed a third lawsuit against Batterman over the same complaint. It looks like this one might have some merit to it, because a judge set it down for a trial date. Man, is Larson going to be fuming once he hears Batterman was murdered in Japan, and that news is going to shoot his lawsuit all to shit on him." Rossie groused to Fugiwara.

"I guess so Rossie-san. Who are you going to give me to interview, sir?"

"I'm going to give you the next two people on the lawyer's list. The first one is a John Keeley, and the lawyer writes this man sold a piece of commercial property to Batterman, and Batterman offered him a deal where Keeley's work crews were going to do the construction of the building Batterman brought for a customer. But once the deal was consummated, Batterman quickly turned around and used his work crews to build the building for the guy who brought the property from Batterman. A few times it was recorded this Keeley fellow threatened to kill Batterman. But he never made any serious moves against Batterman though. The second guy I'm going to give you to interview is Edward Jackson. This guy sold a piece of heavy construction equipment to Batterman, and Batterman never finished paying for the equipment.

"Twice Batterman and this Jackson fellow got into a real donnybrook and in one of the fights Batterman broke Jackson's jaw. They almost got into a few other fights, but they were stopped before they got off the ground by other people who separated the two combatants. There were a couple of minor threats bantered back and forth at each other, but at least the fights ended..."

"Man, this Batterman guy seems like he was a real scumbag type a guy to work with or for, between all the chicks and the fights and screwing this man was doing. It seems he didn't care who he fucked one way or the other in the business world, Rossie-san. What about the fifth guy on the lawyer's list, who is he and what did he have to do with Batterman, Rossie-san?" Fugiwara asked as he shifted his rearend while he also sat on the edge of his bed.

"Oh man, we kind of get a little break with this guy because he comes from Washington D.C., and we can check him out together when we return to Washington after we finish with Batterman's office. This guy's name is James Pochurek and he goes by Jim..."

"What is he Russian, Rossie-san?" Agent Fugiwara asked his partner.

"Naw, I think he's probably Polish or something like that but definitely not Russian, Fugiwara-san It states by the lawyer that this guy Jim brought a piece of property from Batterman, not knowing the property was condemned by the government and classified as a polluted piece of land. This poor fellow was stuck with the property and he lost one and a half million dollars over the transaction, and he was really busting Batterman' horns about the loss and one way or the other, he actually threatened to kick Batterman's ass for him. I see the further we go down the list of names, the less violent the other people were getting against Batterman.

"I'm going to skip the rest of the names on the list for the time being, the four living here in Denver we'll check out first and when we get back to Washington, we'll start to check out a few of the other names on the lawyer's list. I looked at the next few names and three of them are living in

Washington, and the next five are spread out in New York City. Besides, I really want to get back to Washington as soon as possible because I didn't want to leave the state in the first place. I just started something and didn't get it off the ground before Murdock sent my ass over to Denver to interview these names and to also search Batterman's private office for any possible clues on who might have killed the bastard..."

"Who was the chick you were working on back in Washington you can't wait to get back to, Rossie-san?" Agent Fugiwara asked as he gave him a smirk like he was one up on him.

"Man Fugiwara, you just can't get your damn mind outta the stinking gutter for one minute, can you? You're more worried about who's getting laid than you are about getting laid yourself I see, fella." He bitched at his partner as he glared nastily at him for the moment.

"Damn right Rossie-san. All I know is if I'm not getting any then I want to sure as hell know who is. Being married is sure crimping my style with the women you know." He complained.

"Well, who the hell told you to tie the knot and stop playing the field? What am I saying you never did stop playing the field my friend? I guess your wife got married but you didn't didja Fugiwara-san? What the hell ever happened to your fine Japanese upbringing? I thought all Japanese people were very honorable and their honor meant more to them than their own lives meant to them. You sure as hell missed the damn train in the honor and loyalty deal, Fugiwara-san." Rossie smirked at his partner as he gave him the get off my damn back look will ya man.

"I had to get married, Rossie-san. When I first met my Lady Yoke, she told me she was on the pill, and we started screwing around and all of a sudden she announced she was with child, after we were together for a few months or so. So I did the honorable and right thing as you like to say, and I married her which really didn't bother me all that much I tell ya. Because she's a real great kid, good looking and a helluva lot of fun to be with and she makes me plenty happy. But the only reason I still play the field is because I really wasn't quite ready to settle down and start a family of my own. But being with Lady Yoke is making married life real fine, and she even knows I mess around a bit on her and she puts up with it and me. So as long as she has no problem with me, stay off my damn case about how I live my damn life, Rossie-san."

"If she makes you happy then why the hell do you have to screw around on her like you keep doing Fugiwara-san?" He asked his partner with a confused sounding tone of voice.

"What the hell are you all of a sudden, a priest or something around here Rossie-san?"

"Forget it my friend, speaking to you is like speaking to a damn foreigner." Rossie complained at his partner, and then he returned to the list and announced. "Hot damn, the Lawyer included the phone numbers of everyone he put down on the list, along with their addresses and where they work. That's sure as hell going to make our job all that much easier to do. Fugiwara-san, I'm going to place a call to Agent Spaulding and tell him he and Hasler will work on Batterman's office, and we're going to check out these first four names on the lawyer's list. That way we won't even have to meet them at Batterman's office. I'll put Spaulding in charge of Hasler and we can do our own act. Tell you what, why don't you order us supper and I'll call Spaulding."

"You got it Rossie-san." Fugiwara replied as he took his cell phone and ordered pizza.

Rossie got off the bed and walked over to the small chair and table and placed a call out to Spaulding as he sat down and looked out the window. The phone was answered on the forth ring.

"Spaulding here."

"Yeah Richard, Rossie here I'm sorry for bothering you when you're supposed to be off duty. But I have a change in your orders for tomorrow morning, sir. Tomorrow you're to take command of the search of Batterman's office. Fugiwara-san and myself are going to check out the first four names on the lawyer's list of suspects in the Batterman murder case. I don't want anyone not showing up at Batterman's office, or that damn lawyer is going to sneak his ass in there and do who knows what to any evidence there is to find in his office. That's why I want you two to continue with his office, or I'd be giving you two a couple of names apiece to investigate. We now have two points of concern so you two keep at it with Batterman's office, and we'll start checking out the names on the list." Agent Rossie ordered the other agent over the phone.

"You got it Agent Rossie Sir you know anything we can do to help this case move along, we're happy to do, sir. Is that about it sir? I was just about to sit down and enjoy my supper with my wife and kids, Agent Rossie." Agent Spaulding replied to Rossie's last orders of him.

"That's it on my side give your wife my apologies for disrupting her supper on her, Agent Spaulding. I'm make contact with you after work tomorrow night to see how you two guys made out with Batterman's office and that damn pain in the ass company lawyer. And I'll also inform you on how we made out with interviewing the names the lawyer put down on the list. I'm hoping to end this damn investigation within the next three days at the longest, sir."

"Thanks for that information I guess I'll hear from you tomorrow night after work sir."

"That's right and thanks for your help on this one, Agent Spaulding. I couldn't have handled it without you and Hasler on the job sir. I'll speak with you tomorrow after work." With that said Rossie broke off the connection with the other agent and turned to Fugiwara, only to see him already digging into the pizza. Fugiwara looked up from his meal and smiled at Rossie who bitched. "Well I'm pleased to see nothing gets in the way of your eating around here, mister."

"What did you want me to do Rossie-san, wait until you were off the damn phone?"

"Anyway, I have Agents Spaulding and Hasler taking care of Batterman's office for us tomorrow. I wanted someone there tomorrow because I just don't trust that damn company lawyer. He's so damn shifty looking I wouldn't put it past him to wiggle his way into the office and removed some important evidence from the office so we didn't find it. At least this move leaves up free to interview some of these other people who the lawyer thinks was a serious threat against Batterman's life. I can't wait till this mess is over with and we can return to Washington and get back to the case load we were working on before the Batterman murder..."

"And that chick who obviously has peaked your interest in her, huh Rossie-san? Who is she, is she good looking, and how is she in bed anyhow? You have to tell me something about her. I want to know what type of woman who could win your heart, Rossie-san. And don't think for one moment I forgot about our conversation over what you know about this damn case, and yet you still refuse to tell me anything about what you're holding back on me, my so called friend." Agent Fugiwara griped at his partner as he stared and waited for him reply.

"Will you get off it already for crap sake! Who I have waiting for me back in Washington is none of your fricking business, my friend. And yet, I do know something more about this case, but I'm stuck between a rock and a hard place because I just don't know how to tell you what I'm holding back on you. It's too unbelievable and I don't know how I can make you believe it when I don't believe what I know has happened. One day real soon I guess we'll have a couple drinks together and I'll tell you what I truly know about this damn murder case, Fugiwara-san." Rossie replied as he looked down and started thinking about informing Fugiwara about Wind, and who she slaughtered back in Japan, and now she is here in Washington and he's actually guilty of hiding a murderer and he did not know how to get out from under what he was trapped in.

"Dammit, I knew you knew more about this than you were letting on. C'mon, you can level with me, I can keep a secret and if you're caught up in the middle of this thing, I'm certain we can work something out where I can help you square it with Murdock. You didn't kill Batterman, did you? You never really answered me when I first asked you that question, sir?" Fugiwara seriously asked him if he killed Batterman this time as he stared and waited for his reply

"No, I didn't kill Batterman in Japan, Fugiwara-san!" He snapped back at his partner.

"Maybe not, but I'm willing to bet the ranch on you know who killed Batterman, Rossie-san."

FBI Agent Robert Rossie did not reply to Fugiwara's last question of him, and that caused his partner to add with a sharp snap in this tone of voice this time. "I fucking knew it for crap sake. I just fucking knew you knew it for a fact that you know who killed that old bastard over there in Japan. C'mon Rossie-san, now you have to level with me and tell me everything you're holding back on me man." Now Agent Fugiwara was making it very obvious he wanted him to tell all he knew about Batterman's murder, and he was not going to take no for an answer this time.

"I know I have to tell you everything I know about this damn Batterman case, but I can't say anything about the case at this time. Believe me Agent Fugiwara-san, you won't believe me when I start to tell you everything I know, so you're going to be stuck waiting until I finally figure out a way to tell you about it, without you trying to have me placed in a padded cell and locked away, my friend. Look Fugiwara-san, just give me until we get back to Washington and I get my head screwed back on right, and I can prove to you what I'll be soon telling you is the truth. I'm telling you Agent Fugiwara-san, you're not going to believe what I'm going to tell you for one second, let alone what you're going to see for yourself when I finally tell you all about Batterman, the person who killed him, and the other few people savagely murdered over there in Japan. It's a real saga and one you're going to have a real hard time trying to believe my friend.

"Agent Fugiwara-san, just give me until we return to Washington to work this crap out in my own mind before I can sit down and tell and even show you what went on over in Japan, and now it's here in the United States as well." Agent Rossie begged his partner to give him the time he was begging him for because he was that troubled about Wind, and he knew he had to tell someone and it might as well be his partner.

"Okay Rossie-san, I'll give you the time you're asking me for, but you have to tell me everything on what you know of this case, and you're not having me chasing some damn shadows around here because you're obviously trying to protect the person who killed Batterman. But I have to warn you this, my friend. You can't wait too long before to tell me about this case and what the hell is going on with the damn thing, or I'll be forced to go to Murdock and have you pulled in before him, so you can tell him who killed Batterman and the others. I don't like you know who killed that bastard, and you're keeping it to yourself."

"Okay, just give me a damn break before you go off and start pushing any panic buttons around here please Agent Fugiwara-san. I swear I'll tell you everything I'm holding back once I get it all sorted out in my own mind first. C'mon and let's eat I'm starving and let it go for the time being will ya? There'll be plenty of time later on to talk about this case and what truly went down with the damn thing, Fugiwara-san."

CHAPTER NINE

JUNE 15th, 1996 THE BEST WESTERN
HOTEL DENVER CARLARDO
ZERO SIX FOUR ZERO HUNDRED HOURS (6:40 A.M.

FBI Agent Robert Rossie was the first one up on this morning, and he looked over at Agent Shinnosuke Fugiwara who was still fast asleep, so he left the room and went downstairs to enjoy the free meal of some scrambled eggs and bacon, toast and coffee. He just settled in when Agent Fugiwara came walking in and he grabbed a plate and filled it and then walked over to where he was seated and said to him. "I heard you get up this morning so I got dressed and came down to enjoy a meal before we start after the four people we wish to speak with today. When do you want to start going after these few guys we want to speak with today, Rossie-san?"

"Good morning Agent Fugiwara-san, how did you sleep sir?"

"Fine, when do you want to start after these guys you want to speak with Rossie-san?"

"I slept well thanks and I don't think we should start after these guys until after 9 A.M. That's when these types start their workday. I figure about between 9:30 and 10 we can start after them. I plan to make my first call to this Montgomery fellow after 9 A.M. and inform him I wish to speak with him this morning. Once I finished with this guy, I'll call Larson and do the same and ask to have a meeting with him sometime today. I'll speak to these guys today, and I'll make my decision if I want to keep going over Batterman's office, or call it a day and head to Washington and start our search from there again." Agent Rossie offered as he continued to eat his meal.

"Man, you really want to get back to Washington and be with this chick, huh Rossie-san? I'll speak to the two guys you ordered me to meet with today as well then we'll compare notes and like you just said. We'll make up our minds what we're going to do next, Rossie-san." Agent Fugiwara replied as he finished his meal so he could get started with his work for the day.

"Yes, even though I like Denver, I like Washington much better my friend."

"Remember Rossie-san, you promised me you were going to fill in a lot of the missing blanks of this case once we were back in Washington, sir. I hope you're going to stay with that promise, Rossie-san." Fugiwara remarked as he looked deeply into Rossie's eyes, searching for a reply.

"I told you I was going to talk to you when we got back to Washington, once I have been able to put this whole mess in a more believable story line than the way it was going down right at the moment, Fugiwara-san." Agent Rossie corrected the other agent with snap in his tone of voice. He still did not like the pressure the other agent was dropping down on his back, and he was not going to allow Agent Fugiwara rush him until he was ready to tell him all about Wind, and the rest of what had happened to him both in Japan, and since he came back to Washington.

"Yeah, I see you're still going to continue playing this game of keeping some important facts of this murder case from me, until you're good and ready to drop it down on my ass I see, Rossie-san. I'm warning you Rossie, you don't want to keep me in suspense for too long, or you're going to force me to see Murdock over this matter. How the hell can you possible expect me to continue investigating this case, when you're obviously keeping some important facts from my ass, Rossie-san. I'm afraid that's not fair, we have to solve this mess and how can I do it with you tying one of my arms behind my back, and then expect me to find out what you obviously already know about this damn case, man?" Agent Fugiwara actually growled at his partner this time because he was getting that upset with his fellow agent now as he glared angrily at him.

"Calm down a little will you please Fugiwara-san. I promise you to tell you everything I know of this case, once I have all the particulars all worked out first. I'm just not going to tell you what I know then maybe have it change a little later on and I find out I was all wrong on what I had already worked out on this murder case, sir. So keep your damn shirt on and by the time we get back to Washington, I should be able to clue you in on everything I know, and I can also show you the proof of what I'm going to tell you about this case, Fugiwara-san. Just give me the time I need to work it all out in my head first. Then I'll tell you everything I know about the case." Agent Rossie complained as he got up, picked up his tray and walked it over to the table, cleaned it off and put the tray on the stack of used trays, and then he rushed out of the eating room.

Once back in the room, Agent Rossi quickly showered to kill off some more time, and by the time he was dressed, shaved and back in the room. It was near enough to 9 A.M. and he placed a call to Montgomery's office and a sexy woman's voiced announced politely. "You have reached the office of Thomas Montgomery, how may I direct this call please."

"Yes Ma'am and this is FBI Agent Robert Rossie, and I'm here in Denver and was given your bosses name, and I wish to have a meeting with him as soon as possible today please."

"Oh, and I'm terribly sorry to inform you FBI Agent Rossie Sir, that Mr. Montgomery is currently visiting Washington D.C. He's there because he's trying to land a construction project there, and he's scheduled to be spending the next seven days at the least attending a number of meetings with the government and Governor of the State, to try and win this contract sir."

"Is there any way for me to be able to reach him while Mr. Montgomery in Washington from here, young lady." Agent Rossie had to control his tone of voice, because he was that upset he was trapped in Denver, and now his main target was where he wanted to be.

"I can give you his contact number, but I'm afraid you'll have to make the call yourself sir. I know if I told your number to him and asked Mr. Montgomery to return a call to you sir. There'll be no telling how long it might be before he was finally able to return the call to you, Agent Rossie Sir." The concerned sounding secretary replied to him.

"Yes, I see what you mean young lady, and it's that important that I speak to him as soon as possible I'm afraid." Agent Rossie remarked, even though he was aware Wind was the murderer, he still wanted to speak to this man to see if he could find out something else he could sink his teeth into over Batterman and some of his dealings in the United States.

"Once again sir, Mr. Montgomery is currently visiting Washington on a business matter, and if I contact him and give him your message, there's no telling when he might find the time to get back to you so you may speak with him Agent Rossie Sir. That's why I suggest you make contact with him yourself after I give you his contact number, sir. That way when he answers your call, you may speak directly with him, sir."

"I hear ya and you're right with your offer, young lady. If you'd be so kind to give me his contact number, I'll do what you have just suggested, Ma'am." Agent Rossie replied.

"Do you have a pen and paper because here is his number, Agent Rossie Sir?"

He wrote the number down then thanked the secretary and hung up at the same time and looked at Agent Fugiwara and grumbled at him. "Dammit, this Montgomery is in Washington for the next week or so, the son of a gun. Well,

I'm going to make contact with Larson and see if he's available today and meet with him, and depending on how you make out with the two names I gave you to check out, we might find ourselves heading back to Washington by tomorrow sometime. Did you make any calls while I was trying to reach Montgomery, Fugiwara-san?"

"Yes I did Rossie-san. I spoke with Mr. Keeley and he seemed very interested in speaking with me. He sounded like a nice guy and he was very talkative, but not combative thank God. I was just about ready to try and contact Jackson, and see if he was willing to meet with me later this afternoon or tomorrow morning, Rossie-san." The other agent reported to his lead.

"Fine, I'll call Larson and see if I can link up with him today and depending on how it goes with him will make up my mind whether or not we head for Washington tomorrow. Yeah I know so don't start on that crap again Fugiwara-san. I want to see my chick true, but that's not the main reason I was to head to Washington. That's where I belong, I live and work and I think we can get a jump on this case from there, as good as we can from here." Rossie complained as he sort of smirked back at Fugiwara, knowing full well he was not fooling the other agent in the least.

Fugiwara just smile back at Rossie with the look of you're not bullshitting me my friend.

"Arrr..." Agent Rossie mumbled as he picked up his cell phone and quickly dialed Larson's number and on the second ring, he answered the phone himself. "Larson here."

"Mr. Larson, thank you for answering the phone. Allow me to introduce myself to you sir. I'm FBI Special Agent Robert Rossie, sir. I was given your number by Mr. Batterman's lawyer..."

"Oh, that scumbag, what the hell does that lousy prick want with me that he now has the damn Feds busting my fucking horns on me? I thought I was done with that rotten bastard..."

"Mr. Larson, I want to inform you that Mr. Batterman was murdered in Japan last week, and I was making contact with anyone who might have had a work relationship with the man, sir."

"Murdered, wow, though I really hated the sonofabitch and wanted to kick his ass from one side of this country to the other, I never wanted him murdered. Even though he was a real sonofabitch, I'd stop what I was doing and share a drink with him at a drop of a hat. As a friend, he was aces, as someone to work with or for. Naw, he was the biggest prick in the damn world. We're you people able to find the bastard who killed Batterman, sir?" Larson asked.

"Well to be perfectly truthful with you Mr. Larson, I wanted to speak to you about that very remark, sir. I wanted to meet with you today and talk about the murder of Mr. Batterman, and see if you have an alibi for the day he was murdered, sir." Agent Rossie offered Larson.

"Why wait, we can talk right now if you want that is. You just said Batterman was killed a few days ago, well Agent Rossie, I can easily account for my time for the past two weeks, sir. I was up in Alaska and put a bid in on a bridge up there. I can give you at least ten different names of people I was with right up to the day before yesterday. But if you had any fears about where I stood with Batterman, even though he was a real prick to work with, if you check my working relationship with him, you'll see I did over fifteen projects with him. Although we even came to blows a few times, if he called and told me he was working on a project and wanted to know if I would put in with him, I'd jump at any chance to work with him.

"If anyone wanted to make any serious money, all they had to do was grab hold of his shirt tails and hang on and he was going to come out with a fist full of money at the end. That guy could take a shit then do a reach around and grab a hand full of crap and throw it against the wall, and what stuck on the wall would instantly turn to gold, that's how good a damn businessman Batterman was to deal with and work with, Agent Rossie Sir. So I guess I have to ask you now do you have any concerns about my relationship with Batterman, sir."

"Err... I guess you answered many of the questions I was going to ask you about to my satisfaction Mr. Larson Sir. Tell you what I'll do sir, if you get me the list of names of the people you were with for the past two weeks, I'll check them out and if I have any other questions for you, I'll call you back. But if everything checks out the way you have just suggested sir. Then you won't be hearing from me gain, sir. I thank you for your time and patience in this matter and all you have to do is E'mail me those names, and I'll hope not to be forced to bother you again in the future, Mr. Larson Sir." Agent Rossie told the businessman.

"Sure thing Agent Rossie Sir, all you have to do is give me your E'mail address and I'll give it to my secretary, and she's send you the list of names of everyone I was with in Alaska, and when I returned to the lower forties, sir." Larson informed the agent.

"I can text my E'mail address to the phone number I just used to make contact with you today Mr. Larson, is that alright sir?" He asked the man on the other end of the phone.

"That'll do it for me sir." Larson replied.

"Here it comes I'm sending it to you now Mr. Larson." Agent Rossie sent his E'mail address to the businessman, and then he hung up and again looked at Agent Fugiwara and he immediately replied to his lead agent.

"Rossie-san, I made contact with the two people you gave me to interview, and since it seems you just finished with the last one you wanted to speak with. Do me a favor here and you take one and I'll take the other, that way we can deal with these last two people and that'll free us both up in case we end up heading back to Washington sometime tomorrow afternoon, Rossie-san." Agent Fugiwara remarked with a smile, hoping Rossie would take him up on his offer and they both could handle the last two people they wanted to speak with over Batterman's murder.

"Sound like a plan to me, Agent Fugiwara-san."

The two agents interviewed the ones they were interested and decided they both were dead ends. Although both Keeley and Jackson had problems with Batterman, neither of them was angry enough to kill him. The two agents returned to the apartment by 4 P.M. and Rossie immediately placed a call to Spaulding to see how they made out searching Batterman's office.

Spaulding informed Rossie they found nothing that would give them a lead in Batterman's murder, and he reported the lawyer was driving them crazy most of the day. He bothered them ten times in the office, asking when they were going to complete their investigation."

Agent Rossie thought about his response for a few minutes and then he countered. "Okay Agent Spaulding Sir, I guess we're going to end this investigation as of tomorrow morning. So here's what I want you to do. Tomorrow morning you're to show up at Batterman's office alone, and pulled the 'Do not cross' tape down and release the office to the pain in the ass lawyer, and then inform him we're pulling back our investigation of the office and he's free to do whatever the hell he does or has to do with the crap in Batterman's office. Then leave and cancel all further investigations of this murder case unless you people happen to come up with something that need to be looked into a little further. I think everything to do with this case is not going to be found here in Denver, sir. I guess Agent Fugiwara-san and I will return to Washington and carry out the rest of this investigation from our Washington Headquarters.

"Everything we looked into here in Denver led us right into dead ends. With all the work we did here for the past days netted us absolutely nothing. That's why I'm moving the investigation back to Washington, and if we find anything there that leads us back to Denver, I'll request both you and Hasler to be our Denver contacts. That way the case will remain in your hands here in this State, Agent Spaulding. Err..., I guess I'll return the car to your headquarters and make my opening report to your Commander then inform him we're moving the investigation back to Washington, Agent Spaulding Sir." He responded to the other agent.

"That's a real shame because I really enjoyed working with you two guys, and this was a major murder case and it meant a lot to me and Hasler to be part of it. I certainly appreciate the fact you'll use us again if you have to return to Denver for any reason over this murder case, sir."

"Sure thing Agent Spaulding, it was a real pleasure working with you two guys as well, sir." Agent Rossie replied just as kindly to the other agent. Then he hung up with Spaulding and reported to Agent Fugiwara what he just spoke of to the other agent.

Agent Shinnosuke agreed with everything Agent Rossie wanted to do next then both agents prepared to leave for Washington the next morning. After he returned the car and reported to the Commander of the Denver FBI, both he and Fugiwara packed up their stuff, and Rossie requested the FBI private plane to pick them up the following morning at the Denver Airport. He was informed the plane would arrive at 9:20 A.M. sharp.

ZERO NINE HUNDRED HOURS (9 A.M.), MONDAY JUNE 17th 1996,
DENVER CARALDO INTERNATIONAL AIRPORT

Both Agent Robert Rossie and Agent Shinnosuke Fugiwara were at the airport an hour before their scheduled flight back to Washington D.C. was due to arrive at the airport. They were still exhausted from their workload in Denver and looking forward to returning to their home area again. Agent Rossie was dying to call Wind back from the Floating World and see what she was up to while he was away. He was also looking forward to pillowing with her again.

As they were seated in the aircraft, he looked and then smiled at Agent Fugiwara as they got comfortable and he remarked. "Rossie-san, I can't wait to be back in Washington, but when we get back there I want to run up to Jersey and spend the night with my lady and two boys. If you remember right, I lost two days of my off time when you had Murdock call me back to Washington to work with you on this Batterman murder case."

"You know Fugiwara-san, it's going to take me a few days to get back in the grove in Washington, so why don't you take back those two days and make it a small vacation, and stay with your wife until Thursday when you have to report back to Washington to start work back on the Batterman's case." He offered the other agent, hoping to make him forget about their supposed talk about the case, and all he knew of Batterman's murder. He was still having some trouble on how he was going to start the story of the ancient female Samurai Warrior Wind.

"Man Rossie-san, that'd be real cool, are you sure you have the ability to give me back those two days I lost when Murdock called me back to Washington, sir?" Fugiwara questioned.

"Hey what can I tell you Fugiwara-san, I'm the Lead Agent on this murder case, and I think I'm more than able to set the rules on how I want to conduct this investigation? So I believe I can tell you to take those two days back if I see we're going to be down for a little while before we can get going on the case again. Tomorrow I'm going to end up wasting most of the stinking day reporting to Murdock, and you know how he is all the damn time. He's going to want to know everything, even right down to how many times we went to the damn bathroom every day. He's a real stickler when it comes down to making a report to him as you well know, Fugiwara-san. So if I'm going to lose all day Tuesday meeting with Murdock, and I'm probably going to lose most of Wednesday setting up our office again in Patterson's office. Why the hell wouldn't you take those two days back and enjoy your lady and kids for a little while, Fugiwara-san.

"You know once we start work again in Washington, we can sure as hell kiss good-bye any real time off until we can clear up this damn murder case. So you might as well take advantage with any time I'm able to cut you when I can make that time available to you my friend. Yes, take those two days back and I'll clear it with Murdock when I meet with him tomorrow morning, Fugiwara-san." Agent Rossie announced as he smiled again at his other agent.

"Man, I really owe you one for giving me back those two days, Rossie-san. You certain you'll be able to clear it with Murdock, I mean superseding his authority by you giving me those two days back, Rossie-san?" Fugiwara asked his lead with concern lacing his tone of voice.

"What the hell can I tell you Fugiwara-san, once you're on your way to Jersey, I don't see how in the devil he could possibly override me and call you back down to Washington? I don't think he couldn't be that big a prick to order you back here. But I have to warn you once you're back in Washington, I can't guarantee how he's going to treat you, buddy. He might take it out on your ass for us not talking it over with him first, before you reclaimed those two days off you got back." He warned the other agent with a smirk.

"It's like you said Rossie-san, once I'm on my two day vacation, who gives a shit how he's going to react when I report back to work on Thursday. What can he do, take my birthday from me for crap sake." Fugiwara responded, now looking forward to getting those two days off back.

"Knowing Murdock like I do, he just might take your birthday away from you my friend."

"So what, by then I wouldn't really give a damn what he might do to my ass, just as long as I had those two days back, Rossie-san."

Rossie laughed over Fugiwara's response, but they were speaking together for so long they did not realized how long until the pilot of the private aircraft announced for everyone to retake their seats and buckle in for landing. The pilot further said they should be landing within the next half an hour in Washington. Agent Rossie looked at the other agent, and they both started to laugh again, pleased they were almost back to their home base of operations in Washington.

FBI HEADQUARTERS, WASHINGTON D.C.
SEVENTEEN HUNDRED TWENTY HOURS (7:20P.M.)

When the aircraft landed, a dispatched FBI vehicle pulled up to the plane and the agent got out, and waited for the two agents to debark the aircraft. When Rossie and Fugiwara were in the vehicle, the car took off and drove over to FBI Headquarters in Washington. Rossie got out of the vehicle first and he waited for Fugiwara, once he was out of the car, Rossie ordered him.

"Okay Fugiwara-san, here is where we part company for a little while. I know your private vehicle is parked in the rear parking lot of the complex, so go get your car and take off for Jersey as fast as you can leave the area my friend. I'll inform the Agent on Duty that we both have arrived safely back in Washington and because it's so late, we both are heading home for the night and will report to Murdock's office by 10 A.M. tomorrow morning. So take off before Murdock sees you out here and orders the both of us up to his office. See you Thursday, give my best to your wife and kids for me, and have a good couple days off, Fugiwara-san."

Agent Shinnosuke Fugiwara left Rossie as he entered the first floor of the FBI Headquarters and he went right over to the main desk and reported to the Agent on Duty. He informed the agent they both returned and were going home for the night.

The young Desk Agent immediately informed Agent Rossie he had orders to inform Commander Murdock the moment he and Agent Fugiwara reported in at headquarters tonight, causing Rossie to ask the Desk Agent. "Hey man, please don't tell me Murdock was working late tonight while waiting for them to report in." It would be just like the Commander to work later and then expect him to report in and start his report to the Commander this late at night.

"That's right Agent Rossie Sir, Commander Murdock is working late and he's expecting you to come to his office the moment you checked in with me sir."

"Shit, what the hell am I to do now for crap sake?" Agent Rossie used one of Murdock's favorite phases and he stared at the Desk Agent.

"Err... Agent Rossie Sir, as far as I'm concerned, you didn't check in with me yet sir, because you didn't sign in on the long book before you started speaking with me sir. So if you turned and got your ass the hell out of here toot sweet then there's no way in hell I can possibly inform the Commander you reported in tonight as expected, sir. All you have to do is just avoid signing in the log book and then turn and run the hell outta here, sir. I'll never inform Commander Murdock you were here and didn't report in to him as ordered, sir."

"That's some damn good advice there Lieutenant, and that's exactly what I intend to do now sir. Color my ass gone until tomorrow morning. I owe you a bottle of good wine, Lieutenant." Rossie said as he turned on his heels and was already walking away from the Desk Agent.

What Agent Rossie had no idea of was, Commander Ralph Murdock just happened to be looking out his third floor window, and he easily noticed Agent Rossie quickly exiting the building and rushing for his parked car in the rear of the building and he smiled. Because he saw his agent was not going to report to him until the following morning. Something he was going to order Rossie to do anyway, once he reported to his office as he was ordered to do. He was going to forgive Agent Rossie's minor insubordination act and let it go at that.

Commander Murdock smiled to himself as he started to turn out the lights of his office then he prepared to leave the building himself. Please he had such a good bunch of loyal and hard working agents under his command, even though most of them always gave him more trouble than his two young sons did. He was still smiling over Rossie's minor act of defiance as he waited for the elevator so he could leave the building for the night himself.

AGENT ROBERT ROSSIE'S APARTMENT IN DOWNTOWN WASHINGTON D.C.

Agent Rossie could not wait to get back to his apartment he actually sped for home. It took him fifteen minutes instead of the usual twenty minutes to drive from FBI Headquarters to his apartment. He charged up the stairs, opened his door and actually ran into the apartment and threw his one bag of luggage on the sofa, and then rushed over to the closet where he hid Wind's deadly and ancient Katana killing blade. He did not breath properly again until he felt the Kashira or pommel of the sword. He smiled when his hand wrapped around the handle and he pulled the sword free of the closet. He hurried over to the sofa, shoved the one piece of luggage out of his way with his hand then sat down and began to free the ancient sword of its wooden prison.

The sword once again smelled of being ancient and actually rotting, but as soon as the metal of the great blade slid out of the scabbard. The sword instantly started to vibrate slightly in his hand as he dropped the discarded scabbard down on the sofa behind him, not realizing it was rapidly returning to the newness of when it was first created by the master craft workers of old Japan. This time he stared at the sword and was amazed at how it was so quickly returning to its newness right before his eyes. Under his hand he could actually feel the fine braded decorated cord returning to the pommel of the sword as if he was holding onto a hand full of worms, as the rust, nicks and marring scratches sort of melted away from the sword and biting edge, and the almost blinding gleam of the metal returned to the blade of the sword.

As quickly as the sword returned to its newness, the light began to appear in the center of the living room of the agent. His eyes left the sword as he concentrated on the light developing almost at the ends of his feet. He found himself staring at the rapidly growing light as if it had captured and locked his attention to the building, bubbling light. The light grew in its intensity to where he had to shade his eyes from the power of the light. Then as if the light could grow no more, the intensity started to lessen and coolness replaced the heat from the light, the light grew less threatening and the coolness made his blood pressure lessen. Then, as the light turned into a light glow, the sweet, almost song like voice of the ancient female Samurai Warrior spoke to the new master of the sword, and the spirit that was attached to the metal of the deadly sword.

"What is my Master's new bidding? Is there a Teki (Enemy) you wish vanquished my Lord? Is there a new war threatening your domain my Master? I am here to serve all my Master's wants and desires without the slightest hesitation and Toda Cha, total loyalty my Lord."

"Wind-san, I wish to see your true form, your true being immediately, Warrior!"

"If you walk backwards, you will never stub your toe, but you will never arrive at your true destination my Lord. Your wish is my command my Master of time everlasting. I shall rush my spirit to your presence as quickly as I can do as you have ordered me my Master. Everything from the Universe comes out of the Nothing. Nothing, the nameless is the true beginning. Follow the Nothingness of the Yoa, and you will surely be just like it, not needing anything, seeing the world as the root of everything my Master." Wind offered, quoting her Zen training.

"Never mind all that usual babble of yours you keep quoting at me, just do as I ordered you and appear before me at once, Wind-san! I want to see your solid form now, Wind-san." Agent Rossie actually demanded of the ancient spirit of the female Samurai Warrior.

"As you have ordered me, I now appear before my honored and most powerful Lord and Master." Wind replied as the light completely faded and left the beautiful female Samurai Warrior kneeling in the center of the small living room as naked as the day she was born.

"That's much better Wind-san. It's very comforting for me to see you whole and before me once again, Wind-san. I'm sorry I had to leave you dwelling within the Floating World for so long a period of time, but as I told you. I was called away by my work and there was no way for me to possibly allow you to remain in the living world while I was away from your side, Wind-san. It gives me great pleasure for me to see you again, Wind-san." Agent Rossie smiled at the extremely dangerous female Warrior from times long past.

"It is so kind of my wise Lord and Master to think of and be so concerned of me and to call me home from the very lonely Floating World of forever waiting, my Lord and Master of time. But I fear my Lord is in error with your words, it was only a small breath of the stick of time I waited in the Floating world for your call to have me come back to your side again, my Liege Lord.

"Well Wind-san I hate to tell you this, but what you're calling a small breath on the stick of time was almost six full days I was forced away from your side, Wind-san." Agent Rossie corrected, slightly upset Wind dared to correct him in any way.

"Please excuse me but day's my Liege Lord? I do not understand days I fear my Lord and Master. Please explain days to this most inconsiderate Warrior, my Liege Lord."

"Sorry Wind-san but days are what we modern people call what you call sticks of time, one day of my time equals one stick of your way of measuring a full cycle of the sun, Wind-san." Agent Rossie explained as he started to relax now that wind was back in his presence again.

"Oh, this very foolish Samurai Warrior now understands what a day is equal to in my time and belief, my wise Liege Lord. I shall commit a day to my memory, so if you ever refer to a day again in my presence. I shall understand what you are referring to my Liege Lord."

"You do that Wind-san!" He replied with a sort of snap in his tone of voice.

Wind responded by putting her head down and looking at the floor, fearing she had somehow just displeased her Lord and Master in some way.

Getting hold of his slight raise in his temper, Agent Rossie quickly got control of himself and then he asked the ancient female Samurai Warrior in a much calmer tone of voice this time. "Wind-san, do you hunger, are you thirsty and would you like to enjoy something to eat or drink or both, Wind-san. I am prepared to make you anything you might want to eat."

"My Lord is so considerate to this worthless Samurai. I fear I am always in thirst and suffering hunger when I return to the living world from the Floating World my Lord. It would please me so if you would allow this worthless person to enjoy what you call cheese, if I remember correctly my Liege Lord." After asking for something to eat from her Lord and Master, she immediately lowered her head again, fearing she might have just overstepped her bounds by asking her Liege Lord for anything, as if she had a right to ask anything of her powerful Liege Lord.

"I would be most please to prepare you some slices of cheese which is the correct way to request it from me, and would you enjoy a cup of tea, pardon me, a cup of Cha, Wind-san? It's nothing at all for me to prepare you a quick cup of Cha for your enjoyment if you want, Wind-san." He offered the extremely dangerous Warrior from Japan's great past history.

Wind bowed her head politely as she replied. "My Liege Lord, I would truly enjoy a cup of Cha. It has been many sticks of time since the last time I enjoyed a cup of Cha. My last Lord and Master made the Cha so sweet to enjoy, he must have allowed his finger to dangle in the Cha to sweeten it so I believe, my Liege Lord." She offered her new master kindly.

"I'm sorry Wind-san, but I believe your other Master must had sweetened your Cha with what we call sugar in this time. I shall sweeten your Cha in the same manner as he did, Wind-san. What, you suddenly look so stressed out, what is bothering you now Wind-san?" He asked, again not realizing how much Japanese he was speaking and understanding, every time Wind was in his presence, as he waited for her to reply to his last question of her.

"One in all, all in one, if only this is realized then no more worry about not being perfect. I fear my Lord is correct and I am stressed. It is I who should be preparing the meal and cups of Cha for us to enjoy. My Lord, the only time in a true Samurai's life when he wishes to make a cup of Cha for his lover is during the Cha ceremony. When the Samurai is trying to make amends with his mate, or he is seeking to make her with baby. Is that what my new Lord wishes of me, to make me with baby, my Liege Lord?" She was unable to hide the quick smile that crossed her lips, before she was able to cover her mouth with the back of her hand. In ancient Japan, the only time any Japanese person bared his or her teeth to another is during times of war or fighting. It was a terrible insult to bare one's teeth or drink in a clear cup before another Japanese person.

"Wind-san, it does not matter to me who prepares the tea, err... Cha or any snacks for the both of us to enjoy. To tell you the truth, I actually like preparing these minor tasks for the both of us. Here in my time these tasks are done by both male and females, and it does not take away from the male to prepare something for his mate to enjoy, Wind-san." Agent Rossie said to her.

"My Liege Lord, is that what I am to you, your mate my Master? If I am your mate then I shall be happy beyond words and thoughts for you honor me beyond honors. To make the Wind and the Rain is the answer to life." She offered as she smiled up at her new owner of her sword.

"Wind-san, you look tired fatigued, what is wrong with you?"

"I am tired my Liege Lord and I thank you for seeing that. I am weak because I do not have contact with my Katana sword, my Master." She let her breath out in a rush.

"Well why didn't you tell me you had to have contact with your sword, Wind-san? Is this necessary all the time?" He asked the female Samurai Warrior with concern.

"My Lord and Master, I must remain in contact with my sword when I first come from the Floating World, until I get used to the living world again. Once I am comfortable in the living world, I no longer have to remain in constant contact with my killing Katana blade, as long as I am near enough to draw my energy from the great blade, my Liege Lord."

"Then by all means, take the sword in your hands and hold onto it until you're comfortable in the living world again, Wind-san. I need you at your full power anytime you're visiting me from the Floating World. I have many questions to ask you of your past times, and how Hiromoai had used your outstanding skills of the Samurai to eliminate his competition in Japan. I want to know all about your life in both worlds you occupy. So many questions I have to ask of you Wind-san." Agent Rossie mumbled as he could not help himself and he found he was staring at her.

"I shall be most pleased to tell you of my life in both worlds, and of my past times, my most honorable Liege Lord. I enjoyed my life in the past as savage as it was. The only regret I have was being born a lowly female, if I was born a male then all the doors that were closed to me as a female of the time, would have been flung opened, and I would have been happily welcome to walk through them and become a great and honorable Samurai Warrior. The women of ancient Japan were there to take care of our Samurai husbands, look after his daily and spiritual needs and always be ready for when he wanted to pillow with you.

"The female always controlled the money for her honorable husband, because it was beneath a true Samurai Warrior to dirty his hands by handling any money or money matters for his household. The Samurai husband had the right to beat his foolish wife and to also sell her to pay a debt, or if he decided he no longer wanted her he could just banish her to the Willow World. The Willow World is where women wanted to catch an eye of a power land owner, or honored Samurai she wants to attain to the first branch of the Willow. That would mean she would only have to serve the highest standing Daimyo or the Provincial Lord or anyone of high standing of the time. Becoming his first consort or acting wife when he was bored of his wife, or wanted to enjoy the pillowing abilities of another woman.

"If the husband was of mean spirit, he would give his wife to the owner of the Willow and the Mama-san would start her on the fifth branch of the Willow, servicing the sexual needs of the lower class and Heimin or commoners of the Japanese people. She would have to work until the Mama-san felt she had worked long enough to raise her to the fourth branch of the Willow. And then she could work her way all the way up to the first branch of the Willow if she is that good at the art of pillowing. But if she was not good enough to rise from the fifth branch then the Mama-san would order the unlucky ex-wife to servicing the leapers who always have money. But once she is forced to service the leapers, the poor wife will be thought of as unclean and she could never service any other but the leapers, until she is infected by that terrible infection.

"As I offered my Lord, the life of a woman was harsh and at the whim of her Master, Kazoku or the Nobility, husband, or any other male who dominated her spirit. But in my case, my father hid the fact I was of the female line and he trained me beyond durance, making me the best of the best and I won a place in my Lord's Army as General. I proved myself on the battlefield many times and fought side by side by my male Samurai under my Command. I ended up being well honored by my Lord and many of the General's in his Army. But there were always those few angry Generals and lesser Officers who wagged their tongues against me. Some were ordered to commit Suppuku by Kawasomeru-Sama because they were discovered talking insubordination, but at the end as I had once explained to you my Lord. The Shogun ordered his Kebiishi General given the extremely important appointment who is concerned with the arrest and punishment of officials, and this General was sent to your vast encampment with direct orders from the Shogun.

"His order was to bring peace between the two houses of Central Japan, your most noble of houses my Lord Takehiro Kawasomeru and that house of the dog eating foul Lord Motoshige Wakatsuki. He was ordered to bring peace between the two warring Lord of the land and if no peace could be reached, this General was ordered to take the head of the one Lord who would not make peace, or both heads if neither warlord could make peace with the other. Lord Wakatsuki finally relented and offered peace with one condition attached to the offer of peace. He demanded the head of your General who killed his General and that head was mine. That was why you removed my head and cursed my soul and spirit to that of your deadly killing Katana sword.

"That is why I now kneel before my Master of the sword and my Toda-Cha, my Total Loyalty is offered to you and to fulfill every wish and desire, my Liege Lord." She announced proudly as she bowed politely to who she called her Lord and Master.

"Here is your Cha and the cheese you seem to like so much lately Wind-san, and thank you for sharing some of your past lifetime with me. But I'm quite certain I'll have a number of other questions to ask you about your past life. Also what Hiromoai had you do for him since he first found and called you to him from the Floating World, Wind-san. I too am hungry, but I was more interested in getting home and called you back from the Floating World. Please, enjoy what I have prepared for you to enjoy. I want to take a quick shower and get out of my clothes."

Again, Wind bowed politely to Agent Rossie as she watched him put the food and tea on the side table, and then he rushed into the bathroom. She sipped her tea then she rose and went to her small section her new Lord gave her in the hallway closet, and she removed her green Kimono with the gold Obi tie, and then she snuck into the bathroom and laid the Kimono down on the sink for her Master's use. She then returned to enjoying her tea and cheese.

She just got comfortable kneeling on the floor and enjoying her Cha when she heard the water in the shower go off, and she knew her Liege Lord just finished his shower. She tensed up but did not understand why she was feeling this emotion. She wanted to be with him, and even pillow with him tonight, so she wondered why she was tense now.

Agent Rossie came out of the bathroom still tying the Obi around his waist and smiling pleasantly then he said to the ancient female Samurai Warrior. "Wind-san, I take it you had laid out this Kimono out for my use, it's wonderful, beautiful and I thank you for the kind gift. Are you lending me this Kimono or is it a gift for me to keep, Wind-san?"

"Please allow this worthless Warrior to give my most honorable Lord and Master a gift for once, instead of you constantly showering me with great gifts I am far from worthy to enjoy and did not earn. I hope you realize you once gave me that Green Kimono for one of the many battles I had engaged in, when I defeated your hated Teki (Enemy) wherever they tried to hide from their fate my Lord. As you well know, Green with the gold Obi signifies your victory over your enemy my Liege Lord, and it is only proper that you enjoy the Kimono and your many victories you have enjoyed over you countless Teki of our past years my Lord." For the third time tonight, she bowed slightly to her new Master of her great killing blade.

"I thank you kindly for this great gift Wind-san, and I shall enjoy the Kimono, and the many victories I'm suddenly having ever since you have entered my life, Wind-san." With that said, he made such a big deal out of kneeling on the floor alongside Wind that she was actually forced to laugh because of how funny he smuggled to sit down, and he ended up falling over to the side because he somehow caught his foot on the hem of the Kimono.

CHAPTER TEN

Wind continued to laugh at her new Lord and Master, even though it was the height of bad manners, and a serious insult aimed against her new Master to dare laugh at him. But Agent Rossie rolled over on his side and continued to struggle to try and get his foot out of the hem of the Kimono, and this action caused him to roll further on the floor. As he rolled, the Kimono opened, exposing himself to Wind's enjoyment, and she laughed even harder this time.

"Instead of laughing like you are, how about trying to help me out here Wind-san. I have my toe caught in the silk and can't free it, I don't want to rip this wonderful gift you blessed me with tonight, Wind-san." He was also laughing and the more he laughed, the more she laughed as she got up and tried to catch his foot trapped in the exquisite silk fabric of the fine Kimono.

She did not care she was still naked as she got up and tried to help him, and he immediately stopped struggling so much as he took in the lovely vision of the naked beauty trying to catch his foot. He held his foot still and she carefully unfolded the few layers of silk fabric he wrapped around his foot and she released his foot. He suddenly reached up and pulled her down to the floor with him. Immediately, his hands were all over her breasts and then his mouth found the hard nipple of her right breast, and he started to draw the nipple into his mouth and ran his tongue over it. Causing her to laugh with desires this time. He was so full with the want to please her that his hands, mouth and lips were now all over her rock hard body. But when his head got down between her legs, this time she wrapped her legs around his head, actually locking his head between her legs and he went to town driving her wild with desire.

She arched her back to give him easier access so his searching tongue could easily find her small pearl of pleasure, and when he hit the spot she arched her back even more and then her entire body shivered and she relaxed her back as she moaned softly and closed her eyes.

He realized she just came but he had no intention of letting her off so easily as he continued working on the pearl of love, making her getting caught up for a second time with the pleasure he was giving her. He actually pushed one of her legs wider apart and then he did something she had never experienced before in her endless life. He suddenly stuck out his tongue and he vibrated it and did what the modern day man called giving her a bronskie and spraying spittle over the sides of her thighs, but the vibrations was driving her to new heights of sexual pleasure.

She could not help herself and she opened her legs wider to the desires he was awaking in her body. She was so enjoying what he was doing to her she was holding her eyes closed so tightly that a tear escaped her eyes and she shivered again. This time much more powerful and for a longer period of time. Once she finished shivering, she sort of collapsed on the floor and lied still for a few seconds. He got out from between her legs and slowly slid his body up the length of her sweat coated body. Kissing every single inch of her exquisite body as he worked his way up to her lips, and then he stretched his chin and kissed her first on the forehead then he kissed both of her eyes, and kissed the tip of her nose then he planted a tongue to tongue kiss in her mouth. She loved when they kissed with their tongues like this.

For a moment, he laid his full weight on her body and he enjoyed her rapid breathing, and the slight shivering she was still doing, and he felt she was still enjoying what pleasure he just brought to her. She was struggling to get her breathing under control, but her mind kept reliving what her new lover was doing to her body, and each time she remembered it, she would shiver with a new wave of slightly coming. She still held her eyes shut tight as shooting stars filled the darkness of her eyes, and she placed a smile of sheer pleasure crossed her lips.

He was giving her a few moments to enjoy what he just did to her body, as he lightly ran the very tips of his hand ever so lightly over her nipple. Making her still sweat soaked body shiver with this new experience of him so slightly tickling her by what he was doing to her. She just could not get enough of the vast amount of pleasure her new lover was able to bring her with just his lips, tongue and fingertips. She found herself quickly falling in love with this young and very good looking man with round, blue eyes who was naked, and his rock hard body was pressed so tightly up against her body. Without thinking about it, she suddenly reached out and wrapped her fingers around his throbbing shaft, and this brought a groan of pleasure from him this time.

Hearing the slight moan of pleasure from him, snapped her into action and she pushed him flat on his back on the floor, and she untied his Obi and pulled his Kimono opened and smiled when she saw his member standing at attention and demanding pleasure from her. Now it was her turn and she kissed him on the lips then she kissed his chin, and his neck and she slowly dragged her tongue down his neck and across his chest and when she found his nipple, she kissed it, ran her tongue over it and she drew his nipple into her mouth much like he just did to her. With each pass of her tongue over his nipple, she could feel his body jerk slightly and she knew she was bringing him great pleasure now, and this made her do more to him.

She left his nipple and ran her tongue down the center of his breastbone, ever so slowly working her way to his twitching member as it was now caught up between her breasts as her tongue left his breastbone, and she worked her way towards his belly button. Now, every thought in her mind was aimed at bringing her new lover the same amount of pleasure he just gave her. When she found his belly button, she actually dipped her tongue in it and wiggled it around the tiny pool of sweat, and for the first time he arched his back and moved his rearend to the rhythm of her tongue as he let out another slight moan. But this one was much louder and longer than the one a moment before and it increased her want to please her Master all the more.

She left his belly button and slid her tongue from one hip to the other as she still slowly worked her way towards his waiting shaft caught up under her chin. Now his own passion was driving him and he suddenly rested his hands on her head and put slight pressure on her, as he tried to guide her mouth to his swaying shaft. But she would have none of it as she fought off the pressure he was placing on her head, and she continued to run her tongue around in tiny circles just about his pubic hair line. Now she had him squirming all around as he wiggled his rearend and was trying to move his hips so his shaft would find her mouth on its own.

She entered his pubic hair line with her searching tongue and for the first time, the tip of her tongue ran lightly over the very tip of his waiting shaft. This caused him to actually jump and then he arched his back as he tried to use his hips to help guide his dick into her mouth. But her tongue was already by the side of his hip and working its way back across his lower belly, and when she ran her tongue over the shaft just below the head, he again grabbed her head and held it tight as he suddenly thrust his hips up and then tried to force his member into her mouth. Once poking her in the eye, and then hitting her nose with the tip of his shaft. This caused her to smile and laugh as he cried to her in a rather constricted tone of voice.

"C'mon Wind, take it in your mouth before you make me explode with the wait for Pete's sake. I want to feel your mouth around my shaft dammit. You're driving me absolutely crazy with your act of pillowing this time. C'mon and get to it and do me right so I can enjoy all your pleasures Wind-san!" He pleaded to the extremely dangerous female Warrior.

"Hummmm, I never realized my new Lord and Master would be so inpatient to receive the pleasure from this worthless...' Her words were cut off when he suddenly pushed his hips down and then he forced himself into her mouth. Immediately she repeated as best she could with his member planted in her mouth. "Hummmmm." As she hummed, giving him even more pleasure, because the hum caused her mouth to vibrate over his shaft. He now had both his hands resting on the top of her head as he put light pressure and forcing her to take more of him deeper into her mouth as she continued to hum as she went up and down on his shaft.

Now she was surprised over what she was doing to her new owner of the sword, especially since she had only allowed a man's member in her mouth a few times in her life, and yet she was doing him like she was an expert at the act. With the pressure he was placing on her head and the moving of his hips to the motion of her mouth and tongue, was starting to drive her just as crazy as she was driving him in. She started to increase her tempo with her mouth sliding up and down the length of his thickening shaft. Almost as fast as she started to give him pleasure with her mouth, he released and then they both collapsed with her ending up resting her head lightly on his stomach. A smile crossed her lips, she enjoyed the great pleasure she just gave her Lord.

"That was absolutely wonderful Wind-san. You have made me happy beyond happiness."

"I am pleased you have drawn pleasure at my poor attempt to relieve you of the pressures of the day my Liege." She offered to Rossie still have a little problem with getting his breathing under control as he stared at her head being lifted up and then down by his stomach movements.

"You have successfully removed all the pressures I have suffered for this entire day and many more to come I believe, Wind-san. I thank you for the unbelievable enjoyment you have just showered me with on this night..." He was saying when she interrupted his words and added.

"I assure most honorable my Liege Lord, there shall be countless days and nights when I will bring you great pleasures to relieve you of the day's stresses my Lord and Master." She replied as she lifted her head from his stomach, and she looked directly into his eyes and gave him one of her best smiles as she also struggled to get her own breathing under control.

"Of that I'm certain of, Wind-san, and I shall wait with baited breath for those pleasures to be enjoyed by me." He added, trying to be as polite and phrasing Wind as she was doing to him.

She stood, and then rushed into the bathroom and he could hear the water running and just as quick she returned to his side, and she was washing his softening member with warm water and soap. All the while she cleaned him off she smiled and considered herself so lucky to have such a young and very caring new Master of her deadly killing sword.

He had to suddenly fight with himself because he was enjoying her cleaning him so much he was getting so relaxed he was having trouble staying awake. When she finished he got up on one elbow and watched her scurry back into the bathroom and he heard the water running again and realized she was washing herself this time. He decided to get up and slip back into the exquisite Kimono Wind gave him earlier in the night, but he never used the "Obi to keep the fine silk garment closed. Then he sat at the table and waited for her to finish up in the bathroom.

She rushed out of the bathroom still naked and looking absolutely stunning, she smiled when she saw her Liege Lord wearing the gift she gave him. Then she looked around the living room for her own Kimono she left before laying over the arm of the sofa when he was forced to send her back to the Floating World for almost the entire week. Finding it she did as her new Master of the sword did, and never picked up her Obi to help hold her exquisite Kimono closed, and then she sat down across from her Liege Lord and waited to see if he wanted to speak with her.

"Wind-san, I can't tell you how much I was dying to get back to my apartment so I could call you to the land of the living from the Floating World. You were my every thought while I was working in Denver. I wanted to get back to you so I could hear more of your life, and what Hiromoai forced you to do under his command. I wanted so much to pillow with you another night, and for countless nights to come. I have no want of another woman as long as you're with me. I think I'm lucky to have found you, and want to share time with you. From now on the only time you'll be sent to the Floating World is when you have to sort of say recharge your batteries,"

She had no idea what he meant by her needing to recharge her batteries, but she dared not interrupt his words at this time. She knew later on she would inquire what he meant by that phase as she settled in and listened to every word her new Lord and Master was saying to her.

"And when I have to leave Washington to work in another state, those are the only two times you'll ever be forced to revisit the lonely land of the spirits. I promise you if I have to leave the state for any long length of time, I'll take your sword with me so I can call you back to the land of the living much quicker, and then we can again share some valuable time together. But you must remember at all times, you have to stay completely out of sight whenever I have company visiting me. I don't want anyone to know of you until I find a way to introduce you to just certain people I want you to meet. Your presence is going to be extremely hard for me to try and explain to anyone who is as important to me as you are all of a sudden, Wind-san."

"I assure my Lord and Master, I understand the importance of keeping my presence a secret from the rest of your allies. What better way to protect one's self than to have such a weapon as I held in reserve, just in case you come under attack by any of your hated Teki, my honorable Liege Lord." She replied confidently to her new Master of life and death over her.

"I thank you for that understanding Wind-san, that'll make my life all that much easier to carry out with you understanding why I must do certain things to keep you secret from all others until I'm ready to announce to the rest of the world about your presence from the Floating World, Wind-san. Are you still hungry or thirsty, especially after our pillowing?" He asked her.

"Yes my Lord and Master, I am in thirst and also hungry and could stand to eat more of the food of the living again." She replied and then she smiled at him again.

"Well then my dear lady, allow me to tell you that you're in for some treat then. I'm going to order you a Pizza to enjoy, and though I know you have no idea what a Pizza is, the only thing I can tell you is, you'll really enjoy the meal I shall order for your enjoyment."

"This foolish Samurai Warrior has no need for any explanation from my honorable Liege Lord. If your breath says I shall enjoy the meal you are willing to prepare for me. Then that is more than enough explanation I need to hear from your lips my Lord and Master." She replied rapidly without thought, because she had that much confidence in her Master's word.

"Take it from me Wind-san, you're in for a treat tonight, but I must correct you though. It is not I who prepared the Pizza for us. I just have to make a phone call and order it, and it'll be delivered to our door by someone who has prepared the meal for us to enjoy." Rossie offered.

"Then this worthless person shall wait patiently for our meal to arrive, so I can enjoy what my Lord has offered me to enjoy on this night as you call the closing hours of the cock's call. I must say, I truly enjoy seeing the smile that is upon your lips over your want to please this worthless Warrior who does not deserve to be so honored by her Liege Lord like this. Once again you shower this most unworthy of Warriors with gifts she does not truly deserve to enjoy."

They both waited for the Pizza to arrive and when the knock on the door happened, she instantly rose and rushed into the bathroom and closed the door behind her. She did not know which room to run into to hide and she did not dare enter her Master's room without permission so she chose the bathroom. Then she waited for her Lord to call her out of the room.

Agent Rossie paid for the Pizza and then put it down on the table and called out. "Wind-san, our meal has arrived." Then he waited and when she walked out of the bathroom and sat at the table, he placed a piece on a plate and offered it to her. She stared at the unknown food, not liking the looks of it, but she also found the smell of it offensive to her as well. She watched him as he picked up his piece of Pizza with oil dripping on his hand, as he turned his head to the side and chomped off the tip of the ugly looking food and happily began to chew it.

He saw Wind was not eating and he remarked at her. "C'mon Wind-san, pick it up like I did and enjoy it. I'm telling you, you'll enjoy it."

Now she found herself locked in a no win situation, she could not insult her Lord by not eating the food he offered for her enjoyment, but her mind and Samurai training was telling her not to eat the food, because anything this ugly and smelling so bad could not be good for her to eat. She knew her Master would not have went through this much trouble just to kill her, all he had to do was order her commit Suppuku, and she would be honor bound to carry out the sacred act of killing herself under his command. Even though she would only die in her earthly form until he again called her back from the Floating World to live further in the living world.

The only true way for her Lord and Master to completely destroy her spirit was if he snapped the sword in half, and he never allowed the two ends of her sword to once again be mated, because that would allow her spirit to return to the great blade once it was one again.

Not knowing what to do, she suddenly drew in a deep breath and then copied the way he was eating the foul smelling food. To her surprise, the food was fantast, and she found herself really enjoying it though the smell was still hard for her to conquer.

He smiled over the way Wind gobbled down the slice of Pizza, and then he offered her a second slice and she took it greedily. By the time they finished their meal it was late and they were exhausted, they both shared his bed and woke when the alarm clock rang. He showered, ate and then informed Wind she had full reign of the apartment, but she was not allowed to answer the door or leave the apartment for any reason accept for fire. Then he left for work.

FBI COMMANDER RALPH MURDOCK'S OFFICE, WASHINGTON D.C.
ZERO EIGHT THIRTY HUNDERD HOURS, TUESDAY JUNE 18th, 1996

FBI Special Agent Robert Rossie walked into Murdock's office half an hour early for reporting for work, and he plopped down in the chair across from his desk and announced to his Commander. "Agent Rossie reporting in to inform my Commander the trip to Denver was a complete waste of time and effort, sir. We found nothing, but I do have a very slim lead where I have to interview one Thomas Montgomery. It was reported to me by the Company Lawyer that this man was deemed a serious threat to Calvin Batterman's life. I tried to make contact with Mr. Montgomery, but his secretary reported he was visiting Washington on a business trip, that's why we left Denver for Washington early, so I can interview this Montgomery fellow sir."

Commander Murdock suddenly looked around his office, and then he returned his attention on Rossie and snapped at his agent. "Where the hell is your damn partner in crime at for crap sake, that damn Nip Agent I assigned to your lousy investigation of Batterman's murder, mister?"

"I'm sorry I didn't report the fact I allowed Agent Fugiwara-san to pick up the two days of leave time he had coming to him that you erased when you called him in to act as my second on this investigation, Ralph." He offered to his command agent.

"What's this damn 'San' crap from you all about? I think you've been hanging around all these damn Nips for too long because you're starting to speak just like them, mister. And for crap sake who the hell gave you permission to reinstate Agent Fugiwara's two days off I took away from his ass anyway, buster? I'm the only one who can give you people any extra leave time in case you don't understand that fact as yet, Agent Rossie." Murdock growled at his agent.

Rossie smirked as he replied. "I understand that Commander, but I figured it was going to take me the rest of this day to report how it went for us in Denver, and then for me to make contact with this Montgomery fellow, and then meet with him tomorrow some time sir. I believe by the time I finish interviewing this man, it would've killed most of the day tomorrow, and I figured what the hell and I gave Agent Fugiwara-san his two days off back sir."

"Yeah, I see what you mean mister, and perhaps you did the wise thing after all Agent Rossie. I guess I'll let this one go for the time being, but Agent Fugiwara is going to pay like hell for those two days you gave him off. I have a good mind to take two day's pay from your ass to pay for his added two days of holiday, mister. Okay, give me your verbal report on how it went and what you two birds did all the time you killed off in Denver and how much this vacation in Denver cost the company, and then I want the hard copy in my office by the end of the week, mister. Okay, start with your damn report, I'm listening mister!"

"Well Commander Murdock, the first thing we did when we made it to Denver, was to grab ourselves something to eat sir." Agent Rossie gave Ralph the look.

"Yeah, yeah, yeah I picked up the damn message you're trying to shove down my damn throat. Yeah, let's go and get something to eat, I'm kind of hungry myself mister. We can continue with your verbal report when we return from breakfast. Let's shove off, mister."

Rossie followed the Commander to the cafeteria and ordered breakfast and chatted amongst themselves. As angry as the Commander was acting, Rossie knew it was bluster bombing and he was happy to have his two agents back without either of them getting hurt or wounded while they were in Denver. When they returned to Murdock's office he ended Rossie's report by remarking to him. "Keep your verbal report to yourself. I want you to get back to your office, get it set up the way you want it. From this time forward that's going to be your office. I think I'll move Patterson to the second floor and he can have his pick of three offices to work out of down there. He's such a pain in the ass to work with and the less I see of him the better I'll like it, mister.

"When your vacationing Agent reports in for work, I want you two pests working out of that office for the rest of this Batterman case. What I want you to do for the rest of today is, I want you to make contact with this prick some lawyer told you to make contact with. Find out his story and see if he might have had something to do with this case, Agent Rossie. I have everyone who knows about Batterman's murder breathing down the back of my neck for the week, while you two birds were living it up in Denver. I want the two of you working on this murder case day and night if necessary, because I need this case ended ten minutes ago, buster. Get going Rossie!"

He got up and rushed out of the Commander's office and charged for his new office three rooms away from Murdock's main office. He opened the lock and moved in and went to his desk and checked his inbox to see of anything came in on Batterman's case while he was in Denver. There were no new leads for him to check out, so he next checked his phone messages. One was from Agent Fugiwara and he listened to that message. "Hey Rossie-san, did the pain in the ass Murdock stop chewing on your ass yet for giving me back those two days off, my friend. I can't tell you what it means to my wife and I to have these two days back. Somehow I'll make it up to you for this deal. I'll see you on Thursday morning and then we can get back down to business over this damn murder case, Rossie-san, and thanks again for the two days off my friend."

He smiled as he erased this message, and he checked the next one and he was surprised to hear this message. It was from Montgomery's secretary and she informed him she made contact with her boss and told him the FBI Agent was going to be calling him. So now her boss was waiting for the agent's call. He did not erase this message as he skipped to the next one, the rest of the messages did not concern the case he was working on, so he sent them to his save file in his computer then he ended checking his phone, computer or any other communication system.

Still tired from the night before festivities and the stress of meeting with Murdock, he leaned back in his chair and closed his eyes for a few moments to collect his thoughts and rest his eyes. As he was resting his phone rang and he allowed the answering machine to field the call for him. It was for Agent Fugiwara and the case he was working on before Murdock pulled him off that case to work with him on the Batterman's murder. He was pleased with himself because he allowed the machine to answer the call for him. After about fifteen minutes of resting he leaned forward in his chair, and then he went fishing around for the slip of paper that he wrote Montgomery's number on. Finding it he reached for the phone and dialed the number.

On the fifth ring a male answered the phone. "This is Montgomery, who is this and what do you want of me. I'm right in the middle of a meeting and don't have much time to bullshit on the damn phone. Who is this and what do you want from me?"

"Good morning Mr. Montgomery sir, this is FBI Special Agent Robert Rossie, and I'd like to set up a meeting between the two of us so I speak with you about Mr. Calvin Batterman, sir..."

"Why the hell do you want to talk to me about that sonofabitch for? I really hate the lousy big bastard. I think he needs a swift kick right in the damn nuts if you were to ask me, sir. Did the rotten prick fuck you over like he fucked me and about a half a dozen other people over, Mr. Rossie. What the hell did he do this time to get the damn Fed's up his ass for, mister?"

"I hate to be the one who has to inform you of this fact Mr. Montgomery Sir, but Mr. Batterman was murdered while he was visiting Japan, sir."

"You know something Mr. FBI Agent I'm not the least bit surprised that someone killed the lousy bastard. I'm only surprised it took some Jap bastard to do the rotten bastard in for all of us. All he ever did in his stinking life was fuck people over and steal their money and destroy them or their damn companies. He was a real scumbag to deal with sir, work with and be around I tell you Mr. Agent Man." Montgomery snorted into the phone with the FBI Agent.

"It doesn't seem to me that you have any love lost with is death, Mr. Montgomery Sir?"

"No love lost over his fucking murder, I only wish I could've gotten my damn hands around his neck for a minute, I would've saved a Jap all the trouble of murdering him in Japan, sir."

"Be that as it may Mr. Montgomery Sir, I'd still like to set up a meeting with you to discuss a number of problems maybe you can help me get straight about Mr. Batterman and his death, pardon me, murder, sir. It's absolutely imperative that we meet and speak together. I'd hate like hell to be forced to swear out a warrant forcing you to come down to my office and make a full statement about your work relationship with Mr. Batterman and his company, sir. Right at this point I'm more than willing to meet with you at any place you desire to meet, but if you give me any trouble about meeting with me, I'd be forced to go the warrant route on you sir."

"Whoa, calm down a little Mr. Agent Man, I'll be happy to meet with you any time after tomorrow morning sir. I have a meeting scheduled at 9 A.M. tomorrow morning and it should last no longer than two hours, and then I have the rest of the day open, sir. Where and what time do you want to meet tomorrow morning sir?" Montgomery replied to Rossie's threat.

"I'm open tomorrow it's your pleasure when you want to meet, Mr. Montgomery?"

"We can meet at O'Graddies, it's an Irish Pud and it opens for lunch. We can meet there, talk and I'll even buy you lunch at the same time, Mr. Agent Man."

"That's O'Graddies on Fifth Avenue off Summer Street in downtown, am I correct sir."

"You got it Mr. Agent Man, let's say we'll meet there at quarter to twelve so we can talk and enjoy a meal at the same time sir." Montgomery replied and then waited for the agent's offer.

"Quarter to twelve, you got it Mr. Montgomery Sir. I'll see you tomorrow morning sir, and I thank you for taking the time to meet with me under these circumstances, sir."

"Yeah sure, I'll do anything to help out my friends in blue, sir." Montgomery came back with, not understanding the FBI did not dress in blue as Agent Rossie smiled over the remark, and then he hung up with the civilian contractor and let out his breath in a rush.

He happened to look at the clock and was surprised it was nearing noon already and he thought about returning to his apartment to see what Wind was up to, but then he thought better of that move and he pulled out the drawer and removed a slip of paper and began writing out a list of questions he was going to ask Montgomery when he met with the man tomorrow. Once he had his question written out longhand, he went to his computer and entered the questions into the machine so he could print them out and read them much easier than he could read his own hand writing. He knew he could have saved himself some time by using the computer first off, but he wanted to think of his questions first, and once he had them all worked out in his mind. Then he entered them into his computer and had them printed out for himself.

He then busied himself for the rest of the day checking out some of his thoughts, and what he knew of Batterman's murder. He easily understood what Hiromoai was doing by sending Wind out and having her slaughter all his competition in the field, but why would such a powerful Japanese businessman resort to killing anyone who gave him any competition in the construction field. He just could not believe it, Hiromoai had enough money to buy out any other construction company in all of Japan, and for him to resort to murder, just did not make any sense to him. He was stationed in Japan for over three years and he came to understand much of the way the most confusing Japanese people worked, believed and lived out their lives, and as savage as Japan's great past history was. They have come a long way and rarely if ever had to resort to murder to make any headway at what they were attempting to do for a living.

Yes, there was still many gangs operating in Japan, the Bosozoku or the biker gangs, their Kaminari Thunder Tribes and a mess of many different Yakuza or Gangsters, they rare killed with a pistol or sword any longer. Now they tried to kill their competition by hostile takeovers, buy out and a war of attrition by wearing down their competition by starving them out of work or money, having backs turn against the company. The Japanese employed a vast number of many different and novel ways of elimination their competition, but rarely did they employ weapons any longer. He thought to himself as he tried to figure out why Hiromoai had resorted to employ Wind to savagely murder off anyone who stood in his way to accomplish what he wanted on his mind, to become the most powerful construction company in all of Japan.

He returned home by 5 P.M. but he was in a somber mood, because he was deeply troubled with his upcoming meeting with Montgomery. He was concerned over the hatred the man held for Batterman and if he did not know Wind was the person who killed Batterman, Montgomery would head his list of suspected murderers. He enjoyed his meal with Wind and the fussing she was doing to try and get him out of his black mood. Then he announced he was going to bed and she followed him to the bedroom. Though they lied in bed together, there was no interest in pillowing from Rossie, so she made the best of it by hugging him close to her all night. Morning came and he was still in a funk and she did not know what to do to get him in a better mood.

He left barely saying good bye to her and he headed off for work, and he remained in a deep funk for the rest of the day until it was time for him to head off to meet with Montgomery. He checked for his list of questions for the man, and for the first time today, he smiled when he was certain he had the list with him, and then he headed off to meet with the construction man. He was still trying to get himself where he had to be to question the civilian.

THE O'GRADDIES PUB

FBI Special Agent Robert Rossie entered the slightly crowded pud at 11:30 A.M., fifteen minutes early for his meeting with Montgomery. He immediately searched the bar and noticed a table set well away from most of the rest and he headed for it and sat down, and no sooner than he was seated, a waitress came over and asked if he wanted anything from the bar or kitchen.

"I am waiting for someone to meet with me here, and once he arrives we'll order some drinks and food. I'm a bit early and he's due to arrive at a quarter to twelve. If someone comes in and asked for Mr. Rossie, please direct him over to my table, thank you. He handed her a five dollar bill, showing her she better pay attention to his table if she wanted a good tip from him.

She walked off smiling after promising him she would certainly direct anyone looking for him immediately over to his table as soon as they entered the bar.

He made himself busy by studying the many people crowding the bar, and he found himself trying to figure out what the person he was looking at did for work. Two of the young women he looked at, smiled back at him and one of them he thought was going to actually come over to his table until he looked away from her. For the fifth time he looked at his watch and it was just a quarter to twelve and he started looking for Montgomery to come walking into the bar. Though he did not really know what Montgomery looked like, the special agent was sure he would be able to pick this man out of a crowd when he entered the bar.

Two men walked into the bar almost together, but both of them headed off in different directions. Another man entered and he sat down at the bar and did not try to look around the bar like he might be looking for someone. Then a large, powerful and good looking man entered the bar as if he was angry with the world, and he walked right over to the waitress and asked her a question. Rossie smiled as he watched the young lady point him towards his table, and then he watched the large man almost stomp his way towards him. Just as Montgomery reached his table, Rossie stood and offered him his hand and paid the price for trying to be friendly with the man. The agent felt like he just stuffed his hand into a steel bear trap, and he thought this man was breaking some bones in his hand as he offered. "Mr. Montgomery, I'm FBI Special Agent Robert Rossie Sir, and I'm pleased to meet you sir. Please have a seat and we'll talk, sir."

"Yeah and I'm Thomas Montgomery, and I wish I could say I'm as pleased to meet you, Mr. Government Man. I hafta ask you why are you bothering my ass for, I haven't killed the rotten bastard, though I probably would've been first in the line to do so?" Montgomery angrily took a seat and sat like he was going to crush the chair under his weight, and then he openly glared back at the smaller agent as he waited for him to offer why he wanted to meet with him in the bar.

"Mr. Montgomery Sir, this conversation will go much easier and quicker for the both of if you stop being so aggressive against me sir. And that is exactly why I wanted to meet with you sir. Because of your aggressiveness you're clearly displaying and held against Mr. Batterman, sir." He replied as he tried to soften the obviously angry acting businessman up enough, so he could conduct his interview with him in a much better and more productive light.

"Yeah sure, I guess you got a good point and are right at that sir, but anytime anyone mentions fucking Batterman's name to me, I see nothing but red flashing in my eyes. I made that damn man so much money over the years and he always ended up screwing me in the ass at the end of each project I did with the lousy big sonofabitch, I tell you Agent Rossie Sir." Montgomery grumbled just as the smiling waitress came over to the table with a pad and pen, and she asked the two men if she could get them anything to eat or drink.

"Yeah sure baby, I'll have a hamburger, raw with a slice of tomato and pickles on the damn thing, and a picture of beer. Bud at that little sister, and I also want a side of French Fires. Get him whatever the hell he wants to choke down and it's all on my ass, sweetheart. But you gotta make it quick cause I want to get the hell outta here as soon as I done talking with this guy here."

The waitress turned to Agent Rossie almost like she was somehow apologizing for the terrible way this other man was speaking about him in front of her. Then she asked him what he wanted and he ordered a burger and a Pepsi with no ice.

As soon as the waitress was out of earshot of them, Montgomery asked the agent with a snap in his tone of voice. "What the hell's with the stinking Pepsi, man? You're in a stinking bar and here you are asking for a damn soft drink. They sure ain't gonna make much money on you."

"What can I tell you buddy, I'm still on the clock so I'm not allowed to drink any hard stuff, Mr. Montgomery Sir? Now do you mind if I ask you a few questions sir?" He asked loudly as he was trying to be heard over the loud music now blasting in the bar.

"Yeah sure fella, knock your damn socks off and ask away Government man." Montgomery snorted as he held Agent Rossie locked up in an angry glare.

"Okay Mr. Montgomery Sir, why is there so much anger in you when Mr. Batterman's name is brought up before you, sir?"

"I'll tell you why I hate the fucking sonofabitch so much, on the last project we worked on, he bled off all the damn profits from the project, and then the lousy bastard left me high and dry and stuck with finishing the damn project without his crews. I had to finish the project or we would have both been sued and I would've lost my damn shirt on both ends. I fought with him for over seven months for him to at least give me a few of his crews to help me finish the project, and every time I asked him for any help, he told me to go fuck myself. That's why all the damn anger in my voice any time someone mentions his damn name to me, Mr. Agent Man." Montgomery snarled at Rossie this time as he shifted his weight and then took the burger away from the waitress as she put the picture of beer and two glasses on the table, and then she offered Rossie what he ordered from the kitchen. She had to make a second trip to bring him his soda.

"C.mon and eat up Mr. Agent Man these guys make one of the best damn burgers in all of Washington, man." Montgomery grumbled as he took a bear size chomp out of his burger, and then he washed it down with half a mug of beer. He ate the way he looked, like an animal.

The agent took a human size bite of his burger and washed it down with a sip of soda. Feeling uncomfortable with this angry man he wanted to ask him more questions. "Mr. Montgomery, I'm certain you can account for your time for three weeks, am I correct with this assumption?"

"What the hell are you driving at around here Mr. Agent Man? Are you trying to connect me with the murder of Batterman? Look man, true I hated the shit outta that man, but my resorting to murdering the lousy sonofabitch. Naw man, are you barking up the wrong god damn tree here, fella. Yeah sure I lost my ass on the last job I worked with the lousy bastard, but over the years I worked with him made that loss rather easy to get over. It seemed like Batterman would work with you on the up and up for about anywhere from six to ten projects, before he fucked you over on one. But the other projects with the rotten fuck were extremely lucrative I tell you fella. I'll tell you this much, if the bastard would have called me tomorrow to join him on another project, you bet your ass I would've jumped at the chance to work with the bastard again.

"It seems anything that man touched, it immediately turned onto gold. I swear, if that man took a shit and he reached around and grabbed a hand full of the shit and tossed it up against the wall, what stuck would surely turn to gold, the bastard was so lucky at work and with the damn ladies as well, Mr. Agent Man." Montgomery remarked as he took another inhuman bite of his hamburger and then finished off his second glass of beer he was drinking like it was water.

"I heard just about the same remarks from a Mr. Allen Larson. Do you happen to know Mr. Larson, Mr. Montgomery Sir?" He asked Montgomery cautiously as he smiled pleasantly.

"Allen, sure I know Al Larson. I worked with him on a number of projects. I even worked with the man with Batterman at least twice. I found him to be a very honorable man to work with, twenty times better than working with Batterman. If he wasn't fucking over one of his business partners, he was laying the stinking wood to some young chick. There wasn't a woman in all of Denver who was safe when that fuck was out and about I tell you, Mr. Agent Man."

"Mr. Montgomery, I beginning to feel I'm running into a dead end with you on the Batterman case, sir. I guess we're just about done here for the time being. All I'll need from you are the names of any people who can attest to your whereabouts for the past three weeks, and if everything checks out well then there's a great chance you'll never hear from me again, sir."

"How many names will you want? I can come up with at least twenty people I was with, or worked with and out for supper and for some fun and games with, sir. Look Agent Rossie, I'm sorry for coming off so strongly with you over Batterman, but his name is a rather sore subject with my ass. He did me dirty a number of times, but those few times can erase all the profits I made, working with that lousy prick, sir. But I'm certain once you speak with some of the people on the list I'll give ya you'll know real quick I had nothing to do with Batterman's death, sir."

CHAPTER ELEVEN

"But I'll tell you this much for your information Agent Rossie Sir. If you think someone here in the United States was the one who might have killed or had Batterman killed. Then I suggest you check out this David Young fella, sir. If he decided to either kill Batterman himself, or have one of his boys do it for him, he's your man alright. I know he loaned Batterman money on a few occasions, and the last time the scuttlebutt on the street is said Batterman beat this Young guy out of three and a quarter million dollars. From what I know about Young, no one beats him outta any money and live for very long afterwards to tell about it, sir.

"But I'm warning you Agent Rossie, you better watch him real careful like while you're at it sir. He works out of the Black crew if you know what I mean, and these guys are well noted for attacking people like in the old west where they come at you in a group with guns blazing. Young is always surrounded with a horde of his Black Brothers who'll draw down on you at a drop of a fricking hat, and they'll happily go up against any police, or FBI Agents or anyone else they feel is a possible threat, or they just don't like ya, fella. If you try to interview Young, you betta watch your fucking back at all times, and you betta be damn well ready to shoot it out with him and the rest of his Black Brothers if things go wrong with your interview, Agent Rossie.

"I'm telling you in no uncertain terms sir, if you try to interview Young like you just did with me, you better be damn well prepared to have a shootout with him and his Brothers, sir. The guys he has surrounded himself with will come out of the damn woodwork if there's trouble, and they'll start shooting before then know what the hell is happening around them. The entire group is just hell bent on shooting it out with anyone they have a problem with. Hell, I know many of the local police of downtown Washington are so concerned and worried about these bastards. They actually give them a wide birth and allow them to do whatever the hell they want on their beat, as long as they keep the killings down to a minimum, Agent Rossie. I'll give you his phone number and then you're on your own with these damn people. I'm even afraid of these guys. You better put this man at the top of your list of possible suspects in Batterman's murder, mister."

"I'm quite certain of that and I sure will make it my business to interview this Mr. Young, and I'll make damn certain to take along enough support to keep him and his people in check as you have warned me of, and see what he's all about, Mr. Montgomery Sir. I believe I might have even heard about this Mr. Young and the group he pal's around with on a few occasions, sir. Well, I thank you for your time and patience in this matter, and am pleased you took the time to meet with me like this, and I also thank you for Mr. Young's name and phone number. I assure you I'll take the time to check him out thoroughly, and I'll know everything there is to know about him and his Black Brothers before I try and make contact with him, Mr. Montgomery. Again, I thank you for your time and patience in this matter and I shall be leaving you now sir."

With that said, Agent Rossie quickly finished off his coke and he left his half eaten hamburger resting on his plate, and then he stood and threw a twenty dollar bill down on the table for either his share of the bill, or for the tip for the very attentive young waitress who took good care of them as they spoke together. As he left the bar he happened to turn and look back at Montgomery and saw him take his leftover burger and start eating it, and he shook his head and then left the bar with a grin on his face. Even though he knew Wind killed Batterman, he still wanted to meet with Montgomery to sort of feel him out, and see if he could find something else on him to investigate, but he left with no such luck.

His drive back to FBI Headquarters was quick and he rushed back to his office to jot down everything that had transpired between Montgomery and himself, before he forgot anything that might have been said or possibly left out of their conversation. He also checked out Young and the rest of his people and realized Montgomery was not fooling him in the least about this guy and his deadly gang. He included Young and his phone number in his report and left a side note to himself to check him out more thoroughly tomorrow morning when Agent Fugiwara returned for work. Once he finished his hand written notes, he decided to head for home and he was leaving the office a half an hour early, but he felt it really did not matter all that much, because he checked in and started his workday a half an hour early this morning.

He returned home in a much better mood than when he first left for work this morning, and Wind was greatly relieved when he walked back into the apartment, and he actually kissed her hello. Then he went to the kitchen and removed two frozen pork chops and placed them in the microwave to defrost. While they were defrosting he went to the bathroom to relieve himself, and then he took a quick shower and came out of the bathroom wrapped up in the exquisite Kimono Wind gave him the night before and he loved the feel of the fantastic fabric.

Wind was dressed in her favorite deep blue rick silk Kimono with the hand painted large lotus flowers painted on the one side of her Kimono. As soon as he came out of the bathroom, Wind bowed politely to him as she smiled and then nodded at him.

"Ahhh... Wind-san, I can't tell you how pleasing you are to the eyes whenever I look at you. You're like a blue mist on the calm water, and you bring great light to my soul. It's a real pleasure to lay eyes on you every day. How was your day, what did you do all day long with yourself, Wind-san?" He asked as he checked the pork chops and let them go again in the microwave, because they were still quite frozen yet.

"My Lord, this useless person had busied herself by cleaning the dishes leftover from the night before, and from breakfast this morning. Then I cleaned the room with the water in it (bathroom), cleaned this room and then meditated and thought of the many days past in my endless life, refreshing my memory in case you ask any more questions of me about my past times in Japan's history, my Liege Lord. I want to be well prepared for any possible questions that might be still troubling your most honorable mind about my past times, my Lord."

"It sounds like you had a rather busy day for yourself today I guess, Wind-san. I'm pleased you took the time to straighten up the place like you did, it looks great Wind-san and I thank you for your efforts." He actually bowed slight back at her as she stared at him for the moment.

"Do you mind if this foolish Samurai Warrior asks her honorable Liege Lord how his day went for him. I am most interested in what my great Lord does with his honorable day, and if I might fit in anywhere to help make your daily toils much easier for you to deal with my Lord and Master. After all, I am here only to serve and protect you my Lord and Master's every wish and desires. I am so sorry but I cannot help but feel I am failing with my sworn oath to protect and help my Lord and Master with everything he does and toils with for the day."

"Wind-san, with you just being here and waiting for me to return home is more than enough help you offer me. Right now my work has no opening that you might be able to help me with. But if anything comes up that you can do for me, you can believe I shall request your help with the project.

Today Wind-san, I spent most of my day interviewing a most inconsiderate and foul of men. He was so rude he chewed like a horse, and he made enough noise while eating to wake the long time dead. He was a slob and had the most foul of mouths and manners. I was actually ashamed to be seen with him for even the short amount of time I was forced to be with him, Wind-san." He complained to the ancient but beautiful female Samurai Warrior.

"My honorable Lord and Master, aim me at this most foul of men and I shall be most pleased to dispatch him to the Floating World for daring to insult and embarrass my Liege Lord as he has obviously done on this foul day, my Lord." She actually growled as she demanded to be allowed to regain her new Master's face from the lowly animal who had insulted her Lord.

"Take it easy Wind-san, because he didn't insult me enough to lose his foolish life over the minor insults I'm certain he was even unaware he insulted me by his terrible lack of manner. I'm just so pleased I won't have to interact with this foul man ever again in my lifetime, at least I hope I don't have to be with him ever again, Wind-san." He remarked as he sat down on the sofa for a second before remembering about the pork chops. He got up, checked them and they were just right, so he placed them in a frying pan and started cooking their evening meal.

Again, Wind placed a pitiful look on her face and this instantly caused him to ask her with concern in his voice. "Why the look Wind-san, you look like you just lost your best friend?"

"I cannot help be feel that I have failed in my sworn duty to my Liege Lord."

"Let me tell you something Wind-san, you might have let me down in your mind, but I'm telling you if you ever feel like you might have disappointed me, I assure you it won't be the last time in your life you might let me down. But that's life and you can't be perfect with everything you try to make my life happier than it is right now by my being with you like I have been for the past few days, Wind-san. Now how do you feel you have disappointed me this time, Wind-san?" He asked as he turned his attention back to the pork chops cooking on the stove.

"This worthless and dishonored person feels terribly guilty of myself, because I have allowed my honorable Liege Lord to prepare meals for me, and do other things for me that by law, I should be preparing for you and doing for you my Lord." She replied as she immediately dropped down to her knees and bow so low that her forehead actually touched the floor.

"Ha, ha, ha Wind-san, if that's what's troubling you then you're guilty of worrying over nothing at all Wind-san. In my time, it's perfectly alright for me to prepare a meal or do other things that might make your life a little easier to endure, Wind-san. I have no trouble in the least to make you a meal to enjoy. In fact it makes me feel good to do these little things for you. So you see, in reality you're helping me by allowing me to help you by doing these things for you." He said as he again turned to take care of the pork chops he was cooking for the both of them.

She let out her breath in a rush and then she resigned herself to accept all the little things her new owner of the sword insisted on doing for her. But she vowed to herself that she was going to do twice the things for her new Liege Lord to double his pleasure as she watched him cook.

They ate in silence, and then both shared another night of wonderful lovemaking and hugging each other then they turned in for the night.

THURSDAY, JUNE 19th, 1996, AGENT ROBERT ROSSIE'S APARTMENT

Wind was up early and she quickly prepared a meal for her Lord the best she could with the modern day equipment she had to work with. But she watched her Lord cook a few times and she mastered his equipment and made a pretty good meal for him to enjoy.

Rossie came out of the bedroom and he plopped down in his chair at the table, he was still extremely tired because the meeting with Montgomery took a lot out of him yesterday. When he was seated she asked him. "Anata wa yoku nemutta ku?" (Did you sleep well?)

Without even thinking about it he replied in perfect Japanese. "Domo Genki desu." (Quite well thank you) He was speaking better than ever Japanese it was part of the great gift the Kami showered upon the new owner of Wind's deadly Katana killing sword.

"Wind-san, I have to leave for the office early because Agent Fugiwara-san is due back, and I want to make certain I'm at the office before he arrives for the start of our workday. I'm worried because I'm going to carry out an interview with an extremely dangerous bunch of people, and I want Agent Fugiwara-san at my side when we meet with these people. These are the people Mr. Montgomery gave me. Besides, I like working with Fugiwara-san, he knows what he's doing and at least I know he has my back in case I get myself into any trouble out there, Wind-san." He offered as he looked at what he thought was a sad attempt of a plate of scrambled eggs. The eggs looked like they went through a blender and he smiled over her attempt to make him breakfast.

Suddenly, she was acting like she was ready to kill someone as she grumbled and rose at the same time. "What is my honorable Lord saying to this foolish Samurai? Does my honorable Lord and Master fear his life is in any danger on this foul day? If this is a fact then it is my sacred Yoshie, my duty to protect your life no matter where you go on this day my Lord."

He let out his breath in a deep sigh, and then he offered to this extremely dangerous female weapon that looked like she was prepared to kill the world in his defense. "Wind-san, any day I go off for work my life is in danger. That's because I'm working with a bunch of criminals and there is always that strong possibility of one of them trying to harm me…"

"Then it is my sacred duty to be at your side every stick of time you leave my side for your work my Liege Lord. If anything happened to you while you are under my protection, the feared Kami of the Floating World would allow the dreaded Tengu, the Wood Goblins of the forbidden forest to feast upon my foul soul for my failure to protect my Liege Lord's life." She sadly announced as if she was truly in fear of the so called Tengu Wood Goblins.

"How the hell would I be able to carry out my work if I had you hanging around my neck all day and getting in my way when I'm working? How the hell could I possibly explain to my partner and my boss who you are and why the devil you're following me all over the damn place? No Wind-san, it's completely impossible for you to follow me all over Washington while I carry out my own duty to my job. No, you must never follow me when I'm working, to do so would make me extremely upset with you, Wind-san." He groused angrily as he suddenly glared at her as he held her in his angry glare to better drive him point across to her.

"This foolish and extremely troubled Samurai Warrior who has been entrusted to look after my Liege Lord's every want and desire, and his sacred life by the Kami of the Ukiyo (Floating World), is unable to understand why my Lord and Master will refuse me to carry out the very words of the curse you yourself had placed upon my soul and the heart of my sword with your own breath, my Lord?" She cried at her new owner of her deadly killing sword.

"You do have a problem you have to work out for yourself, because I'm giving you a direct order not to ever get involved in what I do for a living. If you ever interfered in my work, it could very well cost me my job, and possible end up with my being placed in jail as well, Wind-san." He warned the ancient Samurai Warrior in no uncertain terms as he continued to glare at her.

"My Liege Lord, you are forcing this worthless keeper of your life to either disobey your word, or the sacred oath and the orders of the Kami who control all earthly and spiritual wonders. What to do, what to do? How can this foolish person possibly disobey my Liege Lord's sacred word, or the orders of the Kami and my true Lord and Master Kawasomeru-Sama? Either way I fear I shall lose my worthless head over either decision I shall commit to my Liege Lord." She grumbled as she fought desperately with her inner self on what to do to protect her Master's life. After going deep into thought for a few moments she asked her Liege Lord with concern in her voice.

"If My Lord is ordering me not to accompany you on your workday then will my Liege Lord at least make certain he shall carry the sacred Amulet the Kami Creator himself had placed within my worthless hand? At least I understand the Amulet will help to keep you safe when out of my sight my Lord." She offered knowing she was deceiving her Lord, understanding if her Master s life was threatened in any fashion, the Amulet would automatically transport her spirit to where her Master was in danger, and then she could dispatch any threat aimed against her ward.

"In case you have not noticed it quite yet Wind-san, I'm always carrying the Amulet you gave to me when I first found you. I have already grown quite accustom to having it on my person at all times lately. It brings me comfort when you're not standing by my side for some strange reason, Wind-san." He offered as his hand automatically went to his neck and he found out he was without the Amulet, and then he remembered he took it off in the bathroom when he showered after returning to the apartment when he completed his workday.

"As the Amulet should do because any gifts from the Creator should and always will bring you great comfort whenever it is hanging around your honorable neck my Lord and Master."

"I guess you have a pretty good point there Wind-san. Either way, all I know is I'm forbidding you to ever come out and interfere with my work under any circumstances Wind-san. It could not only serve to get me killed, but it would be most embarrassing to have you running around and attacking anyone I'm having a slight problem with." He added to his warning to Wind.

"I understand what you are telling me and I shall obey your ever Command to the best of my abilities, my most honorable Lord and Master." She replied, but she put a look on her face that informed him she was agreeing with his orders under distress.

"I see you're upset with me Wind-san, but this is the way it has to be. I just can't have you running all over downtown Washington with your sword in hand and doing what you did in back Japan, to anyone who might give me a problem when I'm forced to deal with the criminals of the state." He fired right back at her, and then he stared at her as he finished eating his morning meal she had prepared for him. When he was done, he stood up and announced.

"Wind-san, as I told you already, I want to get an early start to this day because Agent Fugiwara-san is due back from his short vacation, and I want to be in my office before he arrived and don't understand what I have planned for the day's work." The agent leaned forward and he kissed her on the side of his cheek. He had to put his fingers under her chin to lift her head slightly so he could kiss her on the lips, and he still saw the hurt that was etched in her eyes and he smiled at her and then added. "C'mon Wind-san, it isn't that bad, nothing is going to happen to me while I'm at work and have Agent Fugiwara-san standing by my side and protecting me from all harm. Do you think you could give me a little smile before I leave for work, Wind-san?"

Wind looked deeply into his eyes and then she gave him a weak smile.

"C'mon Wind-san, that isn't a real smile, I want one of your smiles that'll melt butter. You can do much better than that weak smile. I need one to make my day for me, Wind-san."

This time she gave him her best smile, thinking she just could not send him off to work without her smile in his eyes. Then she suddenly looped her arms around his neck and pulled his head to her and she planted a great kiss right on his lips, and she smiled again at him as she let him go and she stepped back a little so he could open the door and then leave the apartment.

Rossie had to actually pry her arms from around his neck then he kissed her again and turned on his heels and left her standing by the closing door to the apartment.

AGENT ROBERT ROSSIE'S TEMPORARY OFFICE AT FBI HEADQUARTERS, WASHINGTON D.C. THURSDAY, JUNE 19th, 1996 AT ZERO EIGHT TEN HUNDRED HOURS

Agent Robert Rossie walked into his new office even before Commander Ralph Murdock showed up for work, and he sat down at his desk and turned on his computer. The first thing he did was pull up David Young's profile, it was chilling to read. The man was arrested fifteen times, eleven of them were felonies and somehow he was always able to beat the charges that ranged from armed robbery to attempted murder. He was also a suspect in six still unsolved murders, and he seemed to have his fingers in every crime that was taking place in Washington D.C. from gambling to human trafficking. He was also offering protection racketeering. He was even suspected in renting out any number of his gang members for any crime someone else wanted to commit. There was a separate warning stating he was a ruthless individual who would kill without thought, and has vowed never to be taken in alive by any police authorities.

The more he read of the report, the more he was considering asking for at least five more agents to accompany him to interview this man, he was getting that concerned over his violence. Just as he leaned back in his chair and let his breath out in a rush, Special Agent Shinnosuke Fugiwara came walking into the office and he was carrying two cups of coffee and a couple of cheese Danishes and he put them down right in front of Rossie on his desk and then announced.

"Hey Rossie-san, I'm reporting in for duty, buddy. I see you arrived at work awful early today, what's going down that has you reporting for work so early my friend?"

"I'm still working on this damn Batterman murder case. Yesterday I interviewed Montgomery and he gave me another lead, one that really is arousing my interest in this other man. It seems this guy is a real sonofabitch who has his damn fingers in every crime in the world. I don't know how we have overlooked this one man and his gang for so long as he was operating right here in downtown Washington for the past ten years as it states in his file, Agent Fugiwara-san."

"What's his name Rossie-san, I might even know this guy already?"

"David Young!"

"Oh man, how the hell did this guy ever get involved in the Batterman murder case, Rossie-san? I tried to put this guy behind bars three different times, but he so well connected the higher ups always ordered me to pull my investigation off of this fuck just as I was closing in for the kill on the lousy sonofabitch. If this guy is involved in this case then you can bet there's a helluva lot more to the Batterman's murder than meets the eye, Rossie-san." Fugiwara complained."

"I'm not certain if he's involved in the damn case or not at this time, Shinnosuke-san. But Mr. Montgomery offered up his name to my ass, probably to get the heat off his ass I was putting on him, Fugiwara-san. Either way, I wanna start checking this guy out, from all I read about him in his file. He and his damn gang need to be pulled the hell off the streets of Washington yesterday, Fugiwara-san. We can't allow this guy to continue his criminal ways for another day." He offered as he took a sip of the steaming cup of coffee then he took a bite of his Danish.

"If you plan to start investigating this guy then you better make damn certain your death bennies are all in order. This guy doesn't take too kindly to anyone poking their damn noses into any of his business dealings. Usually when someone starts checking this guy out that investigator usually ends up dead and dumped in a sewer somewhere down the damn road, Rossie-san." Agent Fugiwara remarked as he picked up his coffee and started to drink it as well.

"Ahhh... how was your short vacation Fugiwara-san?" Rossie asked his partner.

"Just that Rossie-san, too short, I was just getting to know my wife again, and I had to leave her to get my ass back here to help you with this case. I never dreamed you would be expanding the investigation to start checking out Young and his gang of fricking cutthroats, man."

"My investigation of this guy is more than likely not going to have much to do about the Batterman case, but nevertheless I want to start checking him and his gang out, Fugiwara-san."

"Well if you really want to go down this road then include me in on this investigation Rossie-san. I sure as hell am not going to abandon you if you really want to try and take this guy and his damn gang down. Like I said, I was investigating this man three different times and just as I was closing in on him, the case was pulled out from under me, man. I too want this guy off the damn streets of Washington he's that much of a threat, Rossie-san. When do you want to start on this guy, I know where he and most of his gang hangs out, and there's a pretty good chance he might speak with us, because he knows damn well I'm the one who came the closest to bringing his damn ass down, Rossie-san." Agent Fugiwara more or less was bragging over how far his investigation of Young got before he was pulled off the case.

"I was thinking about trying to get to Young as early as possibly today, Fugiwara-san. I don't want any grass growing under my feet on this case, or Murdock is going to make our lives a living hell the longer we take to solve this murder case my friend." Rossie groused.

"I hear you there my friend. What say we get ourselves another coffee and something more substantial to eat, and then let's start beating the damn bushes and see what we can drum up for ourselves, Rossie-san. To tell you the truth, I can't wait to get back on Young's ass my friend."

"He bothers you that much I see, Agent Fugiwara-san?"

"More than you'll ever know, I had him right where I wanted him and the noose was closing around his damn neck twice, and both times just before I could reel him in, I was pulled off his damn case. Once by Murdock who said he needed me on another case and he was going to assign another Agent to replace me, which he never did. The second time I was pulled off Young's case was by the head of the DOJ, (Department of the Justice) stating they had their own investigation going against Young, and I was messing up their case on them. And again, nothing else was done against Young once I was pulled off his damn case. Yeah, before you ask me man, the third investigation on had on the prick, the plot I was following dried up on me, and I ran into a wall before I was forced to give up my last investigation on the prick, Rossie-san. Yeah, I guess you can say he really got under my skin, and I want his ass real bad I can tell you Rossie-san."

"Well this time I promise you Agent Fugiwara-san, no one is going to pull our asses off this guy until we nail his ass to the cross. If I start an investigation on his ass, no one this side of judgment day is going to yank us off the case until we have his carcass hanging on our office door, Fugiwara-san." Agent Rossie bragged then he absentminded reached for the Amulet Wind gave him, and he discovered he left it lying on the bathroom sink and he grumbled to Fugiwara. "Dammit to hell and back again, I have to run home for a few moments, I forgot something that's very important to me, and I need to have it on me especially today, dammit."

"Take off and go get it, I'll hold down the fort until you return. That way it'll give me some computer time so maybe I can find out where Young is hanging at today by the time you return, Rossie-san. I have a pretty good idea where he's been haunting lately, and I'm certain one of my CI's (Confidential Informer) will be more than willing to tell me where Young is staying at right now, Rossie-san." Fugiwara offered as he settled in before the computer on his assigned desk.

"That's good to hear, and it shouldn't take me more than maybe an hour to get there and back, Fugiwara-san." He grumbled as he rose and grabbed the small side bag with is weapon in it, and he was gone from the office in a flash. The traffic was with him all the way and he made it back to his apartment in just under fifteen minutes, and he charged though the door and was instantly stunned by what he found waiting for him inside his apartment.

When he opened the door in a rush, he found Wind kneeling in the center of the small living room, and she was deep in meditation. But she was dressed in her modified ancient battle robe, and her weapons were positioned on her body perfectly, out of her way but at her fingertips if she had any need of her killing Katana blade, or her Wakizashi shorter sword usually reserved to use when she was going to commit Suppuku, or for close in fighting with an enemy. Even her six foot Yumi Agemaki ornamented bow was slung perfectly over her back along with the richly decorated Ebira open quiver that held her special eight Karimata forked tipped arrows with the bamboo shafts. She even had a small Tanto blade held in a loop at her waist, and he could only guess what other weapons she had hidden elsewhere on her exquisite body. Her hair was done up in a long brad, and the very tip of her hair she had an evil looking clip with an extremely sharp blade type implement that she could obviously use her long hair as a weapon as well.

He entered the apartment slowly and then he carefully walked around the still kneeling Wind who was acting like she was unaware he had just entered the room. As he walked around the female Samurai Warrior, he intensely studied her dress. He knew what the Yoroi Hitatare heavy armor battle robe looked like from the ancient past, but this one in no way resembled the old style. Here, the armored robe was cut real short to where it just covered the magnificent rounds of her outstanding rearend. Looking down her legs he could see the also modified Suneate leg protectors, the usual heavy protection was still present and protecting the front of her shins, but behind her legs it was mere fabric that held this protection in place.

Looking at her arms, the same was done here, the heavy Kote sleeve armor protection was there for the protection of outside her arm, the shoulder and the forearm, but the inner areas were covered with a stretchy type fabric as well, allowing her arm great freedom while still protecting the arm where most of the sword strikes would surely take place.

He stopped in the front of her and carefully studied the front of the modified piece of ancient battle armor. Up on her shoulders, the wide and large heavy leather collar protection was still there to protect her throat from the biting edge of the sword, but most of the other heavy protection from this area was removed. Holding the armor closed was a gold throat clasp which displayed Wind's fighting stable honor of the claw, but the front of the armor was cut in a wide diamond where the lower tip of the diamond opening went well down to almost the bottom of her well endowed breasts, and the two wings of the diamond shape went almost to the ends of her shoulders on both sides. It was easy to see how the wide opening would easily allow her all the freedom she would need to fight with her killing Katana blade.

The outfit was mated and held together just below her breasts by about an inch wide piece of the old armor robe of protection, and then a second but much smaller also in the shape of a diamond opening, went from under her breasts and it quickly flared out from just below her ribcage to her hips, and closed again just above her public hair beginning.

Every area of her perfect body that a sword edge might cause her some injury was pretty much covered by the rather flattering but heavily modified in every area battle protection. It was modified not only to protect her body in a sword fight, but it was also obviously modified to show off her exquisite shape as well. Someone had obviously modified the protection not to hide the fact the person wearing the protection was every bit a female person.

What set off the rest of the outstanding picture of this female Samurai Warrior, was the way her hair was cut and shaped. It was cut in the ancient Kami no sagariba, her hair was cut short in the font to just where it passed below her ears, but from her ears back her hair was long, almost down to her rearend. Long braids of her hair outlined the longer strands of hair on both sides of her head, and then formed a large diamond end where the two braided lengths of hair was wound together so they beautifully outline the long length of her hair in the back. The way her hair was cut and shaped, set out her magnificent facial features perfectly, and the black eyeliner outlined and made her eyes look more cat like and narrow. She was the picture of beauty even dressed like she was, to kill anyone who dared to threaten her Lord and Master.

He was stunned by the appearance of this extremely dangerous woman and he was wondering why she was dress for battle. He suddenly coughed to try and break her obvious trance, and it had the effect he was looking for. Wind's eyes fluttered opened and she stared into the troubled looking eyes of her new Master of her deadly killing Katana blade. A flash of embarrassment crossed her face as she continued to stare back at her worried looking Lord.

FBI Special Agent Robert Rossie swallowed hard and then he mumbled at her in a sort of commanding tone of voice. "Wind-san, what the hell is the meaning of this? Why the devil are you dressed like this for? Is there a reason for this that I don't know about, do you plan to do battle with someone on this day, Wind-san? You're not dressed like this planning to attack me when I came home from work later in the day, are you Wind-san? If so, I thought you couldn't do any form of harm to me without suffering greatly by the Kami of your beliefs, Wind-san?"

She immediately bowed so low to her Lord and Master that her nose actually touched the floor then she cried while still holding the kneeling position. "Oh no my honorable Lord and Master, I could no more do any possible harm to you as I could live without breathing my Lord. I fear I have dressed in my battle protection, and I was preparing both my mind and body for possible combat in your defense. If during your workday, one of your hated Teki tried to display any evil treachery against your person, and I had to come to your aide my Liege Lord. If I was foolish as to dare display any treachery aimed against your person, the always angry Fujin. The Kami of my namesake Wind would come from the Floating World to your defense, and he would instantly slaughter my spirit into such small pieces even the dreaded Tengu Wood Goblins would have trouble finding pieces of my body large enough for them to feast upon, my Lord.

"My worthless spirit is only allowed to revisit the land of the living to serve my Lord and Master's every wish and desire. I am incapable of committing any possible treachery aimed against you my Liege Lord. The Council of the Kami would destroy my spirit from the Floating World if I even thought for one breath on the stick of time to harm my Lord and Master in any way, shape or form, My Lord. I am only allowed in the living world to protect you from all harm from the living world, and also sent against you for any unforeseen forces from the Floating World, my Lord." She dared to look up from her kneeling position so she could look into her Master's eyes, to assure him she was in no way a danger against him.

"Wind-san, I'm pleased to hear what you told me. But I'm equally displeased to hear why you're dressed so. I believe I already warned you, demanded of you to never interfere with my work no matter what was happening with or to me, Wind-san. Again I warn you, in no way, shape or form are you to come to me when I'm working under any circumstances. Do you understand Wind-san? If you disobey my order, I'll send you back to the Floating World for thirty sticks or time, and when you return I'll never trust you again. If you disobey me I'll never allow you to remain in the living world while I'm at work. I'll send you to the Floating World every day before I go off to work. Do you understand what I'm telling you, Wind-san?" He laced his words with the hint of anger as he waited for the female Samurai to reply to his latest threat.

"Wakarimasu, I understand, and I shall obey your orders as best as I can, my Lord."

"What the hell do you mean by that shit, you'll obey my orders as best you can? You will obey my orders fully or else, Wind-san." He snorted nastily at her this time.

"What I meant my Lord, if you are in trouble and the Kami who control my spirit order me to come to you. I fear their orders will supersede your order, or I will not be fulfilling my oath you placed on the edge of my sword, my Lord." She replied almost defiantly at her Liege Lord.

"From what I understand of your oath you dare much to take a defiantly tone at me. If I'm not correct, I can order you to commit Suppuku, and you're forced to carry out that painful ordeal. I'm warning you, if you try and defy my word again, I'll order you to commit this act, and then I'll call you back from the Floating World, so you can commit the sacred act a second time then a third time, and I'll keep ordering you to commit Suppuku until I feel you made proper amends for defying my orders, Wind-san. Do you understand what I am threatening you with Wind-san?"

"Wakarimasu, I understand what you are ordering me my Lord and Master."

"Yoi! (Good!) Now that that's settled, I have to retrieve something and then I have to get back to work. I'm still hoping to hold that extremely important meeting with Young today, and I have to get back to my office to see how Fugiwara-san made out locating where Mr. Young is today, so we can both meet with the man. I trust I'll have no further trouble from you, Wind-san?"

"I shall obey your orders as you have issued them to me faithfully my Lord."

"You're not giving me any Nigon (Double Tongue) Wind-san, are you?"

"Iye! (No!) Ieeee, what does my Lord think I am, a lowly Himin, a person of no worth? I am a most honorable Samurai Warrior who has proven my loyalty to my Lord and Master many times over on the field of battle for your honor, my Lord. There is no treachery held in my heart. I never speak with two tongues. If I give my oath then I shall die by my oath, unless it is changed by the Kami who control all things."

Once again she was trying to warn her ward that she was held to the orders of the Kami more than she was locked into her oath she once took for him.

"There you go again dammit. You give me your word not to interfere with my work then you immediately take it back by trying to blame the Kami if you change your mind and come and interfere with my work, Wind-san." The FBI Agent actually growled at her this time.

Again she lowered her head in her bow so low this time she tapped her forehead on the floor as she cried to the Master of her sword. "I fear my Lord does not understand the confusing world of the Kami and the Floating World properly, my Lord. True I have given you my sworn oath not to interfere with your work. But if the Kami see your life is in danger, Fujin will be sent before me by the Council of the Kami, and he will order me to seek you out and protect your life from all harm, whether you agree with his order or not. I must warn my Liege Lord, it would be extremely foolish on your part to dare ignore any order from Fujin, the always angry God of the Wind. He has been known to send out the Dragon's Breath that will destroy all you hold to your heart, my Lord. He does not take lightly to ever have his word questioned or ignored, my Lord."

She did not dare to lift her head from the floor as she warned her Master of the sword of the threat from the Kami. She was scared he would be so angry with her for giving him a slight battle of words over his orders and her possibly following them out as he demanded of her. He stared down at her and then he slowly shook his head as he grumbled down at her. "Well Wind-san, I guess we'll have to cross that bridge when we come to it then, won't we. I won't fight with your namesake for any reason and that was a wise warning you have just issued to me, Wind-san. I shall listen and do as you have suggested when it comes to your Gods. I have enough problems on my hands with my work, to dare start any trouble with the spirit world. Wind-san, I have stayed away from my work for long enough, I have to get back to my office. I take it you'll keep out of anyone's sight until I have returned from my work today, right Wind-san."

She raised her head just enough so she could see his face and then she replied to him. "That is an easy order for me to obey, my Liege Lord."

"Taihen yoi, (Very good) I have to go, I'll see you when I return from work then, I'll bring supper home with me this time, Wind-san." He informed her of his plans for the night.

Wind did not reply, she merely lower her head a third time and waited for her Lord to leave.

He rushed out of the building, jumped in his car and drove like a mad man back to his work. He almost used the siren so he could get through a few areas where the traffic was moving slow. Finally he made it back to his headquarters and twenty minutes to eleven and he rushed inside and jumped in the elevator and went up to the third floor. He was just about to enter his office when Murdock came out of his office and barked at him. "This is a fine time to show up for work. I have a mind to dock your ass for a few hours. What's on your menu for today, mister?"

He stopped dead in his tracks and turned to his Commander and replied crisply. "I received a very good lead from Mr. Montgomery yesterday, and I have Agent Fugiwara checking on our new target. If he was able to locate him, we're going back out later today and confront him, and find out if he had anything to do with Batterman's murder, sir."

"Oh, I see, you must have been on the job already, sorry for jumping on your ass, Agent Rossie. You'll remember to keep me informed on how you do with this new lead once you and your partner are done with his ass, right? I can't tell you how many Politicians I have breathing down my neck looking for news about Batterman's death. Look, I have to get over to the White House, so if anyone's looking for me, just tell them I'll be giving the President CPR, trying to get his damn breathing under control over this damn murder case." Murdock grumbled as he turned, laughing at his own joke as he went back inside his office and closed the door behind him.

CHAPTER TWELVE

FBI Special Agent Robert Rossie charged into his office like he was angry at the world and Agent Shinnosuke Fugiwara remarked as he sat down at his desk. "I see the Big Growl jumped on your ass the moment he saw you coming in. He was in the office at least five times this morning looking for your ass, and each time I told the Big Growl you were out checking out a few new leads on the case. He knew damn well you had already reported in for work today, he was just busting your damn horns I'm afraid, Rossie-san." Fugiwara smirked at his partner.

"Ahhh... he just had to have a chunk of my ass in chew on, now he's happy I guess. Do you know why he has to get over to the White House today, Fugiwara-san? This is the first time he ever told me he was heading for the Big House this early in the morning."

"Yeah, both he and the DOJ lead man have to give their weekly report and briefing to the Boss, the usual thing you know my friend." Shinnosuke replied to his partner, and then he began to inform him on what he was able to find out about Young and the rest of his gang. "Rossie-san, I was able to locate the lousy little prick you want to interview today, he's hiding his ass at a real shit hole of a flop house over on Tenth Street between Tenth and South place and 2014 Port Street. I was able to track him to this location more than once during my past investigation of his ass, so I'm kinda familiar with the dump he's hiding at. It's a perfect setup place for him to have a heavy shootout with anyone he had a finger up his ass with, Rossie-san. I suggest we both wear our heavy body armor if you really want to interview this bastard later today, man."

"That's good Fugiwara-san did you happen to find out where the rest of his damn gang is going to be at? I hope they're nowhere near this guy when we go to interview the bastard. I don't mind tangling with him, but I don't want to get involved in a gang war between us and them."

"My CI I spoke with earlier today informed me he had at least five of his gang members with him mostly at all times lately. I guess this group is supposed to be the cream of the crap so to say. Do you think we should pull in a few of our other Agents, you know just in case this lousy little prick has other ways he might want to talk to us with today, Agent Rossie-san?"

"Naw, but I believe we better inform the local police departments, and maybe have them place a number of their people on standby, just in case this guy is a little hard to talk with, and he wants some trouble before he finally decides to talk with us. I'd much rather work with the local police, they might be better equipped to deal with these pricks than we are. Hell they might even know a number of these people and they might also have an in with some of them. It might be a good idea to pull in at least five of the Police Officers with us when we confront this Young fellow, Fugiwara-san. I have my body armor on already, and I'm ready to go and speak with this guy right now. What say, you about ready to get a little dirty today my friend?"

Agent Rossie asked his partner as he absentmindedly reached and his fingers found the small amulet Wind gave him the other day. For some reason it was giving him comfort to have the medallion hanging around his neck, especially now that he understood the medallion was given to Wind by who she called the Creator of the Eight Islands of Japan.

"I guess I'm ready as I'll ever be, I wish you could've found someone a little easier to interview than this guy, say like maybe Jack the Ripper or someone like that prick. I hope we don't get bloody on this one, Rossie-san." Fugiwara responded as he stood and slipped into his own body armor, and then he slid his suite jacket over his armor vest and was ready to go.

"C'mon, this guy can't be all that bad to deal with, can he Fugiwara-san?" He fussed as he smiled at his Japanese partner this time.

"There can be none worse to try and interview I'm telling you man, this guy will kill his own mother if she even looked at him sideway, Rossie-san. He's the worst of the worst I tell ya."

"Maybe so, but we have to go and interview the little prick anyhow and see what he might know about Batterman's murder. We need some kind of stinking break in this case."

"Hey, that reminds me buddy, when we get back from this damn interview with Young. I wanna talk to you a little about more of what you might know about this murder case, Rossie-san. Remember, you promised me when we got back to Washington you were going to spill the beans of what you know about this case, mister. I'm still gonna hold you to that statement my friend." Agent Fugiwara reminded Rossie of what he offered him when they were in Denver.

"Yeah, yeah, you gonna start that crap all over again mister. Unless you're a damn hemorrhoid you better get the hell offa my backside. Bad enuf I got Murdock riding my ass from morning to night, now you have to start on my ass as well. Hey, what the hell gives around here? I'm afraid I'm hanging around your ass too much and I'm starting to pick up some of your damn Jersey bullshit, Gotta, musta, and crap like that. I used to sound well educated, hanging around you I can feel my IQ going to hell in a handbag, my friend." He complained at his partner as he walked up to him and slapped him on the back, and then he led him towards the door to the office.

The two special agents rushed to the elevators, both of them concerned if Murdock was going to come charging out of his office if he spotted them out in the hallway. They got in the cab and were whisked down to the first floor of the building, and they headed for the rear parking lot. Rossie allowed Fugiwara to drive the vehicle because he knew where they were going. Rossie checked his map and picked out the police station covering the area in question they were heading for, and he called the station and spoke directly with the Desk Sergeant, and requested five of his best officers to serve as a backup for when they went to interview Young.

The kind of upset Desk Sergeant started to give the agent a bit of a hard time with cutting five of his people out to help the two FBI Agents until Rossie actually had to pull rank on the Sergeant. He growled it was not a request he was making, it was an order for him to cut him five of his people to serve as backup for them and that was that. The Sergeant informed him he was going to station a squad car at the head of Tenth Street, and a second squad car at the cross section of Tenth and Courtland, along with two other squad cars stationed at the corner of Tenth and South place and have the fifth car used as a floater, so he could come in from any direction and lend his extra support to any unit that found itself bogged down.

When he was satisfied with how he made out with the Desk Sergeant, he informed Fugiwara he was able to muster police help for their project. The two agents settled in and watched the roads with Fugiwara telling him where they were heading. When they hit Tenth and Courtland coming into the area from the least traveled way, the two agents immediately picked up the police squad car parked by a large mailbox, and both agents nodded to the officer in the car and he kind of saluted to the two agents as they slowly passed by his parked squad car. Agent Rossie breathed out a deep sigh of relief now knowing the backup police personnel were already on the job, and they were acting as their backup. That took a lot of pressure off his shoulder.

Driving down 10th Street Rossie was stunned at what he was seeing. About every building in this area had at least one broken window in the structure, and filth was covering sections of the sidewalk and it extended into the street. There were three cars stripped down to their shells and one of them was flipped over on its side, even the motors were missing. He spotted five women nearly dressed, and two of them were speaking with a drive they stopped in the middle of the street. On one stoop, there were a number of men sitting and angrily eyeing his vehicle as it crawled down the road. There were other groups of young men hanging about or sitting on the fenders or hoods of cars talking. Loud music was blaring, and some people were hanging out of upper windows yelling and screaming at someone on the ground screaming right back at them.

Everything about the area reminded him of a small village in Vietnam that was just one cursed, one stumble, on confrontation from erupting into a rumble between everyone hanging around in the area. Agent Rossie turned and looked at Agent Fugiwara, and he could not understand the look on his face. He was sort of smiling like he was really enjoying what he was looking at, and what he was looking at was actually scaring the hell out of him.

He drew in his breath and then remarked to his partner with concern lacing his tone of voice. "What the hell are you looking at that's making you smile like you are? Am I missing something I'm not seeing out there? Talk about the wild fucking west like you said, man."

"You don't get it Rossie-san, this is great. If anything goes down then all these friggin people you see hanging around out here are going to disappear like ghosts, and the only ones left outside are the ones we really gotta worry about because sure as shit. Anyone left out here is going to be fucking soldiers for Young. You better get ready because his dump is two houses up from our front door on the left, buddy. You can see it from here, it the building with those nine of ten assholes sitting on the steps and porch of the dump. That's Young's dump alright, Rossie-san.

"That's great do we have to fight our way into the building to see this guy, Fugiwara-san?"

"No man, these assholes are not gonna do anything without Young telling them what to do. Half these guys can't take a damn dump on their own, they all look to Young to tell them what and when the hell to do it, partner. Get hot, we're here, I'm gonna leave the car parked right in the middle of the road so everyone here knows we're the heat. I see one of the police squad cars parked out in the open at the end of the block, so this Young character knows we're out here and most likely coming to pay him a fucking visit, Rossie-san. You ready partner, a word of caution, you can't show the slightest bit of fear of any of these shitbirds, or they'll eat your ass alive for breakfast. If one of these flaming assholes steps in your way, you gotta shove him aside like he's the shit he's made of. Or you're just not going to get past any of his soldiers he has guarding the front door of his dump, Rossie-san." Fugiwara warned him as he slammed the car in park and then opened the door like he was ready to kill everyone he seeing standing around outside his car.

Rossie got out of the car and then waited until Fugiwara was by his side, and then they walked to the sidewalk and placed one step on the steps leading to the door of the place. Immediately, everyone hanging around on the stoop stood and sort of blocked the two Agent's way, with one of them stepping forward and taking an extremely threatening stance on the landing of the stoop.

Fugiwara stopped and glared at the black man and then snarled savagely. "FBI mutherfucker, what, what man, you think I'm a fucking fraid of your black ass, think again man. I'd soon place a cap in your bonnet than look at you fricking ass, buddy. Your boss in there buster? You betta get outta my way before somethin bad happens to your shiny ass, mister. I ain't got any time to dance around with your ass. I'll just shoot ya then step on your damn puss as I walk by you, man. And that goes for the rest of you fucking guys. You know what they say, don't be a thug if you can't take a slug, not get the fuck outta my way so I can meet with your boss, fucker."

"I ain't gots me no fucking boss, I'm a made man and think for myself, fucker."

"Whoa what do we have here, you Mafia now nigger? You wanna talk like that then I'll run your black ass in just for some exercise, and don't tell me you ain't got a boss. You'd lick Young's ass after he just took a shit if he told you to, so get the hell outta my way before I show you what I can do to your ass, buster." Fugiwara gave the one blocking his way the look that warned him he was not fooling around with him and he better get out of his way real pronto like.

As concerned as Rossie was over the threatening confrontation raging between his partner and the man blocking their way, he was also well amused over how Fugiwara was speaking. He was equally amazed at how his partner was acting with these ten men who if they took a notion to, they could easily slaughter them before any of their support could arrive and assist them.

"I told you to get the fuck outta my way, and that's what you betta do fast like buster. Unless you want to give up making fucking babies for the government to pay for, because if I have to draw my weapon, my first round is going to blow your left nut off. Then my second round is gonna take your right nut off, and my third round is gonna take off the tip of your dick. I said move." Fugiwara rested his hand on the handle of his weapon still hidden by his suite jacket.

Slowly, the large black man stepped aside and allowed the two agents to walk up the steps, and then past them and walk into the building. As soon as they were inside, Agent Rossie leaned his head closed to Agent Fugiwara and groused at him. "Man you got some fucking balls there Fugiwara-san. I was ready to run back to the car and forget all about interviewing this lousy sonofabitch. Shit, there are more of these bastards on the second floor landing, and they're already giving us the evil eye." He warned his partner as he felt his blood pressure rising.

ROSSIE'S APARTMENT

Wind was still deep in her meditation when her mind suddenly connected to the amulet hanging around Agent Rossie's neck. In her mind's eye she could see at least four men standing on a second floor landing, and they were actually threatening to kill her ward. Two of the men held the metal hands (Guns) that fired the Dragon's teeth (Bullets) that destroyed the mortal fools with the unseen teeth who thought they ruled the world. Instantly, all her reflexes and instincts were on full alert as she got up, and then she began to follow the call of the amulet by allowing the call to pick her up and bring her to where her Lord was suddenly in deadly danger.

As Agent Fugiwara continued to stare at the second group of Young's bodyguards stationed on the second floor landing, Young suddenly parted them and he growled down at the two agents. "What the fuck does two god damn FBI pigs want with my sagging ass for? You two government pigs are on my fucking turf now, and if I say the word, you two shitheads are history. I repeat for you two assholes, what the fuck does the god damn Feds want with me?"

"We want to talk with you for a few minutes that's it, Mr. Young."

"Hey government man I know you, you're the fucking asshole who tried to have me arrested a coupla times before. What the hell's with you man? You haven't learned yet that no fucking cop is ever gonna take me in if I don't wanna go with your ass, government asshole. You betta stop wasting your time trying to find something bad to hang on my ass, buddy."

"Yeah, I tried to take you down before and sooner or later I'm going to finally get my damn way and drag your fucking ass in, so justice could balance the scales of justice with your ass hanging from a tree, fella. I won't give up until I can bring you in, Young. You can only dodge justice for so long before all sorts of hell finally catch up with your ass, mister."

"What about your partner down there, does he feel the same way you do, and he wants to take me down because he has nothing else better to do with is fricking time, asshole?"

Rossie stepped out from behind Fugiwara and snarled at the man on the landing looking down at them. "You better believe it fella. If my partner doesn't find something on your ass, I will."

"You know something government man, I'm done talking, and listening to the bullshit you two scumbags are giving me, dammit. Have some fun talking to my friends here, they don't talk too gooda English, but they know how to talk heavy, with lead." With that said, Young turned and walked through the group standing on the landing with him, and then all hell broke out.

Just as both Agents Rossie and Fugiwara drew their weapon to defend themselves, Wind suddenly appeared just outside the building the two agents entered, and the group of ten men found themselves staring at a female who held a Katana killing sword in her hand, and she was charging right at them as she stepped out of the cloud that brought her to the call of the amulet.

As soon as the men of the stoop saw this crazy dressed woman charging at them, two of them drew their weapons and fired at her. The bullets passed right through her body and did no damage to her as she continued to charge at the ten men. The rest of them drew their weapons and fired at the strangely dressed woman with the sword and charging right at them.

She charged right into the center of the fair size group of men and started to hack away at any hands holding weapons and firing at her. When she had them disarmed, she got down to business and chopped at each man until they fell to the ground and were no longer a threat against her. Two of the men tried to throw a number of kicks and chops at her, but she easily brushed the feeble attempts to stop her with their feet or injured hands aside.

When she had all ten men dead or so badly injured they were no longer any serious threat against her, she turned her attention towards the building and started to enter it.

Just as she appeared outside and eliminated the threat against the two agents inside the building, the group of men on the landing that grew to a number of seven now, started to fire down at the two agents who jumped to the side of the stairwell, and they took cover and started to return fire at the ones firing at them. The group of the landing fanned out so the two agents were unable to see their bodies as they reached into the stairwell with just their hands and weapons, and fired down at the two agents wildly. It quickly turned into a standoff, with each side unable to get the drop on the other, but the weapon fire was heavy. A number of the men stationed on the landing had automatic pistols with twenty five round clips in the weapons.

It was like a thunder storm taking place inside the building from the deafening roar of the weapons going off and the rounds bouncing off the cement first floor. There was so much smoke from the weapon fire that it was almost impossible to see what any of the shooters were doing any longer. Suddenly, a shape of a person rushed by the two agents and the shape ran up the stairs as she roared with angry at the group of men trying to kill her ward.

"What the fuck was that who just ran by us for crap sake? I couldn't make out what the hell it was, but it looked like some nut just ran by us and went charging up the damn stairs to do who knows what. I sure hope whoever the hell it was, wasn't someone helping them scumbags up there out for crap sake. We got enough of them bastards up there without them getting any extra help from someone else. Where the hell's out damn back up dammit? I'm sure they can hear this weapon fire all the way back at out damn headquarters, and these police we have surrounding this dump as still not assisting our asses, for crap sake." Agent Fugiwara called out to his partner as he leaned back and then dropped his empty clip from his weapon and then slammed a loaded clip home, released the slid of his weapon and was firing up the stairs again.

'Jesus Christ' Rossie growled at himself because he was in a much better position to see what was going on around him than Fugiwara was. He immediately realized it was Wind who just went charging by them still dressed in her battle armor, and she was holding her sword out before her as she obviously went to confront the ones firing down at them. He found himself cursing her out for disobeying his orders for her never to interfere with his work under any circumstances, He tried to see where she went, but the heavy smoke from the rounds was clouding the upper are of the stairwell, shielding whatever was talking place up there from his view.

Finally, three Washington Police Officers came charging into the hallway after checking out what happened to the group who was found slaughtered on the front porch of the building. Two of the officers went to Fugiwara's side, while the third officer went over to support Rossie.

The Lieutenant asked him. "What the hell do you have going down in here, sir?"

"We have an unknown number of purps trapped up there on the second floor of this dump, and they're firing down at us. Did you call in for any added backup support, Lieutenant?"

"I sure did sir, what the hell happened outside this place sir? We had a helluva time trying to get through all the damn gore out there, sir." The Lieutenant asked the Special Agent.

"What happened outside? We didn't engage anyone outside the building, all the action is going down inside here. Come to think about it, why the hell didn't the purps outside come in to support these assholes we have trapped up there on the second floor?"

"I don't know if you know it or not, but you have something like eight to twelve purps out there who have been slaughtered like I never saw anyone chopped up like them fools are. They looked like they were run over with a lawnmower. Someone sure had themselves a fricking field day chopping them up like they were a birthday cake or something. Hell, some of their bodies were chopped up so bad that a number of their pieces are out in the middle of the damn street..."

Men screaming in terrible pain drown out the Police Lieutenant's words, and their eyes looked up the stairwell, and then he added to his words excitedly. "What the hell's going on up there for Christ sake? It sounds like them fucking guys are being slaughtered up there sir. Hell, they're not even still shooting down here at us any longer, sir. It seems like all their rounds are being fired up there on the second floor now. What the hell's going on here dammit?"

Up on the second floor, Wind charged into the seven men like an attacking spirit, her sword a blur of silver ripping into the unprotected bodies of the men shooting down at her ward. She was like a spirit possessed, fueled by the fear one of these men being able to kill her Liege Lord. She was wildly but in a controlled manner swinging her sword and anything that moved on the floor. The men were shooting at her and their bullets just passing through her body, not causing her any damage or pain, as she continued to swing her ancient killing Katana sword at anyone she saw moving in the restricted area she was attacking these men in.

The men saw their bullets were having no effect on this crazy acting woman attacking them so wildly, so a few of them decided to try and get away from her before she killed everyone on the landing. Their efforts to escape her wrath was all for naught, she continued to slash and chop at the men now running in all directions, as they continued to fire their weapons wilding at her, hitting mostly the walls and floors with only a few of the rounds hitting her body. She completely ignored the bullets as she continued to go after the men shooting their fire sticks at her and her Lord. Her rage coming out from her mouth in a form of a roar, as she slashed one man across the throat with her sword, and then she allowed the momentum to carry her around and she ended up coming to position that allowed her to stab another one of the men in the chest.

When her sword sank deep into his chest, she lifted up on the Tsuka or hilt of her sword, causing the razor sharp edge to nearly split the man in half from the breast bone up to his throat. The man rolled off the edge of her sword and ended up as a heap lying at her feet as she merely stepped over this downed man, and she charged after another one who was trying to escape her attack. She easily caught up to this man and struck him across the back with her sword, the blade easily cutting through his skin and backbone until it severed his backbone and cut through his spinal cord. Paralyzing him instantly, and she again swung her sword once more at the downed man as she ran past him, cutting his head from his shoulders as she went after another one of the black men now frantically trying to get away from her and the killing sword.

She caught up to this and he suddenly stopped running and dropped down to his knees and put his hands up is a surrender, but she did not recognize his move and attacked him like he was preparing to attack her from his knees. She swung her sword at his face, catching him just below the chin, and the tip of the sword did massive damage to his throat, but her attack did not killing him outright. Still following her Bushido or the Way of the Warrior training of not allowing your defeated enemy to suffer needlessly, she hit him again in the throat with her sword. This man's head jumped into the air, and then tumbled chin over head until it hit the floor. She ignored the still twitching body as she searched the area for another person to attack.

Surveying the carnage she caused as she slaughtered seven men trying to kill her Master, she let out her breath in a rush. She never picked up Young watching the slaughter of his soldiers by this one person. He shook his head, and then he dipped back away from the door and went to the hidden hall and made good his escape of the building, by following the escape route until he ended up in the building next door, and he came out in the backyard. He jumped over a fence and dashed up the driveway and came out on Ninth Street where he crossed the street and went down another driveway and came to a second house he used as a hideout in the area. He hunkered down in this home that had a woman and two young kids in it and he growled at her to hide him.

The young black woman put her son down on the floor, and then she pulled Young's arm and lead him to the bathroom then she pointed up to the ceiling to a metal grill. She told him to reach up and pull the grate down and then climb into the opening and she would replace the grill. He struggled into the opening and she forced the grill back in place as she warned him not to move or make a sound if he heard the police enter her home and demand to search it. Then she left him and went back to take care of her two young boys. She told the older one who was the only one who could talk, not to say a word about the man who was using the bathroom. The boy just shrugged and then he went back to watching the television like it was no big deal.

Wind, not seeing anyone still alive and an active threat against her or her Lord, she lowered her sword, but then she heard footsteps rushing up the stair and she started to concentrate and the cloud returned and immediately whisked her away from the carnage. She disappeared as Special Agent Fugiwara and the Police Lieutenant made it to the top of the landing, and they were being followed closely by the two other police officers and Agent Rossie, who was looking around the crime scene for any sign of Wind. Not seeing any trace of her anywhere, he relaxed and he started to examine the slaughter she had created with her sword on the second floor.

"Holyyyy shit, what the hell happened up here for the love of God? In all my years on the job, this is the worst slaughter I have ever come across. What the devil are you two Special Agents chasing around here anyway? Do you guys have any idea who could have done this and why? Is this something we should know about, and be ready to defend ourselves against, Agent Fugiwara?" The stunned Police Lieutenant said as he carefully walked around the best he could over the hacked to death bodies of the dead men scatted all over the second floor landing.

"I haven't the froggiest fucking idea what the hell happened up her for crap sake. All I know was we were here to interview Young, to see if he knew anything about the murder of Batterman. Crap, I wonder if Young is in this mess of humanity. The world would have been served a favor if he's among the dead up here, dammit." Agent Fugiwara mumbled as he started looking around to see if he could find Young's body among all the mess that was once human beings.

"Mr. Batterman's murdered, how? When did the hell this happen? I just gave the bastard a speeding ticket a few months ago. He's a real bastard, told me he was going to have my damn shield if I didn't tear up the tick. I think the man was starting to believe his own publicity if you ask me. Hell, he must have though his shit didn't stink to be driving the way he was when I caught up with him. I had to chase his ass for several blocks before he finally pulled over." The surprised Police Lieutenant remarked as he also started picking his way over the slaughtered bodies while looking for any sign of who might have been responsible for the attack both up there on the second floor, and also out on the front porch of the building.

Agent Rossie found himself second guessing himself over allowing Wind to remain in what she called the living world. He was beginning to worry if she's this capable of slaughtering nearly twenty heavily armed and well trained to kill men so easily. Then maybe it isn't a good idea for him to continue to try and protect her like he was doing. He would have continued with his thought if it wasn't for Agent Fugiwara who suddenly called out to him, and then asked him if he had any ideas of who might have killed all these men so savagely.

"Huh, what was that you just asked me, Agent Fugiwara-san? I guess I'm a little stunned over all the savagery I'm seeing up here on the landing."

"I just asked you if you had any idea of who might have done this to these fricking guys. As much as I hated these people and wanted to get them the hell off the streets, none of them deserved what happened to them up here, Rossie-san." The concerned Agent Fugiwara replied as he turned his attention back to where he was walking on the landing over the bodies.

"How the hell would I know what happened up here and who might have attacked these people, Fugiwara-san? I don't have a damn crystal ball you know!"

"Man, what the hell crawled up your ass and died? I just asked you a simple question my friend. Just watch where the hell you're walking up here. I don't want you stepping on any possible evidence, or slipping on the blood and go tumbling down the stairs on me, partner."

Agent Rossie immediately felt like an ass by the way he just barked at his partner because he was so upset over the fact Wind had disobeying him, and killed so many people. Because she obviously was following her oath of protecting him from any possible harm as he mumbled back at the other worried agent. "I guess I'm a little upset at what I'm seeing up here, Fugiwara-san. Like the Lieutenant just said, I too have never seen such slaughter of a human being like this before in my life, Fugiwara-san. Sorry I just bit your head off, I owe you a beer my friend."

"And I'll take you up on that beer, after seeing all this mess I think I'm going to really tie one on tonight when we get off duty. It's going to take a lot for me to unsee what I have seen in this damn building. What the hell happened here and who the hell did this? Though they might have done us a service in killing these animals, this is no way for a man to die, especially here in the United States, Rossie-san. I think we better back off and get the forensics people in here and let them do their act and see what they might come up with." Fugiwara offered as he started to back out of the area. He could not wait to get off this floor. The sight of all this blood and gore was turning his stomach and making him sick. He could not even get a good number on the amount of people slaughtered on the landing the bodies were so badly chopped up.

Agent Rossie did not bother to argue with his partner, because much like him, the slaughter on the landing was also making him sick to his stomach as well. He looked around the area and noticed the Police Lieutenant was nowhere to be seen on the second floor landing. He had no idea the Lieutenant was on the first floor and he ran out the back door and he was heaving his guts out over the terrible slaughter he discovered on the second floor of the building.

FBI SPECIAL AGENT ROBERT ROSSIE'S APARTMENT

The cloud carrying the spirit of Wind rapidly developed right in the center of Rossie's living room, and it deposited her and she ended up kneeling on the floor as the thick cloud disappeared about her. She was still dressed in her heavy but severely altered ancient battle robe and arm and shin guard protection, but they was heavily splattered with blood and small pieces of the bodies she had chopped to dead while living up to her oath of protecting her new Lord and Master. She looked at her sword and got up to her feet and went into the bathroom and carefully washed her sword clean of all traces of blood and body flecks.

Once the deadly killing sword was clean, she carefully leaned it up against the sink, and then she struggled out of her robe and proceeded to clean it of all the blood covering the ancient robe. It was quite a chore to try and clean the blood from the body armor, because of the protection and all the braid and heavy leather construction of the robe.

All the while she was cleaning her armor and weapons she did not give a second thought to her own body that was still covered nearly from head to toe with blood and skin flecks as well. Any exposed parts of her body had blood and or flecks of skin stuck to her body. But her first responsibility was to care for her weapons and body armor, and once she had accomplished the care for these items. Then she would turn her attention to her body and her own needs.

As she washed her body armor she worried how her Lord and Master was going to react over her coming to his aide like she did. She knew her Liege Lord had ordered her never to come near him while he was on the job, but her sacred oath to the sword superseded her Lord's own order. She let out her breath in a sigh, feeling she would handle her Lord's reaction when he came home, and he either thanked her for saving his life, or cursed her for interfering with his work.

She lifted her heavily modified age-old body armor out of the tub, and then she started the shower running the way her new Lord taught her to turn the water on, and then she started to wash her body clean of the gore that nearly covered her.

BACK AT YOUNG'S BUILDING

Both FBI Special Agents, Robert Rossie and Shinnosuke Fugiwara was trying to stay out of the way as a horde or crime scene investigators flooded into the building and started examining the slaughtered bodies scattered about all over the second floor landing, as a second group of investigators started checking the bodies slaughtered just outside the building.

Agent Rossie was kind of just standing near the investigators as they dug through all the gore, trying to get an accurate number of dead people that were scattered about. But the remains of the dead were so scattered about the area that it was almost impossible for the forensic people to tell how many dead there were. He was trying to tell if Young was among the dead.

Agent Shinnosuke Fugiwara was speaking to one of the investigators from the FBI when Commander Ralph Murdock came charging into the target building, looking for his two agents. He was immediately informed his agents were caught up in a heavy firefight, and he left the office to check on his people. He did not head for the White House as he offered Agent Rossie earlier in the day, because he felt his agent's lives were more important than a meeting with the President. Murdock marched right up to Fugiwara and pulled him away from the other agent by his arm, so he could speak with him in private. When they were far enough away from the other officers, Commander Murdock grumbled at his agent. "Are you okay mister? You're not hurt are you and how is Agent Rossie and where the hell is he at around here, mister?"

"We're both alright that God for that sir, but it was a helluva mess for a few moments until we got some help from some unknown person, sir…"

"I can see the mess for myself. What do you mean someone helped you and where the hell is that person at, mister? I want to speak with that person!" Murdock groused at his agent.

"I have no idea who the hell helped us out sir, all I know was we were heavily pinned down with weapon fire coming from Young and his gang of assholes, sir. Then suddenly someone ran past us and charged up the steps and attacked the shooters. If it wasn't for this person, we might not be here speaking together, sir. It was that close sir." Fugiwara reported to his control.

"You mean this guy came and helped you two out, and then I guess he just sort of disappeared back from wherever the hell he came from. Is that what you're trying to tell me mister? And you never got a chance to even speak to this savor of yours for crap sake, mister."

"That's just it Commander, if you asked me to describe this person or to even tell you if this person was a male or female, I couldn't say with positivity which he or she was, sir. It all happened so damn quickly. We were dodging a shower of rounds and this person just charged right past us, and then attacked these guys on the second landing, sir."

"You mean to tell me this person just ran up the damn steps under heavy weapon fire, and none of these flaming assholes were able to kill this person before he did all this to these damn fools? How many dead are up here anyhow? From the looked of it, it looks like a horde of purps were chopped to death up here. Hey Sergeant, you have any idea how many god damn people are dead up here yet for crap sake?" Commander Murdock suddenly bellowed out at one the forensic people busy checking on the dead on the landing.

"I haven't the first idea yet how many are dead up here on the landing sir. It's one helluva jigsaw puzzle we're trying to figure out sir, and until we get a better handle on the number of people dead up here, you'll be the first one to know sir."

"Yeah, right, okay, whatever the hell you say buster. And you Agent Fugiwara, if you have no idea if it was a man, woman or beast that helped you two out here! Then give me your best guess on who might have helped you out here, and where the hell is Agent Rossie at for crap sake?"

"I'm right here Commander." Agent Rossie offered as he walked up behind his control.

"It's about time you decided to report to my ass mister. Do you have any idea who might have helped you two birds out here for crap sake?"

Agent Fugiwara cut in and offered. "Commander Murdock, I believe it was a female person who might have helped us out here, and she was dressed like an ancient Samurai Warrior. But in a modern day outfit the best as I was able to tell because she charged by us so quickly, sir..."

"What the hell is wrong with you anyhow? A fucking female Samurai Warrior attacked this group of fricking purps armed with automatic weapons, and they're the ones chopped up like they just went through a damn meat grinder. I think I want you to stop watching so many god damn movies for crap sake. Sheesh a female Warrior attacking heavily armed men with a damn sword. When was the last time you did a drug check, I want you to report in for a drug screen, mister. Or I want you to stop drinking whatever the hell you're drinking lately, mister."

"I saw the same thing Agent Fugiwara-san saw, and I think he's wrong with saying it was some woman who attacked these shitbirds up here, sir." Special Agent Rossie said trying to hide the fact the person who helped them out was a female Samurai Warrior. He was trying his best to protect Wind from discovery by the other agents working on the crime scene.

"Don't tell me you're going to try and tell me some dude with a god damn sword did all this to these men up here, mister. If you try that then I want the both of you reporting in for a drug screen…" Murdock's complaint was interrupted by one of the forensic experts.

"Say Commander I believe your Agent might be right about one thing here sir. I can sure as hell tell you that everyone killed on this landing was killed with a sword, and someone who knew what the hell he or she was doing with the damn think. The best I can tell, the sword attacker went after all these purps hands, disarming them first and then he or she seems to have really enjoyed her craft as he or she took their time with chopping these poor souls up like they were lambs heading for the slaughter, sir. All the wounds I'm seeing on the bodies, all point to their deaths was caused by a sword, or some other large form of a blade, sir."

"You gotta be shitting my stinking ass around here mister. You want me to fucking believe some lone woman armed with just a fricking blade, sword or whatever the hell they used," Commander Murdock stopped speaking at this point, and then he gave a harsh glare at Agent Fugiwara for a moment, before he went on with his angry words aimed at the forensic person. "Killed I don't know how many god damn men heavily armed with automatic weapons, and her or his ass isn't among the damn dead up here mister?"

"I guess that's what I'm trying to tell you at this point sir." The Forensic Agent replied to his Commander.

"When was the last time you had a drug screen ran on your ass, mister?"

CHAPTER THIRTEEN

The forensic man laughed at the Commander's remark about him doing a drug screen as he went back to working on the dead lying all over the landing. Then Commander Murdock turned his attention back to Agent Fugiwara and barked at him angrily. "What the hell went on here and who the hell are all these people slaughtered like this up here? Who the devil did this, and where the hell is this person who did this anyway? Where the hell is he and why the hell isn't he in handcuffs and waiting for my ass to interview the sonofabitch, mister?"

"I don't know who this person who came to our aide is or was sir, all I know is the person charged up the staircase and attacked and killed all these people firing at us from up here sir."

You mean to tell me that one person charged up the staircase while under heavy weapon fire, and he was able to slaughter all these damn purps up here, and none of these bastards hit that person with any of their damn rounds they were firing at you guys? What the hell are you trying to hand me around here mister? I saw all the damage from the rounds these asses were firing at you guys, and there's no way in hell his side of judgment day that anyone could have possible charged up all them damn steps, and not get killed by the heavy wall of lead these bastards were firing down at you two asses. Where the hell is Agent Rossie hiding anyway, mister?" The Commander suddenly bitched back at his agent just as angrily.

"I'm right here Commander, I was busy checking out the crime scene people sir." Agent Rossie replied as he moved up and stood right by the other two agents on the landing.

"Well, I thank God neither of my two Agents was injured in this damn old turkey shoot here. Okay you two, I want to know what the hell took place here, and I want to know about it right this minute dammit? I want to know why the person who helped you two out is not standing here and willing to tell me everything that happened here. I want a complete description of this person if you can't produce the person himself for crap sake. Is this person wounded and on the way to the damn hospital?" Commander Murdock growled as he led his two agents a little away from the area where the slaughter took place, so they could speak more or less in private together. Even thought they were still within earshot of the forensic people checking out the crime scene.

"I really don't know what the hell happened here as yet myself, sir. All I know for certain is as we first entered the damn building we spoke to Young for a few seconds, and he obviously didn't like what we were asking of him. So he allowed his flock of bodyguards do all the talking for his ass, and then they attacked us in force, sir. We instantly got involved in a heavy firefight with these bastards dead up here sir, and as we were defending ourselves. This unknown person suddenly came charging past me in a blur and right up the steps and attacked these people without a word said to either of us sir. It happened so fast I barely was able to see this person go by me sir." Agent Fugiwara reported to his controller in a rather excited voice as he continued to try and piece together what really happened between this stranger and the other people.

"And none of these lousy bastards hit this person with any of the rounds they were firing down at you two bird? Is this what you two want me to believe about the situation you two were involved in?" Murdock asked as he stared at his two agents while waiting for his response.

"I guess they didn't but I don't see how the hell they must have missed the person. The bastards were firing so many rounds down at us during the heavy confrontation, sir."

"I can't believe this crap for one damn second for crap sake. You two want me to believe these purps were firing down at you guys with automatic weapons, and this unknown person ran right past you two and charged up these steps and was not hit by any of the damn rounds these guys were firing down at you two? That's fricking impossible!" Murdock snapped as he suddenly flung his hands up in the air in disgust, and almost stomped away from his two agents.

"I guess that's what I'm saying sir." Fugiwara replied while Rossie was allowing him to do all the talking for the both of them, even though he was the one in charge of the investigation.

"Well then can you at least describe this person to me, so I can maybe put out an APB (All Points Bulletin) on this person and have him arrested so I can question him?"

"The best I can describe this person is, it was a woman and she was dressed as an ancient Samurai Warrior getup, and she attacked these purps like she was a wild person the best I could see through all the smoke raised by the weapon fire, sir." Fugiwara reported to his control.

"What the hell is wrong with your damn head anyway mister? You want me to believe this person who killed all these damn people up here was a female, an ancient Samurai Warrior as you just put it Fugiwara? When the hell was the last time you submitted yourself for a god damn drug screen mister? I think you've been watching too many of you damn Japanese movies lately, and they must've evidently gone to your damn noggin or something mister. And what about you Agent Rossie, what the hell did you see? I want you to describe the person you saw running by you when this little shindig started, mister? And you better not give me the same line of shit as your partner just tried to hand me." Murdock turned his attention to the lead agent this time.

"I saw basically the same thing as Agent Fugiwara-san did sir, but the person I saw was that of a man as best as I could tell for the second I saw this person, sir." Agent Rossie added, still trying to protect Wind from discovery from the other agents for the time being.

"What the hell is going on around here for the love of God? I guess you two jackasses want me to believe some person has ran by you two, and that person had attacked a number of heavily armed purps... Hey Forensic man how many people do you think was killed up here, dammit?"

"I don't know quite yet sir, the bodies are in quite the shape, and I'm having a hard time trying to fix a number of dead up here sir, but I can tell you it's over five at the moment sir."

"Yeah, right, okay you got it Forensic man you just keep doing what the hell you're doing and get me a fricking number on the dead up here as quickly as you can, mister. And as for you two, you guys want me to believe that some damn savior charged up the stairs and killed all these fricking people with a god damn sword, while they were firing at you and this person with automatic weapons, a fucking sword! Dammit, I want the both of you to report for a drug screen the moment you two report back to headquarters as soon as possible..."

"I'm sorry for interrupting you at this time Commander Murdock Sir, but I have to agree with your two Agents here sir. As far as I can tell, all these dead up here have surely been murdered by someone with a sword, or a large knife or something like that, sir."

"What the hell is going on around here for crap sake? Am I losing my damn mind or something, dammit? You two want me to believe someone..." Murdock turned and faced Fugiwara for a second and gave him a look that informed him he thought the agent was going nuts on him, and then he went on with his bitch. "That some possible female bitch with a god damn sword hacked to dead a number of heavily armed soldiers for this Young piece of shit, and none of them were able to kill this attacker. For the love of the Christ Child, how the hell is this possible, some damn broad going up against a horde of heavily armed men with automatic weapons with a god damn sword, and she or he according to my other Agent that thinks this person was a guy, got away without a fucking scratch? Where? How the hell did this person get away from you guys without either of you two trying to stop this person from leaving the damn crime scene?" Commander Murdock added to his bitch at his two agents.

"That got the both of us confused. We both saw this person charge up the stairs, but the person never came down and we checked out the entire area up here and we were unable to locate where and how the person was able to get away from us, sir." Fugiwara reported to his control again.

"I guess this person just evaporated into thin air on you two guys. What else could it be, we got some person who came to the aide of my two Agents, and then this person just disappeared as quickly as he or she appeared to help you two birds out. I want some of the same shit you two are obviously drinking or smoking around here, so I can see the same shit you two people are seeing for a change, dammit." Commander Murdock complained bitterly as he just shook his head in disbelieve over what he was hearing coming from his two grim covered and exhausted agents.

"You also have to remember Commander Murdock. Batterman was attacked and murdered by someone with a sword back in Japan, along with Hiromoai Hatanaka who was also slaughtered with a sword in much the same matter that these guys up here were slaughtered with a sword. Also sir, Asahiko Yurkowa's son and his wife were also killed with a sword, as were a number of his bodyguards, along with Asahiko himself, who was also killed when his head was chopped off with a sword in Japan, sir." Agent Rossie reported mainly because he had to bring up these deaths in Japan, or he would be questioned by Murdock when he finally read his report about Batterman's death in Japan. He hated bringing up these deaths because it was going to connect what took place in Japan to what just took place inside the building they were standing in

"Hummmm, now I'm starting to get the full picture around here good and clear for a change. It's quite evident that this person who murdered Batterman and the others back in Japan, has evidently followed you back here to the United States, and this supposed female ancient Samurai Warrior..." For a second time Murdock turned and looked back at Agent Fugiwara like he lost his mind, and then he went on with is angry words to the two agents. "I'm beginning to see a correlation between the two cases, and either she or he is attempting to silence anyone and everyone who might be able to identify this person to us. So this person you two were bragging was your damn savior might very well turn out to be the murderer in both these cases.

"Okay Agents Rossie and Fugiwara, this is what I want you two to do. I want the both of you to remain here until Forensics has wrapped up their investigation of this mess. You don't have to wait until they clean up the bodies and the rest of this crap. I just want you to stay long enough until you can determine how many of the lousy bastards were killed up here, and also outside this damn dump, and then you're both to report back to Headquarters and we'll go over what you two collected here. Then we'll determine where this case if going to go from that point on. Right now I have to get back to Headquarters and notify the President why the hell I didn't report over to the White House like he had requested of me." Commander Murdock offered as he turned and then he carefully walked around the gore the best he could as he quickly left the building.

The moment the Commander was out of sight, Fugiwara angrily grabbed hold of Rossie's arm and almost dragged him into an empty room, and the moment the door closed he jumped on him with both feet. "What the hell do you call what you did to me in front of Murdock was all about, my so called friend? You hung me out to dry in front of his ass, buster? You saw as much of that person as I did and you know damn well it was defiantly a damn female with a sword that charged past us and attacked those men. Why the hell did you tell him you thought that person was a male for? Look Rossie-san, you're still holding back some important information of this god damn murder case, and for the life of me I can't figure out why you won't take me into your confidence. I'm your fucking partner and I'm working on this murder case with you man.

"If you don't want me to be part of this investigation then I suggest you get yourself another damn partner, one who don't give a damn if you solve this murder case or not. I want to solve it as soon as possible. For some reason you're still holding back so crap from me and until I know what the hell you won't tell me of this case, I feel I'm beating my damn head against a wall. C'mon man, you gotta tell me what you're holding back on me, or kiss my ass good bye and I'm ask Murdock to replace me on this damn case, and you know he's gonna want to know why I want outta the damn case,

Rossie-san." Agent Fugiwara then sharpened his glare and stared Rossie dead in the eyes as he waited for him to explain when he was still holding back on him.

"Look Fugiwara-san, I already told you that you're going to have to stick with me for a little while longer, and when I can figure out the proper way for me to inform you over what the devil is really going down with this damn murder case. Then and only then will I take you into my confidence and clue you in on everything that went down with this case so far. If I try and tell you right now, you're really going to think I lost my mind, and something I think I did over this case. You wouldn't believe a thing I'd be forced to tell you and believe me, you're not ready to see the proof I'll be forced to show you, if I took you into my confidence over this case. You can't go to Murdock and tell him to replace you with this case. Or he's sure as hell going to yank me off the damn case. Then I'd really be placed between a rock and a hard place, and I'd be forced to go to him before I'm ready to give him all my evidence over this case.

"C'mon man, after all the years we have known each other, you have to stand by me until I know for certain you'll be able to handle what I'd be forced to show you, and explain to you over this damn murder case, without my driving you to think I have completely lost my mind over this mess. I can tell you this much though my friend, once I show you what I'm holding back on you, you won't believe either your ears, or your eyes for that matter over what you'll see, and why I'm forced to protect her as long as possible over this mess, Agent Fugiwara-san..."

"There, I knew I was right about you Rossie-san." Agent Fugiwara interrupted his partner, and then went on with his words. "I knew you were protecting someone over this case, and since you said her, now I know that chick with the sword is the one you're trying to protect for some reason that's beating the crap outta me. If this crazy woman who hacked these asses to death is the one you're protecting, who are you trying to protect her from? Hell, if this chick is the one who killed Batterman and the others in Japan, and this horde of assholes in here and outside this building. Then I don't see any reason why you're trying to protect her. Shit, if she can kill these people like they didn't matter crap to her, what the hell is stopping her from turning her damn sword on you and killing you just as easy as she killed anyone else she wanted to silence around here, man?"

"I have no fear of that ever happening to me, Fugiwara-san. Believe me that's no threat to me man. But I guess I have to be somewhat honest with you at this point. You're absolutely correct I am desperately trying to protect the killer of Batterman and the rest of the people killed in Japan and now here in and around this damn building. But there's a reason and as soon as I can figure out a way to prove to everyone in concern over this situation, why I needed to protect this woman like I am. Then I'll bring her out in the open and introduce her to the world, and I'll stun the entire world about Wind." Agent Rossie suddenly announced to his partner.

"Wind, Rossie-san?" Agent Fugiwara asked as he looked at Rossie in a confused state.

"Yes Wind, and that's all you're going to know about this woman who has taken an oath of protecting my life from all harm for the time being, Agent Fugiwara-san." He replied.

"C'mon Rossie-san, you can't possible clam up on me now, not after admitting to me that you harboring a known murderer, man. This has to be some shit to cause you to try and protect a known murderer Rossie-san. What the hell does she have on you man? Did you make this chick pregnant or something man? That's the only reason I can see to dare protect someone who you know beyond a shadow of a doubt is a murderer, man." Fugiwara offered while trying to keep the smile off his life, feeling he now discovered why his partner was trying to protect this woman.

"Man I just wish for once you would keep your stinking mind outta the damn gutter my friend. No it's nothing like that man. She ain't knocked up and I don't think she could get pregnant. I have to try and protect her because she's not really guilty of any murder..."

"How the hell do you figure that way Rossie-san? We just witnessed this chick chop a number of men to death like she was a damn windmill. Seeing what she did here, I'd be hard pressed to say she's not guilty of murder, man. C'mon man, you gotta tell me the whole thing now you can't possibly end this story this way, and leave so many questions unanswered for me. Look my friend, if you don't tell me everything there is to know about this chick then I'm going to Murdock and tell him everything you just told me, Rossie-san." Agent Fugiwara threatened

Agent Rossie just stared back at Fugiwara until he finally smiled, and then bitched back at him. "I see you're not going to buy my threat of going to Murdock, are you Rossie-san?"

"Not in the least my friend. I know you too well for me to believe that lame a threat you just aimed at my ass, Fugiwara-san. Look, if you put up with me until I find the right way to introduce Wind to the rest of the world, I swear you're going to be knocked three steps back man. Then you'll understand it was well worth you waiting until I was ready to introduce her to the world. But I promise you that

I'll introduce her to you long before I do to Murdock and the rest of the world. I promise you, once you meet Wind you're be trying just as hard as I do to protect her until we'll be ready to bring her out from the shadows."

"I guess I went this far with you, so I might as well go the rest of the way until I finally meet this Wind person of yours, and then I can judge her for myself, before I put in with you and start protecting her like you're doing with her. But for now I think I just might…"

There was a knock on the door to where the two agents were talking, and Agent Rossie replied to the knock. "Yeah, what is it we're kinda busy in here, dammit."

"Yeah Agent Rossie Sir, this is Agent Williams from Forensic, sir. I'd like to speak with you for a second sir. I have just figured out how many men were slaughtered up here, sir."

"Give me a second will you please, I'll be right with you Agent Williams Sir." Agent Rossie replied and then he turned his attention back to Agent Fugiwara and asked him with concern in his voice. "Can I count on you over this damn situation Fugiwara-san?"

"All the way as I always am, Rossie-san."

"Great, let's get out there and see what they found for us." The two agents walked out of the room like there was nothing wrong and found Agent Williams waiting for them to come out.

"What do you have for me Agent Williams Sir?"

"Well we were able to reconstruct eleven skulls, finding most of the heavy lower jaw bones left intact sir. But we're not overruling there could be one or two more victims we're unable to uncover in the gore from the slaughtered people. I gotta tell you this sir, whoever did this, really enjoyed their work sir. It seemed the attacker went back and forth over the bodies a number of times, still hacking away with the weapon at the all remains of the dead until there wasn't enough of the pieces left still intact to strike again with the weapon they were using on the dead, sir.

"At first I thought there could have been up to as many as five possible attackers to be able to have done this much damage to these poor people, sir. But all we found with footprints in size seven female, and they were all over every part of the bodies we were checking out sir. There's no doubt whatsoever in my mind that one person was responsible for all the deaths of these people up here on the landing sir. I have also compared notes with the other investigators working on the bodies on the outside of the building, Agent Rossie Sir."

"That was a good report Agent Williams, and I trust before I leave for headquarters, you'll have all your findings down on hard copy for me sir?" Agent Rossie asked the other agent.

"I already have my report ready for your needs, sir." Agent Williams handed him a sealed envelope, and then he smiled at the other agent.

"Very good Agent Williams and I'll make noted of your attention to duty on my report, and include your report in with mine when I file them both for Commander Murdock, sir."

"I thank you for the courtesy Agent Rossie Sir." With that said Agent Williams turned and headed back to the scene of death, and he quickly started wrapping up his equipment as the next crew came in and started cleaning up the body parts from the second floor landing.

Agent Rossie turned to Fugiwara and then announced to him with a smirk on his lips. "Well I guess that's that for here.

We better get over to Headquarters and start preparing our report for Commander Murdock, or we're never going to get back to our homes tonight."

AGENT ROSSIE'S APARTMENT

Wind was kneeling in the center of Rossie's living room meditating. She was praying to Lord Buddha to make her Lord pleased with her poor efforts of protecting his life from the horde of people obviously trying to kill him. She was also praying to have her Lord forgive her for interfering with his work, but she was operating under her oath to protect her ward from harm. She found herself wondering why the male animal found it so hard to accept help for what they classified as the lowly women of their world. She was amused because she could not understand why her Lord or any other male member of the human race could not figure out if it was not for the women the men would never get anything accomplished, and all they would do is die foolishly fighting with their neighbors over land, food or want of what their neighbor possessed.

She had no idea of the time or the length of time she was kneeling while waiting for her Lord and Master to return home for the night. She was hoping he would share her pillow tonight, so she could remove the anger from his mind of her coming to his aide earlier in the day. She did not even realize it had turned dark out, and it was already after midnight.

FBI HEADQUARTERS, ZERO, ONE TEN HOURS (1:10 A.M.)

Both Agent Robert Rossie and Agent Shinnosuke Fugiwara were still busy writing out and comparing their notes together, to finish their report for their Commander. Every once in a while Rossie would peek out into the hallway and noticed the light in Commander Ralph Murdock's office was still burning, and that meant he was going to wait all night long if necessary, for them to finish up with their reports. He just got comfortable back in his chair when he heard a slight commotion outside his office and he got up and checked it out.

To his surprise he noticed Murdock outside his office and he was paying a delivery boy who was holding four Pizzas. Then he looked around and spotted three other agents still working at their desks, and realized his boss just brought food for all the agents working late tonight. He ducked back in his office and announced to Agent Fugiwara some food had just arrived, and he replied he was starving and thinking about ordering something for them to eat himself.

Commander Murdock entered their office and threw a Pizza down on a side table, and then he announced. "If you two guys want, you can eat and then get the hell outta here and go home and get some sleep. Report back to work at 10 A.M. sharp and finish up with these damn reports you're working on, I had no idea it was going to take you guys this long to write up some simple reports. What the hell are you two doing, writing the damn things out in longhand for crap sake?"

"Thanks plenty for the food." Agent Rossie announced but he did not beat Agent Fugiwara to the Pizza, he already had it opened and was removing the first piece and chomping down on it. Murdock left their office and Rossie grabbed a piece of Pizza, and then he asked Fugiwara. "What say my friend, do you want to stay all night and finish up these damn reports for the boss? I feel by the time we finally get home, all we're going to be able to do is kick off our damn shoes and we'll just get comfortable in bed and we'll have to report back to work."

"I feel the same way, and we both don't have anyone waiting for us tonight, so we might as well finish off the damn reports. Besides, I'd like to get out there early this morning and find out if Young was among the dead on the landing. If he wasn't, I'd sure as hell like to make him one of the members of the dead if I had my way about the damn situation, Agent Rossie-san."

"Man, you seem to have a real hardon about this Young fella. Did he do something to you in another life or what, Fugiwara-san? You don't lose any sleep over this damn guy do you Agent Fugiwara-san?" Agent Rossie asked his partner as he smirked at him.

"I do have a kinda personal hardon for the little prick at that Rossie-san. You see a few years back he had this young kid working for him, and he sorta hung the poor kid out to dry, and the kid was killed by one of our Agents in a heavy shootout with Young and a number of his soldiers over a stupid thing that wasn't even worth one life. But the poor kid picked up the tab for Young's friggin greed. Ever since that day, you can say I have it in for the prick, Rossie-san."

"Do you have any idea who the Agent was that nailed the kid you're talking about, sir?"

"Yeah, it was me Agent Rossie-san." Fugiwara snapped back at him, and then he finished off the second slice of Pizza and he then went back to writing out his report for the Commander.

Agent Rossie just put his head down and went back to his report as well.

ROSSIE'S APARTMENT

For the first time since she had returned to the apartment, Wind finally took notice of the time and she grew very concerned because her Lord and Master had not as yet returned home from his day of work. Now her mind was working in overtime, and she found herself worried that her Liege Lord was so upset with her he was not going to return home for the night. She rose and began to pace around the small apartment. She was worried her Master was punishing her for interfering with his work and she was concerned if he was ever going to return home to her.

She dared to look out the front window to see if she could see his horseless wagon returning home. She saw no sign of his or any of the other horseless wagons that were always riding past her Master's home. She moved away from the window and thought about preparing something for her Master to enjoy, if he chose to return to his home and her. She begged to all the Kami to bring her Lord and Master safely home to her. She suddenly closed her eyes tight and tried to link her mind up to the small amulet given to her by the hand of the Creator of the sacred Eight Islands of Japan, Izanagi. But the only way she could communicate with the amulet was if and when her Lord and Master's life was in peril. All her efforts to see what her Liege lord was doing failed, and she resigned herself to waiting for her Master to return to her on his own.

She was even preparing her mind and body to commit the sacred act of Suppuku, the art of slicing one's belly open to appease her Lord and Master for some infraction she might have committed against his person. She was trying to think of every way possible for her to make up to her Liege Lord for disobeying his direct order not to do anything to interfere with his work.

As the night grew later and later the more she got upset with herself for causing any disrupting in her master's sacred Wa. (Harmony) She busied herself by cleaning the apartment again, and again she considered preparing something for her Lord to enjoy when he returned to her.

FBI HEADQUARTERS

Commander Ralph Murdock was no stranger to sleeping overnight in his office, it was one of the reasons he had a couch installed in his office. And this night was no accepting to his rule. He turned in shortly after buying the Pizza's for his agents working through the night, and he woke a little refreshed a few seconds after 6 A.M. He got up, stretched his arms over his head and then realigned his back and groaned over the pleasure it gave him. Then he walked to his door and looked out and saw no one in the outer offices, but he did see the light still on in Agent Rossie's office. Shaking his head he strolled towards the office and then looked in and got angry and barked at the two agents still working on their reports. "What the hell is this crap about? Didn't I tell you two fools to go home after choking down some damn food last night for crap sake?"

Bleary eyed Agent Rossie looked up from his report and he announced to his control. "You sure did Ralph, but we tossed a coin in the air and it came out tails, so we both decided to stay and finish off our report for you. We know how important it was for you to get our reports, so here we are and we're just about finished with both reports for you, Ralph."

"Damn, I don't know what the hell I'm gonna do with the two of you fools? You're the best two Agents I have on the job, yet you give me more trouble than my wife does for crap sake. Shit, since you two fools decided to work through the damn night, here's want you two will do. I want you to finish up the reports, and then I want the both of you to head home and rest for the rest of the stinking day. We start again tomorrow at 8 A.M. as always you two. How far along are you two with finishing off those two damn reports for my ass anyhow, dammit?"

Agent Rossie looked down and then he hit one key on his keyboard, and then he announced with a grin plastered on his lips to his contact. "I'm done Ralph!"

"Ohhh... you're a real funny guy there, mister. I should have known you had a damn..."

"I'm done as well Ralph. I guess I'll see you tomorrow morning." Agent Fugiwara added.

"Hummmm... I'm beginning to wonder to myself if you two smart birds were done with these damn reports, and you two were just sleeping in your office waiting for me to make a first class ass outta myself by giving you two sneaky bastards the rest of the day off, dammit."

"Hey, if you didn't catch us sleeping in here then it never happened I guess, Ralph." Agent Rossie smirked back at the Commander of the FBI Agents.

"Yeah, I thought so I guess I'll see you two birds in the morning. Err... thanks for getting those damn reports done for me so quickly, I really appreciate them being done. Now my part of the job starts on them damn reports. Be safe and

I'll see the both of you tomorrow morning." The Commander offered as he collected the two reports, and then he turned on his heels and headed back for his office as he bellowed out. "Agents Carlson, and Morrison in my office, we have some work to do people." He slapped the two reports in his hand as he stepped into his office.

"Say Rossie-san, I'll buy breakfast for the both of us if you're hungry that is?"

"Naw, I think I want to get home and put my feet up for a change and catch up on some of my much needed sleep. I'm really beat out because it's been one helluva past few days ever since I returned to the United States from Japan. Thanks anyway for the kind offer Fugiwara-san."

"I'm glad you brought up Japan before we left the office for the rest of the day, Rossie-san. I have a few questions I wanna to ask of you if you can spare me the time man."

Rossie sat back down and then waited for his partner to tell him what he wanted to ask him.

"Say Rossie-san, I just wanted to tell you that I got a pretty good look at that chick with the Katana blade, and she looked like a real fox, man." Fugiwara offered with a smirk on his lips.

"Oh brother, I see where this conversation is going in a fast hurry it up, mister."

"Good, then I don't gotta cover my tracks and beat around the damn bush with ya then Rossie-san. As I said, I got a pretty good look at this good looking chick, and I hafta ask ya man, have you been able to get her in the bed, and if so, how was she between the damn sheets, man?"

"Man, you really do love waddling around in the stinking gutter don't ya man?"

"Yeah, it gives me a good hardon every time, but I also noticed that you kinda avoided the answer to the question I just asked of ya man?" Agent Fugiwara smirked at his partner.

"Geese, well if you must know, yeah I got her in bed alright there are you happy mister? You going to be able to sleep tonight now that you know I'm scoring heavy with this fine looking chick as you call her. A word to the wise though, if you ever meet her, I think you might want to refrain from calling her a chick, at least right to her face that is. If you slip and call her a chick, you just might end up looking like some of Young's stinking people, Agent Fugiwara-san."

"Yeah, I thought so, now I know why you're trying so hard to protect her purdy little ass like you're doing man. How is she between the damn sheets, buddy? I bet in her outstanding condition she could go all day and night long, and still go looking for some more, man."

"I guess there's no limit to your debauchery is there Fugiwara-san? If you need know, when I first discovered her she knew little of what she calls the art of pillowing..."

"Holy shit man, she actually used the stinking word of pillowing on you, Rossie-san?" Agent Fugiwara asked with a wide grin on his lips.

"Yeah, why so excited about the word pillowing for my friend."

"What the hell gives with this chick anyway man? She uses a sword to melt out her justice, and then she uses words like pillowing. If I didn't know any better, it almost seems like she might be someone from Japan's ancient past, Agent Rossie-san."

"C'mon man, this conversation's getting a little way off the damn mark here my friend. The next thing I'm going to hear coming out of your mouth is she a ghost from the past, Fugiwara-san. And we both know that's impossible so don't even try going down that road my friend."

"Hummmm... strange you would even bring that kinda remark up in this damn conversation, unless there was something to that last remark that is, Agent Rossie-san?"

"C'mon man, you're allowing your Fed nose getting all worked up over nothing around here, and stop trying to milk me for any more information about Wind, and who she might be and how she might have got here in the United States, wiseguy. I told you more than once already that it's just too damn early for me to start to tell you anything more about Wind and what she's all about, my old friend. Why the hell don't you just let it go for the time being until I work it all out for myself, and then I'd be more than willing to tell you the whole story about Wind, Fugiwara-san." Agent Rossie actually snapped at his partner this time as he let out his breath in a sort of hiss.

"Yeah, I guess I'm going to be forced to wait until you're good and ready to spill the beans about this chick that just saved our lives yesterday my friend. Well if I have to wait then that's what I'm gonna do. How about my coming over to your place and shack out on the couch for the rest of the day? That way we can both come to work together tomorrow morning."

"That's a nice try there as well buster, but I'm afraid you're still wasting your time because no, she's not staying with me and if you come over to my place then neither one of us are going to get any rest. All we'll end up doing is drinking and calling up a bunch of chicks on the phone and see if we can entice any of them into coming over to my place for some fun and games, mister. I already told you I need to rest, because I'm still not even over my jet lag from coming back to the States from Japan. Will you please give me a few days to work this crap out in my own mind, and then I'll tell you everything I know about Wind, and you can then make up your own mind about her and how we'll handle her, once you know everything about her, Fugiwara-san."

"Yeah, yeah I got it already Rossie-san. I guess I'll see you in the morning, I'll meet you in the luncheonette and we can have breakfast together, before we start work again Rossie-san."

"You got it, as long as you allow me to pick up the tab for the meal. I'll see you in the morning my friend." Agent Rossie said as he got up and then he rushed out of his office before Agent Fugiwara could ask him any more questions about Wind and where she might have come from.

He jumped in his car and took off for home, driving as fast as the traffic would allow him to drive and he was quickly losing all his anger for what Wind done, because he wanted so much to check on her and make certain she was alright from the ordeal of going after Young's soldiers like she did. By the time he got home he was excited to see her again. He pulled into his allotted parking spot, grabbed his bag with his weapon in it, and then he rushed for his front door. He jumped two steps at a time, got to the door and opened it and rushed in.

Wind was on full alert and she actually heard his car pull up and she rushed back to the center of the living room, and then she knelt down and rested her nose lightly on the hard oak wood floor, and she waited for her Lord and Master to enter his small castle. She listened as he jumped up the steps to the front porch and she heard him working on the lock of the door.

He stopped dead in his tracks as he looked down at Wind kneeling before him and he offered. "Why this Wind-san? I'm not that angry with you any longer." He moved deeper into the room and added to his words to this extremely dangerous female Samurai Warrior. "This is not necessary Wind-san, get up and sit at the table, because I want to speak with you for a little while. C'mon and get up to your feet and follow me over to the kitchen table."

She did as he told her and she followed him over to the table and took her usual seat, and then she waited to hear what her Lord had on his mind for her. All the while she was waiting for him to come home, she feared he might be so angry at her that he would at least order her to commit Suppuku, or at worst, banish her forever to the Floating World. And when he did not come home all night, she was really worried he was that angry at her, and she was soon going to feel his might wrath falling down upon her neck. Even though he was speaking to her kindly for the moment, she was still very worried he was still angry at her and took nothing for granted.

"Once she was seated, Rossie started in on her. "Wind, even though I ordered you to never interfere with my work, this time I have to thank you for doing so. We were in some serious trouble until you interceded and took control of the situation. Now don't get me wrong here Wind-san, I'm still angry as hell at you for your exposing yourself like you did. Now my partner knows of your presence here, and he's been doing nothing but busting my horns about you."

Although her Liege Lord was using words she did not quite understand, listening close to his words made her understand most of his words and anger that he was aiming at her.

"Wind-san, you have to understand just how serious and how important it is that we keep your presence a secret from everyone but us for the time being. If the authorities ever find out about you, they'll simply throw you in jail and they'll keep you there until they figure out what they're going to do with you. Besides, I can't afford to you coming into another situation you found me trapped in, because one of these times it might just be a training exercise I'm going through, and I can ill afford to have you come charging up and killing anyone who might be giving me a special training sessions, Wind-san. Now maybe you can understand a little better what I'm so concerned about, when I keep telling you not to ever come and interfere with my work." He looked hard and long into her eyes as he waited for some kind of reply from her.

"I must admit that my honorable and most wise Lord and Master had cleared all your concerns up in my mind, and I so much more understand why you are so worried about my exposing myself to any others of this time period, my Liege Lord. In the future I shall be so much better with keeping my presence a secret from all but who you wish to introduce myself to, my Liege Lord. I stand corrected and I shall not be any further trouble to my Lord and his desires." She bowed politely towards her Lord and Master and she dared to give him a slight smile. Being with the modern day males of this time for as long as she had been in their presence was slowly erasing some of her training on how she was supposed to respect others she came in contact with.

"That sounds real good to me Wind-san! I just hope you remember what you just told me, because I assure you if you ever interfere with my business again without my permission. You'll really not like the outcome of that interference to your spirit, Wind-san. Now Wind-san, I want you to tell me why you came to me and how you knew I was in some serious trouble this time, and how you were able to find me as well, when you had no idea where I was when you found me?" He ordered as he settled in to hear what he just demanded of her.

"My Liege Lord, I was able to tell you were in distress because of the great amulet I gave to you as a special present that was once given to me by the hand of Izanagi. The amulet has some special powers that enable me to feel your distress, and then all I had to do was I merely had to close my eyes and think, and you, and where you are and what is happening about you, comes clear to my mind as if I was there by your side. Then all I have to do after that is beg the Kami of the Floating World to deliver me to your side, and then I appear by you and am able to come to your aide and protect your life which is my only responsibility in life to carry out my Lord."

"If that's a fact then all I have to do is leave the amulet home and you'll never be able to find me when I'm working. Is that not correct Wind-san?"

"Yes my honorable Liege Lord, that is most correct as you have just stated. But to carry out what you have just suggested would be extremely foolish on your part to carry off I beg to offer you my Lord. For if you leave the sacred amulet behind so I cannot find and come to your aide, if someone is foolish enough to dare place your life in any danger. Then I will not be able to come to your aide, and if I fail to carry out what the Kami have ordained I do for my Liege Lord. The Kami will then take their mighty wrath out upon my head, and they will end my worthless life as a spirit as my punishment for failing my Liege Lord and my duty to you." She almost cried as she informed him what would happen if he ever left the amulet behind when he went off to work.

"Whoa, I see what is your driving force to be such a pest to me all the time Wind-san, and I must admit to you that I kinda like knowing you're out there, and so ready to come to my aide at a drop of a hat to save my life, if I end up in any danger. Yes Wind-san, I think I'll make damn certain that I have your special gift of the sacred amulet on my person anytime I leave my home for either work, or for any other reason for me to leave this place. Yes Wind-san, I think I am going to like having you around as my safety net and protecting my life from all harm."

"And I assure you my Liege Lord, that is my only true desire in life, and that is to protect your life from all harm. And I do my responsibility extremely efficiently my Lord and Master of time and earth. May I ask my Lord if he would like if I prepared something for you to eat? With you not coming home last night, made me fear you were that upset with me, and you were going to punish me by never coming home again, my Lord." She offered as she finally relaxed for the first time since she went off to destroy the men who were trying to kill her Liege Lord.

"No Wind-san and I thank you for your concern over me. But I had something to eat before I left my work to come home to you. I do have to admit, you were very thorough with dispatching any threats aimed at my person yesterday. Did it bother you killing nearly twenty men yesterday? I still see you attacking the men trying to kill me in my mind."

"May this foolish and worthless Samurai Warrior ask my liege Lord a question?" She immediately bowed politely to her Liege Lord, because it was beneath him to answer any question put forth to him, if he chose to ignore her request to ask him a question.

"What is the question that you wish to ask of me, and if it's possible for me to answer it truthfully for you, I'd be most pleased to respond to your request to answer your question, Wind-san." Once again he did not realize how well he was suddenly able to speak Japanese with her, for some reason he was able to understand anything and everything she was telling him, and he was even able to respond correctly in floorless Japanese, even though before he linked up with her, he was barely able to make a complete sentence in Japanese.

"It is my great honor to be able to ask my Liege Lord a question. My Lord, why were there so many of the hated Ko Ku Jie (Black men) wanting to kill my Lord and Master? And why did not any of your other male Samurai Warriors come to your aide as did I to defend you my honorable Lord?" She then looked deeply into his eyes as she waited for his response.

"Wind-san, you must understand that I represent the law of the land, and there are many who refuse to obey the law properly, and that's where I come in. I enforce the laws of the land..."

"As it was true in my time as well my Lord. The Master of the realm always enforced the laws of the land. If we did not have law and order then we would have had nothing but mayhem as the evil Lord Wakatsuki always tried to create for my most honorable Lord and Master, by always keeping the Ten Provinces of Central Japan in a constant state of war, my Liege Lord."

"Yes, whatever you say Wind-san." He replied as she once again brought up the name of Wakatsuki who he knew was the other Land Baron of the time, who was always warring with her once true Lord Kawasomeru, as he added to his words to her. "Yes Wind-san, without law and order a nation will have nothing to keep the peace in check and balance. And with my enforcing the laws of the land, it creates anger between all the law breakers and then they want to end my life so they can continue committing the crimes that make their living. That is why so many of the black men were trying to kill me and my partner when you came to my aide and ended their lives, before they could do harm to me. Once again I thank you for saving my life yesterday, Wind-san." He offered pleasantly to the ancient Samurai Warrior.

"This I understand this completely my Lord and it was the same when Lord Kawasomeru once ruled over his Provinces of Central Japan. But is it only the Ko Ku Jie men who break the laws of the land and tried to kill my Lord?" She asked him with concern this time.

"No Wind-san, it's not only the black man who breaks the laws of the land. All nationalities of my land at one time or another broke the laws of the land. Some of the laws broken were severe, and that's when I come in, to punish the real bad law breakers. We have other police officials who go after the laws breakers of the lesser laws of the land, and they're put in jail to ponder their crimes and when the law feels he was properly punished. Then that law breaker is released from jail and allowed to go back to his life and make a legal living for himself." He replied as he shifted his weight on the sofa. Then he happened to look at the clock and was amazed that they had talked together for so long a time. It was now half past three in the afternoon and he had to start thinking about making supper for the both of them.

Their supper was quick and great and the special agent was getting tired because he really did not sleep a wink the night before. He started yawning and she instantly picked up the signal and she announced she was getting tired herself. So Rossie smiled as he said he was going to use the facilities and when he was done he was going to take a quick shower, and then he was going to turn in for the night. Although they slept together, they did not engage in making love, they just merely hugged each other for the entire night and enjoyed being so close together.

In the morning, Wind was the first one up and she snuck out of bed and started to prepare the morning meal for the both of them. She was so pleased she was going to make her Lord's meal for this morning, and it placed her in a great mood. She had the eggs cooking and she did a poor job of making the coffee. She placed too much coffee in the pot and it overflowed and made a mess on the counter. But the smell of the coffee did the trick and he came staggering out of the bedroom completely naked, and he was looking for a cup of coffee while stretching and growling like a wounded bear. He smiled when he saw her struggling over the stove.

He walked up behind her and then he gently kissed her on the side of her neck which instantly raised a flock of goose bumps and made her shiver with pleasure, as he gently cupped both her breasts, and then he slowly rolled them around in his hands. He even rubbed his wakening member up against her naked rearend, and she responded by slowly wiggling her backside up against his member and hummed softly while enjoying what he was doing to her exquisite body. Now she was hoping he would take her this morning because they did not pillow last night.

"I'm warning you Wind, if I had the time this morning, I'd enjoy making mad, passionate love to you all morning long, and we'll going well into the afternoon at that my dear. But I'm sorry to offer to you but I have to rush this morning so I'm not late for work today. It's bad enough my boss gave us the day off yesterday, but if I showed up late for work this morning. Then it'd be a cold day in hell by the time I ever got another day off from my Commander and work." He complained to her as he smiled to her over her shoulder.

"Then I must curse your work and this man who makes you leave my side every day my Liege Lord, because it is seriously interfering with our pillowing together. It is said what brings you pleasure you must do often my Lord and Master of life." She retorted as she again wiggled her rearend into his groin, and then she laughed pleasantly as she took the eggs off the heat.

"That's a phase to live by Wind-san. I shall warn you of this then, you wait until I return from work tonight, and we shall share that remark happily all night long."

"Then I shall be waiting happily by your main gate of your castle for when you may return to me tonight with a smile and a wanting heart, my Liege Lord." She replied with a grin as she carried the eggs still in the pan over to the table, and she placed them in his dish to enjoy.

They ate together and then he rose and announced at the same time. "I'm terribly sorry Wind-san, but I must leave you at this time, or I'll end up arriving at my work later." Then he turned and picked up his backpack with his weapon hidden inside, and he left for work.

CHAPTER FOURTEEN

FBI Special Agent Robert Rossie was relieved by her response as he raced for FBI Headquarters. He found himself in a great mood, because here he was dealing with one of the most beautiful women he had ever had the pleasure to be with. One who was an extremely dangerous and deadly persons on the face of the earth, and yet he was able to control her with just words and his smile. A woman who could be a fantastic weapon and an important cog for his company, or she could become a deadly threat to anyone or thing she happens to turn her deadly wrath against. This last concern was the one that confused him the most, and caused him to think about returning her to the Floating World, never to again return to the land of the living.

In his mind, he was confident the world was not ready for her appearance, or trying to control what was not meant to be tamed. He even doubted the world would ever be ready to meet Wind, and then deal with her in the right way. He was worried there would always be another Hiromoai Hatanaka hanging around and willing to take advantage of her abilities in both worlds. A weapon that could walk through walls, bullets had no effect to her life, and she could kill with fearsome hatred for anyone she deemed a threat to the one who commanded her sword, and her spirit.

This very troubling thought was the only thing that was taking down his great mood of the day. As he continued to drive to work, his mind wandered to his partner, and how he was ever going to be able to broach the subject of Wind and her life story with him. Without Agent Fugiwara thinking he had lost his mind or if he would go against what Wind was all about.

He actually had to shake his head to try and clear these rampaging thoughts out of his head, as he pulled to the rear parking lot of his headquarters, and then he rushed for his office on the third floor of the building. The Special Agent arrived for work twenty minutes early, and he was surprised to see Agent Fugiwara was already in the office, and as soon as his partner saw Rossie come in, he asked him. "You still buying breakfast for the both of us today my friend?"

"Yeah, I guess so."

"What's the matter Agent Rossie-san, you seem like you forgot our breakfast deal?"

"I did, I ate this morning, but I can do with a cup of coffee, I messed up my coffee home and went without a cup so far." Rossie offered, covering for Wind messing up his morning coffee.

"How the hell can you even function without a good cut of coffee to set off your day right for ya, Rossie-san? I know I can't do anything until I had at least one strong cup of coffee before I start moving for the day." Agent Fugiwara offered with a smirk as he stood up and waited for Agent Rossie to join him as they headed for downstairs to get breakfast for themselves.

As they were eating, Agent Fugiwara looked at his partner for a few moments, and he could swear he could see something was wrong with his partner this morning, and the longer he looked at him, the more he was sure something was troubling him. Drawing in his breath he asked. "Say Rossie-san, what are we going to get involved in this morning? We completed our reports for Commander Murdock, and all the forensics are in, and the crime scene people have cleaned up all the mess over at Young's dump. I know what I want to do today, I want to go and check on Young and see if he was among the dead from yesterday I sure hope so, my friend."

"I don't know what I want to do because I didn't really give much thought as to what I intended to do today. I was kind of thinking about getting in touch with Lieutenant Kenzaburo Motoshima and see how he's making out with his part of the investigation of Batterman's murder in Japan. I think what you're interested in doing today is a good idea and I'm all for that move, Fugiwara-san. Why don't you do that while I'm speaking with Motoshima-san this morning?"

"Thanks for that, I'm really looking forward on checking on that lousy prick, Rossie-san."

"Do you want any company, you know what happened the last time we had anything to do with that Young and his group of madmen, Fugiwara-san? I think you should have someone accompanying you if you go back to that damn crime scene you know."

"Naw, I'm not expecting any trouble over there today. Someone would have to be out of their minds to create any problems there today or for quite a while to come at that. Besides, I'm certain the Washington PD must have some of their people still keeping an eye on the place, just in case anyone is stupid enough to show back up at that place. As far as I'm aware, the entire building is still being classified as a crime scene, so none of Young's people are going to dare return to the area for quite a while, Rossie-san." Agent Fugiwara offered to his partner.

"Why are so hell bent on returning to that building for in the first place? I'd think you saw enough of that place and all the death that is connected to the place, Agent Fugiwara-san."

"To tell you the truth Rossie-san, I want to find out if Young was able to escape the carnage, and if he did, I want to find out how the hell he was able to get out of the building without us discovering he was sneaking outta the damn dump on us. I also want to see if I can find out how Wind was able to get out of the building without us seeing her going as well, Rossie-san."

His heart actually jumped over Agent Fugiwara mentioning Wind's name to him, as he tried to act like it meant absolutely nothing to him, as he replied to his partner's concerns. "You know something Agent Fugiwara-san, I too would like to know if Young was able to get his ass out of the building alive, and how he was able to do it as well. After all, everything that took place inside that damn building was all caused by him and what he stood for. If we have to still deal with the guy, I'd like to know as much as you obviously want to know, Fugiwara-san." He made certain he did not bring up Wind's name to his partner in their ongoing conversation.

"That's want I'm planning to do while you're speaking with the Japanese Lieutenant. Don't be worried about me I'm certain I'll have company by the building, if I know the Washington

Police Department." Fugiwara offered as he stood by the table and dropped his napkin on the table and smiled at his partner as he gave him a salute and then turned and left the eatery.

Rossie smiled as he shook his head and watched as his partner left to do his act. Then he stood and dropped a tip on the table and paid for their meals and headed for the office. Once there he checked the time and realized it was nearing the time for the Japanese Lieutenant to finish his day's work and he dialed his number. The phone rang five times before an extremely exhausted sounding voice on the other end announced in floorless Japanese. "This is Lieutenant Kenzaburo Motoshima of the Tokyo Police Department, Homicide Division, how can I help you please?"

"Kenzaburo-san, this is Rossie, how are you doing my friend?" He replied to the Lieutenant.

"Well as I live and breathe, Agent Rossie-san, I can't tell you how many times I thought of you ever since you first returned to your country, sir. I'm fine and how are you sir?"

"I'm doing pretty good at that and thanks for asking, but this damn Batterman murder case is still taking up all of my damn time over here in the States I'm afraid, sir."

"It's doing the same thing here in Japan, by taking up my time, Rossie-san. I wonder if your boss is breathing down the back of your neck as mine is doing here to me, sir." Lieutenant Motoshima asked while smiling, because he already knew the answer to his last remark.

"Breathing down the back of my neck is putting it rather mildly if you were to ask me, Motoshima-san. I actually have to sneak by his office and hope he doesn't see me coming in for work, or he jumps on my back with both feel and then he asks me a thousand questions on how my investigation of this damn murder case is going. Then he cries to me that all the higher-ups are constantly busting his damn horns, because they all want answers on why it's taking him so long to solve this case, Motoshima-san." Agent Rossie reported to his counterpart in Japan.

"My friend I hate to report to you, but I ran into nothing but stone walls blocking my every twist and turn I take investigating this never ending murder case, along with the other three murder cases I'm still working on Asahiko's, Tsutomu his son and Hiromoai Hatanaka's murder. But I must offer to you that it seems my boss and your boss must be taking lessons from each other, because of what you're describing to me, is exactly how my boss is treating me over here in Japan with, Rossie-san." Detective Motoshima enjoyed a quick laugh over his last remarks.

"Well, I guess there's no sense in my asking how your investigation of these murders are going for you back in Japan, Motoshima-san. I was kinda hoping you might have found something out I might be able to pick up and run with from over here, to help me with my investigation of Batterman's murder, sir. I'm afraid my Commander is not very interested in helping you solve the other three murder cases you're also working on over there sir. He's only interested in Batterman's murder, and he wants it solved ten minutes ago at that, Motoshima-san."

"Ahhh... so, I see what you mean by those words Rossie-san. I hate to inform you, but my government is not very interested in solving Batterman's murder, as they are solving Hiromoai's murder, along with Asahiko-san's son's murder. They're still not very convinced that the old and proud Asahiko-san's case was murder. They're still leaning towards the honored old man committed Suppuku, because he just couldn't live with his son's murder, along with his son's wife's murder. I do know they want Batterman's murder solved, but they're not so interested in the length of time it's going to take me to solve that murder case, Rossie-san." The Japanese Lieutenant informed his counterpart operating over in the United States.

"I kinda figured that much out for myself because of the lack of communication taking place between our two offices lately, Motoshima-san. But I do trust that if you discover anything that might assist me in any way, shape or form in my investigation of Batterman's murder over here, you'll immediately inform me of that information as soon as it becomes available to you sir? And I promise if I discover anything that might assist you over there in Japan, I'll immediately inform you of what I might have discovered over here, Lieutenant Motoshima-san."

"Yes, yes by all means Agent Rossie-san. If I discover anything that might possibly assist you in your ongoing investigation of Batterman's murder over there, I shall instantly inform you of that information, sir." Detective Motoshima replied to the FBI Special Agent.

"I thank you for that and promise to do the same from my side, Motoshima-san. I must admit I truly miss our many conversations of the past times. A day without a good conversation is like a day without sunshine I'm afraid, Motoshima-san." Agent Rossie offered politely to the Japanese Lieutenant, as he truly missed the work he was doing in Japan for the past three years.

"Well then Agent Rossie-san, there is only one thing I can tell you then sir. You must return to my honored country of the Eight Islands, and allow Japan to grace you with countless more good conversations, my friend. Because I too miss our many conversations we have enjoyed speaking about while you were assigned to my great country, Agent Rossi-san."

"Yes, and I promise when I finally solve Batterman's murder, I shall request to be resigned to your country, so I can once again enjoy the kind hospitality your country has offered me in the past while I was working there, Lieutenant Motoshima-san." Agent Rossie offered politely.

"Then I shall be counting the days for your return to my honorable country, Rossie-san. I am so sorry to offer to you at this time Rossie-san, but I must report to my Captain what I and my partner Sergeant Toshihiro Okamatsu-san intend to work on tomorrow. So I can go home and enjoy my last meal of the day, and my wife's outstanding presence. It is late and my Captain really frowns upon whenever I put in for any extra overtime pay, so I must cut this conversation short at this point sir. But I promise you Agent Rossie-san, when I report for work tomorrow morning, I shall return your call, and then we can talk for as long as you may wish to speak with me, sir. There is much that is taking place in Japan lately, and I cannot wait until I inform you of the countless changes that is taking place in my country. By the time you return here, you might not even recognize my most honorable country any longer I believe, Rossie-san."

"I as well cannot wait until I can return to your country, Lieutenant Motoshima-san. And I understand it's time for you to end your workday, and I apologize to you I placed this call to you so near your end of your work shift, Lieutenant Motoshima-san. You can call me anytime you please tomorrow, and I'd be pleased to hear about the countless changes taking place with your honorable country, Lieutenant. Until tomorrow then sir, have a good night and please give my regards to your lovely wife, Motoshima-san." Rossie offered as he broke off the communication with the Japanese Lieutenant, without waiting for his reply to what he just said to the man that was kind of impolite, but he knew the Japanese Lieutenant was dying to go home for the night.

When he finished speaking with Lieutenant Motoshima, he decided to check on Fugiwara and see how he was making out with his investigation Young's hideout. He picked up his cell phone and quickly dialed Agent Fugiwara's number and then waited for him to answer his call.

"Fugiwara here, what's up Rossie-san?"

"What's up? I'll tell you what's up my friend. I'm calling to see how you're making out over there at Young's dump. What's doing over there Fugiwara-san, and do you have any help there as your backup? If you don't then I'm going to contact the local PD and have the Sergeant send a few squad cars over to that position to lend you any support, just in case you run into some trouble over there, mister." Agent Rossie warned his partner in no uncertain terms.

"I'm doing okay, and I have three Police Officers stationed here until they release this building from evidence. I got here if you must know the traffic was against me all the way, Rossie-san. I have to admit, the cleanup crews did a real shitty job cleaning this place up. It smells like hell of rotting corpses and it's enough to choke a maggot, and it's hot as hell in here to boot. I did speak to the three officers standing a post, and each one confirmed Young was not one of the people slaughtered in here. So that means he's still sliming his way around until justice catches up to his ass, Rossie-san. I'm going to check out the rest of the building until I discover how that worm was able to sneak out of here without us catching his ass when he was trying to get away from us.

"I'm not going to leave this place until I discover how he got away on us, and I also want to find out how our friend was able to get by us, without us detecting how she got away on us as well, Rossie-san. There has to be some sort of a passageway here that Young used to get by us and I'm going to find it. I feel if I find out how he got away, I can back track him and find out where he might be hiding on us right now, Rossie-san. Our missing friend, now she could be another matter though. I don't believe she would know of any hidden passageways inside this lousy dump, if she wasn't working with these creeps. If she was working with them then why did she kill so many of them? Hell, I believe she might even be trying to trail Young to finally bring him to justice for us, Rossie-san." Agent Fugiwara reported to his partner and lead agent.

"Look, why the hell don't you stop worrying so damn much about her and just concentrate your efforts on Young, and where he might be hiding on us in that damn building. Believe me, she's not out there looking for Young, so get that thought outta your stinking noggin. Young is our major problem, and she has nothing whatsoever to do with that lousy sonofabitch."

"You should know about her I guess, Rossie-san. I just made it up to the second floor of this dump and I'm checking out the six rooms up here. The Officers on duty here informed me there's three bedrooms and a sort of library up here, and they didn't know what the last room might have been used for. So that room's where I'm going to start my search for this bastard, Rossie-san. I'll get back to you the first moment I discover anything about this missing bastard, my friend." Agent Fugiwara reported to his lead agent in their investigation.

"You do that Fugiwara-san, but I'm ordering you to remain in contact and if any trouble arises against you, I want to know about it immediately. Dammit, I'll tell you what, I have a few other things I have to look after and when I finish my work here, I'm going to hop over to where you're working, and I'm going to give you a hand. I'm not very comfortable about you working this building over, and my not being with you in case something goes down and you find yourself trapped like we were in that building a coupla days ago, Fugiwara-san. I don't like my partner being out of my sight while you're out on an investigation for us, mister. I'll get out to you as soon as possible. I'll see you in fifteen to twenty minutes from now, Agent Fugiwara-san."

He quickly finished up his last minute paperwork and when he was done, he walked into Murdock's office and announced that he was heading over to the Young crime scene, to lend Fugiwara a hand with trying to discover how

Young got out of the building without anyone catching him as he fled the area. Murdock was upset Rossie allowed Fugiwara to go over to the crime scene without his partner, but when he informed Murdock there were at lead three Washington Police Officers, protecting the crime scene this calmed him down enough to order Agent Rossie to get over there and assist Fugiwara over what he was doing inside the building.

Rossie got over to the Young building as quickly as he could, and he rushed up to the second floor level of the building, and he started searching for where Agent Fugiwara was working inside the structure. The first two doors he opened were the bedrooms, and the third door he opened, he found Fugiwara lightly tapping on the wood paneling of the room, like he was looking for some sort of a secret passageway hidden inside the rather small room.

Upon seeing his partner come into the room he was working in, Fugiwara instantly offered to him. "Wow, you weren't kidding with you getting your ass over here on the double quick I see, Rossie-san. I just about worked over this entire floor looking for how the hell that damn rat was able to get out of this lousy dump without us detecting him trying to escape us. I'm really pissed off at the guy, because he left his soldiers behind to kill us, while he just merely walked out of here safe and sound. I really want this lousy little bastard, and I'm going to get him if it's the last thing I do here in Washington, Rossie-san."

"You don't think he was able to sneak out of one of the damn windows in any of these rooms up here do you, Fugiwara-san?" Agent Rossie asked his partner as he glanced at the window in the room, and then he walked over to it and looked out and quickly discovered if Young went out of the window. If he did not break his neck on the fall, he would have surely made enough noise to wake the dead, and they would have easily caught him trying to escape their trap of him. Forgetting about this possible escape route, he then joined Agent Fugiwara as he checked out each of the panel sections of the wall for any possible escape passageway hidden in the room.

Neither of the two FBI Special Agents realized this room was about four feet deeper than the room right next to it, as they both now kind of lightly started to tap on the walls of the room. As they continued tapping on the wall as they headed towards the rear of the room, Rossie working on the left side of the room tapped on the last panel and it suddenly sounded hollow behind the panel to him. "Uh-oh, I think I have might have found something over here Agent Fugiwara-san. It sounds kinda hollow behind this one panel over here partner."

Fugiwara rushed over to Rossie's side and he joined him with tapping on the last panel on this wall, and then he announced. "I think you might be right Rossie-san, it definitely sounds hollow behind this panel. I wish I had a damn crowbar with me, I'd rip the damn panel down with it."

"Calm down a little will you please Fugiwara, if Young got through this panel without needing a crowbar then we're not going to need one to get the panel opened either. Just keep looking, there has to be some kind of switch or pull to open the damn panel for us. Ahhhh... I think I might have just found it." He bragged as his finger found a slight depression in the panel, and he applied more pressure and the panel instantly sprung open about an inch. Rossie then stuck his fingers into the crack and he pulled and the panel that easily slid open, and then they both looked into the void and saw what looked like a short hidden hallway. Agent Rossie removed his 9mm Colt pistol and then he cautiously started to enter the narrow opening with Agent Fugiwara picking up the rear with his weapon out as well, as they both inched their way into the opening.

"Where the hell do you think this thing comes out around here Rossie-san?"

"I have no idea, but this has to be the way Young got out of the building without us able to catch him as he fled. Hold it a second Fugiwara it looks like a makeshift door here. It is a door." Rossie grumbled as he cautiously opened it and looked down the narrow stairwell that went to the first floor of the building. "This has to be the way the bastard got out of the building on us."

"How do you want to handle this, do you want to go first Rossie-san?"

"Hell, I don't want to even go second, but I guess someone has to go first so it might as well be me. You follow and we'll find out where the hell this lousy prick went down there." The two agents entered the narrow only a little more than a foot wide hidden stairwell down to the first floor of the building, but the hallway continued with a slight turn. He came to a two foot wide by three foot high handmade panel and he gave it a good shoved, and the makeshift door opened and he found himself looking out in the backyard of the structure. The fence of the yard was a few inches away from the opening, and he stepped out and he was easily able to tell which way Young must have went once he was safely outside the building.

The agents followed the fence to the end of the property, and found a gate and Rossie opened it and looked and saw the backyard of the building on the next block. He walked into the yard and towards the home. A child was playing in the yard and Rossie and Fugiwara walked up to the young black child, and Rossie smiled as he asked the kid. "Hiya young man, I'm a friend of your neighbor Mr. Young, and I was wondering if you might know where he might be, son?"

"Yes, he was visiting my mother a while ago, but he left earlier before I came outside to play. He went that way mista." The child pointed towards the street of the next block over from Young's place. Then Rossie asked the kid. "Is your mom at home young man?"

"Yes, but she is watching her show and told me to go out and play so I don't bother her."

"Would you mind going in and asking your mom to come out and talk to us for a few moments, son? I'll give you a buck if you do this for me young man."

"Give me the dollar first, and I'll go and get my moon for you, mista."

He laughed because the kid knew enough to ask for the money first, before he did what he asked the kid to do. "Here you go son, here's your dollar, go and get you mom for us please."

The kid took off like his backside was shooting sparks and Fugiwara moved to Rossie's side and he grumbled. "Man these kids around here learn quick about money, don't they Rossie-san?"

Even before he could reply to Agent Fugiwara's remark, the kid came out of the home with his mother following him. She immediately gave the two men dressed on suites the mad dog look, and then she snapped at them. "What the hell do you two want with me, and how dare you approach my son and give him money and tell him to come and get me. I have a good mind to call the damn police on you two perverts. You better get off my property before I go..."

"Hey lady we are the police." Rossie growled as he flashed his shield at the angry woman.

"Wait a minute I didn't get a good look at your shield mister. It didn't look like any shield I have ever seen before. I want to see that shield again before I call a real policeman to come and kick you two white bastard perverts offa my god damn property, mister."

"Have you seen that many shields in your lifetime that you know the difference between them lady? You're right, it's not a normal police shield, it's an FBI shield and we're both Special Agents, and we're looking for your neighbor Mr. Young. Do you happen to know where he might be at, lady? It's extremely important that we speak to him as soon as possible, Ma'am."

"What do two government Police Officers want with Mr. Young, he never bother's anyone and he's good for the neighborhood. He's always taking care of the kids, and he's always so nice to all his neighbors. Why don't you leave the poor man alone and get out of our neighborhood."

"Ma'am, we have to talk to him as soon as possible, we believe his life might be in danger, and this is why we have to speak to him as soon as possible..."

"You police don't gotta go and try and protect Mr. Young's life around here, he has so many friends in the neighborhood if anyone tied to harm him here in any way, that fool wouldn't stand a chance in hell of hurting Mr. Young, before the entire neighborhood came outta their homes and they attacked the fool trying to hurt Mr. Young. So you see there ain't no need for any of you government people to be hanging around our neighborhood and trying to arrest Mr.

Young. Besides, if the neighbor's ever find out two government policemen are here to arrest Mr. Young, you two might not get out of the neighborhood in one piece you know, mister."

"I don't remember mentioning that we're here to arrest Mr. Young, lady. All I told you was we believed his life might be in danger, and we wanted to talk with him for his own good, lady." Agent Rossie replied as he gave a look at her like he was disgusted with her.

"Don't you go and look at me like that Mr. Government cop, or I'll slap that silly look right offa your miserable face and that taste outta your mouth for you at the same time mister. Besides, whenever any white cops enter our neighborhood, they are always here to arrest one of the brothers, and you two cops are no different than any other police who come here to arrest our men. Now be gone with you two before I alert the neighbors of you two trying to arrest Mr. Young, and then you'll see how we react to the police always trying to arrest our men on us all the damn time. Go! Get off my property at once I told you two white cops if you two know what's good for you." She growled angrily at the two special agents then she glared harshly at them until they turned and went back through the gate that brought them into her backyard.

"Whew, now I know why this damn neighborhood is in the terrible shape it's in." Agent Fugiwara announced as he caught up to Agent Rossie and then got in step with him.

"Well, at least we now know how and where this one got away from us, and where he hid until most of the Officer's left the crime scene, dammit. What's our next step with this damn Young guy, Fugiwara-san?" Rossie asked, all along he knew what he was doing, he was trying to get Agent

Fugiwara's attention off Wind. So he had more time to try and figure out how he was going to introduce her to his Commander and the rest of the world at the same time.

"I don't know quite yet Rossie-san. I guess I'll make contact with my group of snitches and see if any of them knew where the hell Young is hiding at. Someone is going to have to know where the hell Young is in hiding at for Pete's sake." Fugiwara replied to his partner's last question.

"Well my friend, it's starting to get late, what say we put an end to this very trying and exhausting day and go home and rest for tomorrow's drama, Agent Fugiwara-san?"

"Sounds about right to my ass Rossie-san."

"Good, I'll see you tomorrow morning then. I don't see any real sense in our returning to the office. You know what's going to happen to us if we do. Sure as hell Murdock is going to catch us coming in and he'll end up bullshiting with us for a coupla hours, before he finally lets us go home for the rest of the night, Fugiwara-san." Agent Rossie remarked as he looked up at the sky and saw it was starting to show the first signs of getting dark out.

"I know what you mean. I'm going to shut down my cell phone so he can't reach me and order me back to Headquarters. I don't intend to be with him for half the damn night unless he starts shaving a helluva lot closer than he does, Rossie-san." Fugiwara offered as he made a joke about his Commander to the other agents as they both started walking towards their parked cars.

They climbed into their vehicles and each agent went their way for home. Rossie walked into his apartment and immediately found Wind kneeling right in the center of his living room again, and he shook his head. He wished he could break her of the habit of constantly kneeling and bowing before him, and waiting for him to speak to her before she acted like a free person again. "C'mon Wind-san, you don't have to keep constantly kneeling and bowing to me every time I come walking into the apartment. Get up so I can see your face when I speak with you."

She dared to look up at her Lord and smiled when she noticed the look of love in his eyes for her. She leaned back to sitting on her legs position, and waited for her Lord to speak to her again.

"That's much better Wind-san, because I truly enjoy looking at your lovely face instead of the top of your head whenever I come in. It is good to see you tonight, Wind-san."

"It is equally as pleasing for this worthless person to see her most honorable Lord and Master looking so happy when he comes home from his long workday, my Liege Lord. I trust you had a good day at work my Lord? I have taken the pleasure of preparing a fine meal for my Lord's enjoyment, but I fear we are running a little low on that red drink that you and I enjoy so much, and the bubbles of the drink make me giggle so and also makes me want to pillow so much with you whenever I drink the red drink, my Lord."

"That's called red wine Wind-san and fear not, because I have a whole case of the wine in the other closet off the hallway. One thing I never do and that is running out of my wine. I'm so pleased that you enjoy the wine as much as you obviously do, Wind-san."

"I must confess to my Liege Lord, I have never enjoyed such a pleasing drink as your red wine before in my entire life. I admit I enjoy drinking it because it's much like our Sake, but much smoother and is more enjoyable to drink my Lord. This worthless person thanks her Liege Lord for sharing such a fine gift as your red wine with this useless person."

She then bowed politely to her Lord as she held the bow to within honorable time to hold her bow before him.

"I really wish you wouldn't bow to me so damn much, it's becoming rather embarrassing to me all the time Wind-san. Modern day men are not very pleased if a woman bowed to him, and if another woman ever saw you doing this to me. Oh brother will the shit hit the fan then I tell you." He even had to laugh at his own remark this time.

She did not understand what he meant by 'the shit hitting the fan' but since her Lord laughed at that remark, she also laughed like she just understood everything he just said to her.

"C'mon Wind-san, since you brought up the subject of the red wine to me, lets enjoy a glass." He went over to the closet and removed two bottles, opened one and poured them both a glass and then he served one to Wind and then he saluted her with his glass and said. "Bottom's up."

She followed his lead and she smiled back at him and then she started to drink her wine. This was the first time she was drinking the wine warm, and it seemed like it went right to her head and she immediately began to mellow out and grin at her Lord. When she drained her glass he immediately refilled it for her, and then he went into the kitchen and fumbled around as he prepared some snacks for them to enjoy with their wine.

She sipped her wine this time because she was not trying to keep up with her Lord's drinking as she settled back on her legs and straightened up her back. She loved spending close time with her Liege Lord, because every time she did this it always ended up with the both of them pillowing together at the end of the day. She smiled as she dreamed of making love to her Lord on this night, and she was opening her mind to this desire. Her thoughts were suddenly interrupted when her Lord came back in the living room carrying a tray and he said to her.

"C'mon Wind and get up off the floor and join me at the table. I fixed us some snacks."

She got up, her exquisite blue Kimono flowing about her body like a silk cloud as she walked over to the table and sat in her chair. Her head was already spinning because of the warm wine. She took one of the toothpicks stuck in the cheese and enjoyed it while continuing to sip her wine. He saw she drank nearly the second glass of wine and he offered. "Here, let me full your glass for you again, after all you can't fly on one wing you know."

She smiled as he refilled her glass for a third time and she took another sip of her wine greedily this time. She had no idea he was trying to get her drunk, because he had the same idea she had, and he wanted to make love to her as well tonight.

They never ate a full meal as they picked at the cheese and drank nearly the two bottles of wine and when he felt she was in the right mood he made his move on her. He stood and walked around the small table and stopped right behind the dreamy eyed Wind and he started to massage her neck and she moaned with delight. This gave him the okay to get more aggressive with her and he slid his hands down her chest and searched for her breasts. He took one in each hand and started to roll them gently in his hands, as he leaned forward and kissed the side of her neck. She closed her eyes and enjoyed what he was doing to her body, as she leaned her head over to the side to give him better access to the side of her neck. He kissed her a few times and then he went up her neck and kissed the tip of her ear, and then he drew her earlobe into his mouth.

This made her go weak in the knees and she shivered and came. He pulled the front of her Kimono opened to the waist and attacked her breasts again with his hands. But this time he picked up his head and rested his chin on her forehead, and applied pressure until she leaned her head back and he leaned over and kissed her on the forehead then kissed the tip of her nose and then the lips. As their lips met he forced his tongue into her mouth and kissed her passionately.

Again she moaned as she returned his passion. Suddenly he reached down and actually picked her up in his powerful arms and brought her down on the rug and pulled the Obi from her Kimono, and then separated the two ends until he had full access to her naked and lightly perfumed body. His mouth replaced his hands on her breasts as he licked, sucked and moved her nipples with the tip of his tongue. Her hand went searching for the belt buckle of his pants, but he had so much of his weight on her body it was keeping her hands from finding their target.

Now he was lowering his body over hers, all the while he was sliding down her form he kept kissing her body, stopping long enough to dip his tongue in her belly button for a few seconds. Then he ran his tongue over her skin from one hip to the other, trying to bring her to new heights of passion. Now he was running his tongue and kissing her lower belly, making her stomach muscles jump from his kisses, and she automatically arched her back to give him more access to any part of her body he wanted to kiss next. Now he put his full weight on her legs, forcing her to open her legs to his weight and her mind to the thoughts of what next he was going to do to her.

He slid his body further down her exquisite body until his head was at her thighs, and then he started to kiss the outside of her legs, slowly dragging his lips lightly over the front of her thighs, and then putting his head down between her thighs. Suddenly, he lightly nipped the inner thigh of her right leg and then sucked her skin into his mouth and sucked on it then released the skin and breathed on the wet area, making her jump not from any pain, but from the suddenness of the light nip and another moan was her answer to the pleasure he was giving her.

Her response to his efforts increased his own passion and he blew his breath across her Jade Gate and she again arched her back and reached down and tried to guide his head where she next wanted him to kiss and probe with his very skilled tongue. But he resisted her light pressure because he was not going to be rushed until he had her absolutely wild with insane passion. So he moved his head and mouth over to her other thigh and he licked her inner thigh then he kissed her leg until he found the back of her knee and he kissed her there next.

Now he worked his way back up the side of her leg, kissing her here and there as he slowly worked his way back towards the center of her legs. Once he was at the right spot, he breathed out, and then he attacked her Jade Gate with his own passion. Kissing, licking and dipping his tongue in and out the gate and licking the petals of her pleasure. He got so involved in his act that he did not even realize she was arching her back and moving her hips wildly back and forth and up and down to the rhythm of his tongue. She was almost crying with passion over what he was doing to her body, things that had never been done to her before in her long life.

Again she reached down and tried to guide his head where she wanted his tongue to probe next on her, and this time he allowed her to direct him where she wanted his attention aimed at her. When he hit the right spot, he knew what to do and he drove her crazy and she was moaning almost constantly now, and again she shivered as she locked his head in place with both her hands and then held on to his head for dear life until her shivers subsided, and then she released his head and allowed her back to drop back to the floor, and she tried to get her breathing under control again. But he had no intentions of allowing her to stop his act just yet, and he attacked her center with a new passion again as he licked, kissed and probed with his tongue.

When he felt he brought her to the height he wanted her, he suddenly abandoned the area then he slowly worked his way back up her hard body by sliding himself up her. When he was in the right spot, he kissed her the same time his member slid inside her. Another moan came from her as she moved her hips up to meet his first thrust. At first he slowly rolled his hips and he pushed up against her, but as his and her passion mounted, the both of them were lost in the flames of passion. Faster and faster he was shoving himself deeper into her, and she was pushing down with equal force as she met every one of his thrusts with that of her own.

They both were moaning and they both came together, with her still shivering even after he slipped out of her. He completely collapsed and rolled off the side of her and he lied down on the floor and worked on getting his breathing under control. But she still held her eyes shut tight as she enjoyed the last of her shivers, and then she also relaxed her entire body and let her breath out in a rush. Then she opened her eyes, turned her head and looked at her Lord and Master and smiled when she saw he was enjoying the remains of their pillowing.

He got up on an elbow and he reached out and ran the tips of his fingers ever so slowly and gently over her sweat coated breasts as he returned her smile with one of his own, and then he asked her. "I hope you have enjoyed our pillowing as much as I did, Wind-san?"

"I did and more my Lord and Master, you have brought the earth and the moon together, and have brought such endless delight to this worthless Warrior." Again she closed her eyes and within a few seconds, she was breathing deeply, sound asleep.

CHAPTER FIFTEEN

They spend the night sleeping on the floor and Rossie woke when he had to run to the bathroom at 5:30. His entire body was one mass of minor aches and pains from sleeping on the hard floor. He came out of the bathroom and looked at Wind still sleeping peacefully on the floor naked as the day she was born, and he pulled the throw off the sofa and covered her, Then he went to the kitchen to make breakfast for them. He was in such a fantastic mood, mainly because of their lovemaking and he was grinning as he took the eggs and bacon out of the fridge and started them cooking. While they were cooking, he made a pot of coffee and took two cup out and placed them on the table. He wanted to see if she would enjoy a cup of coffee this morning.

Wind woke to his messing around in the kitchen and she got up and automatically sat down in the chair she had claimed as her special chair at the table, and then she waited for her Lord and Master to finish making their morning meal for them to enjoy.

Special Agent Robert Rossie heard Wind get up and he turned to see where she went, and he was surprised she was seated at the table naked from the night before. He smiled at her and then he announced. "Wind-san, the morning meal is going to take another fifteen minutes or more for me to prepare it properly for our enjoyment. You're more than free to take a quick shower and by the time you are done with it, so will the meal be ready."

"I shall do as you have suggested my Liege Lord." With that said she got up from the table and rushed to the bathroom and in seconds, he heard the water running and he turned back to the stove and watched the meal as it cooked.

She came walking out of the bathroom with just a towel looped over her shoulders, because her hair was still wet, and she sat down at the table just as he placed her plate down before her and he offered. "You look great this morning Wind-san. I'm deeply honored to have someone as beautiful as you are, sharing my life with me."

"I am as pleased to be allowed to share your life with you my honorable Lord." She automatically bowed without thinking about it again at her new lover and Master.

This time he bowed back at her just as politely as he sat down and started enjoying their morning meal. But suddenly he looked at her and noticed she looked kind of fatigued and he asked her with concern in his voice. "Wind-san, I can't help but notice, you look rather tired this morning. Are you feeling alright Wind-san? I didn't hurt you last night, did I?"

"I am a little fatigued this morning, and it is the first warning that my time enjoying the living world is rapidly coming to an end on me, and soon I shall be forced to visit the Floating World to do as what you say, recharge my batteries my Liege Lord. As I have explained to you before my Lord. I am only allowed seven full sticks of time (One stick of time was a day) before I must return to the Floating World and remain dwelling there for one full stick of time before I'm allowed to return to the living world and carry out my scared oath of protecting your life, my Lord. I have no power to ignore the call of the Floating World and if I tried to ignore it, with every breath of the stick of time (Second), my body will feel ever increasing pain until I have to return on my own, or cease to exist in either the Floating World or the living world, my Lord."

"I remember you telling me that, when do you feel you must return to the Floating World for one day, Wind-san?" He asked her with concern lacing his tone of voice this time.

"I believe I shall be forced to return to the Floating World within the next stick of time my Lord." She replied sadly, because she never really wanted to return to the very lonely world of the Ukiyo, no matter how short the time she had to remain there was.

"Wind-san, do you mind if I ask you a question that has suddenly popped into my mind?"

"My Lord and Master has the right to ask of this worthless person, any question that might be troubling your wonderful mind my Liege Lord."

"Good, Wind, if you're ordered to return to the Floating World for one full day of time every seven days. Then what will happen say if suddenly I found myself trapped in a life threatening situation, and you're nowhere to be found to come to my aide. What happens then Wind-san?"

"That is a very good question for my wise Liege Lord to ask of this worthless person. If while I am ordered to remain within the Floating World for what you call one day of your time. If my honorable Lord is suddenly trapped in a life threatening situation, the Kami who have command over such things, will instantly send me back to the living world fully charged as you like to offer. And I shall be allowed to come to your aide and carry out my sacred oath of protecting your wonderful life from all possible harm, my Liege Lord. It is just one more of the great gifts that has been showered upon the worthless head of this foolish Samurai Warrior by the God, of the Floating World and the Council of Kami, my Lord."

"There'll be no consequences placed upon your head by the Kami of the Floating World for your having to return to the living world, before the allotting time had expired that you were forced to return to the Floating World, Wind-san?" He asked her, already worrying and then telling himself if she was ordered back to the Floating World for one day. Then that day he would take off from work and hide until she had returned to the living world, so she could protect his life again for him. After what he just went through when he tried to interview Young and got involved in a firefight with his protectors, he was now thankful with having this extremely deadly female weapon protecting his life like she insisted in doing for him.

"The only consequences I will suffer from the Kami, and their punishment is always served by Fujin who is my namesake, the always angry Kami of Wind, or Hachiman, the fearsome God of Warfare, is if I allowed harm to befall you my Lord. Or if I try and not answer the call of the Floating World, when it is the time for me to return for that one stick of time." She offered.

"Then I'm protected by you whether or not you're standing at my side, or if you're forced to visit the Floating World for any reason, Wind-san." He replied, relieved he had her protecting his life no matter where she was at the time any danger found him.

"My Liege Lord is most correct with his last statement to me my Lord."

"Thank you." He replied and then he noticed her shiver a bit and he realized she was still naked, and her hair was wet and he said. "Wind-san, you are cold, not that I want you to cover your exquisite body from my view, but I don't want you to catch a cold and get sick so I think you should put something on to warm yourself. You are able to get sick, are you not Wind-san?"

"My honorable Lord, as long as I am visiting the world of the living, I am in the same dangers as the living people, and I can be affected by the same inflictions you are susceptible to, but if I was to come down with a sickness, that sickness in no way would be able to stop me from my sworn oath of protecting you from any harm, my Lord." She explained to her Lord.

"I'm please to be aware of all this, and if you happen not to be here when I return from work, I guess I'll know you had to go back to the Floating World for your one day of penance.

But I have to ask you Wind-san, how would I know if you had to return to the Floating World?"

"My Lord, if there is any question to where I might be, all you have to do is look to my sword. If my Katana is returned to the scabbard I was ordered to the Floating World. I must warn my Lord, if I am returned to the Floating World, no matter how hard you might try, you will not be allowed to free my sword from the sheath until it was the proper time for me to return to answer your call from the living world. Unless your honorable life was in any deadly danger then I would be allowed to answer your call no matter the reason I was called back to the Floating World."

"I thank you for telling me all this stuff, Wind-san." He replied as he dropped his napkin on the table and then stood and announced. "Wind-san, I'm sorry to say but it's getting late and I have to head off for work, or I'm going to be late and might get stuck staying at the office later in the day than I'm supposed to be there. I hope you shall be here when I return, Wind-san."

"I am in distress to offer my Liege Lord, but I fear as quickly as my energy is being drained from my worthless body, I believe I shall be called home to the Floating World long before you have returned to your castle from your work today, my Liege Lord."

"Then I guess I'll have to take care of myself for the next day or two, Wind-san. I want you to take care of yourself while you're being held in the Floating World, and I'll be looking forward to seeing you again when you're allowed to return to me, Wind-san." He said as he suddenly reached out and pulled her up to her feet, and then he hugged her to him and kissed her with the same passion be showered her with the night before. She returned his kiss just as powerfully, and then he pulled away from her and held her at arm's length for a second as he drank in her outstanding beauty. Then he let her go, turned and walked out the door while cursing himself, because he had to leave her and report to work. He wanted so badly to remain home and be with her until she was called back to the Floating World for the rest of the day.

She had to swipe at a tear that betrayed her as she watched her Master leaving the apartment. Suddenly, she was hit with a staggering weakness to where she was having a problem standing. She looked to her sword her Master left lying on the sofa, and she saw the sword go back into the sheath, and she grew weaker. She looked to the ceiling in the room and saw the small ball of light appear and as she watched, it grew in its intensity until the light filled the room and engulfed her being. Then instantly, she disappeared and the light followed her to the Council of Kami. All that was left behind was her towel she had wrapped around her wet hair lying on the floor.

Again, she found herself standing before the entire Council of Kami naked as she was. She was hit with a flood of questions by Fujin, who was the Kami who was elected to question her about the lives she dispatched while protecting her ward's life. After he heard the reason for her dispatching the living humans, again she was cleared of the slaughter and she was allowed to spend the rest of the time she was ordered to the Floating World, visiting her true Lord and Master, Kawasomeru-Sama and speaking of the old times of ancient Japan. As she relaxed and drew in her renewed strength from the world of wonder, she waited for the time to past when she would be allowed to return to the land of the living and her new Liege Lord in her eyes.

FBI SPECIAL AGENT ROBERT ROSSIE'S
HEADQUARTERS
WASHINGTON D.C., MONDAY, JUNE 23rd, 1996

Rossie reported to work twenty minutes before his start, so he grabbed two cups of coffee and headed for his office. He sort of tiptoed across Murdock's door and heard him growl. "I see you out there. It's about time you showed up for work. I want to talk to you and that partner of yours when you get comfortable to start your damn day of work, mister. Did you hear me buster?"

 "Yeah, yeah your damn voice carries real well in here Ralph. I'll report to your office after I checked my in box and E'mails, sir." Agent Rossie smirked as he picked up his pace and entered his office and saw Agent Fugiwara already sitting at his desk and he complained at him.

"What the hell do you do, sleep at the damn office lately, my friend?"

"Funny, no I was dropped off by the chick I spent the night with. She had to go to work early today so I let her drop me off. I left my car parked back at my place and figured I'd hitch a ride with you to my place after work. I see the Big Growl is in fine tune this morning as usual, Rossie-san. Did he happen to tell you what got his dick hard already today on him?"

"Naw, he was just his old pleasant self today. One day he's going to realized the more he dumps on us, the more trouble we're going to give his ass..."

"So that's the way it is with you two birds I see. Just remember who signs your god damn paychecks around here, before you give me any more trouble." Murdock grumbled as he stood in the doorway to Agent Rossie's office. Then he entered and sat in an empty chair and started drinking his own coffee as he looked right at Rossie as if he did something wrong already.

"What?" He barked at his Commander and when Murdock did not reply to his question he repeated. "What? What the hell did I do already to get you on my ass so damn early man?"

"It's you that rubs my ass the wrong way around here mister. You have all the damn tools to make you one outstanding Field Commander for crap sake, and all you want to do is keep dropping requests to go back to Japan after you wrap up the Batterman's murder case. What the hell do you think I'm into around here, collecting your damn autograph or something? If I get one more damn request signed by you requesting for you to go back to Japan, I'm gonna demand you change your stinking name so I see another autograph from your ass, so I can start a different collection of your name for crap sake. What's all this you wanting to return to Japan? You have a bitch you left behind back there or what, Agent Rossie?" Commander Murdock grumbled at his SPAC (Special Agent in Charge) as he took another sip of his coffee.

"Is that what's bugging your ass this morning Ralph? Look, as long as you tell me you'll think about sending me back to Japan after we finish up with Batterman's case, I'll stop filing another request slip, sir. Anyway Ralph, there's a good chance I might find my ass back in Japan before this case has ran its course, and we solved the damn thing for you sir." Agent Rossie warned his Commander as he also took a sip of his coffee before it cooled off on him.

"That might be right at that there Agent Rossie, so I guess I'll not see another one of these damn request slips in my in box from now on from you, will I mister? If I don't see another request slip from you then I'll consider sending you back to Japan, so you can finish whatever the hell you were working on back there, before the Batterman's case came up on you, sir. Is that a deal between us mister?" The Commander asked his agent with a snap in his voice.

"You got it Ralph." Agent Rossie replied to his control.

"Good, now for the reason I wanted to speak with you this morning. It seems like one of your damn snitches checked in and he somehow left a damn message on my system looking to speak with you. I got his name and phone number and he's looking for you to contact him later on today. What the hell's with this damn snitch of yours and what the hell does he have to offer you, mister. I hate working with damn snitches because they turn my stomach on me for crap sake. The sonofabitches are supposed to be friends with the lousy prick their snitching on, and once they're friends, the damn snitch stabs him right in the back all the damn time. What the hell ever happened to loyalty for crap sake, even between god damn thieves, Agent Rossie?"

"Say Ralph, if it wasn't for these damn snitches, many of our cases would still be open on us. You have his name and number for me sir?"

"Yeah, here you go Rossie, and from now on. Tell your snitches not to leave their messages on my system will ya." The Commander offered the paper to his agent as he drained his coffee, and crushed the paper cup and tossed the debris at the wastebasket, missing it by a good foot. Then he turned and walked out of the office like he did not have a care in the world.

"Well that was easier than I thought it would be. The Big Growl wasn't in that bad a mood after all was he, Rossie-san?" Agent Fugiwara offered and then almost choked on his words when the Commander barked back at him from out in the hallway.

"I heard that and I'll show you who's a Big god damn Growl around here if I ever hear that remark aimed at my ass again, Mr. Fugiwara."

"Not only is the dude a Big Growl, but obviously he has big ears to go along with his big mouth." Agent Fugiwara retorted as the two young agent laughed at their Commander.

"What do we have on the menu for the rest of the day Fugiwara-san?"

"I guess that all depends on what your snitch might have for us. If it's a good lead, I see us working that lead for the rest of the day, Rossie-san."

"That's a good point there Fugiwara-san." Agent Rossie replied as he looked at the clock and realized it was still way too early to try and make contact with his snitch, and then he informed Fugiwara. "Well, it's too early to try my snitch, he's probably still way to damn high from partying most of last night away. This guy won't be functioning right for another three hours at the earliest, so we have some time to kill. Any ideas how we should fill in the time my friend?"

"Hell, we can always bring up your new girlfriend Wind for a little while you know. We can kill off a lot of time talking about her. I'm sure as hell there's a lot more to know about her, and what she has to do with the Batterman's and the other murder cases, Rossie-san."

"I guess you're just not going to let that go until I finally end up giving you one swift kick right in the ass to get your damn mind offa her. I told you..."

"Yeah, yeah I know, when you work out all the details then you'll tell me everything about her and what you're holding back on the Batterman deal, Rossie-san. I heard it all before man."

"And you're going to hear it again and again if you continue bringing her up until I'm ready to tell you everything about her and this damn murder case, buster. Just let it go for the time being will ya please, you pain on the ass you." Agent Rossie growled hotly back at his partner.

It was 10:30 in the morning when Agent Rossie started trying to get in contact with his snitch. He ended up calling him five times in the next half an hour, and each time the phone rang and rang until he finally hung up. The last time he tried and hung up he looked at Fugiwara reading the morning newspaper and he bitch at him because he was that angry over not being able to connect with his snitch. "Man, I guess my damn snitch had himself one helluva time getting high last night, this is the latest I ever tried to contact him and didn't get him, dammit."

"Huh, maybe he's still out there getting high Rossie-san? Do you have any idea where this little prick might hang out while he's out there getting high? We could always get out there and start looking for the sonofabitch if it's that important for you to connect up with the dopey prick my friend." Agent Fugiwara remarked with a smirk across his lips.

"That's all I have to do is go out and start running down all his damn hangouts. How long do you think this dude would live if we did something like that to him, Fugiwara-san?"

"About as long as he's going to live if he keeps screwing around with them damn drugs my friend. Do you have any idea what his choice of poison is, Rossie-san?"

"What isn't his choice of poisons, he's a walking pharmacy. The last time I busted his ass, I got high just logging in the crap on found on his damn body. I can't believe he's still walking around with all the crap he's on." Agent Rossie complained at his partner.

"Then maybe we better go out and find this kid before he craps out on us, and we find him OD's out there somewhere lying in the street. Is he that good a CI?" (Confident Informer)

"Yeah, a coupla times he gave me some good leads that lead to a number of important busts. Besides, it doesn't cost me very much to keep him on my side, all I have to do is flip him a twenty every now and then, and he would turn in his own mother to me. The lousy little bastard has no real religion for anything or one but his damn drugs my friend."

"Yeah, a real work of art I see, Rossie-san. The cream of the crap I take it."

"He's the cream of something alright but I don't know what it is." Rossie came back with as he enjoy a quick laugh over his last remark about his snitch.

"Uh-oh, here comes the Big Growl again." Agent Fugiwara warned him because he had a good angle and he was able to see out in the hallway where he was sitting.

Ralph stuck his head in the office and snarled at his Japanese Agent in a harsh tone. "What the hell did I just tell you about that fucking name mister? If I hear it again from anyone in this damn office, I'm going to kick you so hard in the ass you'll be wearing my toe nails as a necklace. What the hell are you two birds still doing sitting in your damn office like this. You two guys got nothing better to do than sitting on your asses and clocking up the time. Remember you two, I sign the paychecks around here, and I'm going to remember you guys sitting on your damn duffs all day when there's a major murder case that needs your damn attention.

"I'll tell you what I'm gonna do for you two birds. The next time some damn Politician or the President himself calls me to find out how the investigation is going with the Batterman case. I'm going to give them your stinking phone number, so they can start busting your god damn horns for a change around here, dammit. I told you two that this case has a lot of very important people's interest about it, and they're all demanding to find out what the hell happened and who murdered the sonofabitch. My stinking phone is ringing off the damn hook with a horde of people constantly calling me to find out how we're doing on the case for crap sake."

"Yeah, why don't you do that Ralph, why don't you give them Fugiwara-san number?"

"What the hell! Why should he give them my damn number for? Why doesn't he give them your number buster? After all Rossie-san, you're supposed to be the Lead Agent in Charge of this damn murder case. What the hell are you dumping him off on my ass for, Rossie?"

"Errr...." The Commander tried to get a word in edgewise with his two agents, but they completely ignored him as they went off on each other.

"Because your lazy ass is just sitting in the chair doing nothing about the damn case."

"Well what about you, I don't see you going off like a rocket about this case either you know."

"Err..." The Commander tried to butt in for a second time, but they still ignored him as they continued to go after each other.

"I am the Lead Agent in this murder case so that means I don't have to deal with any talking heads about the damn case."

"You being the Lead Agent is all the more important that you handle anyone calling in to find out how the hell we're doing with the damn murder case."

"Err..."

Again the two arguing agents ignored their Commander, and this time he went off on them.

"Ahhhh for crap sake you two pains in the ass are impossible when you two get like this. When either of you two nuts want to get serious about this damn murder case, I'll be in my office throwing darts at your mug shots, dammit." With that said, Murdock stormed out of Rossie's office and charged into his office and slammed his door behind him. But what the two agents did not see, was Murdock was laughing over what his two agents just pulled off in front of him.

As soon as Murdock was out of their office, Fugiwara stood and then he held up his hand and Rossie slapped it, as they both laughed over how they just got rid of their Commander. Once they stopped laughing, Agent Fugiwara turned serious and he asked Rossie with concern in his voice.

"Are you going to try your damn snitch again, because if you're not going to make contact with him then I might go out and do some snooping around for myself man? I have my own snitch and I want to see if I can find out where the hell this little prick Young might have disappeared to on my own, Rossie-san." Fugiwara offered to his partner.

"Yeah, I'll give him another try then I'm going to break for lunch." He dialed the number Murdock gave him and again it rang until he got angry and hung up and then announced to his partner. "Still no answer from the sonofabitch, I guess he really tied one on last night, dammit."

"Then I'm going to skip lunch and go out and see what I can find for myself with my snitch. Do you want me to check in with you before I clock out for the day or what, Rossie-san?"

"I thought you wanted me to take you back to your place being you didn't drive your own car in for work today my friend?" Agent Rossie remarked as he stared back at his partner.

"That was originally my plan, but I decided to call the chick I was with last night, and have her pick me up from work later on today Rossie-san. I think I'll give her a chance to go round two with me for the night my friend." Agent Fugiwara gave Rossie a quick wink of the eye.

"Then how the hell are you going to get around now, if you're going to do some checking on your own, buddy? You don't have your car with you today, and I'm not going anywhere until I make contact with my snitch, and I find out what he wants to clue me in on today. And I'm warning you again man, you better stop doing so much running around on your wife. One of these days she's gonna catch you at it and she's going to cut your damn nuts off on ya, fella."

"That'll be the day I'm going to cut out playing the field with women my friend. I noticed Agent Richardson hanging around outside the office and I'll hitch a ride with him. I know he's going to do some trolling around today, and I can direct him over to the area I want to check out. Color me gone, I'll see you in the morning and if anything comes up with your damn snitch, let me know immediately and I'll come right back and then we can work over the lead together, Rossie-san. I'll let you know how I work out with my damn snitch and between the two of them we should be able to locate Young wherever he's hiding at in Washington."

"You got it, you be careful out there mister, I don't want anything happening to your ass. I don't cherish the idea of breaking in another partner." Agent Rossie groused at his partner.

"Thanks a lot, your stinking concern for my ass is very touching my so called friend. You'll call me if your snitch has something of value for us today sir."

"Sure will and you'll do the same with your snitch if you find out anything useful from him, right Fugiwara-san? I'm heading downstairs and then I'm going to grab me something to eat. I'll call you if I get my snitch and he has something for us to go off on. If not I'll see you in the morning, good luck out there Agent Fugiwara-san." He stood and followed Fugiwara out of their office and then they each went off on their one way.

WIND

Wind was so busy speaking to her well honored Lord Kawasomeru that time got away from the both of them. She loved so much speaking with him and reliving their past times they lived through with him and his rule over Central Japan, and all the trials and tribulations they suffered through together while struggled through life in such a savage era in Japan's proud history. A few of the Kami sat in on their conversation and they were enjoying it as much as she was enjoying being with her old Lord and Master. Not once did she give a thought to the new Master of her sword and spirit, nor did she think about how she was being treated by Agent Rossie.

Although the air was clean but the odors were flat and not as pleasant as they were in the living world, and she was making the best of her time trapped in the Floating World. There was no difference between the night and day it was always the same in the Ukiyo. Bright, and no one was near and the only time someone in the Floating World was allowed to be with someone else in the Ukiyo. Was when a well respected Deity personally requested to speak to one of the lesser members of the Floating World as Kawasomeru had requested to speak to her while she was forced to visit the Ukiyo for the day. Kawasomeru had to wait until the Council of Kami gave him permission to be with Wind while she was visiting the world of wonder.

When he received permission to be with his Wind, he was forced to wait until she was delivered to him. She was dressed in another exquisite Kimono offered her by Amaterasu, the Goddess of the Sun, because she did not want Wind to be standing before the other Gods while naked. She felt it placed Wind at a severe disadvantage when she was forced to speak to the Gods of Japan while she was ordered to the Floating World for twenty four hours.

FBI HEADQUARTERS, WASHINGTON D.C.

Special agent Robert Rossie just got back to his office from eating his lunch, and he was surprised to see Commander Murdock was not in his office, so he got comfortable in his office, and dialed his snitches' number and again, it rang until he hung up. He looked around his office for something to do, and found nothing so he went to his computer and started fishing around for some bits of information he might be able to use in one of his other cases he was still working on, before he was given the Batterman's murder case. The other two cases he was with were now being given over to other agents in the office, so he was even being shouldered out of these cases, so he had nothing else to do. Now he cursed because Wind was not at his apartment, if she was he would have surely left the office early and go home for the day and enjoy her treasures again. If it would have been anything like last night's lovemaking experience, he would have been an extremely happy man for the rest of the day.

He smiled as he remembered how they made love the night before, and how they slept on the floor for the night. He shifted his weight in the chair and got a stabbing pain in his lower back, and smiled again because the pain was from his sleeping on the floor. All the pleasant memories of last night flooded back in his mind, and he loved remembering how she moaned while he was making love to her. Everything about her was wonderful to remember, her outstanding shape, her smell, the way she walked, how she did not mind being naked around him, or how she so respected and protected him and worried about him, made he feel like the luckiest man in the world since finding her. He remembered what she told him of how Hiromoai Hatanaka took terrible advantage of her powers, and he hated the man for doing that to her.

He was being extremely careful because he did not dare want to end up taking advantage of her awesome powers, though it would be so easy to use her as his personal weapon much like Hiromoai had used her for the past few months since he obviously discovered her.

He was so wrapped in his memories about Wind he was unaware of the time until one of the other agents stuck his head inside his office and barked at him. "Hey Rossie, what the hell are you bucking for all of a sudden? You trying to become Agent of the Year working overtime? C'mon man, it's time to head home, unless you're not done sucking up to Murdock, old bean."

Murdock had returned to his office and he walked up behind the other agent and growled at him while almost scaring the life out of him at the same time. "Well it's good to see at least one of my damn Agents willing to do some real work around here. Well Billy, if you're in no rush to get home, I'm certain I can find something for you to do for gratis around here, mister."

"No, no Mr. Murdock sir, my wife and kids are waiting supper for me sir."

"Then I suggest you get the hell out of here before I do find that something extra for you to do, Mr. Wiseass." He smirked as the other agent almost tripped over himself as he tried to leave the office so quickly. Then he looked in Agent Rossie's office and grumbled at him as well.

"And what about you mister? You don't have someone waiting for you to come home. I'd find that rather hard to believe, such a good looking young man as you being forced to introduce your dick to Mary and her four friends for the night. I just couldn't see you jerking yourself off one night, not with the looks you got there Agent Rossie. For the life of me, I can't believe you're still single and playing the field. What's up, there's not one single woman out that who wasn't able to get her damn claws into your hide and forced you up the aisle with her? I'm beginning to worry about you lately mister, you're not going to start chasing a man around instead of finding yourself some lovely young lady to share the rest of your life with mister."

"That'll be the day I even look at a guy that way Commander Murdock, I'm strictly a woman's man and as yet there wasn't one lady that I found to make a wife of. Why the hell are you sticking your damn nose into my private life anyway, you old fart you. You pissed off at me because I can sleep with a different lady every night if I chose to."

"Yeah, go ahead and rub it in on me there buster. Yes, it's true I go home to the same lady every night, but at least I know she's my lady and she's not sharing herself with anyone else like you gotta worry about all the damn time, buster. C'mon mister, I'll walk you down to the parking lot. It's time to lock up the shop for the day and you getting home, son. Where the hell's your damn partner in crime anyway, I haven't seen his ass hanging around the office all day? He did come to work today, am I right Agent Rossie?"

"He went out with Agent Richardson to do some checking on what we were working on when we were jumped by Young's pack of flaming assholes, sir."

"At least he's doing something constructive with his damn time for a change I see. You tell him I want to see him the first thing in the morning Agent Rossie."

"Sure will, why do you want to see him for?"

"If he left for home from the job then he's going to have to clear it with me first, so I can mark down his time correctly for him. They're really starting to come down rather heavy on ass lately with all you guys claiming so much damn overtime all the time."

"He's not putting in for any overtime as far as I know he was just going home right from the job, because he didn't have his car with him today, Ralph."

"Then I don't need to see him tomorrow morning. What's this shit he didn't take his company car to work today? What the hell do I give him a damn company car if he's not going to use it dammit? How the hell did he get to work today anyhow, did you pick him up? Between the two of you pests, you guys are going to send me right over the god damn falls without a barrel."

"He told me he spent the night with some chick he found and she drove him to work today."

"It figures, doesn't the asshole know he's married for crap sake? He's fooling with more chicks now than when he was single. He better knock it off if he knows what's good for himself. Because if he doesn't stop messing around, I'm going to write him up and let Internal check him out to make certain none of these women as setting him up in a compromising situation. The next thing we know, we'll be stuck trying to find a mole in the company. You tell him I still want to see his ass tomorrow. And you can warn him in advance if he doesn't stop messing around with so many women, I'll write his ass up and then Internal will be checking him out from the outside in, dammit. I can't have any of my Agents fooling around on their wives like he's doing for crap sake. We do have an ethics code we all have to live up to if we want to remain Agents."

"I'll inform him you want to see him the first thing in the morning, and I'll also clue him in on why you want his ass in your office tomorrow morning sir. Is there anything else you might want me to tell him, before you get your chance to chew on his ass for a little while, sir?"

"Don't be a wise ass with me wiseass I'm not in the mood for any of your bullshit. Between the two of you birds, you have my losing my damn hair and what's left is turning gray on me faster than I can see it going, dammit. I guess somewhere along the line I must have insulted a gypsy woman, and the two of you birds are my curse from her, dammit. Why couldn't I be what my father wanted me to be, a damn mason just like he was? At least you never get any flack from a damn brick for crap sake." Murdock was still grumbling as he walked away from Rossie.

He had to laugh as he watched his boss leave him, and then he wrapped up his desk, locked the drawer and then he left the office. He was not all that interested in getting home too quickly tonight, mainly because Wind was not going to be there when he got home. He decided he was going to pick up a sandwich at the Seven Eleven, and that would serve as his supper for the night. Agent Rossie was so bored without Wind visiting him that he went to bed before 9 P.M. and slept right through until his alarm went off. He woke with a start, and then automatically looked for Wind sharing his bed. When he realized she was still not home, he got out of bed and went to the bathroom and came out and prepared his morning meal. Everything he was doing on this morning, he was carrying out like he was a robot because he was that sad Wind was not there.

He dropped his plate down on the table, and poured himself a cup of coffee then ate. When he was done, he walked over to the TV and put on the Fox and Friends News station. This was the first time since Wind had appeared at his home that he decided to watch the news in the morning. As he sat down on the sofa, he leaned back and ended up sitting on Wind's Katana sword. He hissed as he reached under himself and pulled the sword out from under his rearend, and then he stared at the ancient killing sword locked in its wooden scabbard prison. He did not remember what she told him, the only way she could come back from the Floating World if her time was done there, was when he released her sword from its scabbard.

The Special Agent rolled the sword around in his hand, feeling and enjoying the heft of the once deadly sword. Then not realizing what he was doing, he grabbed the Tsuka or hilt of the sword with one hand, and grabbed the Saya or scabbard with his other hand and he applied some light pressure on both ends of the aged old weapon. He did remember her telling him he would not be able to separate the sword from the hilt until she was done with her waiting time while trapped within the Floating World. So he had no plans of separating the sword from its scabbard, all he was doing was playing around with the sword a little. But to his surprise, when he applied pressured on the two ends, the Katana sword moved rather easily and then he excitedly yanked it right out of the scabbard then he waited for Wind to again appear before him.

Happy that she was ready to return to him, he did not even realize the handle of the sword was returning to the newness of when the sword was first created by its maker, because he was more interested in seeing her again. He absentmindedly tossed the scabbard back on the couch as he stared at the light growing in the center of the room and in no time at all, he was able to see her spirit taking on the shape of the ancient female Samurai Warrior. He found himself grumbling at her. "C'mon, C'mon will ya and come back to me quicker will you please Wind-san?" He was actually trying to force her to rush making herself whole again.

"I hear your call and I am trying with all my might to return to my Lord and Master faster than the Kami of the Floating World would allow me to come back to you my Lord. Be patient my Lord, for I am coming back to you. To learn to be patient is to learn a lesson, to learn a lesson from life is to give one life. I am here for you my Liege Lord." With that said, her body took on solid form again, and she stood before him naked as the last time they pillowed together, and she was smiling so pleasantly at him. As the cloud of light once surrounding her body, rapidly disappeared and the coolness returned to the room again. Immediately, she dropped down to her knees and she bowed so low that her nose actually lightly touched the hard wood floor, as she now waited for her Lord and Master to start talking to her again.

"I can't tell you how happy I am that you have returned to me from the world of wonder and dreams, Wind-san. How are you feeling? Do you need anything to eat or drink? Do you wish to take a quick shower before you rest in the living world again, Wind-san?"

"I Hitsuyo (Require) some drink because I thirst so from the dryness of the Floating World, and it will please me greatly if I am allowed to wash all the stale dust from the Floating World from my body my Lord and Master." When she left the Floating World, the beautiful Kimono that the well honored female Sun Goddess Amaterasu had loaned her to cover her nakedness before the gathered male Kami of the Council, the magnificent garment was left behind.

The special agent rushed to the fridge and took out the half bottle of wine and quickly poured a glass and handed it to her. Then he rushed into the bathroom while she was enjoying the cold wine, and he started the water running for her shower. When the water was just right, he called out to her. "Wind-san, you can come in now, your shower is ready for your pleasure. I'll prepare you something to eat while you shower and relax some."

"I don't know what this foolish Samurai has ever done in her wasted life that the honorable Kami have blessed me with such an attentive Liege Lord, and I have looking so carefully over me. It is I who should be fussing so over your pleasure my Lord and Master, and not the way you are treating this most unworthy Warrior. I shall enjoy this shower as you call it more than any other I had ever enjoyed before in my life, and that is because my most honorable and wonderful Liege Lord had drawn the water for me to enjoy." She squeezed by him and then she climbed into the flowing water and allowed the water to wash through her hair.

Again he enjoyed hearing her moan in delight as she enjoyed the warm water of the shower. He watched her until she started to wash her body. Then he decided to give her some privacy so she could shower and used the facilities in case she had to go. Already he could easily see her strength rapidly returning to her exhausted looking body as she enjoyed her shower.

As soon as she returned to him, his great mood also returned and he was now smiling from ear to ear as he walked around the apartment while waiting for her to finish with her shower, so he can again be with her. He poured her another glass of wine and allowed it to warm up a bit for her to enjoy. He then picked up the ancient and like new sword and scabbard and put them both by the side of the couch. She was so comfortable at his apartment she no longer had to be in constant contact with her sword to remain solid.

When she was done with her shower, she again looped a towel around her wet hair, and then she came out of the bathroom with the same fever of want to be with her new Lord and Master again. Seeing the glass of wine resting on the small table, she walked over to it and started to enjoy the drink. She so enjoyed drinking the wine he had introduced her to that she could not get enough of it. She loved the fuzzy feeling it always created within her head, and it sometimes made her actually see two of her Lord and Master standing side by side and acting exactly the same. Everything in her life for the first time was as it should have always been all along for her. She did not give a second thought to her being naked and walking around his apartment.

"Can I make you something to eat, do you hunger Wind-san?" He was speaking so much lately with the ancient Warrior that he was beginning to speak much like her himself. He did not wait for her reply as he got up and then rushed into the kitchen and took out the block of cheese and started to carve it up into nice small bite size pieces for her to nibble on. He placed the dish on the table right in front of her because while he was getting the cheese, she sat and waited for him to bring her food.

As he brought the food over to her, she could not help but thank the Kami for bringing her to such an attentive Lord and Master to serve. She watched him with dreamy eyes as she enjoyed everything he was doing for her. Already she felt like she had never had to return to the Floating World for even one stick of time. She could not help herself and she was slowly falling madly in love with her new and young Master. In all her life, all she ever did was take everyone else's feeling to mind, and here she was finally enjoying what she was always did for everyone else, being done for her by this constantly smiling young and very good looking man.

CHAPTER SIXTEEN

FBI Special Agent Robert Rossie was so much enjoying making Wind comfortable back in his apartment that he did not care if he was doing everything she was supposed to be doing for him. If he wanted to, he would be unable to wipe the smile from his lips, he was that happy that she had returned to him again. In the back of his mind, he was extremely concerned once she was forced to return to the Floating World, was the Gods of Japan's past going to allow her to ever return to him. Now, he felt he would die if he ever lost her for good, and that was how much he was starting to rely on her and her protection. He was even having a problem keeping his eyes off her and her exquisite body. She even looked great with the towel wrapped around her head.

As he stared intensely at her, she was becoming a little uncomfortable, because she did not know why her Lord and Master was looking at her like he was doing. Usually in her past life whenever one of the General's looked at a Samurai in that manner, it usually meant one thing. He was going to be ordered to commit Suppuku and end his life for some infraction he might have committed in the service of his honorable Liege Lord. Then he asked her with seriousness in his voice as he continued to stare so intensely at her.

"Wind-san how was your brief stay in the Floating World? What did you do while waiting for permission to return to me in the living world? Were you harmed in any way while you were there? Did the Kami treat you with respect, or were they upset with you because this Gai Jin was now your new Master of the sword and your fine spirit? Were you with someone while there?"

"My stay in the Floating World is always a very stressful ordeal to withstand, until I was allowed to return to you in the living world my Lord. But this time the honorable Kami allowed me to spend my time speaking with my Lord Kawasomeru. He made the time I was ordered to the Floating World enjoyable to withstand. We spoke for many breaths on the stick of time, we spoke of past times and the trouble Wakatsuki gave my Lord and his realm. The Kami as always was very kind to me, and they honored me greatly for my efforts of protecting your life. They questioned me why I attacked the Ko Ku Jie (Black) people, and when I informed them these Ko Ku Jie people were trying to harm your life, they immediately accepted my actions and they honored me for my efforts. I believe this is why they had allowed me to spend time with my Kawasomeru-Sama. I could not wait until you called me back to the living world, my Lord."

"The Kami had no problem with me and the honor you have offered me by protecting my life from harm, Wind-san?" He asked, always worried the Gods who controlled her unconquerable spirit, might recent their permission of her protecting his life like she was doing.

"None whatsoever my honorable Lord, in fact the order that Lord Kawasomeru had long ago placed upon my killing sword and foolish head, is the only reason why I am allowed to return to the living world, and continue protecting your life my Lord. So if the Kami are enforcing my Lord's curse then how could they possibly have a problem with the one who is in command of my sword and spirit in the living world?" She offered in a tone of voice that seemed to question why her new Lord would ever ask such a foolish question of her. Then she smiled without baring her teeth to her new Master of the sword. As it was in the past in Japan, the only time another Japanese person would ever bare their teeth to another, was during battle or in anger.

Agent Rossie was pleased her stay in the Ukiyo was at least pleasant for her to endure. He so wanted to make love to her but he did not want to push her because she just came back to the living world. As he was still kind of staring at her, the phone suddenly rang and he broke his trance and answered the phone, because he was also becoming a little uncomfortable staring at her like he was doing and not know what to say to her next so he was happy to answer the phone.

"Yeah, Agent Rossie here, what's up Agent Fugiwara-san?" He was aware it was his partner calling him because of the caller ID (identification) systems on the phone. He was so concerned with Wind that he did not report to work for the day, and he even forgot all about getting in contact with his snitch, to see if he was able to discover where young was hiding from them.

"Hey partner, I just got in contact with my snitch and he has a positive location for our dear friend Young. The lousy little prick is staying just two stinking blocks away from the building we were attacked in the other day. My snitch warned me that the dude is surrounding himself with another group of killers for bodyguards, but he couldn't put an accurate number on the amount of bodyguards he has protecting his ass now though. I'd like to come by so we can come up with a plan on how we're going to handle this crap tomorrow morning. I sure as hell want to go and get this guy, after him releasing his damn wolf pack on us and almost costing us our damn lives. I guess I have a sort of a hardon for the lousy prick now, Rossie-san. The lousy bastard almost had us iced off when he let his people loose on us the other day. I can't wait until I can wrap my hands around his damn neck and make his eyeballs pop outta his head on him."

"I agree and I want the bastard as much as you do, but I'm kinda busy at the moment my friend. So I guess I'll catch up with you tomorrow morning at the office, Agent Fugiwara-san."

"What! What's this shit all about man? When we get a break with a damn snitch we always talk about it the night before, so we know what the heck we're going to do the next day Rossie-san. What the hell do you have going down at your apartment tonight that you don't want to link up with me now my friend? C'mon man, it's not like I never saw the chick you were boffing at night before. I think this is more important than some baby you want to have her take a ride on your old bologna pony to tuna town, buddy." Fugiwara complained at his partner over the phone.

"I know that but I'm right in the middle of an extremely important situation here, and I can't possibly get out of it at the moment to meet with you tonight my friend."

"Does your important situation have a girlfriend with her Rossie-san?" Agent Fugiwara asked as he forgot all about his snitch and the information he just gave him.

"How come every damn thing about you has to revolve around a damn woman, you pain in my ass you. I wish just once you wouldn't be so damn interested in how much I might be scoring with, and get your fricking noggin outta the stinking gutter my friend. I told you I was involved tonight and I can't possibly meet with you and that's that, Fugiwara-san!"

"Oh brother, if you're threatening me like this then this chick you got in your apartment has to be one helluva damn good looking babe. I don't care what you say, I'm on my way over and that's that to use your phase, my friend." Agent Fugiwara snapped back in the phone at him.

"I'm warning you Fugiwara-san, I have a damn weapon and I know how to us the damn thing, and if you show up on my front porch unwanted tonight. I'm gonna put a damn cap in your ass. I just told you not to come over tonight, can't you give me this one night dammit. It's important for me to handle this tonight, pal." Agent Rossie complained bitterly at his partner.

"I just gotta see this chick you're protecting she has to really be something if you're threatening to put a fricking cap in my ass over her, buddy. Who is she? Do I know her my friend? C'mon man and level with me, you really got me going here Rossie-san."

"It's not a chick at all, it's just something I gotta handle for myself tonight, and I need to settle it tonight, buddy. So give me a break and I'll meet you at the office tomorrow morning."

"In a stinking pig's ear it's not some chick you're trying to protect here, buddy. Hey man, this isn't that female bitch armed with that damn pig sticker that came to our aide the other day is it man? Now I gotta see what the hell this babe really looks like, and why you're protecting her purdy little rearend like you're doing, my old friend. I'm coming over whether you have a weapon or not Rossie-san. It should take me like fifteen to twenty minutes to get over to your place from here. You need anything you want me to pick up a Pizza or something my friend?"

"You're just not going to let it go will you?"

"Nope!"

"Come on over then you pain in the ass you."

"If you think I'm a pain in the ass, you should have heard what Commander Murdock has to say about you not showing up for work today, dog. He was bitching about doing something to your body with a rusty nail and a cattle probe, buddy. And I got your number too. Sure, now you'll send this chick home and I'll never see what the hell she really looks like, man."

"You're gonna be really disappointed when you get here because there isn't some chick here this time, I'm telling you buster. But if you're gonna come over tonight, you might as well pick up a damn Pizza, all I had to eat tonight so far is some lousy nibbles, Fugiwara-san."

"On my way over, this information is hot and I don't want it to cool off on us before we had a chance to go over it together tonight, Rossie-san."

"I told you you won so come on over, you said twenty minutes to get here?"

"On my way, but it might take me a little longer than twenty minutes now to get over to your place. That's because I hafta stop and pick up a Pizza for us now. You have some wine, arrr… never mind that crap, I'll just pick up a bottle for us. I feel like having a little something to drink tonight. What does the chick you got over the apartment like to drink, Rossie-san?"

"That was a nice try there Agent Fugiwara-san, but I'm telling you again I don't have a damn chick here tonight, you thick head you."

"Sure, you won't have a chick there by the time I get there you mean, old buddy."

"You just won't let it go will ya Fugiwara-san. I'll be waiting for you to get here."

As soon as he hung up the phone with his partner, he immediately looked at Wind and announced to her because he was speaking English with his partner, and he knew she did not understand one word that was being said between the two agents. "Wind-san that was my partner I work with, and he has some rather important information that we have to discuss tonight. I'm afraid I'm going to be forced to have you sort of hide in my bedroom until he finally leaves here, and then we can continue our conversations tonight if you'd like to continue talking together."

"I am so sorry that we will be unable to continue with our time together tonight. I was so looking forward to being with my Lord and Master on this night. After my return from the

Floating World, I was looking to be held for a little while tonight my Lord." She complained as she placed the saddest look on her face this time and stared back at him.

"Once my partner leaves, we'll have the rest of the night to hold each other tight. I admit I'm looking forward to being with you in bed. I want to welcome you back to the land of the living."

"To make the Wind and the Rain is the answer to true life and relax my Lord."

"I got it Wind-san, but I'm displeased that I'm forced to ask you to hide in my bedroom, and you must not allow your presence to be discovered by my partner under any circumstances tonight. Or I'll never be able to get rid of him for the rest of the damn night, and he'll drive the both of us absolutely crazy for the rest of the night as well, Wind-san."

"I can always dispatch what you call your partner if you may desire this of me my Lord. That way he will not be much trouble for us tonight. It is that simple to withstand my Liege Lord. It is not what happens to you, it's what you do about it that matters my Lord and Master."

"I'm truly amazed with you Wind-san, you see things so clearly, so black and white with no difference in your thoughts and mind. But you can't go and destroy my partner because he's no real threat against me, he's just a royal pain in the ass every once in a while, especially when a woman might be involved, and he's not part of all the action, Wind-san. Enough of this, I need you to make yourself invisible tonight, I'd really hate like hell to be forced to send you back to the Floating World if you think it might be impossible for you to hide from this man for the rest of the night, Wind-san. Will you be able to hide from him for me tonight?"

"My Liege Lord, I can make myself like a ghost and your partner will never be able to discover my presence no matter how hard he might waste his foolish time trying to locate where I might be hiding from him. One thing I was well trained in that was deception my Liege Lord."

"Good then I need you to go now and hide before my partner arrives, so we can discuss our work for tomorrow, Wind-san." He replied as he rose, and then he waited for her to get up and head for the bedroom. So he could prepare to greet his partner when he arrives, so they could discuss their case and what they would plan for tomorrow morning's workload.

She stood and moved for the bedroom like she was walking to her own death. She wanted so bad to be with her new Master of the sword for the rest of the night, and it hurt her to be banished to his bedroom for who knew how long on this night. It was not what she had in mind for their night back together. When she closed the door behind her, Agent Rossie immediately went into action. He picked up her sword and its scabbard and rushed to the hallway closet and hid the two items in it. Then he rushed around the rest of the living room and kitchen, picking up and cleaning everything he was sharing with her on this night. He even threw the extra cheese in the garbage, rather than taking the time to wrap it up and put it back in the fridge.

Just as he got everything cleaned up, there was a quick knock on his front door and then the door opened and his partner let himself into the apartment. Agent Fugiwara entered with a smile and he walked right into the living room and dropped the Pizza down on the small table, and then he walked into the kitchen and took two glasses and walked back over to the small table and put the glasses down and he operand the bottle of wine with his pocketknife with the small corkscrew, and allowed the wine to breathe for a few second, as he said to his partner as he looked all around the living room and kitchen. He even glanced into the bathroom because the door was slightly open, and he was able to see into the small room.

"Would you like a damn flashlight and do you want to search my bedroom and the closet too. Maybe you might want to walk around outside the building, I'm certain if you look around you'll sooner or later find some poor lady walking around outside, buster." He actually glared at Fugiwara, because he was that upset he was so obviously searching his home looking for Wind.

"I'm sorry Rossie-san I didn't realize you were so sensitive lately about this babe with the sword. I was only screwing around a little with you tonight by searching your place anyway my friend. I took your word for it and when you told me you didn't have some chick in the apartment tonight buddy. I took it for granted you didn't have anyone here tonight it's that simple. I'm sorry also for pressing for this meeting on you for tonight. But my snitch wants to meet with the both of us between eight and nine in the morning, and I felt it was absolutely necessary to talk over what we might be walking into tomorrow when we meet with the snitch.

"We have a lot of shit to go over tonight, so let's take a slice of Pizza and a glass of wine, and then let's get down to some brass tacks around here my friend. I have to warn you though Rossie-san, something about the damn snitch has me on guard some..."

"What do you mean Fugiwara-san, do you think he's trying to set us up for a fall?"

"I don't quite know what it is Rossie-san, but I felt it was a little strange I was trying to get him ever since we left the office, I couldn't get him all day and when he suddenly returned my call, I kinda got a weird feeling from him. I can't really put my finger on what's bothering me about the conversation we had, but he didn't ask me many questions, and he started right off by telling me he knew where Young was hiding. I further feel this Young fella wouldn't have remained so close to the damn crime scene. I woulda figured he would have made his bird far away from the area because of the continuing heavy police presence still hanging around where the shootout had occurred. Like I said, he didn't ask me many questions and for the first time he didn't even ask me for any money for the information he had for me Rossie-san.

"Usually, whenever I made contact with him, his first question is how much are you going to pay me for the information, and then he wanted to know what I wanted from him. He didn't do either this time tonight. Also Rossie-san, I asked to meet with him tonight, but he insisted on meeting with the both of us tomorrow morning, and this is the part that really bugged the crap outta my ass about him tonight. Since when does one's snitch want to expose himself to anyone else when he's ratting out one of his fucking partners in crime? Yes, I feel he might be trying to set us up for a fall, but then I asked myself why he would want to do that. If he wanted to screw around with us, all he had to do was not make any contact with me when I was calling him.

"Yes, once we have gone over everything about my snitch then we'll decide if we want to me meet with him. But I want some of our own people running back up for us this time around, if we have to go after Young again. I have known this damn snitch for over three years now, and on a number of other occasions he fed me extremely important information, information that had helped me solve three different cases I was bogged down on. So I guess I kinda do trust him. But on the other hand, if he's so willing to betray one of his damn criminals, what's to say he wouldn't betray us and sell us down the river at a drop of the damn hat, Rossie-san."

"I'm glad you told me how long you have been working with this snitch, because that was going to be the first question I was going to ask of you. As you were talking, I was trying to figure out what might be in it for him if he hung us out to dry on this one. If Young is paying him to set us up for the kill, I couldn't figure out why and what your snitch would get out of the deal. Knowing Young as I do, if he's paying this creep to set us up. When the jackass goes to get his pay, you know as well as I do and he also would have to know. The only pay he's going to get from Young is a 45 round planted right between his damn eyes from Young.

"Do you really think we should go with your snitch with all the concerns you're raising here, Agent Fugiwara-san. I don't need to get involved in another shootout like we got into when we last went after Young, and all we were going to do was talk to him that time. This time we'll be going after him to arrest him for him allowing his goons to try and kill us, dammit."

"I really don't know what to do to tell you the truth about this crazy ass situation, Rossie-san. You know why I so want this lousy sonofabitch so bad, but I don't want my emotions to get the best of me, and I end up doing something foolish and get both our asses in a sling. But on the other hand, we're just never going to be able to find Young for who knows how long, without any help from the damn snitch world, Rossie-san. I looked at this from so many different ways from Monday to Sunday, and I just can't see my damn snitch selling us out for this bum." Agent Fugiwara stopped speaking just long enough to rip into his slice of Pizza, and down his glass of wine. Agent Rossie immediately filled his glass for a second time for him.

"Thanks Rossie-san." Agent Fugiwara offered as he continued to munch down on his Pizza.

"You know I want Young just as much as you want him Fugiwara-san, so I think we should meet with your snitch. But I'll tell you this much my friend. I don't have any intentions of meeting with him on his terms, especially not after all the concerns you just brought up to my attention. I think we should tell your friend to meet us somewhere we can see all around him, and he can't get us into a corner or trapped. I also want at least two different cars with at least two Agents inside them to trail us no matter where we go to meet this turd. I also want at least two to four cars to follow us if and when we go to meet with this Young creep. I want my ass so well protected when we meet your snitch and doubly protected if we go to meet Young. I'm not going to allow that bastard to get us into a situation like the last one he walked us into, I can tell you that much my friend." Rossie offered as he held Fugiwara locked up in an intensive stare while he waited to see if his partner was going to add anything to what he just grumbled at him.

"I couldn't agree with you more about this crap my friend. I just hope your female protector will be watching over us like she was when Young walked us into that stinking trap a few days ago my friend. If it wasn't for her coming to help us, we both would be pushing up daisies right about now Rossie-san. Is there any way you might be able to communicate this female weapon of yours, and tell her where we might go and meet with Young once we find out where the hell he's hiding at from my damn snitch. I'd feel a helluva lot better knowing that she is watching over us again like she did before. If she was able to hack seventeen people into hamburger meat while they were firing automatic weapons at her then she took off obviously without a stinking scratch on her body. Then she's who I want on my team and protecting my ass if we run into anymore fricking trouble with this damn Young person, and the rest of his pack of assholes."

"I have no special way to communicate with her, she just shows up whenever she decides to get in my way. How the hell did we get back on her? Dammit, shouldn't you be out there stir frying a damn cat of something, instead of bothering me all night long. Once I finished with the meeting I was involved in when you called earlier tonight, I was planning to have a nice, quiet evening, watch a movie. Then turn in and smile all night long as I dreamed of going down to Florida and do some serious fishing in Safety Harbor by Clearwater in Pinellas County. I still don't know why this couldn't wait until the morning to deal with. We could have always put off meeting with your damn snitch until we were ready to meet up with him. By the way, I think that's a good idea as well now that we're talking and you're screwing up my evening on me..."

"What's a good idea Rossie-san?"

"Not meeting with your snitch where he wants to meet. I think we should set the time along with the place to meet. That way it'll be ten times harder for him to possibly set us up for a kill when he meets us when we want to meet with him where we want to meet with him."

"You keep talking like this and I'm going to start believing it was really some chick you had over here tonight, and you only made her beat it when you knew I was coming over here to talk with you about my snitch my friend. I'm going to have another slice of Pizza and glass of wine, and then I'm going to finish up with you and then I'm going to go out and find me a young hen to be with for the rest of the stinking night. You know I only have the weekdays to go out and about, because I always go home to the old lady over the weekends. Unless we sometimes get stuck doing some overtime and I stay in Washington for the weekend, Rossie-san." Agent Fugiwara placed a huge smile on his lips and gave Rossie a wink of the eye.

"You do know that one day that damn snake of yours is going to get you in more trouble than you can possibly get your ass outta, my friend." Rossie smirked back at his partner.

"One day sure I guess." Agent Fugiwara replied with the same kind of smirk n his face.

"You're really getting impossible lately my old friend. Anyway, how the devil are we going to handle this meeting you want to set up with your snitch for tomorrow morning, Fugiwara-san? I don't really relish the thought of walking into a possible ambush you know."

"I think we're gonna do just as you have suggested, and I'm going to set up a meeting with my snitch at a place where we can have some of our people stake out the area, before we meet with him. I'm also going to change the time to our want and need, and not the time he wants to set up a meeting with us. In this way we can throw off any possible ambush, if he's really setting us up for a kill. I'm still a little shaky meeting with him over this Young person, because of what happened to us when we just wanted to talk with this lousy bastard. This time we're going to go after him to arrest his ass, or stop him in any manner we might have to resort to, including killing him and anyone he has surrounding him at the time of our confrontation with the dopey bastard, Rossie-san." Agent Fugiwara offered to his partner as he mulled over any other possibilities they might want to include when they went after Young tomorrow.

"That sounds like a plan to me. When do you intend to make contact with your snitch again Agent Fugiwara-san? Then we can start formulating our own plan on how we're going to counteract any possible ambush this guy might be leading us into, Fugiwara-san."

"I guess I'll make contact with him the first thing in the morning. He wanted to meet with us between eight and nine o'clock tomorrow morning, and that's another thing that raised the hackles on the back of my neck I tell you Rossie-san. My damn snitch is never operating with any true sense of the word until usually early in the afternoon. This is the first time he ever requested to meet with me this early in the day. He just set off too many alarms in my noggin for me to be as comfortable as I usually am with meeting with him this time around, Rossie-san. I think I want Agents Wilson and Parker to be in one of our back up vehicles. The both of them are dead shots and they always have their heads screwed on tight, and if we're running into any possible ambush. I want the very best of our crews for backups for us, Rossie-san."

"You got that right Fugiwara-san, Wilson and Parker are the best shots we have in the entire company. I think I also want Agents David Price and Paul Davenport in the second backup vehicle for us, those two Agents are good whenever they're working together..."

"Yeah, and we might as well put the push on Murdock tomorrow morning, and request Al Johnson and Mark Wesson to be in a third backup unit for our needs, Rossie-san. I want as many of our best people protecting our asses as we can get when we finally meet with my damn snitch, and if we're going to end up confronting Young and any of his damn bodyguards tomorrow at any time of the day, I want these six Agents working with us real close together. I'm also going to request a number of Washington Police Officers to be roaming around the target area, acting as some extra security for us, just in case we run into any trouble with either meeting's we're going to pull off tomorrow morning, Agent Rossie-san."

"You're that concerned about these two meeting tomorrow to request these six Agents, along with a number of Washington Police to be our backups for any action we might get involved in, Fugiwara-san." Rossie asked, showing he was growing more and more concerned over their impending meeting with Fugiwara's snitch, and possibly tangling with Young and protectors he might have surrounding him as well. I guess I'll be busy with giving Murdock some oxygen and CPR when he gets shocked over the other Agents you want to have working with us tomorrow, Fugiwara-san. You know damn well he's going to cry like a spoiled brat over the extra cost this is going to cause, to have the six other Agent's coming in on this case with us, buddy."

"Yeah, I can see Commander Murdock's neck getting as big as his waistline when he hears my request for the extra Agents to be assigned to us tomorrow morning. It should be some fun to watch at that Rossie-san." Agent Fugiwara chuckled over his own comment this time.

"Well let's finish off the Pizza and wine, and then I want to call it a day. We're going to get an early start on to tomorrow's work, and I want to be well rested and ready when we start, my friend." Agent Rossie offered, still trying to get rid of Fugiwara for what was left of their night.

"Yes, it's getting a little late at that I guess. I'm done with the Pizza, it wasn't as good as it usually is tonight anyhow, and whether you realize it or not, the wine is already gone. So if there's no more wine to drink, and there's no naked women running around your damn apartment. Then color me gone for the rest of the night, because I have some things I can get involved in for tonight myself, Rossie-san. Unless you want me to make a coupla of phone calls and get a few hot numbers to come by and give us a good time, buddy?" Fugiwara offered.

"You gotta be shitting me for Pete's sake fella. Didn't you just hear what I said to you man? I wanna get some damn rest so I'm up and ready early for what we gotta do tomorrow morning, asshole? Besides my friend, I'm in no mood to be playing around and doing a little patty cake with some strange women after hearing what you just told me tonight about what we might be facing tomorrow." Rossie actually growled back at Agent Fugiwara, because he was angry the other agent was still looking to interfere with what was left of his night.

The two agents kept slipping ever once in a while in their conversation to their street lingo they were getting so use to using whenever they were forced to deal with the lowlifes of Washington D.C. More and more they were resorting to their ways of talking.

"You got me dead to right and you're right at that, we better put an end to this night so we're well rested for what we might get trapped into tomorrow morning, Rossie-san. If all goes well tomorrow, supper's on me then buddy."

"You got it, it's about time you offered to buy me supper you cheap prick you. If you remember right buddy, I paid for the last three suppers we shared together, brother." Rossie mumbled as he rose, and then waited for Fugiwara to get up. Then he escorted him to the front door of the apartment and actually opened it for him as he rushed him out of the home.

"Wow, why don't you just shove me down the damn steps while you're at it Rossie-san! I'm leaving so there's no reason to shove me like that pal."

"I didn't shove you anywhere asshole, but if you don't get outta here quick like. I might give you a hop in the ass to get you moving faster, buster. I want to get some rest tonight dammit, I'm beat out and you're stopping me from getting any rest. I'll see you in the morning, so go and get some damn rest tonight will ya please my friend." Rossie offered as he smiled at his partner.

Agent Fugiwara smiled back and then he held his hand up and Rossie slapped hands with him. Then Fugiwara turned and started down the steps as Rossie quickly closed the door behind him. He stood by the door until he heard Fugiwara's car finally start up and then drive away. He then turned on his heels and rushed for his bedroom to check on Wind and see what she was doing.

He's happiness instantly left him when he saw she was fast asleep on the bed, so he stripped down and then snuck between the sheets and pulled her close to him. He immediately felt her snuggle up again his chest, and he could swear he could see her smiling in her sleep.

6 A.M. WEDNESDAY, JUNE 24th, 1996 ROSSIE'S APARTMENT

Agent Rossie was up early as tired as he was he did not get a good night's sleep. He was tossing and turning because he was upset with concerns plaguing him over their meeting with Fugiwara's snitch, and then going after Young and his bodyguards. He rolled out of bed and Wind woke over his movement, and he offered to her. "Wind-san, why don't you remain in bed? I have to get up early because I have two extremely important meetings set up for today, and I want to get down to the office so I can be ready to begin these meetings at their scheduled times."

"I am upset my Lord and Master would ever intend to go off to work without a proper meal to enjoy first. What kind of loyal Vassal would I be if I ever allowed you to go hungry for even one breath (Second) on the stick of time? I shall get up and prepare your morning meal for you, and then I shall sit and keep you company until you leave for your work period, my Liege Lord." She then bowed politely and scurried out of the room to prepare his morning meal for him. She knew he would want to enjoy a shower like he always did every morning before going off to work.

Agent Rossie watched as she rushed out of the bedroom, and shrugged and headed for the bathroom. He used the facilities and took his shower and like she always did, he walked out of the bathroom naked. He sat at the table and waited for her to finish cooking his eggs. He was enjoying watching her cook, because she was dressed in an exquisite but extremely short, barely covering the rounds of her lovely rearend light blue silk Kimono, and every time she reached for something, or moved and especially when she bent down, her beautiful rearend came in his view.

She caught him a few times looking at her with lust filling in his eyes and she smiled to herself, being fully aware of what she was doing while she was cooking. She knew if she could not entice him to share her treasures this morning. She would be sending him off to work with the thoughts and dreams of exploring her body when her Lord and Master returned to her after he concluded his day's work. If there was one thing Hiromoai Hatanaka had taught her for the brief time he was in command of her killing sword. Was the new modern way for her to entice her intended target to enjoy what she had to offer when pillowing was locked in her mind.

She carried his eggs to the table and then sat across the table from him. Again she was working on him by allowing the front of her tight fitting Kimono to sag open, exposing the wonderful swells of her breasts to be easily seen by her Master.

Agent Rossie suddenly stopped eating and then he smiled at her as he offered to her. "I have to admit Wind-san you're making it very hard for me to eat like this."

She cocked her head to the side and stared at her Lord for a few seconds, and then she replied to him with confusion in her voice. "I am so sorry to offer to my Liege Lord, but I do not understand what you mean by my making it hard for you to eat like this. Is there something this foolish Warrior is doing that is somehow making something hard for you to be with me, Lord?"

Agent Rossie just slowly shook his head as he continued to smile, and then he stood up and show her what she was making hard for him.

She instantly covered her mouth with both her hands as she started to laugh with glee over his condition, and then she understood what he meant by his remark to her. Here her wonderful Lord and Master was standing up with his rock hard member slowly swaying back and forth in front of her. She was so pleased her plan was working so well for her as she announced to her Master. "Would my Lord feel a lot more comfortable if I was to dress in something that was a lot less reveling? I can always slip into one of my winter Kimono's if it would please my Liege lord."

"If you do, I'll never speak to you again little lady. You're far too beautiful for you to dare cover up even the smallest of your beauty and keep it from my view, Wind-san."

"Then maybe my Liege Lord would be more pleased if I were to expose a little more of myself to your wonderful gaze, my honorable Lord?" She said as she pulled her Kimono a little wider open, exposing one of her perfect breasts, and then she smiled deviously back at him.

"I'm warning you Wind-san, if you keep teasing me like you obviously are doing for some reason this morning. I'm going to end up missing both my meetings today, and I'll also end up losing another day of work with all the distractions you're wisely aiming at me this morning. Although I am so pleased at what you're doing for my pleasure this morning, I must beg of you to stop so I can eat my meal in peace, and then head off for my work day today. I can't believe I'm about to say this to such a beautiful woman, but can you please cover yourself up so I can keep my mind on what I have to do for the day. I assure you Wind-san if it was any other day, I wouldn't care about my workday I'd just stay home and be with you for the entire day. Please." Rossie added as he made a motion with his hands for her to cover herself up for him. Even though he said it, he put a sad look on, and he stared at her beauty until she covered herself up.

All the while she listened and then did what he ordered her to do, she was smiling inside over the power she knew she held over her so powerful Lord and Master. She found herself so amused over the power of her just exposing her breast to her Lord and Master had over his powerful being. She even laughed over how easily it would be for her to rule over her Master with just employing her body as the weapon she would use to conquer his mind. Then she realized how weak the male animal truly was, and how easily any woman could command over him as she relaxed, and then observed her Master as he went back to eating his morning meal.

Agent Rossie quickly finished the rest of his meal, and then he stood while leaving his dish for Wind to take care of as he announced. "I have to go and get dressed for work, and then I'll be quickly leaving once I'm ready to leave, Wind-san. I trust you'll find some things to do to occupy your time until I can return home and we can be together again. I thank you for making my meal, it was wonderful and you're quickly becoming quite the hand with the stove and my meals, Wind-san." He bowed slightly to her, and then he rushed into the bedroom to get dressed.

She stood when her Lord rose, and she returned his bow and watched as he disappeared in the bedroom then she cleaned the table and stove. In what seemed like a few seconds, he returned to the living room and he was fully dressed and he walked up behind her and gently reached around and cupped both her breasts and slowly rolled them in his hands, and he purred in her ear.

"Don't think for one second I didn't know what you were up to this morning, and I truly appreciate all of what you're doing for me, and so pleasantly teasing me before I'm off for work today. You just wait until I return home tonight then it'll be me who'll be doing all the teasing of you, and driving you crazy for a little while before I finally make mad, passionate love to you all night long. Especially if my day goes the way I plan for it to go for me, Wind-san.

She spun around in his arms and she was planning to kiss him, but she was momentarily stunned for her to see her Lord and Master was wearing one of what she always called the iron hand (Gun) hanging so openly under his left arm in plain view of her.

FBI Special Agent Robert Rossie easily caught the slight hesitation in her movements, and then he looked at what she was staring at and he said to her with a smile on his lips, trying to reassure her it was nothing to be overly concerned with. "I'm terribly sorry that you had to see that damn thing Wind-san. I know how you feel about my modern day weapon, but it could turn out to be extremely dangerous with these two meetings I have scheduled for later a little on today. So I must be well prepared and armed at all times today, in order for me to be able to protect and defend myself, if something suddenly turns into being a dangerous situation for me and my partner today."

"Then I too must be prepared to come to your aid if you find yourself suddenly trapped in a dangerous situation with either of these two meeting you have scheduled for today my honorable Liege Lord. I promise you at the first sign that you are in any danger, I shall come to you as my name suggests. Like the Wind that rules the sky, and then I shall engulf you behind my sword and protect you from all possible harm my Lord and Master." She remarked in a commanding tone of voice as she bulked up her chest to show him she was ready to help him.

"I shall be looking for you if I do get myself in any trouble today, Wind-san. That's how dangerous these two meetings I have scheduled today for me and my partner is." That was another thing troubling him so, until he came to terms with this extremely deadly female weapon whose only objective in her life was to protect him from all harm. Now he wanted her to be around just in case something went wrong and he ended up in a life and dead.

"I assure my honorable Liege Lord, at the first feeling you are in danger, you shall find me standing by your side. What about who you call your partner, how is he going to react if I am forced to come to your aide, my Lord?" She asked him with concern in her voice.

"Wind-san, the little my partner knows about you, let me tell you he's already looking for you to come to our aide if we run into any problems with either of these two meetings we have planned for later today. He too was very pleased you came to our aide and he like myself, likes the knowledge that you'll be there if we need your help again, Wind-san. In my line of work, any extra protection we possibly can get for ourselves is well appreciated and needed all the time. I'm sorry, but I have to be off to work now or I'm going to end up being late again." With that said, he kissed her, picked up his backpack after putting on his suite jacket to cover his weapon on his side, and then he was off to meet with his partner.

CHAPTER SEVENTEEN

FBI HEADQUARTERS,
WASHINGTON D.C.
WEDNESDAY, JUNE 24th, 1996,
ZERO SEVEN TWENTY HOURS (7:20 A.M.)

Special Agent Robert Rossie entered his office and was the first one to arrive so early, and he immediately checked his phone log to see if his snitch might have checked in with him yet. He trusted his snitch much more that he trusted Agent Fugiwara's snitch. He grumbled a curse under his breath when he discovered his snitch had not check in with him as yet. Then he went to his computer and checked his E'mails and anything else that was important to him, and then he settled down to wait for his partner to check in for work this morning.

His wait for his partner to arrive at work was not that long because ten minutes later, Special Agent Shinnosuke Fugiwara came strolling into the office, and he was carrying two cups of coffee and three Danishes and he placed the small tray on Rossie's desk and remarked. "Man Rossie-san, what the hell happened to you today? You get thrown outta your place by the babe you disappointed last night or something? What the hell are you doing here this early in the damn morning? Hell, if Commander Murdock sees you in the office as early as you arrived, he'll be crying like a baby thinking you're putting in for a little overtime pay today, my friend."

"I had a real shitty night's sleep and woke early, and I had nothing else to do. So I figured I'd beat the rush hour traffic and I left early for the office, no problem my friend. Thanks for the coffee and cake, I really needed another cup of coffee to get my blood moving this morning. You have everything set in place to get hold of your snitch and get our backup set up for our need for later on today, Fugiwara-san?" Agent Rossie asked his partner with concern.

"I have just about everything we're going toned all set up except for our FBI backup personnel. I have to wait for Commander Murdock to come in so I can get his permission..."

"You need my stinking permission for what Agent Fugiwara? What the hell do you two have up your sleeves that you need my permission for anything around here? And where the hell is my cup of coffee, whoever brought these two cups up to this office? How the hell many times do I have to keep telling you two pests, when you guys come in pick up an extra coffee for my ass once in a while." Murdock complained as he entered the office and then sat down in an empty chair and stared at his two agents, before added to his words for them.

"What the hell are you two doing showing up at the office this early in the morning for? You guys got something going down that I don't know about? I really hate like hell when you two keep any god damn secrets from me, and one day you two are going to pay big time for that sin I can tell the both of you two, dammit. I'm the god damn Commander of this office and anything you guys are working on, I better know about it even before you two birds know about it for yourselves." He growled angrily as he leaned back in his chair and smirked at the two.

"I'm happy you came in the office early yourself Commander that way I don't have to go looking for you hanging around the women's bathroom again, sir."

"Ha, ha Mr. Wiseass, you know one of these days your smartass remarks are going to get you in more trouble than you can possibly get your ass outta, buster. Now what the hell do you need my permission for you had to see me over, Mr. Fugiwara? I'm warning you mister, if this request of yours is well outta hand, I'm going to get you a job as a cook in a Chink restaurant, and let you work your ass off over there for a change and get you outta my damn hair for a while..."

"What hair Commander?" Agent Rossie smirked at his boss.

Murdock turned and glared with anger locked in his eyes as he snarled at his other agent nastily. "Am I going to have some trouble with you now as well, Mr. Rossie? You better watch your damn step around here also mister. I'm certain I can find a job that'll drive you as crazy as you two are always trying to drive me nuts around here the both of you birds. Now what's up and what do you two have going and what do you need my permission for today, guys?"

Agent Fugiwara shifted his weight in the chair and then he leaned forward and spoke directly at his Commander. "This is what we have going down this morning Ralph, and why I had to see you to get you to allow me to put a few extra agents on the job with us for the day sir…"

"What's this all about mister? I've never seen you so damn serious in all the days you have worked for me, Mr. Fugiwara? Why do you think you might need some extra Agents to help assist whatever the hell you two have going down today, and who do you want to pull in to assist you two today, Agent Fugiwara?" Murdock asked as he stared right back at his concerned agent.

"Well, I'd like to pull in Agent's Alan Johnson and Mark Wesson who I know are between assignments at this time sir. Then I'd also like to also have Agent David Price and Paul Davenport as our second backups for this detail if they're available…"

"They're available, Agent Fugiwara."

"Thank you Ralph then I'd also like to have errr…" Agent Fugiwara hesitated for a brief second because he knew Murdock was going to blow his top when he asked for the next two agents, and then he asked. "I'd also like to have Joe Wilson and Eddy Parker…"

"Jesus Christ Almighty, why the hell don't you just ask for the entire company to come out of the woodwork, and hold you guy's hands for the love of the good Christ Child. Do you know how much it's going to cost the company for me to pull in our two sharp shooters to work with you two for just one fricking day, Mr. Fugiwara? What the hell are you two up to anyway that you two birds need all this firepower to assist you two for the day for crap sake?"

"I'm also going to need a good number of Washington Police Officers to also act as our backups for two meetings we have scheduled for later on today, Ralph."

"Jesus, Mary and Joseph! You want what? How about I give the damn President a fricking weapon and order him to come outta the damn White House and pull some duty protecting you two guy's asses while you two are doing who the hell knows what around Washington today, dammit. Do you know how many people are going to jump on my stinking ass when they see the price tab for this detain you two are working on today for crap sake. Jesus, I knew I shoulda pulled today off. I should've called in and told the Desk Sergeant I wasn't coming in today, because I wanted to protect my sanity from you two birds here. Okay, enough bullshitting, what the hell do you two have going down today? I'll order the six Agents in when I hear what you two have?" Murdock asked as he let his breath out in a rush, and then he calmed down and waited for Fugiwara to inform him what he and Agent Rossie were working on for the day.

"Okay Ralph, this is what we have going down. I spoke with my snitch and he has information on the whereabouts of Young. Since the last time we went just to talk to this lousy prick and we ended up in one helluva shootout with his bodyguards, we feel it's going to be ten times as bad when we go after him to arrest his ass. We're expecting another shootout with the little prick and we want our best people on the job with us when we go after him, sir."

"If that's a fact then I'll agree with your request for the extra personnel, and I'll immediately approve the request as soon as I get to my office. But I'm kind of confused here a little Fugiwara. You said you have two meeting scheduled for today, one with your damn snitch, and the other going after Young. Why the hell do you need so much backup support when all you're going to be doing is speaking with your god damn snitch? Do you think you need all this fire power just to speak with your snitch, and if you're so damn worried with meeting with your fricking snitch? Just swear out an APB (All Points Bulletin) warrant on his ass and have him picked up and brought in, so you can interrogate his ass in the safety of this building, mister. That move will save me a ton of extra overtime and money to deal with, buster." Murdock suggested to his agent.

"How the hell can I just swear out a damn warrant on his ass Ralph? If I do that I'll blow his cover for one, and then his life wouldn't be worth a plug nickel, sir. Also, if he had us set up for a fall then pulling him in wouldn't help out either, because Young would just return to the underworld and we'd never find his ass for who knows how long, and my snitch's ass would be blown that way as well. This damn snitch served me very well in the past and..."

"Then how come you're so concerned about meeting with him now, Agent Fugiwara?"

"Because for a number of different reasons I got warning signals from him that drew my concerns with meeting with him, yet the information he has is needed by us if we really want to get our hands on Young, sir." Agent Fugiwara replied to his Commander.

"What are some of these concerns you're dealing with over meeting your damn snitch today, mister?" Ralph asked as he stared at his agent while waiting for his reply.

"Like for the first time since I've been working with the sonofabitch, he never once asked me for some money up front. Then he wanted to meet with both myself and Rossie-san at the same time, and you know damn well no snitch ever wants to expose his ass to another Agent if he could help it, and another reason is; this dude is never up and moving around before twelve noon and suddenly he wants to meet with the both of us between 8 and 9 A.M. this morning. These are the reasons I want so much backup protecting Rossie-san and my ass when we meet with the damn snitch, sir." Agent Fugiwara replied to his concerned looking Commander.

"Those are some might damn good reasons you got there to have so much concern in meeting with this damn snitch of yours, Agent Fugiwara. And I promise you this much, if this sonofabitch is setting up two of my god damn Agents for the slaughter. Then he's going to be the first person who'll be slaughtered on this stinking day for crap sake. I approve of your request for the added support for your meeting with this bastard when, Agent Fugiwara?"

"As soon as I make contact with him and set up a meeting time in our favor and place that's easier for us to stake out, Ralph. I thank you for being willing to give us the extra support we're requesting for this operation. That's important for us to know you have our back on this one sir."

"What the hell is wrong with your noggin anyway, mister. Do you think for one damn second that I'd ever allow two of my god damn Agents to go out on an operation that might cost them their lives, without my doing everything in my power to try and protect the two of you birds while you're both out there, son. I'd never allow any harm to come to any of my Agents as long as I'm on watch of this country, Agent Fugiwara." His Commander actually growled at him.

"Nevertheless thank you again for having our backs on this one sir."

"And you Mr. Rossie," Murdock suddenly turned and growled at his other agent, before he went on with his words aimed at him this time. "Why the hell am I not hearing very much coming out of your mouth on this one, mister? After all mister, you're supposed to be the damn Lead Agent on this entire operation, and here you are, allowing your second in command to run all the interference for your ass. What do you have to say about all this crap about to go down today with this meeting of yours, Agent Rossie? And don't think for one moment I see that we're drifting away from your original investigation of the Batterman's murder case. You two better remember that I have a shit load of damn suck ass Politicians and important people breathing down my damn neck, all wanting to know how we're doing with that damn investigation.

"I'm warning the both of you birds, the fist moment we settled our hash with this Young guy, I want, no correct that last statement. I demand the both of you to put your noses to the grindstone and solve the damn Batterman's murder before you turn your eyes on any other case we might be handling for crap sake. I need that damn case solved as much as I need this damn Young case ended as soon as possible, people. Okay you two, I had just about enough of this damn dumbfuckery to last me a stinking lifetime for crap sake. I'm going to leave the both of you and get back to my office and set up the extra Agents and Police Officers you requested from me. I want to know the very first moment you make contact with your damn snitch, and let me know what time and where you intend to meet with this sonofabitch. See me before either of you two fool's dare to leave this building." Murdock warned his two agents as he stood, and quickly left the office his two agents were using to investigate Batterman's murder.

As soon as Murdock was out of the office, Agent Fugiwara turned to Rossie and smirked at him. "Well that went much easier than I first expected it to go down. I never thought the Big Growl would be so willing to back us with this damn operation. I knew he was going to blow a gasket, but he sure kept his temper in check and he was so willing to support this crap we got ourselves involved in. Well I believe I have put off calling this damn snitch of mine for long enough, I might as well give the prick a call and set him up for a fall this time, Rossie-san."

"Might as well call the lousy bastard and get it over with. I just tried my snitch and he's still not answering my call. I guess I'll try him when we get back to the office after we have dealt with the snitch and Young, Fugiwara-san." Agent Rossie said as he hung up his phone.

"Wish me luck." Fugiwara said as he picked up his phone and dialed his snitch, after three rings a cautious and excited voice replied in the phone. "Man, it's about time you called, I've been waiting for your call for over a fucking hour man. I told you I wanted to meet with you between 8 and 9, now its 9:45. I didn't think you were going to call me and I was about to go out and try and score with no cash. I'm starting to get the damn shakes and I need a fix real bad man. Why the fuck do you think I wanted to meet with you so early in the damn day for? I'm really strung out man, I haven't had a fucking fix for over twenty hours now and I'm starting to get the damn heebie jeebees. I hope you're going to pay me the same amount you always do whenever I have some important information for you man." The snitch nearly cried into the phone.

"I'm really sorry it took me so damn long for me to get back to you, Bulldog. It took me a little longer than I had first expected to get permission to draw the hundred bucks from the cash draw this morning, fella. I have to get permission from my Control to get the damn cash out. I saw no reason to meet with you if I didn't have your pay with me…"

"You're damn right there Grey Ghost, I wouldn't have met with you today if you didn't have my pay, man. I'm really getting the friggin shakes man. I need one real bad now man. I want to meet you where we usually meet all the time. I don't have any wheels to meet you anywhere else and in my condition I wouldn't try and drive a nail in the wood right now. C'mon man, we gotta meet right now before I really lose it man. We gotta meet like ten minutes ago man."

"Calm down Bulldog, as soon as I secure a vehicle from the car pool, I'll be out to see you. But I'm warning you mister, if you don't have the information I needed from you, you won't get a fucking penny from me, buster." Agent Fugiwara warned his snitch in no uncertain terms.

"I know what you wanted to know man and I got what you need alright, you just make damn sure you have the money with you and you get here as soon as you can get here man. I really am strung out bad now man and I need one real fucking bad man."

"I have the damn money in my pocket already and I'm leaving now, it might take me something like ten minutes to get a vehicle, and then another fifteen to twenty minutes to get out to you so be calm. I'm coming to ya, you just be where you're supposed to meet me, or you can go to hell and I'll use this hundred to score me a fine looking bitch, and I'll do to her what you will do to me if you don't show up when you're supposed to be there, buster."

"I'll be there man because I really need one so I'll be there with bells on man." With that the snitch hung up on the agent without saying another word to him

Agent Rossie listened in on the entire conversation and he offered the moment Fugiwara hung up with the snitch. "Well at least we know he's not in Young's pocket and setting us up. I don't think he can think of anything but his next fix. I believe he's still cool, but nevertheless, being we have our backup support all set up for us already. I say the hell with it and we allow the backup to stay in effect, and they protect us when we deal with this sonofabitch, Fugiwara-san."

"I agree with you, let's go tell Murdock where we're going to meet with the damn snitch, so he can inform our backups for us." The two agents got up and they walked into Murdock's office and announced. "Say Ralph, I just talked to my snitch and we're going to meet at our usual place, and I'm going to stretch the time out for an hour from now to give our backup people the time they need to get set in place for us. We're going to meet behind the Publix shopping center over on Front Street and Fifth Avenue and as soon as we get in the car, we're off."

"You got it Agent Fugiwara, I'll make contact with the Washington PD and have them get their people out on the road for us. You can call on your radio and clue your three back up Units, they're waiting your call to inform them where and when you were to link up with your damn snitch.

The backup Units will be set in place long before you two get to the damn shopping center. Good luck on this one and I don't want anyone but the damn snitch to get hurt, if anyone has to get hurt on this one you two. I'm calling the PD right now, get going and good luck."

The moment the two agents left his office, Murdock placed a call to the local Washington PD and he growled at the Desk Sergeant. "I have two of my god damn Agents being placed on the front of a damn dime, and I want your people set in place before my Agents arrive at their location. I'm not talking pretty soon I'm talking about right now mister. My Agents are scheduled to meet with their damn snitch at the Publix Shopping Center on Front Street and 5th Avenue. I want at least five of your squad cars in the area, and I want two Officers in each vehicle, and they're to remain in the area until you hear directly from my ass, and I call the operation off, do you understand my orders Sergeant? Fine, I'm please we understand each other so well here. I'll talk the Police Commissioner and thank him for your needed assistance in this current situation, Sergeant." Commander Murdock quickly informed the Desk Sergeant in an excited tone of voice as he broke off the communication with the man.

Both Agents Rossie and Fugiwara rushed to their vehicle and Rossie was driving, so Fugiwara called in and inform the other three Units where they were heading and when they were supposed to link up with their snitch. Two of the Units were so close to the target area they informed Agent Fugiwara they were just about there, and they would start their surveillance of the area and try and pick up their target and then keep him under their eye. The three Units already had a number of pictures of the known snitch along with a great description of the man as well.

Agent Rossie was taking his time reaching the shopping center, because he wanted to make certain all his support Units and police officers were set in place before they even arrived on the scene. When he was informed all his support backups was set in place, only then did Rossie aim his vehicle towards the shopping center he was circling for the fifth time this morning. Fugiwara was now manning the radio and he was listening to the chatter from his support teams.

"This is Unit Two reporting I have taken up position at the South side of the shopping center, and we have not seen hide nor hair of our intended target so far. Over." Agent Paul Davenport reported to Agent Fugiwara as Agent David Price drove the vehicle for him.

"Roget that, this is Parker reporting we have taken up position on the North side of the shopping center, and we have not detected our target in the area yet, and we have been parked here for over twenty minutes now. Over." Agent Edward Parker reported to Agent Fugiwara while his driver, Agent Joseph Wilson scoped out the area with a pair of field glasses.

"Roget that this is Wesson from Unit Three reporting we have been parked at the East entrance to the shopping center for over a half an hour and we have not yet been able to pick up our target. Evidently he has not arrived at the shopping center as yet. We have been monitoring a number of police reports, and they're all coming in reporting they have not picked up our target as yet themselves. Over." FBI Agent Mark Wesson reported as his driver Agent Allen Johnson paid close attention to everyone coming in and out of the East end of the shopping center in question.

""This is Agent Fugiwara, Roget that last from all Units involved in this current stakeout. I'm pleased to have you guys on board with us on this one. We just entered the parking lot of the shopping center right between the North and South entrance to the shopping center by the East gate, where we're supposed to link up with our target. I suggest the North and South Units move to our sides and watch for the Subject to arrive at our site. Over."

"This is Unit One, we're moving to the North side of your parked vehicle, we have eyes on at this moment. Will be set in position in a few seconds. Over." Parker reported in to Fugiwara.

"This is Unit Two, Davenport here and we're reporting we're moving our Unit to the South side of your vehicle we have eyes on, and we're parking seven vehicles, repeat, parking seven vehicles from Primary Unit from the South side of said vehicle, nine vehicles away and in direct line of Primary Unit. Over." Davenport reported to the lead operator of the stakeout situation.

"This is Unit Three reporting we're staying put because we're currently parked just three vehicles before Primary, and three cars over to the left of Primary. Over." Agent Wesson reported as he made his presence known to the Primary Agents of the stakeout.

"This is Primary reporting we copy all and thanks for your support with this situation. We're expecting the Subject to arrive in the next ten to fifteen minutes. We understand Subject lives nearly twenty minutes from this shopping center, and being he's on foot, this is estimated time of arrival to said position. Who's running the Police support? Over." Agent Fugiwara requested.

"This is Unit Three reporting that's my gig for this one. I'm controlling our police support for this operation. Over." Agent Wesson informed the Primary for this operation.

"This is Primary, good, to all Units be advised, our Subject should be arriving on site in the next ten minutes, so look alive people. You're to report any suspicious vehicles spotted moving around at this time. If this is a set up, now if the time any shooters would be moving around to set up their shot at us. Over." Agent Fugiwara reported as he started to search the massive parking lot to try and spot their walker before he was able to get too close to their vehicle. He had Agent Rossie park their vehicle where he always parked whenever he was to link up with his snitch.

"This is Unit One, I hope this POS (Piece Of Shit) doesn't stand us up and make this all for naught, people."

"This is Primary, be advise, Subject is climbing the walls for a fix, so there's no way in hell he'd not show up for this meeting. There's a hundred in it for him and that's four fixes for the bastard. He'll be here alright. Over." Fugiwara reported to the other agents on the job with him.

"Of that's just fucking great, now we're relying on a god damn junkie for being on time to meet us, dammit!" Agent Davenport bitched in his car mike at the Primary Agents.

"This is Primary, most all snitches are usually junkies. Over."

"And we rely on these types of shitbirds for our information?" Davenport came back with.

"How else do you think we get the information we need on these purps, if we don't get down in the same mud they slime their way around in. These junkies are the ones who pick up all the info we need to make any busts around here." Agent Fugiwara fired right back at Davenport.

"This is Unit One I'm picking up a lone Subject on foot entering the parking lot from dead center of East. The subject seems cold and it's hot as hell out. Can't get a good look at Subject's face at this time, but he's walking like he needs a fix or he has to take a serious dump. Over." Parker reported as he kept the subject locked up in his sight as he removed his weapon from his hip and quickly checked the chamber to make certain he had a round set and ready to fire.

"This is Primary, stay alive people, this might be our target. Hold on, a female Subject seems to be approaching our subject from the left. Whoop they're exchanging spit, man he's sucking her whole face into his mouth. Be advised this is Primary, this is not our Subject, I repeat this is not our Subject. Our Subject is just interested in a fix, not a piece of ass, dammit. Over."

Laughter filled the radio, then.

"This is Unit Two, man you guys have to get an eye full of this lady who just got out of that white vehicle. She's hot enough to start a camp fire off of. Man, if I had the damn time I'd be a happy man spending the entire weekend trying to saddle break her ass down, people." Agent Davenport reported to the rest of the agents working on the stakeout with him.

Agent Rossie reached over and he yanked the mike out of Agent Fugiwara's hand and he announced. "This is Primary, man Davenport, you're getting just as back as Agent Fugiwara is then next thing we'll know is you'll be trying to dry hump the spare tire of your vehicle. Over."

More laughter filled the radios.

"Be advised Primary, this is Unit One reporting in sir, I just picked up another male Subject on foot and he's heading right up the main lane leading to the East doors of the shopping center. This guy is just about tripping over his own feet as he's stumbling his way forward people, and he's obviously checking out a number of vehicles parked in the lot as he's walking if you want to call it his walking. Over." Agent Parker reported as he shifted his weight in the vehicle to get a better look at the subject stumbling his way up the lines of parked cars in the lot.

"This is Primary I just picked up the Subject in concern. Can't tell for certain is he's our Subject until he gets a little closer to our vehicle. Stay on your toes people. Over." Fugiwara reported as he too moved around to get a better look at the person on foot in the parking lot.

"This is Unit Three, I got a good line of sight on the subject on foot, but as of yet I can't make out his face as yet, to compare to our composite of the Subject in question, but this guy can't even fucking walk straight. He just stumbled over what I believe was a damn pebble laying on the floor. I'd bet my dick on it this is our guy, people. Over." Agent Wesson reported.

Fugiwara finally get a good look at the subject's face and he immediately reported to the other agents and Police Officers involved in the stakeout. "To all Agents this is Primary, this is our Subject. I have a positive Moe (Mark One eyeball) on the Subject and he's our boy. Look a live people if anything wrong that might go down, now is the time it will happen. Over."

All three FBI Units instantly checked in with their Primary, and then they hunkered down and prepared to spring into action if the operation went sour on them and their Primary Agents.

FBI Special Agent Shinnosuke Fugiwara turned his body in the front seat so he was better facing the driver side passenger door of the vehicle as he pulled his weapon out and checked the chamber to make certain his weapon was good to go, and then he announced to Agent Rossie. "When I say so, I want you to reach behind you and open the passenger side door, and then let the door swing open on its own, so my damn snitch can slip into the vehicle, Rossie-san."

"You got it Fugiwara-san, just give me the word. You ready with your weapon, the position I'm sitting in I'm completely useless to defend myself if anything bad goes down in this mess.

ROSSIE'S APARTMENT

The instant FBI Special Agent Robert Rossie started to get a little excited over the situation he was operating in, Wind immediately was alerted by the ancient amulet hanging around his neck. She closed her eyes tight and then she focused all her attention on the sacred amulet, and in her mind's eye she was actually able to see what was causing the slight distress to her new owner of her deadly killing sword. Because Agent Rossie was not getting overly excited at this time, she was only feeling his slight tension, but not the fear that usually went with someone who was suddenly trapped in a life threatening deadly situation.

She immediately rushed into his bedroom and quickly dressed in her heavily modified ancient battle armor, and then she picked up her sword and slid in back into her scabbard. She instantly felt slightly fatigued for a brief moment before all her strength returned to her body. When she needed her sword for defensive protection, it did not rob her of all her strength when the sword was placed back inside her scabbard. Then she scattered the rest of the weapons she might need to defend her Master's life on her armor and any pockets the modification created on her body armor. Once she was well prepared to defend her or her Liege Lord's life, she returned to the center of the living room and then she knelt down and began to concentrate so intensely on the amulet then she settled down and waited for her call to defend her Lord's life.

She fell deeply into her meditation while focusing all her energies on the sacred amulet and what it was witnessing. Her breathing went shallow and her pulse lessened as did her breathing. She went deeper and deeper into her trance like feeling and locked all her muscles in place, as she prepared her muscular body for future battle in her Lord's defense. She loved when she was again allowed to employ all her training to defend the person she loved so dearly.

THE PUBLIX SHOPPING LOT SHOPPING CENTER

Special Agent Shinnosuke Fugiwara kept a close eye on the subject walking so slowly towards his parked car, as he tried to will the subject to move a little quicker for them. Finally when the subject reached the back fender of his vehicle, he instantly announced to his partner. "Now Rossie-san, open the back door and let it swing open on its own.

When the snitch called Bulldog noticed the car door swing open, he immediately grabbed the handle of the door and opened it enough for him to easily get inside the parked vehicle. The weak smile he had on his lips instantly disappeared when he saw the second agent driving the car for his contact, and then he snapped at Agent Fugiwara. "What the hell is this shit here man? Who the hell is this uther fucking guy, and why do you have a second Agent with you, Gray Ghost. Since when do you bring another prick with you when you're meeting me man? Shit, if I didn't need a fucking fix so bad, I'd leave you sitting here for bringing another Agent with you man."

"Calm the fuck down man, I only brought him along because you were the one who told me to bring someone else with me, when we were first setting up the meeting for us to get together today, buddy. Don't you remember telling me to bring someone else with me, man? I must tell you Bulldog, I felt it strange you wanted me to bring someone else with me, and I even considered not linking up with you because of that fucked up request, my friend." Agent Fugiwara informed his snitch he was the one who told him to being someone else with him.

"I fucking told you to bring someone else with you when we were going to meet today. Shit, I musta really been fucked up if I told you to bring someone else along with you for this meeting, Grey Ghost. I could swear I told you not to have anyone else with you when we meet, brother." The snitch called Bull Dog looked hard and long at Agent Rossie for a few seconds, and then he shrugged his shoulders and growled at Agent Fugiwara again. "You got my fucking money wit ya man. I really need a fucking fix, I'm about to crawl right outta my damn skin, man."

"I got your money right here," Agent Fugiwara announced and then he added. "But I want to hear what you have for me first, before I give you the fucking money, buster."

Not seen by either the snitch or the two agents meeting with him. The moment the subject entered the agent's unmarked parked car, the three other FBI Units instantly started up their vehicles and moved them closer to the Primary vehicle. Unit One and Two actually parked right along both sides of the Primary car, while the third Unit parked directly behind the Primary vehicle two cars behind it, and both Agents Johnson and Wesson quickly exited their car and then they leaned up against it while staring intensely at the Primary vehicle. Both agents had they weapons out and they were covering them behind their thighs, as they were prepared to spring into action if anything when down on them. They both were staring at Agent Rossie's tail lights on his vehicle, and if they saw three quick taps on the brakes. They were going to charge the car and come to the other two agent's help. That was their emergency signal.

The snitch looked at Agent Rossie to see what he was doing. He was sitting in the driver's seat staring out the windshield and not trying to see his face. But what the snitch did not pick up was he had skillfully removed his pistol, and had it locked in his hand and it was resting up again his right thigh. He was ready to react if the snitch tried anything against him or Agent Fugiwara. The snitch continued to stare at the back of Rossie's head, and then he decided the other agent was not a threat against him and he replied to Agent Fugiwara. "Grey Ghost, when you got in touch with me a few days ago, you told me you wanted to know with Young was hiding somewhere here in Washington. It took me a little while but I was able to find out where he was hiding at, are you sure you got the fucking money with you man? I really need a fucking fix, man."

"I got your god damn money with me, just tell me what you know where Young is hiding, and then you'll be on your merry way with a brand new one hundred dollar bill stuffed in your grubby little hand my friend." Agent Fugiwara growled at his snitch as he glared angrily at him now.

"Yeah, yeah man, I found out he's been hiding in another one of his well known hiding places, over on Mott Street between 1st and 2nd Avenue. He's staying in a three story building on the left side of the street in the fifth building on that side. He's staying on the second floor and the building built like a brick shit house fortress man. As I went down the street, I saw it was not the place for any white man never to be hanging around. Man I need a fucking fix..."

"Enough with you needing a fucking fix already will ya huh buster! The longer you keep stalling me around like you're doing with my stinking ass, the longer it's going to be between your last fix, and the fricking one you're wasting our time with by stalling my ass around like this, buster. Okay, you told me where Young is hiding at. So now I want to know how many fucking bodyguards he might have protecting his ass while he's hiding at this other location. I also want to know if he has any of his people protecting his ass from the outside of the damn building he's hiding in at the same time, and I need this information right now, buster." Agent Fugiwara growled angrily again at his snitch, as he continued to glare at him while he waited for his reply to what he just asked him about.

"Hey, wow, holy shit man, you didn't tell me anything about finding out if this dude was protecting himself with his usually bodyguards, man. C'mon man, I'm dying here I told you what you wanted to know man. I did what you wanted, give me my damn money so I can get out of here and get my fix. Look at me I'm shaking like a leaf on a tree during a windstorm man. Give me my damn money and let me get the hell out of here man." The snitch actually dared to glare angrily at Fugiwara as he waited for him to hand him the money he was demanding from him.

"Who the fuck are you flaring your god damn nostrils at around here buster? I'll kick you right in the damn ass you look at me like that again. You know damn well I need to know what we might be going up against if and when we go after Young. Now if you want your damn money? Then I want to know how many bodyguards Young has surrounded himself with? You can't answer that question for me then you can kiss the hundred bucks' goodbye, and then you can get the hell out of my fucking car, my friend." Agent Fugiwara growled back at his snitch, and then he pulled the hundred dollar bill out of his pockets and started running it between his fingers as he waited for the snitch to break down and tell him what he wanted to know from him.

"Hey man this isn't fair man, you know me for a long time now, and you know damn well I wouldn't hold any god damn information back from you, if I knew what you were asking me, man. C'mon man I'm fucking dying here man I need a fucking fix man." The snitch complained as he stared so intensely at the hundred dollar bill Fugiwara was playing with in front of him.

"Life isn't fucking far man. You want fair, fair is where you go to ride rides, eat cotton candy and step in monkey shit. You're in my world now and fair is what I tell you it is, buster. I'll repeat for your limited intelligence my friend. How many god damn bodyguards does Young have surrounding his ass at this new location he's hiding at, buster. Reach deep into that wasted fucking mind of your and pull up that damn information I'm demanding to know from your ass, mister. You don't tell me what I want to know, no money for you. No tickie, no shirtie." Agent Fugiwara smirked at his snitch, knowing he had him right where he wanted him now.

"C'mon man, how the hell am I supposed to know how many damn bodyguards Young has surrounding himself with. I didn't go to bed with the motherfucker you know man. I'd say he has the usually amount of people around him that he trusts the most I guess, I don't know man. C'mon, I need a fucking fix man." The snitch cried this time at the smirking Agent.

"Well then give me your best guess as to the number of fricking bodyguards you think he might have hanging around him at this new location he's in. C'mon man, you god damn rats know what each other of you criminal types are doing all the god damn time around here, and I'm quite certain you were with this fucking guy more than once in your wasted life buster. So I'm sure you can give me a damn good estimate on how many of his well paid jerks he might have around him at any one given time, Man." Agent Fugiwara accented the word 'man' to intimidate his snitch this time, as he went to offer the hundred dollar bill to his snitch. But when the snitch went to take the bill, Agent Fugiwara immediately pulled the bill back and he growled at him again. "You still didn't answer my last fucking question for me asshole. How the hell many guys does Young usually have hanging around his ass all the damn time, buster."

"I don't know, he usually has between five to eight guys around him every time I was anywhere near the fucking guy I guess, man. C'mon man, I told you all I know about the fricking guy you want to know about from me man, give me my god damn money will ya man?"

"Between five and eight guys huh? I guess that's about right, when you checked on him this time. Did you notice if he had people hanging around the building on outside that might be bodyguards? Did you go over to his new place to find out where he was hiding at? How the hell did you find out where he's staying anyhow, asshole?" Fugiwara demanded of him this time.

"Yeah man, I went over his place with his girlfriend who needed to score also, and he sold her some fucking crack, man. His girlfriend was a little concerned with going into the neighborhood he was hiding in, and she begged me to go along with her. Can I have the damn money now man? I answered all your fucking questions man. I need one real bad or I'm going to start throwing up all over you man." The snitch warned the agent as he stared at him right in the eyes.

"Yeah, here you go, I'm about done with your ass anyhow buddy. But before I give you the damn money, I want your stinking word that if you happen to hear anything else about Young and the rest of his goons that you think would be extremely important for me to know about. I want you to call me and ask for another meeting immediately, buster. I want your fucking word on it that you'll do as I just warned you to do for me man." Agent Fugiwara snarled angrily at his snitch to drive his point home on him this time as he returned his harsh stare.

"Yeah, yeah man I got it alright man, if I find out anything more about Young and the rest of his fucking crew. I'll make contact with you immediately and clue you in on the new shit man. C'mon man, can I have the fucking money now man, I'm really hurting here man?" The snitch cried again at the agent as he put his hand out and then waited for the money.

FBI Special Agent Shinnosuke Fugiwara suddenly reached back in his pocket and he removed a second hundred dollar bill, and then he handed the snitch the both bills and added to his words at the man. "I'm going to hold you to your fucking word, and if you want any more of these damn bills from my buster. Then I expect you to call me the first stinking moment you might find out anything more about this lousy sonofabitch that I might need to know about, man."

The snitch's eyes opened wide as he stared at the two hundred dollar bills for a few seconds, and then he greedily grabbed them both out of the agent's hand as if it was a fix, and then he stuffed them both in his shirt and said back to the agent. "Holy shit man, I really appreciate the extra fucking money man. I promise you man, if I find out anything else that might be important for you guys to know about him and the rest of his flunkies, I'll clue you in immediately on it man." With that said, the snitch opened the car door and he nearly jumped out of the vehicle, and then he actually jogged out of the parking lot like his ass was farting out sparks, and he quickly disappeared from the agent's view.

"Well what do you think about that shit Rossie-san?" Agent Fugiwara wanted to know.

"One thing I do know, I'll bet the stinking bank on it that it wasn't Young's girlfriend that was looking for a score, Agent Fugiwara-san. But I think everything else that ass told us about, was on the up and up. He nearly shit himself when he saw my ass sitting in the damn car though." Agent Rossie laughed at his own words as he tried to see the snitch one last time.

The other agents that were surrounding Agent Rossie's vehicle and part of the operation, immediately gathered around his car, because they all wanted to know what their next move was going to be, and what the other two agents might have found out from their snitch. The group waited until both Agents Fugiwara and Rossie got out of their vehicle, and then the entire group went into the shopping center to find a place to enjoy a quick meal and also talk over what the snitch just told them about.

CHAPTER EIGHTEEN

The instant Agent Rossie was relieved when the snitch got out of their vehicle, Wind got a flush of relief herself, and she broke her meditation and started to breathe properly for the first time since Rossie's amulet sent her the warning that her ward was starting to come under stress.

She leaned back and brought her legs out from under her rearend then she stood and stretched her arms over her head and wiggled her rearend, trying to realign her back properly. Then she started to walk around the apartment while trying to get her circulation going again in her legs. She smiled pleased that her Lord was out of the slight pressure he was suffering from for a while. She walked over to the sink and ran the cold water and cupped it in her hand and drank. She was suddenly feeling so relieved about what she was going through while she meditated about her Lord and Master, while she was waiting for the call from the sacred amulet, ordering her to come at once and protect her ward from all harm. She was not sad that she did not have to go out and help her Liege Lord. Mainly because she knew if she was called to the amulet, someone was going to die when she showed up by her Lord's side with her sword.

She walked around the apartment looking for something to do, it was not even mid-day yet, and she was bored to death and looking for anything to do. She walked into the bathroom thinking about taking a shower, but once she entered the room she decided against it and returned to the living room area. She looked out the window and watched two young children playing with their mother keeping a close eye on the kids as they played together, and she smiled over the pleasant scene. But the mother suddenly looked over her shoulder and she immediately jumped away from the window, remembering her Lord's order not to be seen by any of the neighbors. She pouted and then she returned to the center of the living room and decided to do some more meditation and wait until her Lord and Master arrived home from his day of work. She found herself hoping he would explain to her what happened today that cost him so much stress.

THE PUBLIX SHOPPING CENTER, WASHINGTON D.C.

The small group of FBI Special Agents walked into the Dill Pickle store and sat at two tables they pulled together so they all could sit with each other. The young female waitress walked over to the group of well dressed men, and she asked them what they wanted to drink. They all ordered coffees and she walked away happily thinking of the tip she was going to receive from the eight men seated together. She always made out well when a larger group of people came into the eatery. When the waitress was well out of ear shot, Agent Rossie suddenly looked at Agent Fugiwara and then asked him to inform the others of what went on with the snitch.

"Err... the first thing I found out from him was where Young was hiding at. He was reported by my snitch to be staying at Mott Street between at 1st and 2nd Avenue. Young's believed to be hold up in the fifth building on the left side of Mott Street, and my snitch said the house is a brick place that's built like a damn fortress so that fact might give us some problems and..."

"Say Agent Fugiwara, I'm a little familiar with that building and area sir. I once arrested some damn kid who was knocking the crap out of his girlfriend, and I was waved down by a neighbor and asked to stop him from beating his lady up. I remember the building because I thought I hated to have to force my way into the building, it was that strongly constructed, sir." Agent Davenport offered as he volunteered his information for the group of other agents at the table.

"That's good to know Agent Davenport then we can draw some intelligence from you about the building and area. Now we know where Young is hold up, I think this is what I want to do. Hold up, here come some of Washington's finest. I wanted to speak to the police before we headed off for Young anyway. I'm glad they decided to find us so we can talk." Agent Rossie announced as he stood and waited for the good looking Police Sergeant to walk up to him. When he did, he put out his hand and offered. "Thanks for sticking around like this Sergeant err...?"

"Sorry sir I'm Sergeant Glynn, Thomas Glynn Sir and you are sir?" The Police Sergeant asked as he shook hands with Agent Rossie, because it was the first time he met him personally.

"Now I'm sorry Sergeant, my name is Robert Rossie, sir. I'm the Special Agent in charge of this entire operation, and we have only concluded the first stage of the operation so far Sergeant. Now we're going after the real problem of this situation, David Young, Sergeant."

"Damn, I didn't know he was the one you guys were after today sir. You have your life insurance all paid up, Agent Rossie?" The Police Sergeant smirked as he shook his head no.

"Funny man, how many of your people do you still have on your side assigned to this situation, Sergeant?" He asked as he gave the Sergeant a nasty look for his last comment.

"I still have ten Officers assigned to me and my partner for this detail, sir. Why?"

"I wanted to make certain I know how many of your people I have as backup in this situation, that's why. I might as well tell you where this lousy prick is held up, and I have information he has at least ten of his bodyguards with him where he's hiding, sir. He was reported to be in a building on the left side of the street at Mott between 1st and 2nd Avenues, Sergeant. The target building is the fifth building on the left side of the street. I'm going to have my First Unit of Agents enter Mott Street from the North side, and my second Unit of Agents will come in from the South side much like we did at the shopping center earlier today sir. My Third Unit is going to be held in reserve just in case we get jumped like the last time and we have to fight our way out of the damn building. Here's what I want from your people on this one Sergeant.

"I want most of your Officers assigned to you to be sort of floaters in the area. Use your people to stop any civilian traffic from entering the target area from any directions. Then I want your people to set up and be ready to come to our assistance at a drop of the damn hat, if we run into a possible shootout with this lousy prick and his people, Sergeant. I'm really concerned this mess might turn into a real situation against us if Young decides to make a fight of it, and he aims his bodyguards at us again. We at the company want to end this prick's rule over all the crime going down on the East side of downtown Washington, Sergeant. I have orders from my Commander to place an end to this guy one way or the other, and he didn't care which case it turned out to be, he just wants his fricking reign in this area to end today, Sergeant." Agent Rossie informed the concerned looking Police Sergeant who was staring so intensely back at him.

"It's about time someone is taking this Young character seriously around here, Agent Rossie Sir. You have no idea how many times my Chief wanted to go after this guy, but he has some powerful friends in high places, and we could never get permission to go after this prick, sir. We were always forced to stay away from any place this one was operating in sir. I'll tell you this much Agent Rossie. I know a number of my Officers who have the day off if they catch wind we're going after Young. Sure as shit flows down hill sir, they'll come in on their time off and volunteer to assist us in this operation for free, sir. That's how much we wanted to end this guy's career as the bad ass of Washington, sir." Sergeant Glynn grumbled at the FBI Agent.

"That's fine with me Sergeant Glynn, because I feel we might need all the damn help we can possibly muster on this operation when we go after him, sir."

"Okay Agent Rossie, now that I know our intended target for the day and where this bastard is hold up, I'd like to get back to my people and set up our own support of you guys when you go after Young's ass, sir. I have lot of people I have to move around out here, and once my people find out who we're going after on this operation. You know they're going to be calling in many of the troops who are off for the day sir. We have so many Police Officers who want a piece of Young's ass for all the crap we have to eat over this guy for so many years now, sir."

"Like I already said to you Sergeant, we can sure use all the help we can muster for this operation sir. I have a gut feeling this one isn't going to go down nice and easy like, sir. You might as well shove off and start your people moving around the target area where you want them. Are your people in squad cars or are some of you in unmarked vehicles I hope sir?"

"It's about half and half I'd say, sir. We didn't have enough unmark vehicles to go around for all the Officers assigned to this detail, so some of my people are operating out of their squad cars, sorry sir." The Police Sergeant grumbled as he shifted his weight on his feet and smiled.

"That's no problem there Sergeant, just assign the marked squad vehicles out to securing the area all around the damn target structure sir, and have the Officers keeping all civilian traffic out of the target area, until we have concluded this operation, sir.”

"That's a great idea you just ordered sir, I'll get on it right away for you sir.”

"Fine Sergeant Glynn, I'm make contact with you the moment we shove off and begin our action again Young and the crap he has with him sir. You might as well shove off now and get your people moving around and set in the areas where we need them the most, sir.” Agent Rossie offered and then he watched as the young officer turned on his heels and rushed out of the restaurant and headed for his unmarked vehicle and then leave the parking lot in a hurry.

When the Police Sergeant was gone, Special Agent Robert Rossie returned to the table and other agents he was working with, and he informed them of what the police officers were going to do to help support their operation. Then he listened to what the other agents wanted to do to either support Agents Rossi and Fugiwara, or be an active part of the effort to either arrest or kill Young, before he could escape their stakeout for a second time in less than a week.

Once they had everything all worked out between the ten FBI Agents in the restaurant, they rushed to finish their meals, and then they started to filter out of the restaurant, leaving Agent Rossie to pay for all their lunches. Agent Fugiwara waited for Rossie to finish up with the cashier, and leave the tip then they walked out of the restaurant together and climbed into their vehicle and then they were off to start setting up their operation.

As Rossie was driving the vehicle his blood pressure began to rise as he got excited as their second part of their operation started to get off the ground. The more excited he got, the more his blood pressure rose until the amulet picked up his situation and immediately notified Wind.

FBI SPECIAL AGENT ROBERT ROSSIE'S APARTMENT

As bored as she was, Wind was still on full alert and when the bright light flashed in her eyes, she immediately dropped down to her knees and she went deep into her meditation period, and instantly she was able to see Agent Rossie driving his vehicle. She wondered why the amulet was alerting her to possible danger for her new owner of her killing sword and her spirit as well. So she closed her eyes even tighter and watched as he carefully drove through the street of Washington. From what she was seeing, she suddenly could understand what was distressing her Lord and Master so much, because she was even getting edgy watching him drive the vehicle.

She allowed herself to relax in her meditation as she continued to observe Rossie was getting much better control of himself, and now her vision was kind of going in and out on her because he was calming down now as he continued to drive his car. Now she was able to split her concern and she was pleased she remained dressed in her battle armor, and she still had all her weapons placed in their proper slots in her body armor. Every weapon was in place except for her sword. The ancient sword was resting on the floor next to her right leg, and the hilt of the sword was lightly touching the knee of her right leg. Not that she had to remain in constant contact with the sword at this time, but the nearness of the Katana blade to her body, brought her just that little bit extra comfort, while she was waiting for her Lord and Master to return from his day's work.

SPECIAL AGENT ROBERT ROSSIE'S FBI VEHICLE

FBI Special Agent in Charge Robert Rossie suddenly slowed his vehicle down as he just passed 1st Avenue and was now heading for 2nd Avenue. Now he was looking for Mott Street beginning on his right side of the road, because of the way he entered the target area. Seeing the street sign marked Mott Street, his blood pressure climbed high and his blood started to pound in his ears, and he tightened his grip on the steering wheel to the point Agent Fugiwara noticed the increase in the stress level of his partner and he asked him. "Hey Rossie-san, you want me to drive the rest of the way to the target building. Your knuckles are turning white on you because of the way you're holding onto the damn steering wheel, man. You better calm down a bit before you blow a damn head gasket and pass out on my ass you know my friend."

"Naw, I'm alright to drive, it's just I'm starting to get the damn heebee jeebees about this damn operation. I can't believe this one guy got me so damn concerned and worried about what we might be getting into with this bastard. I can't wait until we settle his damn hash for himself, Fugiwara-san." Agent Rossie complained to his partner staring out the front windshield of the vehicle. He was trying to see if Young might have stationed a number of his bodyguards outside the building, before they turned down the road where Young was known to be hiding on.

"Hey Rossie-san, look to your left side on the next block up from the one we're on. You see those two vehicles parked up there, one of them is definitely an unmarked Police car and the other one is a squad car, and the cop is out of his vehicle and he's directing the civilian traffic out of the area for us, buddy. I don't know if you noticed the other two squad cars we passed when we turned on to this road, and we passed another unmarked vehicle parked at the head of the block we passed. At least we know the Police are on the ball for us this time around buddy." Fugiwara pointed out all the local police vehicles who were lending them support for this detail.

"I didn't pick up the Police vehicles you pointed out Fugiwara-san. But I was able to pick up Wilson and Parker's vehicle across the street from Mott Street when we came up on it. They're where they were assigned to park and wait for us to turn on Mott and then hit the target building.

"We knew we could count on our people to be where they were supposed to be to support us on this operation. But the Police were another matter Rossie-san. One never knows if they'll turn up where they were instructed to take up positions. I'm so used to the damn Police going off on their own every time we use them in any of the details we get ourselves involved in Rossie-san."

"You're talking the truth there Agent Fugiwara-san. That's why I get so worried every time we bring in the local police department personnel whenever we're working on a case together.

DAVID YOUNG'S HIDEOUT

Young was resting in a large bedroom when one of his people dragged Corey Reiser in the building and Young was called out of his room. He looked at Corey and smiled as he asked him. "You need another fix I see right stupid? Do you have any money I ain't no charity you know."

"I have some money, see." Cory was so excited he offered as he pulled one of the hundred dollar bills out of his pocket, and he tried to hand it right to Young.

"You have a hundred dollar bill, where did you get a hundred dollars from? I didn't think you knew what a hundred dollar bill looked like. Who did you rip off, or are you working for the fucking cops?" Young barked at Corey as he put his hands up and refused to take the money, and then looked at the guy who dragged Corey into the room. That guy ripped the bill out of Corey's hand and examined it closely. Spotting the three razor cuts in the top left corner of the bill, he informed his boss. "It has the cuts in the corner this fuck is a fucking snitch for the damn Feds."

"Check his fucking pockets and see what else he has in them, and then check out his body for any damn wires or recording devices. I want to see if he's working for the Feds. If he is then I'm going to make a fucking example out of him for the rest of these damn junkies we're dealing with." Young snarled as he stepped back and three more of his people moved in and started to roughly search Corey's body. All the while Corey was crying he was not a snitch for the Feds.

One of the bodyguards found the other hundred dollar bill and he pulled it out of Corey's pocket and handed it to the other guy who checked out the first bill. The search of Corey's body was stopped as everyone in the room watched as the other guy carefully examined the second bill. The inspector slowly rolled the bill in his hand and then in the same corner that had the three small almost invisible razor nicks in the bill, the same three marks was on the second bill as well, and he immediately reported to Young. "This hundred dollar bill has the same three razor cuts in the same corner of the second bill. He has to be working for the fucking Feds this is their trade mark on how they mark and recognized their money when they give it to one of their snitches."

"Bring the motherfucker over to the damn table and sit him in the chair and then hold on to his ass!" Young growled as he looked at the pretty black girl he was with in the bedroom, and he gave her a quick head movement and she immediately went back inside the bedroom. Then Young turned his attention back to Corey and snarled at him again. "Look motherfucker, if you're working for the damn Feds now, don't make me work on you for who knows how long before you tell me what I want to know, and believe me sucker. You sure as hell will tell me all I want to know from you before I'm done with your fucking ass.

Young then looked at one of his bodyguards and snapped at him. "Heat up one of the long kitchen knives, I want it red hot." Then he turned back to Corey and warned him again. "Don't make me start in on you, because you won't like what I do to you before you tell me the fucking truth. Are you working for the damn Feds, and if you are, what did you tell the fuckers?"

"I'm not working for the Feds man I got the money from my mother. She gave me the money because she felt sorry for me because I needed a fucking fix, man. I swear it man, I'm not working for the damn Feds my mother gave me the damn money man."

"Don't hand me that shit, your mother lives in Boston and she hasn't talked to your ass for years, stupid. Well, if that's the way you want it, so be it. It's been a while since I worked over a snitch. Grab his hands and hold them flat on the table." Then Young stretched his hand out and another one of his bodyguards handed him the glowing hot kitchen knife and he brought the knife over to Corey and allowed him to look at the blade for a second then he asked him again. "Are you working for the fucking Feds and if you are, did you tell the fucks where I was hiding, man?

"I'm not working for the damn Feds man! I swear it to you man."

Young smiled down at Corey's face then he laid the red hot blade on the stretched out top of his hand, and held it there as Corey started to scream. One of his bodyguards wrapped his hand over his mouth and held him tight as he struggled desperately because of what Young was doing to his hand. With just a look from Young, the bodyguard moved his hand from Corey's mouth and he started drawing in huge gulps of air, and was crying as Young snarled at him again. "Hey motherfucker, are you working for the Feds and if you are, did you tell them where I'm hiding?"

"I'm not working for the damn Feds man, I swear to God I'm not working for the Feds. All I wanted was a fucking fix, I'm not working for the Feds or anyone else I swear it man."

"Fuck this scumbag he has to be working for the Feds. I'm out of here." Young threw the knife on the table so the tip of the blade stuck in the surface of the table then announced to everyone in the room. "I'm out of here, you can be sure the damn Feds are closing in on us. Skin this fuck alive, and cut his throat and then get out of the building. I don't want anyone here when the damn Feds arrive. Kill this motherfucker." Then Young called out to his girlfriend and when she was at his side, he and she ran out of the room then the building, after he took a backpack that was filled to overflowing with cash, a weapon and three of his best bodyguards running right behind them.

The bodyguard who checked the marked hundred dollar bills smirked at Corey, and then he moved in on him after he pulled the knife out of the table, as the other three bodyguards held Corey tight in their grasp. All this went down as the Special Agents were meeting at the small restaurant formulating their plans to go after Young and the rest of his people.

AT THE CORNER OF MOTT STREET

FBI Special Agent Robert Rossie drew in a huge breath of air and let it out in small puffs of air, and then he turned onto Mott Street and slowly drove down the street and when he hit the fifth building on the left side of the street, he suddenly spun the wheel of the car hard and drove the vehicle right up and on the sidewalk, and then he slammed the car in park and both he and Agent Shinnosuke Fugiwara immediately jumped out of the vehicle and then they knelt down behind the open doors and aimed their weapons at the building. At the same moment Agent Rossie drove his car onto the sidewall, all three FBI vehicles came roaring down the block and they parked helter shelter in the middle of the street.

The agents in these vehicles quickly poured out of their vehicles, and then they took up positions behind their cars. Both Agents Wilson and Parker were armed with M-16s with powerful scopes mounted on the weapons, and they took over the major security for the rest of the agents involved in the rapidly developing operation. Three other police vehicles came charging down the block from both directions, and the police came out of their vehicles and they added their weapons to the special agents going after Young.

FBI SPECIAL AGENT ROBERT ROSSIE'S APARTMENT

Wind was still deep into her meditation period when her eyes suddenly snapped open, because she was suddenly able to feel the terrible stress level her Lord and Master was suffering from. She had no idea he was about to attack a building while looking for an extremely dangerous criminal and killer. Her breathing was becoming labored as she felt the pressure building on her body, and then in a flash she was responding to the call of the sacred amulet.

BY AGENT ROSSIE'S VEHICLE

Agent Fugiwara called to Rossie across the front seat of the car. "I'm going to call the bastards out of the building, stand by Rossie-san." He reached in the back seat of the car and removed the megaphone, turned it on and growled into the voice amplifier. "This is the FBI, we demand all occupants of 1153 Mott Street to come out of the building with your hands up one behind the other. We're going to call you people out of the building once then we're going to come in and remove you people out of the building one way or the other. I repeat, this is the FBI and we're demanding all occupants of 1153 Mott Street to come out of the building with your hands up. You have five minutes to follow my orders, or we're coming for you people in the building."

"You really think that's going to work for us, Agent Fugiwara-san?"

"Hell no, but I have to do this shit by the numbers then we'll be free to go in the building the way we know we have to enter it, hot and heavy. You know we might get a little bloody on this one. I don't think anyone is going to come out of that damn building in one piece, judging how it went when we went after these fucks the other day, Rossie-san. What the hell…"

Right behind Rossie, a glow of light appeared and then Fugiwara saw a beautiful woman standing behind his partner and he watched as Rossie reacted to the young woman behind him.

Agent Rossie turned the moment he noticed his partner looking behind him to see if something was wrong, and he was stunned to see Wind with her sword locked in her hand, and she was ready to do battle for him. He reached out and roughly grabbed her by the collar protection of her armor, and then he nearly threw her in the front seat of his car. He angrily stuck his head inside the vehicle and snarled right in her face. "What the fuck are you doing for Christ sake? You can't be here, there are too many of my fellow Agents around here and they're going to see you, and then they'll take you into custody and I'll be completely helpless to get you away from them. Didn't I tell you not to come anywhere near me when I was fucking working for God's sake? You have to get back to the god damn apartment before anyone else sees you here dammit. You have to get the hell out of here right this second before I send you away and you know how."

"I came to your side because the call of the sacred amulet informed me that your life was in deadly danger my Lord and Master, and it's my sacred duty to protect your life from all harm my Lord." She replied in an excited voice as she returned his stare with one of her own.

"Jesus Christ, I know all that shit! I've heard it enough from you Wind. I'm not in any danger here and even if I was, I have enough of my Agents here to assist me that no harm could possibly happen to me. You have to get the hell out of here before any of the other Agents sees you and they react to your presence, Wind. Go, go at once and return to my apartment and wait there for me to come home tonight. You have to get the hell out of here immediately Wind, dammit."

"Who the hell is she and what the hell is she doing here with that damn sword in her hand Rossie? Is this the woman who came to our aide when we went after Young? If she is I want to speak to her. Man is she a looker." Agent Fugiwara asked as he took in the beauty of the women dressed in ancient but heavily modified Samurai armor. He could not believe the beauty of this young looking woman who Agent Rossie was growling at in the front seat of their vehicle.

"Not now Fugiwara, I don't need any shit from you right now, I have my damn hands full with Wind at the moment." Agent Rossie turned his attention back to Wind and he started in on her again. "Wind, you have to get out of here before you cause a serious problem for me. With you here you're distracting my attention from an extremely dangerous situation, and I can't have that for one moment. Your presence here is a distraction to me that could cause me to get one of my fellow Agents in some serious trouble, and maybe even killed because you're distracting me from what I have to do here. You can also be the cause of a shootout happening and some of my fellow Agents could get hurt or even killed, all because you had to stick your damn nose into where it didn't belong. You have to get the hell out of here as fast as you came here Wind.

"If you don't get out of here, when I get home I'm going to send you back to the Ukiyo, and I might never send for you again for as long as I live. You have to get out of here right now Wind, get out of here! I can't tell you how upset I am over you once again showing up at my work when I forcibly ordered you never to do this again, dammit. You have to leave and you have to leave right this moment, Wind." He reached into the car and grabbed her by the shoulders and shook her to try and get his point across to her that he did not want her to be near him at this time.

She placed an extremely sad look on her face as she stared back at her upset Liege Lord and then she cried as she pleaded with him. "But my Lord, I had taken a sacred oath to always protect you from all harm, no matter what shape that harm might assume. I cannot possibly ignore my sacred oath and leave your side when you are in deadly danger. The Kami of the Floating World would drive my spirit out to the woods and allow the Tengu Wood Goblins to feast upon my foul remains if I was to allow any harm to befall your being, my Master. How would I be able to exist as a spirit or solid form if I was to allow any harm to come to you my Lord? I would have to immediately commit Suppuku if I was to fail my sacred oath of protecting you my Lord."

"I don't give a good god damn crap about your sacred oath to protect me or any other crap that concerns you right now Wind. Dammit, I might be involved in a situation of life and death, and you're in the fucking way and you're interfering with my duty. If I don't pay complete attention to what the hell I'm here, people are going to die and if anyone dies here, it'll be your god damn fault that they're dead. You have to get the fuck out of here so I can do my job before the other Agents I'm working with become concerned, and they come here to see what the problems is. Then they're going to discover your presence and they'll take you into custody and I'll be unable to stop them from arresting you and placing you in jail."

"Someone who you are here to protect will place me in jail? Why would anyone want to put me in jail if I am only guilty of carrying out my sacred oath and protecting your life from all harm, my Liege Lord?" Wind questioned him with worry etched deeply in her eyes.

As if to support Agent Rossie's complaint to Wind, his radio suddenly burst into life, and Agent Edward Parker asked him. "Hey Rossie, what the hell gives here buddy? When are we going to push on our demand for anyone inside that dump to come out of there with their hands up? Are you having any problems over there that's holding you up from starting this operation against them asses hold up inside the damn building, Rossie? C'mon man, we have to do something even if it's wrong here. You want me to take over the lead of this operation if you're having a problem with getting the damn thing off the ground for yourself, sir?"

"Everything is fine over here I'm just getting ready to jump off. I figured to give them a few moments longer to come out of there peaceful like, before we have to do a hot entry into a compromised structure. And no, I don't want you taking over the damn lead for this operation here, I'm the Lead Agent in the Field, and it's going to stay that way as long as I have a breath still left in my damn body, Agent Parker. Hang tight for a second longer, I was about to make another demand of the perps trapped in the damn building sir. Give me a few seconds to collect my thought before we jump off on them, sir." Agent Rossie fired back at Agent Parker angrily, and then he turned his attention back on Wind and growled at her again.

"You see that Wind, I have my other Agents concerned with why I'm not going in action against the ones we're here to arrest, and you're stopping me from carrying out my duties to my other Agents. You have to get out of here right this second, before I really get angry and I break your sword and end your life even as a spirit on you! You have to go now! Leave at once Wind, this is an order and you don't want to disobey your Lord and Master, because you know what that means to you and your future. So go now before I really lose my temper with you. Go Wind!" Agent Rossie demanded in the nastiest tone of voice he could aim at her, and he had to actually stop himself from striking her to get his point across to the ancient female Samurai Warrior.

"This foolish Samurai Warrior is extremely sorry for interfering with your duties to the others you work with my Liege Lord. I shall leave your side immediately and then wait the punishment from the Kami for my leaving you in a deadly situation my Lord. I shall be waiting for you..."

"Yeah, yeah Wind, just go before I really get angry with you, and I order you back to the Floating World, dammit. Now Wind now! Go god dammit with you!"

She was terribly stunned at the strong anger that her Liege Lord was aiming at her, and she followed his orders and closed her eyes, and then she concentrated with all her might and almost instantly, her form started to fade, and then in a flash she was going from the scene.

Agent Fugiwara was stunned at the form of the woman he was staring at, suddenly disappeared right before his eyes, and he had to shake his head to bring himself back to reality as he grumbled at his partner. "Hey Rossie, what the hell is going on with you and that woman man? I can't believe she just disappeared like a fucking ghost right before my eyes. And since when are you able to speak so perfect Japanese? What the hell are you holding back on me with this damn woman you have protecting your ass with that damn killing sword she had in her hand? Did you see the way she was holding and moving that damn thing around in her hands? It was almost like the sword was actually a part of her body. Uh-oh, shut up both Agents Parker and Wilson are working their way over here to us Rossie. I'm sure as hell they're coming here to see what the hell is going on with the both of us and why we didn't jump off on the purps yet, man."

Agent Parker suddenly grabbed Wilson's arm and stopped him from going forward towards Agent Rossie's vehicle, when he spotted the strong blast of light that instantly filled the other agent's vehicle, and then he asked his partner with concern in his voice. "What the hell was that damn light just them? We better approach the car carefully, that might have been a flair from a weapon going off inside the damn vehicle. Maybe some of Young's bodyguards worked their way out of the building, and they just attacked both Rossie and Fugiwara on us sir."

Still holding on to Wilson's arm, Agent Parker pulled his out handheld radio and then he broadcast for the rest of the agents and police involved in their stakeout. "To all personnel of this operation be advised. We might have a problem with the Primary in this operation. Stand by and I'll let you know what's going down with Primary when we get over to their vehicle, and see what the holdup is about. To all Units, stand pact until we see what the hell's happening with the Primary. We should have already jumped off on the purps, dammit." Then he broke off the communication, and then both he and Wilson took a different approach, and they slowly worked their way over to Rossie's vehicle like they were approaching the one they were there to arrest. With their weapons held at the ready, they both approached Agent Rossie's vehicle cautiously.

Agent Rossie looked over his shoulder and he easily picked up the two concerned agents coming at him in a rush as if he was the bad guy, and he stood up in front of his car door and waved at the two agents coming at him. The moment the other agents picked up Rossie standing up, they were relieved and they let down their guard and walked quicker towards the Primary of the operation. Agent Wilson allowed Parker to jump on Rossie, because he was the one who was so concerned over the amount of time that had passed and they still were not going after the ones held up inside the structure they had so heavily surrounded.

Rossie then got down behind the car door again and both Wilson and Parker got down with him and Agent Parker started right in on Rossie, raising his voice to a loud whisper as he groused at him. "Hey buddy, what the hell's with you man? We should have at least tried to talk these bastards out of the damn building for a second time, or we should have already jumped off on the bastards by now, Bob. We're still going to go after these bastards, unless you got a buster call from Commander Murdock, or something else came up to stop us from going after these guys?"

"Nothing came up that way. The only reason I didn't order us to move on the bastards was because I picked up a female walking with a baby carriage through the alley on the other block, and I was giving her time to get out of the line of fire before

CHAPTER NINETEEN

Immediately, Agents Johnson and Wesson charged the building with weapons out. They were being followed closely by Agents Price and Agent Davenport and Agent Robert Rossie, and Agent Shinnosuke Fugiwara followed them, also with their weapons out. Agent Edward Parker and Agent Joseph Price follow the four other agents into the building with their long rifles held at the ready. They were all heading for the third floor of the building where it was reported Young was held up. The police officers supporting the agents closed in and they took up positions hiding behind the four parked FBI vehicles that were the closest vehicles to the target building.

Agent Rossie watched as the four agents ahead of him charged into the building unchallenged by anyone they felt had to be hunkered down in the building, and they were waiting to attack the agents as they entered. When the agents were on the first floor, Rossie took charge and ordered. "Parker, Wilson, I want you two to follow the rest of us up to the second floor of this structure. You two will engage anyone who fires on us. Davenport and Price, you lead the way and when you reach the second floor, you two break to the right and take positions of support there. Johnson and Wesson, you go next and when you two reach the second floor, break left and take up defensive positions there. Fugiwara and I will follow and we'll take the center of the second floor, and then we'll all cover Parker and Wilson as they come up to the second floor.

"When we're all on the second floor, we'll follow the same routine and work our way up to the third floor of this dump in the same order. You're operating on this detail with weapons free, so if you come across anyone who threatens you in any way, shape or form, you're to eliminate that threat by any means necessary. Shoot the shit out of them then we'll collect their DNA and identify any of the purps that way. I don't want anyone getting hurt on this mission..."

"Hey Rossie, I can't believe we got this far into this structure without having to engage any purps believed to be held up in this dump. What do you make out of that bit of crap, sir?" Agent Johnson offered as he shifted his weapon to his other hand and then scratched an itch on his nose.

"Beats the shit out of my stinking ass, but I'm not going to complain about the lack of any fricking resistance we're running into so far inside this dump. The only thing I can think of is that all the damn purps must be spread out on the two upper floors of this structure, and they're just giving us the first floor of the building to draw us in for the slaughter. So don't any of you guys drop your guards down for a second around here, or you might be eating some lead if you do. Okay people, let's try and get up to the next floor of this dump as easily and safely as we got onto the first floor of the place, people. Let's move out and see what these people are up to in here." Agent Rossie watched the other agents started to move out and he caught up to his partner Fugiwara and asked his fellow agent with concern lacing his voice.

"Fugiwara-san, what do you make out over the lack of resistance we're not receiving by Young or his goons supposed to be held up in here? I don't like this shit, I believe we're heading for an ambush if you ask me my friend. Maybe we should have allowed the police to come into the building along with us that way we have more a helluva more support for this damn thing."

"I feel the same way you're feeling about this shit. Damn, I wish we used a helicopter and placed some of our Agents on the damn roof of this structure. That way we could be working our way against these bastards from down here and from the roof area at the same time, Rossie-san."

"That's a good call and I wish you would've brought that up to my attention before we started into the damn building, Fugiwara-san. It would've made it that much easy for us to have trapped Young and the rest of his people inside the building and gathered them all up at the same time, dammit. Well, it's too late to cry into the breast milk now. Shall we follow the others I want to get this damn operation over before I'm old enough to retire from the company my friend?"

"You want to go first Rossie-san?"

"Hell like I said before, I don't even want to go second in this mess, but we have to support the others during this operation. But first let me raise Officer Glynn and give him some further orders to follow." Rossie pulled out his handheld radio again and clicked it on and grumbled into it. Agent Rossie to Sergeant Glynn, come in, I need to talk to you sir."

"Sergeant Glynn here Agent Rossie, what's up sir?"

"Sergeant Glynn, we have successfully secured the first floor of the building, and I'd like for you to send in four of you :Police Officers and have them continue to hold this floor secured for us in case we run into some stiff resistance on the next floor, and we have to drop back down to this floor. We might need their firepower to help us retreat down to the first floor again, sir."

"That's fantastic that you people were able to secure the first floor of the structure already sir. We were wondering why we were not hearing any weapon fire going off inside the structure, sir. I'll order four of my people into the building to keep the first floor secured, in case you people have to retreat back down to the first floor again sir. Good luck Agent Rossie. Out."

He did not bother to sign off with the Sergeant as he followed Agent Fugiwara over to the stairs that lead up to the second floor of the building and when they reached it, they both charged to catch up with the other four agents already obviously on the second floor of the building. Both Agents Wilson and Parker closed in on the staircase and they covered it with their M16 automatic rifles. Both of the special agents looked at one another, confused over not hearing any weapon fire going off on the next floor up inside the building.

This time Agent Rossie was stunned at what he found lying on the kitchen table on the second floor as he cautiously walked over to the slaughtered body then asked Agent Fugiwara already standing over the body, staring intensely at it. "Who the hell do you think that might be there, Fugiwara-san? It is a human being we're looking at here, am I right partner?"

"I don't have to think who it might be, I know who it is. You see that mark on the shoulder? That mark is where I shot Corey Reiser the first time I have anything to do with the dumb kid. He came at me foolishly with a knife in his hand, and he was as high as a kite. So I shot him in the shoulder to stop him. Then I found out a lot about the kid and the hard life he lived and I turned him and he became my snitch. I don't know why, but they must have killed him when he tried to score a fix from one of Young's bastards. Now I know why we're not receiving any resistance from any of Young's people inside the building. No one is left in the building, they must have picked up the kid when he was trying to score and found the mark on the money I gave him earlier in the day, and they must have figured out he was working for us. They killed the kid and then they all cut out of this dump before we even arrived on the scene, Rossie-san."

Fugiwara offered as he lowered his guard and strolled to the staircase and walked up them as if he was walking up the staircase in his place. When he reached the third floor landing, he started to kick in the closed doors to the three bedrooms and bathroom on this level. He kicked through the closet door and glared into it, and then he turned and watched as the other agents quickly checked out the bedrooms and bathroom, looking for anyone who might still be in the room.

Rossie caught up to his partner and Fugiwara grumbled. "You see, I told you no one was still inside this dump Rossie-san. Now more than ever I want to fry Young's ass. Even though that kid was nothing more than a snitch and junkie, he was still a human, and that bastard slaughtered him like he was shit stuck on the bottom of his damn shoe. I want him so bad I can taste it. I hope the lousy bastard likes the taste of fucking dick, because when I finally catch up to his stinking ass, I'm going to cut his damn dick off and shove it right down his damn throat, Rossie-san."

"And I'll hold the bastard down while you do your act against him partner. Come on man, this shit ain't doing you any damn good hanging around in here like this buddy. Besides, I have to inform the police outside and stationed down on the first floor of this dump that this operation is now a buster detail. Shit, I can see Commander Murdock's face now when I have to inform him we missed the lousy prick for a second time, dammit. This guy has more lives than a damn cat, but we're going to get him and real soon at that Agent Fugiwara-san. Let's get the hell out of here because that body smells, and I have to get the Forensic people working on looking for any useful evidence around here, and then the cleanup people can start to work on the kid's body." Agent Rossie looked at his watch and then complained at his partner.

"Damn, will you look at the time already? There's no way in hell I'm going to return to the office this late. It's already after 6 P.M. and Murdock has to be half way home by now..."

"Bullshit on that crap buster, do you think for one second I'd leave for home while any of my damn Agents were on a possible shootout detail?" Murdock growled as he walked up to the third floor and linked up with his Lead Agent and his partner. Even though he wanted Young either taken in or killed, he was just as relieved none of his agents were involved in a firefight with any of the killers they were out trying to apprehend today.

FBI SPECIAL AGENT ROBERT ROSSIE'S APARTMENT

Wind was so upset by the time she was returned to the apartment that she was near tears. She immediately stripped her ancient battle armor and showered and then quickly dressed in the favorite Kimono, the blue long silk robe. Then she went out to the living room, picked up her sword and walked to the center of the living room and knelt. Once kneeling she crossed her ankles under her and then she bowed and placed her unsheathed sword out before her. Then she sat up and waited for her Lord and Master to return home. The only time she was as upset as she was at the moment and screamed at the way her Lord yelled at her when she went to his aide. Was when Hiromoai was screaming at her in the slight depression in the construction field where she just cut the head off of the American Gai Jin called Calvin Batterman.

She settled in and waited, already preparing herself for when her Liege lord returned to his castle, and she was certain he was going to order her to commit Suppuku for daring to interfere with what he and the others like him, were doing when she went to his side. She was so upset with herself for making her Lord so angry at her. She was actually chastising herself for making her Lord angry. She was also upset because she broke another of her Master's orders by exposing herself to another person in her Master's presence. She could not believe she had committed so many errors in so short a time, just because she wanted to protect her ward's life.

She was struggling to get her breathing under control as she waited for the angry wrath of her Master to fall down upon her head. She even started praying to her namesake Fujin, the God of Wind for his assistance to remove some of the anger held in her Master's heart aimed at her. She did not know what to do to try and please her Liege Lord when he returned that may take some of the edge off his anger harbored against her. She even considered making him supper, but she never prepared that meal for him, and she did not know how to cook the meat he so richly enjoyed eating at night. She searched her mind to find a way to please her Lord and Master and then a though came to her and for the first time since she left her Lord's side, she actually smiled.

She remembered how her Liege Lord loved to look at her when she was almost naked, and being that she was not ashamed of her body in the least, she had no problem exposing herself to her Lord and Master, or to anyone else he might bring home with him. She got up off the floor and rushed into the bedroom she was now sharing every night with the new owner of her killing sword and her spirit, and she started looking through her belongings. Looking for the short light blue Kimono she wore the other morning that had caused his proud member to stand at full attention before her, and swayed with the want to share her treasures again.

Finding the item she was searching for, she quickly stripped the Kimono she was wearing and folded it correctly, and placed it gently back in the small trunk her Lord gave her for her personal belongings. Then she dressed in the short and so beautiful Kimono. She fussed around with the exquisite fabric until the Kimono hung just right on her body, and then she smiled at the reflection of herself in the looking glass she now always used whenever she dressing for the eye of her Liege Lord. Again she smiled at her reflection, completely pleased with the way she looked, and then she turned and headed back for the living room.

She rushed back to where she was kneeling and assumed the same position before her deadly killing sword resting on the floor before her. Then she began praying again to all the Kami of the Floating World to make her Lord forget his anger against her, and making him want more to pillow with her rather than be angry at her. She looked down at her chest and enjoyed the way the swells of her breasts shown through the opening of her Kimono, and she breathed a sigh of relief. Because after looking at herself this way, she could not believe her Master could possibly remain angry at her for long with her looking the way she was while waiting for his return home.

She then wiggled her way comfortably on the floor, struggling slight while trying to lock her ankles together, and then placing her rearend and body weight on her ankles. This was the common way any Samurai Warrior of the ancient past sat, to display to their Liege lord of the time they were in no position that would enable them to spring into action to harm their Master in any way. Once she was completely pleased with the way she looked and was seated, she went back into meditation again as she waited for her Liege Lord to return to her.

She completely cleared her mind of all worry and concerns, and then she spoke to the Kami of her past and drew new strength from this experience because of the comfort she always enjoyed whenever she prayed to the Gods of ancient Japan.

THE BUILDING AT 1153 MOTT STREET

The small group of FBI Special Agents gathered around their Commander and waited to hear what he had to say to them. Commander Ralph Murdock aimed his words at his chosen Lead Agent for this operation and he offered. "Agent Rossie, I understand the disappoint you and the rest of the Agents assigned to you must feel over the complete collapse of your stakeout of Young. I have been out on hundreds of such stakeouts, and I hate to remember how many of them likewise collapsed around my ass when the tire hit the road. Gees, who the hell is this and how did he die? What the hell is that in his arm by his right shoulder? Damn is that ugly."

"It's a bullet wound sir." Fugiwara fired back at his boss as all the agents followed Murdock back to the second floor and he spotted the body of Corey Reiser still lying on the kitchen table.

"No shit wiseguy, I didn't think the fucking thing was a beauty mark. Did you people identify the shooter?" Commander Murdock growled right back at Agent Fugiwara, slightly upset over the way the agent just barked at him in front of the other gathered agents.

"Yeah, I shot the sonofabitch way back when. The kid was my snitch and Young and his bastards killed the kid after they made him tell them we were coming for him today. That's why this dump was as empty as a stinking bird's nest in winter, Murdock, sir." Fugiwara replied.

"Oh, sorry for the smart ass comment Agent Fugiwara, but shit happens to all of us every now and then mister. Okay people, I want Agents Parker, Wilson, Davenport, Price, Johnson and Wesson to cut out for the night. But I want all you birds to report in early tomorrow morning, and I want a fully detailed report sitting on my damn desk by quitting time tomorrow night from each of you Agents. Agents Rossie and Fugiwara will stay behind so I can speak to you two for a while longer, before I finally release you two for the night. Get a move on it people."

Murdock, Rossie and Fugiwara remained silent as they watched the rest of the agents leave the building, and then Murdock turned and looked at Rossie and started. "I have the Forensic people on call and they're heading here as we speak, and they'll more than likely work through the night. Once they're finished with their shit then the cleanup crews are going to follow the Forensic people and clean this shit up. I guess I'll place a call out to the body collectors and have them come and remove this err... body the hell out of here, before we can seal up this crime scene until we're done with this place. When I'm done with you two, then you guys can go home and catch some Zzzzzs. Then I want you two back in the office by 9 A.M. and I want a good report from the both of you on my desk before you two can go home tomorrow night, and I want a good clean report from you this time, Rossie. The last report I got from you, I had to send it down to the code breakers and had them rewrite your report, so I could understand the damn thing..."

"Rossie-san couldn't write you a good report if you spotted him a noun and a verb."

"I see you've missed your true calling around here Agent Fugiwara-san, here you are with twenty thousand comedians out of work, and you're trying to be one, mister. You're a real Jerk Benny here buster." Agent Rossie fired right back at his partner.

"You two never get tired of busting each other's horn I see. How about you two birds growing up a little and start acting like adults for a change? This mess could have worked out to be a real Charlie Foxtrot (Cluster Fuck) we could have ended up on our hands. I shudder to think what the hell would've been the outcome if you guys were successful with trapping Young inside the damn building, and you guys had to engage him in a bloody firefight, dammit. Now, do you guys have any idea why this mess ended up as a fizzle here?" Commander Murdock looked directly at Agent Rossie as he waited for an explanation from either one of his two agents.

"I can explain what went down that screwed up our detail today sir." Agent Rossie started to offer, but he was instantly cut off by Fugiwara as he started to give his explanation of how their operation died on them. "Well this is what happened as I can see it Ralph..."

"You can explain what went down here better than my Lead Agent, Fugiwara? How's that, were you the one running this operation today, because if Agent Rossie was allowing you to be in command of this operation then I can understand why this detail ended up in a cluster fuck, mister." Murdock growled hotly at Fugiwara as he held him in his angry glare.

"Yeah, I think I can explain the mess much better that Rossie-san can, and that's because I know a little more than he does about what went down that messed up our operation, sir."

"And you have nothing to say in your defense, and you're going to stand there and allow your second in Command to tell me what went wrong with this operation, Agent Rossie, and I'm not going to add the damn 'San' at the end of your name mister, because I'm no damn Jap." Murdock turned back and glared at Agent Fugiwara again, just daring him to bitch about him calling him a Jap, but he found Fugiwara just smiling back at him and he asked him why he was smiling.

"I'm smiling boss over the fact that you're not Japanese, because if you were then I'd be looking to change my nationality, sir."

"You're right Agent Rossie this guy here is bucking to be the comedian of the year I see. Okay Agent Fugiwara, tell me how this damn detail ended up in the shitter on us, mister." Commander Murdock then stared at his agent as he waited to hear what he had to offer him.

"Well sir, this body you see on the table was my snitch. Evidently he was brought here to get his fix and Young must have realized he was working with us, and he obviously got the truth out of him, and judging by his condition it took a lot to break the kid down. I figure once Young knew we were on to him and coming for him, he and his friends made their bird before we arrived on the scene, sir. But they didn't leave until they did this to the poor kid, sir. Then we entered the building and while we were on the first floor of the building..."

"Hold it right there Agent Fugiwara, I think I can piece the rest of this mess together on my own." He looked at the terrible condition of the young body and shook his head as he mumbled. "Poor kid, I want his body treated well. Okay you two, I think you guys were put through the ringer long enough today. Call it an evening and head home and get some rest. In fact, you two can report to work at ten in the morning. That way you can rest a little longer before having to report to work. Take off I'll wrap things up for you myself. I'll see you two tomorrow morning."

"You don't have to tell me twice to get the hell out of here sir, I'm afraid I'm beat up from the feet up sir." Agent Rossie moaned and he turned and head for the first floor of the once target building. Fugiwara was on his heels and as soon as they were outside the building, Fugiwara warned Rossie with a snap in his voice. "Hey buddy, I'm coming home with you tonight."

"Now why the fuck do you want to come over to my place tonight for, you pain in the ass you? Didn't you hear the Big Growl telling us he wanted us to get some rest before we reported to work tomorrow morning? If you come home with me tonight, you know as well as I do, we're going to spend the entire stinking night bullshitting about what went wrong with this damn operation tonight and drinking, mister." Agent Rossie complained at his partner.

"You're dead wrong with that bitch Rossie-san. I don't want to come home with you to bullshit about this screwed up operation tonight. I want to come home with you and see this person you called Wind earlier today, when she suddenly popped up out of a damn cloud and she was ready to do what she did to Young's bodyguards the other day. She was going to chop them up for fucking cat food again. That's why I want to come home with you tonight. I want to see what this Wind babe really looks like in person when I can really see her close up, buddy."

Ahhhh... shit I forgot all about her, she's about as big a pain in my ass as you are my friend. What the hell, I guess it's time I spill the beans about her and Batterman and the rest of the Japanese people she slaughtered back in Japan, partner. Well, come on if you're coming home with me tonight, but I want to stop off at the liquor store and pick up something a little stronger than just wine if I'm going to introduce you to Wind tonight, buddy. Let's get going.

"I'm right behind you Rossie-san." Fugiwara replied in an excited tone of voice. He was all worked up over the thought of meeting this female weapon Rossie was keeping all for himself.

FBI SPECIAL AGENT ROBERT ROSSIE'S APARTMENT

Wind was becoming worried because it was getting later and later and her Lord was not home yet. Still kneeling in the center of the living room for over six hours, her legs were starting to really bother her. She was suffering from pins and needles, and now she was getting Charlie horses in her both thighs. But no matter how much pain she was suffering, she ordered her mind to ignore the pains and discomfort, and she would not leave her kneeling position.

Suddenly, she heard the lock on the door being opened and she wondered why she did not hear her Lord drive his horseless carriage drive up. Immediately, her heart started pounding in her chest as she waited for her Liege Lord to open the door and enter his castle. Now she was staring at the door and was able to see his shadow in the glass and she straightened her back, making her breasts look even larger than they were as she stared so intensely at the front door. It opened slowly and the second she saw her Lord and Master, he was looking behind himself and he was obviously speaking with someone else who was obviously with him.

As soon as Agent Rossie turned his head towards her and entered his apartment, she instantly went into her bow. Bowing so low her forehead actually rested on the hard wood floor, as she held both her bow and breath as she waited for her Lord and Master to address her.

Seeing Wind in her bowing position, Rossie hesitated entering is home and his heart instantly softened for the ancient female Samurai Warrior. Agent Shinnosuke right behind him had to give his partner a slight shove to get him to move a little deeper into his apartment. He was dying to see what Wind truly looked like. All he had of her were mere glances, and when Agent Rossie had her in the front seat of their vehicle, he was having a hard time seeing her face and shape.

"Don't push me like that asshole, I hate when you shove me like that, dammit!" Agent Rossie growled at his partner over his shoulder as he refused to take his eyes off Wind now.

"C'mon, I want to see what your girlfriend looks like, besides. I'm starving and want to order something to eat and I want to tie one on after what we went through today." Fugiwara replied as he shoved Rossie on his back to get him moving in the apartment faster than he was moving in.

"You don't stop shoving me like that and you're going to see what Wind looks like real quick like, because she might think you're a threat to my ass and she'll come at you with her sword, wiseass." Agent Rossie retorted as he stepped into the apartment and then stepped aside and allowed his partner to enter, and then he closed the door behind him and they both ended up staring at the bowing female Warrior with their mouths hanging open.

Agent Fugiwara leaned his head closer to Rossie, and he whispered out of the corner of his mouth. "Man, if I had such a beautiful looking lady waiting for my ass to come home, I'd never leave the home in the first place, buddy. I'd keep her in bed and have at her from morning to night. Why the hell is she bowing like that, will ya tell her to sit up so I can see what she really looks like? Hell, I know why she's bowing like that, she acting like the Japanese people from the ancient past, Rossie-san. Does she always do everything like they did back when the Japanese people believed their honor was more important to them than even their life meant to them?"

"I have some news for you my friend she is from the ancient past. Wind was alive back in the years around 1333, and she was the only female Samurai Warrior to ever be allowed into the Samurai Caste. She was in the employ of Lord Takehiro Kawasomeru when the powerful Daimyo was in Command of Eight of the Sixteen Provinces that made up the central area of the main Island of Japan. And that Lord was in constant battles with another powerful Land Baron who went by the name of Wakatsuki, and to this day Wind is still fuming at this other Land Baron, and I know if she ever came across this guy, she'd make mince meat outta the dude."

"Shit, you have to be shitting me old friend, what the hell do you mean she comes from the ancient past, how the hell is that even possible man?" Agent Fugiwara fussed as he continued to stare at the stunning beauty still bowing so respectfully before the two of them.

"C'mon let's get comfortable then I'll explain everything." Then Rossie looked at Wind and commanded. "Wind-san, you may release your bow and look at me. I want to speak with you."

Slowly, painfully, Wind raised her head from the floor, and straightened her back and wiggled her hips to align her spine and let out her breath at the same time, because she was relieved to be released from her painful bow. Then stared at her Lord and waited for his next command of her.

Agent Fugiwara leaned his head closer to Rossie and said again out of the corner of his mouth as he stared at her breasts that seemed like they were struggling to be free of the exquisite fabric of the short Kimono she was almost wearing. He was also glancing at her perfect legs exposed almost right up to her rearend. "Man Rossie-san, she's some damn good looking babe. Does she always do everything you say as soon as you bark it at her, buddy?"

"Yeah, since I found her she's been classifying me as this dead old Warlord Kawasomeru, and she reacts to me in the same manner as she did when she was in his Command. Sometimes it gets kind of old the way she jumps whenever I tell her to do something, most times she has what I wanted her to do finished almost as fast as I tell her to do it. But I have to admit it to you it's really thrilling to have such a beautiful woman so willing to do anything I tell her to do."

"What? You telling me she'll do anything you tell her to do without complaint, buddy?" Agent Fugiwara asked while still leaning his head close to Rossie.

"Yeah, she'll do anything I tell her to do without any hesitation either my friend." He replied as he continued to stare at Wind while still kneeling on the floor before him.

"Anything man? Like if you told her to strip she'd get out of her robe that quick huh? Or if you tell her to get on your Knob (Slang for Dick) and suck it, she would do it man?"

"Like I said to you, without any hesitation, she's not the least bit concerned over her nudity. In fact I think she'd rather walk around naked than be in any clothes. It's rather concerning, because when she's walking around the apartment naked, I can't get any work done my friend."

"You mean to tell me she'd even screw you if you ordered her to do so my friend?"

"C'mon man will you knock that shit off already dammit." Agent Rossie groused as he absentmindedly shoved Fugiwara on his back, but he was unprepared for the reaction from Wind.

When she saw her Lord shove the man he was speaking English with that she did not understand, like he was suddenly upset with the man, she immediately reacted to her sacred oath. Every muscle in her body tightened and she prepared herself to spring into action to protect her Lord and Master. Then she looked down at her sword still resting on the floor and her arm automatically reached for it. She would have picked it up and went to an on guard position and prepared herself to attack the other man if he made any reaction against her Lord.

"No Wind, I'm in no danger that was a friendly shove. This man to my side is my partner who I work with. He's no threat whatsoever against me. I order you never to attack him under any circumstances. If you dare harm him in any way, it'd be the same as harming me. He is to be respected by you the same way you honor me, Wind-san. Do you understand me, Wind-san?" He tried to think of a better way to describe his partner to her, and then he got the idea and added to her. "Wind-san, this man to my right is my Lead General and no harm is ever to befall his head. Wakarimasu-ka, do you understand Wind-san?" He commanded in floorless Japanese to her.

Agent Fugiwara was still amazed over how well Rossie was speaking Japanese suddenly.

Wind automatically bowed within the limits of respect to her Lord and she replied to his last orders. "Hai, Wakarimasu, I understand what you have just ordered of me my Liege Lord, and I shall obey your Command as faithfully as I have always obeyed every order you have issued to me my Lord." Again, she bowed proudly to her Master of the sword and her spirit.

"Very good Wind-san, I knew you would understand what I was trying to tell you. Now you will stand and greet my General properly. I want you to know him and obey his every Command as faithfully as you would do mine at all times. If you remember correctly Wind-san, my General was with me when you came to aide me earlier in the day, and he was also with me when I ordered you to return to my apartment. And that is a bone I shall pick over with you later on, once I have had something to eat and relax for a few moments, Wind-san."

She did not really understand what her Lord meant when he said he was going to pick a bone over with her later, but she figured it had something to do with when she interfered with his word earlier in the day, and she knew she was still not out of his anger yet as she immediately offered to her Liege Lord. "Would my honorable Master like for this foolish Samurai Warrior to prepare you something to eat my Liege Lord?" Again she bowed politely to her Lord, she was trying desperately to try and make him forget his anger of her over her actions of before in the day.

"That won't be necessary Wind-san. We're both so hungry we're going to order food to be delivered so we can err..." He hesitated for a brief moment, and then smiled and added. "We're going to really pig out tonight. I mean we're going to eat and drink our full tonight, Wind-san." He offered as he walked into the apartment, and he placed the bag with the two bottles of Johnnie Walker he was carrying down on the table, and then turned to Agent Fugiwara and asked him. "Do you want a glass, or do you prefer to slug it right outta the damn bottle, partner?"

"Hell Rossie-san, if there was a way to pump it right into my blood stream, I'd drink it that way, I still so damn upset about what went down today. It's going to take me a lifetime to get what they did to Corey's body out of my mind, and I'll hold onto that sight until I get my hands on Young and do the same god damn thing to his ass as he did to that poor kid, Rossie-san."

She was listening to what the other man was saying to her Lord, even thought she did not understand a word he was saying to her Master, he seemed so upset. She was concerned and still worried about his actions, and if he might reach out and harm her Master. So she remained on guard even though her Master ordered her to respect this man like she respected her Lord.

"C'mon buddy, you need a drink." Rossie offered as he went to the kitchen and grabbed two glasses and returned to the living room. He looked at Wind and then said to her as he opened the bottle and poured the two men a stiff drink. "Wind-san, you don't have to remain standing and looking out of place, you can sit or do whatever you want. We'll speak with you once we had something to drink, and I order supper for us later tonight. Make yourself comfortable."

Again, she bowed to her Lord, and then she walked around the men and took a seat by the table they were hovering around and drinking. With each move she carried off, one of her breasts would sneak out of the fine fabric, and that was something Fugiwara did not miss once as he kept staring at her every chance he got to look at her. He was that infatuated with her and her exquisite shape. He was unable to take his eyes off her and adding the drink to the way he was feeling and now he was thinking of making love to this beautiful woman who barely had a stitch of clothing covering her body, it was starting to drive him crazy with want of her.

Agent Fugiwara took a good pull of his drink and then his body shivered, and he asked Rossie. "Hey partner, how the hell did you ever come across this damn female weapon of yours, buddy?" He aimed his chin at her, and waited for him to tell him how he found Wind.

"You remember when I was stationed in Japan? I was there for three years and got to know the Tokyo Police Officers well, especially Chief Inspector Lieutenant Kenzaburo Motoshima-san. He was the head of the Homicide Division. Anyway, when Batterman went to Japan to buy Asahiko Company, started the problems and murders. Well Hiromoai Hatanaka was the one who found her when he dug up her ancient Kofun or crypt by accident. He ended up using her to eliminate all his competition on the Eight Islands of Japan. When Batterman showed up in Japan, Hiromoai went right after him once he found out Batterman brought Asahiko-san's company from him.

"We found out when Hiromoai couldn't buy Asahiko-san's company from Batterman, he sent her out to kill him. How it happened from that point I'm not certain, but she ended up taking Batterman's head at a construction site in Downtown Tokyo, and at the same site. She for reasons I've never asked her about, ended up killing Hiromoai at the same site. Well Detective Motoshima-san was heading the investigation of Batterman's death, and when he discovered he was an American citizen, he called me to the crime site. As we were checking out the scene, I happened to notice this sword stuck in the ground and it looked like it wasn't worth a shit. I gave it to Lieutenant Motoshima-san and he looked at it, and once he was certain it wasn't the murder weapon, he told me he'd make it so I could take it home with me and put it on my mantle.

"When I got back to the States, I took the sword out and started to try and separate the sword from the scabbard. But there were so many little chunks of wood from the scabbard still stuck to the once deadly blade, so I started picking at the flakes with my fingernail. As I worked on the blade, behind my back she suddenly appeared from what she called the Floating World..."

"I know all about the story of the Floating World and up until today, I always thought it was just a romantic wives tale. Nice to know the stories were true, Rossie-san." Agent Fugiwara remarked as the both men looked at Wind's deadly Katana killing sword still lying on the floor where she had laid it, and the blade looked like it was just created by the maker.

"Yeah, well, anyway, I was shocked when I turned and found this beautiful, naked woman was kneeling on the floor and calling me her Lord and Master, and here she is. That's how I found her so to say, Fugiwara-san." Both men turned and look at her like she just did something wrong.

She smiled at them, because she did not know why they were looking at her the way they were.

"Man, I'd give my left nut to turn around and find such a fine looking dish like her bowing behind me naked as the day she was born, Rossie-san." Agent Fugiwara smirked at his partner.

"Don't you ever take anything serious around you, or out of sex as well, buddy?"

"What else is there in life other than sex and work my friend?" he replied and smirked.

"Not very much I guess, anyway, I'm starving, what do you want to eat tonight buddy? I'll order when you tell me what you want." He asked his partner as he poured them both another drink, but nowhere near as big as the first drinks he poured for them.

"I don't know it's kind of later so let's eat light tonight, maybe some wedges I guess, meatball if you can find them this late in the day, Rossie-san."

"I can get the wedges from the same place I ordered the Pizza's the other day. But they won't deliver this late at night I believe, So I guess I'll have to go and pick them up myself which is no big deal, because the Pizzeria's only a coupla miles away from here..."

"I'll go out for them, Rossie-san." Agent Fugiwara offered as he swayed slightly from drink.

"How the hell can you go for them? If you remember right my friend, we left for my place right from the stakeout, and you don't have a vehicle because you rode in my vehicle over here. I'll go and you can get to know Wind a little better while I'm out, Fugiwara-san. Besides, I can see you're getting hit by the booze already so there's no way in hell you'll drive my car."

"Sounds like a plan to me, I'll take that a meatball wedge then my friend."

"Fine, Wind-san, I'm going to pick up supper for us, you're in for another real treat when you get a taste of a meatball wedge, something I know you never had before in your life. I should be gone for about a half an hour. I'll be right back, speak to Fugiwara-san, he understand Japanese perfectly." With that said, Agent Rossie was out of the apartment. He was just starting to feel the drinks so he drove very carefully as he cursed himself for drinking before going out for supper. But he did not know Fugiwara was going to want wedges to eat tonight.

CHAPTER TWENTY

Both Agent Shinnosuke Fugiwara and Wind watched Agent Rossie leave the apartment to pick up their food, and then Fugiwara turned to her and asked her in a very calm tone of voice. "Rossie-san said you came from the past times of ancient Japan. He told me this tall tale of you living back around 1333 which I find awful hard to believe. When did you live back then?"

"My Lord would never tell tales to anyone as you offer of him!" She snapped back angrily at Fugiwara. Even though her Lord ordered her to treat his friend with respect, she was not going to allow this man to say anything bad about her Liege Lord, as she almost glared at the stranger.

"I guess I stand corrected here Wind, I didn't mean anything wrong about my partner. Well your Liege Lord told you to treat me with respect, and to listen to me as you'd listen to him. So Wind, would you mind standing up for me for a few moments, I wish to see what you look like when you're standing at rest." He requested from her as he waited for her to follow his order.

Without the slightest bit of hesitation in her movement, she immediately rose and as usual she stood with her hands resting down by her hips. Standing like she was made the fine swells of her breasts fill the front of the low front and short Kimono she was dressed in. Like a shark slowly circling its wounded prey, Fugiwara walked around her body, drinking in all her stunning beauty from every angle he looked at her. When he ended up standing right in front of her again, he stopped and made no bones about trying to look right down the front of her Kimono. Instantly, angry memories of Hiromoai Hatanaka's old and filthy minded foreman Utsumi, came flooding back into her mind, as she remembered how he tried to get her out of her Kimono, because he wanted to take advantage of her. She stared with angry eyes at Fugiwara as she waited for him to make the same request as the old man wanted from her. She was waiting for him to tell her to remove her Kimono and stand before him naked. Her wait was not that long in coming.

FBI Special Agent Shinnosuke Fugiwara was nearly drooling down the front of her Kimono, and then he actually reached out and untied the narrow Obi that secured the front of her Kimono, and then he allowed it to slowly slip through his fingers and fall to the floor. She did nothing to stop him as she was following her Lord's orders, and she was treating this stranger the same way she would treat her Lord and carry out any orders he would aim at her.

As the Obi was released, the front of her Kimono opened and both breasts were exposed as were the rest of her treasures to his eyes and delight. He stepped back and explored her body with his eyes as would a buyer would look at a cow he was buying for slaughter as the Kimono slid off her body. "Absolutely perfect," he mumbled as he studied every inch of her exquisite hard body.

She could not help herself as he lusted over her body, and she said sexily back at him in a teasing tone of voice. "I trust my Lord's friend is enjoying what he is looking at?"

"Any man in his right mind would enjoy and give his life for what I am looking at right this moment, Wind." He replied as he continued to stare at her nakedness.

She slightly turned her head to the side, a tad upset because this man was not paying her the proper respect she had earned for herself by not adding the 'san' to the end of her name when he was addressing her. But it was not enough of an insult for her to react angrily against the small snub as she went back to watching him enjoy exploring her body with his eyes.

Agent Shinnosuke Fugiwara further insulted her by reaching out and lightly touching her breasts without asking her permission to do so first. At first she slightly pulled away from his touch, but then she remembered what her Lord had ordered her, and she stood straight and allowed him to enjoy himself at her expense.

When he had his full of playing with her breasts, he stepped back from her and announced with a grin on his lips.

"I thank you for your favor and you may get dressed again, Wind."

She bowed to him, and half knelt and picked up her Kimono from the floor and wrapped it around herself. However she did not pick up the Obi, nor did she try to hold the two ends of her robe together, and Fugiwara could see what Rossie mean when he told him she was not the least bit shy as he continued to enjoy her outstanding treasures. Then she turned and sat at her usual seat at the table, and she waited patiently for her honored Lord and Master to return to her.

They both sat in silence as Agent Fugiwara continued to stare at her nearly fully exposed breasts as she sat like she was fully clothed before him. Then he asked her with a little snap in his tone of voice, remembering how the males spoke to anyone back in the day in a commanding tone. "Wind, how do you like my partner? He's really a good man and easy to work with."

"I would die for my Lord and Master." She replied almost in a combative tone of voice.

"I didn't ask you if you would die for him, I would too. But I asked you how you like him? As a person, and as a lover, you know what I mean?" He replied to her with a snap in his voice and for the first time he allowed a slight bit of nastiness to enter his voice while speaking to her.

"You ask of questions that should only be spoken when one is pillowing with his or her lover in private." Again, she replied as if she was ready to do battle with him.

"Why do you seem like you're so upset with me, Wind? Did I happen to anger you and I'm not aware of the crime I might have committed against you, Wind?"

"I am in error if I made you feel I was upset with you in any manner my Lord's General. If this foolish Warrior has relayed such a feeling, it is the furthest thing I wish to make you feel. I shall correct my attitude with you immediately, so I do not insult your person again while we speak together like this." She bowed slightly to the stranger and held it until he spoke to her again.

"Thank you Wind, I appreciate that. Again I ask you how you feel about my friend, Wind."

"I believe my Liege Lord is the kindest of the rulers of Japan. He is kind, and very attentive to this worthless Vassal at all times. He cares for me more than he allows me to care for all his earthly needs and desires and wants. I even have trouble with him for him to allow me to prepare even the simplest of meals for him to enjoy. He barely allows me to do anything to make his life more comfortable and easier for him to endure. But I will persist and I shall win the battle of pleasure for him." She kind of smiled at the stranger seated at the table with her.

Agent Fugiwara suddenly reached out and picked up the glass he was drinking from, and he took a strong slug and then made a funny face, as the harsh liquid assaulted his body. She cocked her head to the side and then she stared at him and he easily picked up the look and asked her with concern. "What is it now Wind, did I do something that had just displeased you?" he asked as he looked at her while waiting for her to reply to his last question of her.

"No, but this foolish Warrior who does not know any better, wonders why when you drink the cha (tea) colored water, you make a face like you just smelt the foulest of odors?"

"I'm sorry Wind, but I'm enjoying a little Johnnie Walker to make myself feel good."

"Cha will make you feel good? If so and you are so easy to feel good. Then I believe you could feel good about a bee sting as well." She offered pleasantly as she really smiled this time at the stranger as she started to relax with him more and more she spoke with him.

"That was cute Wind, would you care to try a little Johnnie Walker, and then you'll see how good it could make you feel." He said as he offered her the glass he was drinking from.

She took the glass and smelt the liquid and wrinkled her nose as the odor made her nose tingle. She took a sip and coughed and having trouble keeping the liquid down while continuing to cough. When she caught her breath she complained. "How do you drinking that it burned my throat. Though it reminded me of Sake, it burns so more than rice wine." She did not even realize the liquor was already affecting her as her head suddenly felt light, and she was slightly dizzy.

"I should've warned you it was a little harsh for a beginner to enjoy, before you took a drink of it. But once you get a little use to it, I'm certain you'll love the drink, I promise you Wind."

"I think it would take all the sticks of time of an eon for me to ever get use to the harsh taste of this foul drink I fear." She replied as she quickly handed him back his drink as she still tried to get the terrible taste out of her mouth, and wondered how anyone could enjoy the drink.

Agent Rossie was back and he walked into the apartment carrying a large bag and he put it down in the center of the table. Then he ripped the side of the bag open and allowed the meals to slip out of the destroyed bag. He then rushed into the kitchen and grabbed three plates and went back to the table and placed a wedge on each plate and handed them out to the others.

Wind looked at the wrapped sandwich as if the wrapping held a hidden severed arm within the wrapping. She was even afraid to look at it for fear of what she might find hidden by the oil soaked wrapping, as she watched what her Lord was doing with his meal. When he took the wrapping from his sandwich and she smelled the delightful smell, her stomach growled in response and she picked up his sandwich and quickly unwrapped it. She took a bit and was amazed at how wonderful it tasted, but she knew she would be unable to eat the whole thing in one sitting, but she vowed to herself she was going to try her best to eat the entire sandwich.

She could not recognize the meat but the gravy that the meat was smothered in was wonderful to enjoy. But she was having a bit of trouble with the cheese, because each time she took a bit, the cheese stretched almost the length of her arm before it broke and ended up hanging from her mouth. Back in ancient Japan, no one would ever eat such a foul thing, especially within the presence of another Japanese person. It was almost insulting what the sandwich was doing to her.

The three of them were enjoying their meal with gusto, when Rossie noticed she did not have anything to drink, he got up and poured her a glass of the chilled wine she was enjoying so much lately, and he brought it to her. She bowed to her Lord and thanked him for consideration and the wine, and he smiled back at her and then he returned to enjoy his meal and drink.

Both of the agents were starting to get a little tipsy from all the drink they were enjoying, as they also enjoyed the slight show she was constantly putting on for the both of them with her so short Kimono that was hiding nothing of her body from their view. Because every time she moved around, either her breasts were exposed, or her other treasure came out for a quick visit.

Suddenly, Fugiwara turned serious as he asked Rossie as he turned his attention at him. "Well I guess I'm going to be forced to ask you flat out Rossie-san. Are you going to tell me what this beautiful little lady here had to do with the death of Batterman, and the others who were also slaughtered in Japan? But I must tell you, I'm finding it hard to believe such a beautiful woman as she, could have anything to do with murder. But then I remember what she did to a number of Young's bodyguards, and I have to believe what I witnessed, and I know she's capable of doing anything she might set her mind to, Rossie-san." He remarked and asked at the same time.

Wind immediately noticed the instant change of her Lord's disposition and she automatically tensed up, not knowing why her Lord suddenly became so concerned over what his friend just told him. She was unhappy the two men were speaking a language she did not understand much of, and they only spoke Japanese when they were speaking directly to her during their talk.

She became extremely concerned over the change in her Liege Lord and she paid much closer attention to how her Master was reacting to what the other man was saying to him. She wanted to be able to spring right into action in an instant, in case the two men ended up in an argument and she had to destroy her Master's friend if he tried to attack her Liege Lord. Many times in the past she witnessed her Lord and Master pleasantly speaking with others, and then in a flash everyone he was speaking to were suddenly beheaded and left to die where they fell to the ground.

So she wanted to be well prepared for anything that might take place any time her Lord and Master was speaking to someone in her presence. She settled down a little and just watched every move her Lord or the stranger was doing while they spoke together.

"I guess the last time Wind had to sort or report back to the Kami who control the Floating World. The one God they claim was the one who create the Eight Islands of Japan..."

"Holy crap Rossie-san, please don't tell me the story about Izanagi and his marrying his sister Izanami, and then the two of them took the time to create the Islands of Japan are true. And she was with these two powerful Gods of Japan and she actually spoke with him and maybe touched him! Damn, I can't think of touching the God who had created Japan, what do I mean Japan. According to the stories I heard, he and his sister created the world from the swill floating among the clouds." Agent Fugiwara cried in an extremely excited tone of voice, because he was just told some of the stories he was told of the creating of the Islands of Japan were true. He was almost hopping up on down on one foot as he waited for Rossie to confirm what he asked him about.

"I guess that's according to Wind and what she told me when she came to me. She was armed with this amulet." He stopped speaking and pulled the amulet out of his shirt and allowed Agent Fugiwara to look at it and then added. "She said the God Izanagi was the one who gave her that amulet, and she gave it to me and it helps her protect me somehow. She told me she can see what I'm doing, and the amulet only activates when I get excited and the amulet makes her believe I'm stuck in a life and death situation. The amulet will deliver her to where I am in any trouble, just like she showed up the two times we went after Young and his bunch of assholes...."

Again Fugiwara interrupted Rossie as he said in his excited voice. "Damn, you mean Izanagi held this in his hand and gave it to Wind and she gave it to you. Do you know what you have in your hands, and what any Japanese person would pay to hold this amulet for a second, let alone what they'd offer for it if you'd be so stupid as to sell it to anyone who wanted it. Damn I can't believe I'm holding something Izanagi was holding in his hands. It makes me not want to wash my hands again I tell you Rossie. So this amulet will inform her you're in trouble and she would come to you and fight anyone attacking you, that's what you're telling me here man?"

"That's what I'm telling you Fugiwara-san."

Agent Fugiwara then turned and looked at Wind who suddenly looked like she was paying attention to what they were saying. But she only perked up when he said the one word she understood in English as well in Japanese and that was her name.

She did not know how to properly react to the look she was receiving from her Lord's friend, so she did the only thing she could think of to do. She smiled back at him as she looked at him just as intensely as he was staring back at her. She was even proud because the stranger was still holding the sacred amulet she gave her Lord and Master in his hand as it hung from her Lord's neck, and he was looking at her as if she was a god herself now.

Agent Fugiwara then turned back to Rossie and asked him as he calmed down some to act nearly normal again. "Can you continue with the story of Wind for me man? I can't believe how damn lucky you are buddy, to have someone like her not only looking after your sagging ass and protecting you like she's doing. But you also have one hot looking babe ready to do anything you want of her between the sheets. You're slipping the old log to her, aren't you man?"

"What do you think buster, if you have to know what's going on between us?"

"Why you lucky little bastard you, what pile of shit did you step in to find someone like her?"

"I don't know but what I do know is. I feel like you just described me, a lucky sonofabitch."

"Damn, I don't believe this shit Rossie-san, and if I didn't see this crap, I'd be calling the Doctors about now on your ass, and have the Doctors to chase you around with a butterfly net my friend. Damn Rossie-san, I remember you saying something about being able to destroy her spirit forever. I forgot how you told me how you were able to do that, and why would you ever want to do that in the first place man?" Fugiwara asked Rossie with a stunned sounding tone of voice.

"Wind told me the only way I can end her life and stop her from living in both worlds, the Floating World and the living world, was to snap the sword in half. That would destroy her spirit, but she also warned me to never allow the two ends of the sword to ever touch each other again, because if the two ends ever touched again. The sword would instantly be welded together somehow, and her spirit would be called back to the living world from the blackness of never as she put it. Let me tell you something about having her around like she is. Although it's a great feeling to know she's out there, and she could just appear if and when I found myself in any trouble. It's also one helluva responsibility to have her hanging around me twenty four seven.

"Yeah it's great that I can tap her any time I want to pillow as she puts it with her. But on the other hand, now all I do is worry if I get excited over any reason, is she suddenly going to come popping out of a damn cloud with her sword locked in her hands, and she starts chopping anyone near me into hamburger meat. It's really a heavy burden to have hanging over my head all the damn time! I'm also worried if I end up in an argument with a friend, is she going to take that as a threat against my life, and she overreacts before I can stop her, and she kills an innocent person, or someone very important to me. I'm telling you, it's a gift and a curse at the same time."

"I see what you're saying to me Rossie-san, but on the other hand, look at what you got going for yourself. If she can protect you like she did when we got jumped by Young's pack of Gombas a few days back, and you can also tap her anytime you want to make love to someone as great looking as she is without any strings attached to the act. Man do you have both sides of the coin going for ya at the same time man." Agent Fugiwara smirked at his partner.

"Yeah, I know that, that's why I called her a gift and a curse at the same time. There are so many good things that come with her presence in the living world, but there are so many problems that also come with her presence. I don't know what to do about her. She caused me some serious concerns when she suddenly turned up at this last mess. Could you see what could have happened if one of our other Agents saw her just pop up with a god damn sword held in her hand? How he might have reacted against her, and how she would have reacted if the other Agent went at her with his weapon in hand. Would she have killed one of our guys without thought, just because she figured he was a threat against me or even against her? Dammit, I don't know what to do about her, but I do know sooner or later I'm going to have to do something about her.

"Another problem facing me is, how the hell am I going to solve Batterman's murder, without bringing her into the case. Can you see how Murdock is going to react when I try to tell him about her, and how she killed Batterman and the others killed in Japan, all dealing with that damn Hiromoai Hatanaka bastard who started this mess off by using her to kill his competition in Japan, dammit? The other thing I have to worry about is, how Murdock is going to feel about me holding back the evidence I knew the killer of Batterman, and I held back that evidence from him until it suited me better when to bring him the evidence on who had really killed Batterman.

"At best I'd be placed on unpaid restriction, at worst he could fire me and I wouldn't blame him in the least if he did. I broke so many protocols because of her and my trying to protect her, and also not telling Murdock about her or all of what I know about the Batterman murder, and the other murders she was involved in Japan. I can't tell you how complicated my life has turned into ever since I found her, and she entered my life and screwed it up like she has, dammit..."

"And also tell him how it feels with you screwing her anytime you want to make love to a beautiful looking chick like her, my friend." Agent Fugiwara smirked as he glanced at

Wind again, and smiled when he saw how she was hanging out of the front of her beautiful Kimono.

"God dammit man, will you ever let that idea outta your stinking mind. There is an awful lot more to life than screwing a chick, or worrying on how much someone else is getting. Dammit will you get off that crap for once. Here I am drowning and you're describing the god damn water to me. I need help with trying to figure out what the hell I'm going to do with her, and how I'm going to tell Commander Murdock about her presence and how she killed so many people and all you're worry about is my screwing her for crap sake." He bitched at his partner this time.

"Hey buddy, now you're starting to sound like Murdock by using his favorite phase. But I see what you're saying, and the problems you're getting over her. Bringing her up to Murdock and explaining to him how she killed Batterman and the others, is going to be a real tough situation to deal with. The other part of how he's going to react when he finds out you could have solved the Batterman murder case right after you returned to the United States from Japan, is really going to set him off I can tell you. Especially because of all the damn heat he's getting over solving that damn case. Yeah my friend, you do have some serious problems on your hands I'm afraid. But we're going to solve all these problems together one way or the other, Rossie-san."

He stopped feeling sorry for himself as he stared at his partner and remarked. "You're going to stick with me and help me out of the damn mess I got myself stuck in over finding Wind?"

"What the hell kind of friend would I be if I didn't stick tight with my partner when he fucked up as badly as you have for the past few weeks? What's the old saying, in for a nickel, in for a dollar? Sure I'm going to stick with you, if not for any other reason but to see what the hell Murdock is going to do to your stinking ass, when he finds out you were holding the evidence back to solve the Batterman's murder for a few weeks now. Man is that going to be a helluva mess, I can see him now going off on your ass with different branding irons, rusty nails and the whip the Big Growl has hanging in his office just for us, when we fuck up like you did with this one, buddy." Agent Fugiwara smirked as he grinned again at his worried looking partner.

"Yeah, you're a real pal, not mine, but you're a pal there buddy. It takes a real friend to stab ya right in the front. But all these are the problems I've been faced with ever since I found Wind." He again glanced at her and smiled when he saw she was looking at him with concerned eyes.

"I don't know how you're ever going to get out of this one with your skin still left on your bones. You know we should or have told Murdock about your little girlfriend here, or we'll never be able to solve the damn murder. But if we bring her before Murdock, he's going to shove her in jail, and then we'll never be able to help her after he gets his hands on her. Damn, we really got ourselves stuck between a rock and a hard place here, Rossi-san. We're going to have to work this out together or we're going to lose her, and I didn't even try her out between the sheets yet."

Rossie ignored his partner's attempt to be a smartass, because he realized he was going to need all the help he can get from him. He shook his head because he did not know what he was going to do about Wind and Batterman's case, as he poured himself the last of the Johnnie Walker from the first bottle, and he topped his drink off by opening the second bottle and filling his glass.

Agent Fugiwara easily got his attention by moving his glass a little closer to his, and Rossie immediately filled his glass as well. Buy now, the both of them were seeing double with all the booze they had consumed, and that was making Wind look all that much better to them both. Because they were seeing two of her and each one of them were dying to bed her for the night.

As if he was able to read Rossie's mind he leaned closer to his partner, and slurred his words. "Man, she's like a painting created by the Master's of old, meant to be touched by eyes, not with the hands, Rossie-san." Then he pitched forward and almost slipped off the sofa. If he did not grab hold of the side of the table, he would have ended up on the floor. Rossie was fast enough to steady the small table, or Fugiwara's weight would have surely pulled the table over with him.

He then laughed at Agent Fugiwara as he groused at him. "Hey man, I think you had enough to drink tonight, you almost hit the floor, stupid. I think I'm going to take Wind in my bedroom, and you can sleep out here on the couch for the night my friend. There's no way in hell I'm going to drive you home tonight, not in the condition I'm in now, man. I don't think I could even find the damn ignition with the key I'm so fucked up. I'll get you some bedding and you can sleep here tonight. That way we can both drive in tomorrow morning and start that stinking report for the Big Growl." He laughed at his joke about their Commander while he also slurred his words.

"Don't give me any of that shit partner, you just want to get her in your bedroom to share her pillow with her, buster. I know what you're up to here man." Agent Fugiwara pointed at the ghost of Rossie, because he was pointing in front of him and missing his body with his finger, as he placed the weirdest looking smile on his lips, and then he belched so loud that Rossie moved away from him, because he thought Fugiwara was going to upchuck.

Laughing himself, Rossie added at his FBI partner. "You're really fucked up buddy, here's your bedding I promised you." He was so drunk himself he held out his empty hand and offered it to his partner, and then he looked at his hand. Not seeing what he thought he was holding the bedding, he turned his hand over and not seeing the blanket he was going to get for him. So he started to look around on the floor, thinking he might have dropped the bedding.

"What the hell are you looking for, you didn't even get up to get the bedding you offered me, you asshole you." Agent Fugiwara slurred his words again as he laughed that funny laugh all drunks always do, whenever they were too drunk to even stand up properly.

"Boy are you shitfaced man, I got up and got your bedding, I just don't know where the hell I put the crap, sleep in your clothes will ya! I don't care I'm going to bed." He tried to get up off the couch, but he could not stand and then he belched and asked his partner. "Am I up man?"

"How the hell do I know, I can't even see you anymore, partner?"

All the while the two men were drinking and laughing together, she watched everything they were doing with amusement. She saw her Lord Kawasomeru as drunk as her new Lord was at this time on a number of occasions in her past, and it was always funny to her how the male animal always got when they were drunk like this. She watched as he tried to get up on his feet, and then he fell right back down in a sitting position on the couch. Then two men laughed at each other again as Fugiwara tried to take another sip of his drink, but he was so drunk he could not find his mouth with the rim of the glass, and he ended spilling his drink down the front of his chest. Then he called out. "Abandon ship, we're going down, the water's up to my chest."

Agent Rossie gave up trying to stand, and he suddenly rolled his rearend on the sofa, and he dropped down to the floor and actually tried to crawl on his hands and knees for his bedroom. Even this feeble attempt failed him miserably and he ended up falling forward on his face on the floor, and then he let out with a fart that almost rattled the windows of the apartment, and he roared with laughter again as he rolled over on his back and stared up at the ceiling.

Wind was now laughing so hard at the two foolish men and the way were acting that she had to wipe the tears from her eyes. Then she rose from her chair and tried to help her new Lord get up to his feet. As she tried to lift him her robe nearly slid off her one shoulder, and this action was leaving nothing to the imagination of both men as Rossie tried to get her breast, but he was reaching a half a foot away from her body, obviously reaching for her double in his eyes. She easily brushed his hand away from her chest as she tried to pick him up, but he was dead weight and almost impossible for her to help him get up to his feet. Then she stood and placed both her hands on her hips and smirked at her Master looking up at her and laughing like a child at her.

The way she was stand exposed her treasures to the both men as she said to her Lord. "My Master, this foolish Warrior is too weak to pick you up and carry you to our sleeping quarters. You have to get up on your own. Then I can help you walk to the room we pillow in." She again bent down and tried to pick and move her laughing Liege Lord still lying on the floor.

Everything she was doing to help her Lord get to his feet, was causing her breasts to bounce and sway to her motions, and Fugiwara was moving his head to the motion of her breasts and grinning like a school boy sneaking a peek into the girl's locker room as they changed clothes, and he wore the widest smile. She straightened up and rested her hands on her hips and snapped at her Master's friend, because she could be angry with him, but she could never display anger at her Master or it would cost her her head after she was ordered to commit Suppuku.

"Are you just going to sit there and watch me struggle with my Master like this, or are you going to help me get him to his sleeping quarters? It is your Yoshi gi (Duty) as his well trusted General to assist me with him. My honorable Lord will be extremely upset with you if he realizes you have allowed him to crawl on the floor like a lowly Heimin, (Commoner) and he will have your foul head taken from your worthless shoulders for your failure to him.

All she received from the drunken Agent Fugiwara was a loud belch, and then he also farted and grinned back at her with a dumb look plastered on his face.

"Oh you foolish male Warriors are all alike whenever you drink too much Sake. You are all totally useless. If we were to be attacked at this very minute, Lord Wakatsuki and his foul Army of lowly dog eaters he calls Samurai, could easily march in to your castle and destroy the two of you fools. We faithful Warriors will always do our duty and protect the fools from their own slaughter. You just remain resting on your backside and I shall do what you should be doing for our Lord and Master, fool." She complained bitterly at Fugiwara, but he was not hearing one word she was barking at him, because he had passed out minutes before she went off on him.

Wind sharpened her glare at her Master's friend and when she realized he had passed out on her, she merely shook her head at him, as she returned to her struggle with trying to move her Lord and Master into their sleeping quarters. After a hard battle with trying to get her Lord into the bed and when he laid down on the bed, she carefully stripped him of his clothes. Then she covered him and walked around the other side of the bed and crawled under the covers with him. He immediately rolled over and pulled her to him and buried his head in the nap of her neck.

FBI SPECIAL AGENT ROBERT ROSSIE'S APARTMENT, FRIDAY,
JUNE 26th, 1996. ZERO, SIX TWENTY HOURS (6:20 A.M,)

Agent Rossie painfully rolled out of bed because he had to go to the bathroom. He staggered to the room trying to more feel his way there than opening his eyes and see where he was going. His head felt like he had an angry mule inside and he was trying to kick his way out of his noggin. He stood before the bowl and half his pee missed the mark and ran on the floor, but he could not keep his eyes open long enough to see what he was doing. When he finished he staggered to bed and dropped down on it like a sack of potatoes that fell off the back of a speeding truck. Wind was sitting up and she watched him stagger around and then drop on the bed and she asked him.

"Does my Liege Lord need me to get him something that will stop the pounding taking place within your honorable hear my Lord, this not the first time I have witnessed my ward when he was foolish enough to try and drink all the Sake from the face of the earth. I have seen the ladies of the Willow help the foolish Samurai who drank too much, and I know the remedy they used to bring the foolish one's back to reality." She offered in a soft tone of voice as she was having a problem with trying to keep the smile from her lips over the trouble her Lord was having with trying to get over the affects of the drink the two men had consumed last night. She could only think her Lord's friend was suffering as bad as her Liege Lord was suffering.

"Gees Wind, what the hell are you yelling at me for? My head is pounding and it feels like it's going to split in half, so I don't need you yelling at me. Ohhhhhh my head." He cried as he grabbed his pillow and pulled it over his head and then he locked it in place with his hands.

Again, she smiled pleasantly over the suffering of her Liege Lord then she got out of bed and searched the kitchen looking for the herbs she would need to fix the drink that would make her Lord's head feel better. Not finding what she needed, she did the next best thing, and she took out two hands full of ice cubes and she dropped them in a towel and then she carried it into the bedroom. She pulled the pillow from his head and he moaned painfully again.

"Ohhhhhhh, my head, please Wind, do me a favor and just shoot me will you please."

She smiled again, and then she placed the cold towel on the back of his neck, and she heard her Lord moan, and then he relaxed as the coolness started to relieve some of the pain in his head. Then she mumbled at him. "Perhaps my most wise and honorable Lord will think better the next time you try and drink the earth dry of all the Sake of the world? It is a very wise man who learns a lesson from his foolishness, it proves he is an adult my Lord."

"Perhaps I'll never take another drink for the rest of my life if I happen to live through this nightmare, Wind." He cried while he had his head buried in the mattress of the bed.

"I shall go out and see if my Lord's friend is suffering so as well. I shall offer him the same help I have just offered my Liege Lord." She offered as he got off the bed, this time she was not going to walk around in the living room naked because of the other man sleeping out there. She slipped into her short Kimono, and then she started to look around for the Obi to tie her Kimono closed. It took her a few seconds to remember she left the Obi out in the living room, where her Lord's friend had removed it from her body. So she grabbed the two end of the Kimono and held it closed with her hand as she went out to check on the other man. She found him sitting up on the sofa, and he looked like he was going to be ill any second, so she made certain she never stood directly in front of the sick acting man and she asked him calmly.

"Does this foolish man need any help from me?" She said in Japanese to the sick man.

"No Wind, I don't need help, this isn't the first time I'm seeing double. But I wouldn't stand in my way if I was you, in case I have to make a dash to the bathroom." Agent Fugiwara replied.

"It's a very foolish person who refuses any help when it is offered to him. Especially when that fool is suffering so as you are. I can get you some ice to help calm the barking Dragon who is making your eyes bleed." She offered with a smile on her lips. She loved to see the men in her life enjoy themselves like they had last night, and it was so pleasing for her to repair what they had destroyed of their minds from all the drink that enjoyed. She liked when the powerful men were so helpless before her like this, and she took care of them.

"Don't worry about me any Wind. You worry about your Master I can take care of myself. I'm going to force myself to heave so I can sober up so I can report to work at least looking like I'm okay this morning Wind." Agent Fugiwara offered and then his skin turned a bright green color and he was up on his feet in a second and made a mad dash for the bathroom, and then she heard him as he heaved his guts out in the smaller visitor's room. Again she smiled over how foolish these two wise men were last night as they drank more than four men should drink.

She left Fugiwara and went back to their bedroom and she was surprised to see her Lord was out of bed and was looking half way human as he looked at himself in the mirror. His eyes were bloodshot and she felt they must hurt him to look out of his eyes the way they looked to her.

"Oh please don't look at me so Wind-san I might scare you to death the way I look this morning. I need a glass of orange juice to help me make it through this."

She smiled as she realized he must have been feeling better now, because he added the 'San' back to his name, and then she asked him with concern in her voice. "Orange juice, my Lord?"

"Yes Wind-san, orange juice, it's in the white and yellow container in the fridge on the top shelf. Hurry, I need a glass so bad so I can get this terrible taste out of my mouth, and then I'm going to take an ice cold shower to help sober me up some for work this morning, Wind-san. Wind-san Isogi (Hurry) please." He cried as he leaned up against the wall with his forehead, the coolness of the wall making him feel a little better for the moment.

She rushed out of the bathroom to the fridge and saw the container her Lord described and wanted a drink from, she did not bother to get a glass as she brought him the whole container, and she handed it to her terribly suffering Liege Lord.

Agent Rossie grabbed the cold container and for a moment he held it up against his forehead and moaned, and then he opened it and nearly drank the entire quart without coming up for air. When he drank his full he smacked his lips and then offered. "Boy Wind-san, this shit's a real lifesaver here I tell you." He then polished off the rest of the quart of orange juice.

She did not understand much of what he was saying to her for two reasons, first; because he was still slurring his words terribly, but no way near as bad as he was talking last night before she had almost drag him to the bed, and for the other reason was; because he was saying words that did not make much sense to her, even though he was speaking to her in Japanese.

"I'm feeling a little better now, I'm going to take a quick shower and then get dressed for work. There's no need for you to fix me something to eat this morning. I doubt I could keep anything down right now, not with the way my stomach is rebelling against me right now. I'll pick something up to eat at work this morning. Did you check on Fugiwara-san for me Wind-san, and if so how is he doing? Is he in as rough a shape as I am, Wind-san?" He asked her as he had to place his hand against the wall to help steady himself so he did not fall over.

"The General you call Fugiwara-san is feeling as bad as you are suffering my Lord. He is in the other water room relieving his stomach in the white bowl we do our business in my Lord. But I think he will survive your night of drinking the harsh Sake I did not enjoy in the least, my Lord." She replied with a smile on her lips she could not hide even if she tried.

"Well, at least I know he'll survive last night, but I'm not so sure about me surviving it Wind-san. Don't ever allow me to drink like I did last night again. I'm taking a shower." He mumbled as he went into the bathroom and she waited until she heard the water running, before she returned to the living room to check on her Master's General again.

Special Agent Fugiwara was out of the bathroom and he was walking into the kitchen just as she came out of their bedroom. He was naked and he did not seem like he cared about it as he went to the fridge and looked in it. Then he turned to Wind and asked her in a slightly slurred voice. "Wind, there was some orange juice in here last night, do you know where it went? I have a terrible taste in my mouth and I need to wash out of it with the orange juice."

"I must report my Lord drank the orange drink this morning, General. My Lord is taking a shower, and then I believe he will dress and come out of our pillowing room and be ready to leave for work. My Lord has already informed me he will not be interested in having anything to eat before he leaves. I do not enjoy his leaving for work without anything to eat." She bowed just within the limits of politeness to who she believed was her Liege Lord's favorite General.

"I don't blame him in the least, I couldn't dare try and eat anything myself this morning. I know it wouldn't stay with me very long before it came up for a revote." Agent

Fugiwara smirked as he turned and searched the fridge again and smiled when he saw a can of Pepsi in the back of the fridge, and he grabbed it like it was the most expensive thing he ever handled in his life. He popped the top and then sucked the soda down almost without coming up for air.

She watched him drink the soda and again smiled, wondering why the foolish male animal would assault their bodies with drink, and then pay for that enjoyment for the entire next day.

After he gulped down the Pepsi, he stood straight and then he announced to Wind. "Damn, that helped me out quite a bit and I'm feeling almost human again thank God. I promise no more of that Johnnie Walker stuff for me again, not until I want to try and kill myself again I guess. I'm going to dress and get ready for work myself, Wind-san."

She smiled at him because he was speaking Japanese and she understood most of what he said except for the slang he used. She also enjoyed him walking around semi-hard, and his member swayed side to side as he walked for his clothes. She even watched him as he dressed in the same clothes he wore last night and when he was dressed, she bowed to him, Satisfied how he looked for work, all he had to do was comb his hair and he would be ready, all but for his eyes. They seemed to pain him when he looked at her. She never looked at herself or she would have realized her Kimono was pretty much opened and hiding nothing from his view. But even if she was aware of the condition of her Kimono, she would not care about it she was far from shy.

Just them Rossie came out of the bedroom fully dressed and he looked so much better than when he went for his shower. Even his hair was combed and he was in a clean suit and when he saw his partner, he immediately asked him. "How are you making out this morning my friend?"

"I'm alive, if that's what you're asking me. What a night, remind me never to overdo it like we did last night ever again. It's like winning a fistfight, even though you win, you spend the next day getting over the war. How are you making out this morning? You look a lot better for the wear my friend." Fugiwara replied as he eyed his partner to make certain he was okay for work.

"I guess I'm just like you and I'm alive, thank God for that much though. You ready to head out? I figured we'll get something to eat at the luncheonette this morning. That way it'll give our stomachs a little more time to settle down some. I don't know how we're going to be able to hide our condition from the Big Growl though. You know he's going to be hawking us all day long. He wants those two damn reports done as fast as we can write them up, Fugiwara-san."

"Just keep your head down and don't let him see your eyes. Then we should be able to pull it off and keep him off our asses today. I think he's going to be more interested in getting our reports than he is in worrying if we had a good time last night, my friend."

"I guess you're right there Fugiwara-san. What say, you want to head off for work and get there early so we can eat and then get ready to deal with the Big Growl this morning?"

"We might as well shove off, because if I stay here any longer and seeing what I'm looking at this morning, you won't be able to get me out of your apartment with a hand grenade, Rossie-san." He warned his partner as he turned and looked at Wind again, standing with her hands resting on her hips, and she was listening to the two men speaking English this time. She was not giving the condition of her

Kimono a second thought, because the front of it was wide open, and the two men were seeing all her treasures as she smiled back at them.

"Wow, I see what you mean Fugiwara-san, seeing her standing there like that. If I wasn't still half ass drunk, I'd take advantage of what she's offering us, buddy."

"And I'd help you with her. The way she looks I bet she could wear down any number of men at the same time, Rossie-san." Fugiwara grumbled at his partner.

"Whoa, I know she loves to pillow and she can't get enough of it. But I really don't think she's ready to even consider doing a coupla guys at the same time buddy. But it'd be awful interesting if she would do the both of us at the same time. Arrr... what the hell am I talking about here, it has to be the damn drink that has me thinking that way my friend. C'mon partner, let's get going. I want to be at my desk long before the Big Growl reports in for the day."

Rossie turned back to Wind and told her. "We're off for work, you hold down the fort and I'll see you right after work. Don't make anything for us for supper I'll pick it up for us tonight."

"Please do my Lord I would like to enjoy that big rice cake with the cheese and meal on it."

"You got it Wind-san I'll pick up a Pizza tonight I guess. I'll see you later tonight. Remember, don't allow anyone to see you while I'm away from the apartment, Wind-san."

She merely bowed back at her Lord in response to his last warning to her.

With that said, both men turned and they left Rossie's apartment.

CHAPTER TWENTY ONE

FBI HEADQUARTERS, WASHINGTON D.C. SATURDAY, JUNE 27th, 1996, ZERO SEVEN FOURTEEN

Even though it was Saturday, both Rossie and Fugiwara reported for work as ordered by Murdock. The overtime meant nothing to the Commander, because he wanted those reports from his two agents while the action was fresh in their minds. He also wanted some time in private to speak with his two agents to see where they were taking the case of Batterman's murder, and how they were linking Young's case up with the one they were working on with Batterman's case. But Commander Murdock was not intending to report to work as early as usual, because he rarely if ever worked on Saturdays. So he was planning to come in when he decided to show up for the extra work, knowing his agents had to get their reports done before he bothered them.

Agent Rossie dropped down in his chair before his desk like he was just shot, and he put his breakfast on his desk and took a good pull of his coffee. He had a second cup of coffee to help sober himself up some, along with a bacon, cheese and cheese bagel. He looked at Fugiwara and noticed he was still suffering from their night of drinking and he smiled as he took another drink of his coffee and announced. "I bet the Big Growl is going to come in late today and that's damn good for us, I need all the time I can get for sobering up before I have to deal with his ass."

"I agree with you there and feel the same way and I hope he does come in late. That way we don't have to deal with him all day riding our asses. By the way, how the hell is this day going to go down buddy? Do we stay in all day, or is it when we finish our reports we go home for the rest of the day? I'm afraid I'm still dying here Rossie-san? You know Rossie-san, I have to warn you of something man. You're getting your ass trapped deep in the swamp, and your surrounded by a heard of alligators and you have your pockets filled with dead fish, trying to protect Wind like you're doing and going against Commander Murdock, the company and the law like you're doing, pal. But what the hell, we'll get you the hell out of this mess together, buddy." Agent Fugiwara offered and then he immediately regretted it, because it hurt his head to even talk still.

"I hear you there Fugiwara-san, I can see the Big Growl going off on my ass when he finds out what I'm doing here." Agent Rossie replied with a smirk on his lips.

"What the hell he can kill us both, but he can't eat us, that's against the law. Well, we might as well start working on these damn reports before the Big Growl shows up, and then he gets on our backs if we're not done with the damn things." Fugiwara retorted as he laughed over his remark.

The two agents went right to work on their reports, and after three hours of writing and comparing notes together, they came up with a complete report covering everything that went wrong with their last operation that fell apart on them. Just as they were about to head down to the luncheonette for lunch, Murdock came walking in their office carrying coffee for the three of them. He smirked at his two agents as he sat down and then grumbled at the two of them.

"How are you guys making out with them damn reports I need done yesterday. I hate when things go wrong for us on a stakeout, and yesterday was one helluva mess as far as I can see. I even have the Captain of the Washington PD riding my case, asking me how the hell things got so wrong for us, and he said the next time we need any of his people. He might think twice before lending them to us. I know he's talking out of his ass because his mouth knows better. Let me tell you guys, if I call for backup from the Washington PD, they'll be there, period." Murdock growled in an angry tone of voice, showing his two agents he had their backs all the time.

Neither agent responded, not because they did not want to say anything to the man, they both were still sort of hurting from all their drinking last night.

"Excuse me did I hear either of you two birds saying something to my ass? How are you doing with them damn reports I asked you people for?" He snorted this time at his agents.

Agent Rossie picked up the two reports from his desk and combined them together, and then he tapped the pages on his desk surface to align them properly. Then he handed them to Murdock as he responded. "I have them both right here, nicely typed up for your approval, sir."

Commander Murdock suddenly cocked his head to the side and he stared deeply into Agent Rossie's terribly bloodshot eyes, and he asked him. "What the hell is wrong with your fucking eyes, mister? Hell, is there any survivors in that damn noggin of yours? You look terrible, how the hell are you operating in that condition mister? What the hell did you two guys drink last night to show up here in this condition? I'm just happy no other Agents are in for work today to see what I'm looking at this morning. Dammit, they wouldn't believe it either you two. You guys have a helluva nerve to show up here in this shitty a condition for work."

Agent Rossie was hurting so bad from his drinking he snapped back at his Commander without thinking what he was saying, and how he was saying it to his Commander. "Say look Murdock, we came in on our day off and I don't even know if we're getting paid for it or not, just to fill out the god damn reports you're busting our horns over. So what the hell do you care how the hell we look or what condition we're in? As long as we got in and we finished the reports as you demanded. Will you cut us some damn slack for a change around here, Murdock!"

Murdock straightened his back and his eyebrows arched as he glared at Rossie, and he snapped at him. "Boy you two must have really tied one on last night to give you the Gonads (Slang for Balls) to talk to me like this. I'm not even going to look at your partner in crime hiding over there, because if you're in this bad a shape I can only imagine how bad a shape he's in, dammit. Yeah, thinking about it, I guess you two birds are doing me a favor to come in on your day off to file these reports with me, and yes, you two are picking up time and a half for coming in today. Did you guys eat any lunch? If not, lunch is on me, C'mon man, let's go get something to eat."

The luncheonette was open twenty four seven, to serve all the civilians who worked in the building day and night, and to also to serve the skeleton crew of Agents who always manned the building during the night, to field any emergency call that might come in after hours.

The three agents entered the luncheonette together, and they took a table near the back of the eating area so they could speak more comfortable. A waitress came over and took their orders, and then they started to speak. Commander Murdock started it off by asking Agent Rossie. "Well, I trust the next time we go after Young, we're going to get the sonofabitch?"

"If I have anything to do with it, he's days are numbered I can assure you sir. After seeing what they did to that poor kid yesterday, we have to stop this bunch of damn nuts." He replied.

"It was a real shame to lose one of our snitches in this operation, now we're going to have some trouble finding Young in his next rathole he's going to hold up in. He's going to be three times as hard to get a hold of now that he understands we're really coming after him this time."

"It might not be as hard as you may think it is to find him again sir, I still have my snitch in operation. In fact Ralph, I'm still waiting for him to get back with me. So far I placed three different calls out to him, and it's unlike him not to respond to my call. I don't know what might be going on with his ass, but right after we eat. I'll give him another call and see if he knows where Young might be held up now." He replied to his control.

"You don't think Young might have got to him and took your contact out as well, do you? If it's like you just said and you don't understand why he didn't get back to you as yet, Rossie." Commander Murdock questioned his favorite special agent as he waited for his reply.

"I really doubt that because my snitch isn't a damn junkie, he just does it for the money I guess. But he never let me down as yet, and he always seems to find out what I need from him, and since I didn't get in touch with him yet, he has no idea what the devil I might want from him. So that would take him out of Young's rotten eye if he thought my snitch was giving me the information on where he might be hiding at, Ralph." He reported to his Commander.

"I guess you have a pretty good point there at that Rossie. But I was going to send you two birds home to sober up right after we had something to eat. I had no intentions of making you two work for the rest of the day, but if you want to try your snitch. Then I want the both of you to put yourselves in for the entire day. I'm not going to have you guys working for free around here you know. Let's eat, and then you guys can decide if you want to put the whole day in trying to get hold of your damn snitch. Okay Agent Rossie and you too Fugiwara, I'm going to give you two putting the Batterman's murder case on the back burner for the time being until you wrap up this Young mess. But once you guys are done with his ass, I want you two to put your noses to the grindstone and work like hell on the Batterman case until you find the murderer for me.

"Don't go worrying any about anyone riding my ass over this damn murder case, I'm a big boy and I can handle any damn candy ass Politician trying to bust my horns over this case, and the day I can't handle them, is the day I give up and quite this damn day job for good." Murdock said as he made room for the waitress to put their plates down on their table.

When they finished eating, Commander Murdock threw three twenties down on the table, and they headed for Rossie's office. Even though he and Agent Fugiwara decided to stay until they finally reached Rossie's snitch, Murdock had no intention of putting in the full day, even though he gets paid for the day even if he showed up for work for only fifteen minutes. He waited for his two agents to get comfortable then he announced to them. "Well guys, stick a fork in my ass because I'm done for the day. I'll see you two guys Monday morning bright and shiny, and sober I trust may I add." With that said he turned and rushed out of their office.

"Well that went much better than I ever expected with the Big Growl today. I guess he's getting a little soft in his old age finally." Agent Fugiwara remarked with a grin, and then he asked Rossie. "Well, what the hell are we going to do, are we going to stay here until you hear from your damn snitch or what, Rossie-san?"

"I'd like to try him at least once before we leave for the day. I want to see if he knows where Young is hiding at. It seems Murdock has the same want for Young's ass as he does wanting the Batterman's case done with. Give me a second so I can try him again, and if he doesn't answer my call this time then we can leave. I'm starting to feel almost normal again, Fugiwara-san."

"Help yourself I'm doing fine just watching you work like this. I can watch you work all day man. You know how I am, I'm a real workaholic, when someone around here mentions work, I go out and get drunk..." Fugiwara smirked before he was interrupted by Rossie offering him.

"Maybe you should give up drinking and running around on your lady like you're doing as well, buster. One of these days she's going to catch you fooling around on her, and she's going to cut your balls off on you buddy. Just give up drinking and fooling around asshole."

"You know I must be suffering from anal blindness all of a sudden, because I just don't see my ass doing either of what you just bitched at me about, my friend."

"You're just plain old nuts I see my friend." Agent Rossie replied as he picked up the phone in one hand, and he dug through his index cards with the other, looking for his snitch's number. Finding it he quickly dialed the phone, and then leaned back in his chair and listened to the phone ringing. On the fifth ring, a sleepy sounding voice offered. "Yeah?"

"It's about fricking time you decided to answer your damn phone Billy, Billy Barnwell. This is Rossie, I need to talk to you, it's very important."

"You got me on the phone, so talk Rossie. What do you want man? I'm busy at the moment? Why are you calling me on a Saturday for man? I didn't know you guys worked the weekend?"

"I work when I have to work! Look Billy listen up I'm looking for a guy and I need to know where he's hold up..."

"I'm sure there's some bars around here where you can go and find a guy for yourself, Rossie." The snitch remarked, trying to be funny with the special agent.

"What the hell are you trying to be around here, a fricking wiseass buster? This isn't a damn joke and I need to find this guy real pronto like, buster. This guy did enough damage and I have to put a stop to him quick." He actually growled at his snitch over the phone.

"Who are you looking for this time Rossie?"

"I'm looking for David Young..."

"Whoa man, why don't you try looking for Jimmy Hoffa while you're at it, because you're not going to find either one, not with the word that's going around on the streets, man? The word's out on the streets, anyone who tries to turn his ass in to the cops, is going to find not only his ass dead, but his entire family is going to pay the same price for his giving Young up to you guys. I didn't know it was the Feds after his ass man. Hell, so many of the usual hang-a-rounds on the street have cut out, because they don't want to get caught in the crosshairs if you guys try and take Young down. I promise if you try, you better have plenty of body bags with you man, you're going to need them." The kid offered to the agent as he tried to warn him to back off on Young.

"I take it you know something about this lousy prick I want. If you know where he's hiding at, I need to know about it right now man. I'll make it well worthwhile to you buddy."

"How much can you pay me this time? Because I have to ask myself how much my life is worth, because if I tell you where this guy is hiding at, I'm as good as dead as soon as I tell you man. I happen to think my life is worth a helluva lot more money than you can possibly pay me, man. I suggest you just back off his ass and hang around and sooner or later he's going to surface then you won't need my help to find him, and I won't get killed for helping you out man."

"I don't have that kind of time to wait for him to just surface someplace on his own. I have to stop him now, before he kills or has someone else killed around here, and I'll tell you this buddy. If you happen to know where Young's hiding at and you don't tell me where he is. Then if he kills another person, I'm going to take you in as another actor in that murder. This is how important it is for me to get this fucking guy, mister." Agent Rossie warned him.

"That's a mighty weak threat there, just look at what Young did to Corey. Word on the street says Corey informed on Young and Young cut his face off. He actually skinned his face off his fucking head man. Do you think you threatening to arrest me worry me as much as having my friggin face cut away from my head? I just wonder if Corey was still alive when they did that to him man. I don't think I can help you out with this one man." Rossie's snitch cried at him.

"Look Bill, if you help me out here, I'll get Young and the rest of his bums and then you won't have anything to worry about from him..."

"Don't hand me that shit man. If you put Young in jail, he has long arms and he can reach out and get me from the jail cell, and I'll be dead and you couldn't help or protect me from him."

Fugiwara listened as Rossie argued with his snitch, and felt if he was a snitch, he would not give Young up either. Not after seeing what he and his bodyguards did to Corey yesterday.

"Look Bill, I don't have the time for this shit you're giving me here, how the hell will Young know if you give him up? The only way he could possibly find out is if you open your own mouth and you tell someone, buddy." He instantly stopped speaking when he thought he heard someone say something to his snitch, and he heard the person speak over the phone.

"Honey, what are you doing on the phone, hang up and come back to bed. I only have off today and tomorrow and then I have to start work again. I want to sleep more. Hang up the phone and come play with me, Billy." The young lady he was sharing an apartment with grumbled as him as she rested her head on his shoulder, and then she tried to hang up the phone on him.

"Will you knock it off, I'm doing something here and it's important. Go back to bed and when I'm done with the call, I have some fun with you." Then the snitch went back to speaking with the agent. "C'mon man, I can't do what you want me to do, it's too fucking dangerous. This guy can hurt you even if he was six feet deep. How the hell can you possibly protect me if he finds out I told you guys where he is? You guys didn't protect Corey and look what they did to him."

"I really hate to go this route on you Bill, but you're not giving me much choice in the matter. If you don't help me here, I can just have a slip of the tongue in the right place in front of the right guy. Then you'll surely have something to worry about from Young and his Gombas. So if you don't help me, you'll have the same problem and fears facing you as you'd have if you did help me out with this one." He actually smirked as he waited for his reply.

"Man, that's really a shitty thing to do to me man. That sucks the big one I'm telling you Rossie. I never thought you would ever hang me out to dry like this man. You suck Rossie, and if you were standing in front of me right now, I'd kick your fucking ass from one street corner to another man. Man, you're really putting my ass out there, if you did that than every Tom, Dick and Harry on the damn street would be looking to collect the bounty Young would surely put on my head, if you ever let that bullshit story lose out on the street man."

"Then you might as well tell me what I need to know and take your chances that way, buddy. Or you can just go down the way I'll sell you out here, Bill. You know I'd never do anything as scummy as this is, if I didn't really need this fucking information from you my friend."

"With a friend like you who the hell needs any enemy? Okay Rossie, give me the weekend and I'll see what I can do for you man. If I find out where he's hold up, one way or the other I'll get the information to you. Keep the front window of your car down about a quarter of an inch at all times man. If I find out anything about your target, I'll slip the paper through the slit in the window and then I'll disappear like I was never around you, man."

"That sounds like a plan to me Bill. You do remember where I live, right buddy?"

"Sure I do, I have been to your crib I don't remember how many times in the past man. You will leave the damn money in the same place as you always, right Rossie?"

"I sure will, but only after you give me the information I want from you, buddy."

"Of course man." Bill snapped back at Rossie.

"Of course." He fired right back at his snitch, and then he hung up the phone on him.

When he was off the phone, Fugiwara sat forward and asked. "How the hell did you make out with the little fuck? It seems like he didn't want to help us out this time around, Rossie-san?"

"He was giving me a hard time that was until I dump the big hurt on his slimy ass. He finally came around and he's going to find out what we need to know as sure as shit flows down hill. He wanted the weekend to find out what we need, so I guess we can go our separate ways and I'll see you back here on Monday morning." He suggested to his concerned partner.

"Hell man, I was hoping to come back to your place for the weekend, and maybe get lucky with Wind, buddy." Agent Fugiwara replied as he perked up a bit for the first time today.

"You have about as much chance of pillowing with her as I have at hitting the six numbers in Lotto and I become rich, man. The only way she'll ever have anything to do with you, is if I tell her to pillow with you, and I assure you Fugiwara-san. You'll never hear those words come out of my mouth no matter what. I'll never tell her to do that with anyone but me. I'm not that type of a guy to use a woman like that. But she's a free spirit, no pun intended, and she can do anything she wants to do, and if you somehow find a way to pillow with her, have at her man."

"Wow that was a punch in the stinking guts Rossie-san. But I'll tell you this much Rossie-san, you could've knocked me over with a pubic hair when you started to tell me about Wind. But remembering how she attacked those guys trying to ice (kill) us last week, and how she just popped up when we were again setting up to take Young down. Then recalling how she looked last night and how she moved and acted. I'll believe anything you tell me about her now man."

"Let's get the hell out of here, I seen the inside of this place enough this week. I'll drive you home buddy. You have wheels home, or do you have to take one of the standby vehicles we have parked behind the building. I noticed three vehicles parked in the last parking lot back there and I can run you over to one of them easy enough so I don't have to run you all the way home buddy."

"I guess I'll collect one of the parked cars out back, I turned my other car in for maintenance two days back. You sure I can't come back to your place for the rest of the weekend, I'm not going to head up home in Jersey for one day that's left of this weekend, Rossie-san." He was almost begging his partner to spend the rest of the weekend with him and Wind.

"Give it up or I'll make you walk out to the back parking lot on foot, buster. I know why you want to come home with me. I'm not going to allow you to spend the rest of today and tomorrow drooling all over Wind's chest. Go to your apartment you have here in Washington and get some sleep, you're still half drunk from our drinking party last night my friend."

"Boy, you're not getting to be much fun any longer I tell you Rossie-san. I know what you're doing. You want to keep Wind all to yourself."

"So!"

"So I'm going to my apartment and seep it off, and then I'm going out tonight and look for my own Wind and have some fun for myself with her, buddy."

"You do that, C'mon and I'll run you out to the back parking lot so you can pick up a car to get around in. I'll see you Monday morning, have fun tonight."

FBI SPECIAL AGENT ROBERT ROSSIE'S APARTMENT

Wind was in a good mood, mainly because she enjoyed watching the two men make perfect fools of themselves last night drinking. While her Lord reported in to work this morning, she spent her time cleaning up the apartment. She hung up his clothes, and placed the soiled clothes in the bathroom so he could wash them in his machine he used, and she cleaned the glasses they use to drink with. When she had everything proper in the apartment, she returned to the center of the living room and she knelt and then went deep into her usual meditation. This was the way she spent her time while waiting for her Lord and Master to return to his castle and her.

Agent Robert Rossie parked in his allotted parking slot, and then he rushed into his apartment. He was concerned with what she might be doing. He opened the door and found her in her usual kneeling position and she had her eyes closed tight. She was so deep in her meditation she did not even realize her Liege Lord had just walked into the apartment. He did not want to startle her by just walking up to her and resting his hand lightly on her shoulder, so he called out to her softly. "Wind-san, Wind, I'm home for the rest of the day."

Her eyes fluttered open and when they focused in on his face, she immediately smiled pleasantly at her Lord, and then she bowed slightly to him.

"You look lovely as every today Wind-san." He offered as he enjoyed seeing her still dressed in the short light blue Kimono. She still did not have held closed with the Obi still resting on the floor where Agent Fugiwara had allowed it to slip through his fingers, when he removed it from her so he could see what her exquisite body looked like naked.

Her cheeks actually blushed red over the beautiful compliment her Liege Lord had just offered her. Throughout most of her life, no one she was involved with ever looked at her as a woman. They always looked at her as a threat again their manhood, or they were in competition against her. Or they were always making up terrible stories about her to weaken her position in the eyes of Lord Kawasomeru. Or she was used one way or the other, sent out to kill anyone her new Masters of the sword wanted dead for any reason they wanted that person dispatched.

She had one true lover in her life, and that was Captain Katsunoke Seisakajo who came from the ranks of the Samurai part of her horse Army. True, she shared her pillow with her Lord Kawasomeru as he grew old many times when he called her for the Floating World, and she also shared her pillow with the hated Hiromoai Hatanaka, and now she was falling in love with the latest Master of her killing sword and spirit. So when he paid her a lovely compliment about her person, she was thrilled to death that someone truly looked at her as a woman and not a weapon.

He moved deeper into the apartment and when he was standing at Wind's side, he reached out and offered her his hand. She immediately took hold of it and he helped her to her feet, and then drank in her beauty because of the way her Kimono hung on her body, barely keeping any part of her fantastic body from his view. Once she was standing by his side he offered her.

"Wind-san, I hope my partner and I didn't insult you in any manner last night. I'm afraid I drank a little too much and might have overstepped my bounds with you. And I didn't keep a close eye on my partner either, and knowing how he always is with women, I'm quite certain he must have thrown a pass at you at least once last night, Wind-san."

"A pass at me my Lord?" She asked confused, not knowing what her Liege Lord meant by the last phase he used on her to describe something to her.

"Yes a pass at you Wind-san. Let me see how I can explain this to you so you know what I mean by that. A pass is when a man says something kind to you, just to try and talk you into his pillowing with you. Sometimes we call it wine and dinning a lady to get her in bed." Agent Rossie smiled at the still confused looking female Warrior.

As she thought over what her Lord said to her, a smile crossed her lips as she figured out what he was trying to tell her. This thought also made her feel more like a woman, to know even her Lord's favorite General wanted to share her pillow with her, and make the wind and rain to her.

He let go of her hand and then he went to the kitchen and made himself a cup of coffee, because he was still feeling a little lightheaded from his drinking last night. She followed and was standing right behind him and when turned to go to the table, he almost bumped right into her. "Whoa, that was close I didn't know you were standing behind me. Let's sit at the table."

She kept her eyes looking at the table top because she did not want to be staring directly at her Lord without speaking. That was considered rude to most Japanese people.

He looked at Wind and then asked her. "Why do you look so sad Wind-san?"

"She looked up and replied. "I'm not sad my Lord, I was giving you privacy to enjoy drink."

"Oh, Wind-san, I think I'm going to go back to sleep as soon as I finish off my coffee, Heaven knows I didn't get very much sleep last night, and what I did get was so deep it has left me overtired today. Will you came back to bed with me, I would really like that."

"I would be most honored to share my Lord's bedroll with him again." She said in an anxious tone of voice, hoping her Liege Lord was asking her if she wanted to pillow with him now. She immediately got up and rushed to the bedroom and turned down the sheets. Then she quickly went into the bathroom and washed herself and when she came out she sat down on the side of the bed. She then waited for her Liege Lord to enter the bedroom and take her, because they did not make the wind and the rain last night, because he was too drunk to make love to her. She was hoping beyond hope she was reading her Lord correctly, and he wanted to make love to her.

He quickly finished off his coffee and he left the cup resting on the table as went into the bedroom and found her sitting on the bed completely naked. He stood right in front of her, her face almost even with his crotch, and then he put his hands on her shoulders and lightly shoved her backwards. She landing flat on her back and he immediately put his head between her legs and went to work on her to her glee, as she enjoyed what he was doing to her.

Sunday was more or less a lost day for both Wind and Rossie who read and watched television and bothered Wind and the both of them shared a very pleasant day together.

MONDAY, JUNE 29th, 1996 FBI HEADQUARTERS, WASHINGTON D.C.
ZERO SEVEN FORTY FIVE HOURS

FBI Special Agent Robert Rossie entered his office with two cups of coffee, one for him and the other for FBI Special Agent Shinnosuke Fugiwara who was not in yet. So he placed his coffee on Fugiwara's desk, and then he went to his desk and checked his phone call messages, to see who might have called and if his snitch checked in with him yet. When none of the phone calls were that important to him, he brought his computer up on line and checked his E'mails. There was not much of interest in those either. So he settled back to enjoy his coffee.

No sooner than he started to relax a little before starting work, Agent Shinnosuke Fugiwara came walking in the office, and he too was carrying two cups of coffee and laughed when he saw his cup restring on his desk already, and then he remarked. "I see we both had the same idea this morning my friend. I brought you a cup of coffee as well Rossie-san."

"Put it down in front of me, because I have a gut feeling today is going to be a two cup day. Did you happen to notice if the Big Growl was in his office yet? When I came in he wasn't here yet, but I figure he'd be right in and busting our horns when he comes in today, Fugiwara-san."

"Then I won't let you two birds down when I start busting your horns this morning mister. And what the hell did I tell you about that damn name you two birds are trying to pin me with? I didn't notice any report concerning you getting in contact with your damn snitch Saturday. Were you successful making contact with him, Agent Rossie?" Commander Murdock snapped as he entered the office and took one of the extra cups of coffee and started drinking it himself.

"Yeah, help yourself we knew you were coming in so we got you a coffee, Ralph."

"In a pig's ass you got me a coffee, don't try and bullshit a bullshitter mister. I asked you if you were able to make contact with your damn snitch Saturday, Rossie?"

"I made contact with him before we left the office Saturday…"

"Then why the hell didn't I see a god damn report from you on that damn connection sitting on my desk this morning, mister?" Murdock shot right back at Rossie in an angry tone of voice.

"I had a long conversation with him Saturday." He replied as he ignored the angry response from his control as he went on with his report. "I'm waiting for a call back from him sometime later today. He was very hesitant to assist me on this one, he was concerned on what happed to Fugiwara-san's snitch, and after a hard push by me he decided to help me out. He told me he was going to call in sometime today, and that's why I didn't make a 353 report on my contact with the snitch, sir. I was planning to make a complete report when he informed me of what he found out for me over the weekend, sir. I didn't see making a half a report to clutter up your desk with."

"I'll take that as a good excuse, even though I don't believe a word you just uttered at my ass, buster. I trust I'll be hearing from you the moment you hear from your snitch later today, mister." Commander Murdock was living up to his name and he growled at Agent Rossie this time.

"Of course you'll be hearing from me as soon as I finished my conversation with Bill, and he has informed me of what he found out about Young and the rest of his stinking group of killers, sir." He again ignored the way his Commander was speaking to him.

"In that case, thank you for the coffee, and I'll be waiting to hear from you later today mister." With that said, Murdock turned and his heels and he left the office and two agents, still sipping on the stolen cup of coffee, proud of himself the way he just jumped on his agent.

"Well I guess you made his day for him, now he'll be in a great mood for the rest of the day since he tore you a new asshole already this morning, Rossie-san. What are we going to do for the rest of the day? I don't see any reason we should still work on the Batterman's murder case, now that we know who killed him and the others back in Japan, my friend."

"Keep your words low will ya buddy, I don't need what we're talking about being picked up by Murdock's stinking radar. That guy can hear a dollar bill falling on the snow. Just because we know who killed Batterman, there's plenty we can still investigate in that murder case, like how Batterman was able to work around all the Japanese laws stopping anyone not Japanese from owning a Japanese business in Japan. Also, what was going on between Batterman and Asahiko Yurkowa-san and Hiromoai Hatanaka, and why he used Wind like he did? All we have to do is just look busy until I finally hear from my damn snitch, Fugiwara-san. Then we'll have something we can really sink our teeth into my friend." He replied to his partner.

"That works fine for me. How was your weekend with that beauty, Rossie-san/"

"I might as well answer that question, because I know you won't stop nagging me until I tell you everything me and Wind did over the weekend. We made love as soon as I got home from the office, and then we went to bed. We woke after six and had supper then we fooled around on the living room floor, and before you ask, she did me with her mouth good and proper, nosy…"

"Holy shit, you mean to tell me she sucks dick too, man does she come well trained, Rossie-san. Man are you one lucky sonofabitch to have such a beauty servicing you, and protecting your ass at the same time, buddy." Agent Fugiwara cried in an excited voice.

"Not only does she, but she does it the best I ever had. Sunday we made love twice and she tried to get me going again for a third time around with her mouth. But I just didn't have it in me to raise to the occasion…"

"She didn't have it in her either I see. You should have called me, I would've come right over and stood in for you, and made her happy." He interrupted him for a second time now.

"I sure you would've. Anyway, that's how I spent my weekend. Are you satisfied, or do you want me to make some shit up to get you off on, Fugiwara-san?" He smirked at his partner.

"No, that's good enough I guess, just knowing she works you over with her mouth was all I wanted to know about her and your weekend at that, my friend."

The phone rang and he nearly jumped out of his skin, and he instantly grabbed it while thinking it might be his snitch finally checking in with him. As soon as he heard the voice on the other end, his shoulder's sagged a little as he replied to the caller. "No, this isn't Agent Patterson, sir. He's working on a case out of Washington at the moment and he's not expected back for quite a while I believe. I'll inform him you called and give him your number when I hear from him, sir.

I'm certain he'll be back to you the first chance he gets when he checks in, sir." Then he hung up and looked at his partner and moaned at him.

"That was someone looking for Agent Patterson, it might have been one of the people he relies on getting his information from by the sound of his voice. He sounded young and kind of excited when I was speaking with him." Then he checked the clock and complained again. "Crap, it's already after ten already, I thought the first call in today would be Billy reporting in to tell me what he found out about Young and his mob of rats, dammit."

"He'll check in soon enough I guess, unless Young found out he was speaking with us, and he did the same thing to him as he did to my snitch Corey. I still want to get his ass for that killing. Why the hell he just couldn't kill the kid outright and be done with it, no he had to hack off his damn face. I want him real bad for that move, Rossie-san." He growled hotly, not even trying to hide the anger he had for Young and everyone he had on his payroll, as he crumbled up a page and threw it at the wastebasket in anger.

"Hang in there Fugiwara-san, we'll get him soon enough. Then you can do whatever you want to him, as long as you leave enough of him left alive so he can stand trial for all his crimes." His partner offered, trying to calm him down a little.

Another agent looked into the office, and he announced to Rossie he was looking for Patterson, and he informed him he and Fugiwara took over his office.

"Agent Patterson seems to be a pretty popular dude all of a sudden I believe Rossie-san." He grumbled as he looked at his partner, and then grinned at Rossie.

"I guess so from the looks of it this morning."

FBI SPECIAL AGENT ROBERT ROSSIE'S APARTMENT

Wind was starting to get absolutely bored to death with all the hanging around the apartment day after day she was doing lately. She knew in another two days she would have to return to the Floating World for an entire day, and she was not looking forward to that experience again. It always made her feel so bad to see so many young Samurai who died in their Master's service. She did not like the new breed of Samurai suddenly showing up in the Floating World. There was so many of them coming in with no honor and respect and terrible wounds on their bodies, and they had no true Master they shared their allegiance with. Even the Kami did not like the new breed of Samurai that killed without the sword, and they killed without thought or honor, they just killed for the sake of killing. So the Kami gave them the lowest areas of the Floating World to occupy, and the jobs no other respected Samurai would ever soil his hands with.

She did not even want to meditate any longer for the day that seemed like it was all she did. She wanted so much to be with her Master and share in all facets of his life, not just pillowing and coming to his side when he was in danger of death. She wanted to meet others that her Liege Lord called his friends and share their lives with. She wanted to be part of his entire life, share everything with him, love him and have him love her as much as she did him now.

Each and every small sound she heard from outside the building, and even inside, always constantly made her jump and instantly to go on guard. She was extremely concern someone might come into the apartment and she would have to hide. Or someone might come to try and attack her Lord or steal from him, and she had to be ready to protect his castle as well as his life at all times. It was fast becoming terribly stressful for her to be in the apartment she thought was her Lord's castle every second of the day. Unless was out with her Lord, or she had to go and protect his life though the eye of the sacred amulet.

She was fast becoming quite stir-crazy, and lately she even found herself speaking to herself more than once, and she was becoming very concern with being cooped up inside the apartment to the point she was becoming slightly looking forward to going back to the Floating World for something else to do with her life. Just to break up the boredom she was suffering from, she so missed the cherry blossoms of her beloved Islands of Japan and the constant sea breeze she so enjoyed when the breeze was up on the Islands.

Above all else she wanted to enjoy, she wanted to be like everyone else in the world, free to go where she wanted, to see what she wanted and to love who she wanted to be with. Above all, she wanted to be with her Lord and Master and enjoy life with him, all matters life with him. She was becoming so confused that she finally had to order herself to go back to the life she knew so well, and wait for the call of the sword to summon her again.

CHAPTER TWENTY TWO
FBI HEADQUARTERS WASHINGTON D.C.

It was almost 11:30 A.M. by the time Agents Robert Rossie and Shinnosuke Fugiwara returned to the office, instead of going to the luncheonette for a break, they both had more coffee and ordered lunch for themselves and brought it back to the office, so Rossie could man the phone just in case his snitch called them around noon.

Both men did anything to eat up their time waiting for the informant to check in. They were becoming just as bored waiting for the call, as Wind was while waiting for her Lord to return to her. Twice, Commander Murdock checked in, and Rossie had to tell him they were still waiting for the call to come in, and he went back to his office mumbling, he was that angry waiting for any word where Young might be hiding at.

Agent Fugiwara was just starting to unwrap his hamburger when the phone rang, and he looked at Rossie and he placed an angry look on his face. Because he was just about to start eating as well and he growled at the other agent. "It figures, this have to be that pain in the ass because my damn lunch is going to get cold on me now." As he reached for the phone

Agent Fugiwara continued to start at Rossie as he waited to find out who was calling in.

"Yeah, this is Special Agent Rossie, who's this."

"Agent Rossie, this is Billy man did you put me in hot water all weekend. I had to talk to fifteen people to find out where Young is at. It was hell, because I had to act like I needed a fix, and most people know I don't go screwing around with that shit, man. The other half of the guys I had to bullshit with, wanted to know why I wanted to know about Young and his people. Two of them warned me I better watch out going around asking anything about Young. I'm telling you Agent Rossie, you better keep your word and make certain nothing happens to me, man."

"Calm down a little will you Billy, I got your back alright."

"Yeah, and I'm certain that's where Young is going to stick a knife in, my back. Agent Rossie, I was never so scared in all my life, this has to be the most dangerous thing I have ever done in my entire life man. I can't believe I ever allowed you into talking me to do this one for you man. I know my life is in danger, and I'm going to end up just like Corey did, with my fucking face cut off and then left to die a very slow death.

I'm scared to death Rossie, sacred I tell you. Agent Rossie, I have the information you wanted, but I really don't want to give it up or work with you on this one. That's how scared I and my girlfriend are over what you had me do for you."

"C'mon man, if you went so far as to find out what I needed then it's too late to stop now. If you're worried about Young coming after you, you did enough for him to do that. So I don't see any reason for you to hold this information back from me. I can't see why you're so scared or concerned over this one. I'm going to take Young and the rest of his killers out of circulation once and for all, and anyone who'll carry out his orders once he's in jail, will go underground. Because I'm sure as hell going to keep the pressure up on any of his people, or anyone else who might want to work with or for him, Billy. C'mon man, I need that damn information you're trying to hold back on me now." He actually started to get a little angry with him on the phone.

"Sure, it's easy as shit for you to say that shit to my ass, because it's not your ass on the line man. No one in their right mind is ever going to try and take down a damn Fed, if he has any brain cells working for him. I don't have that luxury and I don't have body armor to walk around in, to protect myself if some junkie is pissed off at me because as you said, you're going to take Young and his empire down. Do you have any idea how many damn junkies he's supplying, and each one of them junkies will be coming after my ass once you take Young out of circulation man? What the hell happens to me then? What happens to me then? How do I walk around and live when I know one of these days, some junkie strung out because you took Young down, decided to make me pay for that? What do I do then, how do I live under those conditions?"

"C'mon Billy, you're getting all worked up over nothing and you're giving Young and his horde too much credit. I'm telling you, once we take down the head of the snake, the rest of the snake will die, and anyone we missed when we come after him and the rest of his people, junkies included. Will disappear in the woodwork so we don't find the bastards and take them in or do them in. Besides Billy I have to correct something you said. You said no one in their right mind would try and knock off a Fed, but if you remember right. A few weeks ago we got involved in a firefight with Young's goons and they didn't hesitate for a second to engage us in battle.

"So you see, we're on the front of the dime, but the only difference between us and you, we're constantly standing on the front of the dime, and we can get knocked off at a drop of a hat. Yet we're always doing the right thing to get this crap off the streets. So you might as well do the right thing and give me that information you collected. If you intended to hold this information back from me then why did you go through trying to find out what I needed to know for you in the first place, Billy? Now I need that god damn information from you, and if you know what's good for your ass, you'll give it to me right now. I don't want to make this hard on you Billy, but I will do whatever the hell I have to do, if you continue to give me all this damn grief over what I need from you, buddy." He warned his snitch over the phone in no uncertain terms this time.

"I don't give a crap about all that shit and you guys. I'm more worried about myself and my girlfriend. If Young puts the word out on the streets I was the one who fingered him, every drug addict, every small time crook, everyone who might be out to impress him, will be coming after my ass.

And I don't see you guys being able to protect me if he does come after me. Like I just told you, I had a hell of a time trying to find out anything about where he was hiding now. If just one of the people I spoke with over the weekends tells him I was asking about him, he'd immediately put the word out on me, and then my life wouldn't be worth a plug nickel, Agent Rossie. I'm still not comfortable about giving up what I know about where he's hiding."

"I'm beginning to start figuring you out Billy. What's this shit all about, are you trying to jack up the money I give you for any information you give me or what, buddy? You know I always take good care of you when you give me something good, and if you know where Young is held up then I'll take good care of you this time. This is how important this stinking information is to me." Agent Rossie fired back at his snitch as he held him in his angry stare for the moment.

"You really think this is about money to me? As far as I'm concerned, you can shove your money up your ass. What the hell good would any amount of money do me if my face is slit off my skull, and I was left to die a very slow death? Can money but me a new life for damn sake. I'm more worried about my life than the few pennies you plan to give me for what I know about Young, and what he's planning to do to any cops who try and arrest him, Agent Rossie."

"Now you have to tell me what you found out about Young and the rest of his gang of damn thieves and murderers, Billy. If he's threatening any law officials, I need to know about it immediately. I'm warning you Billy, if you don't tell me what you found out, I'm going to have a judge swear out an arrest warrant for your ass. Let me tell you something Billy, if I arrest you, and you give me what I need to know. How long do you think it'd take Young to figure out you're the one who gave him up to us, and he'll surely come after you? Then the only think you can possibly hope for, is we getting to him before he gets to you, asshole."

"You'd really do that to me after all the fricking help I gave you before this one, Agent Rossie? Man do you really suck all of a sudden man. Are you really trying to get me killed or what? And it's not so much for me, but I don't want anything to happen to my girlfriend, she's good people man. I can't believe you're pushing me this hard when it could cost me my life at a drop of a word, Agent Rossie. I still don't think I want to tell you what I know man."

"I'm starting to get real tired of all this damn stalling you're doing here Billy. This is the first time you ever gave me any trouble with what you found out for me. I'm warning you Billy, don't make we get a warrant out for your arrest. That's going to get you stuck in jail for up to five days, and I can more than likely get it bumped up to ten days before you can get bail, and your girlfriend would be able to get you out. But that'll leave your girlfriend out in the open while you're being held in jail, buddy. I'm warning you don't make me go this route with you man." He warned his informant with anger dripping in his voice. Showing the kid he was able done with all the bantering they were doing about the information he had for him.

"You'd really do that to me man? How the hell can you possibly threaten me like that? Isn't this illegal what you're threatening me with here, Agent Rossie?"

"Look Billy, I'll do whatever the hell I have to do, threaten you anyway I have to, to get that damn information you have because that's how important this damn case has gotten, and how much we want to take this Young fella and the rest of his mob down, and get them of the damn streets to make

Washington a safe place to be living in again. Now are you going to tell me what I need to know, or do I have to go down a road I don't really want to travel down with you?"

"What other choice do I have but to tell you want you need to know from me, Agent Rossie?"

"Then stop pussyfooting around with me and tell me for god's sake will ya before I die of old age here, Billy." He demanded over the phone from him.

"I'm going to remember this Agent Rossie and I don't think I'll ever help you out again for the rest of my life. Not with the way you're putting my life in danger here, man."

"You're still stalling my ass here Billy. If you don't tell me what I need to know, I'll leave my office and go down stairs and swear out a warrant for your arrest. Then I'm going to give that warrant to my partner who'll march it over to the courthouse and hand it over to a Judge to sign it. Once its sign, I'll give it to the local Police and within two hours I swear your ass will be in sitting in jail, and your girlfriend is going to be out there all alone without you or us able to help her any. If Young decides you're the guy who put the finger on his ass and he sends a few of his horde out to visit your girlfriend, you'll only have yourself to blame. I'd hate to go this route with you, but I want that fucking information you found out for me, mister. Enough of this bullshit and just tell me what the hell I want to know, now dammit!"

"I hate you because of what you're forcing me to do Agent Rossie, and this is the last time I'll work with your ass. Anyway, this is what I was able to find out. I was told Young and about fifteen of his usual and best bodyguards moved their operation to the commercial trucking area over on West Street and 9th Avenue by the old Wal-Mart district off Rosemount Avenue…"

"That's an awful large area you're talking about here Billy, I'm afraid you'll have to narrow it down a helluva lot more than that if you want me to pay for this fucking information you're talking about, buddy." Agent Rossie actually snapped at his informant as he interrupted him.

"Man I hate you for forcing me to do this shit for you Agent Rossie, and you can stick the fucking money up your ass for all I care about it. I just want to be done with you, and then I'm going to get my girlfriend and we're going to get the hell out of Washington as fast as we can get the fuck out of here, and we'll never return."

"Yeah, yeah whatever just tell me what the hell I need to know, and then you can do whatever the hell you want to do with your girlfriend Billy." Agent Rossie fired right back at his informant, and then he waited to hear what he had found out for him about Young.

"Dammit Agent Rossie, I guess I can now see just how damn important I was to you all this time I have worked with you, man. I can't wait to be the heck out of here dammit. Okay, okay before you get on my ass again on me man. I was told Young and the rest of his friends are hold up at a building 1732 West Street, it's a pretty large blue and white building with two large glass doors and a window on each side of the entrance doors. It's a concrete building with two large garage overhead doors on the back end of the building, and it also has two large windows on each side of the building. I believe it has a number of skylights but I can't be sure because no one I spoke with knew what the roof looked like. There are usually a number of tractor trailers parked on the lot with two tractor machines. I did a drive by the building quickly over the weekend..."

"I'm pleased you went by the building over the weekend, because now I want you to come in today, and you and me are going to take a little ride by the building so I can see what it looks like. Then my people can make up our minds how we're going to attack the place, and what we might be facing when we come after Young and his crew hold up there."

"God dammit Agent Rossie, you really want to me get my damn face sliced off don't you man? How many times do I have to tell you I hate this one man? Now you want me to come with you and do a drive by the damn place? Why not make me sit on the damn roof of the car so Young and his people can get a real good look at me, so they know who to come after when you guys attack them, man? C'mon man, I did enough for you by getting this information you needed, why can't you take that and leave me the hell alone now man?"

"Stop crying and grow up will ya, you'll save us both a lot of time if you did. Look Bill, it's twenty after one now, and I know you're fifteen minutes away by foot. Get your ass in here as soon as possible, and we'll take a quick little ride and once you point out the target building to me, I'll be done with you and you can go dark for as long as you want to hide, buddy. You better get your damn backside in here so we can do this, and then I'll let you go with two hundred and fifty dollars in your pocket, my friend." He ordered his informant with a snap in his voice.

"It's really fricking nice to know you value my life as little as two hundred and fifty lousy damn dollars, Agent Rossie. I leaving now for your office, but I tell you I hate this shit and it's going to be the last time I work with you ever again in my life, Agent Rossie. After this one is over with I'm done with this crap I'm telling you Agent Rossie." The young informant complained bitterly at the FBI Agent over the phone.

"Yeah, whatever just get your ass in here, or would you prefer I come out and pick you up? That way you won't have to waste your time coming in and we'll have to leave from here for the drive by of this place. It'll save the both of us some time, my friend."

"That's a good plan and I'd like you to pick me up. I'll meet you at Lex and 3rd Street."

"I'll meet you there in fifteen be there or else it's the warrant mister." Rossie hung on to his informant and then he turned to Agent Fugiwara and offered him.

"C'mon buddy, you feel like taking a quick ride with me partner?"

"Sure thing where we heading Rossie-san?"

"We're heading for Lexington and 3rd Street. We're going to pick up my snitch and then we're going to go and do a drive by of the target building. So we know what the hell we're going to be going up against when we finally go for Young and his people again, Fugiwara-san." He remarked as he stood, and then he waited for Fugiwara to get up and follow him.

Both agents started to head for the elevators and when they walked by Murdock's office he spotted them and bark at Rossie. "Where the hell are you going mister? Did you get anything and if you did, how come you're not clueing me in on where the hell you two birds are going?"

"We're going out to pick up with my little snitch, and once we get his information I'll send you a full report on how we make out with him, Commander. Right now I don't have enough to bother to make out a report for you sir." He offered his control.

"You do that, no one tells me anything around here anymore, dammit." Commander Murdock complained, and then he went right back to work on his computer.

THE FBI PARKING LOT, JUNE 29th, 1996

Special Agents Robert Rossie and Shinnosuke Fugiwara walk out of the building together, and they headed for where Rossie parked his car when he reported to work today. They got in and Rossie drove out of the lot and turned onto the main road heading for the center of downtown Washington. Both agents were in pretty good moods because they were going to get an eyeball on their target building, and then they could return to their office and work out how they intended to assault the building and get at the occupants. As he came down 9th Avenue heading for the corner of West Street, Agent Fugiwara spotted a lone man looking like he was ready to run if you even looked at him the wrong way, and he immediately announced to his partner. "I believe I got him standing by the Arby's restaurant on the corner of West Street."

Agent Rossie looked at where his partner said was their man and he replied. "That's him alright, look at the stupid asshole, he doesn't want attention drawn to him, and yet he's standing there like he just robbed the damn bank." He pulled right up to the corner and Agent Fugiwara reached behind him and opened the rear door for their informant, and he almost jumped in the rear seat and then he ducked down low and snapped at the agent driving. "Let's get out of the area, there's too many damn junkies hanging around the area looking to make a score. I know some of Young's people will be out and about supplying these assholes with drugs, and I don't want to be anywhere near when they come out of the woodwork to sell their crap to these jerks."

Agent Rossie shook his head as he placed the car in gear and drove down West Street looking for the seventh large commercial building constructed on the East South side of the road. Agent Fugiwara was looking for the building and warned Rossie. "Coming up on your left side, it's the next building. Do you want to stop in front of it and I'll raise the hood like we're having some trouble with the car, so you can get a good look at the building in question, Rossie-san?"

"No way in hell should you stop, someone will recognize me Agent Rossie!"

"He's right Fugiwara-san, we can't stop with him in the car it'll be too dangerous for him. Especially if one of his damn goons comes out of the building to see what the hell we're up to, and maybe even offer us some help. I'll just drive by the dump nice and slow, and you check it out but good. Do you happen to have the toy with you by any chance? I forgot to have you pick the damn thing up when we left the office to pick him up."

"I always have the little toy with me anytime we leave the office. No telling if we might come across some hot looking chick I might want to get a picture of for my collection, Rossie-san."

"Will you give it a rest already, you and that damn one track mind of yours Fugiwara-san. I'm happy you have the camera with you, so snap some pictures of the place and we can have the lab boys enhance them and blow them up at the same time so we can really study the structure, and figure out the best way we're going to handle a hot entry into the building."

"You got it Rossie-san just don't slow down enough to draw any attention to us by these assholes. Keep your arms down so I can get a good shot of the place. I wish I was in the back seat so I could get some really good and clear shots of the place."

"Here we go, start taking the pictures now Fugiwara-san. I'm not going to stop or even slow down any slower than I'm already driving now, and I'm going to maintain this speed down the rest of the road like we're trying to find a place of business. Hell, I might even pull into the business three building down from our target building to really throw this flaming assholes off our asses if they happen to pick us up driving down their road like this, and that's exactly what I intend to do over this situation Fugiwara-san."

"That's a good idea there and I suggest you do exactly what you have just suggested my friend. I'm getting some damn good shots of the place. The toy is a great camera for taking some sneaky ass snapshots man. I got enough, move down to that business and pull into their parking lot and we'll go and see what the devil they're selling, Rossie-san."

"Cool, just protect that camera we're coming up to the business."

INSIDE THE COMMERCIAL BUILDING AT 1732 WEST STREET

One of Young's bodyguard keeping the street covered all the while they were in the building, picked up the slow moving car and he intensely watched it, and for a second he was going to give out the alarm. But when the car rolled past their building he opened the front window and stuck his head outside and watched the car until it pulled into a place of business a few building down from theirs. Then he smiled as he pulled his head in and closed the window, and figured the car was going slow because it was searching for the business they just turned into. Breathing in a sigh of relief he continued his surveillance of the road in front of their hideout.

FBI SPECIAL AGENT ROBERT ROSSIE'S CAR

FBI Agent Robert Rossie also breathe a deep sigh of relief as he pulled his car up to the front of the welding shop, and the two special agents got out of the car to carry out their deception as Billy laid down on the floor of the rear seat of the vehicle. The agents walked in the commercial building and a man quickly approached them and he asked. "Can I help you gentleman?"

"Naw, we're just looking around, that's all."

"Well there's not much to see here unless you just want to watch us work some sir. We have nothing for sale in here. We just prefab work for outside on jobs, sir."

"This isn't a store where you can buy some welding stuff."

"No sir, this isn't a wholesale place, we're strictly a prefab place sir." The foreman of the shop replied to the two well dressed men.

"I'm sorry we obviously made a mistake sir." Rossie said as he did not ask the man any other questions as he turned and both men walked out of the building as quickly as they had entered.

The foreman watched the two men leave and then he shrugged and went back to work.

"Say Rossie-san, did you noticed how that dude looked at you? He looked at you like you had two heads or something.

What say we get the hell out of here and head back to the office? We still have to dump your snitch off where he wants to be let off, buddy."

"Yeah, we have to get rid of him before he has a baby in the rear seat of our car." Rossie got in the car and waited for Agent Fugiwara to get in. Then he stared the car and backed out of the parking lot and asked the informant where he wanted to be dropped off at the same time.

"You guys can drop me off where you picked me up, don't make it obvious you guys are Feds."

Neither agent spoke until they returned to where they picked Bill up and Rossie kept the car running as Billy went to get out and Agent Rossie offered him. "I'll call you man."

"Fuck you will, I'm changing my god damn phone number, and I'm not helping you guys any longer." The informant grumbled at the two FBI Agents.

"In a pig's ear you won't help me any longer mister. You can change your phone number all you want buddy, and I'll still give you a call when I need you again, Billy." Rossie smirked at his informant as he watched him quickly get out of the vehicle.

"You just won't get off my damn ass for nothing, will you Agent Rossie?"

"Nope." He replied as he pulled away from the curb and then headed back for the office.

"Man, he's really starting to become a real stinking cry baby lately Rossie-san. For a while there I really thought he wasn't going to help us any longer."

"He can cry all he wants, but he likes the money too much for him to stop working with us, Fugiwara-san. You need anything before we have back to the office?"

"Naw, I'm fine, let's get back. You know the Big Growl has to be eating the furniture by now while he's waiting for us to get back. The man has no social graces any longer I'm afraid."

Agent Rossie laughed at Fugiwara's remark about their Commander.

FBI HEADQUARTERS, WASHINGTON D.C.

Special Agents Robert Rossie and Shinnosuke Fugiwara tried to sneak by Commander Ralph Murdock's office without any luck. As soon as Murdock saw Rossie walk by his open door, he was up and out of his office and barking at both agents at the same time. "Jesus Christ Almighty and miracles, it's about time you two Agents finally got back here, and I trust the both of you people have a rather lengthily report to make to me. I'll take it verbally for the moment, and after I want a full hard copy of that damn report delivered to my office and on my desk, before either of you two birds leave the building for the night."

Both agents stopped, turned and then entered Murdock's office as he stepped aside and allowed them to enter. Murdock followed them in and walked around his desk and plopped down in his chair with all the grace of a sack of potatoes falling from the back end of a truck. Then he motioned for the two agents to seat themselves then he barked at them. "Well, I'm waiting you two! What the devil have you two birds been up to all day, dammit?"

"Commander, we met with my informant and he took us by the building in concern. We took a number of photos and carefully studied the location and surrounding area. Once Agent Fugiwara and myself are back in our office, we'll have the photos developed and enlarged and enhanced, and then we'll discover the best possible way to attack the structure and how many other Agents and local Police we would need to successfully either take Young and anyone he has surrounded himself with in, or we eliminate said person and persons, sir." He offered his control.

"You informant has located where this major purp is holdup I take it, Agent Rossie?"

"Yes Ralph, he informed us Young and an unknown number of what we labeled bodyguards for a lack of a better term to describe them sir. Are holdup, the structure is located at 1732 West Street and 9th Avenue in the Wal-Mart district of Rosemount Avenue. I spotted the building which is the seventh commercial structure on the south side of the street heading West to East, sir. It's a concrete building constructed like a damn fortress though. From the looks of it, nothing short of a one oh five cannon could possibly penetrate the building."

"That's going to give us quite a bit of a problem with getting at the bastards if they're holdup inside a building as you're describing here, Agent Rossie."

"Not exactly sir, the building has a large front door and a pair of huge plate glass windows on either side of the double doors sir..."

"I still see a major problem with us being able to get at these bastards, because if the double doors and plate glass windows are the only way to enter the building. Then we're going to be forced to funnel down to a stream of Agents doing a hot entry of a compromised building from one area of the building, mister." Murdock came back at his agent with this comment.

"You didn't allow me to finish my description of the target building sir. There's a set of large windows on each side of the structure, and there's also three large commercial overhead garage doors at the rear of the structure, obviously used for tractor trailer deliveries to the structure, sir, So that gives us multiple entry points into the structure from all points of the compass sir."

"How large is this damn structure you're aiming us at, Agent Rossie?"

"I'd have to venture a guess, but I say the building has to be over twenty thousand square feet at the least sir. And it was also reported by my informant that he believed there were a number of skylights on the roof of the building, but he couldn't confirm that observation sir." Rossie added.

"Does this structure have a flat roof, or does it have a round shape like a Quonset hut? You know like an old aircraft hanger that slopes down on each side of the building, and making it look like a huge tube type shape structure, mister?"

"It has a flat roof sir."

"Fine, I'll tell you what I'll do to help you formulate your attack plan of the structure. As soon as you're out of my office, I'll order up one of our helicopters and have it do a flyover of the structure, I'll have the pilot film the flyover and he'll do a survey of the entire area surrounding the immediate area of the structure our purps are holdup in, Rossie. That way you can see an aerial view of the area, and see how you want our Agents to approach the target structure, sir."

"That move would help me out immensely Ralph." He retorted with a grin to his control.

"Consider it done then. Do you have any idea when you intend to make the assault on this building and its occupants, Agent Rossie? I need to know so I can order any extra

Agents from the surrounding areas, if we happen to need more than we have available, Agent Rossie, sir."

"I don't know as yet sir. I fear it's going to take me a few days to formulate a positive attack plan for the building and its occupants, sir."

"I suggest you take a full week to make your plans that way we'll know they'll be successful. Do you believe this pack of assholes will remain inside the structure until we're ready to go after them, Agent Rossie?" Murdock questioned his agent, wanting to make certain he had all his "T" crossed and all his "I" dotted, before he allowed any of his agents to jump off and attack this building and the killers holdup inside the building.

"You know full well now that we know where Young and the rest of his creeps are holdup, I'm going to order the building held under tight surveillance until we're ready to go after the building and the ones hiding inside the place sir. I'm going to order at least two Units to stakeout the structure twenty four hours a day, right up to the day we go after them, sir."

"I was figuring on that because if you didn't order a constant surveillance of the structure in question, I sure as hell was going to ordered it to be carried out myself, Agent Rossie. I want these purps under constant surveillance until we go after them. I don't want any of these bastards sneaking out on us this time around. I want all of them at the same time if we can possibly pull it off successfully. Well, I think this is a good verbal report, so why don't you two go to your office and start on what you have planned. I want everyone we have discussed set in motion before either of you two leave the office for the day. Get going so I can make contact with the airport and get one of my chopped in the air so they can start their flyover of the structure in question." Murdock grumbled as he looked at both his agents, trying to get them in motion with his eyes as he reached for the phone to call the airport.

Special Agent Shinnosuke Fugiwara looked at Agent Robert Rossie, and then he gave him a quick head movement, and they both stood and left Commander Murdock speaking on the phone. When they were out of the office, Rossie smiled at Fugiwara and offered. "Man that went far better than I had dared hope for. It's great when he's working on all cylinders with helping anyone setting up and surveillance and operation, Fugiwara-san."

"Yeah, he's real good when he's on your side, but don't get on his shit side, unless you want to eat a lot of what he's made of."

"Wow, what has you so upset with him, he's always been a square peg with me?"

"It goes way back probably when you were still working up in New York. Murdock was my partner and we were after two purps and we split up and he was supposed to be in one area, and he ended up far away from where he was supposed to be at. Well, I ended up engaging the two we were after and I got nicked because he wasn't where he was supposed to be. By the time he got up to me, I got both purps, but I got nicked twice and lost three weeks. Even though I got paid, it still pissed me off because I lost duty time. But what really pissed me off the worst was, he got a commendation for supporting me and I got time off. I think that was why he was elevated to Commander in the D.C. region, because of what went down at that arrest."

"That was something like four years ago I guess, so why the hell don't you put it to rest already? I was wondering why you're so down on the guy. I never knew about this, Fugiwara-san."

"It's a tough thing to get over, knowing he got the kick up the damn ladder off your ass when you were the one who was hurt in the drawdown my friend."

"C'mon and let it go, we have some work to do here, buddy." Agent Rossie remarked as they both entered their office and got down to their work.

FBI SPECIAL AGENT ROBERT ROSSIE'S APARTMENT

Once again Wind found herself bored to death while waiting for her Liege Lord to come back to her. Lately it was getting harder and harder for her to watch Rossie go off to work, and her being forced to remain behind and not be with the one she was falling deeply in love with. She thought about going into meditation just to burn off some more time so the day would go buy faster for her, but she just could not bend her knees to meditate another minute. She already went deep in thought and remembered her past days when she was so an important General in her Liege Lord's powerful and massive Army. She remembered how she was in command of over a thousand Samurai horse soldiers and she was engaging enemy Samurai Warriors in the service of her Lord and Master's arch enemy Lord Wakatsuki, who was always attacking her Lord or his Armies or the eight provinces that were under Lord Kawasomeru's control.

She could not forget the power she once held in her past, and then the fear she commanded when Hiromoai Hatanaka discovered her, and he was in command of her sword and spirit. In all her life, she was always doing something or in command of other Samurai, or always fighting for her Lord and Master in Ancient Japan, and then in modern Japan, and now here she was once again visiting the living world and she was under the command of a new master of her sword and her spirit. But this time she was not being used to protect her Master, or being sent out to destroy an enemy who was believed to be a threat to the one who commanded her spirit.

Now this new and young Commander of her spirit and sword was angry every time she came to his aide and tried to protect his life when he was in war with the small Army of Ko Ku Jie who attacker her Master and his partner. This still confused her and she could not figure out why her new Master always got angry at her whenever she attacked anyone trying to destroy her Master's life. Her entire life was revolving around her deadly skills with her Katana killing swords, and her ability to protect anyone she was ordered to protect by the curse. Now she was reduced to staying inside an apartment so small it was actually giving her cabin fever, and spending day after day trapped within the walls of this small castle.

So she went from commanding vast Armies of wildly charging Samurai Warriors to hiding behind the walls of this apartment. For the hundredth time she walked over to the front window and looked out and watched the horseless carriages go by before her at speeds she could not possibly run to try and keep up with them.

She looked across the street to what her Master had once referred to as a small park, and she watched as a number of little children played together under the ever watchful eyes of their parents and mothers. She breathed in a deep sight of wanting as she found herself wondering how it would be to carry and then give birth to a child. Though she knew how to make a baby, she was never blessed to become with child whenever she had pillowed with the few men she had pillowed with over the vast years her spirit was linked with her sword. A sound suddenly caught her attention and she raised her eyes up towards the sky and she watched an aircraft fly high overhead, and she marveled at the wonderful machines in command of her new Lord and Master. She wondered how many other things her honorable Liege Lord had developed while she was staying for uncountable years that had passed locked in the Ukiyo.

As she continued to look out the window of her Master's apartment and enjoyed watching the children at play, she suddenly started to feel herself growing very weary and weak, and she immediately realized she was starting to be called back to the Floating World by the Kami Gods who controlled the land of wonderment, to be recharged herself so she could once again live in both worlds of the dead and the living, and spend her full stick of time in the Ukiyo.

She understood her Liege Lord would know instantly she was called back to the Floating World, once he found her sword and saw it had returned to its ancient and crumbling state again. In her chest she felt the heavy pressure of despair rapidly setting in, because she wished with all her heart she could stay in the living world forever, and raise a child and love the man she was with. The more she waited, the heavier her chest grew until the light started to develop right in the center of the small living room, and then slowly drifted over her body and engulfed her form.

Once her body was completely engulfed in the light, she immediately disappeared and the only thing that was left behind to contest to the fact she was once there in the living world. Was her favorite Blue full length exquisite Kimono that ended up in a heap of silk cloth lying in the center of the room where she stood when the call to the Floating World was answered by her spirit.

CHAPTER TWENTY THREE
FBI HEADQUARTERS WASHINGTON D.C.
MONDAY, JUNE 29th, 1996.
SEVENTEEN HUNDRED AND
FORTY HOURS (5:40 P.M.)

Commander Ralph Murdock just closed down his computer and locked his safe, and then he walked out of his office like he was angry at the world. He was feeling slightly upset, and he walked down to the office Special Agents, Robert Rossie and Shinnosuke Fugiwara were working on putting everything they did today down on a hard copy paper report as he ordered them. When they returned to headquarters from working with their informant and scoping out the location where the informant reported David Young and the rest of his hired killers were holdup in. He poked his head into their office and then he barked angrily at the two young agents still working on the requested reports for him.

"Okay you two, let's call it a day, tomorrows another day and I want those two reports finished by the end of the workday tomorrow. I don't give a damn if you guys have to work right through the night tomorrow. I need those two reports done by tomorrow's end of work. Call it a day and go home and sleep this time Fugiwara." Murdock's eyes narrowed to mere slits as he stared at his agent, knowing he was always playing with women while his wife waited for him to return home.

Agent Fugiwara just smiled back at his Commander like he was not paying attention to him.

"Don't give me that dumbass stupid look of yours again mister. I've been meaning to have a conversation with you about you playing around with all the women living in Washington for crap sake. It's not right for an FBI Agent to compromise himself like you're doing, buster. One of these days you're going to fool around with the wrong girl, and then you're going to find yourself in a can of hot soup your ass can't get out of. We have to talk and once these two never ending cases, the Young case and Batterman's murder case are done, we're going to have that god damn talk about this shit, mister. Go home you two and sleep like I said, tomorrow's another day dammit." With that said, Commander Murdock turned and walked away from the two agents.

"Well you heard the Big Growl, let's get the hell out of here because I have a date for the night. I met a new chick last night and I want to try her on for a fit, Rossie-san."

"Didn't you just hear what Murdock warned you about screwing every damn woman in Washington, buddy?" Agent Rossie replied as he stood and closed down his computer.

"Screw him where he breaths from. He's just pissed off because he couldn't get a stinking date for himself outside his wife, if you put his face on a can of dog food, man. Just because he can't go out and have some fun, he's not going to start raining on my day. C'mon my friend and let's follow orders for once in our lives and get the hell out of here before he comes back and changes his damn mind, and he decides he wants these two stinking reports done tonight. Besides Rossie-san, I don't have such a beautiful dish like you have waiting at home for me to arrive, I have to go out and find one to spend the night with..."

"The hell you don't have someone waiting for you to come home to. You seem to forget you're married asshole." Agent Rossie fired right back at his partner.

"You're right, I do have someone waiting at home for me, but you also have to remember she's over a hundred miles from where I'm working, so if I don't want to add four hours, two coming to work and two going home every damn day. Spending an extra four hours to my workday, that's why I sit in Washington every day I work. And since I don't like sleeping by myself, I go out and hunt and find a lady to spend the night with, it's that simple buddy."

"You can find many different ways to try and cover cheating on your lady, but when the tires hit the road, you're still cheating on your lady no matter how you want to try and look at it, buster. C'mon, I'm all locked up, so let's get out of here. It's like you just said, I have some hot great looking dish waiting for me to come home and be with her, and since she's a thousand times a helluva lot better looking than you are, and I'd much rather be spending my time with her than spend another minute with your sagging ass, I want to go mister." Agent Rossie groused at his partner as he rested his hand on his shoulder, and he led him out of their office.

They both looked into Commander Murdock's office, and when they noticed it was empty they both walked normal for the elevators in a much better mood.

FBI SPECIAL AGENT ROBERT ROSSIE'S APARTMENT

He pulled up to his apartment and jumped out of the car, happy because he was home and going to see and be with Wind again and by the time he got home, it was ten minutes to eight. He was exhausted and wanted a glass of wine and see her. He opened the door and was stunned Wind was not in her usual position meditating in the middle of the living room like always when he came home. He shrugged thinking she was in the bathroom when he did not see her, so he headed for the kitchen as he called out to her. "Wind-san, I'm home and hungry, I'm surprised you don't have something cooking for us to enjoy. I'm sorry I got stuck working late tonight, it was a hell of a day for me today and I'm dog ass tired. I'm pouring wine, do you want a glass?"

He listened and when he did not get a reply from her, he placed his glass down on the counter and walked to the bathroom door and said again. "I'm having a glass of wine do you want to join me in a glass, Wind-san?" Again he listened for a replied and when he did not receive one he knocked on the door a second time, now growing slightly concerned from her lack of a reply.

"Are you okay in there Wind-san?" He asked, now really worried if she was alright, and then he opened the door and was surprised she was not in the bathroom. Then he looked in his bedroom then checked his bathroom and when he discovered she was not in either, he started to rush around the apartment. He even went to the rear window and looked out over the parking lot to see is she disobeyed him and she was out in the back getting some sun. Thinking about it he would not be upset if she was put in the back of the place as long as she did not have her sword with her. Not seeing any sign of her in the back of the building, he again searched the apartment.

His breathing started to get restricted as he grew even more worried about where she might be, it was at this point he suddenly spotted the hilt of her Katana sword resting on the floor almost hidden by the leg of the sofa, and he rushed for it. Picking it up he was momentarily shocked by the terrible condition of her ancient killing sword, and then he realized she must have been called back to the Floating World. He immediately went into a minor depression, because he was looking so forward to being with her again on what was left of the night. He did not realize he was actually stepping on Wind's favorite Kimono that fell from her exquisite body with the Ukiyo started to call her back to the Floating World.

THE UKIYO OR FLOATING WORLD

Wind found herself standing before the Council of Kami with her namesake, Fujin, the Kami of Wind once again greeting her as she appeared before the council. She appeared before them naked and again, Amaterasu, the Goddess of the Sun who was ready and waiting for Wind to appear before them. Rushed forward and she handed her the Kimono she loaned her the last time she appeared before the council. This time neither Izanagi, the Kami God who created the Islands of Japan and his sister and wife Izanami, were not seated in their usual place on the council.

Wind bowed politely to Amaterasu as he accepted the magnificent Kimono and immediately slipped into it. Once she was dress, the Fujin in his usually angry tone of voice offered her. "Wind-san, you were again ordered back to the Ukiyo to honor all the Kami who have allowed you to return to the land of the living to the call of your deadly Katana sword. It is we who allow you to return to the living to protect your ward from all harm, as to the curse that was placed upon your killing sword by Kawasomeru-Sama which was his right to curse your spirit to the sword for all eternity, thus stopping us from allowing you to be reborn and returned to the earth to honor a new Master. It was a great honor Lord Kawasomeru had bestowed upon your spirit.

"It was a just honor offered to you because you were ordered to commit Suppuku so that the entire Eight sacred Islands of Japan could have peace returned to the realm. But you have to thank we Kami every seven sticks of time (One Week) for the gifts we have bestow upon you, and if you fail to return to the Ukiyo for one stick of time to honor us as all who dwell within the Floating World. Who honor us every stick of time we allow them to remain within the Floating World, until we allow them to be reborn and returned to the service of their true Lord and Masters of the time we release them from the Ukiyo. If you ever fail to return to the Ukiyo when we call, your spirit will be instantly forfeited, and your spirit will be rendered nothing, neither life in the living world, or the Floating World. You will cease to exist in either of the two worlds you move between now. The only thing we shall allow to remain of you will be the memory of your existence in the past times when you honored Lord Kawasomeru.

"No memory of your existence will be recorded of the times you returned to the living world to protect the new Master of the sword and your spirit. Now, you have a few choices to take up your time in the Ukiyo. As an honor to you for your loyal service to the new Master of the sword and your spirit, we Kami deemed it fit to offer you the ability to visit with Lord Kawasomeru for the full stick of time you are visiting we Kami. We can also offer you the right to visit your four General's you were in Command of during your Lord Kawasomeru when he was defending his Provinces from Lord Wakatsuki's invading Armies. We are prepared to allow you to make the decision on how you want to use your time visiting our Kingdom in the Clouds, Wind-san."

"My Lord Fujin, I would deem it a great honor if I was allowed to visit with Lord Kawasomeru for my time remaining in the Floating World. I find it so comforting to my soul to have the honor to speak to my Lord and Master of all time." She bowed politely towards her powerful namesake.

Without replying to his ward, he merely nodded and instantly, she was brought to her original Lord and Master. Lord Kawasomeru's spirit was seated on a cloud and upon laying eyes on his once and only female General, he allowed himself to smile warmly at her as he beckoned her to his side. Once her spirit was seated on a cloud a little lower than her Lord and Master, Lord Kawasomeru offered to her. "As always it does my spirit good to see you again, my Wind. Tell me my faithful Warrior of everlasting time, has anyone from the living world been able to conquer your so powerful a spirit? Surely by now, there has to be one worthy human who was able to win the heart of my General of all times. Are you happy to return to the living world?"

"My Liege Lord, I am always so pleased to return to the land of the living. I so miss the smells, the air, the countless people who run about like the locus that attack the fields in havoc. But I would give all I have, all I own, all this is offered me to be reborn Samurai, and be returned to the land of the living until my time to be recalled to the Floating World is once again requested of me. I long to have a mate to be wanted by that mate, to have that mate's child, and protect that mate from all harm, I would be happy to own a home, shared by my mate and family, to live what was not allowed me when I was in your honorable service, my Lord. I want the life I was never allowed to enjoy, to love, to want to experience. But this foolish Samurai Warrior is acting the fool and longing for things that no Samurai has the right or want to own, because the life of a Samurai is to serve my Lord and Master alone, honorably, faithfully my Lord."

"Your words ring with the sounds of truth to them, because no Samurai is there to want, but to serve, to serve his Lord and Master faithfully. But you are the exception to the rule Wind, to the Samurai Caste, to the old beliefs of ancient Japan. Because you are a female and you have many different wants and longings for, and it is your right to want what any woman of Japan have and enjoyed. Never be ashamed to have want of such things, because you have served your Lord and Master well beyond all honors one Samurai could possibly offer to his and in your case, your honor to. A Samurai is to serve one Master for his entire life, and then he is sent to the Floating World and his stay here is either long or short, depending on how faithfully he had served his Liege Lord. Then he is reborn. Once the Samurai is reborn, he is ordered to search out a new Master by the Kami to serve for the rest of his life, until he is returned to the Floating World, and then he must wait to be reborn again, to find another Master of life to serve.

"But in the heart of the loyal Samurai who has been reborn, is the want to be honored by the Kami and allowed to become a Lord and Master himself, so he could be served by his Samurai. That is the dreams of the Samurai. But in your case you have faithfully served me twice in my one lifetime, and then you were allowed to serve the evil Master Hatanaka who abused your honor. Now you are again given the great honor to protect another Master of your sword. But as a woman, you have many different wants, needs and loves that a male Samurai Warrior longs for. You have a split honor, one to the Lord and Master, and the other to your womanly needs and desires. I must admit that I am very unfamiliar with these many desires of a woman nor do I or would I waste my time worrying or even thinking about these desires of a woman."

"The ways of the Warrior I am very familiar with, and know how to honor or control or even demand from a male Warrior. But a female Samurai Warrior, Ieeee, I fear what is in the mind and control of a female Samurai. But alas, these worries and concern do not pertain to us any longer, for we are spirits to the world of the living, and as such we owe absolutely nothing to the fools of the living world, all but you that is Wind. You must retain your honor for the one who is the new Master of your sword and spirit. I nor any of the Kami can release you from that honor to the sword and my curse. The only way you can possibly ever be released by the curse I had placed upon your sword that is also placed upon your spirit. The Master of the sword is the only one who can release you from your honor of the sword.

"All this new Master of your sword and spirit has to do is snap your deadly Katana blade in two, and then never allow the two ends to ever be mated back together, and your spirit will be free of all earthly bonds. But I warn you Wind, if your spirit is released from the sword, you will be free to soar with the clouds forever. But if your Master ever needs you, or wants you back, all he has to do is take the two ends of the sword and allow them to touch, and the two ends will immediately become one again, and then your spirit will once again be commanded by the call of the sword and your Master's wants or desires. So even after the sword releases you from its call, you can always be called back to the sword by my Master's command. I never understood the power of the curse I had installed upon your most honorable head, Wind-san.

"Wind-san, the Kami are a unforgiving lot to deal with, they have honored the curse I placed upon your honorable head, but they also refuse to allow the curse to be lifted, and if they finally allowed it to be lifted, they have install an opening to reinstate that curse if your foolish Master realizes he made a mistake by releasing you from your curse. I believe the Kami plan to leave my curse upon your head until the last breath of the Universe, and that punishment was never a thought in my foolish mind when I first cursed your blood to the steel of the great Katana blade. Wind-san, you have to honor the call of the sword until the steel has been erased and returned to the soil it was removed from, and there is no way I can change this decree." The still extremely powerful Lord Kawasomeru stopped speaking at this point and then he looked deeply into the tearing eyes of his honorable and so loyal female Samurai Warrior.

All she could possibly think of doing was to bow so politely to her well honored Liege Lord, and she held her bow until her Lord spoke again to her.

"Ahhh... My forever loyal and respectful Warrior, no other Japanese Lord has ever been so honored as you have respected me throughout your short a life in the living world, and you have served me and my curse for longer than the birds fly in the sky and the fish swim in the Ocean. There shall never be another Master of the Eight sacred Islands of Japan to ever be served by one of his faithful Samurai as you have honored and respected me, Wind-san." Lord Kawasomeru suddenly did something that she had never dreamed he would ever do before her, he bow just as polite as she had bowed to him, and he held his bow to her longer than was necessary to be respectful. She never felt so honored in all her days spent in both worlds. She had all she could do not to dare cry before her Liege Lord, because that would be the worst sign of weakness ever to be displayed before such a powerful warlord as her Lord Kawasomeru was, and still is. Her cheeks actually blushed over the great honor her Liege Lord was delivering to her.

When Kawasomeru-Sama sat up from his bow, he smiled at his stunned looking female Warrior, he was as proud of her as she was of him. He clapped his hands together and a young Samurai walked into the chamber they were speaking in, and he offered the two a cup of Cha (Tea). He bowed properly as he served the Lord and female Samurai, and when he was done serving them, he disappeared as quickly as he had entered the private chamber.

When he was gone, Lord Kawasomeru offered. "Wind, I am displeased to inform you that your time in the Floating World has almost run its course, so I suggest you enjoy your Cha with me, and then prepare your heart to be returned to the living world and the new Master of your sword. I shall look forward with all my heart for your next visit to the Ukiyo, and I shall inform the Kami that I request you to be delivered right to me, and that way you can avoid being brought before the Council of Kami. That way we will have much more time to speak of the respects and the old days when we enjoyed commanding vast Armies of loyal Samurai Warriors, and we did battle upon the sacred honor of the battlefields of Japan. Oh to be able to do battle once again against one's hated enemy, those were the days we really enjoyed the most, my Wind-san.

"I see our time of being together is fast running out for the both of us to enjoy, because I can see the color of your spirit lightening up, and you are beginning to fade right before my eyes, my Wind-san. I shall wait not so patiently for the seven sticks of time to be gone, and we can again share words of the great past of our history together again. Be well and happy my Wind-san, because I see you leaving my presence and you shall soon be gone from my presence. Goodbye my Wind-san." Lord Kawasomeru offered just as her spirit disappeared right before his eyes, and again the once so powerful Liege Lord was left alone in the Floating World.

FBI SPECIAL AGENT ROBERT ROSSIE'S APARTMENT

FBI Agent Robert Rossie was lost in his apartment when he discovered Wind was forced to visit the Floating World. Now he realized just how much he was beginning to depend on this female weapon he found. He did not bother to eat he was so upset when he discovered she was in the Ukiyo, and he did not know how much longer she was going to be held there, before she was allowed to return to him. Suddenly his eyes caught what looked like a flash light that shined at him. Then the small light started to rapidly grow in intensity and he stopped what he was doing, and applied his attention to what was rapidly taking shape right in the center of the room.

The light got so strong that he almost had to shade his eyes with his hand, but he refused to take his eyes off what was happing in his living room, and he did not want to miss a second of it. He always feared that one of these times when she was returning from the Ukiyo, ones of these times she might have a hitchhiker follow her to what she called the land of the living, and that entity would go on a slaughter spree. His thoughts were interrupted when her voice came out of the strong glow of light. One of the neighbors knocked on his front door in concern, because she feared his apartment might be on fire. He called out to her that he was fixing a lamp and his neighbor apologized for bother him as Wind spoke to him.

"My Liege Lord I was in fear you might not have known I was called back to the Ukiyo while you were at work. I was so worried about the concern my disappearance might have caused my Lord. I would be so angry at myself if I ever cause your Wa (Harmony) one breath (Second) on the stick of time. My entire life was created for one reason and one reason alone, and that reason is for my spirit, my soul to protect your every second of your life, my Lord and Master."

"I heard all this before Wind-san, but right now I want nothing more than for you to return to a solid form before me, so I might see you again, Wind-san." Agent Rossie ordered her because he was that relieved she was now returning to be with him again.

"To hear your order is to obey that order my Liege Lord, I shall try my best to rush my return to the living world, and to be by the side of my Lord and Master."

He continued to start and the bubbling, churning cloud of light and he was able to see the first signs of her body taking shape within that cloud. He could easily see she was naked again. The more he stared at the churning cloud, the more her body was starting to take a strong shape again. Then the harsh glow started to fade down to just a bright light as the shadow of her fantastic shape quickly took on a more solid form. Even color was returning to her hair as it was being wildly blown about within the cloud. Then the cloud suddenly disappeared and it left her standing right in the center of what was the cloud and as soon as she was solid again, she instantly dropped down to her knees and bowed so low that her nose lightly touched the hard wood floor. She maintained her bow until her Lord and Master of the sword spoke to her.

"Wind-san, it's a pleasure to see you again. I was so concerned when I didn't find you home when I returned here. But when I found your killing sword and saw the condition of it, I knew immediately that you might have been ordered back to the Floating World." He stopped speaking and glanced at the sword he placed on the sofa, and noticed it had also returned to the shape that it looked like it was just created by the ancient maker of the sword. It never ceased to amaze him how the ancient weapon would always return to the newness of just being made, whenever she was allowed to return to the living world, but when she was called back to the Ukiyo the ancient weapon instantly returned to the well age and almost worthless weapon again.

He returned his attention back to Wind and then he added to her. "Will you please sit back because I wish you wouldn't bow so low all the time so the only thing I see of you is the crown of your head. I want you to relax whenever you're within my presence, Wind-san. I want to see your face when I'm speaking to you, or you're in my presence. It's not necessary for you to bow so much to me every time we are together. I want you to feel as my equal, Wind-san."

Wind sat back and then she rested the weight of her body down on her crossed legs, and then she looked at her Master and offered to him at the same time. "I could no more be an equal to my Lord and Master's presence, as I can change the flow of the river water, my Lord. My Liege Lord stands above the mountain tops and only the Kami are an equal to you my honored Lord."

"I'm not going to get in an argument with you again over this same crap. Do you Hitsuyo (Require) anything, some water, food? I know whenever you return to me form the Ukiyo, you're always in thirst and most times you are in need of food as well."

Dozo (please) Mizu (Water) Isogi (Hurry) Dozo my Lord." She replied pleasantly to him.

Agent Rossie turned on his heels and he rushed into the kitchen and retrieved a glass of water, and he brought it and offered it to her as she continued to sit on her legs.

"Domo." (Thank you) she offered as she took the drink and greedily drank the entire glass without coming up for any air. When she was done, she handed the glass back to her Lord.

Even though he loved looking at the naked woman, he turned again and picked up her Kimono and brought it to her as well. He handed her the beautiful garment, and watched with a smile as she struggled into it and then she carefully spread out the bottom of the Kimono until it looked like a blue cloud surrounding the lower part of her body. This action added greatly to her outstanding beauty, and it also added to the pleasure of Agent Rossie who loved anything she did for him. He moved over to her side and then walked around her back and moved until he was standing right in front of her again, and then he smiled down at her.

As he was walking around her, she had a clear look to the small kitchen and noticed nothing was prepared for her Master to eat, and she asked him as she softly smiled back at him. Has my most honorable Lord and Master had anything to eat on this night?"

"I hate to admit this to you Wind-san, but when I didn't find you home waiting for my return, eating was the furthest thing from my mind. There was no way in hell I would've been able to eat anything without you back here in my apartment, Wind-san." He replied as he cast a quick look into the kitchen and realized how she discovered he did not eat anything tonight.

"Then this lazy and worthless Vassal shall get off the floor and go and prepare something for my Lord to enjoy. I will not allow you to turn in for the night without something substantial resting on your belly for the night." With that said, she struggled to her feet, her knees stiff from sitting in the position of respect she had assumed since returning from the Floating World. Once she had her circulation moving in her legs again, she rushed to the kitchen and began to search for the cheese he always prepared for her whenever she was in any need of any nourishment. Not finding any cheese left for them to enjoy, she began to search the rest of the fridge for something she could prepare for her Lord and Master. Not really knowing what she was looking at, cooking was the least of her abilities, and the way everything was pack at this time and day, she could not discover anything she could quickly make for her Lord.

She turned back to her Lord and put a look of being completely lost, and then she waited for him to come to her aide for a change. She even closed the door to the fridge, and she stepped out of the way as she noticed her Lord was moving towards her

He laughed as he walked into the kitchen and offered her with a smirk on his lips. "Wind-san, why don't you allow me to prepare something for the both of us to enjoy tonight. After all, it had to be a very trying ordeal for you to go to the Ukiyo and then returning back to the land of the living. Besides, I enjoy making something for you to eat if you don't mind that is, Wind-san."

"This very foolish Samurai will be most pleased if my honored Liege Lord came to my aide. I fear I am out of my comfort area when it comes to cooking and preparing good meals for the both of us to enjoy. But I promise my Liege Lord that this worthless Vassal will put all her efforts into discovering the proper way for me to prepare the meals for the both of us to enjoy. By one recognizing what is, just is, and the key to unlocking the prison of self judgment lies within your own mind. I was trained from birth not to allow anything to master me, because I was the master of all and failing was not allowed to enter my mind for even the briefest of moments, my Lord. As I have conquered all that was ever placed before me throughout my life, I shall conquer the art of preparing the meals for my Lord and Master, or I shall die trying. I will not allow my Liege Lord to do all the meal preparations for the both of us, to serve my Lord I must be able to do everything for your enjoyment. I shall teach myself to cook my Liege Lord."

"I have no doubt in my mind whatsoever if anyone can conquer anything that is placed before you. It surely is you who can accomplish that feat, Wind-san. If you don't mind, go and sit at the table and when I'm done making the meal for us, I'll bring it over to you. Do you need to shower Wind-san? I remember how you showered the last time you returned from the Ukiyo. You have the time to do so, because it should take me a good number of breaths on the stick of time to create a meal for us. I know you can shower and be back at the table before I'm done cooking."

Without responding to her Liege Lord, she rose and then she headed for the bathroom to shower. She did so want to bathe but she did not want to leave her Master's side so soon after returning from the Floating World. As she entered the bathroom, she removed her Kimono and hung it on the back of the chair. She did not like how the steam from the shower made the fabric feel on her back and legs. In seconds the water was running and she stepped in the shower.

Agent Rossie smiled as he heard her singing a song in Japanese, her voice was as pleasant as her face was to look at, and the way she sang brought great pleasure to him as he listened to her sing and he cooked their meal.

FBI VEHICLE THREE THREE

Unbeknown to FBI Special Agent Robert Rossie. Vehicle Three, Three pulled into a lot where Special Agents David Price and Paul Davenport could easily see the building at

1732 West Street. These two agents pulled the graveyard watch of the target building. They were scheduled to be relieved by car One Nine and Agents Alan Johnson and Mark Wesson at Zero Six Hundred Hours. The two middle aged agents had black out windows, plenty of coffee and nibbles to last them their term of duty for the night. They could see the lights burning in the large building, but no one was moving about on the outside, and they could spot no one moving around inside the building. Both agents were armed with M-16 automatic weapons and their pistols.

They had enough ammunition to engage anyone attacking them until assistance arrived to help them. These four agents were ordered to maintain a constant surveillance of the intended target building until they decided to act against the Subject's holdup inside the building for the weekdays, and four other agents were scheduled to keep the building under surveillance over the weekend both day and night. All the agents were warned not to engage the Subjects unless they come under attack by the Subjects first. Then they were cleared to return any fire aimed at them.

Agent Davenport was the first one to notice a car slowly coming down the block, and he watched it until it turned onto the property in question. Then the two agents watched as a beautiful young black woman got out of the vehicle and she opened the back door and reached into the car, and she pulled out what looked like at least seven large Pizzas. Then she kicked the car door closed with her foot and walked towards the building like she did not have a care in the world. The main door suddenly opened and the woman quickly disappeared inside the building. But whoever opened the door for her, stepped out of the building and he looked up and down the block, and then he listened for a few moments. He then turned and went back inside the building when he was obviously certain no one was trailing the lady to their hideout.

Agent Price smirked to Davenport. "Man, if I can have a fox like that babe deliver Pizza's dressed like that to us while we're on this damn stakeout, I'd be ordering Pizzas every night we pull this suck ass duty for who knows how long we'll be out here. What the hell do you think is going down inside that dump? I bet the bank they're enjoying a helluva better time than we're enjoying sitting out here like a pair of fricking jerks staring at the building with binoculars, like we're concerned the damn building might get up and walk away on us, partner,"

"I bet they're enjoying eating their damn Pizzas and also that pretty chick that just delivered the damn things to the bastard's holdup inside that damn dump, David. And you can rest assured they're having a helluva better time in there than we're enjoying out here, dammit. I hate these damn stakeout shits we always get stuck doing. You can rest assures that both Wilson and Parker won't be pulling any of this bullshit stakeout duty. They're so far up Murdock's ass they can tell what he had for fricking breakfast. Those two pricks are Murdock's personal pets, and they never pull the shit duty like the rest of us always do." Agent Davenport remarked as he raised the binoculars back up to his eyes and he focused them in again and watched the building.

Agent Price enjoyed a quick laugh over what Davenport was just complaining about, as he went back to staring at the building through his night vision binoculars. For the rest of the night, no one else came to or left the building in question. It was so boring for the two agents it was decided by them that one of them was to sleep while the other agent watched the building, until he was tired and woke the other sleeping agent to relieve him, so he could sleep for a while.

FBI SPECIAL AGENT ROBERT ROSSIE'S APARTMENT

Agent Robert Rossie and Wind enjoyed their makeshift supper and afterwards they remain seated at the table and spoke to each other pleasantly. She was still completely worn out from her very trying ordeal of being called back to the Floating World, and she was trying to regain her strength. He was equally as tired from his dealing with his troublesome informant, and then his drive by of the building in question, and his work on his report for his Commander. Neither of the two young people was very interested in pillowing with each other at this particular time.

It was Rossie who said to Wind. "I wish there was a way we could stop you from having to report to the Floating World every six to seven days, Wind-san. I hate what those visits do to you, sometimes it takes you almost a day, pardon me, one full stick of time to get over the effects of those visits to the Ukiyo. Is there something we can do to make your stay in the living world a permanent thing? That way you'll never be away from me for the day, Wind-san?"

"My most honorable and concerned Liege Lord, you are so kind to think of me in the fashion you always do, my Lord. But I fear I am only a slave to my killing sword, and the curse that was placed upon my spirit by my Kawasomeru-Sama when he also showered me with kindness, by allowing me to become a member of his vast Armies, and he raised me to a General so no Samurai could look down upon me. But despite what my powerful Warlord of the time offered me, there were still many Samurai who spoke behind my back of treachery aimed at my being. Though when any Samurai was found to be guilty of speaking unkind words against me, he was always ordered to commit Suppuku in front of the gathered Samurai, and that Warrior was not allowed to have a second to help guide him on his way to the Floating World. The few still spoke ill of me and they always tried to weaken my position with my Liege Lord of the time."

"I'm aware of the hardships you endured at the hands of the pig headed people of those times in your past, but now it's different. We learned how important our women are to us in this time. We even started to allow our women soldiers to engage the enemy in combat, and we're starting to treat our women as equals in everything they do. Though we still have a long way to go, we are trying to balance the scales. But this is not what I was interested in Wind-san. I asked you if there was a way for us to do something so you never have to report to the Floating World again. I hate when you're away from me for those times you have to go to the Ukiyo. Is there anything we can do to stop you from having to go to the Floating World for even one second, Wind-san?"

"Once again you offer this most unworthy and very foolish Samurai honors that I truly do not earn or deserve to enjoy, my Liege Lord. I am so sorry to inform my Liege Lord that I know of no possible way for either of us to stop myself from having to report to the Ukiyo for that one stick of time. To honor the Gods for allowing me to occupy space in both worlds in which I travel through. For me to fail to respond properly to the call of the Floating World, my spirit will suffer ever mounting and unbearable pain until it becomes so painful that I would either have to report to the Floating World because of the pain, or I am foolish enough to allow my spirit to die from the pain. It is the punishment for anyone who tries to disobey the orders of the Kami."

"I'm so sorry for you that we can't do anything to try and stop you from having to go back to the Ukiyo for even one breath of time in the future, Wind-san. Knowing this then I guess the only thing we can do, is make the most of what times you're allowed to be with me and enjoying what the living world has to off her children." Agent Rossie then checked his watch and was surprised it was already after eleven at night and he asked her. "Are you as tired as I am on this night Wind-san? Because if you are then I suggest we turn in for the night."

Those were the words she was waiting to hear spoken by her Lord since she returned to the living world. To sleep with her Lord and pillow with him would be what she needed, to forget her time served in the Ukiyo. Even though she enjoyed speaking with Lord Kawasomeru, it was always such a strength draining ordeal to be transported from the living world to the Ukiyo, and then being sent back to the living world when her time in the Ukiyo was up. She was unable to hide her smile as she swiftly rose, and then she waited for her Liege Lord to lead her into his private sleeping quarters. It was not right or polite for her to enter his room first, and then she had to wait to be asked to come in with him. She watched him enter through the door, and then he stopped and turned back to her and asked. "Are you coming with me tonight, Wind-san?"

"If that is your true desire of me my Liege Lord then yes, I am coming with you."

"It truly is my desire that you sleep with me on this night Wind-san. I need to feel your body resting up against mine because it'll help me sleep so peacefully tonight." He reached out his hand and she immediately placed her hand in his and he guided her into the bedroom.

They rested together hugging each other for many moments, and he reached out and tilted her head up until he was able to look in her eyes. Then kissed her forehead then the tip of her nose, and then he kissed her so passionately she had nothing else she could do but respond to his hunger and desire of her. She returned his kiss with wild abandonment, and when he slid his tongue into her mouth, she melted in his strong arms. The shared each other's love twice on this night, and then they both fell asleep locked so protectively in each other's arms. She so enjoyed the sound of his breathing that she held her head against his chest for the rest of the night.

CHAPTER TWENTY FOUR

FBI SPECIAL AGENT ROBERT
ROSSIE'S APARTMENT, TUESDAY
JUNE 30th, 1996. ZERO, SIX TWENTY
HUNDRED HOURS (6:20 A.M.)

Morning came too quickly for them. Agent Robert Rossie struggled out of the death like hug Wind had him in, and he slowly rolled out of bed. He had to go to the bathroom so badly he swore he could taste it. Once he finished urinating, he strolled into the living room the day had all the earmarks of being a beautiful day, warm with little humidity. He dug out the bacon from the freezer and started it cooking for them. For some reason he was actually looking forward to reporting to work on this day, mainly because he wanted to see the report filed by the agents watching the target building all night, to see if anything had happened throughout the night. He was sure Agent Fugiwara was going to show up early for work as well to read the same report.

He was about half way through cooking the bacon when Wind came walking out of the bedroom, and she was dressed in her short Kimono, and she failed to use the Obi to hold the robe closed. She sat at her usual place at the table, and then watched what her Liege Lord was cooking for them to enjoy. When he turned to acknowledge her presence in the kitchen, she smiled pleasantly at him and he returned to cooking their morning meal. She made no attempt to close her robe and both her breasts were exposed, she was that comfortable with her body.

He finished cooking their meal and placed the bacon in the plates and walked them over to the table and he placed Wind's dish before her then he sat and smiled at her. He loved to see her eat and the many different faces she always made when she was unfamiliar with the meal he prepared for her. They ate in silence and when they were done, he left the dishes resting on the table for her to look after, and then he announced to her. "Wind-san, I have to report to work earlier than usual this morning, so I'm going to skip my morning shower and head out now. You'll remember to remain out of sight of any of our neighbors as always? I can't wait for the day when I can finally show you off to the rest of the world, and you'll be free to act like anyone else living at this time, Wind-san."

With that said he got up from the table and headed off for work. He was surprised the traffic was so light this time in the morning for him. He pulled into the FBI Headquarters ten minutes after seven, and he automatically stopped and picked up two cups of coffee as usual, one for him and the second for Agent Shinnosuke Fugiwara. Then he rushed for his office and sure enough, Agent Fugiwara was already in the room and he was sipping on a cup of coffee, a second cup was resting on his desk, so he gave Fugiwara the cup he brought for him. Then he sat down and asked his partner with a little concern lacing his tone of voice.

"I assume you have read the night time surveillance report from Agent Davenport already Fugiwara-san? Anything in it worth our time and concern to go over at this time?"

"The only highlight I picked up in the entire report was when the purps had a delivery of Pizzas, and some good looking lady dropped the Pizzas off to the animal's holdup inside the structure. The report never stated if the lady ever left the building, or if she remain inside for the rest of the night, Rossie-san." Agent Fugiwara reported to his partner.

"Did anything come in from the team who relieved Davenport and Price this morning?"

"Not a thing as yet partner, but the second team of Johnson and Wesson just relieved the first team no longer than a little more than an hour ago. I'm quite certain nothing could've happened in that short a time period, Rossie-san." He offered as he took another sip of his coffee.

"I guess you have a pretty good point there Fugiwara-san. I want you to keep an eye on any reports that might come in from the second team, and if anything important comes in, I want to know about it immediately. I'm going to spend the day working out all our approaches against the target building. I'm not looking forward to working all that crap out, but we have to be damn ready when we move against the building and the purps hidden inside the place."

"You got it Rossie-san." Agent Fugiwara replied as he watched Rossie unfold the layout the lab boys worked up for him last night. It was the complete layout of the target area, showing everything, even the roof of the building and the six skylights they could use when the agents assaulted the building they were sure to attack within the next two weeks.

The day dragged slowly on without much happening, so Rossie kept himself busy with working on all the possible attack angles his agents would need to employ, when they finally attacked the killer's holdup inside the target building. Agent Fugiwara helped his partner whenever he was asked a question, but he mainly manned the phones In case the stakeout crew picked up something they needed to be aware of. Even Commander Murdock kind of left the two agents to their work, and only bothered them once since they reported in for work.

Just as Agents Rossie and Fugiwara was preparing to go home for the night, Murdock walked into the office and he started to speak to the Lead Agent of this operation, as soon as he laid eyes on him. "Say Agent Rossie, I need to know if you might be able to take Agents Davenport and Price's place for night surveillance for Wednesday's schedule. It seems Davenport's wife is having some minor surgery done and he asked to be relieved of the duty for that night, so he could be home with his wife in case she needs something after her surgery? I already assure him you and your partner would be pleased to relieve him of his duty under the circumstances, am I correct with this assumption, Agent Rossie. Besides, if Agent Fugiwara pulled night surveillance, it'll keep any number of ladies safe from his wandering dick for the night for crap sake."

Commander Ralph Murdock turned and then he looked right at Agent Fugiwara, and he gave him the look like he was just daring him to say something that could set him off against the Japanese FBI Agent. When he just smiled back at him, Murdock just shook his head and then he returned his attention back to Agent Rossie, and then he waited for his reply.

"Sure thing Ralph, I'd be pleased to relieve Davenport from his duty on Wednesday night, sir. I think I'd like to pull a few days watching this damn building myself, and see if I can get a possible number on the purps holdup inside the damn building with this Young fella, sir. It'd also help me to study the layout of the area first hand sir, and that could help me out enormously when I finish working up our attack plan aimed against the building, and getting at the purps inside the place, sir." Agent Rossie replied to his Commander.

"I knew I could count on you, so I won't expect to see you tomorrow for the entire day, and Thursday, you can just report for duty at 10 A.M. along with your womanizing partner over there, until you catch up and report Friday at your usual reporting time for work, sir. Now if you were not bullshitting my ass about your want to do some of the night time surveillance of that dump. I can set it up where you can pull next Monday, Tuesday and Wednesday night surveillance of the place. So you can get a great feel of the area in question that'll help you complete your detailed plan on how you want to attack the building and the number of extra Agents you plan to pull in for this operation, Agent Rossie. I'll also need the number on the local Police personnel you'll want to pull into this operation as well, sir.

I'd sure like to place a period at the end of Young's name by the end of next week, or the beginning of the following week.

"I understand an operation of this magnitude will need plenty of time in the planning stages of the operation, and working out the number of Agents and Police Officers you're going to need to help you pull off this operation successfully, Agent Rossie. Needless to offer you Agent Rossie, I want this operation finished as soon as possible, so we can once again place our full attention back on the Batterman murder case, mister. I want both these damn cases finished so I can get on with the other duties I have to look after around here, Bob. I'm getting real tired of having so many of these pains in the ass constantly calling me on the phone to see how the Batterman's case is progressing. I'm also getting tired of lying my ass off to all these pains in the ass at the same time mister. I want these damn cases ended once and for all, Agent Rossie!

"I'm warning you for the last time Agent Rossie don't make me regret my placing you in command of these two high profile murder cases, mister. Because if you screw up either of these two damn cases on my ass then it'll be a cold day in hell before I even place you back in command of another operation unless it's for a lost dog or cat. I have a lot of faith in you and your partner hiding behind me, Agent Rossie. So don't let me down on this one or else, mister." Commander Murdock warned his Lead Agent in no uncertain terms this time.

"I have you covered on this one Ralph, and neither me nor my partner will stop until we get Young and the rest of his band of murders. Then we're going to solve the Batterman murder case, along with the other murders that took place back in Japan at the same time. This much I promise you, Ralph." Agent Rossie boasted proudly to his control.

"You sound awful confident over that last statement Agent Rossie. I just hope your mouth isn't writing checks your body can't produce, mister." Murdock smirked back at him.

"Believe me I know what I'm talking about over this one Ralph. You'll see once we have settled up with Young and the rest of his crew. You're going to be damn surprised at the lightening speed me and my partner are going to solve the Batterman murder, along with the murders that took place in Japan that are somehow connected with the Batterman case, sir."

"Okay mister, I'm going to take your word for it. I guess I'll leave you two for the time being. Don't forget Agent Rossie, both you and your partner in crime pulled the graveyard shift tomorrow night so be prepared for it." Murdock nodded and then he left Rossie's office.

"Man, that guy has no social graces at all any longer, Rossie-san."

"Don't I know that, but are you going to be alright with the late night duty we just pulled tomorrow night, Fugiwara-san. I'll bring a large craft of coffee and some cakes. I guess we can go on the one sleeps while the other watches and unless something takes place, we should not lose any sleep on this duty. I can't say I'm disappointed pulling this duty, it'll give me a great chance to see what we're going to have to do to assault that damn building successfully."

"I understand you're not unhappy with pulling the rotten graveyard shift tomorrow night Rossie-san, but I'm sure as hell a little upset by it, and now we pulled Monday through Wednesday of next week with the same stinking graveyard duty. This shit's really going to interfere with my love life prospects you know partner. If you wanted to work at night, why the hell didn't you offer to work with Johnson and let me work my regular shifts? I worked too many years to be pulling the graveyard shift any longer, Rossie-san. With all the years I have in on the job, I should never pull the graveyard shift again. That's shits usually reserved for all the young Agents or for someone who really fucked up an operation..."

"Or he's putting his ass on the line by going out and playing patty cake with a new chick every stinking night while you're supposed to be married, buster."

"Do you really think that's why the Big Growl gave us the shit duty on this one Rossie-san, because I'm out there fooling around on my wife? Man, if he pulled that shit on my ass then he's going to have a real problem with me on this one I tell you Rossie-san. No stinking Commander is supposed to use his position to punish an Agent because of his personal life..."

"Unless that lifestyle might be compromising your damn position as Special Agent for the

FBI, mister! You know damn well this was something that was covered when we were going to the FBI school, and they warned us many times to never get involved with a situation that could compromise your position with the Bureau. Just think what might happen if one of our enemy has a female operative from a hostile nation, and they send that female operative out to screw your damn brains out? Then that same female operative turns around and she threatens you if you don't become her bitch and get what she wants from the company, she'd turn you in to Murdock, and that move could very well cost you your damn job and maybe some jail time, buddy.

"Better yet, let me ask you a serious question Fugiwara-san. Say what I just said becomes a reality and you find yourself stuck between a rock and a hard place, and you have to decide whether to betray the company and get that information, or would you go to Murdock and tell him what you got yourself trapped in? Which one would you do, which one is more important to you? Your job or the security of the United States, and you go to Murdock to turn in this female operative, knowing damn well when you do, the first thing Murdock is going to do, is fire your ass. And in that firing you'll lose everything you worked so hard for the past ten years. Hell, you'll even lose your damn pension. What would you do, go to Murdock or burn the country down?" Rossie asked as he stared so intensely at his partner while he waited for his reply.

"I wouldn't have to think twice over what I'd do my friend. I'd run right to Murdock and tell him how bad I fucked up, and then I'd do everything in my power to make things right, before they had a chance to fire me first. I'd even offer to go deep undercover and work the foreign operative and turn the table on her, and make her compromised her fucking position with her own god damn country, Rossie-san. I'd never turn my back or harm my country under any circumstances. I'd kill any bitch who dares to try and turn me against my country..."

"That's what I wanted to hear coming from your mouth, Fugiwara." Murdock grumbled as he came back to Rossie's office just in time to hear the conversation that was going down between his two agents. He entered the office with a file folder locked in his hands, and then his stare sharpened as he looked directly at Agent Fugiwara and then offered. "Agent Rossie just had the conversation I was planning to have with your ass once these two damn cases were completed by you two birds. It's great to hear you'd never compromise your standing with the company under any circumstances, mister. Well done sir. Now for you Agent Rossie."

Commander Ralph Murdock turned his attention to the other agent and then he went on with his words. "Agent Rossie, here's the latest reports filed by Agents Price and Davenport, and a report that just came in from Agent's Johnson and Wesson waiting to be relieved by the night team of Agents Davenport and Price. It seems there was some action that had just took place at the target building, and they immediately filed a verbal report they just typed up for your information. Here, enjoy yourself, and then get back to me as quickly as possible over what you think about this latest shit going down, mister." He dropped the file folder down on Rossie's desk, and then he left as quickly as he appeared in Rossie's office.

Agent Fugiwara immediately slid his chair over to Rossie's desk, and then he started to look over his shoulder as Rossie opened the file and pull out the section filed by Agents Johnson and Wesson. They both had already read the report filed by Agents Davenport and Price so they were not interested in rereading that report over for a second time. The report stated: 'Wednesday, July 1, 1996: Twenty, Ten Hundred Hours. All lights shining on the parking lot were suddenly shut down. Then we spotted Subject A exit the building in question, Subject A was armed with an M16 with scope and Subject A entered a parked a light green Chevy Sedan vehicle with plate number 17RGC3. Subject A, a large black man dressed in a brown hoodie and bluejeens then quickly exited the property, heading East down West Street.

'Two other Subjects B and C exited the building and watched Subject A leave the site. Both Subject B and C were likewise armed with M-16s. Once Subject A was out of sight Subjects B and C reentered the building. Once Subjects B and C were back inside the building, the outside floodlights were once again turned on. Time used in observation lasted for exactly four minutes and fifteen seconds in duration. Then at Twenty, Twenty Three Hundred Hours, a late model White Ford vehicle slowly turned onto the target property, and we observed a pretty and talk black woman now referred to as Subject D, quickly exit the vehicle while carrying two large paper bags obviously fast food, and as Subject D walked towards the building in question. The door to the target building main door opened and Subject B held the door opened for Subject D. Once subject D was inside the building, Subject B suddenly produced a flash light and began searching the outside perimeter of the large target property.

'Subject B then took a second and he shined the bright flash light down the road, and Subject B actually eliminated our vehicle for a brief second, while he was checking the outside of the target building out. Both I and Agent Wesson ducked down and Subject B must have felt there was no danger outside the building and their property. At Twenty, Twenty Seven Hundred Hours Three Seconds, Subject B returned to the building and quickly disappeared back inside the target building. Report ended at Twenty Thirty Hundred Hours and was filed with FBI Headquarters at same time observation had ended.

"Man, Johnson really knows how to file a fucking report doesn't he, Rossie-san? Well, at least we know there are at least three bodyguards inside the damn building, along with the same women who brought the Pizzas yesterday to these killers. How about we get the wire tap people in on this damn thing, and have them set up their listening gear and tap into any cell phone or land line calls going into and out of that stinking building, Rossie-san?"

"What a great idea, I'm so glad I thought of it my friend..."

"You thought of it huh? Man, it's getting real late, we going to work all night buddy?"

"We're on one helluva roll here so we might as well continue working until we get all our ducks in a row. Why don't you handle the wire tap people for me and get their ass' in gear, while I set up for our night time surveillance of the target building for tomorrow night, Fugiwara-san." Agent Rossie offered as he began to make a number of phone calls of his own.

FBI SPECIAL AGENT ROBERT ROSSIES APARTMENT

Again Wind was extremely worried about her Liege Lord, because it was now so late in the night and he had not returned to their living quarters. She mentally made contact with the amulet, and there was no alarm from it, so she knew her Master was in no danger. But she was still worried because of the lateness of the night. This was the only time she ever allowed herself to get upset with her Liege Lord, when he was late and out of her sight. During these times she worried so if his life ever became threatened, would the amulet bring her to him quick enough to save his life. She knew she would die inside if anything happened to him and she was not there in time to save his life. For what seemed like the hundredth time, she walked over to the window that overlooked his usual parking space in the back of the building, and then she let out her breath in a rush when she discovered he was not home yet.

FBI HEADQUARTERS, WASHINGTON D.C.
TWENTY TWO HUNDRED HOURS (10 P.M.) July1, 1996

FBI Special Agent Shinnosuke Fugiwara just completely his conversation with the wire tap agents on the first floor, and they informed him it was an easy chore for them to be able to monitor all cell phone and land line calls coming out of and going into the target building, but they wanted clearance from Commander Murdock, before they would even consider putting their part of the operation in play. Agent Fugiwara told them he would get back to them right away, and then he broke off his communications with them and waited for the right moment to report this conversation to the Lead Agent, Robert Rossie. Seeing his chance when Rossie stopped looking over a picture of the area and he leaned back in his chair and stretched his back some, he suddenly cleared his throat and then he waited from him to acknowledge him.

Agent Rossie heard the sound and he immediately turned to Fugiwara to see if he wanted his attention, and as soon as he looked at his partner, Agent Fugiwara started to offer. "Rossie-san, I just finished speaking with the Wire Tap crew and they assured me it was no problem for them to do what we want from them, but they want clearance from Murdock before they would go ahead with their orders. I guess they want to cover their asses before setting their crap up for us."

"The pain in the asses wouldn't take your word for setting up their systems, dammit?"

"Nope, they outright insisted in hearing from Commander Murdock first, before they would even entertain sending one of their crews out to set up their monitoring equipment at the target building area for us, Rossie-san." He reported to his partner.

"Well we'll just see about that shit, who were you talking to about this crap, Fugiwara-san?"

"Lieutenant Carlson, just hit line three on the phone and you'll be immediately connected to his office, Rossie-san." Agent Fugiwara smirked back at his partner.

Rossie hit three on his phone and on the forth ring a sleepy sounding voice grumbled back at him over the phone. "Carlson!"

"Yes Agent Carlson, this is Lead Agent Robert Rossie up on the third floor..."

"What the hell is with you people up there on the third floor, don't you guys ever sleep anymore dammit? I just finished speaking to Agent Fugiwara up there, and I guess he must have sic you on my ass now, and you're going to get the same damn answer as he had received from me, Lead Agent Rossie. I need clearance from the Commander before I can even think about sending one of my crews out to tap a phone system, sir. By right, I usually demand a court order before I dispatch one of my crews out in the field. But knowing you people are on the third floor then Commander Murdock has to be aware of what you people are working on up there..."

"Agent Carlson, since I'm the Lead Agent in Charge of an extremely important operation for the company, I'm ordering you to send a damn crew out as soon as possible, sir. I have a number of Agents stationed out in the field, and I need all the damn intelligence I can possible gather on this damn situation, before I can authorize a hot entrance into the target building, sir." Agent Rossie snapped into the phone as he interrupted Agent Carlson on the phone.

"I don't give a shit if you're related to Jesus Christ and you have a direct pipeline to God Almighty, as I said no can do without clearance from the Commander first, mister."

"Look buddy, Murdock went home for the night and since I'm the Lead Agent in Charge here, I'm authorizing you to send out one of you god damn crews, and get that damn surveillance up and running for me tonight, mister!" Agent Rossie nearly yelled into the phone this time.

"And I'm going to repeat the same damn thing to you for a second time Mister Lead Agent in Charge, no can do without clearance from Murdock first, period sir." Carlson repeated again.

"Okay wiseass as the Lead Agent in Charge, I'm ordering you to place a god damn call to Murdock at his home right now, and you get his clearance for you to set up your system at the target building. And once he stops chewing on your ass for bothering him this late at night, and after he finds out you were giving me such a hard time following out my god damn orders. I wouldn't be a bit surprised to find out he busted you back down to a Field Agent again, and you find your ass out there setting up this damn system of yours, mister. So get it done, I expect to hear back from you the moment Murdock is done with your ass tonight, mister."

"You want me to call Commander Murdock at his home this late at night, and it's not an emergency situation? Damn, I don't know. Errr... here's what I'll do for you Lead Agent in Charge Rossie. I want a written request from you in triplicate on my desk in fifteen minutes and upon your personal request, I'll have a team out by your surveillance team by the time the ink dries on your request. But you better remember this Lead Agent in Charge I am ordering one of my crews out under your direct order, sir. If any heat comes down over this order, it's all going to rest directly on your shoulders, sir. You just get me those requests, and I'm having my people setting up and they'll be heading out for your in question situation within five to seven minutes from the time I hang up with you, sir. Is this good enough for you, sir?"

"It works out just fine for me Agent Carlson, and I'll have those request papers down to you within the hour, is this okay with you sir?" Agent Rossie replied with a snap in his voice.

"My team's already loading their van as we speak with their equipment, just get me those request papers down here as soon as possible, good night Lead Agent in Charge Rossie."

"Yeah, right." He snarled back into the phone as he hung up on Agent Carlson, and then he turned to Agent Fugiwara and informed him. "Carlson's sending his stinking people out now, and I need a favor from you. I need you to fill out a 341 file in triplicate and fill them out for me and I'll sign them and then I need you to get them down to that pain in the ass before he has a damn puppy on us, Fugiwara-san."

"He gave you that much trouble? Doesn't the dopey fuck know we're all working on the same side around here, dammit?" Agent Fugiwara mumbled back angrily at Rossie.

"Just get it done for me will ya partner? I need to make a couple of calls."

Agent Fugiwara opened the file cabinet and pulled out the pages he needed, and then he sat down and started to fill in the pages as Rossie made a call out to Agent Davenport who was the lead of the nighttime surveillance team who he was certain had relieved Agents Johnson and Wesson by this time, to see if anything else was happening on their watch.

As Fugiwara was working on the request, the phone rang and since Agent Rossie was on the other line, he answered it. "This is FBI Special Agent Fugiwara, what can I do for you?"

"I know who the hell you are mister, this is Murdock I just got a call from the Lead Agent of the Wire Tap crews, and he reported Agent Rossie really dumped on Agent Carlson, and the ass even threatened to have that Agent busted down to Field Agent again. I want to speak to Agent Rossie before he finds his ass busted down to Field Agent himself, mister!"

"I'm afraid Agent Rossie is engaged at the present moment sir..."

"What the hell do you mean he's engaged? I don't give a flying fuck if he's married for crap sake, mister! I want to speak to his ass right this fricking minute, mister so get him for me!" Commander Murdock almost roared into the phone this time.

Agent Fugiwara made a hand motion to Rossie, informing him he was wanted on the other line and he simply waved him off as he continued speaking to Agent Davenport, forcing Fugiwara to report back to Murdock. "Commander Murdock Sir, Agent Rossie is still on the other line on an important communication over our stakeout tonight, and I'll have him return your call the first chance he gets, will that do for you, sir?"

"That'll do just fine with me, and what the hell are you two asses still doing at the god damn office? Your shift ended nearly six hours ago. I'm not paying any unauthorized overtime mister."

"It got so late on us and we still had a crap load of shit to finish up. So we both decided to work through the night to get what we had to get done, done Commander."

"That's good work because you two know how much I want both these two cases ended as soon as possible. I approve of the overtime and never mind having Agent Rossie call me back. If you two birds are trying to get these two cases over with then I don't care whose toes you guys might step on to complete these nagging cases. I guess I'll see you two birds when I come in tomorrow morning." With that said, Murdock hung up on Agent Fugiwara rudely.

When Agent Rossie finished speaking with Agent Davenport, he hung up and then he turned to Agent Fugiwara and asked him who was on the phone for him.

"It was the Big Growl, I guess Agent Carlson's Control called Murdock and pitched a bitch at him over the amount of pressure you placed on Carlson's ass to get his people in motion, and the Big Growl wanted to chew on your ass for a little while I guess. But I was able to cool him down enough and he told me to tell you to forget about his call. He also approved of our stinking overtime for the night, Rossie-san. How the hell did you make out with Agent Davenport? What's going down with him and that damn stakeout he's working on for us, partner?"

"He reported it was as quiet as a church at night at the target building and surrounding area, but he did inform me the Wire Tap people have already arrived at the target site, and they were busy setting up their equipment. I bet that pain in the ass Carlson had sent his crew out long before he finally agreed to send them out on us, the bastard he is sir. He just wanted to bust our fricking horns for a little while I guess, dammit."

"That happens whenever we have to deal with someone who can't think for himself, Rossie-san. There are so many small people in the damn world, who if they had the backbone they were born with, the world would be a whole lot better off I tell you. What are we going to do now? I'm starting to get a little tired, and don't forget, we pulled the graveyard shift tonight, man."

"You'll have plenty of time to sleep once we're out on the stakeout duty. I'll pull the first watch and that way you can get at least four hours of sleep, unless something goes down and we have to react against it, partner." Agent Rossie offered to take the first watch.

"That'll be great with me because we both have been up since early yesterday, and we're going to pull the duty for tonight. Look Rossie, it's just after midnight, so what say we end this day and get some sleep until we have to report in later tonight. We're scheduled to start out shift at Ten tonight, so that means we have to report in at least an hour early and if we leave now, we should both get enough sleep to make tonight a breeze for us to pull off, my friend." Agent Fugiwara floated his suggestion past his partner to see if he could get him to call it a day, and they could both then go home and catch up on some of their sleep.

"You know partner, I think you have a good point there and that's what we're going to do. Go and clock out and I'll be right behind you. Do you want me to pick you up and bring you to work tonight, that way we can both ride together to the stakeout, Fugiwara-san?" Rossie suggested as he started to close down his computer, and then he secure his desk at the same time.

"Errr..."

"Say no more about it, it's obvious you're not going to sleep as you said was the reason you wanted to end this day. You're going to be able to report to work in time to keep Murdock off your ass, right mister?" He groused as he gave him a sideways glance and smirked at him.

"I guess I'm guilty as charged and don't you go worrying about me showing up for work, I'll be here with bells on when I'm supposed to be here, Rossie-san."

"Just make damn sure you're here when Murdock expects you to be here, and leave the damn bells home will ya buddy. I don't know how Murdock will react if you report in for work with bells dripping from your ass, my friend. C'mon, let's get the hell out of here I'm beginning to have nightmares about my office at night, because I'm here more than anywhere else lately."

The two agents clocked out and then they headed home with Rossie already wondering what Wind was doing and if she was going crazy because he was so late coming home from work.

FBI SPECIAL AGENT ROBERT ROSSIE'S APARTMENT

Again Wind walked to the back of the apartment and she cautiously looked out the window at where her Liege Lord always parked his horseless carriage, and this time as she looked out, she noticed his vehicle pull up and park. The excitement returned as well as her strength and enthusiasm as she watched her Lord climb out of the machine. She stared at him until he was out of her sight. Then she immediately rushed to the center of the living room and dropped down to her knees and bowed until her forehead lightly touched the wood floor. She then held her bow until her Liege Lord entered his small castle.

Rossie entered his apartment completely exhausted and he looked at his watch and saw it with almost two in the morning, and he let out with an exhausted sigh. Then he noticed Wind in her usual bowing position and he smiled down at her, although all he saw of her face was the top of her head. He walked around her and dropped his sort of backpack down on the sofa with his weapon hidden in the small pack. Then he turned his attention to Wind and ordered her. "Wind-san, what a pleasure it is to see you again, but how many times do I have to tell you, you don't have to keep bowing every time I entered the room you're in? To be truthful with you Wind-san, it's almost embarrassing for you to keep bowing before me like this. Look at me so I can see your eyes and know you are listening to what I'm telling you I don't know how many times now."

She raised her head from the floor and then looked at her Liege Lord with pleading eyes as she replied to him. "This worthless Samurai has again insulted my Lord, and for this I should be ordered to commit Suppuku, to make amends for my insult of my Lord. But I must admit my Liege Lord has caused much distress in this foolish but caring Warrior by your returning to your castle so late at night my Lord." Again she bowed to her Master, trying to be extra polite before him while not understanding when she bowed to him like this, it was actually embarrassing him.

"There you go again Wind-san, arrr... never mind, you do what you gotta do to make yourself happy, Wind-san. Err... I'm going to skip any meal tonight, errr... this morning. I need sleep more than I need anything to eat tonight, Wind-san." He was trying to be extra cautious by not showing any form of weakness before this extremely dangerous female Samurai Warrior. He knew never to use the phase of 'please' before her, and he was trying to stay well away from saying anything like 'I'm sorry, or I'm afraid" to her. In ancient Japan, any display of weakness could very well have caused the one making that mistake, his head.

He drew in his breath and then announced. "Wind-san, I'm going to take a quick shower, I smell like a horse, and then I'm going to turn in and sleep for as long as I can. I have to work all night this day, so I need to sleep until I wake so I'm refreshed to start my night of work. It's a special occasion that I have to work at night tonight. But I also have to work three nights of next week as well, Wind-san." When he finished speaking to the confused looking Wind, he turned and walked into the bathroom and almost instantly, she was able to hear the water running in the shower. She rose and then picked up his suit jacket he dropped on the floor because he was so exhausted, and she hung it on the back of a chair like she saw him do time and again.

She then stood in the center of the room, not knowing what else she could do to help her Liege Lord relax. Then she had a thought and she rushed to the fridge and removed the cold bottle of wine and she poured him his usual glass, and she placed it before the seat he always sat at by the table, and she waited for him to finish his shower.

He was still so exhausted he came walking out of the bathroom completely naked, and he walked over to Wind and kissed her lightly on the forehead, and then he noticed the glass of wine and smiled as he said to her. "You're a saint Wind-san, how did you know the wine was exactly what I needed to help me relax a little." He lifted the glass and sort of saluted her with it and then he enjoyed sipping the well chilled wine.

She returned his smile even though she had no idea what her Lord meant when he called her a Saint, but she understood it was a compliment and she was happy he was so pleased with her.

When he finished his wine, he breathed out his breath and then he stretched his arms over his head and wiggled his backside to help realign his back, and this action caused her to smile at him, because as he wiggled his backside, it made his member also wiggle and it also caused it to grow a little hard on him. Then he groaned like a wounded bear, and brought his arms down and he offered to her. "Wind-san I think it's about time we both go and lie down and hopefully I can fall asleep quickly. So I can get as much sleep as I need to make me able to stay up all night to carry out my work properly, Wind-san. I really hate whenever I pull the late shift where I have to work all night. It's hard to remain awake and alert when all you're doing is seeing blackness and your mind is telling you it's late and time to go to sleep. Let's go and get some sleep Wind-san, I'm so exhausted I don't even know what I'm doing any longer."

He turned but before he started to the bedroom he turned back to her and said. "C'mon Wind, I want you by my side all the while I'm asleep. You help me sleep so well at night. I want to pull down the shades and close the curtains so the room stays dark while we're sleeping. Let's go Wind-san." When they entered the bedroom, he went to the windows in the room and pulled down the shades and closed the curtain, making the room as dark as it was in the night.

Rossie woke at three ten in the afternoon, and had to get out of bed because he had to use the facilities. When he walked in the bathroom he realized how bright it was outside, so he knew he was not going back to bed. Besides, he was starving and wanted something to eat and drink. He knew he needed a big meal to hold him over while he and his partner were on the stakeout. His moving around woke Wind and she crawled out of bed and followed him around the apartment, watching everything he were doing. Neither took time to get dressed or comb their hair.

She watched him prepare a meal then she sat and he placed food before her then sat and started to eat. While he ate, he started to explain to her why he was going to work through the night. "Wind-san, I'm not going to be home tonight, so I want you to be on your best behavior and stay well out of sight of our neighbors. I know this isn't fair to be cooped up inside the apartment every breath of the stick of time, but it's necessary for the time being. I promise once these two cases I'm working on have been concluded, I'm going to take you on a vacation with me..."

"Vacation my Lord I am worried I do not understand what this word means to me, my Liege lord?" She asked as she gave him a concerned look.

"Ohhhh... how do I explain this one to you, okay Wind-san, when someone works on something extremely trying for a long period of time, when he finishes that work he needs a break, to sort of say regain his strength and have a little fun and relax, before he has to return to work again. I hope you understand what I'm trying to tell you here, Wind-san?"

"I understand what you are offering me my Liege Lord. Many times in my past after I engaged in battle for my Master's interests, I was allowed to be relieved from my duty for several sticks of time to regain my strength. So I understand what you are telling me very well, my Lord." She smiled at her ward pleasantly it was a smile of victory over understanding what he was saying.

"Exactly, so as I was saying, when I finish with these two cases I'm working on, I intend to take you on a small vacation with me. You're hiding days will no longer have to be so, because as I finish the Batterman case, you'll be brought forward by me and I'll introduce you to the world. Then you'll never have to hide again, and we can start living and having fun like everyone else who lives in the living world. On this vacation, I'll take you down to Florida, to Clearwater, I have a close friend living in Safety Harbor, and we can share his home and do some serious fishing while we're there. I can take you down to the beach and enjoy the water and sand.

"Wow, I can just see you walking around on the beach dressed in a tiny bikini, and I assure you with the shape you have, you'll have every man and many of the women enjoying the beach drooling all over you. Then we can go out and enjoy the nightlife of Clearwater which is fantastic. The weather down there is always perfect, and the people, they're great, friendly and always willing to help you. I promise you Wind-san, once we have enjoyed this short vacation, all you have been put through by me with waiting and hiding for so long. Will be quickly erased from your memory and you'll really learn how beautiful it is to be back in the living world again, Wind-san. We'll have a great life together, once you no longer have to hide and be fearful of your past and how the people of the living world will react to your presence."

"All you are speaking to me of is what I have always dreamed to enjoy in my past endless years of visiting the land of the living, my Lord. When will all this come to reality, and I can once again live like all the other faithful Samurai always lived their lives when they were accepted by their Liege Lord and the rest of the population of Japan, my Lord."

"I promise you it'll all come to past soon enough Wind-san. You just have to be patient and put up with the way you're being forced to act, until I can finally introduce you to the rest of the world. Then you can really start living in this world and be respected for your many outstanding accomplishments of the past, and in this time, Wind-san." Agent Rossie offered her proudly.

"It will be hard for me to do but I shall be patient as the march of time until you introduce me to all your friends of this world, my Liege lord."

"It'll be well worth the patience I tell you Wind-san, because you'll finally be able to live your life as you are, a beautiful woman. I hate to say this to you, but I'm going to leave for my work now Wind-san. I want to get to my office early so I can be well prepared for my night shift of work. It's going to be a long night and I hate to be away from you all night, but I have to do what I have to do for my work. Be patient Wind-san, you time of being alone so much is fast going to come to an end for you. I'll see you tomorrow morning when I'm done with my work, until them Wind-san, I shall miss you. Stay away from the windows and don't allow anyone into the apartment under any circumstances." With that warning issued, Agent Rossie turned and walked out of the apartment and got into his vehicle and then he was off to work.

613

CHAPTER TWENTY FIVE
FBI HEADQUARTERS, WASHINGTON D.C.,
SIXTEEN HUNDRD HOURS (4P.M.) JULY 2nd, 1996

FBI Special Agent walked into his office 4 P.M. right on the dot, and he was surprised to see Commander Ralph Murdock sitting in his chair, and he was speaking with FBI Special Agent Shinnosuke Fugiwara, and both men had coffee and they were sipping it while speaking together. When he walked into the office, Murdock made no move to give him his seat, so Rossie took the empty chair and sat down and waited to be filled in to what the two were talking about.

"Ahhh... its good you showed up early for work as well, Agent Rossie." Murdock offered as he smiled at his agent, and then went on with his words for him. "I was just going over some last minute details of this operation with your partner here, mister. I want you two to be damn careful while on duty tonight. I'm a little concern with the lack of action coming from the assholes held up inside that damn building. I ran a run up in the computer, and it came back with a seventy eight percent possibility that some of these purps would be leaving the building in question sometime today. I figured Young would have to be still protecting his damn drug empire. After all, if he remained out of circulation for any longer period of time. Then most likely he'll have to be extremely concerned with another bastard just like him, moving in and filling the void of him hiding out for so long, and taking over his damn turf on him, Agent Rossie.

"I was also telling Agent Fugiwara that I was thinking of placing Car Seven with Agents Wilson and Parker on duty along with you two agents for the nightshift. I want to make certain I have enough Agents in the area to hold off any possible attack aimed at you guys, until I can get any backup to you people before you're taking out by and of these damn purps holdup with Young. You know Agents Wilson and Parker are our best shots, and they're first class with any automatic weapons. Yeah Agent Rossie, I believe this is exactly what I intend to do for you tonight, mister." Commander Murdock mussed as he thought over what he just suggested.

"You really think Young would put his ass on the line and leave his little rathole just to make certain his jungle was still his, even thought he knows we're out there hunting his ass down? I wouldn't think he would chance it, not with all the heat we've been putting on his ass ever since that shootout we were involved in with the prick and his horde, sir." Rossie came back with, and then he stared at Murdock while waiting to hear what he thought of what he just said to him.

"Yes, and that's what the computer also suggested, and that's why the computer only gave a seventy eight percent possibility of Young leaving his little rathole to check on his criminal empire. It also felt he would hesitate leaving his security of that building and his bodyguards. But on the other hand, it gave a ninety one percent possibility of Young sending out a number of his bodyguards to make certain no one was trying to move in on his damn turf, and to also collect the money owed him from his drug trade and anything else illegal he had his miserable fingers into. He must be spending money hand over foot at a helluva rate to keep his small army loyal to him under these conditions we have forced on his ass. So it's up to me how we react to what Young might do in the next few days, and I intend to be well prepared for any contingency that might crop us when dealing with this guy. This is why I will order Agents Wilson and Parker to be part of your surveillance team for the night, Agent Rossie."

"If you feel this strong about what Young and his batch of murderers might do then by all means who am I to try and argue with you over your decision, Commander. I have to admit, I'll sure welcome all the extra help I can muster with our stakeout. I always felt just one team keeping an eye on these people wasn't enough to get the job done properly for us, sir."

"Good, you organize what you need for tonight, and I'll notify both Agents Wilson and Parker they just pulled the graveyard shift along with the both of you two. I'll be back to you before you head out to relieve Johnson and Wesson. Once you link up with them to relieve them, inform them they're on call if anything goes sour with this stakeout tonight, and we need any extra assistance. I'll also have the Washington Police Department to be alerted for any possibility for the next few days. I want everyone on the alert from this point forward, until we go after Young and his people. I have to go and alert Agents Wilson and Parker." Murdock got out of Rossie's chair, and then he headed out of the other agent's office so he could contact his other two agents.

"I have to say this much about that sonofabitch, when he's on your side he's on your side all the fricking way, Rossie-san." Agent Fugiwara announced proudly about his Commander.

"It's good to know he's that concerned dealing with Young and his group, now I feel a helluva lot better facing him this time around. Okay Fugiwara-san, this is what I you to do while I'm looking after a few last minute items I have to handle, before we set out to relieve Johnson and Wesson. Head down to the arsenal and check out some long rifles for us tonight. M-16s and enough ammunition and extra clips to support a strong response from us if we end up with any problems for tonight, five hundred rounds should be enough. By the time we expend that much ammunition, we should have enough backup support showing up to hold off a small Army."

"I'm on it, I'll collect the weapons and ammunition we're going to need and store it in your vehicle. I'll also look at what else is available for our defense, and if I feel we might need it, I'll pull it from the armory and store it in our vehicle also, Rossie-san." Agent Fugiwara stood and then he rushed out of their office to carry out his orders.

Agent Rossie watched his partner leave, and then he went to work on his computer he wanted to give the entire area surrounding the target building one last check over. He wanted to make certain he did not miss a thing. Just like Murdock, he was starting to feel something might go down in the next few days, and he wanted to be well prepared for when it came his way. By the time he finished working on his computer, the time was twenty after six and he still have over an hour and a half before he was to relieve Johnson and Wesson on stakeout. So he decided to check in with Murdock to make certain he made contact with Agents Wilson and Parker, and he had also alerted the local police department to place them on ready standby for the next few days.

He closed down his computer and left his office and went down the three offices on this side of the building and entered Murdock's office just as he was hanging up the phone. "I'm glad you stopped in, I was just going to send for you. I wanted to let you know how I made out with what I wanted to set up for you tonight for you and that pain in the ass partner of yours. I alerted the local police department and they assured me they would increase their patrols in the area, and they could also shut down all civilian traffic in the area whether on foot or vehicle rapidly. Also Agent Rossie, I got hold of Agents Wilson and Parker and they're prepared to stakeout with you and your partner tonight. I also put Agents Johnson and Wesson or standby for a call in if we run into any trouble tonight. So I guess you're all set for tonight, Agent Rossie."

"I really appreciate it Commander Murdock, you took a lot of weight off my shoulders for this stakeout duty tonight sir. I guess you're right and I'm all set for the late duty tonight, sir. I think we're going to leave early and relieve Agents Johnson and Wesson, so we can set up and take over their stakeout duty sir. Will you be stopping by to check it out with us tonight, sir?"

"Where the hell's your damn partner at for crap sake? He should be here and listening to all I have set up for you two tonight, dammit. And I don't think I'll be stopping by tonight, I don't want too many of our people showing up in the area. It might alert those damn assholes holdup in the damn building of theirs, Agent Rossie. Yeah, and I agree with you wanting to show up at the stakeout early. That way you can talk to Agent Johnson and he can fill you in if anything when down, and he didn't get a chance to run a report in to my office yet, mister." Murdock smirked as he grinned at his agent, and then gave him a quick head movement to get him on the go.

"Before I leave you Commander, I sent Agent Fugiwara down to the armory to get us a pair of long rifles and enough ammunition so we can hold off any attack before backup arrives on the site sir." Agent Rossie then went to turn and head out but Murdock stopped him by offering.

"It's about time that one's doing something useful with his damn time, Rossie. You know you're the only other Agent in my command who doesn't seem to mind working with that trouble maker. I even considered having him transferred to another office because he's always creating so much damn trouble, or taking about me behind my back. I'm getting kind of tired of hearing the other Agents complaining about him all the time, dammit. You were his last chance, if he fucked up with you then he was heading for a post somewhere overseas where he could have rotted for all I care." Commander Murdock complained about Agent Rossie's partner.

"What the hell is with you two for god sake? He bitches about you and you bitch about him. I think the two of you should go out and hit the bar and get blind stinking drunk together and work out your differences, so there would be peace in the office again. A number of other Agents have picked up the animosity between the two of you." He fired right back at his Commander.

"Yeah, and one of these days that's what we're going to have to do I guess. That way if the conversation goes sour on us, only one of us will return to work if you catch my drift."

"C'mon Ralph and put it to rest, I'm getting a little tired of hearing both of you bitching about the other. Either bury the hatchet or have him transfer and be done with it. That way you can get off the rest of the other Agent's asses every time Agent Fugiwara pisses you off again, sir." He complained again as he just turned and walked away to catch up with his partner.

Agent Rossie rushed downstairs and picked up his partner standing by their vehicle and he was speaking with a pretty and young woman who worked at the luncheonette inside the building. He immediately smiled as he approached the two, and then announced. "Are you about ready to get working Agent Fugiwara-san?"

"I'm ready as I'll ever be Rossie-san." He replied as he watched the young lady walk away the moment Agent Rossie started speaking to him. She worked in the building long enough to know when to leave any of the agents hitting on her when it was time for her to go.

"Man Rossie-san, I don't mind telling you, but you're getting to be a real drag lately, buddy. I'm been trying to get her in bed for the past three months, and this was the first time she seemed open to my suggestion, and you had to come out here and throw water on the fire I was trying to start under her purdy little ass, man. What's the word, buddy?" Fugiwara asked his partner.

"One of these days that damn Japanese serpent of yours is going to get you in more trouble than a little bit. By the way buddy, the word is you better find a stinking way to make peace with Murdock, or you might find yourself stationed in Alaska trying to run down a damn snowman that broke the law up there. Murdock's really getting on your case and I'm not the only Agent from the company that's picking up the bad vibes the both of you are sending off at each other."

"The Big Growl is getting that upset with my ass, huh, Rossie-san?"

"More than you can possibly imagine I'm telling you my friend. You have the weapons and ammunition we're going to need if the shit goes down on us tonight partner? I have to tell you Fugiwara-san, Murdock's really concerned that something might go down on us tonight, and now he has me worried some about the same damn thing as well. He does have Agents Wilson and Parker coming in tonight and helping us with the damn stakeout. I guess we better get a move on it, it's getting rather late and I want some time to speak with Agent Johnson before his watch ends tonight." He groused as he opened the door and climbed into the vehicle.

Agent Fugiwara quickly rushed around the car and he jumped into the passenger's seat as Rossie carefully backed out of the parking lot, and then he drove off. Now he was deeply trouble over what Agent Rossie had just told him about how Murdock was starting to come down on his ass lately, and he started thinking of a way to cool it down some with the Commander. He loved his work and did not want to get fired over something stupid.

Rossie fought the downtown Washington traffic all the way until he came up on Rosemount Avenue, and then he slowed down and started working his way to West Street. When he came up on 9th Avenue, he shut off his car lights and approached West Street and Johnson's vehicle. He went past Agent Johnson's car and pulled into a spot under a wide Oak tree. He then got out of his vehicle and walked like he was out for a stroll as it was getting darker out. He liked the spot Johnson had his vehicle parked, and decided to move his car in that slot when Johnson pulled out to go home. When he was right by Johnson's car, he suddenly ran and opened the rear door and jumped in the back seat and asked Johnson with concern in his voice. "How are you guys making out tonight? Anything going down that I should know about? I have Parker and Wilson coming in to back us up tonight, Murdock has convinced himself something with these pricks is going to go down in the next few days and he wanted more Agents on the job in case it happens."

"That's just great, the sonofabitch left our asses hanging out on the fucking breeze for the past few days, and now he wants to add more Agents to the damn stakeout because he's suddenly worried something might go down now! Remind me to thank the bastard with the end of my foot the next time I see him for all the concern he showed for mine and Wesson's asses out here, Rossie." Agent Johnson actually snarled at Rossie, he was that upset Murdock was now more worried about the stakeout that he was putting a few more Agents on the job suddenly.

"I'm sorry he didn't cover you and Wesson's ass a little better than he did, but he's doing it now and thank God nothing went down on your watch, Agent Johnson."

"That line of bullshit didn't make me feel any better I tell you, Agent Rossie. Murdock should keep his damn mind on the job and protecting all the teams out in the field, or he should hang it up and find something else to do, and let someone who's more concerned for his Agent's welfare, to be in command of this damn office, Agent Rossie." Johnson bitched as he angrily glared out the front windshield of his vehicle, while trying to get his temper under control.

"Cool down some Johnson, you're watch is over with so there's no fault no harm, buddy. I'll have a talk with him when my shift ends and see if I can make him see where he screwed up n this stakeout, Agent Johnson." Rossie offered, trying to calm the other agent down some.

"Yeah sure, you'll have a little fucking talk with the prick, and then he'll do as you say because he's nursing your ass along to take over his office when he finally decides to give us a break around here, and he retires, Agent Rossie. All you guys on the third floor have it made with that fuck, man." Agent Johnson snapped, he was that angry with the latest call from Murdock.

"Hey man, that was a shot blow the belt, one thing I can tell you about Murdock, he's behind all his Agents the same, and he doesn't play any damn favorites. He's an equally opportunity bigot, he hates all of us the same, man." Agent Rossie offered while trying to lighten up the mood by cracking a joke about their Commander, but Johnson ignored his attempt to be funny.

Agent Rossie shook his head sadly, and then he repeated. "Did anything go down today that you didn't have a chance to send Murdock the report of yet, Agent Johnson?"

"Naw, the lousy scumbags didn't come out of their rathole once during my whole watch. The chick that delivered the sandwiches came out of the dump a little after nine this morning. She hopped in her car and drove away, that was the only excitement we had throughout the entire shift. Even their watcher didn't come out of there this time when the bitch came out to leave, Agent Rossie. Other than that, it's like I said, not one of the bastards showed their damn pusses out of the damn building for a second. I think they're acting like they're worried if they poke their heads out of there, they're going to get it shot off, Rossie." Johnson growled this time.

"Man, you have to cool off a little, or they're going to have to burry standing up, buddy."

"Cute man, you don't have to try and make me lighten up man. The only thing that's going to make me happy after hearing Murdock's latest order is him retiring. Are you relieving me and Agent Wesson a little early, all of a sudden I want to get the hell out of here? I might file a request to be transferred to another fricking office now, I'm that pissed off Murdock left me and Wesson with our dicks hanging out in the breeze like he did on this stakeout, Agent Rossie."

"What the hell can I tell you buddy, you have to do whatever you have to do, but I caution you not to act to rashly and you end up making a mistake you can't correct, just because you're pissed off right now, Agent Johnson? I'm certain Murdock didn't single you and Wesson out to leave you two hanging out in the open like you feel he did. I know he did increase the local police presence in the surrounding area well before your shift ended tonight, Agent Johnson. So you weren't being left hanging out in the open as much as you might feel you were."

"Are you certain about that last statement, Agent Rossie? Because if Murdock did increase the police presence around the area then I feel like he did have my back after all, dammit. I just wish the sonofabitch would've told us beforehand about the local police. That way we didn't feeling like he might have thrown us to the damn wolves on this fucking stakeout, Agent Rossie. I can't tell you how many times we heard a noise, or a damn car come flying down the block that we both ended up feeling like our ticket came up, and these bastards were attacking us. We didn't put that crap down in our report to Murdock, because it had nothing to do with our stakeout, or these lousy bastards we're out here and they discovered us and they were here to kill us, man."

"I know how you feel Agent Johnson I've been on enough stakeouts in my life to understand how you had to feel about this one. Look my friend, why don't you and Wesson take off a little early and catch up on your rest. Agent Fugiwara and I have it from here." Agent Rossie offered to the other agent, easily seeing the exhaustion etched deeply in his eyes.

"Yeah, I think I'd like to get the hell out of here early at that Agent Rossie. You sure you don't mind relieving us a little early?" Johnson replied as he let his breath out in a rush.

"Fine, take off, we got it from here. Besides, I want your car out of this slot so we can pull in the same place. This is one helluva perch to observe the target house from here, Agent Johnson. You guys did real good finding this place to operate from, buddy."

"You got it Agent Rossie, as soon as you're out of the car, we'll take off. I want to thank you again for letting us get the hell out of this area a little early. Watching that dump for so long gives one the fucking heebie jeebies I can tell you Agent Rossie. Every stinking sound you hear out there immediately gives you a hardon on, and then your eyes bug out while you're staring in the damn binoculars trying to see if the bastards discovered you, and they're coming after your ass, man. Like you I've been on my fare share of fricking stakeouts myself, but this one will sure get to you after a few hours of staring at that damn dump out there. Besides, this isn't the safest place to be hanging around. We picked up a number of young kids roaming around just looking to get themselves into some sort of damn trouble, Agent Rossie. Good luck with the stakeout I'll have a cold one for you tonight for relieving us a little early. Catch you later man."

Agent Robert Rossie got the message and he quickly climbed out of Johnson's vehicle, and then he watch him pull out of the well hidden slot and turn on the road and take off like he belonged in the area. Then he walked to the sidewalk and waved his hand at Fugiwara who took the driver's seat when he got out of their car. He pulled out of his parking spot and drove slowly towards his partner then he passed the slot, stopped and placed the car in reverse and backed into the vacated hidden slot. He drove to the slot with the car lights off to not draw any attention to his vehicle moving down the block. Once the car was parked, Agent Fugiwara moved over and allowed Rossie to get in on the driver's side and as soon as he was comfortable he asked him. "How were Agents Johnson and Wesson doing with the stakeout? You sure spent enough time speaking to them two birds, buddy. I was beginning to get a little worried that something when down and he was cluing you in on the problem, Rossie-san?"

"Arrr… nothing but the usual grips from someone you're relieving from an extremely boring stakeout, Fugiwara-san. I'll tell you one thing though, those two guys sure picked out one fine place to do a stakeout of that damn dump out there. Where the devil did you put the binoculars, I want to focus them in on that building before we need the damn things. From the looks of the sky, we might get hit with a few showers tonight. It's getting darker out there than three feet down a cow's throat. I'm kind of hoping for some rain tonight, it'll surely keep the damn creeps holdup inside their hideout tonight. Rain might be a break for us tonight, Fugiwara-san and I think we need all the breaks we can possibly get with this mess we're out here on, my friend."

Just as he said the words, it started to drizzle and he ended up smiling over the heavy mist. He even spotted two young kids running for shelter, and he realized the rain will help keep the kids off the streets as well tonight. So the two FBI Agents settled in for their long vigil of the night.

As the night slowly started to drag along, nothing was happening on the entire long block of commercial building, outside of a few kids digging around in the garbage for anything they could pick up to sell even though it was still drizzling out. Then it happened, at exactly 12.21 A.M. someone came strolling out of the building and he looked down the block in the opposite direction where Rossie had his vehicle parked. The guy had a flash light and he gave a number of signals with it, and almost instantly, a vehicle obviously on the next block down flashed his headlights and when he did, he lit up Rossie's parked car in the process. As soon as the headlights hit his vehicle, the two agents immediately ducked down in the front seat.

Agent Rossie picked up the sound of a car motor and he slowly raised his head and looked between the steering wheel and the dashboard of his car and easily picked up the car that flashed his headlights, was now coming down the block slowly with its headlights off and he ducked down and reported to Agent Fugiwara what he just noticed going down outside. At the same time, his radio squawked and he opened the communication and heard. "Hey Bob, I got a fucking vehicle heading for the fricking target building with his headlights off. Over."

"We picked up the same thing from this side of the block, but the sorry sonofabitch lit up our vehicle like a Christmas tree with his headlights when he flashed them, I just hope they didn't pay any attention to the way we were parked over here, dammit. Over." He responded with a snap in his voice as he chanced another look at what was happening by the target building.

"Who do you think is coming to the damn place, could it be our stinking target? Over." Agent Parker asked as he was manning the radio while Agent Wilson was the driver.

"I haven't the slightest idea, I just took another peek, we're in direct line with the oncoming vehicle, and it's hard for me to see what the hell's going on out there. Do you still have a good MOE (Mark One Eyeball) on the moving vehicle, Agent Parker? Over."

"Yeah, we have a clear view of the bastard, and it looks like the vehicle is about to turn onto the target property, yep, there he goes. He's turning onto the property alright and Subject One has moved out of the vehicle's way and it seems like Subject One is now directing the vehicle where to park. Errr... head's up, three more Subjects have just came rushing out of the building, and it looks like they're now surrounding the Subject who just got out of the parked vehicle. The exiting Subject is a large black man. Isn't it reported this Young character is supposed to be a large man, Agent Rossie? Over."

"That's a Roger, Young is reported to be a large black man could it be the sonofabitch was never inside the building until now, dammit? Or could it be Agents Johnson and Wesson missed our target when he exited the building, and he's now returning to his little rathole? Over."

"I seriously doubt that last Agent Rossie, Johnson might be a real fuckup, but there's no way in hell he'd ever miss one of our targets as he left the target building, Agent Rossie. He's too good at what he does to ever make that large a mistake on any stakeout he's assigned to sir. Over Agent Rossie." Agent Parker offered in Johnson's defense to the Lead Agent of the operation.

"What the hell's going on out there? I can't lift my head high enough to get a good look without possibly compromising my position at this time, Agent Parker. Over."

"The Subjects are walking cautiously back towards the building and all Subjects are well protecting the one Subject who just exited the vehicle. There they go they're all inside the building. You two guys can relax a little now it looks like all the rats are back in their hole for the night, hopefully, Agent Rossie. Over." Parker reported to the Lead Agent.

"Thank God for that, I really thought something was going to go down on us tonight. I'm happy I didn't punch the panic button and alert or revolved police presence in the surrounding area over this damn stakeout. I would've surely ended up looking like the south end of a north bound horse if

I did, dammit. I hate these fucking stakeout duties. Over." Rossie complained.

"I hate to admit this to you Agent Rossie. But I was just about to push the panic button myself, until all the bastards when back inside the damn building, so we both could have looked at what you just said, the south end of a north bound horse. I like that one... Uh-oh, hang on a second Agent Rossie, the front door light of the subject building just went on again, and it looks like someone's standing in the doorway now. He's still inside the building, but there's definitely someone standing in the doorway of the subject building sir. Have no idea what he might be up to so standby and when I see what he's up to, I'm report same to you Agent Rossie. Over."

"Standing by, I have a pretty good look at the target building again myself, but I don't have a good MOE on the front door of the damn place though, so I'm forced to rely on what you can observe of what's going on by the front door, Agent Parker. Over."

"I roger that last, standby because something looks like it might be going down by the front door of the place. I can't make it out clearly at this time Agent Rossie. But something is definitely up, because I'm picking up a number of shadows now passing by the front door on the inside of the target building. I'm happy there's a large window on each side of the front doors. It's enabling me to see a little deeper into the target building. It sure looked like something is cooking in the dump I'm picking up some increase in the activity inside the dump, Agent Rossie. Over." Agent Parker reported as he concentrated his binoculars on the front door of the building.

"Keep me informed because I can get a good look at the front door of the place without compromising my position to the Subjects, Agent Parker. Over." Agent Rossie offered as he stretched his neck, trying to see if he could get a look at the front door of the building.

"Roger that last, I'll keep you advised. So far all the activity is being contained inside the subject building at this time, Agent Rossie. I see no one coming out of the damn building, or any other lights going on inside the building. All the activity I'm picking up is still happening at the front door of the subject building at this time Agent Rossie. Over."

Rossie turned to his partner and grumbled at him this time. "Crap, I wish to hell I knew what was going down inside the damn building. I'm one breath away from pushing the panic button and alerting the local police to tighten up their backup security for our stakeout, Fugiwara-san."

"I don't blame you in the least for the tension you're suffering Rossie-san. My balls are bugging me, and that only happens when my ass is in any danger, partner. Do you think you might want to get in contact with Murdock, and inform him of what might be going down, or at least have him order Agents Johnson and Wesson back here before any shit goes down on us, Rossie-san? This I why I hate these damn stakeout duties so much. You never know when the shit's going to hit the fan on ya, dammit." Agent Fugiwara complained at his partner.

"I don't know; on one hand I need to see what the hell is happening with this damn situation before I go and start pushing any panic buttons around here. But on the other hand; I don't want to wait too long before calling in any of our backup Units until we're dick deep in purps trying to kill us, Fugiwara-san. Damn, what to do, what to do? Shit, I think we're going to remain still and wait and see if anything goes down on us. But I'm telling you this, at the first sign of any trouble coming our way I'm calling in the troops. Shit, I think Murdock started my goose bumps and now I'm starting to see trouble coming our way from all angles dammit." Agent Rossie groused as he looked out the car windshield, still trying to get an eye on the front door of the place.

"Say Agent Rossie, It looks like there is more activity happening, I'm picking up much movement inside the target building. I see many Subjects running back and forth before the two large plate glass windows on either side of the front doors of the structure now sir. Over."

Agent Rossie moved his weight around in the front seat of his vehicle, while trying to get a better angle on the front door. He discovered the only why he was going to be able to clearly see the front door of the subject building, was to exit the car and then walk out to the sidewalk and then look down the block with his binoculars, and he knew that move was completely out of the question. If he exposed himself that much, the purps holdup inside the building would easily detect his presence and attack him and his partner without question.

"Be advised Agent Rossie, it seems whatever the hell was creating all the activity inside the target building has reached its peak, and it now seems like all the activity is dying down inside the building at this time sir. Two of the outside light just went out, and it seems like the Subjects who were making all the movement by the front doors have either went back to whatever the hell they were doing inside the building, or whatever was causing all the concern has dissipated, and everything seems to be getting calmed down inside the structure again, sir. Over."

"Roger that last Agent Parker keep me informed on any possible changes. Over,"

"Immediately Agent Rossie. Over."

"Well what the hell do you make out about all that crap that just went down inside the dump, Fugiwara-san?" Agent Rossie asked his partner with concern in his voice.

"I have no stinking idea what all that crap was about just then, all I know is I'm damn glad I didn't push any panic buttons and pulled in our backup personnel. Or we would've surely blown this stakeout, and then we'd be swimming around in purps trying to kill us, Rossie-san. I don't know for certain who just showed up at the target building, I'd like to think it was Young, so we know for certain where the sonofabitch is truly holdup, and that was what caused all the activity inside the target building. But I truly don't know at this point, so I say we stay alert and be ready for anything coming our way. We also have to keep our finger on the so called panic button in case the bastards come flooding out of there, and we're forced to engage them. I want all the help we can surround ourselves with, judging by the number of people we just saw come out of the damn building and protect the bastard who just showed up at the building, Rossie-san."

"I hear you there my friend. I just wish this night was over already. With the stakeouts I've been on, I'm beginning to believe this one was the most stressful of them all. Maybe it has something to do with the constant drizzle we're dealing with and also the bastard we have to deal with on this one Fugiwara-san. I don't know which one is driving my hackles wild the most. I don't think I'm going to bother Murdock until the last possible moment if anything goes down. I can just see his face if I make contact with him and that contact turns out to be nothing. The Big Growl would never let me forget that one as long as he was in Command of the company."

"Yeah, but I'd give a stinking day's pay just to see his stinking puss turn that so lovely deep red it always turns whenever he gets upset with us, Rossie-san. It's the only way I can get back at him, by always trying to drive him nuts, Rossie-san." Agent Fugiwara smirked at his partner.

"I'm not going there with you again Agent Fugiwara-san. I already warned you that you were starting to push him a bit too far lately over all your screwing around with women. And you have to remember that he's the one in command of us, and it's what he says or does that counts with us, so I suggest you get off his ass a little for your own sake around here man. Then maybe he just might get off your ass a little bit in return my friend. But you're so damn stubborn you never pay attention to anything I warn you about when it comes down to Murdock and you, mister. One of these days you're going to pay big time for being such a pain in the ass with him when you have to find a new line of work. Or you have to transfer to a different post, or he banishes your ass to an outpost somewhere in bumfuck Egypt my old friend." Once again Agent Rossie tried to talk Agent Fugiwara to get off Murdock's back so peace can return to the company.

"You know something Rossie-san I think your words are starting to get through to my noggin after all my friend. Maybe you're right for a change, and I should get off Murdock's case a little and see if he gets off my ass in return. I'm getting a little tired of always banging heads with him every time we met my friend. I'd really hate to be transferred from this station, unless he might do me a huge favor here and he transfers me to the Jersey FBI office. That way I'd be a helluva lot closer to home, and that just might stop me from fooling around so much on my lady." Agent Fugiwara stopped speaking and then he went deep in thought for a few minutes, and then a wicked smile crossed his lips as he added one word to what he was thinking.

"Not!"

"Not what?" Agent Rossie asked his partner with a grin on his lips this time.

"Not nothing is ever going to stop me from playing the field like I do. I just love women too much to be faithful to just one of them for the rest of my stinking life, Rossie-san."

"I thought you were talking out of your ass because your mouth knew better, buddy. I know nothing this side of judgment day will ever stop you from cheating on your wife, asshole."

"You got it all wrong there Rossie-san. I'm not cheating on my wife. I'm just sharing myself with all the ladies of the world. If I was cheating on anyone, I'd be cheating the women of the world by staying truthful with just one lady, and depriving all the other women of me and the pleasures I can offer them, Rossie-san." He replied with a smirk of his own this time.

"Oh brother, are you suffering from a case of the big balls around here buster, you feel you would be depriving the women of the world of your pleasure? You really believe that load of tripe you're spilling outta that mouth of yours, buddy?"

CHAPTER TWENTY SIX
FBI AGENT ROBERT ROSSIE'S VEHICLE

"Sure I do Rossie-san. Just think of how many broken hearted women of the world will be fumbling their way around out there, if they knew I was out of the running with them?"

Agent Rossie just shook his head at his partner, but their light hearted moment was suddenly interrupted by a call in from Agent Parker.

"Agent Rossie, I have a lot of activity at the target building suddenly. The outside lights were just flipped on and I see a lot of movement by the front of the stinking door again. Stand by, something happening in there..." Agent Parker reported to the Lead Agent of the operation.

"What the hell do you see going on out there I need more Intel before I can react properly to any possible threat, Agent Parker. Respond!" Rossie growled into the mike of his radio.

When no reply came back from Agent Parker, he growled again into his radio in an angry voice. "I just ordered you to report to me what the hell you see going on out there mister and you have failed to report to me. What the hell do you see happening and is it a threat against us at this time, Agent Parker? Report in immediately to me mister that's a direct order, sir."

"Agent Rossie, I have a large number of Subjects pouring out of the building at this time in a rush. All Subjects are heavily armed with automatic weapons, M16's and AK 47's to be sure. A good number of them are taking up defensive positions right in front of the building, and a few of them are rushing towards the curb of the road. Be advised Agent Rossie, one of the Subject's has a flashlight in hand, and it looks like he's going to be aiming it at your vehicle, sir. I believe we have been uncovered and we have an active situation on our hands. Call in our backup support. I make at least seventeen purps have just taken up positions on the outside before the front of the target building, sir. Over." Agent Parker reported to the Lead Agent of the stakeout operation.

Just as Agent Parker warned Rossie about one of the Subject's with the flashlight, the light instantly eliminated his vehicle, and then the second Subject started to fire at his car with the M-16 he had locked in his hands. The windshield of his vehicle instantly shattered, and the stream of rounds ripped apart the interior of the parked vehicle at the same time, if it was not for the motor of the car, the two now trapped FBI Agents would surely be dead.

FBI SPECIAL AGENT ROBERT ROSSIE'S APARTMENT

Wind was trying to keep busy to stop her boredom by cleaning her equipment when she was suddenly hit with a feeling of being a little lightheaded. Then she closed her eyes and she dropped down to her knees as she realized her Liege Lord was suddenly suffering great stress from something that was happening around him.

She closed her eyes tighter and she concentrated with all her might and then in her mind's eye, she was suddenly able to see what was going on with her young Master. Seeing he was in terrible danger, she wanted to immediately rush to his side and protect him from all harm. But her Liege Lord's angry words of warning for her never to intervene with his line of work was still ringing loudly in her ears. Never the less, she got off her knees and she rushed into their bedroom, and she quickly changed into her heavily altered battle robe and she carefully started salting her body with the extra weapons she would need in order to better protect her Liege Lord's life. Once she was read to do combat, she returned to the center of the apartment and again she dropped down to her knees and immediately went deep into her meditation.

She was concentrating with all her might and what her Liege Lord was seeing, she was also seeing at the same time. Her heart started pounding wildly in her chest because she realized the enemy Samurai were attacking her Liege Lord with the hated metal hand and firing the unseen dragon's teeth that so easily ripped into the ancient and heavy battle robe. Every fiber in her body was driving her to follow the call of the sacred amulet, and rush to her Liege Lord's side and protect his life like she was trained from birth to do. But her feet were anchored to the apartment by her Master's orders for her not to come to him while he was working.

She now tried desperately to calm down her fast beating heart and she want to go to her Lord's side and defend him from the lowly attackers trying to destroy him. Now she was praying to the all the Kami of the Floating World, so they could change her Lord and Master's orders so she could go to him. She called upon her namesake, Fujin, the always angry God of Wind to intercede and speak to the Council of Kami, and see if he could have them change her orders so she could rush to her master's side and save his life.

She was so concerned that her Master was on the verge of being slaughtered by the attackers, she even considered forgetting her Master's orders and rush to him and protect him before he was killed by the attackers. She was so torn in what to do, so all she could do for the moment. was to watch and when she had enough and could no longer stand it and she rushed to his aide, she would react and the Kami could do whatever they wanted to do with her spirit once she saved her ward for death. So did not even care if the angry Kami killed her spirit and her being no longer existed in either world. All she knew was when she could no longer stand it she was going to come to her Master's aide no matter what.

BACK AT THE STAKEOUT

When Young's horde of bodyguards started to fire on Agent Rossie's vehicle, both Agent Parker and Wilson jumped out of their vehicle and they started to open fire on the gang members with their own M-16s. But their weapon fire was much more controlled than the way the bodyguards were just spraying their rounds wildly at Agent Rossie's vehicle.

When the other two agents started firing on the gang members, they immediately turned their attention on them. One of the gang members with the flashlight was the first one hit by Parker's rounds. The gang shooters was now wildly pounding rounds down the block at both Parker and Wilson as they returned his fire with that of their own. Suddenly, the sounds of sirens also filled the night air as a horde of responding police vehicles reported to the scene of the shooting.

FBI Commander Ralph Murdock's phone rang and he answered it in a sleepy voice. "Yeah, Murdock here, who is this?"

"Commander Murdock Sir, this is Sheriff Bill Wagner Sir, I just received a report that all hell just broke out at you FBI stakeout over at West Street sir. It was further reported heavy, and I mean heavy automatic weapon fire was reported being fired. I just dispatched our helicopter so they can better light up the entire area in question with their huge floodlight sir. I also have every spare squad car I can spare responding to the scene I can order there sir. I'm going to report to the scene so I can take command of my Officers and also coordinate them with your Agents you have working on this operation sir. From all the reports I have flooding in sir, it sounds bad, real bad sir. I might even be forced to pull in Police Officers from other offices to better handle this situation before it really gets out of hand on us, sir."

All the grogginess instantly left Murdock's body as he jumped out of bed, and he started dressing with his free hand, as he held the phone to his ear with the other and he listened to the Sherriff's report. His wife was up and she started to make him some coffee, because she realized her husband was going back to work tonight. Murdock looked at the clock and was surprised it was only ten minutes past one and he informed the Sherriff. "Look Sherriff Wagner Sir, I though the regular Washington Police Department was going to handle this one for us? I'm also going to respond to the scene, but first I'm going to alert a number of my other Agents. I want every hand I can possible get out there trying to end this damn thing before it all blows up in our faces sir. I'll get back to you when I'm on my way to the scene, Sherriff."

"Yes sir, I understand and I'm heading out now for the scene. I want to be with my people when they respond to this mess, sir. I'll be expecting to hear from you when you arrive on the scene as well, sir. Also Commander Murdock, the local Washington Police have and are responding also, but they reported to me they were underhanded and informed me of this stakeout you had in operation, and I informed him I'll have my deputies cover the stakeout for him. But they do have their vehicles involved in this mess as well, sir." The excited Sherriff Wagner responded to the FBI Commander's minor bitch at him.

"You got it Sherriff." With that Murdock broke off the connection with the Sherriff, and then he immediately dialed Agent Johnson. Three rings later. "Yeah, this is Johnson."

"Agent Johnson, all hell just broke out at the stakeout, we have Agents in harm's way sir."

"I'm on it, I'll contact Agent Wesson and we'll meet you at the scene, Commander. We both have 16's in the trunk of my vehicle sir. It's about time we put the period at the end of Young's fricking sentence for him sir. He has screwed around with us for long enough and he killed enough kids with that god damn poison he peddles, sir. I'll be leaving to pick up Agent Wesson then we'll head for the scene as quickly as we can get there, sir."

"I'll link up with you there, glad to have you on my side, Agent Johnson you're one of my best Agents, sir." Murdock offered as he broke off the connection and then he rushed downstairs while still struggling into his shoulder holster and weapon. His wife met him at the foot of the stairs and she offered him the cup of coffee that he gulped down as he continued to walk towards the front door, He stopped just long enough to finish his coffee, and then he kissed his wife goodbye and went out into the darkness of the night.

BACK AT THE STAKEOUT

The instant the gang members turned their attention and started firing at Agents Parker and Wilson, both Rossie and Fugiwara jumped out of their vehicle and they started firing at the other gang members from actually behind them now. The gang members now found themselves caught in a cross fire, but that ended real quick when more of the gang members poured out of the building, and they started to fire in both directions, driving all four of the FBI Agents back to seek better protection against the horde of deadly rounds being fired at them.

Agent Parker continued to trade rounds with the gang members, but Agent Wilson stopped a round in his shoulder and he went down hard. So Parker stopped firing and he lent aide to his downed partner as he asked him with concern. "How bad you hit buddy?"

"Not good, I'm down for the count and I'm fighting to stay..." Wilson passed out in his partner's arms as he growled at his partner. "God dammit, I'll get them for you buddy." Parker then grabbed his radio and roared into it. "Agent Rossie, Wilson's down and he's out. I can't tell if he's still alive or not, I'm still receiving heavy weapon fire, and I have to reply or I'm going to end up like Wilson. Where the fuck is our god damn backup for Christ sake?"

Just as he cursed over the radio, the first two squad cars came roaring down the block and slammed to a stop and two Sherriff's from each car got out, and they started firing at the gang. A third Sherriff car came in from the other end of the road and linked up with Parker, with one of the Sherriff's aiding Wilson. After discovering he died, he added his weapon fire to the fight.

Both Murdock' and Johnson's vehicles arrived on the side of the road where Rossie was firing at the gang members from almost at the same exact moment. Both Agents Johnson and Wesson fanned out on Fugiwara's side of the vehicle, and they opened fire on the gang members with their M-16s While Commander Murdock got out on Agent Rossie's side of the vehicle and he ran to him and started firing with his service weapon at the hunkered down gang members. Rossie laughed at his Commander and then he smirked at him. "What's this crap with the damn service weapon, Commander? You can't handle a 16, sir?"

"I hate them damn things, they make my top plate fall and the last time I used one of the damn things, I lost my plate, it fell out of my mouth and I ended up stepping on my teeth and breaking the damn plate. Since then I never used another one of those weapons if I can help it, mister." He yelled at Agent Rossie over all the weapon fire going off all around them.

Agent Rossie had to laugh over why Commander Murdock refused to use another M-16 in this shootout. More Sherriff cars came down the road and they quickly circled around the agents. Rossie was the first one to see an Ambulance put up behind where Parker was firing at the gang members from. The brave paramedics got out and they started working on Wilson, trying to bring him back to life, but everything they did for him did not help. The bullet traveled up his shoulder and ended up in his neck and ripped it up beyond repair.

Weapon fire now broke out from inside the building as windows were kicked out, and other gang members began to shoot at the police firing at their other criminals on the outside of the building. The return fire from the more and more Sherriff, regular police officers, and a number of other FBI Agents who heard what was going down, and they came in and supported their fellow agents by lending their weapon fire to the minor war going down right in the center of the commercial district of downtown Washington. The Sherriff helicopter was doing a fine job of lighting up the gang members, but it was forced to move off when some of the gang members began to fire at the hovering helicopter, trying to knock out the powerful floodlight giving away their hiding places to the officers trying to get at them.

Then he finally got a chance to speak safely with Agent Rossie, and Murdock asked him in an excited tone of voice. "What the hell happened to have set this mess off like this, Rossie?"

"Someone who we believe was Young came down the road, and he entered the building. When he was coming down the block, one of his people came out and when who we believe was Young's vehicle responded to the flashlight signal from the first Subject who came out of the building. The car flipped his headlights on and when it did, it completely eliminated my thought to be well hidden vehicle, sir. Then a mob of his damn friends came out and surrounded him, and they walked him into the building. Evidently they must have spotted my car, and once they secured Young inside the damn building. The purps poured back out of the building and they opened fire on Agent Fugiwara and me first, and when Agents Wilson and Parker opened fire at them from the other side of the road, they immediately turned their attention on them."

With a deep breath in, Agent Rossie continue with his report for the Commander. "I hate like hell to report this to you Ralph, but I believe Agent Wilson is dead. He was killed when the purps opened fire on him and Parker after they opened fire on the bastards, sir."

"Shit Joe's dead, god dammit, I really want Young's fucking hide now. I don't want him to come walking out of that damn building alive, do you understand? I want him to be dragged out and dumped down the fucking sewer. I can't believe they were able to kill Wilson for crap sake." Murdock was obviously extremely shaken by the news one of his agents was killed in the firefight raging almost out of control in the commercial district of Washington.

Their conversation was suddenly interrupted by heavy weapon fire, this time it was turned on them from the gang members, because this area was were the heaviest weapon fire was coming from the police and being aimed at the gang members. Agent Rossie had to put a loaded clip in his weapon, and then he started to fire in short three round controlled bursts at the criminals. The weapon fire was so heavy that the surviving members of Young's gang was forced to move back inside the building for their own protection, and they immediately started to shoot at the police from any area they could fire from inside the building.

Two heavy armored Sherriff vehicles pulled up by Agent Rossie's parked vehicle, and the driver of one of the heavy machines stuck his head out of the port and he barked at who he thought was in command of the officers firing so far away from the target building. "You guys want me to approach the building and you guys can use my vehicle as cover, so you can get a lot closer to all the action and maybe break this mess up some?"

Agent Rossie looked at Commander Murdock and he immediately nodded yes, and then he replied to the young Commander riding inside the armored vehicle. "That's sounds like a damn good plan to me buddy." He then ejected the half empty clip and slammed a full clip home. He did not want to start to shoot with a clip with just a few rounds left in it. Agent Fugiwara followed suit and he placed a full clip in his M-16, and then the three FBI Agents and Four Sherriff Deputes and two regular Washington Police Officers all got behind the heavily armored and slow moving vehicle as it slowly approached the target building.

The armored vehicle came under direct heavy weapon fire, and Agent Rossie could hear many rounds pinging off the heavy steel hide of the once war machine. One police officer went down, he was hit in the ankle and he dropped to the ground, but he rolled over until he ended up hiding behind one of the commercial trucks parked on the side of the road, and once he was out of the line of fire, the armored vehicle started to move towards the target building again. The officers knew they had to get closer to the building to be part of the action.

Agent Rossie cautiously looked around the massive machine and he noticed there were no gang members still outside the building still alive. He counted six downed bodyguards for Young. He suddenly slammed his hand against the back of the machine and it stopped and the driver opened the hatch using the cover as protection for his head as he looked to see what the FBI Agent wanted to either tell him or what he might want from him at this point.

"This is close enough to the fucking building, now if you can turn onto the property and move us near that parked car to your right, we can use that as a cover and see what these bastards are up to in there. You don't happen to have a voice amplifier in this machine do you, sir?"

"I can get you guys close enough to that car for you to get behind it without them being able to get a round off at ya and yes, there's a megaphone on the rear of the machine on the left side in that metal box back there sir. You're more than welcome to use the damn thing, sir."

FBI Agent Robert Rossie looked for the box the driver was talking about, spotting it on the tail end of the machine he quickly opened it and removed the megaphone, and then he followed the machine until it pulled right up alongside the parked car that delivered who he thought was Young to the building. When the three FBI Agents, four Sherriff's and one police officer made a dash for the cover of the parked car, they got down low and almost instantly, the gang members held up inside the building, started to pound away at the car with their weapon fire in hopes of either killing the police officers, or driving them away from the building. It did not take the officers long to realize the car did not offer them enough cover to keep them alive, so the small group of officers and agents got back behind the armored vehicle, and decided to keep that machine parked where it was. Rossie picked up the megaphone, flipped it on and then barked into the machine after he adjusted it to the proper volume.

"You guys inside the building, why don't you people do the right thing here and knock off all the weapon fire, and then come out of the building with your hands locked behind your heads nice and easy like. If things keep going like this, not one of you guys will get out of that building alive. So do the right thing here and give up now, before anyone else has to die here tonight."

His answer from the gang members was a new hail of deadly rounds fired at them, forcing Agent Rossie to drop back down safely behind the armored vehicle, and he complained at Murdock. "Well, that didn't go the way I wanted it to go down sir."

"You think?" Murdock fired right back at his smirking young agent.

Agent Parker placed a call to Rossie, because he had no idea Murdock had came in and he was working with Agents Rossie and Fugiwara. "Hey Rossie, you took all the weapon fire off me and the few Police Officers working with me over here. How the hell are you doing up there? If you want, we can try and work our way up to you and lend you guys a hand."

"I was meaning to make contact with you, I saw the medics working on Agent Wilson, any luck there, Agent Parker?" He asked the other agent with concern in his voice.

"No luck at all I hate to report, Agent Wilson is gone and I want some payback for the rotten bastards who just killed him on me, Rossie..."

"Control yourself, Agent Parker I can ill afford to have an Agent working on a vengeance mission, not with what we're current faced with here. We're facing a group of assholes who think nothing about killing any authorities, and we have to stop then here and now. But we have to be operating with clear heads here on this one, not on vengeance, Agent Parker."

"Is that you Commander Murdock, I can't believe you came to assist us with this one sir. I'm glad to have you on board for this mess, this way you can see everything that goes down first hand sir. I'm not operating on a vengeance angle here sir. But when we finally get our hands on these damn purps, I want first dibs on Young's fucking head. I owe that to Agent Wilson sir. All I want to do is speak with him for just five minutes sir. Then I'll give you what's left of the sonofabitch so he can stand trial, if he can stand at all after I'm done with his ass that is, sir."

"I promise you Agent Parker, if we take him in alive, I'll allow you to put the cuffs on him while I get everyone else out of the damn building. That way you can have your five minutes with the bastard. Then I'll take my five minutes with him, and then I'll hand his ass over to Agent Rossie and see what he leaves of the lousy bastard, and if there's enough left off him. I'll allow Agent Fugiwara to have a few moments with the bastard, and then every other Agent involved in this mess will get their bit of time with the fuck as well."

Agent Edward Parker smiled to himself, because he knew there was no way in hell Murdock was going to allow anyone from the company to get their hands on Young for a second.

But he was still hoping Young would be stupid enough to make a fight of it and if he was lucky, he would be the one to end his life because of what he done to his partner.

Once he was finished speaking with Parker, Commander Murdock turned his attention back to the task at hand. He poked his head around the armored vehicle and a round went whizzing by his head and he pulled back and thought for a moment. But before he could make a decision, all the police hiding behind their squad cars parked in the center of the street facing the target building, opened fire driving the gang members away from the front of the building.

When most of the heavy weapon fire slackened down enough, Murdock grabbed the megaphone and he warned the purps still held up inside the building. "Listen up in there, I'm giving you people ten seconds to come out of there with your hands up, and at the end of that time, we're going to storm that building and if you people don't give up real peaceful like then you'll be carried the hell out of there, feet up."

Then he looked at Agent Rossie and asked him. "Are you ready if we have to make a hot entry in there, sir? I can't allow this shit to continue the way it's going down. The longer it takes us to root these assholes out of there, the harder it's going to be for us when we go after them."

Rossie had to blow his breath out in a rush, and then he rapidly shook his hands to get his circulation moving again, he was that worried about them forcing their way into a compromised building with who knew how many heavily armed purps were hiding in there, and ready to fight it out with anyone to entered the building. His blood pressure was going sky high, and his breathing was becoming labored at the same time, and he was sweating profusely as well.

FBI SPECIAL AGENT ROBERT ROSSIE'S APARTMENT

Wind was deep in mediation feeling every bit of the pressure and concern her Lord was feeling at the same time he was suffering through the hard time at the target building. As hard as she was trying to remain at the apartment following her Liege Lord's order not to intervene in his work, she was having so much trouble obeying his orders. Every fiber of her body was crying out for her to run to her Master's side and protect her ward like she was trained to do for her whole life.

Every time Agent Rossie got a little more excited over the deadly situation, the amulet would automatically send her another flash of pain as a building warning her Liege Lord was in danger, and she should go to him immediately. Each time her Master got excited again, the flash of pain would be much sharper as the amulet tried to order her to his side. Her mind was being ripped apart with the want to go and protect her Liege Lord, but she was also fighting with herself over obeying his order not to come to him when he was working. Another shot of sharp pain and she suddenly sprang up to her feet, and then she began to pace the apartment, wanting so bad to rush out to her Liege Lord's side and protect him.

Then she felt a wave of relief as she sensed her Lord had suddenly relaxed and calmed down a bit. Now she was happy she did not rush to his side, because she would have surely upset him and then she would have to make good her mistake by committing Suppuku, and be forced to go back to the Floating World for another stick of time, as a further punishment from the Kami Gods for her failing to honor and protect her Liege Lord properly. Lately, she was growing rather resentful over always having to worry about everyone else's feeling and safety. Again, she felt more comfort coming from her Liege Lord and since he was calming down, so was she and she was deciding if she wanted to go to her meditation or not.

THE STAKEOUT

FBI Lead Special Agent Robert Rossie leaned up against the stopped heavy armored vehicle as Commander Ralph Murdock was taking more and more pressure off his shoulders, and he was perfectly fine with that. Even Agent Shinnosuke Fugiwara was relaxing and he was likewise allowing Murdock to takeover command of the entire operation which was his duty all along.

Before he ordered his agents and the police officers and deputies supporting their action, Murdock offered to his Lead Agent. "Bob, when I'm done waiting for these assholes to come the fuck out of that damn building, I'm going to order this armored vehicle to crash through the front of the building. Once he rips an opening wide enough for us to enter the structure, we're going to follow the machine into the building. Once we're inside, were going to immediately fan out and then start to search for every scumbag hiding inside that dump. I'm giving you the direct order and I want you to pass it on to the rest of our backup support Units. I don't want any of my Agents or Police playing with any of these bastards in there. It they don't give up as soon as you come across any of them then in there you're to take them out and hunt for your next target.

"I'm not going to lose another Agent or Officer because one of you guys hesitated for a second not wanting to kill these bastards and the pricks were able to get the drop on them because of that hesitation. The answer to this present situation is hot, and if they don't give up. Then they don't want t live a second longer in this world. Do you read my last ordered, Agent Rossie Sir?"

"I got you loud and clear and as for my passing that order on to our backup Units, that's easy sir. I had my handheld radio opened and everyone attached to this operation, heard your last orders as you issued them to us Commander. So I guess we're as ready as ever to get this mess over with. From the looks of it, our backup Police Officers obviously heard your last order, and they looked geared up and ready to follow us into the building, sir. Look at them sir, I'm certain they all heard we lost one of our own already, and they look like they're just foaming at the mouth to get some payback for our dead Agent, sir." Agent Rossie drew Murdock's attention to the police officers still positioned being their squad cars in the middle of the street, and he could easily tell they were all hopped up and ready to jump into action as soon as he did.

"I see what you mean Agent Rossie, well then there's no sense in putting this shit off for a moment longer. The damn fools in there used up every bit of the ten seconds I gave them to come out of there and then some. You better get ready, we're about to jump off, you got your vest on and what about your partner, does he have his vest on as well, mister?" Commander Murdock asked his agents if they had their bulletproof vests on.

"We're both protected we put the vests on as soon as we reported for the stakeout duty as was the standing orders, sir." Agent Rossie offered as his blood pressure shot up to the top of the scale, and he started breathing heavily as he prepared his body for action.

"Very well, I guess now is as good as any to get this damn mess over with, so let's get going. Commander I want you to rev this damn thing up then I want you to charge the building. Keep your foot to the metal and drive this damn thing as deep as you can inside that dump. Then you're ordered to hunker down inside the damn machine and leave the rest of this shit up to us. Did you get my orders, sir?" Murdock asked the drive, he wanted to make certain there was no doubt in his mind what he wanted him to do with his heavy armored machine, and then he added to his orders to the driver of the armored machine. "I want you to floor this damn thing when I slam my hand down on the tail end of the steel hide of this thing, mister. You got it right sir?"

"Yes sir, I'm waiting for your signal, and then I'll ram the damn building for you sir."

"Very good, I'm going to communicate with the rest of the Unit's part of this operation." Murdock adjusted his handheld radio and then he barked into it when he was certain everyone attached to his operation had their ears on. "Okay people listen up I'm only going to say this one time so if you didn't hear my fucking words then you people better be damn able to read my fucking mind, because I won't repeat my order a second time to anyone. I'll be too busy entering this damn building with the rest of my Agents. To all personnel, when you see this machine start forward, follow us because he's going to rip the front of the building open for us. Once we're inside the building, it's a fox hunt and I don't want any of you people getting hurt. Don't play around with these scumbags, they give you any trouble ice them off toot sweet. If you people are ready give me a beep and then we're active."

Commander Murdock listened in and his handheld radio was instantly flooded with many beeps from the other Units involved in his operation, and when he felt everyone was operating on the same page, he immediately slapped his hand down loudly on the steel backside of the armored vehicle. Instantly a thick black heavy cloud of diesel bellowed out of the exhaust pipe of the machine, and then it lunged forward, picking up steam as the machine charged right for the pair of heavy glass front doors of the building. Without the slightest bit of hesitation, the metal monster had no problem crashing into the building, and almost as fast as it was traveling, the large machine disappeared deep inside the building.

Commander Ralph Murdock, along with Special Agents Robert Rossie and Shinnosuke Fugiwara and Alan Johnson and Mark Wesson, and the four Sherriff Deputies and one remaining police officer, charged right behind the vehicle. Behind them was a horde of other police officers and their elite SWAT Officers. As soon as the horde of officers entered the building, they fanned out and went searching for any targets. Weapon fire erupted in many areas of the building. There was a small second floor landing with two large offices and that was where Young found himself trapped as he and nine of his best and heavily armed bodyguards were holdup with plenty of ammunition. The rest of his bodyguards had orders to stop any of the police officers from getting at Young, who planned to get out of the building the first chance he got to leave.

The extremely concerned Drug Kingpin David Young was keeping a close eye on what was going on at the first floor of the building, always looking for the first chance of him getting out of the building alive. He found himself cursing his luck, because he just returned to the building from visiting his girlfriend to share a meal and her bed with, and now he was trapped in a life and dead struggle with the police he could not get an accurate count on.

Agent Rossie broke off from following Command Murdock and both he and Fugiwara went deeper into the building, and when he was confronted with three of the mob, then engaged in a heavy firefight. Rossie fired first, hitting one of the bodyguards, while Agent Fugiwara engaged another one of them. Rounds were flying in all directions and the quarters were so close it was hard to aim a weapon, so the agents were firing more or less from the hip. Agent Rossie had to disengage as he ejected the empty clip from his M-16, and then slammed a full clip home. He was cursing up a storm and shaking like a leave in the wind, he was so scared of what was happening all around him as he again engaged the third gang member. Then it happened.

FBI Special Agent Shinnosuke Fugiwara cried out and then he went down hard. He also got hit in the shoulder and the round got through his armored vest and came out at the back of his neck. The wound was bad, but it was not a mortal wound, just a very painful one. When he went down, Agent Rossie got a clear shot at the one who just hit Fugiwara and he took him out. His blood pressure was so high it was actually pounding in his ears, and he bent down and checked on Fugiwara's condition. "You hurt bad Fugiwara-san?"

"You ever see someone hurt good you fucking idiot you?"

"I guess you're not hurt all that bad for you to be in such a shitty mood my friend. Did you just experience a sharp pain in the neck?"

"No wiseass, I just experienced a blow job. What the hell do you think I experienced, buster?"

"Testy, testy. It's amazing how much a little bullet can change the disposition of the one who was hit. All joking aside, how are you doing my friend?"

"I hurt like a mutherfucker Rossie-san. Look, leave me here and keep going. I don't want you worrying about me any, because it could cause you to get tagged as well. Keep going buddy, I'll be okay, go get that fucking Young cocksucker for Wilson, man." Agent Fugiwara raised his good arm and he actually shoved Rossie away from him to get him moving again.

"I'm going to go, but first I'm going to shove you under that table to keep you out of sight of any of the bastards we're in here trying to cap. You keep quiet and when this mess is over, I'll come back to you and get you help. I'll call in you're wounded on my handheld, and as soon as the medics are cleared and they can enter the building. They'll find you easy enough my friend. You stay safe and quiet if that's at all possible, buddy. I'll be back to you as soon as I can break free of this mess and check on you. I'll clue Murdock you're wounded, maybe that'll get him off your ass some, partner." With that said, Agent Rossie moved on, he too wanted to get Young.

FBI SPECIAL AGENT ROBERT ROSSIE'S APARTMENT

When Agent Fugiwara was wounded, Agent Rossie's blood pressure responded and spiked so high that Wind had no other choice by to respond to the painful call of the sacred amulet. She allowed the amulet to lead her to his side and when she ended up standing on the outside of the large commercial building behind a wide tree with her sword locked in her hand, she cautiously entered the building. She was not getting a good read on where her Liege Lord was inside the vast building, so she went carefully searching for him. She realized who was the ones working with her ward, so she stayed well out of their view. The interior of the massive commercial building was as black as night, and there was debris scattered about all over the place. It was obvious the ones who were a threat to her Liege Lord's life, were the ones who put so much of the stuff in the way, making it almost impossible to move around the building freely.

She was using all her ancient training as she continued to search for her Lord and Master, she turned a corner and spotted a man with a long thing locked in his arms and when he spotted her, he immediately aimed the thing directly at her, but before he was able to pull the trigger of his rifle, she attacked him with her sword. Her first blow cut his left arm off and it forced him to drop the M-16 and her second blow freed his head from his shoulders. She moved on without giving a second thought to the death she had just caused. She was staying moving in the darker areas of the building, and whenever she picked up one of who she believed were her Master's loyal Samurai, she gave them a wide birth as she continued to move forward. The thunder of so many weapons being fired inside the building was very disconcerting to her, and she was having a little trouble keeping her mind on what she was doing.

As she continued cautiously moving forward inside the massive building, she suddenly came across a door and she opened it and moved into the room, instantly she was set upon by five gang members as they attacked her with their small arms fire. Two of them fired their 9mm Colt pistols at her, and then they expected her to fall dead before them. But they were shocked when instead of falling to the floor she attacked all five men with her sword.

Windsbreath, her sword was a blur of silver as it hacked through limbs, hands, shoulders and necks as easy as the deadly killing sword cut through the air. As she attacked them, blood was splattered all over her body and ancient armor, making her look more like a wild spectra sent from the very pits of hell. Men screamed out in terrible pain while not understanding why their rounds did not stop this wild woman from killing them, as she continued to hack them to death. She never once cared where she struck any these enemy Warriors with her sword, or the terrible damage she was doing to their bodies.

When she killed all five of who she had classified as her Liege Lord's enemy, she cautiously opened the door and reentered the larger area of the massive building. Again as she cautiously moved forward she immediately picked up another man she considered a serious threat to her Liege Lord's life, and the man was hunkered down using a piece of heavy machinery to hide behind. He was obviously waiting for one of the other men dressed in her Lord's uniform to come near enough to him, so he could spring out and kill the unsuspecting Warrior.

So she steathfully worked her way up behind the hidden man and then she attacked him without warning. Wishing to kill this man quickly, she swung her killing Katana blade at him and cut his head from his shoulders, even before the unsuspecting man could possibly react to what was happening to him. He died silently and swiftly and she moved on.

CHAPTER TWENTY SEVEN
THE EARLY MORNING HOURS OF JULY 3rd, 1996

All the while she was moving around inside the building, she continued working her way where more of the thunder from the weapons was happening. She came to another man who did not seem to be a threat and she felt he was working with her Lord, but he was dressed differently than the others obviously helping her Lord. So she worked her way up behind this man and crashed the hilt of her deadly blade on the top of his head, knocking Murdock out cold, and she moved forward. Then she was finally able to pick up her

Liege Lord and he was surrounded by at least six men with ugly metal weapons, and they were all trying to get a clear opening to attack her ward. Immediately she roared as she attacked, running she swiftly passed one man and struck him on the side of the neck with her sword, the man was dead even before his body hit the floor.

Then she rushed by a second hunched down man and she struck out at him, easily chopping his arm off, and then bringing her sword around as she passed him and caught the man a second time with her sword, chopping through his body from between his shoulder and neck, leaving him to suffer a slow death, but he was out of the action. A third enemy Warrior saw this woman kill one of his friends, and he turned his weapon on her and sprayed her body with seven rounds, and then he stared at her in stunned disbelief as she continued to run directly at him.

He was so dumbfounded over why his rounds did not kill her he did not react when she came at him and attacked, cutting him across the throat with the edge of her blade. She kept going and hit a forth man with her blade, chopping his right leg off just above the knee, and then she struck out at him for a second time and also caught him in the neck, leaving him behind to die a slow and agonizing death. She carefully worked her way up behind Rossie as he fired on one of the guys trying to kill him, sending three rounds into the man's body, and dropping him where he was hiding. He did not pick her up standing behind him as he rushed for the stairs leading to the small upper landing with two offices at the top of the stairs.

She did not want to get in his way, so she kind of just silently trailed him up the stairs as quiet as possible and when he reached the top landing, he cautiously moved forward and opened the door carefully to the first room that was obviously empty. So he moved on to the other office much larger than the first one. Again he cautiously opened the door and from what he was able to see from where he was standing on the landing, the room looked totally empty. But there were many places inside this room for anyone who wanted to stay out of sight to hide in. So he took his time looking into this room to the point he actually entered it and cautiously started to search it. When he moved a little deeper into the room, a sudden sound alerted him to the fact someone else was hiding inside the room. So again he carefully moved to his right while holding his weapon at the ready for anything that might come at him.

She decided to remain standing on the outside of this large room, and she had all her feelings on full alert, while her mind prepared her body to react to anything that was aimed at her Liege Lord's life. She vowed to herself as long as she was able to stand, nothing would be able to harm her Lord and Master in any way while he carried out his work.

When Young saw Agent Rossie enter the room all by himself with no backup, he stepped out from behind a file cabinet and aimed his pistol directly at his body. Two more of his bodyguards came out of their hiding place and also aimed their weapons right at him. Then two more stepped out and circled him. Rossie felt he was as good as dead, so he aimed his weapon at Young and ordered him. "Look Mr. Young, there's no chance in hell of you getting out of here alive, so you might as well give up to me, and I'll protect you and bring you in alive. So why don't you order your people to drop their damn weapons and you give up to me, and we can all live through this mess. No one has to die here today. I don't want to shoot you or anyone else..."

"Why not, I want to shoot you mister." Young snapped right back at the FBI Agent.

That was all Wind had to hear, a threat aimed against her Lord and Master, and this large black man was aiming one of the iron hands (Pistols) that fires the dragon's tooth at him and she reacted without hesitation in her actions. She charged into the room as she yelled out in anger.

Young instantly took his eyes off Agent Rossie and looked at this crazy acting woman with a sword in her hand, and she was attacking his people like she had a real purpose in mind. He went to aim at her, but Agent Rossie fired three rounds at him first and he went down in a heap on the floor. But one of Young's bodyguards charged forward and wrestled Rossie down to the ground as Wind continued attacking the other bodyguards. She was hacking and chopping anyone who was in her way. As far as she was concerned, anyone who was in the room besides her Lord was the enemy, and she had to dispatch them immediately before they harmed her ward. She killed three of the total of nine bodyguards in the room protecting Young's life.

When she killed the first three bodyguards, the others came out of hiding as she continued attacking the others. She just wildly kept hacking away at anyone who crossed her path, and when she was down to just two bodyguards still alive in the room, she stopped her attack and then carefully stalked the one still a threat to her Liege Lord as she also watched and saw Rossie had his captive pretty well in hand. She stepped forward and the last bodyguard did not hesitate, he opened fire and seven of his rounds ripped through Wind's body. By now she was so use to the bullets passing harmlessly through her body she barely noticed the slight pain they caused her as she struck out and her sword nearly split this man's head in two down the center. He instantly dropped down to the floor, and she immediately turned her attention back to her Liege Lord.

Seeing she had a clear shot at his throat with her blade of the one who was fighting hand to hand with her Lord, she carefully lowered her killing blade until it barely touched the struggling bodyguard's chin. Then she made a swift move and the edge of her deadly blade easily slit his throat, spraying her Lord with his blood. Her Lord immediately released the death like lock he had on the bodyguard's body, and then he struggled up to his feet and just as he was about to lace into Wind for disobeying his order for her not to come to him whenever he was working. Agent Johnson, who heard the weapon fire going off on the second floor landing, came charging into the room. Picking up Agent Rossie standing with someone covered from head to toe with flesh blood, he instantly rushed for the two of them.

Wind, who was still on guard and charged up and in the mode of protecting her Lord and Master against any possible threat aimed against him, picked up the sudden movement of a man wildly charging at them, and instantly she considered him a threat against her Liege Lord and herself, and she swiftly turned to engage him in battle. As she turned, Rossie picked up Agent Johnson rushing towards him and he immediately called out to Wind in a commanding and excited tone of voice. "No don't harm him, he's one of my people, don't kill...

Wind, reacting on pure instinct and immediately attacked the man she thought was in the process of attacking her Lord. With three quick swings of her deadly killing blade, Johnson's head jumped a foot in the air, and then it tumbled head over chin until the head crashed onto the floor, and then slowly rolled to a stop coming up against a different file cabinet.

Rossie was absolutely beside himself with anger as he growled savagely at Wind. "What the fuck did you just do? What the fuck did you just do god dammit? You just killed one of my people for God sake Wind! I told you never to come to me when I was working for just this worry, dammit. What the hell am I going to do now? How the hell am I going to be able to explain how Johnson was killed and by who? God dammit Wind, you have to get the hell out of here before any of my other people come in here and they see you standing there with that sword locked in your hands, and your body covered from head to toe with blood. Get the hell out of here, get back to the god damn apartment and I'll settle up with you when I get home. You go back to the apartment and you stay there and you wait for me to come home, and then we'll talk. Get out of here right this second. I hear people rushing up the steps. Get out of here dammit!"

Her shoulders sagged forward over the terribly angry way her honorable Liege Lord was yelling at her, and the terrible face he was aiming at her at the same time he was roaring at her, shook her to her very soul. She closed her eyes and then concentrated with all her might and in an instant her body disappeared and was returned to their apartment.

The first one who charged into the room was Commander Ralph Murdock, his head was still bleeding from the strike of Wind's sword and he was out of breath and scared to death. All the weapon fire from below had ended and they had five prisoners, and when the agents and police heard new weapon fire going off on the second floor landing of the building. They charged up the steps fearing what they were rushing into. Murdock walked up to Agent Rossie and rested his hand lightly on his shoulder and then he looked at the body of Young and asked. "Who's that?"

"That's Young, he's dead he was shot sir."

"Oh, I thought he might have died from old age, of course he's shot you shoot the rotten sonofabitch?" Murdock smirked as he gave Agent Rossie a weird look at the same time.

"Yes sir, he didn't want to give up to me, Commander."

"Outstanding, I just wish you left him a little alive that way I could have had the pleasure of putting his lights out for the bastard. What's all this other shit and how the hell did they die? Wait a minute, oh my God, is that Agent Johnson on the floor over there Agent Rossie?"

"Yes sir I'm afraid it is, and I have no idea how he or the rest of the people in here died sir. All I know was when I first came in here to search the room to see if anyone was hiding in here. I found all this slaughter, and then I saw Young and he was hiding in the corner by a filing cabinet and I ordered him to give up to me. He refused and aimed his weapon and fired at me..."

"We heard the weapon fire going down in here, and that's why we charged up here to make certain none of our people were still locked in a firefight with any of these bastards held up in here." Commander Murdock offered as he interrupted his agent's verbal report.

Agent Robert Rossie hesitated for a second and then he drew in a gulp of air, and started to finish his verbal report to his Commander Ralph Murdock. "Yes sir, anyway sir, when he fired at me and obviously missed, I immediately returned his fire and ended his life for him sir. When I got my breathing back under control I was just about ready to start to search the rest of the room out when you guys charged in here and stopped me from doing what I planned to do sir..."

"If I remember correctly Agent Rossie Sir, when you were assigned to the Japanese FBI Branch no more than a few months ago, didn't a number of people there get slaughtered in much the same way we see these people slaughtered here in this room, sir? Hell, even the American businessman Calvin Batterman was killed by someone with a fucking sword back in Japan. From the looks of what I see here mister, it seems quite evident that the damn killer working in Japan, has obviously followed you back here to the States, and that person is now doing what he or she was doing in Japan while you were stationed there, mister. At least we have one leg up on this killer this time around. You were on his tail back in Japan, and now he's working here in the States, it should make it a little easier for us to get a damn handle on this fricking mystery killer. But I'm also wondering why this killer only attacked Young and his pack of animals.

"Dammit Agent Rossie, I wonder if we have a fucking Vigilante on our hands, and he's only interested in killing anyone breaking the law? That's all we're going to need, some damn civilian taking the law into his own hands and killing anyone who he thinks is a law breaker..."

"I can't see that is the case here in the least Commander, after all sir, what law did Batterman break, to have what you're calling a Vigilante, turn his attention and sword loose on him for, sir? What laws do you think he broke in Japan, sir?" Agent Rossie asked Murdock as he let out his breath and he started to calm down some from all the action he was just involved in.

"I don't know, but I do remember you saying something a while back about it was supposed to be illegal for any what you and the Japanese people like to call a damn Gai Jin, a stranger a non-Japanese fellow owning any stinking Japanese business in Japan? If that's true then that might be the law Batterman might have broke to bring this killer's attention and his damn sword down on Batterman's foolish neck, Agent Rossie."

"I never looked at it that way Commander. I think you might have a good point there, sir." All the while he was speaking to Murdock, he was still fuming inside over the fact Wind killed one of his fellow agents, even though she did it in the heat of battle, she still did it.

"I always have good point to make anytime I'm speaking to anyone around here, mister. God dammit, I can't believe I lost two Agents in this here mess for crap sake. I'll tell you this much though Agent Rossie, asses are going to fry over this one I assure you, mister. God dammit, Johnson was killed in just about the same exact fashion as Batterman was killed back in Japan. He had his damn head lopped off as well, but at least the damn murderer didn't take off with his head like he did with Batterman's noggin. Agent Rossie, I want this god damn murderer or Vigilante or whatever the hell else he or she or whatever is, dammit. Now we have a much larger reason to find Batterman's murderer, because if you find who killed him, you'll also find whoever just killed Agent Johnson, and the rest of the people dead inside this damn room, sir."

"Okay people, we have a wounded Agent downstairs we have to look after, and then we have to get the crime scene people in here so they can start going about their damn business, and find out what the hell these lousy bastards were doing all the while they were hiding out inside this fricking building. I want to know who owns this fucking property, and I want to know why that person was allowing a bunch of god damn murderers to use his place as a hideout from the law. I want answers and I want them yesterday in fact, people!" Commander Murdock growled as he turned and he walked out of the room in a huff. The sight of so many people being so savagely hacked to death was starting to turn his stomach ill on him.

"Agent Rossie, I want you to go over everything you possibly know about this damn sword murderer killing a number of people back in Japan, and now here in the States as well sir. I want to know everything you know about this damn killer, and I want it put down on paper as fast as you can jot it down for me, mister. This fucking person killed one of ours this time around, and I what his damn hide on a wall for that fucking killing." Commander Ralph Murdock called back to his agent following him down the narrow stairs to the first floor of the building.

"You'll get it I assure you sir, but first I want to check on my partner and see how he's doing sir. Then I have to get back to my place and handle a few things I have to look after immediately. I'll report in around noon I guess after I got some rest for the day, sir."

"Sounds like a plan to me Agent Rossie. I want you to get some rest before I pick your brains about this murderer with a god damn sword, sir." Murdock stepped aside and allowed Rossie to lead him over to where he left his wounded partner. When they got there all they saw was the remains of the emergency medics who obviously looked after Fugiwara, and they removed him from the site to transport him to the local hospital. "Well, it looks like the medics removed Agent Fugiwara, why don't you go home and rest and I'll head for the hospital and see if they'll allow me to see him. I'll report to you on his condition as soon as I know something certain about his condition. I don't think you want to waste your time hanging around the hospital he's probably in surgery anyhow. Going Agent Rossie, I want you rested because you know the reporters are going to want to know what the hell went down here last night and this morning, mister."

"Yes, I'm really beat out and want to rest some. I know there's no sense heading down to the hospital right now, it's more than likely what you just said, he's probably in surgery and it's not going to do any of us any good hanging around and staring at the walls while waiting to hear anything about Fugiwara's condition." He offered, what he really wanted to do was get back to his place and dump on Wind for killing Johnson. Even though he was aware it was a reflex sort of accident she killed him, but if she listened to his orders in the first place then this death would have never happened. He was burning up inside and wanted to get at wind for her blunder.

"Yes, when we get outside I want you to leave the area immediately. If there are any damn news reporters hanging around out there and I'm certain there are many by this time, I don't want you to stop and speak to any of them. I'll handle anything we're going to release to the reporters myself. I don't want any of our people speaking to any of them pains in the ass for nothing about this situation. You just push your way through them like they aren't even there, Agent Rossie.

Agent Rossie drove like a wild man to his apartment, and when he slammed his car in park he rushed into his home as if he was angry at the world. He opened the door and found Wind in her usual spot of kneeling in the center of the living room, and he angrily stomped his way past her and when to the kitchen and grabbed himself a beer. Then he returned to the living room and took a slug of the beer then put the can on the table and glared at Wind. He slowly walked around her while studying her locked in her bow with her face close to the floor. She exposed her back to him in case he wanted to lash her for her mistake by killing one of his Generals.

When he was standing before her head he finally growled savagely at her. "God dammit Wind I told you not to come to me whenever I was working, and in doing so you killed one of my fucking people. I can't believe you disobeyed me, and that failure to listen to my orders you ended up killing a fellow Agent of mine for Christ sake. I don't know how the hell I'm ever going to be able to explain how you came about, and how you been killing everyone my Commander wants to know about, and now this. Dammit, I don't know what the hell I'm going to do with you now. You just can't follow my fucking orders, and this is extremely concerning to me. I have to do something with you. I can't afford to have you keep showing up anytime I'm involved in a damn shootout. This time you killed one of my Agents, the next time you could cost me a few Agent's lives, and maybe even my own. What the hell should I do with you?"

She slowly raised her head and went to reply, but she was immediately shouted over by the still fuming agent. "Don't you dare say anything to me? Don't you say one fucking word to me, dammit? I have to do something with you, I can't possibly have you hanging around any longer, no telling what you might cause the next time I run into a stinking problem at work." All the while he was yelling at her, he was still holding onto her killing sword, and now he was actually using it to lean on while he stared down at her with anger locked in his eyes and words.

Suddenly he reared up and then began wildly pacing around the still bowing ancient Samurai Warrior, he was still fuming over the fact she was the cause of Agent Alan Johnson's death, and he could not get over his anger and disappointment in his female weapon and lover. He had all he could do not to strike her with her sword, knowing all that would happen is her spirit being called back to the Floating World, and when the Kami finished punishing her for her failure to him, she would be returned to him again. He felt that was not enough punishment for her, all he could do is see Johnson's face when she first hit him with the killing sword. The look on his face and the pain locked in his eyes would never leave him memory for a second. Seeing his death again in his mind, gave his anger renewed fever, and he stomped around her for a third time.

His chest was actually hurting him because he was that angry at her, and for the first time since he found her spirit locked to the steel of her ancient sword. He looked down at her and marveled at her beauty and loyalty, and if it was not for her loyalty to him, she would have never ended up killing Johnson by accident. Remembering the look in Johnson's eyes as she struck him with the sword, instantly removed the love he was still feeling for her, and in one sudden and extremely foolish move, he spun the sword around in his hands and then raised his knee at the same time. Then he smashed the ancient sword's flat side on his knee and snapped it in two. Almost instantly, her spirit disappeared from her bowing position in the middle of the floor. The only thing that was left of her for him to remember was the two ends of a rusted and ancient sword and her favorite Kimono lying on the floor where she was bowed to him.

For a brief second, he almost put the two ends of the suddenly rusted sword together again, feeling he might have punished her too severely, but then he thought better of it. He dropped the end of the sword with the hilt still attached to it on the sofa, and then he walked over to the table, actually stepping on her Kimono as he walked. He placed the other end of the sword down on the table then he went in his bedroom and found an old tie box and returned to the table and placed the other end of the now rusted sword in the box. He removed a slip of paper from the drawer and wrote a note to Detective Motoshima and told him to guard the tip of the sword with is life, and not to allow it out of his sight or let anyone else to have it. He further wrote when he got the chance he would call him and explain everything to him so he understood just how important the tip of the blade was to the drama suddenly controlling his life for the moment.

Then he got up and went over to his desk and removed a roll of scotch tape and some ugly leftover wrapping paper and first wrapped the narrow box tightly. Then he taped it all together. He returned to the desk and found his address book, and opened it to the M's and found the name and address he was looking for. He pulled a sticky label apart and stuck it to the face of the box and quickly addressed it to Lieutenant Kenzaburo Motoshima, in care of the Detective and Homicide Division, Police Department, Tokyo Japan.

His anger over Wind killing Johnson, even though it was more an accident, it was still fueling his rash actions and anger. As he was filling the label out his phone suddenly rang and broke his concentration and he answered it, it was Commander Ralph Murdock and he reported in an excited voice. "Bob, I just wanted to let you know that Agent

Fugiwara was taken out of surgery a few moments ago and everything looks great, he's reported in no danger of dying and the Doc's are going to keep him for a week, and then we'll get him back for crap sake. But he has to be placed on light duty for at least two weeks or more, and then I can get back on his ass again. The only hang-up is the Doc's don't want any visitors for up to two days.

"The Doc's stated they don't need him to get excited, and they were kind of worried if any of our Agents started to flood the hospital, Shinnosuke was going to get excited and want to be released from the hospital to get back to work. I know how you must feel about this shit and I'll see what I can do about getting you in there before the two days are up, so you can visit your partner even if it has to be under the table so to say. But if not, you'll be the first Agent allowed to visit him on the third day, Agent Rossie. This is good news for us to hear Bob."

"That's real great to hear Commander Murdock Sir, and I'll be reporting back to work a little later on today, and then we can talk a little more about Agent Fugiwara's medical condition. But right now I'm completing the few things I have to get handled before I report back into work, sir." Agent Rossie replied to his FBI Control over the phone.

"Sorry I bothered you so much I see Agent Rossie, I just thought you might be a little interested in Agent Fugiwara's medical condition, that's all, sir."

"Don't be like that Ralph, or course I'm concerned about Shinnosuke-san's medical condition sir, it's just I had a few extremely important things that I had to look after immediately, and then I can put my full attention of his medical condition, along with the other things we're concerned with over all these murders and crap." Even though his partner was going to be okay, his anger for Wind killing Agent Johnson was still controlling his rash actions, and his emotions would not calm down even a little until he finished what he set out to do.

"Got ya, you go and get those so damn pressing and important matters taken care of, and then I want you to rest up some and report in after you had a chance to calm down a bit from this mess. Then we'll start going over all that had transpired at that damn stakeout earlier this morning. I'm not happy we lost two of our Agents in this damn mess, and I want to know where the hell it all went so damn wrong for us at the stakeout for crap sake. I'm not use to losing any god damn Agents on any operation we're involved in sir, especially any I'm in command of."

"Neither am I and I assure you Commander Murdock Sir, I'm sure as hell doing something about the situation as we speak sir..." Agent Rossie said into a dead receiver and then he hung up and finished preparing his package. He took a second and looked at Wind's exquisite Kimono still lying on the floor where it fell from her body, and he sadly shook his head. But he went too far with his angry actions to stop now. He resided himself to think once he was done with the Batterman's case and all the rest of this nightmare was behind him, he can then mate the two ends of her sword back together and call her back from the Floating World. Then he could put his full attention on her and form a strong and working relationship with her.

When he was finished with the package, he stuffed it in the pocket of his suit and stood. He gave one last look around the apartment and everything of Wind's had returned to the well aged, rusting and crumbling state. He even walked over to the once exquisite Kimono and moved it with the tip of his shoe and it went right through the once fine fabric. He decided to leave everything where it was until he finished with his day's work then he would move her stuff to a safe storage for her. Deciding he was still too worked up to rest properly, he left for the office, but he planned to stop by the post office and sent off the package to the Japanese Detective.

FBI HEADQUARTERS, WASHINGTON D.C.
ELEVEN HUNDRED HOURS (11 A.M.)

FBI Special Agent Robert Rossie reported to Commander Ralph Murdock's office as ordered and he plopped down in a chair and let his breath out in a rush. His hair was a mess and his eyes were heavy and bloodshot, and he looked like he had not slept in over a week.

Commander Murdock stared at his disheveled agent for several long moments, and then he mumbled at him. "Man, you look like a fucking train wreak mister. Didn't I tell you not to report in to work until you had a chance to rest up and calm down some? I don't need any of my Agents collapsing on me because of a lack of sleep, or you're suffering from exhaustion over a situation you were just put through for the company, Agent Rossie. To tell you the truth Bob, I wasn't expecting you to show up at the office until tomorrow morning after all you went through earlier today. At least I had some sleep before I was awoken to report to that mess earlier today. You sure you want to stay here, I'm happy to give you the rest of the day off you understand, sir."

"There's nothing for me to do back at home, so I might as well stay and start my report of this morning's actions for you, Ralph." Rossie announced as he let out his breath in a rush.

"You can always catch up on your sleep you know, Bob. On second thought, maybe it's a wiser idea if you were to stay here for the rest of the day that way I can keep my eye on you, and I'll know you're not over at the damn hospital trying to find some way for you to check on Shinnosuke's condition. Knowing you like I do, you'd sure as hell find some way to breach their security and get in to see that Japanese asshole friend of yours, mister. Anyway, if you get tired, you can crash in your office on the couch, and I'll cut off your phone service so you can sleep until you're strong enough to start the report I need from you, mister. Thinking about this a little further that's exactly what I'm ordering you to do, go in your damn office and sleep as long as you need, I still don't understand why you're here so early anyway Bob. I'll hold down the fort until you wake on your own. That's not a request I making here mister, that's a fucking order!"

Commander Murdock continued to stare harshly at his exhausted looking agent, until he got out of the chair and almost stumbled back to his own office. Then Commander Murdock turned in his chair and opened a draw and looked at the phone lines, and when he found the one to Rossie's office, he flipped it off to give him some privacy to sleep in peace.

Agent Rossie slept right through the rest of the day and through the night and finally woke when he heard a noise outside his office the following day. It was the cleaning crew, and being it was the Fourth of July, none of the other agents outside the ones who pulled the weekend duty, were in the building along with the cleaning people. He looked at the clock and was stunned it was past 10 in the morning. He slipped into his shoes and rushed for the bathroom. When he came out he was starving and went to the first floor to the luncheonette that was always open twenty four hours a day, every day and ate breakfast. After eating he decided to go home and rest, looking forward to tomorrow when he would be finally able to check on Fugiwara's condition.

As he opened the door to his apartment, he half expected to see Wind kneeing in the center of the living room waiting for him to come home. He could not hide the disappointment in his eyes when he realized she was no longer going to be there to greet him when he came home. His shoulders sagged over the disappointment as he walked through the apartment, making sure he did not accidently step on her Kimono again, and he plopped down at the table and then looked at the sofa and saw the half of her once deadly killing Katana sword. Now he was sorry he broke the sword in two, and sent the one end off to Detective Motoshima. He knew if he still had the two ends of the sword, he would have surely allowed the two ends to tough and become one again, and then he would have sent for Wind and enjoyed her treasures again.

Not having anything to do, he decided to lie down and continue to rest and regain his strength. He almost instantly fell off to sleep and did not wake until he had to use the bathroom again, and now it was after 7 P.M. and he was over tired. He checked the TV and as always, there was nothing on, so he raided the icebox and fixed himself something to eat. He never realized how lonely it was to eat alone until he got use to sharing his meals with the beautiful female Samurai from the ancient past. Nothing seemed interesting to him and after midnight, he decided to try and sleep. He ended up tossing and turning all night long and when he finally gave up trying to sleep, he rose and went to the living room and cursed when he saw it was only 4:23 A.M.

He made himself a pot of coffee and looked out the window as he sipped his coffee. He could not help but feel sad because he send Wind back to the Ukiyo until he retrieved the other end of the sword from lieutenant Kenzaburo and then joined the two ends together again, so he can again be with Wind. He looked at the calendar and realized it would take at least another three to four days at the least, before the Japanese Detective received his small package, and then another three to five days for him to send it back to him. So he had at least a full week or more of not seeing his Wind again. Now, he found himself cursing himself for acting so foolishly for snapping her sword in two, and then sending one end of it to the Japanese Detective.

Letting his breath out in a disgusted sigh, he went and had another cup of coffee. He ended up daydreaming and thinking of how it was to be with the ancient woman from the past, and how much fun he had with her. Teaching her of the many new and different things he was sharing with her, and how she always looked at him when she did not understand what he was showing her, or telling her about. The eye's her eyes was the most striking looks of Wind, and he saw them every time he closed his own eyes now. Again, he was angry at himself for breaking the sword and sending her away to the Floating World.

He lit up a cigarette, something he did only when he was really upset, and he was plenty angry at himself for sending Wind away. He left his coffee and table and reached behind himself and picked up the half of the ancient sword. He looked at the terribly rusted sword with the hilt and unraveled brocade that once adorned the handle. Missing were the six small gold emblems on each side of the hilt that held the fine silk brocade in place on the handle of the sword.

Seeing the terrible condition of her sword shook him to his soul and added to his sadness. He laid it back down on the sofa and finished off his second cup of coffee. He looked at the clock and cursed because the time was crawling by so slowly, and he wanted to get down at the hospital and check on his partner's medical condition. He still had over an hour to kill before he could head for the Walter Reed Hospital, so he decided to wash his FBI vehicle and clean it out from the stakeout duty he just went through. There were a number of empty coffee cups and wrappers from the food they ate while on stakeout cluttering the back seat of the car.

When he finished with the car he checked his watch and it was close enough to 9 A.M. for him to head out for the hospital. It took him just short of a half an hour to get there and he parked and rushed for the third floor. He was looking for room 315 and when he found it and entered, he was the only one there. He walked into the room as quietly as he could move for fear Agent Fugiwara might be sleeping and he did not want to wake him. But as soon as he saw him, his partner smiled at him and called out at the same time. "Come-on in, you bring any smokes with ya?"

"You know you can't smoke in here, asshole. How the hell you feeling? I was surprised when you were hit and fell down you didn't crack your head open, because if you did, nothing but empty beer cans and half eaten pussies would have rolled out the opening." Rossie smirked.

"Yeah, I went down pretty hard at that I figure. Kit sucks to be wounded my friend." Agent Fugiwara responded as he ignored the smart ass remark from his partner.

"What's with you anyway, the last time I saw a face looking like that it was in a jar of Formaldehyde, buddy." He smirked again at his partner, trying to make light of his condition.

"Yeah I can imagine, I hit the side of my head on the damn floor when I went down, it's swollen up some on me, will you leave me the fuck alone already, buster." Agent Fugiwara fired back at him and then he asked his concerned partner. "How's Murdock doing?"

"Arrr… he's doing okay I guess, but he asked about you in words that ain't in the dictionary. He's really upset you were hit though, the first question he asked me was if you had your vest on properly when he remained with me and he asked the both of us if we had our vests on."

"I bet he did, what about that scumbag Young, is he dead I hope so dammit?"

"If he ain't we'll have to come up with a new word for what he is I tell you my friend." Rossie smirked as he relaxed a little please Fugiwara was doing so well.

"Good thank God for that. That sonofabitch didn't deserve to live, he created so much sorry and pain for people while he was peddling that poison, Rossie-san. No one's going to miss that little prick very much I can assure you my friend." Agent Fugiwara snapped without showing any emotions of Young and the rest of the ones who died while trying to protect his life.

"Hey how about you, how the hell are you making out buddy?" Rossie asked as he turned serious for a moment and then waited for his reply.

"I'm doing okay I think, but the Doc's told me the bullet clipped the bone in my shoulder, and that's why they want to keep my cooped up in this dump for a few more days. But I'll tell you this much, my friend. Just as soon as I can find my damn clothes they have hid on me someplace around here, I'm going over the fucking wall and escaping this damn prison they have me locked up in and I'm going to get me some real food to eat for Pete's sake. Did you ever try and eat any of this slop they call food in this stinking place, Rossie-san?"

"Nope, and I hope to hell I never have to try some of their food now, or in the future buddy. Wow, I bet that must have hurt like hell when the bullet hit your bone, buddy. You know something? You're now a prime candidate for medical Marijuana, Buddy." He offered, trying to lighten up the mood some and take Fugiwara's mind off his pain.

"HaHa, you're being a real Jerk Bennie buster so knock it off and give me a break will ya? What's going on down at the office and thanks for coming by and checking on my ass, partner?"

"Arrr... Murdock is waiting for me to clue him in on everything that went down at the damn stakeout that really turned into a stinking mess on us..."

"What went down, I was kind of out of it from almost the very beginning of the mess you know, Rossie-san?" Agent Fugiwara asked as he moved a bit to get more comfortable in the bed.

"I hate to be the one to have to tell you this shit, but we lost two Agents in the shootout with Young and his pack of goons. We lost both Johnson and Wilson..."

"We lost Agent Johnson, how the hell did we lose him? I was aware we lost Wilson he was hit before I was Rossie-san. But I never thought we lost Agent Johnson. I always thought he was like a fricking cat and he had nine lives, dammit." Agent Fugiwara started to get a little upset over Johnson's death and it set off one of the machines.

A nurse obviously monitoring the machines from the nurses' station came rushing in and she warned the two men at the same time. "I can't have my patient being upset like this and if it continues, I'll be forced to ask you to leave the room sir, and you." She turned her attention to her patient and warned him in no uncertain terms. "If you continue to allow yourself to get upset like this then your stay with us is going to be a lot longer than it was first expected. Can I trust you to calm down or do you want me to send your visitor packing for you, sir?"

"I'll be a good little boy I promise you so can he stay."

"Yes he can remain as long as you remain calm and you better be, it's been a long time since I last put a bad boy over my knee." She smirked back at the good looking Japanese FBI Agent.

Then two men watched the young nurse leave and Rossie asked him. "Who's that?"

"That's the floor Nazi, it's said she got so angry at one of the patients she actually tossed him out a third floor window. But she takes damn good care of you when we're hurting man."

The two laughed together until the nurse returned and she announced in a pleasant tone of voice this time. "I'm afraid your visitor is going to have to leave now. The doctor set up some x-rays he wants of your shoulder again. He's a little worried and wanted to see how you're healing, Mr. Fugiwara Sir." She looked at Agent Rossie and then she waited for him to leave.

"Well I guess that's my cue to go, and since I don't want to get pitched out a third floor window I better leave quickly, partner." He smiled at Agent Fugiwara and then he started out of the room with the nurse calling out after him.

"I see you're a very wise man sir, and that only happened once while I was on duty. It seemed the rather upsetting visitor didn't want to leave when I ordered him out of the room, so I showed him he couldn't fly, sir." She smiled at the agent as he rushed out of the room.

Agent Rossie left the room laughing and rather happy Fugiwara was in such good hands, and as he was leaving he bumped right into Murdock coming to check on the health of his wounded agent and he stopped him and asked. "How's Agent Fugiwara doing, and I'm happy to see you visiting him today Bob. I was a little worried about the dumb prick."

"He's doing real good and wants out of the hospital already, and he has a great nurse taking care of him sir. She's a real doll and told me she hated seeing me leaving because she didn't want her patient to be left alone in the room, sir. Go in and talk to Agent Fugiwara and when the nurse comes back, blow her a stinking kiss, she really loves when you screw around with her, she has a great sense of humor, Ralph." Agent Rossie left his Commander while laughing again, knowing he just got Murdock in some hot water with the floor nurse already.

CHAPTER TWENTY EIGHT

JULY 6th, 1996, FBI HEADQUARTERS
WASHINGTON D.C.

FBI Special Agent Robert Rossie reported for duty at his regular reporting time, and as he was walking by Commander Ralph Murdock's office he bellowed at him. "Hey you, get your lousy ass in here double quick, I got a bone to pick over with your ass, mister."

Agent Rossie stopped walking and then turned and entered the Commander's office with a hug smile on his lips and was acting like he owned the world while he was at it.

"That's right buster, you grin at my ass. You got me in some hot water with that damn floor nurse yesterday. Hell, she even tried to pitch me ass out the damn window because I went in Fugiwara's room and started talking to him, and she wanted to take the prick somewhere for some kind of test. Man was she some helluva spitfire, I could've used her on our stakeout a few days ago. I bet she would've cleaned out all those sonsofbitches single handed. All kidding aside, how are you doing today, you get enough rest over what was left of the weekend, mister?"

"I'm really fine sir."

"Good, good then I want you to write out a full report on this sword swinging maniac we have suddenly running all around downtown Washington and hacking people to death and enjoying it while he's doing it. By the way Agent Rossie, I was going over some of the reports filed about this sword carrying nut, and in a few of those reports, the damn killed was described as a female, could this shit be true, mister?" Commander Murdock asked his agent with concern.

"That was what I was told as well sir. But each report I covered was different, one stated it was a female, the next referred to the murderer as a male and another reported the killer as a person, so I didn't know what to really make of the very confusing reports sir. That was what was making Batterman's murder case so complicating and hard to crack for us sir." Again, he was already trying to protect Wind by denying the killer was a female.

"I see what you mean, I just got my fingers into this case and I'm already confused by it. I couldn't believe it was some damn female who just hacked a total of seventeen well trained bodyguards to death using just a fricking sword to get the job done. When most of these pricks were armed with automatic weapons and not one of the dopy bastards were able to kill this supposed bitch with a sword as her weapon. It's all bullshit if you ask me, mister."

"Me as well Ralph, I'll get on that report for you as ordered, but I don't know how much more I can possibly add to it for you sir. Like I said, when I entered the room in question, they were all already chopped up and the only one still alive in the room was Young, and I nailed his ass as soon as he confronted me in the room, sir." Agent Rossie reported to his control.

"You don't worry about that, you just write out that report and let me decipher what I was to bleed out of that report for my knowledge, mister. You put down what you know went down and I'll take it from where you left off, sir." Murdock replied with a snap in his voice.

Agent Rossie got up and headed for his office to work on the report, and for the next two days that was what he worked on for most of his time in the office. The entire third floor of the FBI building was all in somber moods over the deaths of the two agents, and their funeral was to take place later on Thursday, and there was a rumor floating around that Agent Shinnosuke Fugiwara was going to attend the funeral. But it never happened because the doctors would not allow the wounded Special Agent to leave the hospital yet.

Even though Agent Rossie had visited Fugiwara at the hospital even day after work, he never once told him what he did with Wind, nor did the wounded agent ever ask him anything about the ancient female Samurai Warrior, it was the furthest thing from both Agents minds.

The rest of the week past rather quickly by and on Tuesday the 14th, it was a great day for the FBI Center in

Washington. Because this was the day Agent Shinnosuke Fugiwara was finally scheduled to be released from the hospital. Agent Rossie was elected to be the one to pick up the wounded agent and bring him to their headquarters, and it was his pleasure.

Everyone in the building was standing on the outside of the building as Agent Rossie's car slowly approached their main headquarters with his emergency lights blinking away, and the moment everyone saw his car coming down the road, they all began cheering for the injured agent. Even Commander Ralph Murdock was outside and he seemed to be cheering the loudest of everyone outside. This energized all the agents, even agents who had the day off, showed up to welcome Agent Shinnosuke Fugiwara back into their fold.

When Agent Rossie pulled up before the building and the horde of FBI Agents, they immediately opened the path Agent Fugiwara could use to walk into the building, and as he exited the car, the crowd started clapping again. Even a number of the agent's wives and children were also at the gathering, and they were just as happy as the agents were to get Fugiwara back. As the two agents entered the building, they were followed in by the others gathered outside to welcome Fugiwara back, inside it was just as crazy as everyone came up to the wounded agent and offered him their best. It was hell for Rossie to get Fugiwara into their office.

Once they were in the office, Rossie closed the door and asked Fugiwara how he was doing with all the excitement his appearance caused the rest of the agents. "How you doing my friend?"

"I'm doing good enough I guess, hey man, did you see Murdock out there, I thought he was going to bust a gut the way he was cheering for me. I never thought that guy would ever respect me the way he was doing out there, Rossie-san. If he keeps this shit up I just might be forced to change my mind about the fricking guy." Agent Fugiwara said, and then he wince from a sharp and sudden stab of pain he just received from his wound, and Rossie picked it up and asked him again with some concern in his voice.

"Are you sure you're doing okay my friend? I saw the look and your reaction to the pain you're still suffering from the damn wound you received at the stakeout. If I see it again I'm going to force you to leave and rest up more before you end up back in the damn hospital..."

"What the hell do you mean he might end up back in the fricking hospital again, Agent Rossie? What the hell's going on with him Agent Rossie? Did you pick up something I should know about mister? There's no sense my bothering to ask him anything, because he'll only lie his stinking ass off to me if I try to find anything out from him, mister." Commander Murdock grumbled as he started to enter the office and stopped dead in his tracks and he still was holding onto the doorknob and he stared at both of his agents in the room.

"Arrr... I just noticed a wince of pain from him and I warned him if I see it again, he's going either home or back to the hospital, Commander."

"That tares it for crap sake, I thought it was a little too early for you to report back to work, mister. I'm going to send you home, you do have someone there who can look after you, or at least check on your ass every now and then? If you don't then I'm sending your ass right back to the stinking hospital and that will be that buster." Murdock growled at his injured agent.

"I'm fine for Christ sake, I just moved the wrong way and I paid for it. That was all it was sir."

"You're lying like I said you would to my ass mister."

"I'm not lying to you Ralph, why the hell would I bother lying about the damn wound to you? You and every other mother's son knows I was wounded, so I can't lie about that and I'm certain they all know I'm still suffering pain from the damn wound still. So there's no sense my lying about anything to you guys man." Agent Fugiwara offered to his Commander.

Ralph finally moved deeper in their office and he stared hard and long at his wounded agent for a few seconds, and then he groused at him as he continued to stare him right dead in the eyes. "Okay mister, I'm going to take your stinking word for how you're feeling for the time being for crap sake. But if I or anyone else inside this building sees you wincing in pain again then your ass is going to be shoved back in a stinking ambulance, and you'll find yourself back in the arms of that nasty ass old nurse who nearly threw me out of the third floor window of the stinking hospital." Commander Murdock stopped speaking at this point and he shot a nasty glare back at Agent Rossie for not warning him about the nurse in the first place.

"I'm really fine I'm telling you Ralph, and I don't need to go back to the damn hospital for nothing, and if you try and send my ass back there. I'm telling you I'll go over the wall and make it back to the office before you even return here. Then we can start to play Ground Hog Day and do the same crap over and over until you finally get tired of paying for a fucking ambulance, and let me stay in the office so I can get back to some kind of work for my partner around here, sir."

"Okay, okay, I hear you but I'm warning you mister. I don't need any damn heroes around here, you hurt and I want to know about it immediately, mister. Immediately I warn you, and I'm also going to work out for someone to be with you until you're completely over suffering from this damn wound, buster. A male someone, I wouldn't trust you with that damn nurse from the hospital for a second, buster. Okay you two, I'm certain you both can find something to do around here that needs doing, so you can earn the pay I'm forced to give you two lazy peckers. Find something to do the both of you. I'll be back to check on you off and on for the rest of the day. All kidding aside Agent Fugiwara, it's great to have you back to work mister. The office wasn't the same without you screwing everything up on everyone here." Commander Murdock gave the agent a quick wink of the eye, and then he turned and rushed out of the office.

For the next two days Agent Rossie's office was busy as hell, Wednesday Fugiwara went home by 9:30 A.M. because he was uncomfortable and in pain, and Thursday neither he nor Rossie were alone with each other so they could talk together with everyone coming in and out of his office. Everyone wanted to check on Agent Fugiwara and they were coming up with any and every excuse to enter Rossie's office to speak with the wounded agent.

ZERO EIGHT FORTY FRIDAY MORNING,
JULY 17th, 1996
FBI HEADQUARTERS WASHINGTION D.C.

For the last three days Agent Robert Rossie was trying to talk Agent Shinnosuke Fugiwara into staying at his apartment, but Fugiwara kept refusing because Commander

Ralph Murdock had his wife brought down to Washington so she could take care of her injured man. But she had to go home to take care of the kids for the weekend and headed back to Jersey. So today Rossie was keeping the pressure on Agent Fugiwara to spend the weekend with him. Lately, Fugiwara was getting around pretty well, and most of his strength had returned to his body and there was little if any further pain from the wound to his arm and shoulder any longer. He was even thinking about calling one of his female friends to spend the weekend with him.

Agent Rossie knew the other agent was in no shape to fool around with any women at this time, so he kept the pressure on him to come and stay with him for the weekend. He still never mentioned anything about what he did with Wind, and Fugiwara was still somewhat confused over what happened to him, and he never once thought to ask about her either. Agent Rossie kept nagging the still slightly wounded agent for the entire day and as the end of the day approached, Fugiwara finally relented and he agreed to stay with him for the weekend.

Commander Murdock just appeared at the office door and he was going to speak to Agent Rossie, and see if he would not mind taking Fugiwara home with him. Even though he was getting around okay, he still did not want the hurting agent to be alone for the full weekend. But even before he could ask if Rossie would not mind looking after Agent Fugiwara, he offered.

"Commander Murdock Sir, I'm planning to take Agent Fugiwara home with me and look after him for the next few days sir. But mind you sir, I'm going to put in for some extra hazard duty pay if I have to deal with this guy for the whole weekend, Ralph. No telling what kind of stinking trouble he's going to cause me and my place, sir."

"I can't argue with you there Agent Rossie, to be truthful with you mister. I was thinking about doing the same exact thing, because you only have to deal with our wounded hero here. I have to deal with thirty three of you Agents who act just as bad as this one does all the damn time around here for crap sake. Well, it's close enough for you two jackrabbits to head home for the weekend, and I don't want either of you two trying to drink all Washington dry of booze, and leave a few of the women unmolested for someone else to have a little fun with, dammit. Okay you two take off and enjoy the weekend, because next week we're going to put our noses back on the grind wheel and get something done with the damn Batterman murder case. Now that we successfully dealt with that pain in the ass Young, and the rest of his bunch of lunatics." Commander Murdock leaned against a file cabinet and he watched as the two young agents quickly wrapped up their desks and then headed off to the sound of Murdock bitching at them.

"If anyone doesn't believe the dead don't rise from the grave, they want to be hanging around here at quitting time, and watch you two birds move getting out of here for crap sake." Then he started laughing at them as they both rushed for the elevators.

Once they were in Rossie's vehicle they both relaxed and joked over how Murdock was riding them all day. As they turned onto the main roan to his place, Agent Fugiwara finally asked. "How are you doing with that little spitfire of yours doing anyhow my friend? Is she still as hot as she looked the last time I saw her man?"

"I'm afraid that's something we're going to have to discuss a little later on when we get back to my place. Things happened you need to know about buddy, but now is not the time to try and go into it. I want to get you over to my place and comfortable, and then we'll talk about all that went down while you were stuck in the hospital. You want me to stop so we can pick up some Johnnie Walker. I'm plum out of anything but wine at home to drink, and I don't have very much of that left. So if you want to get buzzed tonight, we better stop somewhere along the line and pick up something to drink. Come to think about it, do you want me to cook something or should we pick up something for supper?"

"I think we should stop and pick up something, I'm in no mood to watch you blacken a steak on us. I saw you cook a few times in my life and that was enough. Why don't we pick up some sandwiches, like meatballs maybe? I'm not in the mood for Pizza, I'm kind of sick of that crap for a while Rossie-san." Agent Fugiwara replied as he struggled to get comfortable in the car seat.

"Sounds like a plan to me buddy, we can pick up the sandwiches at Publix, they make a damn good wedge and meatball wedges sounds real great at that. We can also stop at their liquor store and pick up some Johnnie to drink while we're at it, buddy." Already, he was trying to think of a proper way for him to try and explain to his partner what and why he did what he did to Wind and her sword. He understood Agent Fugiwara was going to get real pissed off at him when he found out he snapped the sword in two pieces and sent her back to the Floating World until he got the other end of the sword back from Detective Motoshima, and then he could join the two ends of the sword together again. Now he found himself pleased that he kind of hid the half of the sword he held onto before he left for work this morning. He wanted to tell Fugiwara about the sword before he saw it resting on the sofa when they entered his apartment.

He finally pulled into his parking slot and they got out and rushed into the apartment with Agent Fugiwara half expecting to see Wind dressed in her exquisite Kimono, and her bowing to the both of them as they entered the room. As soon as he entered he started looking for Wind when she was not kneeling in the center of the living room, he turned to Rossie and snapped at him. "Well where the hell is she at? I wanted to see that fine looking fox again as soon as possible. She was all I was thinking about as we drove to this dump of yours man. Don't tell me she's stuck back in the damn Ukiyo for twenty four hours? Hell that means she'll be gone for half the time I'm staying here, Rossie-san."

"You hit the nail right on the head and I'll explain it all to you as we enjoy our supper and a few shots of Johnnie, Fugiwara-san." Agent Rossie replied as he placed the bag of sandwiches and bag with the bottle of Johnnie Walker on the table. Then he rushed into the small kitchen and took two glasses and rushed back to the table and opened the bottle of booze and poured two good glass of the booze, he then handed one to Fugiwara and held his and suddenly saluted his partner with his glass as he offered to him. "I'm damn glad you didn't die on me my friend, I'd hate like hell to have been forced to break in a new partner to work with, mister."

"Oh, it's so nice to be loved, not by you, but it's nice to be loved buddy. Thanks partner, I'm happy I didn't die as well, Rossie-san."

They both took a good slug of booze, and then Agent Rossie unwrapped the sandwiches and handed one to his partner and he took the other. After they ate, they shared another drink, and then Fugiwara asked Agent Rossie with much concern lacing his tone of voice this time. "Okay partner, you said after we had something to eat and get comfortable, you were going to tell me where and what happened to Wind. So start talking to me my friend."

"You got it, well after you got wounded I continued on after Young. I followed him up to the second floor landing of the building and entered a room and he and a shitload of his bodyguards were hiding inside the room. When I entered I was confronted by Young himself, and we got into it and he fired at me and missed, but I didn't miss his ass though. I got him then all hell broke loose. Wind followed me into the room and she immediately attacked any and everyone hiding in the room. Murdock said seventeen of Young's bodyguards I think it was, was killed by Wind. But she was still so worked up with the killing fever that when Agent Johnson happened to enter the room in a rush to help me. His sudden actions confused her and she thought he was attacking me, so she reacted and chopped his head off his shoulders and I started..."

"Arrr... damn, please don't tell me she was the one who killed Agent Johnson on us Rossie-san? Jesus Christ Almighty, I can't believe she was the one who killed our Agent, dammit?"

"I'm afraid that's how it happened, Fugiwara-san."

"Geees what a mess then what did you do with her? I'm certain every one of our people were rushing for you by this time, Rossie-san."

"I jumped on her with both feet and sent her back to the apartment, and as soon as I was able to get away. I returned to the apartment and really got on her case. I was so fucking angry at her I didn't even realized what I did until it was too late to do anything about it, Fugiwara-san."

"What the hell did you do with or to her Rossie-san?"

"Shit, before I could stop from reaction in anger against her, I snapped the sword in tw..."

"You did what? Please don't tell me you snapped the damn sword in two? That means you sent her back to the Floating World for good. Well not really for good, all you have to do is put the two pieces of the sword back against themselves and they'll automatically heal themselves and become one again, and that would mean she can come back to us. Where the hell are the two ends of the fucking sword at Rossie-san?" Agent Fugiwara nearly yelled at his partner this time.

"If only it was that easy..."

"What the hell do you mean by that fucking remark, Rossie? It's real easy to do, all you have to do is to allow the two ends of the sword to touch, and it'd automatically become one again, what's the problem?" His partner growled at him as he interrupted him for the third time now.

"Well, I have one end of the sword here with me." Agent Rossie replied as he walked to the back of the sofa. Then he bent down and pulled his end of the sword out from underneath the sofa and showed it to Agent Fugiwara like it was supposed to calm him down some.

"Where the fuck is the other end of the damn thing at? Go and get it and we'll call her back to the living world and then we can enjoy her charms together, buddy."

"I can't do that Fugiwara-san?"

"Why the hell not, what the hell did you do with the other end of the damn thing, Rossie?"

"In my anger, I sent the other end of the sword out to Lieutenant Motoshima back in Japan for safe keeping..."

"Whatttttt! Why the hell did you do that for, dammit man." Agent Fugiwara suddenly roared angrily as he interrupted Rossie for the fourth time in their conversation as he reached out and yanked the broken end of Wind's sword out of his hand, and then he slid his hand on the hilt of the sword and held it like it was a complete Samurai Katana blade.

"All we have to do is wait and when Lieutenant Motoshima get's the other end of the blade in the mail, I'm sure as hell he'll contact me immediately and ask me what this was all about. Then all I have to do is tell him it was a mistake and ask him to send the other end of the blade back to me, and then we can join the two ends back together and call her back to us from the Ukiyo." Agent Rossie replied to his partner in a simple and matter of a fact tone of voice.

"You really think that's as easy as it's going to be for us to get that other end of the god damn sword sent back to us from that damn Japanese Detective? You don't think Lieutenant Motoshima isn't going to demand a full explanation over why you would send him the end of an ancient Samurai Katana blade in the first place man? If you don't think for one second he's not going to drag your ass over the coals trying to find out why you sent him an end of a Katana blade then you're stupider than you look, mister."

"Who, you better calm down a little before you go and blow a damn head gasket, buster! There's nothing for you to get this fucking upset about, he'll send me back the sword nice and easy man. I'll tell him it was a piece of evidence and I need it back and he'll send it back to me that easy." Agent

Rossie replied, getting a little upset himself over the way his partner was reacting to him sending Wind's sword to the Lieutenant.

"Don't worry about me and my damn head gasket buddy. Why don't you call the fucking Lieutenant and see if he got your damn package yet, mister?"

"There's no need for me to go and bother the Lieutenant yet. I checked on the package by the tracking number and right now it's on a slow boat heading for Japan. Its ETA is scheduled for Monday morning. Here, I'll prove it to you my friend." Agent Rossie grumbled as he turned his back on Fugiwara and opened his computer and then had his hands dancing across the keyboard while he went looking for the tracking information on the package he sent out to the Japanese Lieutenant.

Agent Shinnosuke Fugiwara was actually shaking he was that upset with his partner as he slowly rolled the short end of the once so deadly killing sword around in his hands. And before he even realized what he was doing with the weapon, he suddenly attacked his partner with the broken end of the ancient and rusted once deadly killing blade in a wild rage over what he did to Wind. He jammed the broken blade deep into the back or Rossie all the way in his body to the Tsuba or sword guard. Then he pulled the blade sideways, slicing and opening a wide and ugly gash in his back. He knew he went too far to stop now, so he continued to attack Rossie's now helpless body like she had attacked the bodyguards at the first stakeout they had set up to speak to Young when they wanted to interview him.

In his insane rage he continued to chop and slash at his partner's body, cutting chunks of flesh and bone from him. He stabbed the areas he could not slash and cut away with the not as sharp ancient blade. He did not stop attacking Rossie's body until it looked almost as bad as when she attacked a body. Then he stepped away from Rossie's body, rushed into the bathroom and showered the blood of his partner from his body and clothes. All the while he was showering he was cursing his partner, and actually blaming him for what he just did to his body. In his madness he could not blame himself for anything he was doing, all he understood was, he wanted to be the one who called Wind back from the Floating World, so she would be forced to carry out his bidding for a change, and he could then become a power in his own right.

Once he had finished showering and washing his clothes in the shower, he searched and found and took a gallon of harsh cleaning solution along with a gallon of bleach, and he thoroughly washing down the tub, walls and floor of the bathroom. When he cleaned it up to his satisfaction, knowing the Forensic people would have no reason to really check out the shower area of the apartment in any investigate they would carry out of the crime scene. He carefully backed out of the apartment while making certain he did not step in any of the blood, and start to track it around the apartment and leave any evidence he might have been in the apartment when his partner was killed. Then he locked the front door and rushed for Rossie's parked car while hiding her broken blade in his pants. He went to the rear of the vehicle and placed her broken sword in the trunk of the car and then he started the car and slowly pulled away from the structure. He drove away at a controlled speed, not wanting to draw any attention of his leaving the building.

He headed for the last lady he picked up the day before he was shot at the stakeout while still fuming at Rossie for snapping the sword in two and sending the other end to that Japanese Detective, and he headed directly for her home. He smiled to himself when he saw the lights on in her home and knew she lived alone so he realized she had to be home for the night. He parked the car and walked up to the door and rang the bell like he did not have a care in the world. Brenda answered the door and when she saw who it was, she immediately fell in his arms. She read the newspapers and watched the news and knew he was wounded and she was so worried about him. She nearly pulled him into the home and closed the door behind them. As soon as he was in the house, he went to her phone and called Commander Murdock.

The Commander answered the phone himself and the instant he head his voice on the phone, Agent Fugiwara immediately offered to his control. "Commander Murdock Sir, this is Agent Fugiwara, sir. I'm terribly sorry for bothering you at home this late at night sir, but I found Agent Rossie to be an extremely boring person to be with for even one hour of the day. So I borrow his car and I'm going to spend the night with my new girlfriend. I left Agent Rossie telling me he was going to look up an old flame himself and have some fun for a change, sir. I'm sorry again to offer you sir, but I just couldn't spend a full weekend with that so boring ass guy, sir. He would've driven me to go back to the hospital just to get away from the guy that is how boring he is, sir."

"Boy you two guys are going to send me right over the fucking falls yet, buster. Okay I understand, I had to admit it myself, but there were times I also found Agent Rossie to be a little boring myself every once in a while, Agent Fugiwara. You just take care of yourself and don't overdo it and screw yourself up on me. But if you have his car then how the hell is he going to report to work on Monday morning, mister? Dammit you two guys are really getting to be royal pains in the ass lately."

"I don't know, I guess I'll go back to his place and pick him up and drive him in on Monday morning, sir." Agent Fugiwara offered, trying to make it sound like it was no big deal and he was not worried about returning to Rossie's apartment for any reason.

"That won't be necessary I guess Agent Fugiwara. I have to run out to Home Depot my lady gave me a helluva long honey to do list for the weekend. Agent Rossie lives just three blocks away from the place, so I'll just stop by in the morning and have him drive me back to my place and he can use my car to get to work, and I'll have my wife drive me to work on Monday morning. You're lucky you were wounded or I'd make you drive all over the damn place over all the extra trouble you're giving me lately, mister. Have a good time I believe you earned it Agent Fugiwara. I'll get over to Agent Rossie's place tomorrow morning, maybe I can enlist his help with all the crap my lady wants me to do over the damn weekend. I'll call you if anything comes up with Agent Rossie, or this damn Batterman murder case, mister." With that said Commander Murdock hung up on his injured Agent and then he went about his business.

Agent Shinnosuke Fugiwara smiled as he hung up, and then he mumbled to himself. "As soon as I can convince Murdock to send me over to Japan to investigate who had killed Rossie, I'll start my search for the other end of your god damn sword that stupid fool sent to that damn Japanese Detective, and then I can start my search for you. Then Wind, I can become your Lord and Master and control you and have you carry out all my bidding for a change while I'm screwing your lovely little ass off, lady. Are we going to have a lot of fun as I become one of the most powerful men in the world, and I'll owe it all to you and this god damn sword of yours, Wind! I'm coming for you

WIND-SAN!"